The EAGLE
and the
ALBATROS

Deke D. Wagner

A Novel of the Imperial German Air Service

The Eagle and the Albatros © 2014 Deke D. Wagner

Edited by Elizabeth A. Rainwater

Cover design by Deke D. Wagner
Illustration courtesy of Rise of Flight®

Printed in United States of America

ISBN-13: 978-1491272725
ISBN-10: 1491272724

FIRST EDITION

For more information please address Deke D. Wagner at:
dekedean@gmail.com

Wagner, Deke D.
The Eagle and the Albatros: a novel / Deke D. Wagner—1st ed.

1. France, Germany—History—World War One—Fiction. 2. Imperial German Air Service 1916-18. 3. Air combat—France—Fiction.
Title-4158207

Printed on demand by Createspace Amazon

DEDICATED TO:

"Mutti" Almut Wagner-Wilson,
Without her loving support help and patience,
nothing in this life would have been
possible.

ACKNOWLEDGMENTS:

In acknowledging the help he has received in the writing of this novel the author expresses a debt he cannot adequately repay. In gratitude he can but name those people from whom he has received encouragement and whose time and effort have been freely and graciously given. In the instance of my best friends, Mack and Katrina Blauvelt, "Auntie" Edda Wagner Woolard, Catherine Prysiazny Jerry McKavitt, Aurelio Cadenas, Daniel Pirkel, Fellini's Pizza, and the entire staff of the Atlanta Buckhead Library. Without their support, advice and forbearance, this novel would not have been possible. Thank you all, from the bottom of my heart.

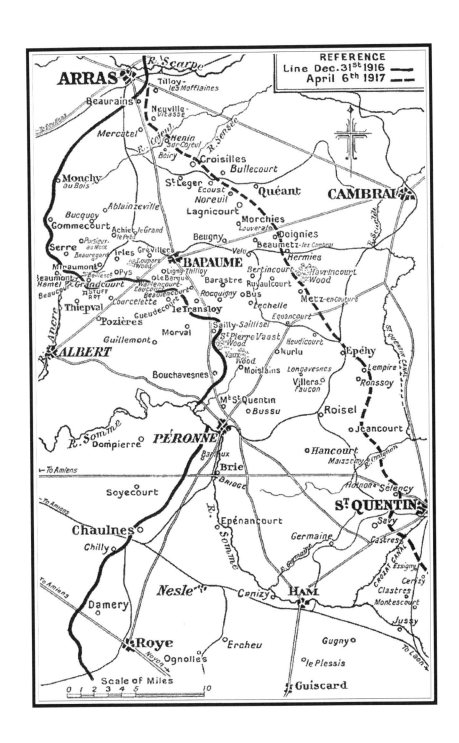

THE SOMME SECTOR (1916-17)

Ah! well a-day! What evil looks
had I from old and young!
Instead of the cross, the Albatross
about my neck was hung.

**—The Rime of the Ancient Mariner
Samuel Taylor Coleridge**

The EAGLE
and the
ALBATROS

May 1917
An unknown aerodrome
Somewhere in France

Prologue

✠

MAY 7, 1917. A COOL NIGHT HAD SETTLED over the embattled purlieu of France, and the spirits of vanquished airmen lingered longingly amid the moonlit shadows of canvas hangars. It had rained earlier that day, and in the depressions of the tarmac remained reflective little pools of water. The air was stirred by the faint breeze drifting in from the west, rippling the puddles of this shoddy tableau, mirroring its secretive scenes. The pilot mounted the aeroplane, like a knight throwing a leg over the withers of a favored warhorse, and nestled into the cockpit, ensconcing himself squarely amidst an archaic array of gauges, switches and valves. A mechanic labored over him, strapping him in, while another shuffled to the nose of the two-seater Sopwith and seized the wooden propeller. The pilot and mechanic barked the usual litany, and shortly, the 9-cylinder Clerget sputtered to life.

Once the Sopwith was throbbing with full power, the mechanics yanked the chocks away, the pilot guided the slender, snub-nosed aeroplane down the darkened airfield. Seconds later, he was airborne. He tinkered with the fuel mixture briefly then ascended to one thousand meters altitude.

He was quite nervous. But once comfortably airborne, he calmed his nerves with a neat shot of cognac from a flask of cheap, junky stuff he'd bought at a local canteen, and it did the trick. The pilot smiled anxiouly, grinning with comprehension; it'd been a long time since cognac had given him such a glow as had the wine of adventure.

He smiled, suddenly realizing the soothing humming of the Clerget motor—its constant pounding and vibrations probing deep into the fillings of his teeth—did more for his nerves then any cognac could. It was good to finally get underway.

It was barely past midnight as he guided the tetchy little Sopwith across the ink-black sky, higher and higher and further away from the secret aerodrome of *Fl. Abt. 99*, hidden deep inside German held territory. Destination: Paris!

Also aboard the two-seater was a tight-lipped passenger named "Agent X", who sat stiffly in the observer's seat of the British built biplane. The pilot, always an astute officer, assessed Agent X as quite unimpressive, an odd looking individual, a small, frail man with a twitchy little mustache. How he'd survived as a spy this long was anybody's guess. The pilot leered back at Agent X, wondering how this feeble little creature could possibly be an operative of the renowned German Secret Service.

After a mild protest from Agent X, the pilot climbed to three thousand meters, disregarding orders to stay low. He wanted to get as high above the Front as he possibly could, where the droning revolutions of the Sopwith's rotary would not be heard. Minutes later, he crossed the front lines north of Verdun and proceeded southwest to Épernay, dropping back down to the prescribed five hundred meters. A mollified Agent X sighed restlessly and snuggled down into the cockpit.

The Sopwith was performing perfectly.

A refulgent moon lit up the Marne River, just as Intelligence had said it would, and the pilot followed its meandering path through the countryside, its cold waters glistening in the pale moonlight. He'd done very little night flying during his one-year career as a pilot, and for very good reasons. Most aviators rarely flew once the sun went down. Things looked very different at night. Typically, airmen used maps or local landmarks to orient themselves, but in the darkness of night, those landmarks weren't so easily visible. Nor did the maps offer much help. And the old Sopwith? Well, it only had a directional compass, that was all. The pilot was quite thankful this cool, dark night, for the moon and its radiant attributes.

It was a welcomed beacon.

After a trouble-free hour and thirty minute flight, the unlikely pair of Germans arrived at their destination. The pilot landed the Sopwith safely in a patchy beet field parallel to a narrow roadway just a few kilometers east of Paris. He noticed a strangely glowing skyline. He had assumed the City of Light would have been blacked out because of war. Not so. Wise to the Parisian proclivity of unbridled gaiety and its love of nightlife, he knew the good people of Paris would never allow something like a silly little war to get in the way of their everyday lives. Singing, dancing, drinking, eating, making love, celebrating—everything had to continue. The pilot chuckled; sometimes the French were as arrogant as any German.

Once the Sopwith's noisy rotary shuddered to a halt and the wheel chocks were set in place, Agent X bounded from the rear cockpit. An idling car was already waiting for him. And before the little man darted off for his destination, he gave the pilot terse, laconic instructions. A determined expression beset his pale face.

"Wait here," he ordered. "Back in an hour!" Agent X sprinted to the waiting sedan. He slid into the backseat and was immediately driven away.

The pilot watched the sedan accelerate down the road and disappear in the darkness. Moments later, another man came out of the farmhouse. The pilot felt tense and ill at ease, not sure whom he could trust.

The man approached him slowly.

The pilot kept a wary hand on his 9-millimeter Luger, just in case. He wouldn't hesitate to use it if the need suddenly arose. He whispered his line. "Poincaré is a bigot."

The stranger spoke his line, muttering in a hoarse Breton dialect. "Clemenceau is the man in chains." He stepped out from the shadows.

The pilot recognized him, remembering him from the Secret Service briefing. He'd seen all the dossiers of the men participating in the mission, complete with current photographs and sobriquets. The mission, as it had been explained to him, was an exchange of military intelligence. He got no further information than that. Intelligence had simply stated that certain aspects of the mission were confidential and on a "need to know" basis, and he didn't need to know.

"*Bonjour, monsieur.* I am Agent Z," said the man.

"*Salut, Enchanté,*" the pilot replied. He knew "Agent Z" was just a sobriquet, a codename.

"Alright, this way, *monsieur,*" said Agent Z. "I'll assist you with the refueling and such."

"Of course." The pilot nodded. "Lead the way."

Agent Z led him to a barn, where he was instructed to wait. Waiting was always the most nerve-wracking part of any mission, and this situation was no different.

Damn! The pilot grumped silently. Those pesky old butterflies were fluttering about his gut again!

Agent Z offered him something to eat.

The jittery pilot refused politely. "Thanks. But no," he said. "Couldn't eat a thing right now."

"Oh, I understand. Too nervous, eh?"

The nervous pilot sighed. "Shouldn't we go ahead and refuel the aeroplane?"

"Sure, in a moment. Relax for a minute, that was a long flight."

"Relax? Sure."

"How about a drink?" Agent Z pulled a green bottle of mineral water out of a haversack.

"Hmm, got anything stronger?" The pilot asked.

"Of course." The compliant agent reached into a jacket pocket and tossed over a flask. "Take a deep pull, my friend."

The thirsty pilot unscrewed the top, sniffed the contents, and smiled. "Schnapps?" The pilot took a hearty gulp then gave it back to the agent. He suddenly remembered the flask of cognac; but he was saving that for the return flight. *"Merci, monsieur. That's really what I needed."* His face flushed a pinkish glow as the bite of needful spirits took effect.

"Hals-und Beinbruch," Agent Z uttered, in a sharp Berliner's accent, revealing his German heritage. He took a swig from the flask then replaced the cap and stashed it back into his breast pocket.

"Ah, your deutsch makes me feel a lot more comfortable," the pilot replied in his typically prim Bavarian accent, a reassuring grin forming on his face. And from that moment on, both men gladly cast aside their Gallic patois and spoke in High German.

"I take it, this is your first operation with *FlugM?*" Agent Z asked.

"Ja."

"Do you normally fly with a *Jagdstaffel* ?"

"Uh, just trying to do my part."

"Aha! A patriot, then?"

"Not exactly." The pilot shook his head, scoffing softly. He felt more like a high-flying chauffeur than some high-flown nationalist. He coughed roughly—that feverish grippe was beginning to take hold of him. He plopped down on an old wooden box, a light sweat breaking out on his forehead, his breathing becoming laborious and strained. He could feel his temperature rising ever higher.

"Got the bug, eh?" Agent Z said. "The weather's been dreadful around here lately."

The Bavarian sniffled and nodded, reaching into a jacket pocket, pulling out his cigarette case. He offered the agent a smoke. *"Willst du eine Zigarette, mein Herr?*

"No thanks. Don't smoke."

"Good man. It's a nasty habit. But, you know how it is?"

Agent Z's head bobbed in agreement, grinning. He rifled through a brown paper bag and pulled out a sandwich and began eating.

The pilot lighted the cigarette and puffed quietly, thinking to himself: I hope Agent X gets back sooner than later. This is absurd! What in the hell am I doing here? Disgusted, he rose to his full height, the cigarette dangling from his lips. He gestured impatiently to Agent Z, saying: "C'mon. Let's get that machine refueled, eh?"

The agent frowned. "Oh, all right." He bagged his sandwich and got up. "You worry needlessly, my friend—"

"Let's just get it done now."

Agent Z led the pilot to a shed where a cache of 10-liter petrol cans was stored. A moment later, both were striding from the shed to the Sopwith two-seater, each burdened with two full petrol cans, and began the refueling process, an interminably laborious task.

Lightning suddenly flickered. Thunder rumbled.

The pilot's eyes jerked to the sky as cold petrol spilled over his hand, drenching his tunic sleeve, gushing over an already full tank, stinging his nostrils with acrid forty octane fumes.

"*Verdammt!*" he swore. "They said no rain! No rain!"

The pilot capped the Sopwith's tank as rain began to fall, and fall steadily. He stared up at the darkened sky and wondered if all aerologists were just a bunch of bumbling stuffed shirts with meaningless meteorological degrees. And yet as the rain fell in steady droplets, he began reviewing the past few hours in his mind. He'd always felt suspicious about fortuity; would it manifest itself as ill-timed luck or would it bestow an unpredictable grace? As it appeared, luck had been on his side thus far. But the synchronicity of a timely rendezvous, mechanical efficiency, good intelligence, and above all, agreeable weather, had given him a sick feeling inside; was it unusual luck or a fateful harbinger of some unseen doom? Perhaps. But then the peril of the situation struck him all at once. The pilot gladly heeded the sudden spatter of falling rain, welcoming it as a sign of normality. But his mind kept wondering back to thoughts of catastrophe as he dashed back to the barn, his face glistening with angry dampness, his leather jacket shiny with rainy wetness.

Agent Z followed closely.

Once inside the barn and out of the rain, they sat and waited.

"Damnable French weather!" The pilot spouted.

"Oh, don't worry, my friend," the agent affirmed as he supped on his half-eaten sandwich. "This will pass. It's just a little shower."

But the rain fell harder and heavier and the pilot began to pace about, back and forth, more anxious than ever, puffing a cigarette like a condemned madman, smoking one after another, even though his distaste for them deepened with every puff. He glanced at his pocket watch for the tenth time then gazed out of the barn doors at the glistening field. It was getting soggier by the second. He shook his head in disgust and stalked back to the rear of the barn where he unbuttoned his fly, relieving himself in one of the empty horse stalls.

He stood for a moment in deep thought. What if Agent X doesn't get back in time? What then? What if I take off, like the Major instructed, and he's just running late? What if he's just had car trouble? The pilot sighed heavily. What if? What then? What If... It was all quite maddening! He finished his business and buttoned up—

"*Mein Herr*, come quick!" Agent Z shrieked suddenly. "I see lights. Agent X is coming back. Look there!"

The nervy pilot hustled back to the front of the barn. He peered carefully out the two barn doors, which were now fully open. Indeed! There were headlights of an approaching car. They flashed twice as the car neared the entrance of the field. The signal! Both men sprinted out to the Sopwith and commenced start-up procedures. The pilot climbed in the cockpit and Agent Z took a position at the prop, as the black sedan sped up the gravel driveway, skidding to a halt, sending rocks flying through the air. The Sopwith, which was at that moment, just belching to life, shuddered and shimmied, the cold Clerget rotary struggling to crank up. Thunder clapped and the rain continued to fall in heavy sheets.

Agent X dashed up to the pilot. "Hurry, let's get out of here!" he shouted frantically. "I'm being followed!"

"What!" The pilot yelled back in a shocked voice.

His eyes jerked to the roadway. Sure enough! The German aviator saw three sets of headlights growing more rapidly in size every second as they approached the field. Agent X hastily climbed into the observer's seat and jerked his flight helmet on. The pilot primed the fuel cock for takeoff, then yanked the goggles over his eyes, then placed both feet on the rudder bars, clutching the control stick tensely, ready for takeoff. "Get that Lewis gun ready, *Herr X*!" he ordered "We may need it!"

The pilot's voice was scarcely comprehensible under the roar of the steadily thrumming Clerget engine. He increased the fine-fuel adjustment to full, and signaled Agent Z to remove the chocks, just as the headlights, now recognizable as black police sedans, broke through a gate at the far end of the field, racing straight for the

Sopwith. The pilot heard the faint crackle of gunshots and thought he saw Agent Z fall to the ground, firing his sidearm in retort. But he wasn't sure; the penetrating white beams from the car's headlights were nearly blinding. He threw an arm up, against the bright lights, shielding his eyes, and guided the Sopwith across the rain-soaked field, directly towards the oncoming cars. Bullets whizzed by his head as he slewed the Sopwith down the field, keeping it on a collision course with the police sedans.

"Hang on, *Herr X*. This is going to be close!" he shouted.

The pilot gripped the stick firmly, accelerating down the wet field still fumbling with the fuel regulator. Closer and closer, he converged with the three sedans, feeling bullets bouncing off the Sopwith. Suddenly, a sharp stinging pain bit into his right shoulder; blood spurted from a nasty bullet wound, then quickly dissolved in a pink mist in the prop wash.

"*Agh-h-h-h!*" He gasped, blood spattering all over the cockpit and instrument panel. He grasped at his injured shoulder, instinctively yanking the stick back at the same time. The Sopwith flitted into the air just as the landing gear cleared the roof of the first oncoming car. But the engine was still sputtering, the Clerget still choking for fuel, still gasping for air, struggling for power, spinning weakly, but gaining altitude nonetheless.

"Airborne!" The pilot exhorted grimly.

Agent X pelted the passing sedans with the Lewis gun. Miraculously, he hit one of the drivers with his hastily aimed volley, killing him outright. The car swerved and flipped over, cartwheeling out of control across the field, trailing a welter of debris. Then, inexplicably, the Sopwith's Clerget engine, choked for lack of fuel, spluttered, misfired and died. The aeroplane canted up and over the hedgerow at the far end of the field in a near stall. The pilot, stricken with dread, frantically fumbled with the fuel mixture as his consciousness faded. But his adjustments failed miserably.

The prop ticked over twice, then shuddered to a halt.

"What's the matter?" Agent X yelled at the top of his lungs.

"Damnation!" shrieked The pilot. "We're—going—to... crash!"

From: Secret Service HQ, Berlin
      Ministry of War
      2300-hours, 7 May, 1917

To: Kommandeur der Flieger (Kofl)
    1st Army, 3rd Army, 7th Army, 9th Army.

<u>URGENT BULLETIN!!</u>

INTERCEPT IMMEDIATELY! Sopwith two-seater leaving
vicinity of Sivery/Verdun. Occupants, both double
agents (Agent Y and Agent X) have appropriated
classified battlefield documents of German unit
strengths and artillery locations,and are attempting to deliver such to French Intelligence.

STOP AT ALL COSTS! The assailants are considered
dangerous, and traitors and criminals of the German State. Use all means necessary; ruthless, merciless, summary—immediate retaliatory action is
required. Conspirators have commandeered Allied
aircraft for this purpose. Stop at all costs!

Oberst Hermann von der-Lieth Thomsen, Kogenluft
General Konrad von Linkhof, Deputy War Minister

Book One

✠

Eagle's Blood

April 1916
Munich, Germany
Mossbacher's Inn

Chapter 1

✠

APRIL 20, 1916. *OBERLEUTNANT* Willi Wissemann tilted the brandy snifter back and finished off the last dregs of cognac, an old vintage Courvoisier, one he had been savoring for this special occasion. And tonight was a special occasion. Not only was it his twenty-ninth birthday, he'd recently passed his pilot's certification test at Schleissheim Flying School, a school just south of Munich; he was bound for the Western Front in the morning. He'd received orders from *Idflieg* a day earlier to report to the 6th Army *Flugpark* at Valenciennes. Once there, he would join the pilot pool, ferry new aircraft to outlining airfields, adding some much needed flying time to his nascent flight log, waiting his turn for a permanent posting to a reconnaissance and bombing section, gaining valuable flying experience. But that was all in the hopeful future. Tonight, he would have to enjoy himself!

"*Herr Ober...*" he beckoned to his waiter.

The waiter, a corpulent, middle-aged man, strode over to the table. "*Mein Herr?*"

"Another cognac, please."

"Of course. Back in a moment."

"Thank you."

The waiter paced away for the kitchen.

Willi Wissemann reached for his silver cigarette case laying on the table, extracted a fag, struck a match and lit the Halpaus, his preferred brand of cigarettes. As he inhaled deeply, he happened to glance at his wristwatch again, for about the umpteenth time, noting the hour; it was 9:30 p.m. already.

Hmm, what's keeping her? he thought. That girl! Couldn't be on time to save her life.

A moment later, the waiter returned with the cognac. He set the half-full snifter down on the table and pulled out a pad and pen.

"Ready to order now, sir?" he asked.

Wissemann sighed. "I suppose so." He glanced at his wristwatch again and shook his head dejectedly. "I guess she's going to be late."

"I see. Go ahead, sir. What will you have?"

"Uh…" he picked up the small booklet-like menu, the cigarette dangling from his lips, and perused it quickly. "I guess I'll have the schnitzel with red cabbage, and… potato balls." He inhaled some smoke, then exhaled a blue sigh. "Yes. That will do nicely."

The waiter scribbled hastily. "Very good, sir."

"Some bread would be good, too."

"Of course." The waiter smiled. "Do you want to order for the tardy young *Fräulein?*"

"Hmm, better not. I made that mistake once before. Never again."

The waiter chuckled. "I know exactly what you mean, sir.

"Women, eh?"

The waiter smiled. "I'll put this in right away, *mein Herr.*" He folded his order pad and stuffed it in his apron. He gave a faint nod and darted away for the kitchen.

"Ah, Ilse. You sweet, wonderful creature. Where are you?"

Wissemann gazed around the dim, candle-lit restaurant, picking up the cognac snifter, noting how empty the place was. He was a bit surprised, it was usually very busy, it being one of the few places in Munich that hadn't been affected by the war's harsh food rationing. He took a little swig of the cognac and grimaced blissfully. Such good spirits—and to drink it all alone? A pity! Smoke rolled from the cigarette, dissipating in a thoughtful haze.

"Wissemann? *Oberleutant* Willi Wissemann?" a deep, boisterous voice resounded, breaking in on the Bavarian's brooding reverie. "I'll be damned. It *is* you!"

Wissemann turned around in his seat to see who was hailing him. "*Ach Gott! Hauptmann* Ulbricht. So nice to see you, sir," he said, sliding his chair back to stand up.

"Nah-nah, keep your seat, Wissemann," said *Hauptmann* Ulbricht, gesturing deprecatingly. "No need to get up. Just thought I'd say hello. I won't keep you from your dinner."

Hauptmann Rudolf Ulbricht was the *Kommandant* of the Schleissheim Flying School. He was a lean, thirty-nine year old from Rosenheim. He smelled of cheap tobacco, schnapps and musky hair tonic. He stroked his waxy, red mustache, smoking a pipe, holding a strapping young blond in his arms. "Fancy meeting you here."

"Uh, tonight's my last night in town, sir. Shipping out for the Front tomorrow morning."

"I see." Smoked curled from the pipe. "Russia, I hope not?"

"No, no, *Herr Hauptmann.* France, thankfully."

"Good. Good." Ulbricht nodded, relieved. "Russia is a frozen, godforsaken wasteland. A frozen hell on earth."

"Yes, sir. So I've heard." Wissemann stood up and motioned to a chair. "Have a seat, *Hauptmann?*"

"No thanks, Wissemann." Ulbricht smiled puckishly. "Me and the young lady here, were just heading out. We're going to have a drink at the Ratskeller. Or maybe we'll just go over to Gretchen's place first and make our own music, hmm?" Ulbricht winked, popping the buxom blond on her firm, round rump. She winced, smiling.

"Aha." Wissemann brushed some ashes from his tunic sleeve.

"You alone, *Junge?*"

"No, not really, sir. My date is just, well... a little late."

"Aha." Ulbricht sucked his pipe bemusedly. "Oh, by the way, this is Gretchen. Just met her a few hours ago. Nice girl. Likes to have fun, it seems." He grinned lewdly, his eyes flaring.

"*Fräulein...*" Boot heels clicked. Wissemann bowed gallantly and gestured with an upturned hand.

Gretchen, a big, busty blond with rosy cheeks and a cherubic face, giggled coquettishly, proffering her hand, which Willi Wissemann promptly kissed. "Oh, my. Such a fine gentleman. Pleased to meet you, *Herr* Wissemann."

"My pleasure, Gretchen."

Ulbricht guffawed. "Hah, he's a real high-flown ranker, he is," he quipped, laughing at his own irony. "And a damn good pilot to boot as well, Gretchen. My best student, all around. Tops in his class."

"Really? He's quite handsome, too," the girl cooed.

"You're very sweet, Gretchen. Thank you." Wissemann's face blushed a little.

"Well, Wissemann," *Hauptmann* Ulbricht said in a puff of smoke, "I'm off for some fun. Take care, *Junge.* Keep on your toes up there in France. Those Brits are fine gentlemen. But watch out for the Frenchies. Those snail-eating bastards are crafty devils, I tell you."

"I will, I will." Wissemann nodded. "Have a good evening, sir."

Ulbricht seized his date by the waist and drunkenly drifted off for the door. "Send me a postcard or something, Wissemann," he said as he opened the door. "Maybe they'll let you fly an Eindecker, if your lucky. *Auf Wiedersehen, Junge!"*

The door slammed and Ulbricht was gone.

Wissemann sat down and picked up the snifter. "Hmm, an Eindecker? Hmm, that would be something." The Bavarian leaned his head back and sucked down the cognac as if it were his last. *"Ahhh!* Good vintage, this is." He belched softly, the high-quality, distilled cognac stinging hotly in his gut.

It was a good feeling.

So was the fact that he'd finally finished flying school. Now he was off for the front lines, and in a few hopeful days, in the cockpit of an aeroplane. Flying school had been a breeze, much to his relief. Initially, he worried he'd have trouble learning the art of banking, turning, and of course, landing. But it all came quite naturally to him. It seemed as if he were born to fly, at least that's what *Hauptmann* Ulbricht had said. In fact, he did so well, he was offered a flight instructor's position at the school after he graduated. But he quite assuredly turned it down. He wanted to fly combat missions, bombing and reconnaissance jobs, maybe even shoot down an Englishman or a Frenchy, scoring victories like the great Max Immelmann or Oswald Boelcke. Both of those gents were renowned aces by now, both were currently tied with thirteen victories apiece. Each man wore the prestigious Order *"Pour le Mérite"* around his neck. It was the Fatherland's highest award. The Order—literally "for merit"—was instituted by Frederick the Great and bore a French name because French had always been the language of etiquette in the courts of western Europe.

Wissemann remembered his own miserable existence as an infantry officer in the mud-filled quagmire of the Marne, scarcely a year ago. He recalled the frustrating stalemate and the battles of attrition for a mere few meters of murdered landscape—featureless gouges of blood-red and brown littered with thousands upon thousands of casualties. After a full year of blowing France to bits, the entire countryside between Compiègne to Reims had been reduced to a unrecognizable moon-cratered landscape.

Then one day during a lull in the action, the distant buzzing of an aeroplane engine caught his attention. A mere thousand meters above the battlefield, quietly, almost politely, a German biplane drifted by, surveying the human carnage below. Wissemann stared up at it for a long time that day until it disappeared from sight. That neat little aeroplane lolling along so peacefully imbued him somehow with a new sense of hope. That would be a decent job for a man like himself, he decided then and there.

Yes! The career of an aviator was respectable work, an apposite image, something becoming of a German officer. On that day, the intrepid Bavarian decided he wanted out of the infantry—the intransigent existence of an army mired down in the muck. Aviation was a means to get back in the war and out of the mud. He wanted in that tiny mechanical bird; to soar above the war-torn landscape of France into the rarefied air of the atmosphere would be like reaching for heaven. The only other alternate exit from the inimical misery of trench warfare would be on a stretcher, or worse, in a pine box. Indeed, he decided, aviation it would be!

He rubbed his lower backside. His wound was almost healed now, just a little stiffness now and then. Ulbricht was right, the French were feisty devils for sure, Wissemann had the stitches to prove it. During the Battle of Artois, in May of the year before, a determined "Frenchy" had stuck him good with the point of his bayonet. He'd spent the next six months in a hospital. That's when he'd decided it was time to get out of the infantry. After his wound healed, he applied for a transfer to the Air Service. In November '15, he was accepted and said good-bye to the infantry and the trenches forever, a decision much appreciated by his mother, a decision satisfying his sweetheart as well. Indeed, it gave her much elation—keeping her Willi safe from random artillery shells and bayonets. War in the air, it seemed to her, was a lot safer. Of course, crashing down from three thousand meters had obviously never occurred to her!

Willi Wissemann glanced at his watch for the tenth time. *"Lieber Gott!* Where is that girl of mine? Am I to spend my last night in Germany, alone?"

The waiter reappeared with a piping hot plate of schnitzel, red cabbage and potato dumplings. "Here you are, sir. Your bread will be out in a moment." He set the piping-hot plate of food down before Wissemann and stepped back. "Anything else, sir? Another cognac, perhaps?"

Wissemann inhaled warily. "Hmm... better bring me a bottle of beer, instead. Doppelbock, please—with a glass." The hungry Bavarian seized his linen napkin and stuffed it down his tunic collar. "Don't want to be besotted when the *Fräulein* gets here, you know?"

The waiter grinned. "Of course, sir. One Doppelbock, coming up." The waiter strode away in a meaningful gait.

Wissemann picked up his knife and fork and delved into the veal like a condemned man eating his last meal. The food was excellent, as always. He wondered how the fare would be in the Air Service. It had been terrible in the infantry. Downright nauseating at times! The

German Flying Sections were reputed to have good field kitchens on their aerodromes. They also had cozy billets, too, he heard.

The life of the airman was indeed a step up from the mud-slogging infantryman. Cowering in rain-soaked trenches had not been his idea of how to fight a war, staring out over a pile of sandbags for hours upon hours across a wasteland of muck, blood and barbed wire, wasn't either. Now he'd be soaring over that sloughy quagmire known as "No-Man's Land", flying straight into enemy territory, bombing, raining hellfire from the sky above, flying daily reconnaissance missions, a tedious but required necessity, engaging in aerial combat. Yes, the life of the airman, that was the life for him!

"HERR WISSEMANN... OBERLEUTNANT? Wake up," said the waiter. He nudged the sleepy airman out of his languid stupor. "Uh... pardon the intrusion, sir. We're closing in five minutes."

"Huh?" Wissemann awoke, yawning sleepily. "Closing? Is it that late already?"

"Eleven o'clock, sir."

"So sorry, must have fallen asleep."

"I understand. Shall I call you a cab?"

"No, no. I'm not drunk. Just very sleepy. Thank you, though."

"Are you sure?"

Wissemann yawned again. "Absolutely sure. My hotel room is just two blocks from here. I'll walk. I can manage it, I think."

"Very good, sir."

"Oh, the bill? How much do I owe you?"

"Not to worry. *Hauptmann* Ulbricht took care of all that."

"What? Really?"

"That's right, *Oberleutnant*. He called about a half hour after he left. He had us put it on his account. You see, he's quite the regular here." The waiter smiled and patted Wissemann on the shoulder. "He seems to like you very much, he does."

"He paid for my dinner and drinks?"

The waiter nodded. "That's right."

"How nice of him."

"Yes, he's a fine gentleman."

Wissemann roused himself. He opened his cigarette case and popped a Halpaus in his mouth. He struck a match and lit it. He glimpsed at his wristwatch. "Well, I guess I better be off, then."

"I'll fetch your coat and hat—"

"Oh, that's not necessary. Thank you, though."

"Very well. Good night, sir."

"Good night."

The waiter paced away.

Wissemann rose from the dining table and straightened his tunic tails. He looked around the restaurant. He was the only one left. Everyone was gone except for the staff. A busboy was already flipping the chairs up, setting them down on the cleared tabletops. The sleepy-headed Bavarian laid out a handsome tip for the waiter, then sauntered into the lobby where he was met by the coat-check girl.

"Here you are. Your coat and cap," chirped the young girl, a cute-looking brunette with sparkling hazel eyes. "Have a good night, sir"

"Much appreciated. A good night to you, too." Wissemann smiled and took his service cap and nestled it firmly on his head, cigarette dangling from his mouth. He shrugged into his *Steingrau* overcoat and popped the collar up. He was just about to head out the door when the waiter came stalking up.

"Sir! Wait! You forgot something." The waiter handed over Wissemann's sterling-silver cigarette case. "Don't want to leave this fine piece behind, do you, sir?"

"No, I don't. Thank you. You're absolutely right, *Herr Ober.*" Wissemann took the case and stashed it in a coat pocket. "It was a Christmas gift from my fiancée. She would hang me out to dry if I ever lost it." The Bavarian lieutenant grinned mirthfully.

"The same girl who never showed up, sir?"

"The same. She must have gotten held up somewhere. She was coming from Berlin. Took a train all the way down, you know. Slow going, I'm sure."

"Aha, I see. That explains everything."

"Does it?" Wissemann smiled. Twin jets of smoke rolled from his nostrils. "If you say so."

"Of course. The trains never run on time anymore—because of this blasted war."

"*Ja*, the war..."

"Well, good night, sir," the waiter said again. "Give 'em hell out there at the Front."

Wissemann laughed. "I certainly will!"

The waiter opened the door for Wissemann and waved Good-bye. The lanky officer paced off down the cobbled sidewalk towards his hotel room. The April air was brisk and cool and the tall Bavarian buried a pair of clammy hands deep into his coat pockets.

A late winter thunderstorm had pelted Munich with cold rain, drenching the environs of the fabled Bavarian city. Little puddles of water still lingered in the crevasses and potholes of the cobbles. The street was wide, brick-paved and cheerless in the dim glow of street lights and there was a peculiar lack of traffic along its fringe.

The war had dampened the party atmosphere here in Munich. Nightclubs and cabarets rarely stayed open late anymore. Some restaurants had even gone out of business. Food rationing had limited the fine fare once available on their celebrated menus. Even some of the bigger and more famous beer halls had taken a hit in revenue. Munich, just like the rest of Europe, was in an anxious holding pattern. True "living" would have to wait until the cessation of hostilities. And that didn't seem near in the future.

Wissemann turned down Maximillianstrasse, striding stiffly to his hotel, which was just a further two blocks. His footsteps echoed urgently, almost ominously, as he traversed a quiet intersection. Things were indeed hushed at this hour. A few pedestrians drifted by, the occasional motor car, a police officer walking his beat. But that was all. It was all too strange for Willi Wissemann, much too subdued for his liking.

Nevertheless, tomorrow he'd be bound for northern France on an overcrowded, noisy, shuddering train car. The continual embarking and disembarking was sure to take a toll on his nerves. He hated trains, train stations and anything associated with them. Better take an extra bottle of "something" for the trip, he thought. Who knows how long it might take.

He found the Kempinski Hotel and swiftly made his way to the entrance, snuffing out his cigarette underfoot before he went inside. He removed his service cap and stepped up to the check-in counter, announcing himself.

"W. Wissemann. Room three-oh-three, please."

An old, bald-headed night clerk with a ratty mustache, slumbered half-asleep at his desk, supporting his head on a propped arm. The clerk stirred groggily, grunting and snorting, but did not move. His eyes remained shut. His mouth hung wide open.

Wissemann smiled. "*Entschuldigen Sie bitte!*" he shouted, his voice echoing loudly. "My key, please!"

The thunderous articulation jolted the sleepy night-clerk into abrupt consciousness. His head bolted erect and he jumped up excitedly. "What? Who? Huh?" he stammered.

"My room key, please. Number, three-oh-three."

"Three-zero-three?"

"Yes!" Wissemann hissed.

The night clerk nodded sleepily and turned around to his key rack. He alertly found Wissemann's key. "Here you are, sir. Sorry, just fell asleep, I guess." He handed over the key.

"Not a problem. I nodded off myself just a little while ago."

"Good night. Have a restful slumber, *Herr* Wissemann."

"Thanks. I shall."

Wissemann turned for the stairwell leading to the upper floors. He had just placed a boot on the first step, when the night clerk beckoned him back with a lusty utterance.

"*Herr* Wissemann!" he exclaimed. "I almost forgot!"

"What did you forget?"

"There's a telegram from Berlin, here for you."

"Berlin?" Wissemann's head snapped around. He stalked back to the check-in counter.

"Yes, sir. Came in about an hour ago."

"Let me have it, then."

"Of course. Just sign here, please." The night clerk slid a heavy, black logbook forward, onto the check-in counter, and handed over an ink pen. "It's from an... Ilse—"

"*Ja-ja.* I know who it's from," Wissemann interjected impatiently.

He scrawled his name on the line indicated, then the clerk handed the telegram to him, which was in a yellowed envelope. Wissemann tore it open straightaway and unfolded the creased paper. He read the teletype note, nodding knowingly, absorbing the telegram with hurried interest, his eyes darting over the print like a man possessed.

He read:

```
               IMPERIAL TELEGRAPH SERVICE
                  BERLIN, GERMANY

Lieber Willi:                              21.APR.1916

     Sorry to miss your big send off. The trains are awful
here. Berlin is a horrid mess. Even Papi's influence
couldn't do a thing for it. Hope you are well. Please
telephone from your headquarters when you arrive. I need
to know you are safe. Please be careful at the Front. I
love you very much. Happy Birthday, Willi. Good luck!

                                      Liebevoll, Ilse
```

"*Verdammt!* As expected," he grumped. Willi Wissemann felt elation and disappointment all in the same instant.

"Not bad news, I hope?" asked the curious night clerk.

"No. Just a disappointing good-bye note, that's all."

"Oh." The clerk shrugged languidly and went back to his desk.

The dejected German airman trudged heavily up the staircase, rereading the telegram twice more before he reached the door to his room. He stabbed the key in the keyhole and opened the door, went inside, slamming the door behind him. He clicked on a lamp and heaved his rummy backside onto the cushy double bed mattress. The old brass bed creaked and groaned under his weight but held fast. He undid his tunic collar, laid the telegram down on the nightstand and reached for his bootlaces. In a few flustered seconds the boots thunked noisily to the floor.

He reached into the kitbag that was at his bedside and pulled out a bottle. The brand new, uncorked bottle of Courvoisier, glistened enticingly in the dim lamplight of the little hotel room. He broke the seal and popped the cork, seized a courtesy drinking glass from a set of four arranged neatly on the nightstand, and poured himself a healthy shot. He held the glass up to the light, nodding contently.

"Here's to you, *Liebchen*." He shot back the cognac in one gulp. He sat up and glanced in the mirror over the bedroom bureau. "Ahhh! Happy Birthday, old man. May you see many, many more!"

He refilled the glass.

"And here's to the German Air Service—the best damn bunch of aviators and nut-and-bolt crews in the world." He gulped down that shot greedily too. "Here I come, you French snail-eating bastards! And you... you, snotty English poseurs! God bless the German Air Service... the Kaiser... and the Fatherland!"

He swigged a third neat one and collapsed in the pillow, sighing, belching crapulently, glowing. And so it went...

WISSEMANN SWUNG DOWN from the rail car onto the platform at Valenciennes, almost colliding with a stout fellow in *Feldgrau* who had been coming the other way. The two men stopped. The other, like Wissemann, wore the airman's badge of the Air Service. He displayed the shoulder boards and *Litzen* neck ruff of a basic Saxon lieutenant.

"Afternoon, sir," he said cordially. "You must be... *Oberleutnant* Wilhelm Wissemann?" He popped off a crisp salute. Boot heels clicked. "My name is *Leutnant* Jakob Herzog."

"*Leutnant* Herzog? Charmed." Wissemann returned the salute with a snappy one of his own. "I am Wilhelm Wissemann. I reckon you're with the aircraft depot at Valenciennes?"

"That's correct, sir. I'm in charge of the Pilot Pool."

Wissemann nodded. He reached into his tunic pocket and produced his order packet, which he handed over to Herzog. "Here are my orders. Just finished my pilot training at Schleisshiem."

"Very good, sir." Herzog took Wissemann's order packet and clamped it to a clipboard. "Follow me, please, sir." He about-faced and stalked off down the platform.

Oberleutnant Wissemann trod hurriedly behind, bags in hand, a grim expression of forbearance on his face. The train ride through Germany and France had been as expected; bumpy, too long, and exasperating. It had stopped many times along the East-West railway, finally reaching the city of Valenciennes, a small town near the Escaut River, a place very close to the Belgian border, at five o'clock in the afternoon. Of course, making the trip with a bad hangover didn't help matters much. But his spirits were high nonetheless.

Herzog led him to a dirty, Mercedes *Kübelsitzer.* "Toss your kit in back, sir, and I'll drive you over to the aerodrome."

"How far is it."

"Just down the road a bit." Herzog opened the driver's side door and slid in behind the wheel. "The depot is right next to the rail line. Makes it easier to unload equipment and supplies. Convenient, eh?"

Wissemann nodded. "Quite convenient, I'd say."

"Yes, expedient for pilots and aircraft, too." Herzog hit the ignition switch and the Mercedes sputtered to life. "And you'll be glad to know, sir. We've been receiving shipments of the new Roland two-seater. Damn good machine, I tell you."

"Ah, yes. I've heard about it. It's a fast machine, I hear."

"You got that right, sir. Clocks in at 165-kilometers per hour."

"You don't say?" Willi Wissemann stowed his bags in the backseat, got in the front and closed the door. He reached into his tunic pocket and flipped open his sterling cigarette case. "Care for a smoke, *Leutnant?*"

"No thank you, sir."

"Don't smoke?"

"Well, not cigarettes, anyway." Herzog revved the engine twice and gunned the gas and the Mercedes peeled away from the curb. "Never acquired the habit, I guess."

"That's a good thing." Wissemann took a deep drag.

"I do like an occasional cigar, though."

The Mercedes sped down the slushy thoroughfare to the aircraft supply depot. The weather here in France was still invariably cold and damp this time of year. Wissemann noticed there were still frosty hints of snow and ice on the ground everywhere. The sky was gray and overcast, burdened with cloudy strata. A chill breeze blew across the landscape, artillery echoed, guns cracked—the Western Front!

Inside the Mercedes, Wissemann sat stiffly, calmly smoking his Halpaus, feeling good to have a purpose again. The Air Service would give him a chance to really prove himself. Of course, he realized, getting posted to a section might take a few days, weeks, or maybe even a month. But it would give him time to acclimate himself to the lay of the land, give him time to adjust to life in the *Fliegertruppen*—as the German Imperial Air Service was known at that time.

Herzog swung the staff car around a curve and the aircraft park came into view. It was basically a large aerodrome complex next to a busy rail terminus. Wissemann could see huge wooden-constructed hangars, smaller huts and tents, and rows upon rows of parked aircraft, maintenance crews milling about in a purposeful manner. The outer perimeter was surrounded by thick hedgerows and a tall barbed-wire fence. A truncated, cloth cone mounted on a sturdy upright pole, known as a windsock, fluttered limply in the breeze, next to the red, white and black *"Reichskriegsflagge,"* the Imperial German War Flag. The flag flapped and curled masterfully on its tall, metal mast, its eagle seemingly willing to take fight at any moment.

The Mercedes braked to a halt at the front gate. A guard in a over-sized helmet and a Mauser rifle stepped out of the guard house, raising a halting hand. He was a thin youngster in a baggy *Bayern Bluse* uniform. He looked to be about seventeen or eighteen, in Wissemann's estimation.

"Halt! Password, please," said the guard stiffly.

"Ach! It's just me, Schiller... *Leutnant* Herzog," Herzog said in a half-annoyed voice. "Got a new man for the Pilot Pool—*Oberleutnant* Wilhelm Wissemann."

The guard snapped off a salute. "Of course, sir. Drive on!" Schiller tipped the barricade bar up and waved the staff car through.

Herzog accelerated, scoffing. "Schiller, that little idiot, he ought to know me by now."

"Formalities, I suppose?" Wissemann interposed.

"Nah. That kid's just playing too hard at soldier, that's all."

Wissemann grunted carelessly. He was driven through the gate down a perimeter road that rimmed the southern edge of the aerodrome's expansive field to a rectangular, two-sectioned building labeled: *6. ARMEE FLUGPARK-OBERKOMMANDO*—the 6th Army Flight Park, Commander's Headquarters. A little feeling of anticipation swelled up inside him. Today, he was officially an airman of His Majesty's Imperial Air Service, an aviator for the Fatherland; soon his career as a pilot would begin. The cigarette perched proudly in broad smiling lips. He was finally in his element.

"We'll have you check in with the *Kommandant*, first," Herzog said, as the Mercedes rolled to an abrupt stop. "He likes to personally greet each new pilot." He hopped out of the car, snatching up his clipboard, striding over to the entrance. "After that, we'll amble over to Stores and get you suited up with some proper flight gear and a cozy billet."

"Right." Wissemann extricated his lanky frame from the uncomfortable bucket seat and grabbed his bags—a leather valise and a canvas musette bag. "How long do you think it'll be until I'm posted to a flying section?"

"Maybe tomorrow, next week, next month. Who can say?"

Wissemann groaned. He hoped it wouldn't be a whole month.

"Probably very soon, I'm sure. The Brits have been thrashing us lately. We've had quite a few losses lately. I'm sure there's a section that needs a replacement pilot." Herzog bounded up the steps to the *Kommandant's* office and reached for the door. "This way, sir."

"I hope so. I want to get into action as soon as possible." Wissemann took a final puff of his Halpaus and flicked it to the ground. He was just about to stamp it out when Herzog interjected with a terse warning.

"Uh, I wouldn't do that if I were you, sir," said he.

"Huh?"

"The *Kommandant* would have a fit if he saw that."

"Oh. Right. Sorry." Wissemann wisely picked up the smoldering butt, cupping it in a gloved hand. "So careless of me."

"There's a butt-can right here at the door, sir." Herzog pointed with a wagging forefinger.

"Of course." Willi Wissemann grinned sheepishly and tossed the butt into the old army coffee tin at the edge of the doorway. "The *Kommandant*... is he a stickler for regulations?"

"Mostly." Herzog gestured with an urgent wave. "In you go, sir.

Wissemann launched up the steps and trod across the threshold into the hut with Herzog right on his heels. Inside, Wissemann was greeted by a tubby little noncom with a crew cut and round red face, who was parked comfortably behind a small desk and typewriter. The noncom immediately rose to attention, clicking his heels, nodding.

"Afternoon, gentlemen," he said respectfully.

"*Unteroffizier* Maier—this is *Oberleutnant* Wissemann," Herzog announced. "He's just joining us today. Straight from flight training. Get him squared away after his little chat with the *Kommandant*, aye?" He handed over Wissemann's order packet. "Here's his paperwork, Maier." Herzog sighed irritably, suddenly. "Ach! I just remembered something. I've got to run a quick errand."

"*Jawohl, Herr Leutnant,*" Maier replied. Boot heels clicked. He took the packet and set it down on his desk.

"I have to get back over to Personnel and get some clothing requisitions done, filled out, before mess call." Herzog turned for the door. "Nice to meet you, *Oberleutnant* Wissemann. Good luck. Hope you get posted quickly."

"Thanks, *Leutnant* Herzog—"

"Oh, and mess starts at eighteen hundred hours, sharp."

"Right."

"Perhaps I'll see you there?"

"Yes, yes. Probably so. I'm famished."

"Sir!" Herzog saluted.

Wissemann returned the salute.

Herzog exited the office.

"Alright, *Herr Oberleutnant,*" Maier said officiously, "I'll check with the *Kommandant,* see if he's not too busy. Have a seat there, for a moment. It'll be but a minute or two."

"Thank you, *Unteroffizier.*" Wissemann unbuttoned his overcoat and sat down in one of the two chairs provided. He peeled his leather gloves off and stashed them in a pocket.

Maier strode down the hallway leading to the *Kommandant's* office and gently tapped on the door. "*Herr Major...*" he announced briskly. "Do you have a moment, sir?"

There was a noisy grunt and then a reply: "What is it, Maier?"

"A pilot from training school, sir—here for your compulsory briefing?"

There was another noisy grunt, then: "*Ja, ja.* Come in. Let me have his paperwork."

"Yes, sir." *Unteroffizier* Maier went in, saluted, and handed over the order packet.

"Leave the door open, please," the *Kommandant* ordered gruffly.

"Yes, sir." Maier left the *Kommandant's* office and clumped back into the antechamber. He said to Wissemann: "He's going to look your packet over. Give him a moment, sir."

"Of course. Uh, may I smoke?"

"Hmm... better not, sir. The *Kommandant* isn't 'big' on cigarettes."

"Oh. Right." Wissemann fidgeted nervously.

Unteroffizier Maier sat down behind his typewriter and began pecking away, humming tunelessly.

A minute or two passed by...

"Maier!" the *Kommandant* shouted.

"Sir?"

"Send in *Oberleutnant* Wissemann!"

Maier turned to Wissemann. "He'll see you now."

Wissemann stood up and seized his bags. "Right."

"Leave your gear, sir," Maier instructed. "It'll be alright there."

Willi Wissemann nodded and dropped his bags. He straightened his tunic tails and stalked off down the hallway. His throat suddenly became very dry and his hands felt a little clammy. He stopped at the threshold and announced himself. "*Oberleutnant* Wilhelm R. Wissemann, reporting as ordered, sir!" His voice was crisp and clear.

"Come in, come in," the *Kommandant* replied hurriedly.

Wissemann tramped in stiffly, came to a crashing halt in front of the *Kommandant's* desk, saluted and then stood at attention. His chest swelled proudly and his chin rose square and stern. He blinked nervously and cleared his throat. He tried his damnedest to look calm and composed.

"Afternoon, *Oberleutnant,*" said the *Kommandant*. "I am Major Otto von Gottschalk.

"Afternoon, sir!"

"Very good, very good. At ease."

"Thank you, sir." Wissemann spread legs wide and clasped his hands behind his back.

The *Kommandant* looked the young officer over.

Oberleutnant Wilhelm Reinhardt Wissemann was a tall, slender man with broad shoulders, a ramrod posture reminiscent of a parade ground drillmaster, deep-set, blue eyes, eyes that possessed the icy gaze of an eagle soaring skyward for a kill. A well-formed, aquiline nose offset fiercely chiseled facial features and high cheekbones. There was a jagged scar which spread diagonally from his lower lip, ending up at the bottom of his chin, hinting at some forgone injury. A forelock of dark hair, pomaded and barbered neatly, balanced a fair complexion, which gleamed radiantly from a recently completed shave. Even in repose, Willi Wissemann was every bit the high-flown Teutonic warrior and certainly a fine looking example of Bavarian manhood—a gentlemanly German officer.

"Well, *Oberleutnant,* I see you've completed your training course with flying colors."

Wissemann smirked, wondering if the stern old Prussian realized he'd just quipped a little pun. But on second thought, probably not. He didn't look like the kind of man who made off-handed little jokes. Wissemann stiffened awkwardly. "Thank you, sir. I always try to do my best," he replied with a grim smile. He looked the *Kommandant* straight in the eye and took stock of the man who would be his commanding officer for a hopefully short stint at 6th Army *Flugpark*.

Major Otto August von Gottschalk, formerly a long-serving veteran of the Prussian 1st Lancer Regiment, cast a rather bluff and avuncular image. He was a hoary-haired man with a trim, snowy mustache and sullen, hazel eyes. He looked to be in his mid-forties, his bronzed complexion deeply lined and wrinkled with years of military service and middle-age. His red-piped M1910 Lancers officers' tunic was cleanly pressed and festooned with the Iron Cross, 1st-Class, a pilot's flying badge, and a row of highly polished brass buttons. His left hand ring finger was adorned with a shiny gold wedding band.

"That's what I like to hear, *Oberleutnant*." Von Gottschalk folded his fingers atop the desk and leaned back in his chair. "How many hours on single-seaters?"

Wissemann sighed. "None, sir."

"Hmm. No matter. We have plenty of two-seaters here that need to be ferried back and forth. The Eindeckers are always in short supply anyway. So, tomorrow, at zero-six hundred, sharp, we'll go up for a little test flight—see what you've learned. I'll take a 'backseat', let you put the aeroplane through its paces. Then after you've satisfied my sense of propriety, performed your duty efficiently here, I'll attach you to a flying section in the field. That clear?"

"*Jawohl, Herr Kommandant*." The edgy Bavarian stiffened, coughing, and inquired: "What will I be flying tomorrow, if I may ask, sir?"

"An old Aviatik B.II, I believe. Can't have you new lads cracking up the latest equipment."

"Oh. Right. I understand."

"Any more questions?"

"Uh... well—"

"Good. See *Unteroffizier* Maier, straightaway. He'll get you in a billet at the Officers' Barracks, get your paybook up to date, outfit you with some flight gear, etc, etc. Do your duty to my satisfaction here at AFP-6, and I'll see you get posted as soon as possible. Screw up, and you'll find yourself at the bottom of the queue. Is *that* clear *Oberleutnant* Wissemann?"

"*Jawohl, Herr Kommandant!*"

"Good. Dismissed."

"Thank you, sir. I'll do what—"

"Dismissed *Oberleutnant*." Von Gottschalk bit off Wissemann's reply quite curtly. "And close the door behind you, please."

"Yes, sir. Of course." Wissemann saluted, about-faced and paced out. He closed the door gently and returned to the antechamber, passing by *Unteroffizier's* Maier's desk, picking up his bags with a disquieted sigh. He shook his head gloomily. "Hmm..."

"All right, then. Is the *Kommandant* done haranguing you?" the tubby little noncom asked playfully. "I mean, for now, that is."

"For now?"

The chubby noncom laughed softly. "Oh, he's quite the martinet. But don't you worry, sir. You'll be fine."

Wissemann grumbled uneasily. "Well, if you say so, Maier."

WILLI WISSEMANN SLEPT fitfully that night at the Officers' Barracks, and rose at the sound reveille, 0500-hours sharp. After roll call, he dressed and went to mess. He did not eat much, just a black cup of coffee and a piece of canned fruit. Both were none too appetizing. He reported to Hangar D, on the farthest side of the aerodrome, as *Leutnant* Herzog had instructed him. He waited there for the *Kommandant* to appear.

The mechanics had already rolled out the old Aviatik and were prepping it for the flight. Wissemann stood around nonchalantly, puffing a cigarette. He was quite nervous. Then, exactly at 0600, Major von Gottschalk came tramping up, *Leutnant* Herzog in tow. The *Kommandant* was clad in a heavy, double-breasted leather jacket and flight helmet, goggles cocked up, a faded red scarf dangling loosely around his neck. He held a pair of wool gloves in a clenched hand, a grim expression on his face. He was ready for a morning of flying.

"Wissemann..." he said brusquely.

"*Herr Kommandant!*" Boot heels clicked. Wissemann saluted.

"Now, *Oberleutnant* Wissemann. Let's see what you've learned at flying school, hmm?" Von Gottschalk returned the salute. He turned to Herzog. "Is all his paperwork squared away, *Leutnant?* Pay booklet, life insurance, legal will, etc. etc?"

"*Jawohl, Herr Kommandant.*" Herzog's heels clicked assuredly. "*Oberleutnant* Wissemann is now officially a member of His Majesty's Imperial Air Service."

"Good." Von Gottschalk tied his scarf and buttoned up his jacket.

"He's by all odds, ready for his test flight, sir."

"I hope so."

Wissemann nodded, the Halpaus bobbing conspicuously.

Von Gottschalk grimaced detestably. "Get rid of that damned cigarette, Wissemann! Let's get ready for take-off."

"*Jawohl, Herr Kommandant!*" A nervous Willi Wissemann flicked the butt to the ground. He cringed immediately, realizing Major von

Gottschalk's aversion to cigarettes.

"Pick that up, immediately!" Von Gottschalk barked. "Or I'll have you on kitchen fatigues so damned quick, you won't know what the hell happened!"

Wissemann blushed bright red. *"Yessir!* Sorry, sir." He bent down and picked up the smoldering butt, crushed it and stashed it in his pocket. His throat went completely dry.

"Get in, Wissemann. You're the pilot."

"Jawohl, Herr Kommandant." Wissemann did as ordered and heaved his lanky frame into the rear cockpit of the old Aviatik two-seater. He situated himself uneasily and glanced over the control panel and cockpit, acclimating himself with the controls.

Major von Gottschalk climbed in the front cockpit.

The mechanics began the start-up procedures. A fitter took hold of Wissemann's harness straps and buckled him in snugly. He did the same for Major von Gottschalk. Now, both men were strapped in securely. The crew chief took up a position at the nose of the old aeroplane, grasping the propeller with both hands.

"Aus?" he called out. "Switch is off?"

"Switch is off," Wissemann repeated.

The chief turned the propeller through its full arc, drawing air into the cylinders. Wissemann turned the compression release handle back and announced: "Free." He then switched the magneto on. Soon dancing sparks formed their essential arc as he turned the magneto crank as rapidly as possible. The cylinders picked up these sparks, and the fuel ignited as the crew chief heaved the propeller. The Mercedes six-cylinder engine sputtered over in a cloud of blue smoke. The Aviatik shook itself like a wet dog, throbbing with tentative life force, then roared to full power. With the motor running, the air pump supplied enough pressure from the petrol tank so that the fuel flowed steadily to the carburetor.

Wissemann allowed the engine to warm for a full five minutes.

Von Gottschalk signaled for the chocks, and the crew chief yanked them clear of the wheels. "Alright, Wissemann!" he yelled, under the din of mechanical rumblings. "Let's go!"

The leather-clad Bavarian pulled the goggles down over his eyes and cocked his head to the left, so he could see out over the vertical exhaust stack, now exuding thick fumes, and advanced the throttle to the maximum. The Aviatik began rolling out onto the field. He kicked the rudder about and turned the old two-seater into the wind. The Aviatik traversed the field, bouncing gently, and after a run of three hundred meters, lifted into the air.

"Take her up to two thousand meters, Wissemann!" Von Gottschalk yelled, as he turned around in the seat to face his pilot. "Then we'll go through a few basic maneuvers!"

"*Jawohl, Herr Kommandant!*" Wissemann shouted back.

He eased back on the control stick and the Aviatik B.II began a slow, shuddering climb into the high blue. The three-bay, khaki and brown reconnaissance biplane responded stiffly to the controls. It was easy enough to steer around the sky, as the gangly Bavarian soon found out. He remembered flying an even older Aviatik at Schleissheim, and it seemed that this one handled no differently. It was not a maneuverable machine, flying more like a boat or a balky "apple-barge," as many German pilots liked to refer to the slow, unwieldy machines of the Imperial Air Service. The 120-horsepower Mercedes pulled the eleven-hundred-kilo barge across the sky at a ponderous one hundred kilometers per hour.

Climbing over the gloom of a thawing April countryside, composed mostly of dun and green woods, Wissemann gazed around the sky. There were but few clouds drifting about that morn. The heavy overcast from the day before had dissipated overnight. The sun was just a glowing red ball at that hour and it lit the sky in a pinkish hue. He looked down upon the expansive aerodrome below and got a rare birds-eye view of the buildings and hangars. Tiny ant-like figures milled about among white flyspeck aeroplanes. AFP-6 was certainly a busy place at the crack of dawn.

Already that morning, a train from Germany had chugged into the rail yard, its weighty freight cars packed to the gills with supplies and plane parts for the *Fliegertruppen;* disassembled aeroplanes chained to flatcars; fuel-tankers and ammo stores. Nearly everything a flying section could want, was being unloaded with uncanny speed and organization. The war on the Western Front was in high gear.

Fifteen minutes later, the old Aviatik B.II was buzzing along blissfully at two thousand meters.

Von Gottschalk shouted: "All right—put her into a few figure-eights, Wissemann!"

Wissemann obliged; the old Aviatik banked and turned about clumsily.

"Now a slip-turn!"

The Aviatik skirted into a neat little slip-turn.

"Good. Now, a barrel-roll!"

Wissemann rolled the old biplane over and around. It slowly corkscrewed through the air.

"Excellent!" Von Gottschalk nodded, quite pleased.

"Thank you, *Herr—*"

"Now let's see what you're really made of, *Oberleutnant!* A loop!"

A loop? Wissemann grimaced. The B.II wasn't really designed for such maneuvers. He nodded reluctantly and shoved the stick forward, putting the Aviatik in a steep dive. The balky biplane would need a lot more speed if it was to perform the maneuver properly. Down went the Aviatik. Down! Then, after the proscribed distance, Wissemann hauled back on the stick, easing it into his stomach. The aeroplane pulled up, curved over upside-down, and then slid into a shallow dive. He chuckled. A loop!

"Very good! Another!"

Another? Wissemann thought warily. Okay, whatever you say, *Herr Dummkopf!*

The Aviatik looped again.

"Not bad, *Oberleutnant!* Not bad at all!" Von Gottschalk elated spiritedly. "Now... how about stalling the machine into a spin!"

"A spin, *Herr Kommandant?*" Wissemann shouted, quite taken aback. "Really?"

"Yes! A spin!"

"*Jawohl!*"

Wissemann did as ordered. He cut the throttle, pulled back on the stick, stamped down on the rudder bar, until the aeroplane lost forward momentum and flicked into a spiraling tailspin. The Aviatik shuddered, spun around thrice, bumped, bucked and twirled, until it had fallen one thousand meters. At five hundred meters, Wissemann reversed the effects of the spin and leveled out. But to his lamentable chagrin, the old Mercedes engine suddenly sputtered and conked out. The propeller just ticked over slowly, windmilling powerlessly in the slipstream.

"Ach! Restart the motor! Quickly, Wissemann!" Von Gottschalk shrieked. "Restart the motor!"

"*Ja-ja, Herr Kommandant*—attempting that now!"

But the little six-cylinder would not start.

"Restart! *Verdammt! RESTART!*"

"Nothing doing, sir!"

Wissemann calmly jerked the old barge around in a wide, gliding turn and put the nose on course with the aerodrome. He was about a half a kilometer from the far edge of the field, drifting along at four hundred meters altitude. He figured he could just about make it.

"*Gott!* We're going to crash!" Von Gottschalk screamed.

"Don't worry, sir! I think we can make it!"

"Please, Wissemann! Get this barge down in one piece, and I'll post you anywhere you like! Quick as Mercury! I swear!"

Wissemann grimaced. He gripped the control stick firmly and kept the Aviatik on an even keel. The wind had shifted in his favor and it pushed the gliding two-seater along as if some great hand were guiding it. The wind whistled in the wires as the biplane drifted down another hundred meters, now on a beeline for the field. Up ahead a bosky hedgerow loomed directly in his path. But that was not the Bavarian's real worry. Telephone wires stretched across his glide path. Telephone wires! And down he went; three hundred meters; two hundred meters; one hundred meters. He was very close to the edge of the field now.

Von Gottschalk was squirming restlessly, grumbling, cursing, bobbing his head about worriedly. *"Lieber Gott! Ah-h-h-h-h-h-h!"* he muttered frantically. "Wissemann! Please!"

"Hang on, *Herr Kommandant!* Almost there!"

The Aviatik crossed the road delineating the far end of the field and zoomed over the telephone wires by barely a meter. The wheels skimmed the top of the hedgerow, snagging a few branches, finally coming to a rest on the frosty turf of the field after a jarring bounce. The aeroplane coasted along a few more meters before the tailskid came down, biting hard into the earth with a noisy jolt. The ancient bird finally came to a rolling stop. Mechanics, fitters, armorers, pilots and everyone else were already making a mad dash for the grounded Aviatik. They'd all heard the aeroplane's engine quit unexpectedly.

Von Gottschalk gasped. Wissemann sighed.

"Stupendous, Wissemann! Stupendous!" the old Prussian exalted.

Wissemann smiled. He whipped out his sterling cigarette case, flipped open the spring-loaded hinge and popped a Halpaus in his mouth. A match flared.

"Danke, Herr Kommandant. Care for a cigarette?"

Passed by FlugM Censor # 2677
Frau Ilse Magdalena von Linkhof
c/o Supreme Headquarters
6th Armee Flugpark-Valenciennes, France
To Berlin (Please forward)

Liebe Ilse!   4. May 1916

I hope this letter finds you well. All is fine here at the Front. Everything is working out as planned, I will soon be posted to a flying section. I passed yet another flying test a few days ago. I went up in an old Aviatik with a very fussy Prussian major and showed him that the Bavarian airman is as good as any. The flight, though, did not go without mishap. During a few basic maneuvers my motor conked out! But do not fret my dear, your sweet Willi dear got everything back down to earth in one piece...machine, the Major, and myself. It was quite the feat, I must say. The Major was honestly impressed. He says I have a great future in the Air Service. I think he is right.

How are things in Berlin? I'm sure the flowers are all in bloom by now. And I'm sure you and your parents are planning another fine summer vacation in Vienna. I trust your mother is well? And the General too? Sorry I spouted off a bit. I hope he wasn't too offended by my crude jokes. I am a bit of a wag sometimes. Please forgive me? Tell your mother I was very pleased with the chocolate and bottle of cognac she sent to the hotel after my graduation. It was a very thoughtful thing to do! Kiss her for me, will you dear? Give her my regards!

Once I arrive at my permanent base, dear, I'll send a telegram. But don't worry if it comes a bit late. I shall be very busy at the Front, I think. There may be little time for letters to friends, family, and fiancees. One day soon, my dear, we shall be together. I haven't forgotten my promise. War or no war, we shall wed and be the loving husband and wife! Mark my words, Liebchen. We will enjoy the bliss of holy matrimony very soon

Hochachtungsvoll, Willi

Chapter 2

✠

MAY 14, 1916. VON GOTTSCHALK WAS TRUE to his word. Willi Wissemann had only to spend a short, ten-day stint in the Pilot Pool. Early one morning, after ferrying an Albatros C.III to a front line combat section, he was called into the old Prussian's office. He was told, in all seriousness, he was to be assigned to a reconnaissance bombing section located in the Somme sector, near the French town of Quéant. Wissemann had to hold back a smirk. The Major's imperiously bluff announcement seemed comically at odds with the frantic mutterings of a fortnight ago. Von Gottschalk had displayed an uncharacteristic frailty when it seemed as though he might lose his life. As an eleven year Army veteran, Wissemann had known and seen plenty of officers who'd displayed an austere comportment in ideal situations, but seemed to fall apart quickly when things got too dangerous. He couldn't help but stare at the Major's Iron Cross and marvel. How had he won such a magnificent medal, what high-ranking fool at Staff had recommended one of Germany's highest decorations? And what brave deed had he done to garner such accolades? Wissemann could only stare and wonder.

Stuffy old pensioner!

"*Oberleutnant* Wissemann," von Gottschalk said. "Tomorrow at zero-six hundred, you will fly a new Roland to the aerodrome at Quéant. You've been posted to FFA-4b, 6th Army Sector. Your new section commander will be *Hauptmann* Hannes Hochstetter, a Bavarian, like yourself. He's an ex-cavalryman of good stock, I hear."

"I see," Wissemann replied huskily. "Thank you, sir."

"*Nah, nah,*" Von Gottschalk's hand fluttered deprecatingly. "Don't thank me, Wissemann."

"*Herr Kommandant?*"

"You can thank your lucky stars."

Wissemann scoffed silently. "Sir?"

"That was quite a miraculous landing you pulled off, *Oberleutnant* Wissemann. Quite miraculous!"

"Yes, but—"

"I was sure we had breathed our last, Wissemann. But the divine hand of God intervened."

"Well, *Herr Kommandant,*" Wissemann met Gottschalk's eyes grimly, defiantly. "I'd like to think my steady piloting hand had a *little* something to do with it. Don't you think, sir?"

"Whatever the reason, Wissemann." Von Gottschalk sniffed. "You displayed a cool head under the circumstances. You'll live a long time, have a long career, if you truly possess innate piloting skills and good fortune. Here's some gratuitous advice: if you insist on playing the wag, insist on bucking the system, go against the German Army's established ethos, you won't last a day. Obey and conform, and you'll go far, Wissemann. Understand?"

"*Jawohl, Herr Kommandant—*"

"Dismissed."

"*Sir-r-r-r!*" Boot heels clicked. Grim-visaged, Wissemann saluted, about-faced and left the *Kommandant's* office. He strode off to his quarters with a buoyant feeling; it was a good day and not a bad little war after all. So, it called for a quiet celebration. He was done for the day, his duties complete and that vintage bottle of cognac would do nicely now. His face was beaming proudly. Tomorrow he would once again be in the thick of things, soaring over the battlefield. Not as a common "potato-head" or just another company-level field officer, but as an aviator. That was something to be proud of, indeed. No more slogging it out in the trenches, no more crawling around on hands and knees, no more skirting barbed-wire entanglements or dodging shellfire. No more feeling dirty and helpless!

AT EIGHT O' CLOCK in the morning, May 7th, as the bloody battle of attrition for Verdun waned on miserably in its fourth month, Willi Wissemann was preparing to fly his first mission as pilot of a Roland two-seater. He had reached the aerodrome near Quéant just an hour before. He was a little tired, grimy and unshaven, but he believed in starting hard; he didn't expect himself to do otherwise. He met briefly with the operations clerk and stowed his gear in his assigned billet, a simple canvas tent, then reported to the mess tent. The members of FFA-4b sat before him in the mess. There were eleven of them—six pilots and five observers. The squadron owned five Albatros two-seaters and one brand new Roland C.II. Willi Wissemann looked the men over reticently. They had not solicited friendliness and he expected none. In the midst of men who should have been his comrades and countrymen, he felt alone—as he often was. He picked up the slip of paper which heralded the orders of the day and glanced over it: a bombing sortie in enemy territory.

"I am *Oberleutnant* Willi Wissemann," he said evenly. "Just in from the Pilot Pool at Valenciennes." He leaned forward, his eyes challenging the indifferent stares. "Who's leading the eight o'clock mission? I noticed that we're slated for a bombing sortie on the bridge at Cappy."

"You're leading the mission, *Oberleutnant*," one of the pilots spoke up. He was a ruddy-faced young man with blond hair and a pencil thin mustache. His name was *Leutnant* Landsberg.

"Me?"

"You're the ranking officer now."

"Oh, I see."

"We lost our *Flugzeugführer* yesterday, over Péronne."

"But I've never led an aerial formation. I mean, I'm basically fresh from flight school."

"No matter, *Oberleutnant*," another said. "You'll learn soon enough. We're all basically novices here."

"What about *Hauptmann* Hochstetter?"

"He doesn't fly any more."

"Why not?"

Landsberg smiled. "He's a 'pencil-pusher' now, you know. He's done his duty—grounded."

"Grounded?"

"That's right. Enemy anti-aircraft got him in the leg. He's under orders not to fly for a while."

"Oh." Wissemann nodded dumbly. "Retired, eh?"

"Uh, something like that."

Wissemann lit a cigarette. "Who's going to be my observer?"

"Ah, that's right," a fellow named Fritz Bärmann replied. "You need a back-seater, don't you?"

"That would be *Leutnant* Zemke," Landsberg interjected.

"Zemke? Who's he? Where is he?"

"Oh, he'll be here in a moment."

"He's an old hand. *Hauptmann* Hochstetter's former observer."

"Zemke's an expert gunner," declared Bärmann quite assuredly. "He's already got a claim pending with *Idflieg*. Shot down a Vickers just a few days ago."

Wissemann nodded. Zemke sounded like the perfect flying companion. He took a deep drag from his Halpaus, feeling a little nervous, wanting to get going as soon as possible. Waiting around idly always made him a bit edgy.

He remembered the waiting game in the trenches. A blistering artillery barrage always preceded the attack—a tactic often used for softening up enemy positions before the infantry assault. Round after round of high explosive shells would sail over the heads of the cowering infantryman and end up somewhere in the enemy trenches or, hopefully, well beyond. But sometimes they landed in the German lines. That was always a heartbreaker. It was always some poor slob who was due for a rest or a long leave that got it. Friendly fire didn't happen often but it did happen from time to time. Sometimes a "friendly" got hit by German gunfire.

Wissemann remembered one incident especially. A younger soldier had forgotten the password one night, on his way back from a rations-run, and was shot by his best friend. The poor soldier died the next morning. The lad who'd shot him was so distraught, he put a bullet in his own head the next day. Bad business. Alas, Willi Wissemann grimaced. War was a never-ending hell.

"*ACHTUNG!*" Landsberg yelled.

Everyone bolted to attention.

Hauptmann Hochstetter strode in. "At ease, gentlemen," he ordered. "Here's the latest intelligence from 6th Army *Kofl*."

Hauptmann Hannes Hochstetter was a tall, broad-shouldered man. He almost seemed too old to be a pilot, in Wissemann's estimation. A seriously receding hairline, a trim, graying mustache, a fine face creased with deep lines, betrayed him as a middle-aged man. And as former cavalry officer, he wore the uniform of the 5th Bavarian Light Horse. Hochstetter laid a grid map out on the table, smoothing out the creases with a steady hand, then leaned over, resting his willowy forearms and elbows on the tabletop.

"Okay. Gather round, men," he enjoined calmly. "We've been tasked with another bombing sortie."

The eleven men congregated around the table.

Hochstetter looked around. "Where is Zemke?"

"Uh, the latrine, sir?" Landsberg replied, shrugging.

"Still with the stomach problems?"

Leutnant Bärmann nodded. "I guess so, sir."

"Poor lad—"

"Here I am, *Herr Hauptmann!*"

A short, stocky man in flying leathers threw the tent flap back and came tramping in. He was a pale-faced, peaked-looking twenty-four year old with blond, close-cropped hair and a lantern jaw. Zemke strode up to the table, gloves and goggles in one hand, flying helmet in the other.

"Just spreading some latrine rumors," he quipped.

Hochstetter and Landsberg chuckled. Wissemann smiled.

"Zemke..." said Hochstetter, "this is *Oberleutnant* Wissemann. Your new *chauffeur*, see?"

"Aha!" Zemke turned to face his new pilot. He gave a quick nod and clicked his heels. *"Herr Oberleutnant,* glad to make your acquaintance. I am *Leutnant* Franz Zemke." The diminutive observer-officer proffered his hand affably.

Wissemann bowed gallantly then shook Zemke's hand. "The pleasure's all mine, *Leutnant.* Willi Wissemann—at your service. Glad to meet you."

"So. We'll be flying together today, eh? Dandy."

"That's right, Zemke," Hochstetter interjected. "And *Oberleutnant* Wissemann will be leading today's sortie against the bridge at Cappy."

"Cappy?" Zemke groaned. "Again?"

"That's right. *Kofl* won't rest until it's knocked out, *Junge.*"

Wissemann grinned, admiring Hochstetter's jaunty bearing.

Hochstetter's towering frame rose up from the table. He was a legendary commander among the men of the flying section, a fine gentleman and a dashing figure. Even though he was a good five years senior to Wissemann, and ten years older than most of the men under his command, Hochstetter always maintained a lighthearted, youthful interaction with all his subordinates, including the noncoms.

"And this new fellow is going to lead the *Kette?*" asked Zemke.

"He is the ranking officer under me." Hochstetter patted his right leg. "I can't lead it. That bit of Limey ack-ack didn't leave much, now did it, Zemke?"

"Nah, Herr Hauptmann. I guess not," Zemke replied, a little grin forming on his cheeks. He turned to Wissemann and said: "Ever lead a bombing sortie, *Oberleutnant?*"

"Well, not really." Willi Wissemann reddened, suddenly becoming very self-conscious of his lack of experience. He sighed anxiously, folding both arms over his chest. "T-This is my... first duty-posting to a flying section."

Zemke scoffed softly, his eyes widening a bit. "Hmm... I see. Well, just stick to the flight plan, okay? I'll lead you through the whole thing. Nothing to it, really."

"Yes, Wissemann," Hochstetter said with a broad grin. He clapped the Bavarian tyro on the back. "Follow *Leutnant* Zemke's directions to the letter and you'll come out just fine."

"*Danke, Herr Hauptmann.*"

"Okay, gentlemen, let's take out that bridge, aye?" Hochetter's eyes scanned over each man's face. "You'll have no support from the Eindeckers today. It's our show, men. FFA-4b has been given the sole responsibility for destroying that bridge."

"Same attack routine, sir?" Landsberg asked.

"Correct. Get up to three thousand meters before you cross over in enemy territory, then slip down below one thousand and release your bombs over target. Drop the whole load at once. I don't want you men lollygagging around with all that damned ack-ack the *Engländers* are bound to throw up at you. And keep on the lookout for enemy scouts. They're sure to be lurking around that sector. And get back safely, right? The crew that knocks out the bridge will receive a bottle of champagne from me. Clear?"

Boot heels clicked. "*JAWOHL, HERR HAUPTMANN!*" the assembled men shouted in near unison.

"Man your machines, gentlemen." Hochstetter clapped his hands. "It's time to earn your flight pay. Good luck, lads!"

Twelve men marched out of the mess tent out to their waiting aircraft. Wissemann found his machine, and he and *Leutnant* Zemke clambered aboard. Within minutes, six German two-seaters were throbbing at the chocks, ready for takeoff: five Albatros C.I's and one brand new Roland C.II. A signal gun cracked and a green flare arced across the dewy field. Six machines roared with power.

"Here we go," Wissemann said to himself. "*Hals-und Beinbruch!*"

AT THREE THOUSAND METERS the sky was a vivid blue, and the patches of cumulus drifting below hovered like idly grazing cows. The Roland's throaty rumble was powerful and even and the wind whispered lazily through the rigging. Up here, Wissemann discovered, with deep satisfaction, his senses were finely tuned and alert. The Mercedes six-cylinder seemed to purr with a throbbing contentment as it turned over and over at twelve hundred revolutions per minute.

The pale blue two-seater's all-wood fuselage had earned the

aircraft the nickname "Walfisch" or whale. The fuselage had a sleek, oval shape made up of the normal wood formers and longerons. An unusual feature of the Roland was the placement of the upper wing; it was integrated with the fuselage. Of course, Wissemann found upward and sideways viewing quite outstanding. But downward visibility on landing was seriously compromised. He'd nearly cracked up the "Walfisch" landing at Quéant, the large single inter-wing struts blocking his view. The purpose of the little side windows was to facilitate viewing and defense. But he found these lacking too. He couldn't quite "feel" the ground at the end of the glide path to landing. The nose-heavy aircraft almost plowed in and flipped over.

For early May, it was a fine day as the *Kette* of six German two-seaters spread out in a loose wedge across the sunny sky, gently rising and falling on invisible air currents, on a direct southwestern heading for the Somme River. *Leutnant* Zemke hunkered down quietly in the rear cockpit; Wissemann saw him in the rear-view mirror that was mounted on the forward-aft section of the fuselage. Zemke periodically glanced at his wristwatch, likely noting the time it was taking to reach the target area. He was a peculiar sort, Wissemann quickly realized, seeming to have a nervous energy bordering on compulsive anxiety. Zemke was constantly readjusting himself in his seat, checking and rechecking his Parabellum machine gun, glancing at his compass or map, doing everything but sitting still. He was quite the fidgety type, almost too comical to watch.

Wissemann was still grinning from ear to ear when something flashed off to his right, erupting in a ear-splitting echo. Ack-ack! The British gunners had seen them! They were ranging their shots from hidden artillery guns down below in the brumous gloom of the front lines. Little blossoms of red-black erupted all over the sky around the formation of German two-seater biplanes.

Zemke bolted upright and rapped Wissemann on the shoulder. "All right, *Oberleutnant!*" he shouted. "It's going to get a little rough for a few minutes. But don't worry. It's all harmless enough!"

Wissemann scoffed and thought to himself: how can someone shooting artillery shells at you be harmless? The shelling was almost as bad as what he'd endured on the ground as an infantryman. He glanced across the sky at the other aircraft in formation and noted the ostensibly calm bearing of the crews. They plowed on through the curtain of fire as if nothing were happening as puffs of black smoke began to dot the sky around them.

"Okay, *Oberleutnant!*" Zemke shouted again, "Take evasive action with some zigzagging and banking! Let's not give them too easy of a target, eh?"

"What?" Wissemann yelled huskily. The noise of the engine and the buffeting slipstream was nearly deafening.

Zemke leaned in closer. "*I SAID:* take some evasive action with some slow zigzagging and banking!

Wissemann nodded. He jerked the stick over in a bank and began a series of masterful maneuvers designed to throw off the British gunners. The Roland wafted via the air like a great blue whale swimming through a sea of roiling fire, banking and rolling gracefully while shell after shell exploded around it. The other machines in the *Kette* began to follow suit. Six German aeroplanes lolled through the blackening sky—six canvas kites on a lazy Sunday afternoon.

Then as quickly as it had started, the guns fell silent. Only to be replaced by another disquieting sound. Machine gun fire! Wissemann shot a glance over his shoulder and saw the trouble. Six de Havilland D.H. 2 scouts were sliding down a sunbeam, their Lewis guns spewing hot lead. Zemke had already seen them and was hacking away with his Parabellum. His 7.92-millimeter machine gun barked fitfully, slinging slug after slug at the dark brown, lattice-tailed scouts.

Wissemann saw the D.H.'s fan out into three pairs, wheeling into position behind their potential targets. They were ugly little birds with frail-looking tail booms and bathtub-like fuselages. Their exposed rear-mounted 9-cylinder rotary engines "pushed" them along nimbly and gave their pilots a clear and unobstructed field of fire. Drum-fed Lewis machine guns blinked angrily as .303-caliber tracer rounds streaked across the sky.

CR-TAT-TAT-TAT-TAT! CR-TAT-TAT-TAT-TAT!

Wissemann heard a few rounds zing through the wires and one thud into the fuselage.

"Take evasive action!" Zemke shouted.

"Say again?"

"*Gott Verdammt!* Shake this Tommy off our tail! Now!"

"Of course!" Wissemann shouted back, a bit riled by Zemke's terse invective.

He heeled the Roland over in a tight bank and fishtailed into a slewing skid, almost stalling into a spin. Zemke lurched backwards clumsily, grasping for dear life, swearing bitterly. The attacking D.H. tried to follow but its forward momentum caused it to overshoot. Zemke watched it zoom by and pull up in a climbing turn. He swiveled the Parabellum and squeezed off a quick burst. The smoking bullets marched up the lower wing and bit off a piece of the wingtip. The D.H. rolled over in a dive and sped away in the opposite direction, minus a few centimeters of wing.

Zemke jerked his gun around and popped off another burst at the second Britisher, but missed. The Roland banked awkwardly. "C'mon, Wissemann! Stay on course for the target! These Tommies won't hang around forever." He cocked and cleared his gun.

"Right! Staying on course!" Wissemann glanced at his compass and steered to a southwestern course, towards the Somme. "How much further now, Zemke?"

"Maybe five kilometers! That's the Vaux Wood down below us! We're almost there!"

Wissemann saw the nearest Albatros two-seater suddenly stumble out of level flight, flames gushing from its engine compartment, a D.H. clinging close behind, its gun operating with deadly efficiency. As he watched, he saw the observer of the Albatros crawl free of the smoldering cockpit, slide along the turtle-back, and roll off into empty sky. The Albatros appeared to bulge at the seams, then literally disintegrated in a fiery explosion. The spinning pieces dissipated in the buffeting wind, burning out quickly.

"GOTT! Those poor slobs!" Wissemann cursed.

"Damned Tommies!" Zemke snorted rancorously. "That was Mayer and König!"

"Friends of yours—"

"Stay on course!"

Wissemann's mouth clamped down tightly. He eased the stick forward and put the Roland in a long dive; he'd seen the Somme River looming below, its glistening green waters reflecting in the morning sunlight. The remaining four Albatroses nestled in behind and slid into a long dive too, slowly losing ground to the superior speed of the new Roland, the D.H.s still in hot pursuit. Then the ack-ack started up again. Puffs of blackened smoke began exploding in the sky close by.

"All right, Wissemann!" Zemke barked as he leaned in close over his pilot's shoulder. "Get this crate down to one thousand, level off, and make a beeline for that bridge!"

"Right!"

"Steer to, two-seven-five! Follow the Somme—west! It'll lead right up to the bridge!"

"Two-seven-five. Got it!"

"Keep this buzzard as level as possible once we make the attack run! Then I'll release the eggs, hopefully on target. The rest of the Kette will do the same. They're following your lead, Wissemann. So keep it steady as she goes! Okay?"

"Steady as she goes!" Wissemann replied comprehensibly.

A D.H. zoomed in close, rattling off a quick burst. Bullets whistled around Wissemann's ears. He heard his observer swear and then the Parabellum answered in retort.

"Ach!" Zemke grunted and fired. *TOK-TOK-TOK! TOK-TOK-TOK!* "Take that, you Limey *Schweinehund!*"

The British-built biplane rolled wildly to avoid the return gunfire. Zemke's volley hit the enemy aeroplane square in the nacelle. The flaming bullets chewed up the cockpit coaming and shattered the tiny windscreen the pilot was hunching behind. Blood sprayed up in the slipstream. The pilot, obviously wounded, slunk down in his seat and the D.H. spun down out of control briefly. It tumbled down about a thousand meters, then leveled out, apparently still under control but flying north now.

"Ah-hah! That volley got him! Saw the blood!" Zemke reloaded his machine gun.

"Look! There!" Wissemann shouted, pointing. "The bridge!"

Zemke spun around in his cockpit. "Finally! What's our altitude?"

"One thousand!"

"Excellent! Alright, keep it steady now! We're on the attack run!"

Zemke signaled frantically, jerking his arm down in a preset hand signal. The other machines zoomed down above the river following Wissemann's Roland, closing the five hundred meter gap slowly. The D.H.s suddenly cut for home, the British flight leader firing a green flare from his Very pistol. The Britishers re-formed, climbing away, seemingly content to abandon their attack.

But Zemke knew the real reason.

Suddenly, every gun in the Somme River valley seemed to open up—artillery, machine gun fire, small arms, everything! Smoking shells whizzed through the air from every direction like a swarming hive of bees. But the Roland droned on, not a round struck it. Wissemann's hand held the control stick firmly, gripping the throttle with the other, a grim figure of determination. Zemke left the gun and crouched down in the cockpit.

"I'm going to arm the bombs!" he shouted. "Once we get close enough, I'll pull the release lever. Pray for a hit!"

"What? Say again!"

"I'm going to arm the bombs!"

"Right!"

Zemke armed the Roland's four 12.5-kilogram, high-explosive bombs by pulling the pins from their noses, which were arranged horizontally in a rack near his right knee. This would free the screw-type fuse, which was actuated by centrifugal force; the necessary spinning motion of the bomb being imparted by fins in its tail helped stabilize the bomb in its fall. Once the bombs were ready, he sat upright, his head barely above the edge of the cockpit. He reached for the bomb release lever.

"Steady on, Wissemann!" he shouted. "Almost there..."

The anti-aircraft was deafening.

Willi Wissemann hunched down over the stick. The Mercedes was at max power, its pistons and rocker arms hammering steadily. He saw the bridge, it was jammed with traffic. Trucks, cars, troops and horse-drawn wagons of all kinds scurried across hurriedly, alerted by now of the impending aerial attack. Rounds of all calibers continued to spiral towards the German formation, which was now down below a thousand meters, one aeroplane behind the other, engines roaring magnificently.

"Here—we—go!" Zemke announced shrilly. He yanked the bomb release lever. *"BOMBS... AWAY!"*

Four high-explosive bombs whistled down towards the bridge. Wissemann banked and climbed the Roland north so he could hopefully see the results. He jerked his head over a shoulder just in time to see four fountains of flying foam jet high into the sky. All four bombs had missed!

"*Scheisse!*" Zemke cursed bitterly. "Damned goose-eggs!"

"Couldn't you have aimed them a little better?"

"What?"

"Couldn't you have aimed them a *little* better!"

"Aimed them better?" Franz Zemke scoffed. "And what the hell with, eh? "

"I don't know? Something! You mean to tell me, we don't have some sort of aiming device aboard this apple-barge? "

"*NO!* Just my little blue peepers! That's all!" Zemke's reply was as bitter as it was ironic.

"*Lieber Gott!*" Wissemann huffed angrily and grit his teeth. "Well, that's just plain ridiculous!"

"Kiss my foot!"

"Take a running jump at yourself!"

Just as Zemke was about to hurl another abuse, he saw Bärmann's Albatros zoom in low and release its payload—square on target. A tremendous explosion, then another, rocked the bridge. A cloud of smoke and debris leaped into the air. Two of the four bombs dropped hit the target. The bridge buckled violently then collapsed in a smoldering heap of splintered wood and crumbling concrete. All sorts of pedestrian traffic and mechanical transport slid into the murky waters of the Somme. Men moaned and horses shrieked. A cloud of thick, black smoke roiled up into the morning sky. The three other Albatroses flew over and dropped their bombs but with little effect. The bridge had already been knocked out.

A successful mission indeed!

"Hey-ho!" Zemke cheered. "That was magnificent!"

"Right. Mission accomplished." *Oberleutnant* Willi Wissemann grumbled and banked the Roland back on a course for the aerodrome at Quéant. The sudden reversal of fortune had tempered his anger. But only a little. He stewed silently. Zemke! That damnable little jackass, he raged mutely. *Gott Verbot!* I'm a superior officer!

Franz Zemke kept his eyes glued to the burning bridge, nodding gleefully. "Well-well-well. Looks like 'ole Fritz Bärmann and Georg Vordemfelde will be sipping champagne with Hochstetter, tonight." he said, then cracked: "Guess they didn't need a bomb-sight, eh?"

An enraged Willi Wissemann bit his tongue.

HAUPTMANN HOCHSTETTER poured champagne into two crystal flûtes, handed one to *Leutnant* Bärmann, then handed one over to *Leutnant der Reserve* Vordemfelde. He sat down in a mess chair and poured himself a glass full. The champagne, a glistening green bottle of Moët and Chandon, sparkled like liquid gold in the delicate stemware. The officers of FFA-4b had all gathered in the mess, a large canvas tent next to the orderly room, after a special meal of stuffed cabbage rolls and potatoes, all to toast the two lost crewmen and the destruction of the bridge.

Willi Wissemann sat alone, sipping cognac, smoking a Halpaus and trying his best to appear nonchalant about the whole affair. Somehow, he thought, it ought to be himself savoring those effervescent little bubbles. No aiming device? Unbelievable!

Hochstetter raised his glass high and made a toast.

"To Mayer and König," he said. "May they rest in peace."

"*Pros't!*"

"*Bottoms up!*"

"And to a job well done—Bärmann and Vordemfelde!"

"*Pros't!*"

"Hear, hear!"

Wissemann eyed the lucky squadron members with resentful eyes. He was still fuming about the day's action. *Leutnant* Zemke's rather off-handed manner had irked him to no end. He'd wanted to tear into Zemke when the Roland finally touched down, making up his mind to do so. But a whirlwind of elation had swept over the squadron once Bärmann and Vordemfelde deplaned and explained their success in wild, hubristic running commentary. Everyone was in a state of euphoria. Wissemann wisely held his tongue. And now the little man from Diessen was absent from the festivities. He had promptly skirted off to town looking for a little action and some female companionship after the debriefing and a quick scrub. Wissemann sighed heavily and shrugged. Oh well. A new man must abide by the codes of patience and probity until the *Staffel* atmosphere was thoroughly sniffed out.

"*Oberleutnant* Wissemann!" Hochstetter beckoned loudly, "Come. Sit. Have a glass of champagne with us, won't you?"

"Well, I..."

"Yes, Wissemann. Please join us," Bärmann pleaded.

"C'mon. There is plenty. You led a successful bombing sortie today. You're a bona fide member of this flying section now." Hochstetter produced another flûte from a rickety, old bar cart and proceeded to fill it up. "This is a fine vintage. I've been saving it for just such an occasion."

Wissemann stubbed out his cigarette, rose from his chair and sauntered over to the three men, pulled up another chair and sat down. "My, my, champagne. The Air Service certainly does have its advantages."

"It certainly does!" exclaimed Vordemfelde.

Hauptmann Hochstetter slid the bubbling stemware over to Wissemann. "A job well done today, Wissemann. Drink up."

"Thank you, sir." Wissemann took a little sip. "Ahh... excellent."

"Zemke told me that you handled yourself quite well today, for a tyro, *Oberleutnant* Wissemann."

"He did?"

"That's right. The new Roland is not an easy bird to fly, I hear."

"But he—"

"Zemke said you're the best he's ever seen, hands down. To fly against such heavy anti-aircraft and overwhelming odds is one thing..." Hochstetter grinned, "but to go up against the great Major Hawker, is quite another."

"Major Hawker?"

Bärmann added: "Those D.H. scouts we ran into over the Somme were part of Major Hawker's elite Squadron No. 24—he himself is an ace with many victories. Much like our Boelcke and Immelmann. A very dangerous man."

"Really?" Wissemann was dumbfounded. He had to honestly

admit he knew nothing of this Major Hawker fellow or his elite Squadron No. 24. "I suppose I'm a little ignorant when it comes to the enemy air services and their aces. I really didn't know such a man existed."

Vordemfelde and Bärmann laughed.

"Well, anyway, Wissemann," Hochstetter said with a big grin. "Zemke was quite impressed with the way you handled your machine in combat today. *Pretty smooth*—those were his exact words."

"*Humph...* I thought he was annoyed with me."

"Nah!" Bärmann interjected. "Remember: Zemke is a real hard-ass up there in the sky, a real hothead sometimes. But on the ground, he's a charmer—harmless as a kitten."

Everyone laughed and nodded.

"Welcome to FFA-4b." Hochstetter's champagne glass rose up in tribute. "Keep up the good work, and *you* may even one day become a great Hawker or Boelcke. *Prost!*"

"Maybe, perhaps."

"*Prost!* To the aces, Hawker and Boelcke," Bärmann exhorted bathetically.

"Hear, hear!" Vordemfelde cheered.

"To the aces." Wissemann tilted his flûte upwards and drained it.

The tent flap flew open and *Unteroffizier* Dieter Dietz strode in, holding a piece of paper. Dietz was the squadron orderly. He came to a halting step, saluted, and said: "*Herr Hauptmann*—the message center just received orders from 6th Army *Kofl.*"

"Oh?" Hochstetter looked up, eyes squinting warily.

"Yes, sir. They want photos of today's little bombing exhibition, first thing tomorrow morning." Dietz handed Hochstetter the typewritten order.

Hochstetter glanced over the order. "Hmm, so they do."

"The *Kommandeur* also commended us on a successful mission." Dietz smirked impishly. "He said Field Marshall von Rupprecht was certainly pleased."

Hochstetter scoffed softly. "Indeed. That's why I'm here in France. To please his Majesty, Field Marshall von Rupprecht," he quipped, his words bitingly ironic. "Anything else?"

"Yes, sir." Dietz nodded. "We're to ferry all the old Albatros C.Is to AFP-6 for disposition, in exchange for newer C. III models. Not all at once, of course."

"Of course." *Hauptmann* Hochstetter rolled his eyes. He turned to face Wissemann. "*Oberleutnant* Wissemann..."

"*Herr Hauptmann?*"

"You want to be in charge of that duty? You, and uh... *Leutnant* Landsberg?"

"Yes, sir. Of course," Wissemann replied instantly.

"Since you know the route to AFP-6, and all?" Hochstetter rose from his chair and moved to the exit. "Don't worry, you'll get to fly a combat sortie somewhere in between."

"Not worried, sir," Willi Wissemann replied evenly. "After today's action, I'm not in such a hurry to get shot at again." He chuckled. "Well, not so soon, at least."

Hauptmann Hochstetter winked. "Good man, Wissemann. We don't need heroes around here. Just pilots."

Chapter 3

✠

JUNE 10, 1916. OVER THE NEXT FIVE WEEKS, Willi Wissemann flew countless reconnaissance flights as well as several artillery-spotting sorties, all in support of 6th Army. When the Western Front settled into static trench warfare at the end of '14, the role of artillery became increasingly more important, being one of the few ways to get at the British trenches, machine gun emplacements, supporting battery positions and supply lines. Balloon observation had grown rapidly and assisted greatly in spotting for artillery barrages. But even at one thousand meters and higher, it was difficult at long range to see into or through solid objects such as thick woods, villages, and terrain.

During the early phases of the campaign, Wissemann and the aircraft of FFA-4b were increasingly used as spotters against hidden ground targets, although the process was severely hampered by the clumsy coordination between aircraft and battery. The spotting aircraft had to fly back to the battery and drop written messages that adjusted the artillery fire. It then had to return to its spotting position and repeat the process all over again, until the target was destroyed. Incredibly tedious work!

But the miracle of wireless transmission was not unknown to the German airman, and FFA-4b began receiving wireless transmitting hardware to use in cooperation with batteries that were equipped with receiving units. The size of the wireless equipment had been too ungainly and heavy for the earlier unarmed B-type aircraft. With less powerful motors, they'd had a load limitation and only the wireless receiver could be carried. When these cumbersome aircraft had proven the technique of wireless spotting, enemy aircraft and anti-aircraft soon posed a serious threat. Better aircraft were needed.

The new Rolands and Albatros two-seaters, with larger engines, had more power and could carry a wireless sending unit, defensive machine guns, more fuel and better photographic equipment.

Nevertheless, the existing Field Aviation Sections had not been trained for the specific task of artillery spotting. Therefore, by April, FFA-4b had been re-designated, FAA—*Feldflieger Abteilung Artillerie.* Then, much later, the designation was just shortened to FA-4b, for ease of record keeping. The unit was listed with a strength of three Roland C.II's and three Albatros C.III two-seaters, and the crews retrained accordingly. That "retraining" was more like on-the-job-training.

FA-4b had been commissioned in January by the War Ministry, by a special army order. Several other squadrons were authorized too. A large number of recruits had been processed at the basic and advanced training levels so that organization did not begin until the end of March '16 at FEA-2 (Flying Replacement Section No. 2) in Schneidemühl, Germany, and was completed by mid April. During this recruitment period, *Hauptmann* Hochstetter was appointed squadron commander. He was a qualified pilot and observer, and his experience included service with several other aviation units, as well as his original cavalry regiment. The squadron received a draft of one hundred noncoms and enlisted men from the 2nd Army Corps district. Initial equipment issued included three Opel motor cars, two BMW motorcycles, six Daimler aircraft-carrying flatbed trucks, a wireless truck, and a covered workshop vehicle.

The aircraft and crews had been sent to the Front ahead of the convoy of men and material. *Leutnant* Landsberg had been responsible for the convoy which left Schneidemühl on the morning of April 16, 1916. The column arrived at the aerodrome at Quéant two days later and FA-4b was officially mobilized. *Unteroffizier* Dietz told Wissemann all this during his initial familiarization briefing. The Bavarian airman realized relievedly he had not been so "new" after all!

On this Friday morning, he found himself in the cockpit of his Roland, high over Fricourt, flying escort for *Leutnant* Bärmann and his observer, Georg Vordemfelde. They were directing an artillery barrage via wireless in a two-seat Albatros equipped with a new transmitting unit. One of the purposes of the new Rolands, in addition to its regular duties, was to provide escort for the *Staffel's* three Albatroses. The idea of escorting artillery spotting aircraft, particularly during an artillery shoot, as Wissemann understood, was to permit the observer in the spotting aircraft the chance to concentrate on plotting the drop of shells and transmitting results without having to worry about enemy scouts. If they did show up, Bärmann had been previously instructed to join up with Wissemann and the mission would be aborted. If the enemy scouts persisted, Wissemann had been ordered to break off and engage the offending aircraft, while Bärmann's aircraft dived for the safety of friendly lines. The "Walfisch" was well suited for limited offensive action. It was a good enough escort aircraft, as fast or faster than most Allied scouts, and its forward-firing 7.92-millimeter Maxim added extra firepower to the already potent rear-mounted Parabellum. Most Rolands were issued in ones and twos for this purpose.

FA-4b now owned three Rolands.

Wissemann leveled off at two thousand meters. The long flat rays of the dawning sun were pinkish-orange, the landscape below was a mosaic of acutely contrasting greens and purples. The thick, pungent exhaust mixture rolling back from the Mercedes was, in the rarefied air, an ambrosia of oil and lacquer and new metal odors that spoke of the Roland's virginal newness. Wissemann was again piloting a new machine. LFG—the aircraft's manufacturer—had already modified the original design with a major change to increase the tail plane's surface area. The newly painted dark-green and red-brown machine was designated the C. IIa, and it was the first model of a batch of ninety-five to reach the Front. It was especially delivered by Major Gottschalk himself! And since Wissemann was the ranking flying officer of the section, he was always invited to have first dibs on all new aircraft. His original Roland had been wrecked by a novice pilot who'd been making a routine test flight, gauging the aircraft's newly overhauled Mercedes engine.

Both plane and pilot were lost.

Circling back towards the Front, Wissemann moved the control column forward, and the rounded pug-nosed spinner and the odd "ocarina" shaped exhaust stack sank away. The deep earthy colors of high summer came rushing up at him, the buffeting slipstream puffing out his cheeks, the wind howling in his ears.

Franz Zemke, as usual, was quite restless. He generally hated escort sorties, as they gave him little to do but keep on the lookout for enemy aircraft. And so far, none had appeared, much to his chagrin. But his Parabellum stood, loaded and ready, nevertheless.

Bärmann's Albatros methodically motored along the front line directing artillery fire into the British lines. Shells arced across the pale blue at regular intervals. It seems that a recently snapped reconnaissance photo had uncovered an interesting development in the enemy's troop movements. Reinforcements were pouring in at an alarming rate. This could only mean one thing, Hochstetter had announced during the morning briefing: The British were planning a major offensive!

The foxy old ex-cavalry officer surmised it was an answer to General von Falkenhayn's monumental assault on Verdun. Verdun had been selected because of its exposed flanks and relatively weakly held front line on either side of the Meuse River. The Somme sector had been uncannily quiet since then. Hochstetter knew this period of supposed inactivity on the part of the British marked a calm before the impending storm. It was never known to fail. And as for the Frenchies, he knew their hubris would never permit the ancient fortress city of Verdun to fall, and they would, therefore, commit all of their reserves to defend it. France, he averred confidently, would be "bled white" and ultimately sue for peace.

So. The British had to do something to relieve the pressure on Verdun. The French knew it, Hochstetter knew it, the German High Command knew it. And every German soldier down to the lowliest private knew it. The airman of FA-4b certainly knew it too. Day after day they had flown over the battle lines and witnessed the curious build up—little ants hard at work—all visible from three thousand meters; a lofty bird's eye view.

Franz Zemke cocked and cleared his gun. He was ready for action.

"Wissemann!" he shouted hotly, "we've got company. Look, there!" He was pointing to two gnat-like specks approaching from the west, about a thousand meters higher.

Wissemann craned his neck, adjusting his goggles.

"Aha! I see them!"

Zemke fired a warning flare from his signal pistol, alerting Bärmann and Vordemfelde. They immediately broke off their transmission and made a long banking dive for the German lines. The Roland, in turn, banked sharply, following the Albatros' descent.

The two specks grew larger and became quite recognizable. Nieuports! Their pallid olive and brown paint jobs and red, white and blue cockades glinted dully in the expanding sunlight. Their buzzing Gnome rotaries grew louder and louder and more threatening as they approached. They were both armed with single, wing-mounted Lewis guns; Wissemann could already hear the Britishers test firing them with short warming bursts. He advanced the throttle to full power and the Roland thundered forward at a more quickened pace. He also cleared and charged his single Maxim, hoping he might use it this morning. Already, Zemke was using his. Wissemann could hear the retort of quick, staccato bursts crackling from the Parabellum. He knew the Nieuports were drawing near. Out front, he could see Bärmann's Albatros winging low for the German lines. The new, pale-blue C.III seemed to lumber along lackadaisically. Nevertheless, Vordemfelde was at its rear machine gun, poised for action.

The guns below were strangely silent now, as they seemed to sense aerial combat was about to commence. A hundred thousand eyes were certainly staring into the pale blue yonder that was to soon become a stage for brutal aerial combat. Willi Wissemann could sense their presence; he felt their curious eyes glaring up at him, in awe, waiting to hail the victor and mourn the fallen, surely collecting on bets made in sport. And he did not want to disappoint them. He would give them a good show. Here, you poor slobs, you poor pitiful "potato-heads," he thought. Here is the glorious airman at work. Watch and be awed. Cheer! We fight for you! C'mon! Cheer, you dumb bastards!

Wissemann jerked the Roland around in a tight bank and turned to meet the Nieuports head-on. Zemke bolted upright in his seat and clapped his pilot on the shoulder.

"That's it, Wissemann!" he exhorted lustily. "Let's meet those Tommies face to face!"

"Hang on, my little friend. It's going to get interesting!"

Wissemann's thumb tensed over the trigger. The Maxim was ready to deal out its 7.92-millimeter warload. His eyes watched the Nieuports grow in size. Closer they came, now at the same altitude as the Roland. Closer! Ever closer! Five hundred meters—four hundred meters—three hundred—two hundred—one hundred—fifty meters! Open fire! Wissemann squeezed the trigger.

TOK-TOK-TOK-TOK-TOK-TOK-TOK-TOK-TOK-TOK!

A blazing volley of flaming rounds spat from the single machine gun. The bullets arced across the gap and zipped through the left-most Nieuport's rigging, punching a few holes in the upper wing. Splintering debris flitted into the slipstream. A piece of shredded canvas tore free.

"Sah-ha!" the Bavarian pilot cheered. "A hit!"

The Nieuport fired in retort. *CR-TAT-TAT-TAT!*

Wissemann snapped to a crouch above the control stick. His slitted eyes saw a piece of the windscreen break off. A bullet had sliced by, not more than a centimeter from his left ear. Then the Nieuport zoomed up, hurdling the Roland by a few meters, pulling up in an abrupt climbing turn. The other Nieuport roared by a second later and Zemke gave him a squirt. The tracers curved low as he misjudged the Britisher's speed. The Nieuport corkscrewed up in a zooming climb. Zemke kept fire on him. His bullets sailed through the air like flaming darts but hitting empty air. And all the while, Bärmann kept his Albatros on a course straight for Quéant.

The Nieuports looped around, like hawks circling for a kill.

"Get this crate turned about, Wissemann!" Zemke barked. "They're coming round now!"

"Right!"

Wissemann jerked the stick over and heeled the Roland into a wide turn. The Nieuports were closing fast. Their guns were already spitting hellfire.

"Hah! Those Tommies must be fledglings!" Zemke averred. "They're nowhere near in range yet, and they're already firing!" He cocked his Parabellum and began tracking the closest one through his ring-sight. "C'mon, you *Schweinehund!* Come to Papa Zemke!"

He sighted carefully and fired. The Parabellum shook steadily and the wooden stock thudded into his shoulder. The fiery volley of smoking bullets burst from the barrel and flashed towards the Nieuport like a bolt of lightning. They slammed into the propeller and cowling of the British biplane in ringing ricochets and clanging thuds. The Nieuport wobbled and dipped. The wooden propeller suddenly changed from a blurred disc to a splintered, windmilling paddle, vibrating violently. The pilot yanked the aeroplane out of the line of fire and slewed into a wild skid, greasy smoke pouring from the shot-up cylinders.

"*Lieber Gott!* I got him!" Zemke spouted excitedly.

Indeed he had. He could see the pilot in the shattered Nieuport jerking his head about frantically, a face white with fear. The frightened Englishman lost control of the machine and slipped into a spiraling nosedive as the cowling, propeller and engine tore loose from the nose-end of the fuselage. Its upper wing ripped off and the Nieuport tumbled down to the cloud deck below.

"Look, Wissemann," Zemke shouted. "He's going down! Out of control! A victory! A victory!"

"A victory? Yes—*YES!*"

A victory indeed.

The Nieuport broke apart, falling to pieces, the lower wings folding back, snapping off suddenly, tearing loose from the fuselage, fluttering away in the slipstream. The rest fell like a rock.

Wissemann's head jerked around just in time to see the stricken scout go down and disappear in the murky haze below, somewhere near Delville Wood, on the outskirts of Longueval.

"Good shooting, Franz!" he shouted. "Good shooting!"

The remaining Englishman gave the Roland a halfhearted burst and then pulled up in a half-loop, rolled, and sped away in the other direction, apparently losing his nerve. His gunfire had come nowhere near the German two-seater. And in a few seconds, he had doubled back to the west on his way to his own territory, tail between his legs.

"Run, you Limey bastard!" Zemke snarled, shaking a fist. "Run away, why don't you!"

Wissemann nodded. "Well done, Franz! Excellent work!"

"Damned excellent, Willi! Thank you."

Wissemann suddenly realized something. He'd called Zemke by his first name, twice now. And Zemke had replied in kind. It seemed the two were finally hitting it off. Both men were smiling proudly. They had finally turned a corner towards a lasting friendship.

The Roland gracefully cut through the air towards Quéant, its Mercedes roaring at a comfortable one hundred sixty kilometers per hour. Down below in the German trenches, the "potato-heads" were cheering now. A dull roar rolled up from the muddy morass below. The exultant soldiers of the Fatherland cheered lustily and waved proudly to their victorious airmen.

Imperial German Air Service: 1. Royal Flying Corps: 0.

POISED ABOVE THE GRASSY AERODROME, the little Eindecker looked like a bird of prey, its khaki wings gleaming in the warming rays of mid morning sunlight. There was a gracefulness in its flight, but no danger. The man in the cockpit gazed over-side, a lean, pale-faced, eagle-eyed warrior whose little mustache twitched curiously and whose eyes flared lively and blue. There was an acute assessment of the aerodrome below and a sure, inexorable consciousness of everything that moved. But the airman seemed as innocuous as his machine, perhaps more like a naive child. That was the jest of Mars, the god of war—the investiture of favor and grace to the Eindecker and its famous flier.

For in the cockpit sat a man that was known on both sides, from the coast of northern France to the Swiss border. A man who had forged his name profoundly upon the anvil of war, with the hammer blows of his Maxim machine guns.

The preeminent perpetrator of the "Fokker Scourge!"

Christened Maximilian by doting parents, others named him "*Der Adler von Lille*" or the Eagle of Lille. "Max" had a lonely devotion to his pet dog, Tyras, who often slept within or on his bed. He didn't smoke or drink and wrote daily to his mother. When he flew, he wore old velvet trousers but on the ground dressed at his best. He loved having his photo taken whenever he had a new medal. And the glistening *Pour le Mérite* always hung from his tunic collar these days—the Fatherland's highest military honor.

Now, descending down in easy banks upon the aerodrome, the Eindecker's Oberursel blipping officiously, he guided the slender monoplane in for a landing. The aerodrome's location was unfamiliar to him. But he saw the Roland and Albatros two-seaters parked in neat rows, and knew it was German. And as he touched down gently, he saw the ground crews racing out to greet him, faces fused with awe; a real celebrity was visiting Quéant!

"Someone notify *Hauptmann* Hochstetter, straight away," the chief maintenance NCO, *Vizefeldwebel* Fromm, gushed. "The great Immelmann is among us!"

Unteroffizier Deiter Dietz bolted up and dashed off to the Operations hut, shouting frantically as he went. "*Achtung! Achtung!* Immelmann is here! Immelmann is here!"

"The mighty Max Immelmann, here?" gasped Wissemann, as he clamored down from his Roland's cockpit, having spent the afternoon attending to a faulty tachometer gauge.

"Who?" a clueless Franz Zemke questioned, popping his head up over the coaming of the rear cockpit, his face soiled with soot and gun lubricant. He'd been in the process of dismantling his Parabellum machine gun, trying to discern its recent tendency for jamming. "Good Heavens! A real aviator in our midst!" He extricated himself from the innards of the Roland and hopped to the ground.

"Wonder what he wants?" Wissemann questioned.

"Maybe he's lost?" Franz Zemke grinned. "He's a bit far south of his 'drome, I think."

Wissemann scoffed. "Doubtful."

"Let's go meet him, eh?"

"Oh, Franz. Let's not make a fuss. I really don't understand what all the flap is about—"

"*Ach,* c'mon, you old stick-in-the-mud. Don't be shy." Zemke flipped his wrench into an open toolbox and wiped greasy hands off on his coveralls. "I, for one, am a great fan of the man from Dresden, our—Ace of Aces."

"Well, whatever. I guess we need a little break, eh?"

"That's the spirit, Willi.

Both men girded their woolly *Feldgrau* tunics and buttoned up. The afternoon was hot and humid, and they'd worked laboriously all morning in shirttails and braces. Wissemann donned his peak cap and lit a cigarette. Zemke swiped his face with a hanky and shoved it in a back pocket. They paced off slowly, following the converging throng to the now parked Eindecker and elbowed their way to the front of the gang of sweaty, star-struck airmen and mechanics. Hochstetter was already standing by the Eindecker and its pilot, his towering frame standing a good head and shoulders above all the rest, which seemed to diminish, tellingly, the stature of the gallant *Oberleutnant* Max Immelmann—Germany's answer to Major Hawker and France's *Capitaine* Guynemer.

"Greetings," *Hauptmann* Hochstetter was saying, grinning ear to ear. "Welcome, *Oberleutnant* Immelmann, to the humble environs of *Flieger Abteilung Nr. 4b.*"

Max Immelmann peeled off his leather flight cap. "Thank you, *Herr... Hauptmann*—" he quickly snapped off a crisp salute and clicked his heels when he recognized the two pips on Hochstetter shoulder boards. "Uh... what aerodrome is this, sir, if I may ask?"

"Quéant—6th Army Sector," Hochstetter replied instantly. "Why do you ask?" He pursed his lips suspiciously and squinted.

Immelmann's face blushed. "I think I'm lost. Quéant, you say?"

"That's right."

Franz Zemke, who was now standing near the front of the crowd, elbowed Wissemann in the ribs and snickered. He whispered: "See! I told you, Willi."

Wissemann smirked and shook his head petulantly. "Quiet, you!"

"I was chasing two B.E. two-seaters across the lines when my guns malfunctioned," Immelmann explained. "I'd followed them down all the way from Arras. Didn't realize how far I'd gone, I suppose."

"Aha, I see." Hochstetter nodded, smiling. He glanced at the nose of the Eindecker and saw the twin Maxim machine guns. "Hmm, didn't realize they were putting two guns on the Eindeckers these days? Quite novel."

Immelmann smiled. "Indeed! This is the newer E. IV model. The twin Maxims—they're standard equipment. But Anthony Fokker hasn't quite worked out the bugs yet. This is the second time I've had trouble with them." Immelmann unbuttoned his leather jacket and undid his scarf. "I've even flown Fokker's three-gun version, too."

"Three?" Hochstetter's jaw dropped.

The assembled noncoms and officers gasped in a chorus of awe.

"That version didn't work so well either." Max Immelmann laughed. "Shot my propeller to pieces one afternoon."

Wissemann eyed Immelmann closely.

So. Here was the magnificent "Eagle of Lille."

Max Immelmann was a man of middling height, quite frail looking and of delicate facial features. His pencil thin mustache was trimmed neatly and his hair was dark and barbered closely around the temples and nape. A dashing cleft chin and full lips seemed to contrast sharply with the large ears and thoughtful eyes. He was a slender, pale fellow and had the refined manner of genteel upbringing. And when he peeled off his gloves, Wissemann noted the delicate shape of his hands and fingers. The amazed Bavarian also noticed the fabulous *Pour le Mérite* dangling at the young Saxon's neck. It glittered in the afternoon sunlight like expensive jewelry. Wissemann stared dumbly, awestruck.

"Well, I suppose you'll need to call your aerodrome, then," Hochstetter interposed. "Your comrades are probably wondering about you."

"Yes. They'll send a car for me." Immelmann nodded.

"Would you care for a drink or cigarette, *Oberleutnant?*"

"Oh, no. I don't drink or smoke. But I thank you all the same."

Zemke frowned. "No drinking? No smoking?" he grumped quietly. "Well, there goes our party for the Ace of Aces." He glanced at Wissemann, sighing.

Wissemann humphed softly, gazing thoughtfully at his cigarette, then took a deep drag. Well, Willi, he said to himself. There's your answer to success: no drinking or smoking. Bah! How can one live at the Front in these conditions without some sort of vice?

Ridiculous, indeed!

"Oh, *Oberleutnant* Immelmann," Hochstetter said, as he directed the great ace to Operations with a sweeping right hand. "I'd like you to meet my second-in-command—*Oberleutnant* Willi Wissemann, a crack pilot himself."

"Why, yes, of course." Immelmann nodded.

"Wissemann?" Hochstetter waved. "Come here a moment, if you would, please?"

Willi Wissemann froze for a second. His faced reddened. "Um..."

"C'mon, Willi," Zemke prodded. "Hochstetter has called you out."

"Zemke, please—"

"Let's meet Max Immelmann, *ja?*" The little man winked and pinched his friend's elbow.

"Stop that! Let go of me, Franz," Wissemann fussed.

He shushed Zemke and then strode warily over to Hochstetter and Max Immelmann. He wisely flicked the cigarette to the ground, stamping it out, a size-twelve boot heel grinding it into the ground.

Zemke chuckled and sauntered after his self-conscious pilot.

"Good afternoon, *Oberleutnant* Immelmann," Wissemann said

cordially. He snapped his head and clicked his heels. "A pleasure to meet you, sir." He proffered his hand.

Immelmann gave a nod and smiled. Both men shook hands firmly. "Nice to meet you too, *Oberleutnant* Wissemann." The young Saxon retracted his hand, smoothing his bangs back out of his eyes. "This is a—Bavarian outfit?" He gazed at Wissemann's uniform for a clue.

"That's right," Wissemann replied. "What section are you with?"

"FA-62, Brayelles, southeast of Douai."

"Aha. And how is the great Oswald Boelcke?"

Immelmann smiled. "In the lead, I'm afraid. He just shot down No. 18, a few days ago. I've not been able to catch up with him."

"Hmm, he's quite the marksman, I hear."

"That he is."

Zemke nudged Wissemann.

"Oh, sorry... pardon me, *Oberleutnant* Immelmann," Wissemann said clumsily, pointing to his inseparable sidekick. "This is *Leutnant* Franz Zemke, my observer and gunner. A good fellow to have around in a tight spot."

Boot heels clicked. Zemke popped off a stiff salute. *"Herr Oberleutnant!* Glad to make your acquaintance, sir!"

Max Immelmann sketched a simple salute. *"Leutnant* Zemke..." He gave a curt nod, a gentlemanly air beaming from his persona.

Hochstetter interceded. "Well, Immelmann, let's get to Operations and make that call to your aerodrome, hmm? I'm sure they're wondering about you by now."

"Yes, I should do that, I suppose." Immelmann bowed. "So nice to meet both you gentlemen."

"Likewise, *Herr* Immelmann," Wissemann replied.

"Yes!" Zemke exclaimed. "G-Good luck in the race with Boelcke. I'm rooting for *you*, sir!"

Immelmann smiled awkwardly.

"Thank you," he said. "Thank you—"

"Okay, my good lads," *Hauptmann* Hochstetter interjected. *"Oberleutnant* Immelmann has some important telephone calls to make. Dismissed, off you go."

"Yes, sir."

"That goes for all of you men!" Hochstetter gazed at the gawking throng of *Feldgrau* and officers' peak caps. "Back to work now. We've got a photo-recon patrol at seventeen hundred hours." His hand fluttered impatiently. "Back to business now. *Los! Schnell!* Dismissed!"

Hochstetter then whisked the great Saxon ace away, arm over shoulders, leading him to Operations. The men of FA-4b grumbled disappointingly and sauntered off, returning to their duties. Wissemann about-faced and walked to his Roland. He shrugged and glowered grimly. He really couldn't see what all the fuss was about. So the man had shot down more than a few enemy machines? *Pah!* So what. The feat seemed easy enough with the right equipment. The twin-gunned Eindecker appeared a potent enough machine. And with three machine guns, the feat ought to be even easier. Quite!

The thought stirred Wissemann's supple mind. Perhaps I need to fly an Eindecker, he thought. Perhaps then too, I shall become a great German ace!

Zemke followed closely, hands jammed in his coverall pockets. "So that's the great Max Immelmann, eh? What a neat fellow. A real killer! Bet he'll pass Boelcke soon."

"Really?" Wissemann said with a wry grin. "How much, hmm?"

"Twenty Marks!" Franz Zemke spouted, rising to the bait. "Twenty Marks says he'll pass Boelcke by the end of next month!"

"Twenty?"

"All right—fifty!"

"You're on, Franz!"

"Fifty Marks!"

"He's got to pass Boelcke by the thirty-first of... July, alright?"

"Fair enough, Willi. The thirty-first of July!"

"Fine."

"It's official then."

Both men spat in their palms and shook on it.

Wissemann nodded. "Good deal."

"Ooh! You're going to be sorry come payday, Willi."

ON THE 18TH OF JUNE, it was back to business. Wissemann and Zemke rose at dawn and suited up for the day. Down the line, the *Startwärter* gangs threw their weight against the props, and Mercedes motors droned with fitful life. The night before, 6th Army *Kofl* had called for a photo reconnaissance of the rail yards at Albert. The German High Command was getting restless for intelligence on the British buildup. And as had been the common practice, two Rolands would escort a camera-equipped Albatros. *Leutnant* Landsberg and his observer, Hans Hasslbeck, were slated to snap the photos. Bärmann and Vordemfelde, who had recently transitioned from their Albatros, would man the other Roland two-seater.

The trio roared into the wind, turning a wide circle as they climbed. Soon they were winging west for the Front.

It was humid-hazy and from two kilometers above Bapaume, Wissemann gazed westward and could see very little of the Somme valley verdure. To the east, clouds rolled up in thick cumulus thunderheads near the earth, their shining edges alluding to some heavy rainfall. Wissemann gripped the fine-fuel adjustment lever and slid it up a few notches to compensate for the humid air. It was uncomfortably warm even at two thousand meters. Below him the huge, unwieldy silhouette of the Albatros C.III cruised steadily for British soil. Poor slobs! It was a rotten job—steering a lumbering apple barge into British territory after pictures. It made escort work in a Roland seem like a field trip.

The *Kette* was swinging southwest now, over the Ancre River, their objective the northern boundary of Albert, where the rail line and the main highway intersected. Slowly, the smudgy outskirts of their target came into view. And as they slid down a gusty thermal over Aveluy Wood, English anti-aircraft began raising hell. Some of it was reaching the higher levels and tossed the German two-seaters about like butterflies in a windstorm. A glint of light flashed on high, and Wissemann's lips tightened. British scouts patrolled high up; a vic of three khaki-brown biplanes. He could see the defensive effort the English were putting up for whatever secret they were holding behind the "Leipzig Salient."

The first biplane launched its attack; the English flight leader peeled away in a wing-over and came zooming down. Each of his comrades did the same, and three Bristol D-Scouts came plunging downwards in a screaming dive; Wissemann could easily make out their boxy silhouettes. He had no decision to make, it was already made. Orders! He had to protect the photographer. He rocked his wings and a hand went up over the cockpit coaming. *Achtung!* Bärmann and Vordemfelde saw it. Their Roland instantly heeled over in a little side-slip and dovetailed aft of the Albatros' larboard beam. In the Albatros, *Feldwebel* Hans Hasslbeck cocked and cleared his Parabellum, standing stiffly in the cockpit, ready for action.

Wissemann jerked the stick forward. He felt the wicker seat sink from beneath him, and for a split second, it felt like he was going to retch. The sudden drop in altitude had jolted his stomach. The sickening taste of soured coffee crept up in his throat. The slipstream buffeted against the little half-moon visor.

Through squinted eyes, the Bavarian airman saw three shadowy Bristols blurred against the wind in a mad charge for the Albatros. His legs steeled with muscle as he kicked heavily against the rudder bar. The controls were stiff with the velocity of the frantic dive, and there seemed steel bands across his chest. He had reached the limits of his webbed harness.

But Wissemann's Roland was aft of the Bristol now, and a little below. The first Englishman ranged his victim at fifty meters. His .303 Vickers machine gun barked savagely. *TAC-TAC-TAC! TAC-TAC-TAC!* Bullets danced up the Albatros's tail assembly and marched down the turtleback. Hasslbeck returned fire but suddenly convulsed jerkily amid the hail of bullets and a ghastly pinkish mist. Bloodied and wounded, he lurched backwards and slid down inside the cockpit, suddenly gone from sight. The flaming barrel of his Parabellum jerked skyward, ratcheting off a few rounds before falling silent. Landsberg banked the Albatros hard and the Bristol skidded wide, right into the line of fire of Vordemfelde's gun. Smoking bullets clawed out across the gap for the stumbling biplane. And when the red, white and blue cockades leaped clear of Vordemfelde's fusillade, a cockade was now a perfect target in Wissemann's sights. His single Maxim bucked. The force of the slipstream obscured the tracers. But Wissemann didn't need them. He saw the Bristol stand on its tail. His muscles tensed, and he raised the nose, ranging his sights along the upright aeroplane, and squeezed down once more on the trigger. His mouth was a stiff, straight line. He didn't miss.

TOK-TOK-TOK-TOK-TOK! TOK-TOK-TOK-TOK-TOK!

The Bristol shuddered violently as the bullets thudded into the cockpit and upper wing. Pieces of wood and canvas tumbled into the air. The pilot jerked his head about madly as if he had to wonder where the onslaught was coming from. Then the fuel tank belched fire and flames quickly engulfed the cockpit. A dirty band of black smoke curled out from behind the tail, and as Wissemann's Roland hurdled the flaming wreck, the Bristol spiraled down in a whining nosedive, minus its pilot, plunging down in a fiery corkscrew.

"Victory!" Wissemann cheered exuberantly.

"Hah-ha!" Zemke exhorted. "That's showing 'em, Willi!"

The remaining Bristols weighed in now, a good deal of fight still left in their guns. One rolled in behind Wissemann's tail. Zemke was already hammering away. The Roland fishtailed. The Englishman couldn't draw a bead and wisely broke off, but not before a few bullets scarred his Bristol. The other Englishman made for Bärmann's observer-less Albatros, his Vickers gun doing further damage. The Albatros stumbled and coughed but flew on nonetheless, a thin vaporous line streaming from its radiator.

Vordemfelde had the Bristol bracketed, and his Parabellum spewed hot lead across the sky, near enough, hotly enough, to make the Englishman give up his plaint. The Bristol pilot broke off and zoomed down after his comrade, who was already down low, scarpering for his aerodrome. Both Tommies had had enough. They'd sagely decided these German eagles were too nasty and too sharply clawed. Somewhere down below, the smoldering wreck of their leader's Bristol lay in a twisted heap. And somewhere close to that, the broken body of a brave English officer lay dead. He'd chosen a death of free-fall instead of one by fire. The leaderless Bristols turned west for their 'drome, a hard lesson learned.

Meanwhile, Wissemann had kept an eye on Bärmann's Albatros in hopes of seeing a revived Hans Hasslbeck. But the poor lad never emerged from his cockpit. With no one to operate the camera equipment, the mission would have to be aborted. The signal was given, and all three machines turned out abreast the wind and headed east. Wissemann had a sick feeling in his gut. He knew young Hasslbeck might be dead or dying. And if he was still alive, with those horrid multiple bullet wounds inflicted upon him, he'd, in all likelihood, just bleed out right there in the cockpit.

Bärmann couldn't help him. He was strapped in his seat, nursing the battered Albatros back to base. Vordemfelde couldn't help him either. Wissemann grimaced. No one could help him.

The Gods of War could've helped him... had they been watching.

BACK AT THE AERODROME, the bloodied body of Hans Hasslbeck was lifted from the cockpit of the Albatros. A sticky pool of blood on the cockpit floor confirmed Willi Wissemann's fears. He had bled to death on that seemingly interminable flight back to Quéant. He was laid out on a stretcher and carried to the Operations hut where the last rites were performed. Then his body was sealed in a canvas body bag and driven to a local field hospital. Wissemann and Zemke were remorsefully quiet during the debriefing. So much so, they nearly forgot to register the claim for the Bristol shot down; a very distraught *Leutnant* Bärmann had to remind them. It was the first time ever that a pilot of FA-4b had put in a claim. *Hauptmann* Hochstetter questioned his second-in-command on the day's events.

"*Oberleutnant* Wissemann," he asked solicitously, "what happened out there today?"

"We were attacked by a flight of Bristols, north of Albert."

"I see. Go on..."

"They came down very quickly, three of them. I rallied the *Kette*, and we formed up in a defensive formation. The English flight leader attacked first after securing a tail-end position on Bärmann's Albatros. Hasslbeck got it first in the exchange of gunfire. He went down, and I never saw him after that. I alertly maneuvered behind the Englishmen and managed to gun-sight the Bristol and fire two quick bursts that ignited his fuel tank. He went down in flames after that. The other two Englishmen pressed their attack, but not for very long. Zemke and Vordemfelde beat off their attacks. The Bristols quickly disengaged, sir."

"Where did the Bristol fall?"

"Somewhere southwest of Méaulte, I think."

"Hmm, that's on their side, I'm guessing?"

"I believe so, *Herr Hauptmann*. Maybe two or three kilometers?"

"Fine. I'll call 6th Army and see if their observers saw it crash."

"Sorry, sir," Wissemann apologized. "We couldn't complete the mission. Well, with Hasslbeck—"

"Forget it, man. You did your best. That's all I can ask of you."

"Danke, Herr Hauptmann."

"All right, that's all for now. Dismissed."

"Sir!" Boot heels clicked.

A crestfallen Willi Wissemann marched off to mess, a cigarette dangling from his lips, somber thoughts echoing through his mind. Somehow he felt responsible for Hasslbeck's death. The poor lad had only been in the squadron a fortnight, barely falling into the routine of things, barely getting his feet wet. Somewhere in Germany, a heartbroken mother would be crying tonight. Or maybe a girlfriend or fiancee, or even a wife. Wissemann knew nothing of Hans Hasslbeck save his name and age. He was just twenty.

Hardly a man at all!

Later that night, Wissemann ruminated over his future as an airman, stretching out on his cot, writing a letter to Ilse by candlelight. A distraught Franz Zemke suddenly burst into his tent, red-faced and embittered, shaking his head disbelievingly.

"He's dead! He's dead! I can't believe it!" Zemke bawled. "Those rotten Limey bastards finally got him." He paced about stiffly, digging deep in his pants pocket, looking as though he were about to burst into tears,

"I know, Franz. It's horrible. Poor Hasslbeck, just a kid, aye?"

"Hasslbeck?" Zemke snorted wearily. "No, no, no!"

"What are you talking about, Franz? Who—"

Zemke tossed a wad of *Deutschmarks* onto Wissemann's cot.

"Immelmann! Shot down! Today! Dead..."

Passed by FlugM Censor # 2680
Frau Ilse Magdalena von Linkhof
c/o Supreme Headquarters
6th Armee, Quéant, France
To Berlin (Please forward)

Lieber Ilse!   *18. June 1916*

    You shall be eminently proud of me, Liebchen. I have shot down my first Englishmen! It happened over the Somme battleground on a routine reconnaissance sortie. My comrades and I were ordered by Army on a photo reconnaissance of the rail yards of a certain town, which I am not at liberty to tell you, due to military protocol. Three enemy scouts attacked from on high and zoomed down upon us. It was a nasty fight which saw the loss of a comrade, a new man in the Abteilung. Nevertheless, I shot down the English flight leader and saw him go down in flames, behind enemy front lines. I await official confirmation now. My fingers are crossed!

    By the time you receive this letter, you, and all of Germany, will have learned of the loss of one of our greatest airmen. Oddly, he visited our aerodrome the day earlier, before his untimely demise... by accident. His machine was having mechanical troubles, forcing him to land. Zemke and I got to meet him personally. Now he is dead. Strange. The synchronicity of his visit and sudden death was a chilling reminder of how one's destiny can change so quickly. And I assure you, Ilse, I do not intend to suffer the same fate. I am as careful and cautious as ever, taking no foolish chances. Worry not, your "Willi dear" is in good hands here at the Front. With God as my co-pilot, and Franz Zemke as my gunner, I am well-insulated from danger. Be ever so assured, my darling!

                              Always Yours, Willi

Chapter 4

✠

JULY 14, 1916. AFTER THE DEATH of Max Immelmann, the German Air Service slipped into a gloomy funk. The aura of mystery that surrounded his demise seemed a bit surreal, if not cooked-up, in the mind of one Willi Wissemann. Reportedly during a fight with British F.E.2 biplanes, Immelmann had sustained hits from a sharp shooting aerial gunner and was manifestly shot down and killed. Not true, German authorities claimed. Instead, he had indeed shot off his own propeller due to a malfunctioning interrupter gear. His Fokker Eindecker had apparently shaken itself to pieces and thusly crashed to earth. An unlikely scenario, Wissemann thought to himself that day, after reading *Flugmeisterei's* officially circulated report. In view of the interrupter gear the Eindecker came equipped with, an experienced—even superb—pilot like *Oberleutnant* Immelmann would have simply shut his engine down and glided to earth. Wissemann suspected the Supreme Command was just trying to sustain the myth of Immelmann's invincibility.

The incident, nevertheless, brought about a substantial loss of morale to the squadron, especially to Franz Zemke, who had thought the "Eagle of Lille" indestructible. And as German air losses began to mount, the tide of aerial superiority seemed to shift to the Allies. In response to Immelmann's death, the German High Command ordered the great Oswald Boelcke away from the Front at the behest of the Kaiser. He was now commanded to tour the front line units and select his own men for one of the first all-fighting scout squadrons.

DEKE D. WAGNER

The German Air Service would soon be undergoing some important changes and reorganization. War in the air was going to get sophisticated. And a certain airman named Willi Wissemann fully expected to be apart of those changes. However, on the ground, the same old war raged on.

Commencing on 24 June, the British Fourth Army launched an intensive week-long artillery bombardment on German trenches. The next day, the Royal Flying Corps attacked German observation balloons and knocked out the "eyes" of the 6th Army. Then at 0730 hours, on 1 July, the long-awaited infantry attacks began. Thousands of English Tommies poured over the embattled Somme countryside into German territory. Swarms of low-flying British scouts, klaxon horns blaring, swept over the battlefront in support of the infantry attack. Losses for the RFC were relatively low in this opening phase of the battle. But on the ground, it was a totally different story. Wissemann heard a rumor that the British Army had suffered over fifty thousand casualties on the first day of the attack, a very high price for a mere two kilometers of territory.

On a blistering hot Monday morning, Willi Wissemann and Franz Zemke were flying a reconnaissance sortie over Maricourt, just behind enemy lines. It was an extremely cloudy day. Thick altostratus hung high in the sky above three thousand meters and puffy, cottony cumulus drifted along lazily at around two thousand. This was ideal weather for a lone reconnaissance machine. Plenty of concealment could be found in the peaks and valleys of giant, anvil-head clouds and the broken cover of the lower stratosphere.

At 0700-hours sharp, *Leutnant* Franz Zemke was already snapping pictures of the British rearguard. Willi Wissemann was in a foul mood. His victory claim over the Bristol had been denied by *Idflieg*, listed as unconfirmed in Army communiqués. The official ruling said it had fallen too far behind enemy lines to be observed by ground observation. This was an insult to his pride and sense of justice. Poor Hans Hasslbeck's death had gone unavenged. *Hauptmann* Hochstetter tried to get the ruling overturned, saying four other airman had witnessed the action. But Inspectorate's ruling held firm: no physical proof, no confirmation.

It was a ridiculous judgment in Wissemann's estimation. He almost felt like flying over to the crash sight, land, and abscond some piece of the Bristol to essay his claim. But the lanky Bavarian gave up his plaint and got good and soused instead. The "stuffed-shirts" at *Idflieg* could just kiss his bony, white rump.

Unconfirmed indeed!

Zemke tapped Wissemann on the shoulder. "We're done here!" he yelled. "I got all the pictures of Tommyland I need!"

"Right!" Wissemann nodded.

He wheeled the Roland in a wide turn and turned east. At about the same time anti-aircraft artillery started up again. British 3-inch and 13-pounder guns began lobbing shells up into the sky. Puffy, black shell bursts began erupting all around the two Germans, tucked snugly inside the relative safety of their cockpits. At this stage of the war, neither was too worried about ack-ack. Wissemann went into his usual evasive maneuvering to avoid the shelling, and the shell bursts began to fall short and wide of their mark. Zemke secured his photographic gear and prepared for the hour-long trip back to base. Ho-hum. Routine work. Just another day at the office.

But Fate had other ideas.

WHOOP-O-O-SH !

The Roland suddenly flipped over upside down as a rocketing 3-inch British shell tore through its lower wing and sheared off the left aileron on its way through the top wing, leaving a smoldering, gaping hole next to the wing strut. The aeroplane stumbled into a spin and began spiraling down, out of control. Wissemann, white-faced and white-knuckled, seized the control column with both hands and tried to pull the wounded "Walfisch" straight and level. The two-seater was steadily losing altitude!

"Lieber Gott, Willi!" Zemke shrieked. "The Tommies sure got our number that time!"

"Will you shut up! I'm a little busy right now!" Wissemann stood up on the rudder bars and yanked the stick with all his might. "Come, come, you wretched old fish! Pull out! Pull out!"

Zemke howled fearfully. *"Aghh-h-h-h! We've had it now!"*

"Verdammt! Will you have a little faith, man?"

Wissemann jerked the stick over with a mighty heave and righted the spiraling aeroplane. With one aileron missing, it was a superhuman feat to get the machine back in level flight. But somehow, he had managed it. The damaged Roland finally leveled off at one thousand meters. The herculean Bavarian eagle gasped a sigh of relief. His heart drubbed frenetically; his face was white as a ghost.

"Bravo, Willi!" Zemke exclaimed elatedly, pounding his pilot on the shoulders. "You did it! You got this wounded buzzard back on an even keel!"

"Mein Gott! We're still in the soup, Franz!"

"How much further, Willi?"

"How should I know? You're the observer! Read your map!"

"No need to get snappy!" Zemke went digging into his map case.

Wissemann wrenched the control stick to the right to compensate for the shot-off aileron. The machine was slewing and yawing wildly as he tried to maintain straight and level flight. The strain was nearly unbearable. He could feel his arms and shoulders stiffening with an aching pain. But the damaged Roland two-seater lumbered forward, nevertheless, towards German territory on a downward slant, losing altitude ever so slightly. He dipped the aeroplane's right wing, eased the stick down, all the while English ack-ack continued its insistent barrage. Down to a thousand meters the Roland sank, rigging wires wailing.

Franz Zemke had finally pinpointed their position. "That's Bernafay Wood down there!" His gloved finger pointed to a thin tree line bracketed by two railroad tracks. "On the far side of those trenches is the village of Guillemont—the German lines. Just a little further, Willi!"

Willi Wissemann nodded, too exhausted to give any kind of answer. His arms were aching terribly now, the Roland teetering precariously, its weight upon the shoulders of one determined man. Down to five hundred meters, at present. The churned up earth and wire entanglements were quite visible; the contested territory of No-Man's Land was under his wings. He throttled back the Mercedes and came swooping over the woods holding the battered two-seater as level as possible. The big Bavarian was panting heavily, groaning bitterly. "Ach! This is madness! *Gott helfe mir!*"

Suddenly the staccato knocking of machine gun fire and the hissing of glowing tracers curved up from a trench line. A German gunner was tracking the two-seater! The radiant, yellow volley traced a path straight for the Roland's engine. A loud metallic clanging and banging followed as the bullets played a little tune on the engine panels. The motor gasped and coughed and the stench of burning oil wafted back into Wissemann's nostrils. The prop clanked to a halt, pointing straight up, like a middle finger. The spray of petroleum anointed his goggles.

The Mercedes was done for. Silence reigned.

"Those stupid idiots!" he cursed. "Now we're finished!"

"So close! Hang on, Willi!" Zemke's head was bobbing frantically.

The Roland drifted down to one hundred meters, tottering wildly, the ground rushing up much too fast. Wissemann banked the faltering machine over a tangle of barbed wire, winging for the outskirts of Guillemont. There, next to a highway, he saw a patch of plowed field, and he shoved the nose down in a steep descent. He barely noticed the advancing motorcade of staff cars and motorcycles motoring along the nearby highway. His goggles were up and the taste of oil was in his mouth. He cringed as the wings took out the telephone wires stretched across the roadway, then slammed into the field, careening through a little fence, slewing, scattering wheels and landing gear, smashing the lower wings. And as Wissemann watched in dismay, the Roland spun around, slid backwards a short distance, then came to a grinding halt in a cloud of dirt and dust and a jumble of torn canvas and teetering wings.

Wissemann snatched the goggles from his head. "Out my friend! Quickly! I smell petrol!" He undid his harness straps, stood up in the seat and jumped overside. "This thing is going to blow, Zemke! *OUT-OUT-OUT!*"

Franz Zemke clambered from the cockpit, groaning and moaning, but not before trying to loosen the camera and its photographic plates from the side of the Roland's fuselage. "Got to save these things for headquarters!"

"Forget it, Franz! Leave it! The petrol tank is going to explode!"

"No! We must save the plates and camera, Willi!"

Wissemann snatched Zemke by the collar and jerked him away from the Roland. The engine was now smoldering with the sickening, sweet smell of petrol. "C'mon you little idiot! Forget the damned camera!"

Zemke pulled away and seized the Ernemann 13 x 18 camera and jerked it from its mounting bracket. *"Nein,* Willi! We must preserve our work. Headquarters will need these exposures!"

Wissemann didn't argue anymore. He dashed to the roadside with Zemke stumbling behind him. They reached the fence parallel to the road in good order. They stood for a long moment, watching the smoldering Roland, fully expecting it to go up in a terrific explosion. But as they watched and waited, mouths agape, nothing happened. The smoke slowly cleared and the dust settled and the two Germans were left relieved and stunned. The smashed Roland did not blow up or burn. It was about this time Willi Wissemann finally noticed the Army motorcade braking to a halt along the roadside.

"Ahoy, there!" A voice called out. "Are you gentlemen all right?"

Wissemann turned around to face the voice. "Yes, thank you. We're fine, no injuries." The sweaty, oil-splattered Bavarian saw who was hailing him. It was an elderly officer with the shoulder boards and collar braids of a *General der Kavallerie*—a Prussian cavalry general. The man was standing up in the backseat of his staff car, waving. Wissemann stiffened. A Prussian general? He pulled the flying cap from his head and mussed his hair into some kind of order, reached in a jacket pocket, and jerked his service cap on.

"I wonder who he is?" Zemke inquired, panting feverishly, clutching his camera photo plates with grim urgency. "Oh, curses! He's coming over."

Wissemann groaned. "Ach! That's all we need now. A general breathing down our necks."

The moustachioed cavalry general extricated himself from the staff car, easing down from the seat onto the floorboards then to the shoulder of the road, just as his driver came around to open the door for him. The general paced off smartly and approached the two grounded airmen. He leaned against the fence. He was smiling.

"Good day, gentlemen," the General said cordially. "Looks like you had a close call, eh?"

Wissemann stiffened to attention; his hand instinctively came up to a salute. Boot heels clicked. *"Jawohl, Herr General,"* he replied nervously, sweat draining down his neck. "I believe our anti-aircraft gunners mistook us for Englishmen, I'm sorry to say."

Zemke snapped to, saluting, nodding. "Yes, sir, they certainly let us have it, that's for damned sure!" The little observer cradled his camera awkwardly, sighing, quite exasperated.

The General grinned. "I saw that. I must have a little talk with those fellows. Can't have them blasting away at our own machines, now can we?"

Wissemann cringed. "No, *Herr General.* Certainly not."

"I'm General Ernst von Hoeppner, by the way..." he proffered his hand, amiably, leaning over the fence, "currently commander of the 75th Reserve Division."

Wissemann reached over the fence and shook the General's hand. "A pleasure, sir. I'm *Oberleutnant* Wilhelm Wissemann," he turned to Zemke, "—and this is my observer, *Leutnant* Franz Zemke." Hmm... he thought. This general is quite informal and cordial.

"General," Zemke replied with a nervous smile. He jerked a salute.

"I watched you lads from the road. Looks like you were already in a bad way when our gunners began potting away at you. Were you lads in some kind of trouble?"

"Yes, sir," Wissemann spoke up. "We were hit by English anti-aircraft over Maricourt. A shell nearly took our wings off."

"I see. No one hurt, I hope?"

"No, *Herr General.* Just a little shaken up, that's all."

"Excellent. Glad to hear it."

Zemke frowned. "Those idiotic trench gunners are the ones that shot us down, sir. Not the English. *Oberleutnant* Wissemann nearly had that thing landed proper!" he gazed at the smoldering wreck of the Roland. "Well, at least we saved the photographic plates."

Von Hoeppner chuckled. "Very '*unfriendly*' friendly fire, eh?"

Wissemann coughed. "Yes, sir." He hid a little smile under clamped lips.

Zemke laughed. "*Very* unfriendly!"

Von Hoeppner gesticulated to his staff car. "Need a lift, gentlemen?"

"Uh, well... yes, *Herr General.*" Wissemann nodded. "That would be much appreciated—"

"Absolutely, sir!" Zemke hefted his camera equipment to his shoulder. "Our regular mode of transport is out of action, as you can see. Look at that wreck, will you? What a mess!"

"Where is your squadron, *Oberleutnant?*" von Hoeppner asked.

Wissemann bent down, straddling the lower fence pole, squeezing his lanky frame through the fencing to the roadside. He dusted off his trousers and smoothed his tunic tails. "Quéant, *Herr General.* About twenty kilometers from here, I would think."

"Here, Willi." Zemke handed over the camera and slid through the wooden fencing.

Wissemann took the camera. He and von Hoeppner began walking to the staff car. "I'm sorry, sir. But I don't recall hearing of the 75th Reserve Division operating in this sector. Have you been transferred to this area?" He had taken a little chance to hazard a guess on behalf of his curious mind. Why was a Prussian cavalry general in this sector of the front?

"No, no. I'm just on a inspection tour, sussing out potential *Flugmeldedienst* observation posts. The Army wants to establish a flight-reporting service in this sector," von Hoeppner replied frankly, then said with a sigh: "I'm being considered for a different kind of— transfer. An appointment, I'd say."

"Oh?"

"General Ludendorff has suggested that I might be in the running for the new Supreme Command he's creating for the *Fliegertruppen.* The Air Service is going to be reorganized very shortly. It needs a General Staff of its own."

"I've heard that, sir—"

"*Hauptmann* Boelcke has returned from his tour of the East—he is to reform the *KEK staffels* into self-contained fighting squadrons. He'll hand pick the men for the job, I understand."

Von Hoeppner directed the two airmen to the backseat of the waiting staff car and both men climbed in. Zemke secured the camera then reclined comfortably. Von Hoeppner took a seat in the front. The driver closed the doors, then slid in behind the steering wheel and started the motor. The staff car rumbled to life; the General's motorcade was rolling again.

Wissemann's eyes lighted. "Really? Well, I hope *all* pilots are eligible."

"Of course. We'll definitely need all the best fliers we have."

"I certainly hope so, sir."

"*Ja, Herr General,*" Franz Zemke chirped gleefully. "*Oberleutnant* Wissemann is such a man for the job. He's a crack pilot. That's for damned certain!"

General von Hoeppner grinned and nodded. "I'm sure he is, *Leutnant* Zemke. I'm quite sure he is." He gazed at Wissemann with amused, scrutinizing eyes.

Wissemann's face reddened.

LATER THAT AFTERNOON, after General von Hoeppner returned the two displaced airmen to their aerodrome at Quéant, the old Prussian officer was given a special tour of the facilities. He departed all the wiser. Wissemann and Zemke retired to the mess for a few drinks. The day had not been without harrowing escapades, for certain. But Wissemann couldn't forget the friendliness of von Hoeppner. He was not used to Prussian officers being so kind and accommodating. It was quite refreshing and unexpected.

Von Hoeppner's potential appointment to the "new" Air Service stirred his mind. He would be a great ally to have in one's corner. Willi Wissemann knew if he could win the General's favor, he could get into Boelcke's new fighting squadron. It seemed as if history was being written; a new chapter in German aviation was in the making. And this plucky Bavarian officer wanted to be part of it.

Wissemann sipped his cognac and lit a Halpaus, contemplating the possibilities. Blue smoke rolled from the cigarette like the thoughts of being a scout pilot rolled over in his mind. I could be an *Überkanone,* he thought to himself. I'm as good as Boelcke or Immelmann. He could clearly see the *Pour le Mérite* dangling at his throat.

"Zemke," he said, "do you think I'd make a good scout pilot?"

"*Ach, ja!*" Franz Zemke exclaimed. "No doubt about it, Willi"

"Yes, I think I would."

"Are you thinking about what General von Hoeppner said?"

"H'mm." Wissemann nodded. "I must get a transfer to Boelcke's new fighting squadron. I must!"

The tent flap to the mess suddenly swung open. *Hauptmann* Hochstetter came striding in heavily. A frustrated look seemed to contort his normally mirthful visage. He marched straight up to the table where Wissemann and Zemke were sitting. He stopped short of sitting down and placed a gentle hand on the big Bavarian's shoulder.

"Wissemann," he said evenly. "I've got a little job for you."

"*Herr Hauptmann?*"

"Since we need a new Roland for tomorrow's recon of the Combles Sector, I need you to go up to AFP-6 and get another one."

"I see. When?"

"As soon as you can."

"Of course. I'll have duty driver take me straightaway."

"No, no. I want you to take the Eindecker."

"The Eindecker?"

"That's right—the Fokker E.IV Immelmann left behind before his untimely demise. *Kofl* has been harassing me about that machine for days. Well, they want it back. They want to put the damned thing in a museum, or something similarly absurd."

"A museum?"

Wissemann and Zemke exchanged odd glances. Zemke shrugged.

"You're the only man I can trust for the job, Wissemann."

"Thank you, *Herr Hauptmann*. I appreciate the vote of confidence."

"*Vizefeldwebel* Fromm has got the Eindecker on the line, prepping it for flight. So... whenever you're ready, Wissemann."

"Of course. I'll get my flying kit straight away, sir. I'll report to the tarmac immediately." Wissemann stirred from his seat and corked his bottle of cognac. He took a final puff from his cigarette and then crushed it out in an ashtray.

"Willi's the man for the job, sir," Zemke threw in.

Wissemann grinned keenly. "It'll be my pleasure and honor to fly Immelmann's old bird, *Hauptmann*. A pleasure, indeed."

Hochstetter looked at the half-empty bottle of cognac and snorted. "You're not too soused yet, I hope? Because this is an important job, Wissemann. *Kofl* wants that Eindecker in perfect order, understand?"

Wissemann stood up and clapped Hochstetter on the shoulder. "*Ach, Herr Hauptmann,*" he uttered in a whimsical tone, "I'm surprised... hurt. I thought you knew me better than that, sir. I'm as sober as a priest at morning mass. Please, don't worry."

Hochstetter rasped his chin cagily. "All right then. Get going. They want that Eindecker by nineteen hundred hours." He glanced at his wristwatch. "You've got three hours yet. Straight to Valenciennes, okay? No fooling around, see?"

Boot heels clicked. "No fooling around, sir!" Wissemann nodded.

Zemke smirked as he caught sight of the Bavarian's flaring eyes.

Hochstetter turned on a heel. "I've got to go up to Barelle—our new aerodrome. We're being moved further back from the front lines in a week. I've got to shore up the details with the 6th Army *Kommandeur*. I'll be back tomorrow at noon."

"Yes, sir."

"Okay, *Oberleutnant*. Get it done. Carry on."

Hochstetter stalked out of the mess tent in a hurried pace.

"Well, Zemke," Wissemann said, grinning. "Guess I'll see you later this evening. "

"Have fun, Willi. Remember now... no fooling around, eh?" Zemke winked, holding up his glass. "*Hals-und Beinbruch!*" he gulped the cognac down, then folded his arms over his chest. "See you, tonight."

A wry grin toyed with Wissemann's slender face. "I'm off then. *Tschüss!*" He strode out of the mess tent in a determined gait. A nice, little jaunt up to Valenciennes. Ach! Just what the doctor ordered.

WHEN OBERLEUTNANT WILLI WISSEMANN took to the high blue that late afternoon, his face was a stern countenance of determination. His smile had vanished. A thin line remained. A fierce heat burned inside him. Out to the north, a dull heat-haze hung on the horizon, a cloud mass that was, at the moment, but a summer menace. He wasn't troubled with the weather, though. Neither did he feel the rising atmospheric heat. The burning sensation was emanating from his heart, his soul. A new purpose had suddenly beset him. Now he wanted to become a scout pilot; a single-seat flier; a fighting airman. A man whose sole duty and purpose it was to shoot down enemy aeroplanes.

Before Wissemann had left the aerodrome at Quéant, he'd convinced *Vizefeldwebel* Fromm to arm the twin-gunned Eindecker with its typical war load. The old line chief protested, complaining the machine was only to be ferried to Valenciennes for delivery to the *Werft Kompanie* and its residing engineer officer. Not girded for some "joyride," or more aptly, a combat sortie. In the end, Wissemann got his way. The Eindecker was gassed up, its synchronizing gear checked and its ammo boxes were armed with one thousand rounds of 7.92

millimeter ammunition. The equivocating Bavarian claimed it was for safety's sake only. Just in case a roving enemy patrol happened to intercept him on the way to Valenciennes. "One must never throw caution to the wind," were his exact words.

Of course, Fromm didn't believe any of that. The old line chief was ultimately plied with a full bottle of Martell and told to keep his mouth shut. Franz Zemke had played an integral part in this little charade, the little man from Diessen convincing the argumentative Fromm that Wissemann was just being overly careful. He knew how badly his friend wanted to test his mettle. Finally, after much finagling, the khaki-colored buzzard took to the skies, ready for anything and everything.

Now, twenty minutes into the flight, Wissemann yanked the stick over, banking to the prevailing winds, turning westward. It was time to go hunting, time to try out a few of Immelmann's theories. He eyed the twin machine guns keenly—they looked thoroughly menacing mounted right there in front of him, their snub-nosed barrels pointing directly at the mahogany-blurred disc that was the propeller. Wissemann smiled and pulled the charging handles, then placed both thumbs on the trigger buttons, took a little breath, held it, and squeezed. The resulting flashing and knocking startled him at first. But as he triggered two more warming bursts, he became used to the knocking—the unsettling kicking and vibrating of twin Maxim machine guns.

He made an adjustment to the fine-fuel mixture. The two-row, 14-cylinder Oberursel rotary pulled the Eindecker along at a modest 170-kilometers per hour. Not what Willi Wissemann had expected at all. Likewise, he soon discovered, the inertial and gyroscopic forces of the large spinning motor, seemed to make the machine even less maneuverable than his old Roland. Turning and banking under these conditions proved exceedingly laborious. Wissemann chagrined, the E.IV still used wing-warping instead of ailerons. But all that aside, the Bavarian airman was still determined to test his mettle.

He leveled off at three thousand meters, putting the compass on a southwesterly heading, winging for the skies of the Somme battlefield. He glanced at his wristwatch and figured he had about forty-five minutes to find and engage an enemy machine. Then he'd have to head back to Valenciennes and get Immelmann's Eindecker back to the flight depot for disposition. All this before anyone was the wiser. And more importantly, before the petrol tank went dry!

Another twenty minutes came and went.

He was over Le Transloy presently, skimming over the broken

stratocumulus, two kilometers up, the sun on its way west, painting long shadows against the landscape, casting crepuscular rays, slowly fading to dusk. Wissemann had been patrolling the sector along the cottony cloud base all the way from Pérrone and was heading back north now. He'd thought several times of just dashing straight into British territory, trying to flush out some Tommies, provoking the enemy anti-aircraft in announcing his presence, inducing an enemy patrol into a dogfight. But his sense of better judgment told him no. You must be patient, Willi, he said to himself. The quarry must come to you. Boelcke had said: "Stalking enemy aeroplanes is much like stalking wild game. One has to be willing to wait for the perfect moment to strike." And good things came to those who waited.

He glanced at the fuel gauge and sighed bitterly. Ach! Time to head back. Willi Wissemann gazed longingly at the western sky, and then, reluctantly, turned east, shrugging. Well, at least he had given it a try. He gassed the Eindecker and eased the stick back, climbing through the milky strata, the sun settling over his shoulders. Seconds later, he broke through and was winging towards Bapaume, his mouth a grim line. His eyes swept the sky one last time—

"There! A shadow! A silhouette!" An aeroplane?

He banked around and saw that he was wrong. Three aeroplanes! Pusher biplanes—held together by a mass of flying wires and struts, elongated wings with a large bathtub-like fuselage containing a pilot and an observer in between, both sitting in front of a whirling rotary engine. A single Lewis gun stuck out from the nose, looking more like an afterthought than a piece of defensive armament. The trio was winging west, back to British territory, flying in a neat vic formation.

Wissemann's heart skipped a beat; three F.E. two-seaters! The F.E.2b—a lattice-tailed birdcage and flying bathtub—a *"Gitterrumpf"* in German jargon. They were obviously plodding back to base after a little jaunt over German territory. Did the English intentionally design these aircraft to look so peculiar and fly so slowly, he thought? And how in God's name did they induce the crews to go aloft in such outmoded contraptions? The wide-eyed Bavarian snorted; the British airmen certainly weren't lacking for courage.

And who was responsible for designing such ludicrous looking machinery, he wondered? No matter. It was time to test his nerve!

The German airman eased the throttle back to match their pace, circling around to the aft quadrant, still a good thousand meters above them. As he cruised in a bank behind the British biplanes, Wissemann turned the matter of attack over in his mind. What would Immelmann do, he wondered? How would the late "Eagle of Lille" go about grappling with three enemy machines at once? Better yet, how would the great Boelcke go about it? Immelmann might go charging in headlong, surprising the formation with the boldness of his attack. But Boelcke would probably seek all the advantages of stealth first, then, carefully make an assault. Both equally proven methods. Yet the latter method seemed safer, less dangerous. Wissemann gazed at his beckoning fuel gauge and sighed.

It would have to be Immelmann's way!

Down, like a bolt of lighting he flashed. The Bavarian Eagle dived through the moist cloud bank, charging his guns, hunching over the stick, squinting through the sights. And as the Eindecker's prop sliced the outer fringes of the clouds, he saw the rearmost F.E. fill his gun sights. The Englishmen did not appear to be wary of his Eindecker, for they flew on in a near straight line. Wissemann figured they were probably on their way back to base after a lengthy recon flight, and in all likelihood, not expecting an encounter with enemy aircraft so late in the day. Two thumbs hovered over the trigger buttons.

TOK-TOK-TOK-TOK-TOK-TOK! TOK-TOK-TOK-TOK-TOK-TOK!

The quiet of the lazy afternoon was suddenly broken by the rapid-fire bursts of twin Maxims, the sky spattering with staccato fire of flaming orange-red. Tracer rounds lashed out over the hundred meter gap, slamming into the tail assembly of the F.E. Canvas punctured, wooden pieces splintered off in the slipstream, a section of the tail's elevator tore loose. The British-built biplane staggered but flew on. Three rudely alerted crews bolted into action. The gunners stood up and swung their Lewis guns around.

Wissemann zoomed past the formation, circling back in a climb. He gazed at the fuel gauge once again. *Gott!* Time left for one more attack. He jerked the throttle to the max and the 160-horsepower Oberursel roared with power. Back around he went, the balky wings of the Eindecker banking slowly. Seconds later, the British biplane came into sight once again.

The F.E.s had spread out now, the gunners manning the rear machine guns, standing upright in their seats. How ridiculous they looked, thought the Bavarian. One bounce, one shudder, one jolt, might heave the hapless Englishmen overside. Who had designed such absurd-looking aeroplanes? Why were brave men forced to make due with such laughable equipment? It did not seem fair. Poor lads! What crack-brained engineer was responsible for these silly-looking flying bathtubs? What greedy, self-serving capitalist had fabricated such aeronautical lunacy?

Wissemann pitched the Eindecker's nose down and dived. He

targeted the same F.E., aiming from fifty meters. It was yawing wildly, slewing, staggering about the sky with a damaged tail assembly. The gunner was firing, but his bullets were nowhere near the converging monoplane. His rear machine gun was quite useless in a stern attack.

The Maxims flashed again.

Hot lead spewed forth as Wissemann held down the triggers. Twenty rounds impacted, slamming into the whirling propeller and rear-mounted engine, bullet strikes flashing all over the F.E. biplane's stubby fuselage. The splintered propeller began warbling clumsily, smoke began pouring out of the engine compartment. Then the battered machine stumbled in a jerky left bank, wheeling around suddenly in the opposite direction, just as Wissemann zoomed by. The other two F.E. machines swung around in wide right turns, gunners blasting away. A few .303-caliber rounds whizzed harmlessly past the Bavarian's ears. But one British bullet struck Wissemann's instrument panel, smashing the glass-faced fuel gauge, sending a sliver of glass flying, nicking his upper lip. He winced as blood spurted from the tiny cut, then leaked into his mouth. He could taste the salty liquid as he turned round after the smoking F.E.

"*Verdammt!*" he spat, cursing his bad luck.

Now he really had to break off and head back to Valenciennes. With no fuel gauge, he wouldn't know how much petrol was left in the tank. He groaned irritably. Nah-nah-nah! That *Gitterrumpf* had to go down no matter what! It was already halfway to hell, smoking and staggering all over the sky, a few more shots would send it there for certain. The Eindecker quickly closed the gap and the German lined up his gunsights again. The F.E. was a giant silhouette now—a fat goose for the slaughter.

"*Auf Wiedersehen, Herr Engländer!*" Wissemann spouted cockily, open firing, this time, at a mere twenty-five meters.

The guns stuttered briefly—then stopped. Jammed. "Ach!" The bloodied Bavarian jerked the charging handles to clear the jam, then pressed the trigger buttons again. Nothing. Silence reined.

Bullets whistled around his head. The other two F.E.'s were attacking! Wissemann pounded the gun butts with his fists, yanked the charging handles, swore, spat, did everything possible but dance a jig on top of his jammed guns. Nothing worked.

More bullets whistled by his ears. He shook a fist at the sky above and uttered a hoarse curse, then jerked the Eindecker wide of the now circling F.E.'s, zooming down in a dive for German territory, his face ruddy with anger, his lips red with blood. He gnashed his teeth, continually pounding the gun butts until his hands were sore and bruised. And the Oberursel droned on, the two-row rotary slowly putting some distance between Wissemann and the Englishmen, who were now turning back for their own lines, one nursing his damaged engine back to base, still quite airborne. Wissemann glanced over his shoulder and saw the tiny silhouettes of three biplanes winging into the orange sunset, a little trail of smoke streaming from the last one.

He shook his head bitterly. He almost wanted to cry. Such a golden opportunity lost, lost to idiotic, malfunctioning guns. A bad synchronizing gear, indeed! Who had designed that lousy piece of equipment, eh? What man was responsible for that design?

"*Agh-h-h-h-h-h!*" a howling cry echoed across the darkening skies.

At exactly 1900-hours, a gliding Eindecker touched down at Valenciennes, its engine silent for lack of fuel. It coasted onto the hangar tarmac and rolled to a dead stop. An enraged Bavarian officer clambered out of the cockpit, stalking off to the Officers' Mess, a grim, bloodstained line where a smile should have been. Nostrils flared, eyes flashed. A stiff, stalking stride hinted at some deep, embittered animus. Hands were balled in tight fists. Alas, the perfect picture of utter disgust. Willi Wissemann was a miserable man!

Chapter 5

✠

AUGUST 25, 1916. OBERLEUTNANT Willi Wissemann wanted to retch. The sudden jolt of turbulence had forced stomach-soured cognac into his mouth. With a grunt of disgust, he swallowed it back down. He exhaled slowly, shaking his head as the revulsion deepened, fighting the urge to throw up, sweat draining down his face. He leaned over the side of the cockpit and spat.

Wissemann swore an oath.

"*Verdammt!* No more late night parties. No more drinking."

His hands trembled. He took a deep breath and closed his eyes for a moment. That second seemed to last for an eternity. But once the nausea faded, the German officer quickly regained his composure. He peered through the windscreen and concentrated on the whirling blades of the propeller. They spun in a fine mahogany-blurred arc. The bombilation of its 160-horsepower Mercedes engine was a deafening but reassuring sound. An exhausted Bavarian pilot reached for the petrol cock and fine-tuned the fuel mixture valve, setting the carburetor for the rarefied air of the upper atmosphere.

Behind him in the rear cockpit, sat his duteous comrade and friend, *Leutnant* Franz Zemke. The diligent observer glanced over a route map clamped securely to a clipboard, then checked his Parabellum machine gun, cocking the charging handle, clearing it for action. Within a few moments, they would be over the target area— the Bray-sur-Somme Bridge—six kilometers southeast of Albert.

Below the cruising Roland, refulgent expanses of altocumulus clouds drifted along idly, almost static against the backdrop of a pastel-colored sky. This murky mass occasionally obscured the two aviators' view. But these men knew the lay of the land well. They had flown this route many times in the last six weeks, nearly every day—thirty-five sorties total! Cloudy obstacles or not, they knew where they were going.

Today their mission was a simple, routine one: photograph the road and bridge and return safely with the photographic plates. The photos would be very useful to German Intelligence, who hoped to get significant proof the British 4th Army was still staging in that area. This birds-eye view of the British infantry would be exceedingly helpful in gauging troop strengths of a waning British offensive. Moreover, at high noon, with the sun at its zenith, the ground shadows would be at a minimum, thus revealing more of the actual landscape to the camera lens. This would produce unequivocally precise photographs.

Franz Zemke scanned the landscape carefully. At three thousand meters, the expansive fields of the Somme, gouges of dun and green, was a somber plain ringed by a featureless milieu of downland umber. He glanced at his map once more, coordinating it with their last known position. He nodded; this was the place. The dutiful observer turned around and apprised his pilot with a gentle tap on the shoulder. They were over the target area!

Craning his neck backwards, Wissemann could see Zemke pointing at the Somme River, its majestic roiling waters glistening in the noonday sun. He nodded in acknowledgment, throttling back the engine, gently easing the control stick forward, pitching the Roland into a shallow dive. Concurrently, Zemke prepared the camera, which was firmly affixed to the side of the fuselage.

Wissemann banked the Roland, making a wide turn towards the south, plowing through a thick patch of wispy cumulus. Seconds later, the little two-seater emerged from the circumfluent cloud, heading straight for the bridge, cruising at two thousand meters. Today the two Germans would be fortunate. There were no clouds over the immediate target area. Nevertheless, as soon as they became visible to the gun batteries hidden below, bursts of red-black anti-aircraft shells exploded around them. None of these explosions came close enough to cause any real concern, but it definitely made things a bit more nerve-wracking. Nevertheless, Wissemann kept a steady course, while scanning the sky around him. He was more afraid of enemy scouts he couldn't see than of the ineffectual shelling.

The trusty Roland droned on while the enfilade of anti-aircraft burst around its slender brown and green wings. Between Zemke's feet on the floor of the rear cockpit sat a large 250-mm box camera and six glass plates stored in slits at the back of the box. He hoisted the camera and placed it on the cockpit side, holding the pistol grip and trigger, leaning over, pointing the camera down, gazing through the viewfinder—finally snapping the picture. Quickly, he inserted the plate cover and withdrew the negative, storing it in the rear of the camera, slid a new plate in position, and shot again.

Meanwhile, Wissemann monitored the aircraft's performance. Everything was running smoothly. If only I had a few bombs, he thought. I could take out that rotten bridge right now. But that was a job for tomorrow. Today was just a photo-shoot.

After a few anxious circuits over the target area, Zemke had all the reconnaissance photographs he needed. He tapped Wissemann on the shoulder, signaling for the flight back home. Wissemann banked the Roland and turned to the east and the German lines. The mission was nearing two hours and Wissemann was already pining for the addictive taste of tobacco. Of course, that would have to wait. In these days of open cockpit flying, he ruefully conceded, lighting a flame was virtually impossible. And try holding a fragile thing like a cigarette against a brisk slipstream? That was quite impossible too!

Wissemann coughed roughly, feeling his chest tighten, smiling, thinking to himself. He'd smoked a whole pack of cigarettes the night before. His throat was raw and irritated. But worse than that, he was dog-tired. He didn't get to bed until late. It was well after four in the morning before he was able to collapse on his cot. There was a rumor going round in the *Abteilung* that he might be transferred. So, the good lads of FA-4b threw an impromptu party in his honor. It'd been difficult to extricate himself from the revelry. Most squadron parties could last well into the wee hours. And this one was no exception. During the height of the festive merriment, he sneaked out of the mess tent and stumbled back to his quarters.

Leutnant Landsberg had actually been scheduled to fly the photo-shoot. But he was so utterly hung over the next morning, he was stricken from the roster. The reconnaissance flight was nearly canceled. But a duteous Willi Wissemann volunteered to take the mission in his stead, even though he'd suffered through a fitful slumber. Every mission was important to him. Personal discomfort didn't matter. So long as he had the will to do battle, to fight, a war to win, only victory mattered. "If one hasn't given everything," he'd said, "then one has given nothing!"

He bit at his nether lip and thought: such a good German officer you are, Willi. Mars had to agree. Obedient, faithful and foolhardy!

As the minutes passed, the Roland finally approached friendlier territory, climbing higher every second. As the two-seater leveled off at its max altitude—4,000-meters—high over Morval, Wissemann scanned the shell-torn landscape below for a familiar landmark. These days, No-Man's Land was a cratered expanse of highly contested terrain. He was glad to be inside the cramped confines of an aeroplane cockpit and not in some rat-infested trench. Life in the Air Service certainly had its advantages. He imagined the embattled terrain below him as if it were a giant chess board, where kings and queens waited in the wings as the sacrificial pawns were sent forward in mass slaughter, while the knights of the air zoomed high overhead, doing battle in their lofty steeds.

As he was daydreaming and admiring the St. Pierre-Vasst Wood below, Wissemann happened to notice two amorphous specks approaching from the north, zooming down from greater heights. Zemke noticed them too, and alerted his pilot with a forceful rap on the shoulder. And as the specks grew larger, both recognized them as enemy scouts. Nieuports! "Ach! Here come the Tommies now," Wissemann muttered to himself. He knew these nimble scouts were dangerous weapons in knowing hands.

Zemke seized his Parabellum and swung it around. Wissemann adjusted his goggles and took a deep breath. He wrenched the control column right and banked towards a large layer of clouds, tracking the path of the Nieuports with a wary eye. The drab scouts continued on a course directly towards them, now closing with greater speed. He knew the Tommies had seen his lumbering barge sailing across the sky. He rammed the throttle forward, the Mercedes bellowed richly, the manifold crackling, blue flames licking out from the bulbous exhaust stack. The Roland excelerated.

Seconds later, the Nieuports zoomed past. Zemke rattled off a volley as they streaked by the stern but with little effect. Both Englishmen had misjudged the distance and their speed and overshot. Wissemann banked hard to give Zemke a continued field of fire. The Englishman in the leading Nieuport quickly recovered from his gaffe and rallied back to the German machine in a tight barrel roll. But he couldn't maneuver his Nieuport into the Roland's blind spot.

Zemke took aim and opened fire. *TOK-TOK-TOK-TOK-TOK-TOK!* He peppered the drab little Nieuport from stem to stern. The coruscation of impact should've been symptomatic of a well-aimed shot. But the apparent damage had no effect on the English scout. The Nieuport broke off, diving under the Roland's tail. The Tommy in the second Nieuport launched his attack from fifty meters, firing a single drum-fed Lewis machine gun. It barked unevenly.

CR-TAT-TAT-TAT! CR-TAT-TAT-TAT!

A smoking salvo of .303 caliber ball-rounds slammed into the tail assembly of the Roland. The slewing two-seater shuddered under the impact. Splintered plywood, canvas and paint littered the slipstream. Zemke, undeterred by the effects of the Englishman's attack, continued hacking away with his Parabellum and hit the Nieuport with a well-aimed shot. The Nieuport staggered, yawed, reared up— suspended briefly on its tail—and as it lurched skywards to avoid a collision with the Roland, stalled in midair. A hanging target! Zemke hosed the biplane with a smoking stream of 7.92-millimeter slugs. Once again his aim was true. This time Franz Zemke's marksmanship hurt the little English bird badly.

The Nieuport's engine took the brunt of the hellfire. The disabled Le Rhone rotary, riddled with bullets, clattered to a halt. Its shattered wooden propeller windmilled impotently, oily smoke streaming from shot up cylinders. The stalling scout stumbled on its side, yawing wildly, the Englishman wrestling for control. Seconds later, he managed to regain forward momentum, pitching the nose down, plunging earthward in a dead-stick glide. But the powerless rotary was just dead weight now—the Nieuport, a hopeless, helpless cold-meat carcass.

Suddenly, from the high-blue above, a Fokker biplane streaked down upon the hapless Nieuport. It was lancing down like an arrowhead toward the British single-seater. The Fokker's single Maxim machine gun spat out vicious staccato bursts of smoking bullets. Two more Fokkers zoomed after the other Nieuport, their guns blinking angrily too.

The wily German pilot took up a point-blank position behind the faltering British scout, and fired a long salvo, mortally wounding the pilot. The dead Englishman slumped over his controls. The Nieuport began to spin earthbound, out of control. A long, twisting pall of black smoke trailed after it. The top wing broke off halfway down. The Nieuport eventually crashed on the outskirts of Lesboeufs, near the German rear trench line, after a long, uncontrolled crash-dive. From three thousand meters, it looked like a flashing pinpoint of light.

In the meantime, the remaining Englishman beat a hasty retreat, winging through a drift of clouds, hiding, heading back to his aerodrome, eluding his attackers. The desperate Tommy generated enough speed in his escape to outdistance the two Fokkers. Wissemann watched all this from an envious distance. How he longed to be in a hunting squadron.

The Fokkers regrouped. The flight leader pulled alongside the Roland. He saluted amiably. *"Wie gehts?"* he seemed to be saying. But his face was all but hidden by a fold of scarf and the blankness of tinted goggles. Grim faced, Wissemann's hand rose to a salute so nonchalant, it was more like a wave. He recognized the green and brown Fokker D.II. It was from KEK-Vaux, an old scout squadron based at Vaux Aerodrome. The pilot rocked his wings, then banked away in a slow, diving turn, his two comrades maneuvering in close to his flanks. Moments later, they disappeared from sight.

Angry with the Fokker flier for stealing his thunder, Zemke swore bitterly. *"Gott verdammt!* That damned *Schweinehund* snatched a sure victory from me!"

"Glad he did!" Wissemann yelled back. "Saved our poor heinies!"

"Those Tommies were reckless idiots, for sure!"

"Indeed!" Wissemann agreed. "They were far too reckless! Those half-wits attacked first without checking the sky above!"

"It seems as though our wily Fokker-friend used us as cats-paw, Willi! Unbeknownst to us! That dastardly old cheat had stalked the Nieuports—waited for the Englishmen to make their play, and..."

"And then mercilessly pounced on them!"

"Scheisse!" Zemke spouted, cursing the Fokker driver, feeling the situation had been well under his control. However, the fickle hand of fate had intervened, snatching a sure kill from his snare. Credit for aerial victory seemed unlikely now for poor Franz Zemke. His lips parted. Something unspeakable escaped through that narrow slit.

THIRTY MINUTES LATER... the Roland descended earthward for a landing, awkwardly bouncing a few meters, then touched down on the grassy turf of Baralle, the squadron's new airfield. Wissemann reduced power and the two-seater rolled to a halt just on the edge of the cinder tarmac. The engine sputtered and died when he switched off the magnetos, watching the propeller tremble to a sputtering halt.

Franz Zemke snatched the flight cap and goggles from his head, unstrapped himself from the rear cockpit and peeled off his gloves. He turned to Wissemann, who was still seated in the front cockpit.

"Another frustrating mission. One more for the books, eh, Willi?"

"Yes, one more. Do you have a cigarette, Franz?" Wissemann asked as he undid his safety harness and pulled himself out of the cockpit. He hopped to the ground.

"Here, Willi. It's my last one."

"Danke shön."

"That was some fine flying, Willi," Zemke said as he clambered down from his cockpit.

Wissemann took the cigarette and lit it with a match. "Thank you, Franz. That was some fine shooting. What happened?"

"It's not worth discussing, really."

"You seem a little disgusted. Don't be angry."

"That *Engländer* was done for, Willi. I shot him all to pieces—*kaput!*" Zemke smacked his fist in the palm of his hand, emphasizing his point, however moot it was.

"You had him dead-to-rights, *nicht?*"

"That fathead in that Fokker polished him off after I'd already knocked its engine out of commission. That Nieuport was mine!"

Wissemann grinned, took a deep drag from the cigarette and then handed it to Zemke.

"Oh, forget it, Franz," he said, exhaling in a smoky sigh. "Put in a claim with *Idflieg*—I'll corroborate it."

Franz Zemke shook his head bitterly and took a final drag from the cigarette. "*Quatsch!* It's doubtful they'll award a victory to me. Those single-seat jockeys get all the credit." He handed the smoldering butt back to Wissemann, then unbuttoned his flight jacket and pulled a handkerchief from his pants pocket. He swiped the sweat from his reddening complexion. "*Gott!* It's really hot today."

"Maybe *you* should put in for pilot training, Franz." Wissemann clapped his flustered comrade on the shoulder. "Stop putting it off, eh? You too, could be one of those 'fatheads' flying a Fokker."

"Right," Zemke grumbled bitterly, placing the handkerchief back in a pocket.

Wissemann greedily finished off the cigarette, taking several deep puffs just as the chief maintenance NCO, *Vizefeldwebel* Fromm, strolled up. Fromm was continuing his afternoon inspection, checking all the aircraft in the *Abteilung*. A gritty expression contorted his lean face, a patronizing tone soured his words.

"I see you two made it back in one piece," he quipped."

"*Humph!*" Zemke replied. Wissemann just smiled silently.

"Any battle damage?"

Zemke pointed to the tail assembly as he undid his scarf. "There... a nice bit of handiwork by one of our English friends."

Fromm inspected the damage. Numerous blackened bullet holes pockmarked the rudder post and tailplane. Some of the canvas fabric was in tatters.

"*Verdammt, Engländer!*" he cursed.

"Will she live, Fromm?" Wissemann wisecracked.

"*Ja.* Some damage. Nothing serious. I'll take care of it, as usual," Fromm remarked dryly.

Vizefeldwebel Alfred Fromm was the chief maintenance mechanic of FA-4b, and a short, frail, middle-aged man. He was a little long in the tooth for aviator's antics, long lacking in forbearance too, often working endless hours on the overburdened aircraft of the squadron. His hectic schedule usually kept him up late in the night, so he mostly slept during the day.

He squinted through thick, round wire-rimmed spectacles, prodding the bullet holes with his stubby fingers. "So, what happened out there today, eh?" he asked.

Wissemann nudged Zemke with an elbow and winked. "Nothing serious. We took care of it, as usual." His voice was full of sarcasm and irony as he mimicked Fromm's squeaky voice.

Zemke grinned, nodding in playful agreement.

Fromm bolted up from his inspection and glared at Wissemann, shaking his head in dejection. "You know, sir. A bit of appreciation might be in order now and then!" He stomped away annoyed, a laggard gait betraying his exhausted frustration.

Pilot and observer smiled at each other, then burst into raucous laughter. "Poor old Fromm!" Wissemann jibed. "No sense of humor,"

As this little scene had played itself out, two section mechanics had begun dismantling the camera from inside the Roland's fuselage, but clumsily at best. One lad nearly dropped the photographic plates on the ground.

"Hey, *Dummkopf!*" Zemke's eyes nearly popped out of his head. He threw his arms up tetchily. "Watch it, you idiots! Be careful with those plates. They nearly cost me my ass today!"

The two mechanics exchanged indifferent glances, grunting inaudibly.

Franz Zemke grabbed one by the arm. "Hey! Nice and easy, *bitte?*" His tone was more patronizing than it was pleasant.

The mechanic stared back, blinked blankly, shrugged, and trudged off with the photographic equipment under his arm. Zemke escorted the ham-fisted pair of mechanics all the way back to the Operations hut, fussing at them bitterly, making sure they didn't drop the photo plates.

Wissemann had to laugh—

"*Herr Oberleutnant! Herr Oberleutnant!*" a voice called out, suddenly. It was *Unteroffizier* Dietz beckoning with a lusty wave. Dietz was now adjutant to *Hauptmann* Hochstetter.

"Yes, Dietz. What is it?"

Unteroffizier Dietz saluted. "Some good news, sir—from *Kofl.* Your transfer's been approved."

"Approved?" Wissemann's eyes brightened. "Finally! No more schlepping around in these old nags. It's a fighting scout for me!"

Willi Wissemann slapped the side of the Roland's fuselage likening it to an old horse. He marched off to Operations, his head suddenly in the clouds. FA-4b wasn't the best flying section in the Air Service, nor the worst, but nothing compared to the new, well-equipped *Staffeln* and their single-seat scouts—the thoroughbreds of the sky.

"Good luck, sir," Dietz called out after him, watching Willi Wissemann make his way down the tarmac. A little smile formed on his lips as he shook his head remorsefully. *"Ach,* another fine officer gone off to join a *Jagdstaffel."*

Wissemann found the Operations hut, went in, traversed the main map room, making his way to Hochstetter's office. He knocked on the door with a heavy hand.

A deep, gruff voice beckoned from within. "Who is it?"

"Oberleutnant Wissemann reporting as ordered, sir."

"Enter."

Wissemann pushed the door in, stamped to a halt, saluted crisply, clicked his heels—more for his own amusement than protocol then snatched the service cap from his head. He smiled broadly.

"Will you knock off all that parade ground clap-trap already?" Hochstetter replied jocularly, smiling. "At ease, Willi."

"Danke, Herr Hauptmann." Wissemann relaxed his posture.

Hochstetter clapped his hands together with glee. "Well, Willi, looks like your requests for transfer have been granted," he said, in his usual cheerful manner. He held the official communiqué in his hand, waving it about, back and forth.

"My prayers have been answered, *Herr Hauptmann?"* Wissemann was standing casually now, his weight balanced forward.

"So it seems, *Junge.* Looks like you've impressed the right people."

"The right people, sir?"

"The great Oswald Boelcke has summoned you for an interview."

"Boelcke's summoned *me?* Let me see that."

Hochstetter nodded and gave Wissemann the communiqué. He returned to the camp chair behind his desk and lit a cigar.

Wissemann read the message silently. "I'll be damned. It's true!"

"Yes! It's a potential appointment to a new squadron he's formed at Bertincourt. It's an all-fighting scout *Jagdstaffel—JASTA,* they're calling them now."

"Hmm? I wonder why he chose me."

"I know Boelcke, Willi. I recommended you."

"*You... recommended... me?*"

"Your efforts haven't been in vain here, lad." Hochstetter offered up a cigar. "Here, take one."

Wissemann nodded agreeably. "Thank you, sir. So, when do I leave?" He lit the cigar and took a puff. It was one of those fine Dutch cigars the *Staffelführer* coveted so fondly.

"As soon as you can get packed, *Junge.*"

"Really?"

"A truck leaves tonight for Cambrai. Twenty-one hundred hours.

"Twenty-one hundred, sir?" Willi Wissemann questioned, then recovered. "Splendid!" Funny, the way the German Army ran the day on the basis of a twenty-four hour clock, just as the English did. He never could quite get used to it. He had to figure back each time. Hmm. Let's see, twenty-one hundred. Yes, that would be... nine o'clock in the evening. "Splendid, *Herr Hauptmann.* Can't wait.

"You'll meet *Hauptmann* Boelcke on Monday."

"Boelcke? *Gott!* Truly?"

"Truly. So, Willi, you'll have a few days of leave before your interview, hm?"

"And my release papers—"

"Your orders have already been cut, *Junge.* You're a free man."

"I'll miss you and this bunch terribly, I mean—"

"Rubbish!" Hochstetter smirked. "Get the hell out of here, Willi! Get drunk. Go find a girl, have some fun. Just get out of my hair already, will you?"

Hochstetter's jocular nature and sage advice certainly appealed to Wissemann's inclination towards leisure. "I damn well intend to, sir."

"Boelcke is a tough bird, so you'd better go all out and enjoy yourself. You've earned it."

"Thank you, sir." Boot heels clicked.

"And don't be so damned sentimental, Willi."

"Of course not."

"This is a war, remember?"

"How could I forget?"

"The next time I see you, *Junge,* I want to see the *Pour le Mérite* hanging around your neck." Hochstetter bolted to his feet, waving the cigar in a circle, laughing. "Now off with you!"

Wissemann flipped a salute.

"*Au revoir, mon vieux!*

"Good-bye, Willi!"

HE HAD FINISHED HIS BUSINESS at the *Kommandeur der Flieger's* office in a rather brief meeting, then passed a enjoyable half-hour with the cavalry captain who served Army as its staff aviation officer. A high-keyed Willi Wissemann was temporarily transferred to the German 1st Army, *Kofl* essentially setting up a meeting with *Hauptmann* Oswald Boelcke. Willi Wissemann was to report to AFP-1 (Cambrai), Monday, August 28th, at 0700 hours. Until then, he was on his own. He had a whole weekend to enjoy—two full days of uninterrupted leisure, rest and relaxation.

He checked into the Le Mouton Blanc, a hotel in the heart of Cambrai, a place currently run by the 1st Army Quartermaster, and was assigned a room on the second floor. The elated Bavarian airman could hardly stop smiling. It all seemed quite surreal to be granted a meeting with the renowned Oswald Boelcke. The man was a living legend. He'd practically written the book on combat aviation. All men marked for single-seat squadrons would be measured by this magnificent man's mettle. His personal tally of nineteen victories was currently tops in the Air Service. Only the late Max Immelmann had come close to that record. Now Boelcke was forming a squadron solely set up for "hunting" sorties. This *Staffel,* and seven others just like it, would be exclusively equipped with the latest single-seat scouts. Fokkers, Halberstadts and the new Albatros D-scouts would be assigned in groups of a dozen or more. And to be handpicked by Germany's greatest ace was an honor Wissemann had been dreaming about for a long time. The best tactics, the best aeroplanes, the best pilots—an unbeatable combination.

He couldn't wait for Monday!

After a short nap, then bath, Wissemann decided to go out and treat himself to a sumptuous dinner. A quiet, celebratory meal of sorts, a special reward for a job well done. He'd noticed a few restaurants on his way in to Cambrai; the city was still intact in spite of the war, a few eateries were still in operation, and decent food could still be had, so he hoped. He'd just received his monthly pay hours before and had money to spare. A fine bottle of wine, a good meal, maybe some coffee afterward, even dessert, would be the order of the day. Later, when he returned to his room, he'd uncork that new bottle of cognac Zemke and the good lads of FA-4b had given him as a going away present. He planned to sleep in late on Saturday, do nothing but lounge around the whole day through. And on Sunday, he'd write Ilse a long letter detailing everything that had happened.

He left the hotel around 8 o'clock, making his way down the boulevard in search of a nice restaurant. It was a fine night, cloudy but still very nice. A cool breeze stirred the thinning August air. A cigarette dangled from his mouth, a thin smile tugged at his lips, his eyes twinkled with gay assurance of a bright future, his hands nestled restively in his pants pockets and the service cap upon his head was tilted at a rakish angle. He'd removed the stiffening ring to give it a fashionable crushed effect. If he was going to be a scout pilot now, he wanted to look like one. Membership certainly had its privileges, he thought merrily.

After about fifteen minutes of walking, he found a quaint little bistro on the Avenue de Quesnoy. It had a nice look about it. Big glass windows, white tablecloths, candles. Cozy.

He went inside.

It was a dimly lit place, only half full, servicemen mostly. He didn't see a host or hostess, so he found a table on his own and sat down. He ashed his cigarette in an ashtray and looked around, noticing mostly noncoms and enlisted men. He saw one officer, a *Hauptmann*, sitting with a cute little blond. The two appeared to be in love. Their hands were coupled over the tabletop in a fond embrace, a half-full bottle of red wine graced their dinner table.

A moment later, a waiter came to Wissemann's table. He was an elderly gentleman, a Frenchman, and he spoke fluent German, much to the hungry Bavarian's surprise. *"Guten Auben, mein Herr,"* the waiter articulated evenly in German. "How are you, this fine evening?"

Wissemann smiled and jerked a nod. *"Très bien, merci,"* he riposted adroitly, once more displaying a good command of the French language. *"Comment allez-vous?"*

"Hah-hah-hah!" the old Frenchman chuckled, amused by the German's unmistakable patois, then replied in kind: "I am well, sir. Thank you. Would you like to start off with an apéritif? What can I get you, *monsieur?"* The waiter leaned over slightly, pen and pad in hand.

"Hmm... a bottle of wine, to start with."

"Red or white?"

"Red. A Beaujolais would be nice. The best you have."

"Very good, *monsieur.* An appetizer, perhaps?"

"Um, the wine will suffice. Let me peruse your menu a moment."

"Of course, *monsieur."* The waiter nodded and handed Wissemann a small paper menu. "Here you are. Take a long look. Everything's available except the *Escargot de Bourgogne.* Oh, the *potage au cresson* is very good, tonight. All right—back in a moment with your wine."

"Merci, garçon."

91

"De rien, monsieur." The waiter turned about smartly and darted off for the kitchen.

Escargot? Wissemann grimaced. Snails in a melted butter and garlic sauce were not his idea of recherche cuisine. He couldn't see how Frenchmen enjoyed such peculiar delicacies. He'd tried them once, years ago, before the war, while vacationing in Paris. He'd found them to be rather tasteless and gummy. Although his palette was quite refined, Wissemann just couldn't bring himself to enjoy the edible, terrestrial snail.

He glanced over the menu and made some careful selections.

He gazed at the doting couple again. They were still holding hands. Ah, what a loving couple, he thought. The young girl reminded him of Ilse. She had a petite figure and pale white skin, just like Ilse. Her sandy blonde hair was the same, too, but much shorter. She was dressed in a simple pleated skirt and blouse, plain low-heeled shoes and dark stockings. She looked to be much younger than the man, at least fifteen or twenty years younger. The officer, a captain, was a slender, well-built man with graying temples and a neatly trimmed goatee. Even though the bistro was dimly lit with just candles, Wissemann could clearly see the distinctive regimental insignia on the left forearm of his *Feldgrau* tunic. The officer was an artillery commander—the 267th Field Artillery—to be exact.

The waiter returned. "Your wine, *monsieur.*" He set a glass down on the table along with an *amuse-bouche of Tepanade* and bread, and then pulled the cork from the bottle and offered it up for inspection.

Wissemann waved him off. "Oh, that won't be necessary. I'm sure it's fine."

The waiter sighed, a bit disappointed, and poured a small portion into the slender stemware, anyway. *"Monsieur, S'il vous plaît?"*

Wissemann grimaced, shrugged, picked up the glass and sampled it. *"Mmm... Ça me plaît.* Excellent. What year?"

"Nineteen-fifteen—a very nice *Côte de Brouilly*—eh, *monsieur?*"

"Aha. Nice indeed." Wissemann picked up the menu and rasped his chin. "Let me start with the *potage au cresson,* please. Then, perhaps, let's follow that with... hmm, *filets de poisson pouches au vin blanc. D'accord?*

"Très bien, monsieur." The waiter filled the discerning airman's wine glass halfway to the top, bowed cordially, then paced away.

Wissemann picked up the wine glass and took a healthy swallow. "Ahh... splendid." He then popped open his cigarette case and lit a Halpaus. Bluish smoke rings soon curled up to the rafters. He reclined comfortably and stole another glance at the young blonde.

She caught his eye and smiled, just as the artilleryman happened to be looking the other way. Wissemann winked. She coyly dropped her eyes and twitched her head back to her date.

The Bavarian airman chuckled. He took a deep drag from his cigarette and then exhaled the smoke in a long, wispy sigh. *"Ach,* Ilse. I wish you were here, my dear. The world is so lonely without you." He took another sip of wine and began to contemplate his dinner.

Outside the bistro, Wissemann suddenly heard the raucous crackle of a motorcycle pulling up, its noisy motor puttering to a stop. A helmet-clad soldier hopped off, looked around a moment, nodded, then stalked into the dining room. He paced right up to the artillery commander's table. The rider was obviously a courier, and he had a message for the artilleryman. He came to a crashing halt. Boot heels clicked. He saluted, then reached in his courier pouch and handed over an envelope. The commander snatched the envelope from the courier's hand, ripped it open, and hastily read it.

Wissemann inhaled cigarette smoke, still watching curiously.

The artillery commander cursed, yanking the napkin from his tunic collar, shaking his head. He shoved his chair back and stood up, his face flushed now. He waved off the courier. The courier saluted again, marched back to his motorcycle outside, kick-started it and motored away, leaving behind a wake of noxious fumes. The artillery commander leaned over to the young girl and kissed her hand. He said something, but Wissemann couldn't hear what it was. He guessed it was something close to an apology. The commander donned his service cap and stalked out of the bistro. Wissemann watched him cross the street, get in the Opel staff car that was parked near the curb, start it, then jerk it into gear. A moment later, he was halfway down the avenue.

Wissemann stole another glance. The little blonde sat eyes forward, seemingly unperturbed. She reached for her purse and pulled out a gold cigarette case and plucked out a slender cigarette. She lit it and began puffing. She smiled—

"Monsieur—soup du jour!" The waiter stood over the table with a piping hot bowl of watercress soup. He set it down before Wissemann, along with a spoon and an extra napkin.

"Merci," replied the Bavarian airman.

"Il n'y a pas de quoi, monsieur." The waiter gave a quick nod and was gone in a flash.

Wissemann took another glance at the young blonde. But she wasn't there, now. Gone? Where'd she go? He thought.

"Monsieur? " a soft voice murmured over his shoulder.

Wissemann turned around in his seat abruptly and glanced over his shoulder. The young blonde came gliding up. She smiled impishly and took a little puff from her cigarette. He bolted to his feet and took the young lady's hand and promptly kissed it.

"*Bonsoir, vous allez bien, Madmoiselle?*"

"*Bonsoir, monseiur.* Good evening to you, as well." The girl curtsied daintily, smiling coyly.

"My name's Willi, *mademoiselle.* Willi Wissemann. And you are...?"

"Babette. Babette Jourdan. *Enchanté, Monsieur* Wissemann."

"*Mon Dieu!* Oh, Please, call me Willi." Wissemann said, waving his cigarette about deprecatingly.

"All right... Willi."

"So. I see you've been abandoned this evening. What happened?"

Babette frowned. "Oh, '*Herr Big-Shot*' was called off to his artillery company again. It happens quite often, really."

Wissemann nodded. "I see. Will he be back?"

"Maybe." Babette shrugged. "But I don't think so. He left me here last Friday night. He never came back then."

"Well, then" Wissemann grinned broadly. "I shall keep you company, my dear. Will you sit with me a spell?" His outstretched hand directed her to the empty chair across from his, pulling it out in a gentlemanly gesture. "Sit. Please."

"Ah, a fine gentlemen, you are." She sat down.

Wissemann slid back into his chair. "There we go."

Babette leaned back, folding her arms over her chest. "Are you recently posted to this area, Willi?"

"Maybe." Wissemann took up his soup spoon and took in a mouthful and swallowed. "I don't know where they're going to put me just yet. I find out Monday."

"Are you an aviator?" She saw the shiny, silver airman's badge dangling from his tunic.

"Yes. Soon to be a scout pilot, *mademoiselle.* I hope."

"*Oooh...*" she cooed. "How romantic."

"Romantic?"

"Oh, yes. Most certainly. You airmen are like knights of old."

Wissemann chuckled. "Hmm, I've heard that before."

"What squadron are you with?"

Wissemann's brow narrowed. "I hate to talk shop, *mon chère.* Forget it. Tell me about yourself. What's a pretty young thing like you doing with that old front-hog, eh?"

Babette exhaled a cloud of smoke. "Well, he's entertaining sometimes, I suppose. He takes me out frequently. Buys me things.

You know, a girl gets lonely. Until General Joffre pushes you German so-and-so's back into the Fatherland, I'll just have to sit and wait around for my big, strong Frenchman. Now won't I?" She chuckled.

"Sure," Wissemann replied, then took a sip of wine.

He looked the French girl over. She was quite young, her eyes were pale green, and she had a cute snub-nose. Her skin was perfect. Her lips, daubed in rouge, were full and pouty. Narrow shoulders supported a slender, angular neck. She was proportionally endowed and had beautiful, slender fingers, tipped in pink polish. She wore no jewelry save the simple gold locket hanging near her cleavage.

"By the way, how old are you, Babette?" he asked.

"Twenty. What about you?"

"A year out from thirty. How old is the front-hog?"

"Uh... forty, I think? Maybe older? I never really asked him."

"Hmm, quite an age difference between you two, I see."

"I'm kind of a an old fashioned girl, I guess. I like older men."

Wissemann smiled salaciously, winking. "So, I guess you haven't, uh... well, you know, h'mm—"

"I don't talk shop, Willi." She winked back. "So forget it, *hein?*"

"*Touché, Mademoiselle!*" Wissemann raised his glass.

They both laughed.

The waiter returned with the *filets de poisson.* But Wissemann was already too distracted to finish his soup, much less start on the fish filets. He waved the waiter off, a polite gesture, and poured himself some more wine. He turned to the young girl with questioning eyes.

"Some wine, Babette? It's very good."

She nodded.

"Bring the lady a glass—will you, *garçon?*"

"Of course." The waiter smiled and gave a little nod. He left the filets and trotted off the kitchen.

The hungry Bavarian seized a fork and sampled the entree. He swallowed and grinned. "*Mmm...* good, this is!" He took a sip of wine. "So... you want to know about ole' Willi Wissemann, do you?"

"As much as you dare, Willi."

"There's not much to tell, Babette. I'm just a country boy from the Allgäu. Just trying my hand at flying these days. Earning my three hundred *Deutchmarks* a month—saving it for a rainy day."

"A rainy day?"

"One day soon, I'll marry my fiancée, Ilse, settle down, and have some children. Perhaps start my own business? I don't know, actually. I haven't really given it much thought. There's a war on, you know. First things first, right?"

"Yes, the war." She nodded. "Everything's in limbo these days."

"And God only knows when it will all end."

"You're engaged, then?"

Wissemann nodded. "For over a year now.

"Oh." Babette suddenly looked a little crestfallen. "And when will you marry, Willi?"

The waiter returned with a wine glass. "*Mademoiselle,* your glass."

Babette gestured. "*Merci, garçon.*"

The waiter poured her a glass of wine.

"And how is the entrèe, *monsieur?*" he asked.

"*Magnifique!*" Wissemann exclaimed spiritedly. "My compliments to the chef."

The waiter nodded snappily. "*Très bien, monsieur!*" He bolted away.

"So. When will I marry, you ask?" Wissemann leaned back in his chair and studied the young girl's sullen face. "Don't know, really. Like I said, there's a war going on. Many things hinge on its outcome. My future is one of them."

"Why do you wait? You could be killed tomorrow, you know." Babette sipped her wine thoughtfully.

"True. But if we were married now, and I was killed—God forbid— my girl would just become another sad little widow. Germany has too many of those, these days. I couldn't do that to her and her family."

Babette scoffed softly "How admirable. But somehow, I don't believe all that, Willi."

Wissemann took another fork-full of fish. He chewed in a thoughtful manner, swallowed, then said: "Well, you're right, there— just a bit. She comes from a very upstanding family. Rich, I might add. Her father's a Prussian general, head of the railway, or something like that. Say, you're not a spy, are you?" He chuckled and dabbed his mouth with a napkin.

Babette smirked. "No. Don't be silly."

"Well, anyway... the old Prussian isn't too keen on his daughter marrying a commoner from Bavaria. Even a dashing, flying one. He'd rather see her married off to some count or baron, I'd imagine. Willi Wissemann isn't quite good enough for his little princess."

"Oh, that's nonsense, Willi. You're being dramatic—"

"You see," Wissemann returned, retrospectively. "My father was a nobody. His father was a nobody, a commoner. I don't have a drop of noble blood in me."

"Then you have risen purely on merit," Babette argued. "Surely that is... commendable, isn't it?

"My fiancée is the daughter of a Prussian aristocrat, my dear.

She'll not be married to the son of a—*commendable*—nobody."

"So why do you love this... this—*little princess,* then? Sounds like you're putting yourself through a lot of unnecessary heartache."

"Perhaps, I truly love her."

Babette humphed. "True love. Now *there's* an old fashioned idea."

"You've never been in love, Babette?"

"Once."

"Ah, so you know what I'm talking about, then."

"Yes. I was very young, sixteen. A boy from school."

"What happened?"

"We married."

"Oh? Well, where is he now?" Wissemann sensed the worst.

"Dead."

"Ooh... sorry to hear that."

"*C'est la guerre.*" Babette shrugged. "He was killed during the first months of the war. I never found out what really happened to him. The War Office in Paris only told me he was killed in battle, near Mons. No further details."

"Hmm. That's sad. Sorry to hear that, Babette."

"Don't be, Willi. I'm all over it now—ready to start anew."

"With a middle-aged German officer?"

"Oh, we're just friends, Willi. That's all."

"I see. Is he in love with you?"

"Probably."

"Doesn't 'Herr Big-shot' know the penalty for fraternizing with the enemy?" Wissemann smiled.

"Enemy? I am no one's enemy, Willi."

"*Ach,* You know what I mean. If the brass hats knew, they wouldn't be too happy about it, I assure you."

"People are people, Willi. You can't stop romance, or love. Not even a war can do that."

"True. True. But the German High Command doesn't look too highly upon fraternizers. Especially its officers." Wissemann took another bite. He washed it down with some wine.

"And you? Are you not fraternizing right now, Willi?"

Wissemann laughed. "And I'm loving every minute of it, *mon Chère.*" He held up his wine glass up high. "*Santé!* To love!"

Babette smiled. She picked up her glass. "*Santé!* To love!"

Glasses clinked. They both drank.

As Wissemann set the wine glass down and dug into his dinner once again, the faint sound of a motorcar caught his ear. He looked up and saw the artillery commander had returned. The Opel staff car shuddered to a halt and the commander got out and made his way back through the front door. He had a befuddled look on his face.

"Ah, your friend returns," Wissemann said, as he speared another piece of fish, shoving it in his mouth. "Perhaps—he'll join us—in our conversation—of love, hmm?"

Babette jerked around in her seat. She gazed across the bistro. Her face blanched. *"Mince!* He's back. Oh, Willi. This is bad. Very bad!"

Wissemann made a little face.

"Bad? Why? We're just talking, my dear. That's all."

"I know. But he's the jealous type. He'll think that I've been flirting with another man."

Wissemann smirked. "Well, haven't you?"

"Willi!" She hissed. "Be quiet. Here he comes."

The artillery commander stalked up. His face was flushed, a hostile look toyed with his features. "Babette? What's going on here? What are you doing?" The commander's French was clumsy and full of venom.

"Wolfgang—this is Willi Wissemann," Babette said with a nervous smile. "Willi... this is Wolfgang Deissel, a good friend of mine."

Wissemann half stood up. "Charmed, *Hauptmann*—"

"Willi Wissemann?" Deissel snorted. "An idiot, I'm sure!"

Wissemann scoffed, mildly stunned. His brow arched crossly. "Idiot? You could've at least said *'gentleman'*, same amount of wind!"

"Listen, *OBER-leutnant*," the commander rejoined acidly, making it a point to emphasize Wissemann's subaltern rank. "See here! Mind your manners. You're speaking to a superior officer."

"Oh, please, Wolfgang!" Babette pleaded. "Don't make a scene now. We were just talking, that's all."

"Talking? Don't you lie to me, Babette!" the commander spouted, hands on his hips. "Every time I turn my back, you're fooling around with every muckrake in town. And now, an aviator? *Gott!* Have you lost your mind? A lousy airman? Really!"

Wissemann scowled crossly. "Listen here, I don't have to take that kind of disrespect from you. superior officer or not. We airmen fight just as hard as you artillery jocks, or potato-heads, see? We dodge just as many bullets up there as the lot of you." He flicked his fork down and rose slowly, staring the artillery commander straight in the eye.

"I'm warning you, *Oberleutnant!* Stay away from my Babette."

"We were just having a friendly conversation, *Hauptmann.* Nothing is *going on* here, I assure you." Wissemann's chin came up. His chest swelled balefully.

The commander grunted. "Damned airman! You think you can

steal all the women, don't you! Think you can just waltz in anywhere and take your pick because you wing across the sky in those fancy little kites, eh? Well, forget about it! Keep your lousy aviator's paws off my girl!" He grabbed Babette by the wrist and jerked her out of the seat. "C'mon!"

"OW-W-W! You're hurting me!" Babette shrieked. "Let go of me!"

"Easy there, *Hauptmann.*" Wissemann put a firm hand on the commander's wrist. "Let's not get grabby now, all right? Calm down."

"*Verdammt!* Unhand me, you bumptious little shit!"

He slapped Wissemann's hand off, shoving him back, causing the lanky Bavarian to stumble backwards, causing him lose his balance. Wissemann staggered into a table, nearly knocking it over. Clumsily, he braced himself on a chair and regained his footing.

Everyone in the restaurant went silent. All conversation halted.

"Wolfgang! Stop it!" Babette shouted exasperatedly. "Stop it!"

The artillery commander let go of Babette's wrist and lunged for Wissemann. He lurched forward with a wild haymaker, just barely missing the Bavarian's chin.

A startled Willi Wissemann recovered his balance and swung back. There was a dull, spatting thunk as flat knuckles smashed against commander's cheek, bringing him down in a crashing thud; smashing a table; knocking over glasses; laying him out on the floor. Wissemann knelt down, straddled the supine man, and fired again. A fist landed squarely on the commander's nose, causing it to explode in a spatter of blood. He struck again. A hard punch blackened the man's right eye. Another punch glanced off his chin.

But the man fought back. The commander threw the big Bavarian off and got to his feet. "Damned son of a bitch!" he snarled, swiping at his bloodied nose. "You're going to get a nasty thrashing from me now, flyboy!"

Wissemann was up. "Come on, already! Do your worst, old man."

The waiter and proprietor came dashing into the dining room. "What's going on!" the proprietor exclaimed.

"Stop it! Stop it!" Babette shrieked. "Both of you!"

Wissemann and the artillery man squared off like two prizefighters going at it, moving around in a little circle, each eying the other angrily, both panting exhaustively.

A totally frantic proprietor ran out of the bistro, out to the sidewalk, gesticulating wildly. "Call the Gendarmes! Call the military police!" he uttered frantically. "Somebody! Quickly! Quickly!"

Wissemann landed another punch. The old commander staggered backwards, his lip busted, bloodied. Deissel regrouped and danced forward and caught his opponent in the ribs. Wissemann gasped and hunched over. He jerked sideways and took another nasty lick.

"Bastard!" the battered Bavarian cursed, uncoiling like a released spring. With a twist of his hips and a hard right, he sent the commander to his knees, then threw another right from a half-crouch. His knuckles smacked hard against the thickset jaw, driving the old front-hog into a wall.

Babette was crying now. *"No! No! Noooo... aghhh-h-h-h!"*

Stupefied servicemen gawked at each other, wild-eyed and frozen with indecision. Suddenly, a shrill whistle chirruped! The servicemen backed away from the door. The fighters paused. Four German military policemen came stomping in, their whistles shrieking loudly. They stalked over to the two combatants, truncheons drawn.

"ACTUNG! HALT! Both of you! Desist immediately or face the wrath of my stick, I say!" one bellowed loudly, waving his truncheon about with minatory intent. "Stop it! You're both under arrest!"

"The rest of you men, clear out of here. Now!" another policeman said, barking at the gawking throng of *Feldgrau*. The place began to empty out. Anxious servicemen spilled out into the street.

Yet both antagonists still faced each other with hands up, fists bloodied, each unwilling to yield, both gasping for breath. For a long moment nothing happened. Both men stood poised, sweating, panting, grumbling. There was a sound of heavy breathing.

Both men were near total exhaustion.

Wissemann puffed, lowering his fists. "So. Had enough, old man?"

The front-hog grunted. There was a quick, gasping intake of air as he stepped backwards, feinted with his left, then connected with a hard-right. Wissemann was too tired to cover up, and he took it clean. Everything went white for a split-second. He fell backwards onto his backside, blinking dazedly. Then... everything went black.

Chapter 6

✠

DECEMBER 31, 1916. BERLIN WAS KNEE-DEEP in snow. War waged on all fronts. Millions were dead or dying. And yet, the von Linkhofs were having a party. It was New Year's Eve now, and Willi Wissemann trudged heavily along the sidewalk of a nearly deserted city street. The cold cab ride from the Adlershof Test Facility had taken longer than usual, only because he'd stopped off at a local wine shoppe on the outskirts of Charlottenburg to purchase a bottle of cognac. The wind howled, snow fell in icy flakes. Snow had continued to fall in heavy, white flurries on the eve of 1917; Berlin was totally blanketed in an icy white powder. He shivered. It was cold but not nearly as cold as Silesia. He'd spent the better part of the last three months there in that godforsaken place. Compared to the hinterlands of East Prussia, Berlin looked like a veritable paradise to a warmth-loving Bavarian.

Wissemann, package in hand, found the address he was looking for, and walked up to a large iron gate. A guard in a security uniform stirred at his post, unlocking and opening the gated doorway halfway, waving the shivering Bavarian through.

"*Guten Abend, Herr Wissemann*," he said. "Go right in. It's just starting up."

"*Danke*, Ludwig." Wissemann gave a nod, doffing his cap slightly.

He paced up the snowy driveway towards the front entrance. Along the edge of the driveway, he saw several big luxury cars parked one behind the other; Mercedes, a Hispano-Suiza, a Gräf & Stift Double Phaeton, a Duesenberg, even an English Rolls-Royce, and some others he could only guess at, lined the circular driveway. Chauffeurs stood by stiffly, waiting, smoking, chatting, passing the time in idle conversation. A grand affair was definitely in the making here.

Wissemann trod up the steps to the front door and rang the bell. A moment later, the door opened and a little white-haired man with a bushy mustache dressed in a butler's uniform answered.

"Ah, Willi. Come in, come in," he said amiably, bending at the waist respectfully. "Greetings. I see you've finally made it?"

Wissemann chuckled. "Yes. Better late than never, aye, Marten?"

"Oh, don't worry, Willi. These affairs never really get going until the apéritifs."

"I suppose you're right—"

"Willi! Willi!" a young woman squealed as he entered the foyer of the mansion. The butler, Marten Zangler, closed the door on the snowy weather. And before Wissemann could even take off his coat and cap, a young woman wrapped him up in a big bear hug and kissed his reddened cheeks. "*Ach,* I'm so happy you're here, finally!"

Marten smiled tenderly. "Well, well. Someone is glad to see you." Wissemann embraced the young woman, laughing merrily. He returned her kisses with equal enthusiasm.

"*Liebchen,*" he cooed. "I'm so glad to see you, too!"

"Oh, Willi, I'm so happy you're here!"

"And I'm happy to be here, believe me."

"*Gott!* You wore your dress uniform. Splendid!"

Wissemann vetted his reflection in the pier glass. "Hm? So I did."

"You look so handsome and dashing. Doesn't he, Marten?"

"Yes, indeed." Marten nodded. "So he does, my dear."

"Me? Handsome?" Wissemann scoffed mockingly.

"He reminds me of myself, back in *my* youthful days," Marten replied, reaching for the dapper Bavarian's overcoat. "I'll take that for you, sir."

Wissemann nodded politely. He set the packaged bottle down and went through the standard routine of admittance. "Oh, stop it, you two, you're embarrassing me." He handed Marten his *Stein Grau* greatcoat and dress blue service cap.

"Don't be silly, Willi," she replied. "You look magnificent!"

"Marten, take care of *that* for me, will you?" Wissemann winked, pointing to the bottle of cognac.

"Certainly, sir. I'll keep it in a safe place." Marten nodded.

"Wait until Mother sees you!" The young woman clapped her hands. "She'll be delighted to see you all decked out in your fine dress uniform. You hardly ever wear it."

Wissemann simpered, quipping: "And for good military reasons, my dear." He tugged mechanically at the stiff tunic collar, grimacing.

She made a little face, shrugging uncomprehendingly.

Willi Wissemann turned to the old butler, heels clicking. *"Herr Zangler*—happy New Year's Eve, good sir."

Marten Zangler bowed reverently, nodding, grinning. "Thank you, Willi. Happy New Year's Eve to you, too." He paced away for the coat check closet. The old butler reminisced. He too had once been a soldier, winning the Iron Cross for bravery, serving with distinction in the Franco-Prussian War, some forty years earlier. He was proud of his twenty year Army service and sergeant's stripes.

Wissemann paused a moment, standing arms akimbo. "Ilse, stop! Let me look at you, my dear." He nodded, awe inspired. "Oh, my, my. You are as beautiful as ever, especially this evening. Breathtaking!"

The young woman smiled, slightly abashed. But she was beautiful!

Elisabeth "Ilse" Magdalena von Linkhof was a hazel-eyed, honey-haired, slender woman of twenty-two years. She wore her hair up in the traditional Victorian style and always dressed in the current fashions of the day. Tonight she wore a resplendent white evening gown, diamond tiara, and long white gloves. She bore an uncanny resemblance to Czar Nicholas' daughter, Tatiana Romanov, a Russian princess; people always remarked on the fantastic similarities. Although she did have a predilection towards fashionable finery, Ilse was always careful not to appear too garish or extravagant.

She taught music at an elementary school in Charlottenburg—a wealthy upper-class borough in Berlin. And as a talented musician herself, she played piano and sang, being an accomplished contralto of local acclaim. Ilse was also a highly educated and open-minded woman. But sometimes her scholarly education put her at odds with her peers. All too often, she'd vocalized her objections of the war and its negative consequences to friends and family. This of course, did not always please her parents, who were conservative German royalists, staunch supporters of the Kaiser and the German monarchy. Nevertheless, she was the apple of her father's eye.

Ilse von Linkhof, of course, fretted perpetually over her fiancé, Willi Wissemann. She couldn't understand his inherent predilection towards self-destruction. Repeatedly, he had returned to the fray of the war zone, constantly putting himself in hazard, much to her distress and vexation. She had a notion to keep him from harm's way. But how? What could be done to preserve her Willi dear from danger? Something had to be done!

Ilse von Linkhof took her man by the arm and hurriedly escorted him to the main dining room, where the other guests were preparing for a dinner feast and New Year's Eve celebration. It was an annual affair hosted by General von Linkhof and his wife Helene. Many dignitaries were there from the General Staff and the Imperial Cabinet, as well as certain members of the German Reichstag.

Wissemann always hated these kinds of affairs, planning to extricate himself before the stroke of midnight, taking Ilse with him. He'd be more comfortable in the Officer's Kasino at Adlershof, drinking toasts with regular army officers instead of rubbing elbows with snobby, high society aristocrats. Until then, however, he would have to play the role of the charming, officer and gentleman—a role that came quite naturally to him.

The jaunty Bavarian officer felt a bit stiff and uncomfortable in his pressed dress uniform. Tonight, Willi Wissemann wore a light blue dress tunic with ponceau red cuffs in the Brandenburg style. Both collar and cuffs were decorated with silver Litzen. The resplendent blue tunic and trousers, complete with slender red stripes, made him feel quite like a character in a certain Tchaikovsky ballet. He was unaccustomed to the black dress shoes as well—they felt a bit rigid and a half size too small. Yet, nonetheless, and all distractions aside, Willi Wissemann felt quite merry this evening. He was at Ilse's side and that was all that mattered to him.

Fumbling for a match and a cigarette with one hand, he lit the Halpaus and inhaled anxiously, feeling quite nervous negotiating the assemblage of distinguished *de bon ton*, who were all gathered around the fireplace for a before-dinner toast. Ilse smiled blissfully; she certainly was proud of her handsome aviator-officer. A dapper-looking servant carrying a silver serving tray offered them a glass of wine—a fine vintage Riesling. They both took a glass. She held her's up and made a quick toast.

"To a happy New Year, Willi, and the best of times."

"Hear, hear!" someone yelled.

Another lucubrated: "To the Fatherland and—"

"And to victory!" Wissemann replied, sarcasm tainting his tone.

"Oh, Willi. Don't be so sardonic. Not tonight. Please?"

"All right, *Liebchen*." Wissemann raised his glass. "*Prost!*"

"*Prost!*"

They touched glasses and then took a little sip. Willi gazed into Ilse's beautiful hazel eyes and then kissed her gently on the lips.

Ilse cooed with deepening affection. "Oh, Willi. I do love you so."

"I, I... love—oh, look! There's your mother."

Wissemann promptly doused his cigarette under a heel. Ilse's mother, Helene von Linkhof had suddenly appeared from across the room. She swanned over to the loving couple, grabbing Ilse's hand.

"Here you are, my dear. I'd wondered where you'd gotten off to," she remarked glassily. "Ah... Willi is here too. Splendid!"

"Oh, mother, doesn't he look grand? He's so handsome tonight."

Wissemann blushed with boyish awkwardness, grinning timidly.

"Yes, indeed. He certainly does, my dear. Dashing! Debonair!" *Frau* von Linkhof smiled at the young officer standing before her. "A fine Bavarian officer and gentleman."

Wissemann gently seized the old woman's white-gloved hand and kissed it. "Seasons greetings, *Frau* von Linkhof. It's so good to see you again—a pleasure, as always." Heels clicked. Wissemann jerked a nod.

"Thank you, Willi, she replied. "I'm glad you came. It's so nice to see you again as well."

Wissemann smiled politely. *Frau* Helen von Linkhof certainly looked quite elegant in her evening gown and sparkling tiara, all festooned in diamonds and pearls. Yet, Ilse looked even more stunning than her mother. Her satin evening dress and long white gloves made her look so beautiful, like a princess of Charlottenburg Palace. Her slender and diminutive figure made all others pale in comparison. Wissemann knew he was with the most beautiful woman in the whole mansion, if not the whole of Germany.

"H'mm, *Oberleutnant*," a gruff voice rumbled, and somewhat patronizingly said: "uh... so pleased you could join us this evening?" It was Konrad von Linkhof, Ilse's father. He had walked up while the trio had been exchanging their evening cordials. The old general reluctantly proffered his hand for a handshake.

Wissemann responded instantly, and the two men shook hands stiffly, indifferent expressions constraining their faces.

"Good evening, General von Linkhof. Thank you for inviting me."

"Hmm, yes. Well, it was Ilse that invited you, not I."

"It is an honor to be here tonight, sir. Really," Wissemann replied glibly. He leered at the old man, disdain burning in his eyes.

General von Linkhof, who was fully clad in a pristine Prussian dress uniform, grunted cagily, stroking his mustache, eying Wissemann with the same distrustful comportment, a look of contempt quite evident in his expression.

"Well, I hope you enjoy yourself, *Oberleutnant*," he replied in a glib tone. "Her happiness is my happiness. Enjoy your dinner."

"Indeed. Thank you, sir..." Wissemann trailed off. He wanted so badly to tell the old man off. But that wouldn't do considering the time and place. No. No! He must hold his tongue.

"Now. I must see to our guests, Helene," Konrad von Linkhof

announced icily to his wife. "Make sure dinner is served promptly at eight. I must talk to General von Hindenburg before he departs for Army headquarters." The old man bowed his head perfunctorily, turned about and stalked off, disappearing in the thronging crowd of dress uniforms and evening gowns.

Wissemann made a little face and sighed. *"Pfft!* Now that that's out of the way..."

"Willi! Behave yourself," Ilse warned.

"Oh, don't mind him," *Frau* von Linkhof enjoined. "Papi's just an insufferable old bore! Pay him absolutely no attention at all, Willi."

"Sage advice, *Frau* von Linkhof. Sage advice."

Ilse rolled her eyes and groaned anxiously. Wissemann grinned.

Frau von Linkhof patted Wissemann's forearm, nudging him, gently jerking her head, motioning him to follow her. "Come, Willi. I want you to meet someone." She led him to a remote corner of the room, towards a gayly decorated, giant-sized Christmas tree, where two distinguished staff officers, one a cavalry general and the other a tall, mustachioed naval officer, were standing, conversing in quiet conversation.

Ilse followed curiously. *"Mutti?"*

"Excuse me, gentlemen. Sorry to interrupt you," *Frau* von Linkhof said, smiling, bowing. "Ernst, I'd like to introduce someone to you, if you have a moment?"

"Yes, of course. Absolutely, Helene," replied the distinguished cavalry general.

"Ernst, this is *Leutnant*—"

"Um, uh... OBER-leutnant, Herr General," Wissemann interjected awkwardly, correcting *Frau* von Linkhof's little gaffe, trying to emphasize his higher commissioned grade.

"Oh, dear. I'm so sorry, Willi," she apologized in a hoarse whisper, squeezing his forearm in embarrassment, her mouth tightening awkwardly. "This is—OBERLEUTNANT—Wilhelm Reinhardt Wissemann, my daughter's fiancé. He's a instructor at Adlershof."

Wissemann chuckled, unruffled by *Frau* von Linkhof's second, innocent little mistake. He was actually a test pilot at Adlershof.

"Willi, this is General Ernst von Hoeppner."

Wissemann clicked his heels sharply, nodding respectfully. "Good evening, *Herr General*. It's a pleasure to meet you again."

"He is the new commander of the *Luftstreitkräfte.*"

"Good to make your acquaintance, *Oberleutnant*," von Hoeppner replied cordially. And then remarked, a little surprised: "You're instructing at Adlershof?"

"Well, not exactly, sir. I'm a test pilot there." Wissemann sighed inwardly. The General had forgotten they'd met once before, on the Somme, during that failed British offensive. No matter, he thought. He knew von Hoeppner was a very busy man these days.

"Really?"

"Yes, sir. I've been instructing at the Stutthof Flying School, in Silesia, for the last four months," Wissemann replied nervously. "I'm on temporary loan for a few weeks. Just test flying a few captured Allied aircraft at Adlershof for the intelligence folks at *FlugM*."

"I see." Von Hoeppner smiled. "That must be very convenient."

"Convenient? I beg your pardon, sir?" Wissemann was puzzled.

"Now you can be closer to your lovely fiancée, for the holidays."

"Hmm?" Willi Wissemann was befuddled momentarily. Then, his brumous mind quickly cleared. "Oh! Yes, of course! It's nice, indeed," he stammered bashfully. "It's turned out to be quite pleasant. Wonderful!" He turned to Ilse and smiled nervously.

Ilse von Linkhof began to laugh. "Oh, Willi! You're such a absent-minded blockhead sometimes!"

Wissemann gazed at her, his cloudy eyes now sparkling with amusement, bursting into laughter. Then General von Hoeppner joined in on the merriment. And so did the naval officer, *Frau* von Linkhof too. A moment later, all were chortling hilariously.

Then once the hilarity died down, *Frau* von Linkhof interjected forcefully: "Come, Ilse. Let the men talk." The wise, old house-*Frau* was privy to the ways of men and the military. It was time to bow out. Her purpose was complete. "Come along, my dear. We must check on dinner. Papi wants everything ready by eight o' clock."

"*Ach, Mutti*, please..." Ilse protested.

"Now, now. You know how he is. Come along, *Mädchen*."

"Oh, all right," Ilse replied with a frustrated sigh, and gave Wissemann a little peck on the cheek. "Okay, Willi. I'll be back later. Behave yourself, all right?"

Willi winked. "Of course, my dear."

Ilse and her mother strode down the hallway, hand in hand, heading for the kitchen.

"Charming girl, *Oberleutnant* Wissemann." said the tall, dignified stranger in the handsome naval uniform. "You're a very lucky man."

"Good heavens, where are my manners!" General von Hoeppner gushed apologetically, rolling his eyes. "Forgive me, Peter."

The naval officer chuckled. "Oh, don't make a fuss—"

"Wissemann, this is *Korvettenkapitän*, Peter Strasser. He's the commander of our Naval Airship Division. He's a veteran of numerous

Zeppelin raids over England and France."

"*Kapitän*," Heels clicked. Wissemann sketched a polite nod.

"Glad to meet you, *Oberleutnant* Wissemann," Strasser replied.

"Likewise, *Kapitän* Strasser."

Both men shook hands.

"*Kapitän* Strasser is here in Berlin, Wissemann, persuading the War Ministry to approve the production of more Zeppelin airships," von Hoeppner elaborated. "We were just talking about the new Gotha bombers coming into service in the new year before you walked up."

"Ah, yes." Willi Wissemann replied knowingly. "I've seen a few of those big-winged monstrosities at Adlershof."

"They're a good deal cheaper to produce than giant airships," von Hoeppner quipped.

"*H'mm...*" Strasser winced, clearing his throat, stroking his goatee solicitously. "Well, the War Ministry doesn't seem to understand, *Herr General*—the damage inflicted on the enemy by our airships. It's only a small part of the strategy."

"Only a small part?" Wissemann replied inquisitively.

"Indeed. Our Zeppelin raids are seriously tying up tremendous amounts of enemy military potential—"

"Oh, Peter! Don't start in on all that business again."

"Nevertheless, Ernst, Air Intelligence now believes nearly twelve RFC squadrons are in England. Not to mention all the anti-aircraft guns and manpower needed to operate them."

Wissemann agreed. "Then our Zeppelin threat *is* causing more than just material damage? A very good point, *Kapitän*."

Von Hoeppner chuckled and took a sip of his wine. "Well, Peter, our older bombers, the A.E.G. (G-series) have successfully bombed Paris. And the new Gotha G.IV's will have the range to reach London, making your floating behemoths... quite obsolete, I'm afraid."

The naval officer's brow narrowed. "Obsolete? I think not—"

"We can operate them in far greater numbers, Peter," General von Hoeppner interrupted bluntly, "instead of sending out just one vulnerable—giant gasbag over England."

Strasser scoffed. "Ernst, the new L-40 is nearing completion. It will reach up to heights of six thousand meters where no British aircraft can reach as of yet, much less attack. Furthermore, the L-42 will be able to reach seven thousand meters."

"That's fantastic!" There was a hint of awe in Wissemann's tone.

"*Gott!*" von Hoeppner countered. "The new Gotha bombers are much faster than any Zeppelin. They can sneak in for low altitude attacks—they're not so easily damaged by enemy scouts or incendiary bullets, mind you."

Kapitän Strasser smiled. Von Hoeppner's fervent fencing was quite comical. He lit a cigarette and then offered one to Wissemann. "Care for a smoke, *Oberleutnant?*"

"*Ja. Danke, Herr Kapitän.*" Wissemann popped the fag in his mouth and smiled. Strasser lit Wissemann's cigarette.

He gestured with a kindly hand. "So, *Oberleutnant*. What do *you* think of the new Gotha bombers? You've seen them buzzing around at Adlershof. Can they carry more bombs than a Zeppelin airship?"

The tall Bavarian officer hesitated a moment, puffing thoughtfully, then said: "Well, *Kapitän* Strasser, I really don't know. I would imagine a Zeppelin could carry more bombs. Hmm... that's a very tough question." Wissemann waffled, unprepared to answer such an objective query—he truly didn't know much about relative bomb loads or the Gotha itself. It was an aircraft he knew little about. He graciously took the middle ground. "Well, I think both have great potential, sir. Personally, I'm more partial to aeroplanes, smaller ones, especially. Like our new Albatros."

"The Albatros, eh?"

"Indeed, *Herr Kapitän*. It's a pilot's dream."

"Really?" Von Hoeppner interjected, quite surprised. "So you've flown our new scout?"

"Yes, *Herr General*, I have. The Albatros D.II is an excellent machine. It handles extremely well." Wissemann puffed his cigarette. "Its two machine guns are a tremendous advantage."

General von Hoeppner chuckled and clapped Wissemann on the shoulder. "Well, well, well, Willi. You obviously haven't seen the *latest* Albatros. It's even better than the D.II. It's a new design—much more streamlined, I can tell you."

"There's a newer model?" Wissemann gasped.

"Yes. The Albatros D.III, Wissemann. It's much faster, lighter and more maneuverable than its predecessor. They're coming off the production line in swarms—as we speak."

Kapitän Strasser sighed wearily. He was feeling a bit left out now, reluctantly realizing the conversation had drifted away from the subject of airships to aeroplanes. He decided to bow out, his knowledge of aeroplanes was quite limited. Alack and alas, the debate with von Hoeppner had dissolved into a fruitless exchange of words.

"Excuse me, gentlemen," he said suddenly. "I need to refresh my drink." A chafing *Kapitän* Strasser clicked his heels, bowing, and extricated himself from the degenerating colloquy, drifting off, in search of more wine and a more sympathetic audience.

Once out of earshot, von Hoeppner said to Wissemann: "Willi, those Zeppelins are costly and ineffective, I tell you. Germany can ill afford to invest her limited resources in such clumsy and vulnerable contraptions—giant, floating targets, for God's sake!" The General shook his head petulantly, finishing off his wine.

"I hope he wasn't offended by what I said."

"No, no, Willi. He's just trying to drum up support wherever he can, that's all. He already has Admiral von Scheer's endorsement. He'll get what he wants in the end, I'm sure."

"I see."

Von Hoeppner motioned to a servant. He wanted more wine. "So. I didn't realize you had such an interest in scout planes, Wissemann. I figured you to be a career instructor pilot, or a two-seater man." A servant gave the General a fresh glass of wine. *"Danke, Herr Ober."* He nodded gratefully and took a swallow.

The servant bowed and moved on.

"Well," Wissemann explained. "I've been trying to get transferred to a front line *Jasta* for some time now, sir."

"A *Jasta?"*

"Yes, sir. But I feel like *Oberst* Thomsen's just been giving me the runaround."

"It's nothing personal, I'm sure.

"Well—"

"He is a very busy man these days, you know."

"So I've heard. But—"

"As a matter of fact, we've both had our hands full reorganizing the *Luftstreitkräfte."*

"That's what he's been telling me." Wissemann chagrined.

"If you're truly interested, Willi, I'll see what I can do for you."

"Really?" Wissemann's eye's widened.

"H'mm." Von Hoeppner nodded. "There are still a few *Jastas* in need of some experienced leadership."

"That would be most appreciated, sir. Thank you, *Herr General. "*

"Don't mention it, Willi," von Hoeppner replied with a genuine smile. "Come by my office at the War Ministry building, say—Tuesday morning? Oh-nine hundred? We'll discuss it further. Don't be late. I'm a very busy man."

Wissemann smiled broadly.

"Oh, I'll be there early, sir. You can count on it!" he exclaimed elatedly. An exuberant Bavarian airman shook the Prussian general's hand. "It's going to be a great year. I just know it!"

But the Gods of War would ultimately decide that...

BACK TO SILESIA WILLI WISSEMANN WENT. After a fabulous holiday in Berlin and a short stint at Adlershof, he was back in the cold climes of East Prussia, and back to the grind of a daily training routine. His meeting with General von Hoeppner had gone well. But the confluence with his chief of staff, *Oberst* Thomsen, was quite a different thing. *Oberst* Hermann von der Lieth-Thomsen was a gruff, temperamental man with an obvious contempt towards any soldier or airman not Prussian. He bluffly cited that Wissemann's slug-fest with the artillery captain made him a debatable candidate for a *Jasta* posting, much less a *Jastaführer*—as the Imperial Air Service now officially titled the rank of squadron leader. Even though Wissemann had been exonerated of all charges, the artillery man admitting to striking him first, Wissemann serving his fifteen days in a military jail without incident, the old Prussian formally denied his application. He was told to reapply in thirty days. This was the official reason.

A dejected Willi Wissemann sat in the passenger car of an eastbound train, on his way back to Silesia, sullen and resentful. The train ride was long and laborious, giving him plenty of time to think about his past. The bitter Bavarian mentally sketched the past three months of his less-than-stellar military career...

The interview with Oswald Boelcke never happened. Due to his arrest and incarceration, he missed the meeting with the great air ace. After Wissemann's release, his adept piloting skills led *Idflieg* to believe he might be more useful as a flying instructor. It was more a form of punishment than anything else, officially mandated as a probationary period. Wissemann adamantly fought the appointment to the flying school, but his repeated requests were denied. So the transfer to a "hunting squadron" never materialized.

Then in late October, Boelcke's accidental death completely upended his plans for the future. *Jasta 2* went on to make history without him, while he labored as a flying instructor in a remote training facility called the Stutthof Flying School, in East Prussia.

Those were long, wearisome days. He languished bitterly at the flying school. The days turned into weeks, into months, and soon his mood became gloomy and reproachful. Would he ever have the chance to prove himself? Would he ever fly combat again? It wasn't that he was so anxious to get back to the war and all the killing, it was more about satisfying his aspirations as an airman, doing something meaningful. Willi Wissemann wanted to contribute to the war effort, to fight the enemy from the cockpit of a fast moving scout aeroplane, aiming a pair of finely tuned machine guns at the Fatherland's enemies, scoring victories, winning medals, garnering fame, becoming an aerial hero.

On the other hand, he thought humbly, maybe it was just about satisfying his vainglorious self-image. Perhaps he just wanted to grab some glory for himself? Wissemann was never one to be motivated by altruism—the gnawing egotism of his Teutonic mind prohibited that from ever happening. He was an officer and he fully understood the duties of his commission. His job was to lead, to fight and to vanquish the enemy. Kill. There was no room in his heart for melancholy, no room for remorse. That longing rhetoric that so many poets often tried to explain away in twisted, prosaic prose just did not exist in him. He wanted to fulfill his destiny, and that destiny was to be a *Jasta* pilot, a *Jastaführer*, a *Kanone*, a great ace, a champion to the cause of his beloved Deutschland.

Finally, on December 1st, after instructing for two grueling months at Stutthof, the powers-that-be decided to send him to the Adlershof Test Facility. He was given a special thirty day leave and told to report to Adlershof, the aerial testing aerodrome just outside of Berlin. For nearly a month, he'd flown experimental and captured enemy aircraft, evaluating and appraising their strengths and weaknesses. He was elated. It had given him time to be with Ilse. That was the best reason. And Christmas in Berlin was always a treat!

There in Berlin, he also realized chances of reassignment to the Front would be much better. Being closer to Supreme Headquarters meant more opportunities to fire appeals at the brass hats, the men who called all the shots, made all the decisions, meted out all the rewards and assignments. Indeed, chances should've been better there in Berlin than from that remote backwoods flying school where he was shuffling papers, pushing pencils, steering some rosy-cheeked student around the sky in a lumbering old apple-barge. A front line posting was the opportunity he had so coveted.

"NIX!" the reply had been. All hope had been quashed by some boorish Prussian neanderthal. Willi Wissemann vowed to go over Thomsen's head, and von Hoeppner would be his trump. He knew he deserved the chance to prove himself, and at the age of twenty-nine, the change for this Bavarian eagle was long overdue. Whilst he only had sixteen months experience in the Air Service, transferring from the infantry in September '15, he knew he had all the makings of a *Jastaführer. Oberleutnant* Willi Wissemann was now a *Zwölfender*—a "Twelve Year Man." He was unquestionably qualified.

All Prussians be damned!

✠

THE TELEPHONE ON THE BIG, OAKEN desk rang twice. A burly hand seized it before it rang a third time. A heavyset man in a snug-fitting uniform tunic put the handset to his ear and listened. Rich, aromatic smoke curled up from his pipe's bowl. He sucked in a little puff of smoke as his teeth clapped down on the stem, clearing his throat.

"Yes, Greta?" he said in a husky voice.

"It's the Deputy War Minister on the line, *Herr Oberst*," said the secretary. "Calling from the Reichstag."

"Oh?" He cradled the pipe in a free hand and sat forward. "Well, put him through, please."

"Yes, *Herr Oberst*."

The man nodded, grunted, glancing at the clock on the wall. It was 12 o' clock. He heard a little click as the operator patched him through, connecting his Berlin office on Wilhelmstrasse with a line from the Reichstag. He adjusted himself in his seat, reclining comfortably, waiting for the call to connect.

Feldflugchef Hermann von der Leith-Thomsen, the high-minded aristocrat from Flensburg, the founder of the modern German fighting squadron, was a very busy man these days. Everyone knew that under his willful powers, he'd almost single-handedly unified all the various air units under one command structure, organizing all single-seaters into self-contained squadrons. And up to now, he was nearly finished with that task. The old Imperial *Fliegertruppen* was now designated the, *Luftstreitkräfte*—Air Strike Force.

"Hermann..." a voice said. "It's Konrad. How are you?"

"Fine, fine, Konrad. And how are you, today?"

"Good. Just glad to finally get a chance to talk to you."

"The Cabinet has got you running around like a madman, eh?"

"*Lieber Gott*, yes! This new appointment is going to be a handful."

Hermann chuckled. "So. What's on your mind, Konrad?"

"Willi Wissemann! That's what's on my mind!"

"Oh, of course—

"Did you take care of everything?"

"It's all taken care of, Konrad."

"Really?"

"*Ja.* All taken care of, my friend. I formally denied his request for front line service, yesterday morning."

"Good! He's going back to Silesia, then?"

"That's right. Back to Stutthof."

"Excellent. And what about von Hoeppner?"

Thomsen took another little puff, smirking. "Don't worry, Konrad. He's ass-and-elbows deep in paperwork right now. He'll never get around to signing anything concerning one, Willi Wissemann. He's got his hands full with the new Albatros scout coming into service."

"So... there's no chance of Willi Wissemann getting posted to a *Jagdstaffel*, is there?"

"None. No chance. Not on my watch."

"*Wunderbar*, Hermann! Good work!"

"He can stay right there in Silesia and freeze his little Bavarian butt off, for all I care—"

There was a pause as a little interference crackled over the line, then von Linkhof said: "I also want to thank you for averting that mess in Cambrai, Hermann. I never really got around to thanking you for that. Was he really going to be court-martialed?"

"Well, General von Below certainly wanted it, my friend. Seems the artillery commander Wissemann locked horns with, was the General's son-in-law-to-be. I pulled a few strings, Konrad. Called in some favors. I convinced von Below to drop the charges."

"Really? He dropped the charges?"

"H'mm. It seems Wissemann was acting in self-defense, Konrad, according to several witnesses. Diessel recanted this under threat of demotion, likewise. Then, Wissemann was cajoled to drop his plaint."

"I see."

"Von Below is a reasonable man. We understand each other very well, if you know what I mean." Thomsen laughed. Smoke rolled up from the pipe in a roiled cloud.

"True. General von Below is a very sensible man."

"So why do you care? I thought you hated Wissemann's guts?"

"I do. But I'm doing it for my daughter's sake, Ilse. She wants him out of harm's way. I just want him out of *my* way. And Silesia is far enough out of the way as any place. For now, at least."

Hermann chuckled. "Well, he'll be there for quite a while. That's for sure."

"I don't know what she sees in that Bavarian upstart." Von Linkhof scoffed. "Really, I don't."

"Indeed. He's a loutish type, all right."

"I must find a way to turn Ilse away from him. He's a bad influence on her. He's got her head all turned around. She's all of a sudden concerned with this, this... 'class and social unrest business' that's going around Germany these days."

"*Ach*, Don't worry, Konrad. A fine girl like your daughter? She'll get over him, eventually. All that bourgeois nonsense types like

Wissemann try to purvey—it's just a load of cow-plop. It doesn't mean a damn thing."

"Humph, I'm not so sure about that, Hermann."

"Stop worrying. Ilse will see the light. She's a smart girl."

"And if this war drags on, *ALL* of Germany will have to start worrying."

"Listen, my old friend. We nobles have nothing to fear from this war and middle-class louts like Willi Wissemann. For God's sake! We practically built Germany—made it what it is today—not little crumb-bums like him. Types like Wissemann always self-destruct anyway. Mark my words, Konrad."

There was another momentary pause.

Konrad von Linkhof sighed. "Well, anyway, thanks again for everything, Hermann. I certainly appreciate it. I really do. Good work, I must say."

"It was nothing, Konrad."

"Will I see you at the Cabinet meeting on Thursday?"

"Um... no, I don't think so. I'm off on a little inspection tour."

"Oh?"

"General von Hoeppner and I are visiting the Albatros Works in Johannistal."

"I see. The new Albatros scout?"

"Correct. They're just about ready for deployment."

"Ja! The Allied air services will be in for an unpleasant surprise."

"They certainly will." Thomsen laughed haughtily. "And with this new fellow, *Rittmeister* von Richthofen, leading the charge, our Air Service will be invincible!"

"Hmm... von Richthofen? Haven't heard of him."

"Oh, you will, Konrad. You will."

"Is he a good pilot?"

"Uh... more like a great marksman, my friend. He's an avid game hunter in his spare time. That lad never misses once he takes aim, I tell you what."

"Well, that explains the marksmanship."

"He's one of Boelcke's hand-picked airmen. A real killer!"

"That's what we need right now—killers."

"Von Hoeppner is going to pin the *Pour le Mérite* on him in a few days. Von Richthofen is our *new* Boelcke. And of *our* class, mind you."

"Von Richthofen, you say?"

"That's right. I think he's going to be a top-notch pilot."

"That's good to hear."

"We'll finish off France and England this year, Konrad."

"You think?"

"With all this new equipment, unrestricted submarine warfare, men like von Richthofen and a new grand strategy, we'll be sipping champagne in Paris by Christmas. Mark my words. Germany is on the verge of victory!" Thomsen's fist slammed down on his desktop.

Von Linkhof winced. "G-Glad to hear it." He cleared his throat with contented finality. "Well, Herman, it's been nice chatting with you. I suppose I'll see you at the next General Staff meeting?"

"Perhaps."

"Take care, Hermann *Auf Wiedersehen.*"

"Good-bye, Konrad."

Thomsen hung up the telephone and grunted blissfully, the fate of one man now officially put to rest. Or so he thought.

Chapter 7

✠

JANUARY 25, 1917. WILLI WISSEMANN SAT on his bunk in the officers' billet at Stutthof reading *Kriegzeitung,* a military journal, sipping a tin of warm coffee. He was reading about Manfred von Richthofen—the peerless Prussian had recently been given the command of a *Jasta* and had been awarded the prestigious *Pour le Mérite.* Wissemann cringed. Why couldn't it be himself he was reading about? Why couldn't he be the man in the article? Why not give him command of a *Jasta*? Damnation! Prussian cronyism, that's why!

A gust of winter wind found its way inside his little room, causing him to shiver uncontrollably. He bolted up and paced around stiffly, cursing his predicament foully. Outside, the wind howled ominously and frequently. It was winter in Silesia and snow covered the hard ground in great icy drifts. All flying had been canceled, all training halted. And here was Wissemann, stuck in a veritable frozen tundra while others received accolades upon accolades, not to mention commands of their own fighting squadrons. It just didn't seem fair, he groaned bitterly. Something had to be done!

Wissemann tossed the journal down on a ragged little table and finished off the coffee. He shrugged into his greatcoat with hurried impatience, donned his crush cap, then bolted for the door. He would have to do something about his situation, something drastic. He could not sit around in an icy wasteland and while away the twilight of his career whilst a glorious air war raged on the other side of Europe. He had to get back into the fight somehow.

His brief stint on the Somme had only whetted his appetite for aerial combat. He'd lost his chance before, missing the interview with Boelcke and a potential posting to *Jasta 2* because of unnecessary shenanigans. He'd funked, bungled badly, screwed up. He would not allow that to happen again. No, no. Not again!

Wissemann stalked over to the Operations hangar, his boots slogging clumsily in the snowy drifts, a cigarette burning in his mouth. The sun was just coming up and the snowfall seemed to be diminishing. But not enough though, the lanky Bavarian surmised, to commence operations—it would be another dull day of classroom instruction. The "classroom" was a small, drafty dispersal hut with a cantankerous wood-burning stove, stacks of wooden crates serving as chairs. Day in and day out, Wissemann had stood before "*CLASS 10/16*" explaining the merits of the old Aviatiks and Albatros two-seaters they trained on. There were a couple of Fokker-D scouts around at the Stutthof School, but none were equipped with guns or reliable engines. Just as well, he scoffed inwardly. Nothing could get off the ground in this glaciated landscape anyway.

Wissemann pushed through the side door of the Operations hangar, entering the small office that served as the school's clerical hub and message center. It was sparsely manned at this hour, only one clerk was on duty. Activity usually began at 0700-hours and the clock on the wall said 6 o'clock.

Wissemann inhaled a puff, then sighing smokily, said:. "Well, Baldamus, what's the weather forecast for today, eh?" But he knew what the answer would be.

Albert Baldamus, a stocky, pale-faced lad with blond hair, rose clumsily from his seat as the Bavarian officer strode in. "Uh... well, you know, sir—"

"Keep your seat, *Unteroffizier*," Wissemann replied crisply. "Don't pull a muscle on my account. Where is Ziegler?"

Baldamus sat down. "He's on sick call, sir. The flu, I think. That bad virus that's going round finally caught up with him, I guess."

The cigarette glowed bright orange. "And you? Feeling all right?"

"Yes, sir. I've been keeping to myself."

"Good man, Baldamus. Any news from Berlin?"

"Just the usual, sir. Another new class is due in, in a week, a safety bulletin from headquarters, a few letters, a new winter maintenance directive, etc. etc."

"Anything for me?"

"No, sir."

"I see." Wissemann doused his cigarette in a nearby ashtray.

"Well, Baldamus, I need you to patch a call through to Berlin for me. *Kogenluft*, this time."

"Von Hoeppner's headquarters, sir?" Baldamus' brow rose.

"That's right. Straight to the top this time."

"But it's next to impossible to reach him, sir. He's always out and about these days, inspections and meetings and such—"

"No harm in trying again and again—*nicht?*"

"I guess not. But, sir—"

"That's an order, *Unteroffizier*." Wissemann's tone sharpened a bit. "Get on that switchboard now and connect me please, Baldamus."

Baldamus gulped. "Y-Yes, sir."

He got up abruptly, stamped into the communications room and sat down. He patched through a telephone connection. Wissemann followed him in and stood by, arms folded in front of him, a hopeful expression beaming from his rosy, wind-swept face. A moment later, Baldamus had made a connection with the main telephone hub in Danzig and was waiting for a link to Berlin.

"Just a moment, sir," Baldamus said, glaring warily over his shoulder at a very impatient Bavarian officer.

"Oh, no hurry, Baldamus," Wissemann replied, outwardly unperturbed. But inside he was boiling like a copper teapot. "We've got all day to do this, you and I, my fine young friend."

"All day, sir?" Baldamus winced. "Uh—yes, of course."

"All day—"

"*Ah! Kogenluft*—Berlin!" Baldamus said with a start as the line suddenly connected. "Yes, yes... is General von Hoeppner available? This is *Unteroffizier* Albert Baldamus calling from Stutthof Flying School, Silesia..."

Wissemann smiled.

"Oh?... No?... When will he be in? Later? I see," Baldamus replied, adjusting the headphones over his ears. "Yes, yes, I understand... it's concerning one of our instructors, *Oberleutnant* Wilhelm Wissemann... right. Oh. Well... uh, it's about... hold on a moment." He cupped the mouthpiece and turned to Wissemann. "Sir, what's this about? What's this concerning?"

Wissemann's lips clamped down frustratedly. "My transfer to the Western Front, you little idiot!" He sighed bitterly.

"Oh! Right!" Baldamus nodded densely. "It's about a transfer, sir," he said into the telephone. *"Oberleutnant* Wissemann wishes to transfer to a front line *Jasta* on the Western Front."

Wissemann's eyes kindled.

"What?... In writing?... Oh, I see. So, the General isn't there?... Oh, he is there? But all transfer requests must be submitted by form? Yes, I see. I understand. An official request must be submitted by—"

"Give me that!" Wissemann snarled short-tempered, snatching the phone from the clerk's hand. He jerked the headphones to his ears and huffed irritably. "Hello? Who is this? To whom am I speaking? *Leutnant* Dietrich? Well, this is—hello? Hello?" Wissemann cursed through a sigh. *"Verdammt!* The line went dead! Get my connection back, Baldamus. Now!" He bolted upright and stripped the cumbersome headphones from his head.

"Yes, sir!" Baldamus replied quite rattled, fiddling with the phone jack nervously. "Right away, *Herr Oberleutnant!* Right away!"

"This weather is impossible!" Wissemann scoffed angrily and turned for the door. "I'll be in the mess, Baldamus. I must eat something or my stomach will twist itself into horrid little knots. Send a runner when you've reconnected. Understand?"

"Yes, sir. I'll send a runner, posthaste."

"Good! And stay on that blasted switchboard until you've reached Berlin. I must speak to General von Hoeppner—today!" Wissemann turned on a heel and bolted for the door, mumbled expletives boiling over into a flaring tantrum. The door slammed a second later.

Baldamus sighed wearily. "Ach! What an overbearing man."

He frantically re-patched the telephone line, beginning the connection process once again, humming anxiously. *"Gott!* I hope he gets his transfer. My ailing heart couldn't handle another day with him lurking about." Poor, pathetic Albert Baldamus, his clammy hands couldn't work fast enough!

✠

AS THE CLOCK STRUCK NOON, Willi Wissemann was still sitting in mess awaiting word on a connection to Berlin. In his inordinate frustration, he'd given his morning classes the day off. Classroom instruction would begin again at 2 o'clock. Until then, he'd hoped to resolve his problem or, at the least, have talked to General von Hoeppner. But no such thing had happened yet. He'd smoked one cigarette after another and gulped down umpteen cups of black coffee, and was so jittery now that his hands were trembling. He needed to hit upon some kind of solution soon, or he feared he might go quite mad.

As Wissemann sat restlessly at a table, absently thumbing through an Army journal, glimpsing at it while keeping a watchful eye on the clock hanging on the wall, he read an interesting article. The journal reported on a story about General von Hutier's 11th Army, bogged down on the Eastern Front, suffering the winter doldrums. Troops had tried to occupy themselves with musical shows, dramatic plays, and occasional raucous soccer matches, weather permitting. The war in the East had settled down to a dull waiting game as the Russian Army regrouped, all under the threat of possible revolution. Things were deteriorating badly in Russia and it looked as if the great Motherland might capitulate soon. So, the German High Command decided to sit back momentarily and wait for the situation to unravel. No sense in wasting valuable manpower, they reckoned warily, if the Russians were about to fold—

"Oberleutnant Wissemann?" a meek voice called out suddenly. It was *Unteroffizier* Baldamus. He came striding in the mess cautiously.

Wissemann jerked to his feet. "Well?"

"Sorry, sir. Nothing yet. Telephone lines currently out of order."

"Out of order?"

"Yes, sir. Must be some trouble up the line somewhere."

"Verdammt!" Wissemann's face reddened. "You mean I've been sitting here waiting for a connection..." he glanced at the clock "... for six hours? And the phone lines have been out of order the whole damned time?"

"Uh, well... sorry, sir."

"Unbelievable!"

"Um... it only happened an hour or so ago, sir. Before that, I was actually making headway. I found out that General von Hoeppner *is* in his office all day today, in meetings and such. His adjutant said he'd be there until late in the evening."

Wissemann's eyes brightened. "Well, then. We must get that telephone switchboard working. What can be done to fix the problem, here Baldamus?"

"Nothing can be done *here*, sir. It's up the line somewhere. A relay station is experiencing some technical difficulty, I understand."

"Which relay station?"

"The one in Graudenz, I believe."

"Graudenz? Hmm..." Wissemann stroked his chin cagily.

"Yes, sir."

"Are we able to communicate with them at all?"

"Well, yes. But the trouble, it seems, is just beyond their reach. Calls to Berlin are temporarily blocked."

"Temporarily, eh? Aha..." Wissemann nodded. A neat little idea had just brightened in his brain. He snorted superciliously: "Well, we'll just have to fix that now, won't we, Baldamus?"

"Sir?"

"Come along, Baldamus." Wissemann grabbed the journal and jetted for the door. "Let's get to that switchboard of yours, lad, and rectify this situation immediately!"

"I don't understand. What do you intend to do, sir?"

"I'm just going to light a little fire under somebody's heinie, Baldamus. I must get through to von Hoeppner's office today. He must grant me a transfer immediately." Wissemann stormed out of mess heading for Operations, Baldamus following closely.

"But *Herr Oberleutnant*," Baldamus grumped. "All transfers must be submitted in writing... uh, *Army Form A-1-A-0—*"

"Bah! I don't have time for all that nonsense anymore, *Junge.*" Wissemann's hand was fluttering dismissively. "No more paperwork, for God's sake."

A few icy footsteps later, Wissemann was standing in Operations. Baldamus was sitting at the switchboard, powering it up.

"Just a moment, sir," *Unteroffizier* Baldamus said, donning the headphones. "I'll have the relay station in Graudenz on the line shortly. Hang on..."

"Fine. Just hurry it up already," Wissemann enjoined tersely, leaning over the noncom's shoulder. "Those lads in Graudenz are going to wet their pants when they find out who's calling."

Baldamus made a little face. "Sir? Who *is* calling, if I may ask?"

"Just patch the line through, eh. Hurry it up, will you!"

"*Jawohl, Herr Oberleutnant!*"

A minute drifted by and Baldamus had finally made a connection.

"Graudenz? This is Stutthof, calling again... yes, that's right." He listened a moment, then looked up at Wissemann, shaking his head disparagingly. "They're still having problems, sir. But they do have a repair crew out checking the phone lines."

Wissemann frowned.

"They said they could probably have the phones up and running by oh-eight hundred tomorrow. The snowfall will slacken by then."

Wissemann huffed, sighing impatiently. "Give me those damn headphones, Baldamus. Get up. Let me talk to them. C'mon, get up!"

Baldamus hurriedly handed over the headphones, hefting himself out of the chair. Wissemann jerked the headphones on and plopped down, then leaned in closer to the mouthpiece. He cleared his throat officiously. "Hello, Graudenz? This is... GENERAL VON HUTIER, 11TH ARMY. Can you hear me?"

Baldamus gasped. His eyes widened. *"Oberleutnant! Mein Gott!—"*

Wissemann shushed him away. "Quiet, you!"

Unteroffizier Baldamus backed away, shaking his head gravely.

"Yes, that's right—General Oskar von Hutier here." Wissemann affected his voice artificially, making it sound gruff and husky. "I demand to know the meaning of all these technical difficulties! I've been trying to reach General von Hoeppner in Berlin for the better part of a day now! I'm losing my patience here!"

Wissemann listened. He smirked impishly

"Sir—" Baldamus made to say.

Wissemann's hand waved testily, forestalling the noncom's interjection. He leaned in closer to the mouthpiece and barked: "I don't want your damned excuses, *Feldwebel!* I want that line fixed by sixteen hundred hours. Do you hear me? *Verdammt!* Or by God, I'll come over there myself and put a boot to everyone of your sorry asses —demote each one of you, summarily! Do you understand?" Wissemann turned away from the mouthpiece and chuckled. *"That certainly got their attention."*

Baldamus groaned sickly.

"I'll give you one hour to rectify the problem, *Feldwebel!"* Wissemann roared into the phone line, railing on the sergeant at the Graudenz relay station. "If you fail, all hell will break loose! I assure you. You'll be sorry you ever heard the name—Oskar von Hutier!"

Baldamus threw his hands up and walked out of the room.

Wissemann chuckled, leaning back in the chair, smirking. "Get it done, see!" he waxed theatrically, really pouring it on now. He lit a cigarette and inhaled deeply, quipping to himself: "This should do the trick, alright. Nothing like a general calling to shake things up a bit."

LESS THAN AN HOUR LATER, Wissemann was speaking with General von Hoeppner, relaxing comfortably in a chair, smoking another cigarette, grinning from ear to ear. The Graudenz repair crew had gotten the telephone lines working again, at the angry insistence of one old general "Oskar von Hutier."

"I don't understand what's going on, Wissemann," von Hoeppner was saying. "I thought General von Hutier was trying to call me here in Berlin. But instead, I'm talking to you. What happened?"

"Hmm..." Wissemann grumbled artificially, still playing his little game of charades to the nth degree. "Yes, that's very strange, General. I don't know what happened either. Perhaps the operator got the calls mixed up or something? Damned phone company, always fouling things up."

"Indeed." Von Hoeppner coughed. "So, Wissemann, what's on your mind? Why'd you call me? Everything alright there in Stutthof?"

"Oh, everything is fine, sir. The weather is atrocious, of course, as one might expect."

"So I've heard."

"Training has been temporarily postponed." Wissemann inhaled deeply. "But that's not why I'm calling, sir."

"Go on, Wissemann. Get to your point. I've got an early dinner party I must prepare for—General von Hindenburg is in Berlin, along with General Ludendorff. I don't have a lot of time here."

"Right, sir, of course. I'll be brief." Wissemann leaned forward and cleared his throat. "It's about my transfer to a *Jasta*, sir. You and I discussed it when I was last there at the War Ministry. You said there were some front line *Jastas* in need of strong leadership."

"Yes, I remember. I passed the paperwork on to *Oberst* Thomsen for finalization. Have you not been gazetted yet?"

"Uh, well, he officially denied the request, sir. Didn't he tell you?"

"No... he did not!" Von Hoeppner sounded annoyed.

"Thomsen said I wasn't fit to lead a *Jasta*," Wissemann elaborated theatrically, inhaling smoke. "He told me to reapply in thirty days."

"He did, did he? Well, I'll be damned."

"That's right, sir. He did." Wissemann exhaled a lungful of smoke. "Is that proper protocol, *Herr General?*"

Von Hoeppner did not reply.

"General...?"

"*Nein!* It is not!" Von Hoeppner suddenly roared, startling Wissemann. "I shall have to have a word with him, I see."

"I don't want to cause any trouble, sir. I mean—"

"That man has usurped my power once too many times, he has! Ever since I've taken command of the Air Service, he has fought me on every issue. Foiled my every effort to reorganize things—*my way*, argued with me incessantly!"

There was a brief pause as Wissemann heard von Hoeppner shuffling some papers, then the sound of a cabinet draw jerking open.

Wissemann grinned and chuckled quietly. "Well, if it's not too much trouble, *Herr General,*" he said coyly. "I'd like to get transferred back to the Western Front as soon as—"

"Wissemann..."

"Yes, sir?"

"Pack your bags immediately! I'm going to post your orders over the wire, tonight. You're going to the Western Front, my good man. I'm posting you to a *Jasta*. *Oberst* Thomsen be damned!"

Willi Wissemann smiled. "Thank you, *Herr General*. Thank you very much." Smoke jetted from his nostrils. He nodded gleefully. Yes!

Book Two
✠
Eagle's Jasta

February 1917
Laon, France
Champagne Sector

Chapter 8

✠

FEBRUARY 17, 1917. THE SKY WAS OVERCAST and gray. Tiny snowflakes drifted down lazily on an already snow-blanketed ground. Somewhere in the vicinity, a lonesome train whistle echoed and the thumping of heavies could be heard from the west. There was a forlorn anxiety suffusing the surroundings, and a dispirited German officer felt the sadness of a dreary afternoon creeping up on him. The officer shivered uncontrollably while subzero gusts of wind tugged at his coat tails, standing silently, hands in pockets, the collar of his *Steingrau* greatcoat turned upright against the elements, a heavy wool scarf swaddled snugly around his neck. An officer's crush cap, tilted rakishly over a brow, shielded his eyes from the mounting snowfall. Both legs were neatly wrapped in cloth puttees, and the once lustrous black ankle boots were now dull and damp from snow and ice. And somewhere, under the heavy folds of that flocculent greatcoat, pinned on a freshly pressed tunic, hung a silver airman's badge. This officer was an aviator, a veteran of His Majesty's Imperial German Air Service, a man desperately determined to fulfill his destiny.

He pulled a Halpaus from his sterling cigarette case and placed it between his windblown lips. He fumbled through the capacious pockets of his greatcoat searching for a matchbox, but to no avail. Mumbling quiet expletives, he undid the top buttons of the heavy greatcoat, ruefully remembering he had stashed the matches inside one of his tunic's hip pockets. He found them, lit the cigarette, and took a deep drag. He exhaled slowly, frowning.

Oberleutnant Wilhelm R. Wissemann gazed upon the snowbound surroundings with increasing contempt. The platform at the Laon train station was nearly empty that dreary Saturday afternoon, only a few station porters lurking about, waiting restively for the next train to arrive. The Bavarian's spartan belongings rested at his feet—a leather valise and a canvas musette bag. In the inner pocket of his greatcoat were orders from Supreme Headquarters. After completing a ten-day conversion course on single-seaters, he was officially attached to the 7th Army in Champagne.

He'd finally been brevetted to a front line *Jasta*—as all Imperial German Air Service scout squadrons were now formally known. He was replacing *Hauptmann* Fritz Traurig as *Jastaführer*. The erstwhile Traurig, suffering from sudden stomach problems, transferred to a home defense *Jagdstaffel* near Freiburg, a German city located close to the Black Forest. And after reading the Inspectorate's disciplinary reports, Wissemann knew why.

Wissemann glanced at his watch. It had been well over an hour now since he'd telephoned the operations adjutant at Pusieux Ferme airfield, announcing his arrival at the station. Where was that transport? Wissemann grumbled impatiently, lacking the forbearance to withstand the harsh weather. The would-be *Jastaführer* grudgingly sat down on a frigid wrought iron bench next to the ticket office. The metallic bench sent cold tremors through his torpid body. Even though he wore long underwear, thick trousers and a wool overcoat, the biting cold metal bench still sent shivers through his bony rump.

Gott! How he hated cold climates. This was no better than Silesia. "This is no way to fight a war," he chattered to himself. "I have been banished to Jotunheim, it seems. The Gods of War have succumbed to the throes of winter." Wissemann chuckled—the powers-that-be had enough to worry about. One more freezing officer? Nah!

His hands felt numb and clammy inside the old leather gloves. He intermittently pulled them off and huffed on them, trying to warm them up, but it was a futile attempt. It was just too cold to do anything productive. He sat shivering, wondering again when that transport would arrive. Where was that transport? He reluctantly longed for the warmth of that dirty, overcrowded train car now.

The winter winds buffeted him again, and he trembled. He flicked the smoldering cigarette butt onto the railroad tracks, shaking his head sullenly, contemplating the events of the past year. Just as the revolving seasons changed, his world had changed too, finally to his liking. He stared dejectedly at the fobbed pocket watch in his hand—4:15? His nerve was waning, he wanted to get on with his career!

An elderly, hoary-haired porter ambled by. Wissemann stopped him. *"Excusez-moi, monsieur,"* he asked politely. "Where can one get a decent cup of coffee around here?" Wissemann's French was good, it had always stood the test of time.

The porter glared at him, stunned. Clearly he was not accustomed to Germans who spoke French so fluently. The old man's voice was high-pitched with surprise.

"A decent cup of coffee? *Sacre bleu!* There's a small café in the plaza. They sell coffee—if you can call it that." The old Frenchman's accent hinted at a common, Alsatian dialect.

"Merci, monsieur."

Wissemann drew himself up stiffly and stalked off the platform, bags in hand, in the direction of the café. He carefully negotiated the icy steps leading down from the platform on to the boulevard. The streets were mostly empty; his boots crunched clumsily on the frosty ground, tramping out a steady cadence. As he marched towards the café, which he spotted immediately after turning a corner, a couple of German soldiers saluted as they passed by. They were tired and blowsy looking. Poor bastards, Wissemann thought. It's a rotten job, skulking about some frozen, rat-infested trench in the dead of winter.

He opened the door to the café, brushing some snowflakes from his shoulders, nodding politely to two women dining at a table near the front window. He reverently removed his service cap from his head. His dark, pomaded hair glistened in the golden half glow of the café oil lamps, as the warmth of the potbellied stove in the corner of the room soothed his frigid arms and legs, the warm air making him realize, in pure appreciation, that he had been uncomfortably cold. He stamped his feet a few times on the floor to get the circulation going, then noticed two German majors sitting at the opposite end of the counter. They grumpily looked up from their newspapers, giving him indignant stares, annoyed, then went back to their quiet reading. Wissemann cringed, blushing with mortification, realizing he'd unwittingly disturbed them. He edged up to the counter.

Behind the wooden counter, an old, gray-haired woman busied herself with the ignoble duties of her trade. She addressed him in a gruff, impersonal voice, but in her stolid coldness, there was the kindliness that asked no questions of the wandering stranger. She didn't smile or make eye contact either. Alas, he was beyond caring at this point. The French could not be counted on for their friendliness these days, not to a German, anyway.

"Bonjour, monsieur. What will it be today?" She asked.

"Je voudrais café, s'il vous plaît," Wissemann replied.

She nodded, tramped over to a coffee pot and poured a steamy, black brew into a plain ceramic cup, then placed it on a saucer. She pushed it across the counter to Wissemann. He gave her two francs, thanked her, and picked up the steaming cup, wrapping his hands around the simple crockery, finding pleasure in its warmth. However, the pleasure was fleeting. He grimaced reprovingly after taking a sip.

"*Igittt!*" Wissemann cursed quietly to himself. "*Blümchenkaffee!*"

It was bland, bitter and weak—a rationed, beetroot coffee. Yet, still, it somehow felt good going down his throat. He looked around and found an old magazine, unbuttoned his greatcoat, sitting down at a small deal table. Wissemann read quietly, glancing over an issue of *L'Illustration*—a French photographic journal of the war, picking up a few bits of news. He'd studied French since his youth, so interpreting the stilted text was easy for him.

The war seemed to be going well for the French Military, according to the press. Their army censors saw to that, of course. The French High Command would never allow the truth to be known to the public, just as the German censors wouldn't allow it either. Wissemann scoffed. The truth was always the first casualty of the war. Although certain pundits in the French popular press presaged eminent disaster, as yet another Army offensive ground to a halt, they were quickly silenced by windy political blustering and more hollow promises from the Generals. Theirs was a paper war. And if things didn't look good on paper, they'd make it look good. It was the same with the German Army. The home front was confident the war was going well. He shook his head and read the headlines:

"FRENCH TROOPS AT VERDUN CAPTURE GERMAN POSITIONS!"

The headlines certainly trumpeted confidently, Wissemann thought. How little the people really know. The censors have been hard at work here. He glumly remembered his own censoring duties, bowdlerizing the letters of the men of his old infantry company. As an executive officer, it was his duty to censor the enlisted men's correspondence, blacking out certain phrases, names and places, making sure they didn't divulge military secrets. Military secrets. Really? What military secrets?

"Preposterous!"

Censoring the men's letters, though, oft gave him a profound insight into their personal views and thoughts on the war. It was a task this Bavarian officer had utterly detested. It had made him seriously uncomfortable; reading another man's private thoughts was really none of his business. He lit another cigarette and continued reading the magazine, another anxious hour drifted by...

THE DOOR OF THE LITTLE CAFÉ SWUNG OPEN SUDDENLY. A short, ratty-looking corporal came trundling in, bundled up in an oversized M1915 *Feldgrau* greatcoat. He was wearing a noncom's field cap with a traditionally crushed crown. His face was gaunt and unshaven, beady eyes, framed in tight fitting, round spectacles, scanned the small dining room. A moment later, those beady little eyes fell upon a tall, Bavarian officer.

"*Herr Oberleutnant?*" the noncom strode in slowly.

"Yes. I am *Oberleutnant* Wissemann."

"Sir. I'm *Unteroffizier* Grimm, *Jasta 23*, Pusieux Ferme," the little man said. "I'm the staff orderly and clerk to the adjutant."

"Right."

"I'll drive you to the aerodrome. I hope everything is—"

"Something wrong with your arm, *Unteroffizier?*" Wissemann snapped testily, noticing Grimm had forgotten to salute.

"Sir?"

"Did you forget I'm an officer—your superior?"

"Ah, where are my manners, *Herr Oberleutnant.*" Grimm saluted jerkily, his face turning ruby with mortification, averting his gaze.

Wissemann's eyes flared. "Yes, *Unteroffizier.* Where are your manners?"

"S-sorry, sir. It won't happen again."

"I should hope not—" Both men exchanged awkward glances.

"H'mm..." Grimm cleared his throat. "Ready to go, sir?"

Wissemann frowned, glancing at his pocket watch; it was already half passed five o'clock. "Quite ready. What took so long?"

"Well, the weather is turning foul again," Grimm stated meekly, "I had a little engine trouble on the way over here."

Grimm removed his cap and scratched his head. Wissemann quickly noticed the noncom's untidy tresses and receding hairline. This man seemed a bit old to be a corporal, and one who was in dire need of a decent haircut. He was quite unimpressive looking—a small, dowdy-looking little man who couldn't have weighed more than sixty kilos clad in dirty, over-sized coat that reeked of sweat. Impressions, however, Wissemann chagrined, seemed to count for little these days.

"Engine trouble?"

"Yes, sir."

"I see. Well, let's get my bags loaded."

Wissemann handed Grimm the canvas musette bag containing his flying gear. It seemed a little heavy; Grimm tucked it under his arm, masking his discomfort with a sick smile.

Wissemann asked: "How far is it to the aerodrome?"

"Ah, maybe seven or eight kilometers, sir?"

"That's not far."

"The roads are very bad, though."

"Oh? Well, I'm not surprised—"

"And the snow is starting to come down again."

"Let's get going then."

"It'll be an interesting drive, *Herr Oberleutnant.* I assure you."

Wissemann grumbled. Grimm's bleak remarks didn't interest him. He just wanted to get to the aerodrome posthaste, weather be damned! He hated traveling—dingy passenger cars, the needless asperity of railroad employees, the weather. The cold, nasty weather! He hated that the most. It always put him in a bad mood.

Both men trudged out of the café, Grimm leading the way towards an idling truck. A dilapidated, old Daimler shimmied and quaked, its pistons clattering irregularly. Grimm tossed Wissemann's musette bag into the back of the truck. The wind howled, the little corporal groaned. Not only was the weather turning foul, so was his attitude.

Wissemann handed Grimm his leather valise.

"Here, take this one, too."

"So... how was your trip, sir?" Grimm asked, feigning concern, lashing both bags to the rear compartment of the truck, securing the tailgate with a noisy clank.

"Miserable. Quite miserable, I say. This damned weather slows everything down." Wissemann glowered at the gray skies above. There seemed to be no respite in sight for days to come.

"Yes. Miserable," *Unteroffizier* Grimm parroted. "It's certainly curtailed *Jasta* operations."

"Well, it'll clear—"

"I'll bet the *Jasta's* grounded again tomorrow, sir—the snail-eaters too, for that matter."

Grimm's forecast sounded gloomy and pessimistic, his mood seemingly as foul as the weather. Wissemann's face flashed a sour look of ingratitude. He was really beginning to detest this vile little man, shaking his head detestably. This *Unteroffizier* Grimm was already trying his patience!

Both men climbed into the truck. The little noncom started the motor and shifted into first gear. He pulled out on to the Rue de la Fére, proceeding down the snow-covered roadway heading east, the old Daimler lurching and shimmying every time Grimm shifted the gears, riding the clutch with klutzy, uncoordinated motions.

"Well, let's see what the aerologists have to say about that, Grimm," Wissemann rejoined, finally, a bit exasperated.

"I don't know, sir. It doesn't look good."

"A little snow shouldn't stop a *Jasta*—"

"Oh, no, sir. Not a little snow. But a lot will!"

"Grimm... oh, never mind."

Wissemann had stopped short of berating the little corporal, not really in the mood to bandy with surly noncoms today. He needed to conserve his energy for the task at hand, dishing out discipline to an incorrigible fighting squadron, all too aware of the *Jasta's* dubious combat record since its creation by the War Ministry in October '16, before its official front line deployment on January 1st. His thoughts drifted back to the Supreme Headquarters briefing...

In six weeks, *Jasta 23* had only gunned down seven enemy aircraft, three of those being credited to one man, the acting *Jastaführer*. And according to *Idflieg's* field report, this *Staffel* was evidently a collection of misfits and troublemakers. Wissemann sighed inwardly, what a sorry excuse for an aviation unit! Reports of belligerency, insobriety, disorderly conduct, insubordination, filled the information file at Supreme Headquarters. It was as if all the wayward castoffs of the Air Service had been lumped into one squadron. Wissemann knew he had an onerous task ahead of him. To transform these nonconformists into a true fighting force would be a real herculean feat.

Oberst Thomsen, Chief of Staff of Army Field Aviation, had been calculably reluctant to put him in charge. But Wissemann's personal appeal to General von Hoeppner had changed all that. Thomsen was forced to post him to the Western Front at the helm of a fighting squadron. It seemed quite evident, Wissemann realized. Thomsen had exacted a good measure of revenge by sending him to *Jasta 23*, arguably the worst front line *Jasta* in the Air Service. Perhaps I am the perfect candidate for this outfit, he said to himself.

Indeed, he thought. He'd seen enough of the war in the trenches to realize this conflict was being fought with outmoded battle tactics and bad military policies. Modern warfare was won with machines, gasoline and sound tactics—not horses, wagons and swagger sticks. It was more than just a military conflict, it was a war of the classes as well, the war only widening the gulf between the elite and the lower class, the German officer corps seemingly wedged right in the middle. A titanic clash of social upheaval was in the making here. Wissemann wondered how much longer Germany could wage a war of attrition with just old-fashioned jingoism and Victorian battle tactics.

Grimm stared at the overcast sky above and sighed; it was

snowing much harder. "Um, I don't know, sir," he drawled. "Things aren't looking so good."

"This *Jasta* will be operational, Grimm! Bad weather or not."

"We've already lost too many aircraft due to accidents, sir."

"Accidents?"

"The *Jasta* is down to half strength."

"How many aircraft are available for operations?"

"About four or five, I think, not counting the Halberstadts."

"Halberstadts? Dear God!"

The Halberstadt scout, as Wissemann recalled gloomily, was a decent but unwieldy machine, deployed during the previous spring. Compared to the newer Albatros scout, it was underpowered and under-armed. The Halberstadt was also plagued by overly sensitive elevators—it was a balky buzzard in fledgling hands, and a handful for an old hand. While elite Prussian units, especially those serving in Flanders, were receiving the new Albatros, the lesser *Jastas* were still getting the older Albatros D.II and the occasional Halberstadt. All the same, the new *Jastaführer* professed: the old D.II was still an excellent aircraft, better than anything the French could get into the air. Well, except for the Spad. The Spad was to be avoided at all costs!

"I'll see to it myself, I will," Wissemann vowed. "This *Jasta* will be properly reequipped, the High Command be damned. Things *will* be different under my command!" He grumbled inwardly. Imbeciles!

Grimm stared at Wissemann. Ach! This new squadron leader, he could see, was going to be a real hard ass. This man really intended to transform the *Jasta*. Grimm grimaced—the poor blighters of *Jasta 23* were in for a rude awakening! Things were going to change. Grimm suddenly felt ill. He leered at the new commander from the corner of his eyes, taking his attention off the roadway for just a second.

Suddenly, Wissemann lurched forward, clutching the dashboard, buttressing himself against the forces of eminent collision.

"*LOOK OUT!*" he bawled.

Grimm swerved, just in time, jerking the truck back onto the road, almost hitting a truck parked on the snowy shoulder. His thick features reddened again. He swallowed hard, muttering, chiding himself for being careless. "Sorry! Sorry!"

Wissemann cursed through a sigh. He lit another cigarette and puffed nervously, shaking an angry fist.

"*Dummkopf!*" he snarled. "Will you watch the road already!"

"S-Sorry. So sorry, sir, " Grimm muttered, exhaling fretfully, his face looking red and feverish now.

"I'd like to arrive in one piece, if you don't mind!"

HALF AN HOUR LATER. The clattering Daimler truck veered around a bend in the roadway and the aerodrome came into view. Beyond the crossroads, where the road entered the aerodrome, there was a gated barrier flanked by a sentry box which stood empty and covered in snow. A wooden gate, which should have been secured at this hour, swayed loosely on its hinges. Someone had left it open. There wasn't a guard on duty either.

Wissemann scoffed. "Shouldn't there be a guard on duty?"

"Yes, *Herr Oberleutnant*—"

"*Unglaublich! Vor die Hunde gehen!*" Willi Wissemann rasped his forehead. Yes, this *Jasta* was certainly going to the dogs!

The truck motored past the guard shack and through the gate, down a tortuous snow-covered lane with rocky stonewalls on each side. The walls were covered with patches of ice and slushy snowdrifts. The lane snaked down a shallow hill and led to the outskirts of the airfield and the *Jasta* Operations hut. Also at the bottom of the sloping drive stood a large old chateau, framed on three sides by a bosky acreage. The aerodrome, Wissemann quickly noted, had once been an old vineyard.

Grimm carefully guided the truck through a pillared archway, turned into a small gravel courtyard, parking in front of the Operations hut. Wissemann noted that the hut was actually a stone high house with a dovecote of flat tiles. Adjacent to the high house, he saw a large two-story, half-timbered chateau of wattle and daub. It was ancient but solidly constructed. And with plenty of rooms and a large dining room, it most certainly served as the officers' quarters and mess. He nodded. "Good. Decent..."

Out beyond the main structure, Wissemann noticed an expansive airfield surrounded by thick hedgerows. This flat tract of land had once been a vineyard. Parallel to the winding gravel driveway stood six decrepit-looking Bessaneau aeroplane hangars. These quondam French structures were obviously seized when the German Army overran the area two years prior. The ragged looking hangars were large canvas tents, structures typically supported by a wooden framework. Each held two or three aircraft. And of course, to Wissemann's grave disappointment, no aircraft were visible, anywhere, on the snowy field.

Next to the hangars stood a dilapidated dispersal tent. The tent's modest little chimney pot gave no hint of activity. Along the southwest edge of the airfield, Wissemann could see an old, maison bloc longhouse that probably served as the maintenance shop. Undoubtedly, all repairs took place there. Other smaller tents, near the Operations hut, made up the enlisted billets. These grayish, conically shaped tents, draped in white snow, looked remarkably like little Eskimo igloos. He groaned. The aerodrome was even less remarkable than the file photos at *Idflieg* had shown it to be. The amort *Jastaführer* hastily flicked a smoldering cigarette butt out the window and swung down from the cab of the truck. He saw steam boiling from the radiator cap as the engine shuddered to a halt. Hmm, he thought. Perhaps the little noncom really was telling the truth about his engine trouble.

"Up the steps there, *Oberleutnant*, you'll find Operations."

"Right. My—"

"Don't worry. I'll take care of your gear, sir," Grimm replied instantly. "And watch your step, sir."

Wissemann strode carefully up the icy steps and opened the door and entered. A blast of warm air overwhelmed him as he stepped inside. Heat and warmth at last, he thought. Mmm... and someone is brewing coffee, too.

"Afternoon, *Herr Oberleutnant*. Cold, nasty weather we're having today, eh?" said the odd looking man sitting behind a cluttered desk. The man was obviously underwhelmed by the arrival of the new *Jastaführer,* choosing to rise slowly from his chair and strike a pose midway between attention and sloth. He sighed miserably, arching his achy back.

"Indeed—"

"*Oberfeldwebel* Albrecht Schutzling, *Jasta* adjutant—at your service, sir. Welcome to Imperial *Jagdstaffel* No. 23, and beautiful snowbound Pusieux Ferme Aerodrome."

Staff Sergeant Albrecht Schutzling was a typical, mild mannered "old man" of thirty-three years and a thin fellow with a bloodless face. He seemed to be possessed with the well-bred manner of genteel conservatism. With oily, ginger hair and a ridiculous red mustache, he bore an uncanny resemblance to Kaiser Wilhelm, the Emperor of Germany. Schutzling smiled easily but was typically a serious-minded man with parochial middle-class views. He was married with two children and always kept a locket with photos of his family in his pocket. Albrecht Schutzling patiently awaited the end of the hostilities and the resumption of the mediocrity.

"Thank you, *Oberfeldwebel* Schutzling," Wissemann intoned, amiably as possible. "I am *Oberleutnant* Wilhelm R. Wissemann—the new *Jastaführer."*

"Yes, yes. Of course."

"I believe we spoke on the telephone?" Wissemann abruptly shifted his casual tone, uttering curtly: "Isn't there suppose to be a guard on the front gate, *Feldwebel?*"

"Oh, uh... well..." Schutzling dithered, hesitating to give an explanation.

"Who is supposed to be on guard duty?"

"Uh—well, sir. Let me check the duty roster." His guilt suddenly became panic. He began a dispirited rummaging. "Well, looks like someone must have misplaced it. Hmm... can't seem to find it?"

Wissemann's gaze raced around the room. It was a pitiful composite of massive clutter and disarray. "Well, I'm not surprised, *Oberfeldwebel*, given the condition of this *Schweinerei*—pigsty! When was the last time this place was cleaned out? And look at the filth on those windows. Shameful, shameful! A sad commentary on what the German Air Service has become."

"Um... *Jawohl, Herr Oberleutnant?*"

"What do you mean '*Jawohl, Herr Oberleutnant*'?"

"Uh, don't know, sir? It seemed like the thing to say?"

"*Lieber Gott!*" Wissemann rasped his face.

"D-don't worry, s-sir," Schutzling stammered. I'll get this mess sorted out posthaste." He turned to the door and shouted: "Grimm! Get in here. Now!"

Grimm stumbled in, bags in hand. "What? What!"

"Where is *Gerfreiter*—what's his name?"

"You mean, Hippel?"

"Yes! That's the blockhead."

"Don't know. I'm not my brother's keeper."

"Isn't he supposed to be on guard duty right now?"

"I believe so."

"Any lowly snail-eating Frenchman could waltz in here and blow us to kingdom come!"

"And what do you want *ME* to do about it?"

"Go find him!" Schutzling bolted out from behind his desk. "Tell that half-wit to report to me as soon as you find him. Go. Now!"

"Now? This minute?" Grimm's face sagged.

"Yes! Get moving. Now!"

"Jesus von Christ—"

"Get going!"

"Alright, alright, I'm going!"

Thoroughly annoyed now, Grimm tossed Wissemann's bags down on the floor and stalked out the door, the door slamming noisily.

Oberfeldwebel Schutzling seemed ready to burst, his pale face reddening with embarrassment. He turned back to Wissemann and shrugged, grimacing with uneasy misgivings.

"I know this must look awful, sir. So sorry," he apologized miserably. "Security has been a bit lax around here lately. With the weather turning so bitterly cold, it's difficult to keep the men at their posts. I know that's no—"

"No excuse? This is a war zone, *Lieber Gott!* The security of this aerodrome should be of the utmost importance. Have *Gerfreiter* Hippel report to *ME*—once Grimm finds him! Regulations will be enforced." Wissemann gritted his teeth angrily, his normal sangfroid seemingly slipping away by the second.

"*Jawohl, Herr Oberleutnant!*" There was a kind of faint convulsion on Schutzling's stolid face. A light sweat broke out on his forehead.

The baleful Bavarian took a deep breath and exhaled, reminding himself to remain calm. He looked around the Operations hut and saw a half-opened door marked: *JASTAFÜHRER,* stenciled in faded, black letters. Wissemann strode across the room to the door.

He turned to Schutzling. "Is this my office?"

"Yes, sir. It is. *Hauptmann* Traurig used it as his office," Schutzling explained nervously. "I'm sorry it's in such disarray. He left us in quite a hurry, you see."

Wissemann opened the door and clicked on a light. He gazed in, nodding, surveying the room. "And where are my personal quarters?"

"In the main chateau, sir, on the second floor. It is a very spacious old house—"

"And the officers' quarters?"

"*All* the officers' quarters are in the chateau, sir." Schutzling nodded. "Two men per room."

"Aha. How many officers?"

"Eleven." Schutzling chagrined. "Oh, wait... make that twelve, *Herr Oberleutnant*—counting you."

"Twelve. Do I share a room with someone?"

"No, no, of course not. You have a private room, sir."

"Excellent. Amenities?"

"Oh, yes," Schutzling clicked his heels. "Thankfully, we have electricity here, *Herr Oberleutnant*," he replied quite assuredly. "The fine French folks that once roosted here were well-heeled provincials of the wine trade, you know."

"I see."

Wissemann stepped into the dimly lit office, gazing about. It contained a desk and two chairs. Hanging on the wall, crookedly, was a ragged-looking chalkboard roster; it recorded the comings and goings of the *Jasta*. On the opposite wall, a crudely tacked-up campaign map of the Champagne region displayed the unit's sphere of operations: west to Montdidier, east to Rethel, and south to the front lines near Reims. The *Jasta* routinely patrolled this breadth of territory and each pilot was required to fly two missions a day. And from a small window one could see out over the aerodrome—a good view of the facilities. Hanging next to the window, a framed photograph of Kaiser Wilhelm adorned the wall.

Wissemann grumbled, pacing up to the picture, shaking his head in deepening repugnance. He pulled the picture down and handed it to the moustachioed adjutant.

"Here, Schutzling," he said, "you may hang this in your office, if you like. I'm afraid it's a bit too mawkish for my taste."

The ginger-haired adjutant scoffed silently, looking stiffly virtuous. He nodded and reluctantly took the picture, leering at Wissemann in disbelief, tucking it under an arm. Unbelievable! He thought. This new *Jastaführer* seemed to lack the proper decorum typically established in a Prussian commanding officer.

Wissemann took stock of the office. A field telephone and a few loose papers cluttered a dilapidated, old desk. Two camp chairs sat dusty and idle. The room had a fusty odor about it; a stale gloominess hung over the office like an ancient crypt. He swung about and cracked open a window to air out the fetid room, sighing heavily, resigning himself to the grim reality of the conditions.

"All right. Bring me the dossier files of all the pilots," he said, a bit offhandedly, "the enlisted men as well. I want to have a look at them. A cup of coffee would be nice, too." Wissemann removed the service cap from his throbbing head and ran stiff fingers through his hair. Damn, he thought, this is far worse than I imagined.

"*Herr Oberleutnant!* Right away." Boot heels clicked.

"Who is the maintenance chief?"

"That would be *Vizefeldwebel* Peltzer, sir."

"Peltzer?" Wissemann jerked a nod. "Right. I want to see him right away. I have a lot of questions for him."

"He will have questions too, sir," Schutzling parried.

"I'm sure he will," Wissemann countered, and strode back to the operations office, retrieving his valise. "Just tell him I want to see him —now, *Feldwebel!*"

"I'll fetch him right away, *Herr Oberleutnant.* Perhaps—"

"Thank you, *Feldwebel.* That will be all."

"Yes, sir."

The adjutant nodded and scurried away, grumbling. Imperious officers always made his stomach churn. This persecution must be some sort of penance he had to pay, he thought, for all those years he'd tormented his subordinates at the accounting firm in Augsburg. Alas, kismet's exacting retribution never ceased to amaze him. The nettled noncom marched straight to the Operations telephone, muttering implacably all the way.

Wissemann went back into his office and took his overcoat off, draping it over a chair. He cracked open a bag, pausing, listening. The bumptious Bavarian could hear Schutzling talking on the telephone in the other room. Wissemann smiled; he was already making an impact on the *Jasta*. The new *Jastaführer* then went about meticulously removing all the items from the musette bag. He placed each item on the desk: an ink well, books, a letter opener, a clock paperweight, etc. Finally, he set a finely framed photograph of his fiancée on the desktop, Ilse von Linkhof. Wissemann smiled tenderly as he gazed at the picture. Ilse had such a kind and alluring face.

"Now this, is suitable for hanging!" he declared proudly.

He did miss her very much. Both had hoped to marry soon, but with the war on, they'd waited. And wait they did, for nearly two years now. Wissemann knew she was growing ever more impatient everyday, obsessively worrying. She'd warned him to be careful and not take foolish chances, and Wissemann had told her repeatedly not to fret. "Those things that we hold to be precious," he'd said that day at the train station, "are only saved by sacrifice." But Ilse could not consoled by those words. She cried unabashedly.

Wissemann had spent his remaining leave with her in Berlin in December. He reminisced fondly: the quiet dinner at their favorite restaurant, *Zur Letzten Instanz,* the gay Christmas party at the officers club, the New Year's celebration; it all seemed so far away now. The loneliness of the train and now these dismal, unfamiliar surroundings put him in a morose mood. He suddenly became very depressed.

He lighted a cigarette, thinking.

"As soon as I get things under control," he said to himself, "get this *Jasta* reorganized, I'll put in for another leave. Perhaps then, I can finally marry my little *Liebchen.*" He promised himself to make the necessary arrangements—this blasted war could go on forever. "I must not wait any longer!"

Moments later, there was a knock on the door. Schutzling had returned with the personnel files and a cup of coffee. "Here are the files you wanted, *Herr Oberleutnant,*" he said. "They're in alphabetical order. Officers on top—enlisted and noncom underneath."

"Excellent."

"And your coffee, of course." He set the cup down on the desk.

"Thank you, Schutzling."

"We do have a little sugar, sir. I'm sorry, no cream, though."

"Don't bother. I take mine black."

"Black?" Schutzling nodded suspiciously. He laid the files down and sighed. There seemed to be distress in that sigh. *"Vizefeldwebel* Peltzer will be here in a few moments, sir. He was just closing down the maintenance shop when I rang." Schutzling happened to notice Ilse's photo perched on the desktop, and smiled. Hmm, a fine girl, he thought. At least this officer has good taste in women. Coffee? Well... And that business about the Kaiser?

"Have Peltzer come in as soon as he arrives."

"Yes, sir—"

"Thank you, Schutzling. That will be all."

"Jawohl , Herr Oberleutnant."

Schutzling nodded and returned to his duties.

The tall Bavarian officer sat down behind the desk and sipped the coffee. Ach! He made a little face, more rancid ersatz! He glanced over the files of the *Jasta,* and within a few moments realized his troubles were only beginning. The personnel files he studied contained countless instances of insubordination, misconduct, violence, and just plain old disregard for military protocol. The information was disconcerting.

He glanced over the *Jagdstaffel* duty roster first.

There were ten officers in the *Jasta*, eight of whom were pilots. There were forty-one enlisted men of varying maintenance skills, mechanics, armorers, riggers, fitters, who were directly responsible for the care of the *Staffel's* typical complement of twelve aircraft. The rest of the personnel were devoted to the countless auxiliary services of supply, communications and mess service.

Wissemann thumbed through some of the dossiers...

Vizefeldwebel Adolf Auersbach, born in Ulm, a career noncom and reservist of thirty-eight years of age, father of seven girls, was a cobbler in civilian life. Wissemann scoffed, Auersbach was obviously a bit too old to be a combat pilot and could have probably gotten a waiver from active service on the account of his large family. Wissemann shook his head in disbelief.

Ludwig Eckhardt, was from Rosenheim and a *Kettenführer.* He was an intellectual type with a degree in philosophy from the University of Munich. He was an able pilot but apparently a lousy marksman. An armorer's report stated that, on many occasions, he came back from missions with all his ammunition spent but without ever filing a victory claim.

Eduard Fleischer, born and raised in Munich, was a reputed coward, being cited for lack of courage in the infantry, transferring to the Air Service eleven months ago. Fleischer had hoped to quell his demons from the cockpit of an aeroplane. But so far, according to, *Hauptmann* Traurig, he had not.

Jacob Frankenberg, a handsome, Jewish playboy from Lindau-on-the-Bodensee, was the son of a wealthy banker. He was a romantic and a dreamer, never holding a real job, just living off a trust fund while barely graduating from the College of Art in Vienna. Although he boasted being an avid angler and was reputedly quite handy with a rifle, he hadn't scored a single victory in twenty-five aerial combats.

Otto Gutemann, a Swabian born in Nordlingen, an engineering graduate of the University of Ingolstadt, the one shining star of this refractory unit, was the acting *Jastaführer*. His four victories were tops in the unit, three occurring on the same mission—all Spads. He was a competent individual, when he wasn't helping his mechanics fine tune his aeroplane, he was in the mess fixing the gramophone or doing some other menial task. He apparently possessed remarkable flying skills and excellent marksmanship. But something was amiss here; why hadn't a better *Jasta* snatched him up yet? Wissemann wondered. Why he was still in this *Jasta*?

Then there was Edwin Prandzynski, an Austrian officer, serving as an observer of sorts, learning to fly and fight in a German air combat unit. Despite his abstemious Catholic background, Prandzynski was a distressingly narcissistic man, flaunting his medals ostentatiously, wearing them on his flight jacket during combat missions. It seems he'd been decorated for bravery during the Trentino offensive on the Italian front, the year before. But Wissemann knew well what the German hierarchy thought of their Austrian allies. Not much! And Prandzynski's piloting skills were equally appalling; he'd wrecked or crashed five machines since his arrival in December. That technically made him a French ace, Wissemann chuckled inwardly. Alas, the Austrians—our allies? Humph!

"Perhaps I could recommend the Croix de Guerre." The *Jastaführer* sighed, thinking about that fine French medal, shaking his head mockingly. "Hah! Just one more medal to add to his collection."

Paul Kindlich, a youngster of nineteen from Garmisch, was an Olympic skier of gold medal potential before the war, winning many competitions on the slopes of the Bavarian Alps. He'd scored his first two victories on the same day. And according to his dossier, was a career oriented lad, doing everything by the book, with an eye towards promotion. However, his innate shyness kept him from expressing himself properly, and he stammered insuperably. This was a butt of many jokes by the more indiscreet members of the *Jasta*.

Johann Neubauer, a former journalist from Nürnburg, was a garrulous misanthrope with a bitter sense of humor. *Flugmeldedienst* finally confirmed his one and only victory claim after an inflammatory letter to *Idflieg*. There was a lengthy investigation. Another pilot from a neighboring *Jasta* had also filed a claim for Neubauer's Caudron, a French two-seat reconnaissance machine. Both men had attacked it during the same air battle. Both had made a claim but only one confirmation could be granted. Neubauer's caustic but erudite petition won the day.

Feldwebel Josef Schäfer, a burly noncom from Völklingen, the squadron alcoholic, was currently on probation. He'd been recently arrested by the military constabulary for stealing a bottle of liquor from the field supply commissary in Laon. Schäfer was a devil-may-care maverick and incorrigible ruffian. No one trusted him either. He was constantly under suspicion by the other *Jasta* members. Every time something came up missing or mislaid, he was suspected or blamed. No one dared confront him though, for he was a burly ex-steelworker and an amateur boxer, "The Ironman from Völklingen," and had a wicked reputation for brawling and womanizing. Schäfer claimed to be the undefeated champion of the Crown Prince's Bavarian 6th Army. No one really believed him though, yet no one ever openly disputed it.

Finally, there was Tomas Winkler, currently overdue from leave. He was born and raised in the United States. A music student of classical piano; he was studying in New York City when the war broke out. Late in 1914 when the war escalated, his German born parents decided to return to the Fatherland, taking the then eighteen-year old Winkler with them. Wissemann saw the *FlugM* communiqué attached to Winkler's dossier. It was a report from the chief of Air Intelligence in Berlin. Winkler was under suspicion—a suspected Allied sympathizer because of his American citizenship—even though he'd scored one of the *Jasta's* eight victories.

The beleaguered Bavarian moaned, poring over the rest of the dossiers, taking mental notes, distressing warily. What a collection of blockheads and oddballs, he thought. *"Mein Gott,* Willi," he grumbled to himself. "What in the hell have you gotten yourself into this time?" He sat in quiet misery, reading on for another twenty minutes, wondering when he was going to wake up from this horrid dream...

WILLI WISSEMANN WINCED SUDDENLY. There was a thunderous slamming of a door and a sudden rush of cold air. The *Jagdstaffel* maintenance chief, Maximilian Peltzer, had just arrived.

"*Oberleutnant...*" Schutzling announced, popping his head around the door jamb. "*Vizefeldwebel* Peltzer, here to see you."

"Send him in, please," Wissemann gestured beseechingly. "Bring the weather forecasts for tomorrow too, will you?"

"Right away, sir."

"Maybe we can get a *Kette* up—knock down a Frenchman or two."

"I can already tell, sir—operations will likely be suspended again."

The *Jastaführer* scowled. The weather seemed like another excuse for the *Jasta* to shirk its duties.

A portly, blowzy-looking man stood framed in the doorway.

"*Vizefeldwebel* Maximilian Peltzer, reporting as ordered, sir," said the portly man in mechanic's coveralls, addressing his new *Staffel* leader with a limp salute and a hoarse cough.

Wissemann grumbled, motioning him with a jerky wave. "Come in, come in, *Vizefeldwebel.*"

Wissemann immediately noticed Peltzer's grubby appearance and unshaven face. Greasy locks protruded out from underneath a tatty Feldmutze, and he was still in coveralls, which were covered in oil and soot. Peltzer, a heavyset man from Würzburg, and an old-looking thirty-one years, had thick eyebrows that nearly hid deep-set brown eyes; a long protuberant nose dominated swarthy facial features. His hands were black with grease, fingernails bitten to the quick. An acrid nub of a cigar dangled, clamped between thick, chapped lips. He also reeked of sweat and petrol. This sweaty temperament, matched with a foul body odor, petrol fumes, cigar smoke, and who knows what all else, made Wissemann wince woefully. The *Jastaführer* cleared his throat, trying to maintain his composure. He drew a little breath.

"Good afternoon, *Vizefeldwebel* Peltzer. Have a seat, please." He returned the sergeant major's salute, directing him to a chair.

"Afternoon, *Herr Oberleutnant.*" Peltzer sat down.

Wissemann took a cigarette from his sterling case, lighted it, then flicked the matchstick into the ashtray he'd just set out. He took a long brooding drag. The high-minded Bavarian thought of berating the slatternly maintenance chief for his unkempt appearance, very tempted to cast aside the formality of courtesy and tell the shabby-looking noncom what he really thought. However, he wanted to get on solid footing with the old chief, the man that virtually kept the

Jasta running, before going off on some savage, spittle-flecked tirade, which is what he felt like doing at that point. "I am *Oberleutnant* Wilhelm Wissemann..." Smoke streamed from his nostrils in twin jets; he manufactured a glib smile. "I am the new *Jastaführer.*"

"I know," Peltzer replied, shifting the cigar to the corner of his mouth, "Schutzling just briefed me a few minutes ago..." and the cigar shifted again.

Wissemann ashed his cigarette, staring at that soggy nub with growing impatience, watching it bob about restlessly, up and down, side to side, around again. *"Vizefeldwebel,* when you address me," he enjoined curtly, "take that damned cigar out of your mouth!"

"S-sir?" Peltzer stammered, staring at the *Jastaführer,* suddenly red-faced and dumbfounded. "Oh, yes, of course." He shrugged haphazardly and tossed the soggy nub onto the floor.

Wissemann's brow arched peevishly, his eyes flaring. "Peltzer. Do you mind? This is my office."

"Sorry." Peltzer grumbled, his face now paling with mortification. He picked up the nub and shoved it into a pocket.

"Thank you, Peltzer," Wissemann replied reproachfully.

An awkward moment of silence ensued. Both men traded uneasy glances. Peltzer sank deeper into his chair, brooding, thinking: This new *Jastaführer* is in a real foul mood. Damn! I hope he's not gonna to be a hard ass.

Wissemann moaned, rasping his face, feeling a bit disconcerted himself. "Now..." he began, folding his hands atop his desk, "what's the status for all aircraft, currently?"

"Status, sir?"

"I mean, how many are available for operations."

Peltzer stared absently at the ceiling, studying its moldy tiles, as if the answer could be found among the cobwebs. "Well, let's see... when my men finish overhauling that ancient Halberstadt we received from 7th Army *Flugpark* yesterday—we'll have... six, sir." Peltzer rested his hands on his lap and shifted himself restlessly in the chair.

Wissemann sighed miserably. "A Halberstadt?"

The *Jastaführer* knew a man could do many things wrong in an Albatros, but in a Halberstadt? The possibilities for cracking up were limitless. Ach! One would expect the French to stumble about in antiques that could have been designed by da Vinci, but a German?

"A new Albatros could arrive tomorrow, sir, if the weather holds out," Peltzer said, then added diffidently: "Maybe more?"

"Seven, then—a D.III, perhaps?" Wissemann was hopeful.

Peltzer chuckled. "Oh no, sir. Most definitely a D.II."

"Aha."

"This *Staffel's* at the bottom of the list for the new D.III scout, sir."

"I see—"

"The Prussians always get their greedy little hands on the latest equipment first, as you probably already know."

"Yes, so I understand." Wissemann rasped his chin. "And how are we on spare parts and supplies?"

"Um... we have two wrecked Albatroses for spare parts."

"Wrecked? Explain."

"One was recently written off by our Austrian guest. Damned fool, bounced it right into the side of the munitions shed, thought the whole place was going to go up in flames—" Peltzer suddenly broke into a nasty coughing spasm, gasping, grunting, groaning.

Wissemann leaned far back in his chair, grimacing, trying to avoid the mechanic's sickly spasm. He took a drag from his cigarette and exhaled—sighing really—half-annoyed. "Anything else?"

"We have plenty of props, tires, high-tensile wiring, machine guns, patch kits—that sort of thing. We've got plenty of spare parts."

"What's the condition of the aircraft? Are they in good running order, Peltzer?"

"No, not really, *Herr Oberleutnant.* For the most part... they're all sewn, patched and out of plumb. I mean, they're all flyable and combat ready—just too many hours on the motors. Army isn't sending us new motors, just reconditioned ones—overhauled of sorts."

Wissemann grumbled; Peltzer's assessments didn't sound good.

He glanced over the maintenance report again, frowning, noticing one entry in particular—several aircraft were indeed overdue for major overhauls, and in another—some should've already been retired. He wondered how this unit could wage war at all, with ham-fisted mechanics, slapdash maintenance, shoddy equipment, reckless pilots; it truly amazed him that the *Staffel* had even shot down eight enemy aircraft! Somehow, someway, he'd have to convince 7th Army *Kofl* to re-equip this *Jasta*. But how?

Apparently, 7th Army appeared to regard this *Staffel* with a high degree of contempt. Willi Wissemann believed this wholeheartedly. Even though Bavaria supported the war effort as much as Prussia did, Bavarian staffed units were often treated with downright disrespect. *Jasta 23* was suffering because the officer in charge of Army Aviation, the 7th Army *Kommandeur de Flieger,* a Prussian Major, despised this particular unit with a passion. He'd repeatedly, perhaps purposely, disregarded all Peltzer's maintenance requests, saying, for example: "a transportation logjam" or "foul weather" was to blame for supply hold ups.

Wissemann didn't believe any of that. Things were being held up on purpose, supplies were being held back, requests were being ignored. All these elements were contributing to a serious dearth of morale. The *Jasta* wasn't just a collection of misfits and rejects, it was a forgotten, undisciplined military mob left to fend for itself. It was all very frustrating; Wissemann realized he had a sobering task ahead.

Schutzling returned with an intrusive rap, peering around the door jamb. "Just got off the telephone with our wonderful weather forecasters in St. Quentin. *Wetterdienst* has issued a severe weather warning—all flight operations have been suspended for the next twenty-four hours."

"Of course." Wissemann sighed gravely.

"Just as well, we need the respite, eh, Peltzer?" Schutzling put in sarcastically.

"Uh, um..." Peltzer stammered.

Wissemann shot Schutzling a sour look. The facetious adjutant just smirked and went back to his duties. Peltzer grunted and broke into a violent coughing spasm, turning bright red, gasping for breath. He was looking dreadfully peaked and feverish.

The leery *Jastaführer* shook his head, stubbed out his cigarette and said with a sigh: "Okay, Peltzer. That will be all for now. There will be a *Staffel* briefing tomorrow morning, and a maintenance briefing after that. I'll let you know the exact times later. And since the weather has the *Jasta* grounded, we'll iron out some of the finer details of discipline, aye? We'll re-familiarize this unit with the Army manual once again? Understood, *Vizefeldwebel?*"

"*Jawohl, Herr Oberleutnant.*" Looking sheepish and bloated, Peltzer rose to leave the office.

But before he even got to the door, Wissemann had a final remark. "Peltzer, I recommend you get some rest and take care of that cough," he said, picking up his coffee tin. "A hot shower and a shave might be in order as well, *ja?* Dismissed."

"Yes, sir." Peltzer, nodded, saluted and tramped out of the office.

Wissemann returned the salute and stood up. He shook the dregs from the coffee tin in one hasty gulp, then strode around his desk and stood by the window. He thought quietly as the falling snow swirled about in the buffeting wind, noticing, suddenly, a cold draft was circulating through the room, making him shiver. He closed the window. Heavy gray clouds hovered over the horizon, the wind began to howl. He felt lonely and depressed, having second thoughts now, wondering if he'd done the right thing transferring to a front line fighting squadron.

Willi Wissemann groaned, thinking.

He knew he had plenty of practical experience and flight time under his belt, but the hours spent on single-seat machines had been fleeting. He'd taught others how to fly and was an excellent pilot himself, but there was a disquieting dearth of experience concerning single-seater combat nagging at him. He'd flown Aviatik utility trainers in Silesia, Roland two-seaters on the Somme, locking horns with the Royal Flying Corps many times. English pilots fought with a gentlemanly, hell-bent bravado, sportsmen to a fault. Wissemann had been forewarned though. Here in the Champagne Sector, the French *chasse escadrilles* fought with élan, the wily Frenchmen quite finicky about engaging in wild free-for-all melees, fighting with great guile and caution. Their Nieuports were quite maneuverable and their Spads much too fast. And if the *Jasta* ever ran into the likes of Guynemer and the Storks, the elite pilots of the French Air Service, Wissemann distressed, he'd be writing more and more condolence letters every night.

His thoughts drifted back to the New Year's Eve Party. Ilse was so tipsy that night, he had to literally carry her back to her house. She pleaded with him to stay the night. But he begged off politely, concocting some half-baked story about how he had to fly a certain General back to the Zeppelin base at Schneidemühl at the crack of dawn. He drove back to the officers' barracks and slept restlessly for the rest of the night. What a fool, he thought of himself later, for not taking advantage of his *Liebchen's* amorous advances, as any other normal man might have. Wissemann knew he was desperately in love. He couldn't spoil her virginal purity with one alcohol-fueled tryst. He was proud of himself for being a gentleman.

Wissemann sighed with a shiver, the pangs of loneliness and the cold overwhelming him, his stomach rumbling, aching under the constant barrage of coffee and stale cigarettes. He needed to find the mess and get some food in his belly. Or perhaps, he averred, something a little more potent than coffee. A neat shot of cognac would do the trick nicely! A little smile formed on his face. He grabbed his coat and cap and got some directions from Schutzling.

"It's in the chateau, sir," the adjutant conveyed.

"Right. Got it."

"First floor, on the right. You can't miss it."

"Thank you, Schutzling," Wissemann replied. "Please, schedule a *Staffel* formation, oh-eight hundred tomorrow, in the dispersal tent."

"Everybody, sir?"

"Just the officers—the pilots, I mean."

"Right."

"It will be mandatory for *all* pilots to attend. No excuses."

"Jawohl, Herr Oberleutnant."

"And... let's have Peltzer's gang come in at—oh-nine hundred. I want to speak to his crew separately."

"Yes, sir. As you wish."

"Also..." Wissemann added innocently, "have my personal orderly meet with me in my office in an hour."

"Personal orderly, sir?" Schutzling scoffed inwardly; this officer obviously didn't understand how things worked in a Bavarian *Staffel*. Personal orderlies, or "batmen" in British jargon, were not to be had here at *Jasta 23.* "Uh, anything else, sir?"

"Yes. Put *Gerfreiter* Hippel on report."

"Already done."

"Excellent. Have him report to me at..." Wissemann glanced at his pocket watch—eighteen thirty-five—6:35 p.m. civilian time, "...um, nineteen hundred hours?"

"Yes, sir. Nineteen hundred."

"That will be all, Schutzling. Thank you."

"Herr Oberleutnant!" Schutzling clicked his heels.

Wissemann donned his cap and traipsed off to mess, the door slamming behind him. It was strangely quiet outside as he traversed the walkway to the side entrance of the chateau from Operations. But he welcomed the tranquility. The howling of the wind had died down and snowflakes fell silently from the sky, and now he could hear his stomach grumbling. He wondered what the cooks had planned for supper. But the fare mattered not to him. The broad-shouldered Bavarian hungered for a large helping of success. Ja-ja! He would gladly have a second helping of that!

DEKE D. WAGNER

Passed by FlugM Censor #2765
Frau Ilse Magdalena von Linkhof
c/o 7th Army Headquarters Laon
Berlin (Please forward)

Liebe Ilse!   17.Feb..1917

I have arrived at my destination, finally. The weather conditions are atrocious, as you may have imagined. The train ride was also terrible. I sat crammed in amongst many other soldiers in a tiny coach. The stench was horrendous! My accommodations are quite modest here, but I shall not complain one bit. I am happy to be here and take command of this Jasta. Hauptmann Traurig, the former Jastaführer, seems to have left things in a bit of a shambles and the discipline of the cadre is a fright, but rest assured, I will instill a sense of order and discipline! Please do not be upset with me for requesting combat duty again. I love you dearly, but the love for my country is stronger still. I have my duty as a German officer to fulfill and to see this bloody war to its end.

I hope everything is well with you. I couldn't help but notice that strained expression on your face as you waved good-bye to me at the train station. I could see the hurt in your eyes. I know it wasn't easy for you to say good-bye to me again. Forgive me? It's not easy to love a military man, I'm sure. But please understand that an officer's duty is very important to him. We live in chaotic times these days, and there isn't much solace in promises of the future. But I am sure that the cause we fight for is just and necessary. There will be a place and time soon when we can attest our vows and make plans for a long and permanent future. And that future cannot wait until the end of this blasted war!

Fondly, Willi

Chapter 9

✠

FEBRUARY 18, 1917. "YES—RECONNECT ME WITH Oberst Thomsen's headquarters, please!" snapped a frustrated *Oberleutnant* Willi Wissemann to the army operator on the other end of the telephone line, pacing his office floor in stiff strides. "I was cut off a moment ago."

"Can you hold, sir?" the operator replied. "It'll just be a minute."

"Yes, yes, I'll hold," Wissemann uttered in a throaty snarl.

The testy *Jastaführer* had spent the better part of the last hour on the telephone. Now his patience was really wearing thin. After getting off the line with 7th Army *Kofl* in Laon, with some disheartening denials to his supply requests, Wissemann decided to override the *Kommandeur's* terse rejection with a call to *Kogenluft's* Chief of Staff, *Oberst* Hermann Thomsen. Earlier that morning, his call to General von Schubert's headquarters had been rudely rebuffed, and the adjutant suggested he should call AFP-7 regarding replacement issues. *Gott!* He was getting the run around from all the staff offices, and he wasn't getting a thing done. And now it was nearing 0800 hours, almost time for his first *Jasta* assemblage.

A voice crackled over the line.

"Hello, *Leutnant* Junck speaking. What can I do for you, sir?"

The line crackled with buzzy interference.

"This is *Oberleutnant* Wissemann, *Jasta 23*, Pusieux Ferme. Is *Oberst* Thomsen available now? I must speak with him. It's very important."

"Oh. Is it urgent? He's very busy at the—"

"It's most urgent! May I speak with him, please?"

"All right, all right. One moment. I'll patch you through."

The bumptious Bavarian's lips compressed in a thin line of annoyance; Supreme Headquarters' insipid indifference maddened him. He was tired of dealing with pretentious Prussian commanders and their haughty adjutants. No one seemed to care that his *Jasta* needed to be re-equipped, especially *Oberst* Thomsen. Wissemann remembered his meeting with the old Prussian two months earlier in Berlin at the War Ministry. Wissemann certainly hadn't endeared himself to Thomsen with offhanded remarks about the sorry state of the training facilities at Stutthof. Of course, what he really wanted back then was an assignment to a *Jasta* on the Western Front.

So a week later, once back in Silesia, he began an endless barrage of handwritten transfer requests and telephone calls, all aimed at the puffed-up Prussian Chief of Staff. But those requests were overtly ignored. Then when he finally got hold of General von Hoeppner, all that had changed, of course. Thomsen relented, but unwillingly. He agreed to post the insistent Bavarian to a *Jasta*. This was due to von Hoeppner's express, written endorsement. And any endorsement by the General was to be taken as an order. He knew, though, Thomsen would never allow that order to stand without some form of revenge or retaliation. Wissemann had only to count the days before the old colonel enacted some boorish edict, basically relieving him of his command or concocting some absurd charge to get him court-martialed. It was only a matter of time.

General von Hoeppner was Thomsen's new superior and Commander in Chief of the German Imperial Air Service and a man not to be trifled with. Rumors had it that Thomsen was embittered over the fact that he'd been passed over for the position of Chief of the Air Service. He'd practically been running things for over a year, long before anyone ever heard the name Ernst von Hoeppner.

The story going round said that Thomsen resented von Hoeppner's superior ranking. A mild friction apparently existed between the two men. Not a good way to run a business, Wissemann thought. Initially, Thomsen had brevetted him to a Bavarian *Jasta* in the Alsace. But he changed his mind at the last minute.

He flatly informed General von Hoeppner that Wissemann had no real command experience, so a command position was out of the question. And just for spite, the hateful old Prussian sent Wissemann to the FEA Army depot at St. Quentin with no official orders, basically relegating him to a state of bureaucratic limbo. Once again, Wissemann spent a frustrating week ferrying aircraft to and from various airfields—

The line buzzed with a gruff voice.

"Yes? Hello? This is *Oberst* Thomsen... "

"Herr Oberst, Oberleutnant Wissemann here, listen—"

"Oh, you again! What do you want, Wissemann?" The old Prussian's voice growled with loathing. "Make it quick, see!"

"Well, *Herr Oberst,* I have some supply issues—"

"Out with it, Wissemann! I am very busy right now!"

"I'm calling about the new Albatroses—the D.III's? They were supposed to be delivered to my *Jasta* days ago. When should I expect them, sir?"

Thomsen scoffed. "When should you expect them?"

"The 7th Army *Kofl*—informed me that—I was to receive D.III scouts." This was a blatant prevarication and Wissemann knew it. He heard his own voice saying the words evenly, but they still sounded feeble. The equivocating *Jastaführer* was at his wits' end. He had to do something. He took a little breath and held it.

Oberst Thomsen laughed, quite unimpressed with the Bavarian's glib falsity. He knew a bluff when he heard one. "D. III's? No! You will not receive new Albatroses of that mark—not by my records. What are you trying to—"

"But, the *Kommandeur* said—"

"Do you take me for a fool, Wissemann?"

"Ah—"

"Those machines are for the Prussian *Jagdstafflen,* Wissemann. For von Richthofen's *Jasta* and such. "

"But, *Herr Oberst,* I need new aircraft here."

"Bavarian *Jastas* will not receive new aircraft until April or May."

That reply made Wissemann sigh with exasperation. He decided to play a trump card. If he couldn't get what he needed through official channels, then he'd have to resort to more "unofficial" means.

"Herr Oberst," he said forcefully. "I have a conformation order in my hand. It is signed by General von Hoeppner..."

"What? Who—"

"He officially approved it, sir."

"Why, you—"

"And further delays may result in queries by *Idflieg, Herr Oberst,"* Wissemann smiled. A mischievous chuckle escaped from his lips.

"Goddamn you, Wissemann!" Thomsen cursed.

"Herr Oberst..." Wissemann replied, then after pausing for effect said: "Where are my new Albatroses, sir?"

"Listen here, you little jackass! If you go over my head once more, I'll come down on you so hard... I'll... I'll... you, you—"

"I need my Albatroses."

"For your information, you blockhead!" Thomsen snarled, deciding to play his own little trump card, an undeniable fact. "The Albatros D. III is temporarily grounded for wing failure!"

"What? Wing failure?" Wissemann wasn't sure he believed the querulous old colonel. This, he thought, was more of Thomsen's stalling tactics. The new Albatros already having mechanical problems? Wissemann scoffed. He thought: Aha! Thomsen is playing my little game now, eh? Goddamn liar! *"Herr Oberst,* I am now down to eight operational aircraft—"

"Enough!" Thomsen snapped, now thoroughly worn down.

In his frustration, the old Prussian had let the Bavarian get the best of him. But it was a calculated ruse. He was more concerned with Wissemann's threat, idle as it may have sounded. He knew the Bavarian had befriended General von Hoeppner, they'd become quite chummy, it seemed. Thomsen worried; he didn't want von Hoeppner involved in any of his activities. The double-dealing old Prussian knew he couldn't legally deny Wissemann aircraft, knowing purposely blocking the original order for the Albatros D. III, before the recall, would be tantamount to criminality. It could be perceived as a gross illegality by the General Staff. The folks at *Idflieg* might even get wary. Or worse. The stuffed shirts at *FlugM* might launch an investigation. He certainly didn't want any of that. And he certainly didn't want von Hoeppner's aids snooping around his offices either. Thomsen wanted to remain in good standing with everyone.

Nevertheless when the new Albatros was grounded for wing failure after several untimely accidents, all deployments were canceled—for all German *Jastas.* The latest version Albatros D.II would substitute all orders for the grounded D. III. So there was really no need to obstruct the order anymore.

Thomsen ruminated; there were always ways "official ways" to add to the red tape! He chuckled, changing his mood artfully.

"All right, Wissemann," he said smoothly. "I'll send you three new D. II's, as soon as possible?"

"What?" Wissemann, stunned by Thomsen's sudden, complaisant reply, caught his breath. Then as reality set in, he nodded slowly. Aha! He was now quite pleased with himself. "Oh? Really? So... when can I expect them?"

"I don't know."

"Will more be sent later?"

"That's all you'll be getting, Wissemann!"

"All right. And how about some new replacements? When—"

"Stop pestering me with your petty little requests!"

"With all due respect, *Herr Oberst*. My requests are not petty." Wissemann's tone was playful and sarcastic. He was basking in a small triumph now.

Thomsen barked: "I'm coming down there in three weeks to inspect your *Jasta,* Wissemann! So you better get things in shape, by God. Or I will assign you to a field kitchen on the Russian Front! Or something worse!" He slammed the phone down, disconnecting the telephone call abruptly.

A grim scowl creased Wissemann's drawn features. "Old blast of wind." He hung up the telephone, rasped his face and sighed. His thoughts began to ramble. The D.III, grounded? He could hardly believe it. He lighted a cigarette. "We shall see. I will find out the truth, even if I have to go up to St. Quentin myself."

A sharp knock sounded at the door. It was Schutzling. He'd overheard the conversation with *Oberst* Thomsen. *"Herr Oberleutnant,* is everything all right?"

"Everything's fine. The *Oberst* can be very—stubborn, sometimes."

"Hah, that's an understatement." Schutzling was then gazing at the watch on his upraised wrist. "Uh, its oh-eight hundred, sir. The men are gathering for the briefing?"

"Right. Let's head to the dispersal tent. I'll deal with this later."

The resolute Bavarian officer reached for his cap, placing it on his head at a jaunty angle, and gave it a pat. He threw his overcoat over his shoulders and stamped out of the Operations hut with the cigarette dangling from his mouth. The thick personnel file was tucked carefully under his arm. He paced hurriedly to the dispersal tent, which was on the northwest side of the aerodrome. On the way, he passed by the three Bessaneau hangar tents, their tattered canvas flaps were wide open to the breeze. All three hangars were in ramshackle condition, and so were the aeroplanes inside of them. Everything around Willi Wissemann was a bleak reminder of the incontestable decay of morale. But he wouldn't let it bother him anymore. His recent victory over bureaucracy had taken the edge off a miserable condition. The *Jasta* woes could be fixed; he knew it. It would just take time and a lot of hard work. And a little finagling, too!

After a steady pace, he reached the dispersal tent. He took a final drag and flicked the smoldering butt to the ground. Schutzling opened the wood framed door to the dispersal tent for him, and Wissemann went in. He lingered at the doorway a moment, his eyes raking over the group of assembled pilots. Smoke and heady laughter rolled up to the low ceiling and no one moved a muscle. Wissemann shook his head, disappointed. Schutzling pursed his lips dubiously.

SCHUTZLING PURPOSELY slammed the door—hard—jolting everyone to their senses. He cleared his throat, bellowing, quite brusquely: "*JAGDSTAFFEL—ACH-TUNG!*"

Wissemann marched up to the head of the assemblage, laid the cumbersome personnel file down on a small tin table, stood legs akimbo, and waited, hands in coat pockets. Eight dozy airmen stumbled to attention. Each pilot rose and stood up stiffly, each gawking about in wild wonderment. *Feldwebel* Schäfer, the last man to rise, wobbled to attention, pie-eyed and mumbling bitterly, as he tried to shake off a hangover from his addled brain. The *Jastaführer* then took up a ramrod posture, hands clasped behind his back.

"As you were, gentlemen. As you were," he commanded calmly. "Take your seats, please."

The men sat down. And after a restless shuffling, mumbling and coughing, the hum of voices gradually quieted down. Wissemann stood patiently in front of them. All the *Jasta* pilots were there. A typically garrulous *Oberleutnant* Wissemann would usually tend to expatiate unnecessarily in these instances, but this time he averred to keep it short and sweet. He warily gazed upon the contrasting group assembled in front of him, sighing glumly. Ach! A motley collection, indeed! He picked the personnel file up and smiled. It was a thin little smile, the smile of a newly brevetted *Jastaführer*.

But the pilots did not smile. Their eyes were impassive slits, they dared not express their true feelings; their lips were clamped shut in a properly solemn line.

"*Guten Morgan, meine Herren,*" Wissemann began.

A low rumble of voices replied, an indiscernible dissonance.

"To those men who haven't met me yet... I am *Oberleutnant* Wilhelm R. Wissemann, your new commanding officer. I'm originally from Kempten, a small town in the Allgäu. I'm a former flight instructor and reconnaissance pilot. Before that, I served in the infantry and saw plenty of action in the trenches. Now. I called this briefing to introduce myself and go over a few things concerning the function of this *Jasta*. I've read your personnel files extensively..." he paused there for a moment, scanning the glaring faces. An air of indifference seemed to suffuse the gathered throng.

"And, well..." he added heavily, waggling the file ominously, "It's not good, my friends. Not good at all—"

Someone guffawed; a short stabbing laugh had broken out over the concourse of strained silence. *Leutnant* Gutemann spun around in his seat and searched for the impertinent culprit. He leveled his eyes at Josef Schäfer—the trenchant toper's equine laugh was distinctive enough to be recognized from anywhere in the room.

"For God's sake," he drawled. "Listen up, you blockhead!"

"Piss off, Gutemann!" Schäfer growled bitterly.

Gutemann shook his head, eyes aflame. "Listen here, you—"

"Eyes forward, gentlemen," Willi Wissemann ordered curtly, suppressing the urge to raise his voice. "Let's get down to business, men." He folded his arms over his chest, glowering at Schäfer, neck stiff, boot heels together.

Schäfer grinned, quite amused.

"Anyone who knows me..." Wissemann began, commencing his harangue in a solemn, pedantic tone, " ...knows I run things by the book. Everything put in the book has a purpose. So when in doubt, remember—we always do things by the book. Deviate from the book, and you had better have some very good reasons. I do not make terms with the incompetent. And I do not lose arguments in my *Jasta* either. That's one of the nice things about being a *Jastaführer*." Wissemann relaxed his posture. "I want you to remember this, gentlemen: excellent performance is standard, standard performance is substandard. And substandard performance is not allowed... NOT ALLOWED." He paused a moment to let that sink in, scanning their faces for a reaction.

"Pay attention, lads," Schutzling urged in a persuasive tone.

"Now, that said, does anyone have any questions?" Wissemann asked, looking upon the solemn faces before him with hope.

Schäfer stood up slowly, looking about, gazing at the assembled men around him, his lips twitching with soundless glee. A smug look brightened on his face.

"With all due respect, sir," the cockeyed churl simpered. "I don't want to seem out of line—but it's been a long time... a long time, since anybody did anything by the book around here."

The assembled airmen snickered. Wissemann's eyes flickered with annoyance. He cleared his throat, lips clamping down in a tight smile. He said: "*Feldwebel* Schäfer, there are four ways of doing things in my *Jasta*—the right way, the wrong way, the Army's way... and, my way. Do things *my way*, Schäfer, and we'll get along just fine. Any more questions?"

Schäfer mumbled something sounding like: *Scheibenkleister!*

The rest of the airmen squirmed uneasily, stunned to disbelief.

Wissemann then added: "Most of you are officers of the *Luftstreitkräfte*, and I expect you to act accordingly. Some of you may even remember what life was like in the trenches. You should be thankful for the opportunity to serve in the Air Service. Besides, where else can you find such fine food, free accommodations, and a holiday on the beautiful Champagne countryside."

That drew a few chuckles. Even Wissemann smiled. The Bavarian's balky *bon mot* had nearly broken the tension. But it was apparent his hackneyed humor went mostly unappreciated. The smiles quickly returned to tight, thin frowns.

A runner from the *Jasta* message center suddenly appeared with a communiqué and gave it to Schutzling. The adjutant glanced over it and then passed it to the new *Jastaführer*. Wissemann read it silently. The message was from *Kofl*. In curt, official phrasing, it informed him on the weather. His face brightened.

"Well, we're in luck, gentlemen," he said, his mouth curling up in a wry smile. "It seems as though the skies will clear up this afternoon."

Some of the men grumbled.

"*Ugh!*" Schäfer winced like a man hit in the head with a sand bag.

"According to the aerologists, the weather will be ideal around late afternoon. Patrols should be scheduled," Schutzling added.

"And just to show you that I'm not a hard man, gentlemen, this will only be a voluntary patrol." Wissemann studied the group for a response. "Volunteers—anybody?"

"I'll go, sir," Gutemann replied, volunteering immediately.

Another hand shot up. "M-me too, s-sir," Bubi Kindlich, the stuttering officer muttered.

"Anyone else? " Wissemann asked.

The assembled pilots looked around at each other, all shaking their heads, mumbling indistinctly. Wissemann saw no more hands.

"Very well," he said. "A barrage patrol will be scheduled for seventeen hundred hours. You two fine fellows see me after the briefing. Everyone else may have the day off."

Some halfhearted murmurs rumbled up from the seated pilots.

"But, I'm restricting you to the confines of this aerodrome for the duration of the day—with one exception."

More grumbles reverberated. Schäfer rolled his eyes.

"Those of you who wish to, may attend the religious mass held at the *Cathédrale de Notre Dame* in Laon. *Feldwebel* Schutzling will issue you a two-hour pass for the service. I expect you all back by eleven hundred hours. Do not be late."

"That's right, gents. Two hours," Schutzling lucubrated, and then quipped vindictively: "*Feldwebel* Schäfer—report to mess for potato peeling."

The nettled noncom slammed his cap down angrily and groaned. He drew a line across his throat and stuck out his tongue. Schutzling's chin jutted out, chuckling, staring back coolly.

"All right, gentlemen. Dismissed!" Wissemann ordered.

The men rose slowly. A low murmur of despair seemed to suffuse the motley gang as they shuffled toward the door. They were not happy. Things looked bleak. Gutemann and Kindlich approached Wissemann. Both men were smiling amiably.

"Morning, sir. Gutemann said, saluting snappily, then proffering his hand cordially. "Outstanding briefing,"

Willi Wissemann pumped the young officer's hand. "Thank you, Gutemann."

"Yes, v-very inspiring overture s-sir," Kindlich stuttered. "I've been l-looking forward to m-meeting you." He shook hands with the *Jastaführer.*

"Well, thank you, gentlemen."

"Inspiring stuff, indeed." Gutemann nodded.

"Oh, it was nothing, really. Just trying to instill a little buoyancy."

"T-they d-definitely need it, s-sir."

"I hope I wasn't carping too much."

"On the contrary, sir," Gutemann drawled, his Swabian accent coming through. "I think a bit of castigation might benefit some of these half-wits. They're not all a bad bunch, really. But *Hauptmann* Traurig couldn't motivate them. Hopefully your strong leadership will inspire them."

"Yes, perhaps so." Wissemann nodded and agreed. He studied the young officer for a moment.

Leutnant Otto Gutemann was an averaged height, fair-haired, young man with better than average looks. His green eyes were very focused and piercing. A pencil thin mustache, just a fuzzy, blond line above two thin lips, almost seemed pretentious. His complexion was rosy and vibrant.

As the acting *Jastaführer,* he'd been handling all the *Jasta* affairs since *Hauptmann* Traurig's headlong exit. He was glad that Wissemann was here now to take command. Although Otto Gutemann was a good pilot and certainly a decent fellow, he didn't relish commanding a *Jagdstaffel.* His censorious criticisms of certain individuals in the *Jasta* certainly didn't endear him to those subordinate to him.

His reluctance to act in concord with the more incorrigible members of the *Jasta,* excluded him from many after hours festivities. But he didn't care about all that. He was here to fly and fight.

"T-they're all a b-bunch of id-idiots, if you a-ask me," Kindlich stuttered.

Wissemann leaned back on the table, crossed an arm over his chest and placed a thumb under his chin. He gazed at the youngster with heedful interest. Hmm, so this is our young Alpine champion, he thought.

Leutnant Paul "Bubi" Kindlich was a small and frail looking lad of nineteen years, merely a boy in Wissemann's eyes. The "boy" carried the ignominious moniker of "Bubi" by the *Jasta* cadre, a title he reluctantly accepted. He was short, wiry, and had effeminate facial features. His delicate hands seemed perpetually sweaty, and they trembled ever so slightly whenever he used them to express a point. His hair was jet black, slicked straight back and shimmered with a high-gloss sheen. His face was smooth. Wissemann figured he probably didn't even shave yet. But young Bubi Kindlich's most obvious physical trait was an insuperable stammer. He was constantly stumbling over syllables, hesitating, halting—trying to find the right words to say. He preferred the twin Maxims mounted on his Albatros to do the talking for him. His guns never stuttered. They only killed.

"I'll get them straightened out," Wissemann articulated evenly.

"One can only hope so, sir."

"You two fellows seem to be okay."

"Th-thank you—s-sir."

"Danke, Herr Oberleutnant."

"I read both your dossiers. I was quite impressed."

"We're here to fight, sir." Otto Gutemann jerked a nod. "And not with each other, mind you."

"Indeed. Three Spads, Gutemann. Impressive! That's not easy."

Gutemann blushed. "It wasn't *that* difficult, sir. They were all duds, it seems."

"Duds?"

"I mean, they must've all been novices or very scared."

"Scared?"

"They didn't put up much of a fight, sir. Really. They seemed confused when we—Kindlich and I—I should say, surprised them." Young Gutemann spoke in diffident tones, obviously downplaying his achievements. Modesty, it seemed, was one of his finer qualities.

"Never underestimate your abilities, Gutemann," Wissemann said.

"I was lucky, sir. I think I killed the flight leader outright. My initial burst must have mortally wounded him. The other two just froze, I guess."

"Yes, G-Gutemann is a d-dead shot. He never m-misses."

160

Wissemann smiled. "And you, Kindlich. Two in the same day? One on your first patrol? Not bad, *Junge*. Not bad at all."

"Got l-lucky, s-sir. I—I suppose. He f-flew right in f-front of me."

"You men are too modest." Wissemann replied, and popped a cigarette in his mouth and lit it. "A trait I dearly admire though."

"Then later t-that eve-n-ning," Kindlich stammered on, "I shot down a F-Farman, t-two-seater, low over the tr-trenches. He b-burst into flames."

Kindlich's halting speech patterns certainly didn't reflect his aggressive spirit. And Gutemann's easygoing drive was unmatched. The inseparables, Wissemann thought with ludic bemusement. The both of them, matched like a perfectly paired set of dueling pistols. He would have much to learn from these two—*Kobras*. He realized if the rest of the *Jasta* could be this aggressive, his job would be that much easier.

"There's no luck in good shooting, Kindlich," he said, cigarette smoke rolling from his mouth. "Don't be so modest."

"Well, s-sir..."

"I know you're an avid sportsman—a sharpshooter. I'm sure it comes quite natural to you."

"I wouldn't have any other man in my *Kette*, sir," Gutemann remarked, patting Kindlich on the shoulder. Kindlich nodded.

Wissemann smiled then raised an important issue. "Before we leave for the patrol, Gutemann, I'd like to go over a few things with you, okay? Hand signals, procedures, tactics, et cetera, et cetera."

"Absolutely, sir."

"You—*Leutnant* Gutemann—will lead this patrol. Not me. Show me the ropes, *Junge*. So I can get the *feel* of things? I have little experience in *Staffel* operations. Understand?" Wissemann spoke honestly, his modesty showing through. He really hated to admit he had very little single-seat combat experience. However, in light of the current circumstances, he really had no choice. Could he trust Gutemann to teach him the basics of aerial combat? Wissemann winked. "Teach an old dog a new trick?"

The junior *Jastaführer* chuckled. "Oh, most certainly. I'll be glad to help out. I follow Boelcke's Dicta to the letter."

"Of course. I've read Boelcke's Dicta as well." Wissemann retorted quite matter-of-factly and with a hint of rancor. This Bavarian officer most certainly remembered Boelcke's Dicta, the German Airman's Bible. It was a published work of eight air combat guidelines, designed to teach scout pilots the rules of engagement and basic scout tactics, written by the great Oswald Boelcke himself.

"There's no better advice than Boelcke's rules for air combat, sir."
Kindlich interjected. "S-sir. You m-may not r-remember. B-but,
you were m-my instructor at Stutthof... back in S-September. Do you
remember m-me, sir?"

Wissemann winced. "No. I'm sorry. I do not."

"I, I was in Class 09/16, s-sir."

"No, too many trainees—can't remember a thing from that time."

"Oh, t-that's all right."

"I apologize for my awful memory."

"Oh, n-no apology n-necessary s-sir," Kindlich stuttered. "I'm s-
sure you h-had your h-hands full. You were a very g-good instructor."

"Thank you, Kindlich. You're very kind. But, unfortunately, those
were frustrating days for me. I'm just glad to be here at the Front
now, where I belong."

"And, I'm honored to serve under such a noted officer as you, sir"
Gutemann added.

"Thanks," Wissemann replied, blushing just a little.

"Y-yes. A d-distinguished off-officer, indeed!"

"Well, gentlemen, I've enjoyed our little chat," Wissemann said,
clearing his throat, a bit embarrassed. "But I must get ready for the
next briefing. *Vizefeldwebel* Peltzer's group is coming in now."

"Good luck with that, sir," Gutemann replied, grinning jocosely.

"Luck? Yes, we'll certainly need some."

"M-more than just l-luck, s-sir. A m-miracle!"

"Indeed. We have some serious maintenance issues to discuss."

Gutemann and Kindlich both nodded, smiling, holding back a
good laugh.

"So. I will see you on the flight line at, say... sixteen-thirty? We
can go over a few patrol procedures before the flight, yes?"

"Certainly, *Herr Oberleutnant*. That will be fine."

Gutemann and Kindlich saluted crisply. Boot heels clicked.
Wissemann returned their salutes, and the two men paced out of the
tent. Then he turned to Schutzling, who had just returned from
Operations and was standing by eagerly. His face was aglow with a
prideful grin. Wissemann acknowledged him with a suspicious stare.

"Yes, Schutzling?"

"Good news, sir."

"Oh?"

"Three new Albatroses just arrived by truck, sir, via Laon. You'll
have to sign the release form first, before Peltzer's men can begin
unloading them."

"New Albatroses? Really? *Oberst* Thomsen wasn't kidding."

"The truck convoy was redirected here by *Kofl*, according to the Motor Transport Officer. A last minute order, I understand."

"*Oberst* Thomsen, no doubt."

"I think these might be factory fresh, sir. The ones with the new wing mounted radiator? The flush-fitting, Teves and Braun design."

"Splendid!"

"Our *Jasta*, sorry to say, sir," Schutzling chagrined, "is still flying the... well—the old Windhoff design.

"Oh? Hmm..."

"These are straight from *Armee Flugpark Nord*. Sign here, sir."

Schutzling happily handed the lading manifest to the *Jastaführer*. Wissemann glanced over the document, which was in carbon copy triplicate. Yes indeed, he read with elation; they were definitely factory fresh Albatroses. Three brand new aeroplanes! The new D. II's *Oberst* Thomsen had so irately informed him about had arrived. The baffled Bavarian could hardly believe what he read. The three Albatros scouts had apparently been scheduled for delivery to nearby AFP-7. But Thomsen rescinded the order and diverted them to Pusieux Ferme instead. Four Daimler flatbed trucks loaded with new Albatroses and engine parts suddenly rolled into the Operations courtyard. All in less than an hour! The Imperial German Air Service could function with utilitarian rapidity, if need be.

"Your pen, Schutzling..." Wissemann beckoned.

The ginger-haired adjutant handed over his fountain pen; the *Jastaführer* scribbled his initials at the bottom of the form then gave the pen and document back to Schutzling. The German Army prided itself on its military efficiency and good record keeping. Wissemann felt like he must have already signed a thousand documents since his arrival a mere day ago. Nevertheless, he was feeling pretty good about things now.

"My first 'official' victory," he quipped sardonically. "Maybe Peltzer can get one of these machines ready for the afternoon patrol."

"Quite possible, sir. In spite of what you may think of him, *Vizefeldwebel* Peltzer is an excellent mechanic."

"You think so, eh?"

"The best in this sector. I'll wager a month's pay on that!"

"Well, that's one wager I'd be willing to lose."

Schutzling did admire the portly sergeant major's mechanical prowess. When it came to aircraft maintenance, Peltzer certainly was a maestro. A magician. He could even work wonders with the inferior equipment of *Jasta 23*. This adulation came easy for the redheaded pencil pusher because he and Peltzer were the best of friends.

Peltzer and his group tramped in and took their seats. The heavyset maintenance chief plopped down in the front row, his cigar twitching restlessly. "Morning, sir."

"Good morning, Peltzer! Let's begin, shall we?"

"WELL, THAT'S ABOUT IT, HERR OBERLEUTNANT. Just watch for my hand signals and you'll be fine, sir. Nothing to it, really," Gutemann articulated confidently.

"Excellent," Wissemann replied.

"And if we get separated, somehow..."

"Yes?"

"Return to this rendezvous point—here, sir," Gutemann pointed to the coordinates on the grid map, "then we'll re-form and proceed with the patrol."

"Right." Wissemann nodded.

He girded his well-worn leather jacket, donned his flight cap, wrapping a scarf tightly around his neck. He nervously fumbled into a pair of fur lined gloves then extinguished a final cigarette before striding out of the dispersal tent for the flight line.

Outside the dispersal hut, three Albatros scouts stood ready, parked on the near side of the field. The two older machines looked worn and faded. Their reddish-brown and olive-green camouflaged wings looked dull in the pale afternoon light. But Wissemann's Albatros had a glowing newness about it. It stood ready, practically shining in the knot of three aircraft, first in line. The Bavarian beamed blissfully. He likened it to a wistful warhorse waiting for its gallant knight.

Peltzer labored quietly with two other mechanics. The chubby sergeant major turned around to look upon the *Jastaführer,* as if some sixth sense warned him of an approaching thunderstorm; he was already wary of his *Jastafürer's* moods. He'd learned long ago that many an officer was lacking in forbearance—only stark efficiency could placate them.

His face glowed from a recently completed shave, and he was sporting new coveralls. Peltzer looked a sight better than he had the day before. And of course, that reeking cigar, ever a permanent fixture of *Vizefeldwebel* Max Peltzer's countenance, was still firmly clenched in the corner of his mouth.

The bitter cold air nipped at Wissemann's nose as vaporous wisps of air curled from his mouth. It was cold. Bone chilling cold. But the new *Jastaführer* didn't seem to mind. Here at last, he thought, today is the day. He tugged at his chinstrap for about the tenth time and strode up to the stocky maintenance chief. Both men exchanged salutes. Peltzer even clicked his heels, much to Wissemann's surprise.

Peltzer had a few instructions to iron out with Wissemann regarding the operation of the new Albatros. *"Herr Oberleutnant,* she's all ready," he said. "We busted our heinies to get her ready for you. Everything should be in order."

"Very good, Peltzer."

"Just go easy on the throttle. That engine needs time to break in."

"Understood."

"One hundred and sixty horsepower, for you, sir."

"Yes. The Mercedes D. III. It is a fine engine."

"I fine tuned a few things, sir, so that thing ought to hum nicely."

"Well done, Peltzer. I had my doubts. But you put them to rest."

"Thank you, sir." Peltzer grinned. "You won't find a finer steed in the whole of France."

"I know. The Albatros is an excellent machine."

"Yes. She's a fine piece of machinery, sir." Peltzer nodded briskly.

Wissemann smiled. He could tell Peltzer was at least enthusiastic about his job. There was a twinkle in the hefty noncom's eye.

"Carry on, *Vizefeldwebel.*"

It amused him that Peltzer like to refer to the *Jasta* aircraft in anthropomorphic terms, oft comparing them to a finicky woman or a temperamental horse, not unlike an old sea captain referring to his ship. He had pet names for many of the machines in the squadron, and had a few "nicknames" for certain squadron members too. And according to Adjutant Schutzling, Peltzer was probably the best maintenance chief in the whole Bavarian war effort.

Wissemann's mind drifted back to Peltzer's dossier...

Once a former auto mechanic from Würzburg, Max Peltzer ran his own repair shop before the war. His reserve unit, a transportation outfit activated at the start of the war, fought at Verdun, where he labored as a truck mechanic. After a year of languishing in the motor pool of 9th Army, he transferred to the Air Service. Peltzer served in various two-seat reconnaissance sections before settling down at *Jasta 23* the previous October. Then on January 1st, he was promoted to the rank of *Vizefeldwebel* and made maintenance chief.

The *Jastaführer* pounded the rotund noncom on the shoulder for a job well done, feeling reassured by his talented capabilities.

Peltzer smiled proudly.

Wissemann perfunctorily tugged on a bracing wire for personal assurance and then clambered up a small, wooden stepladder which was propped up against the side of the fuselage of the new Albatros. He slid into the cockpit. The crew had just removed the timber maintenance support trestles so now the new Albatros rested in its customary takeoff position—on two wheels and tail skid. One of Peltzer's assistants strapped Wissemann in with the webbed seat harness and then began the preflight procedures. Peltzer hopped up onto the stirrup. A fat finger gesticulated officiously.

"Okay, sir," he uttered. "Note the control panel instrumentation. Tachometer—here. Throttle lever—there. Auxiliary throttle control, along with firing buttons—right here. Fuel tank switches, magneto switches"—he pointed with little jabbing gestures—"compass, fuel gauge- right there. Your machine gun charging handles are... there and there—"

"Peltzer!" Wissemann interjected testily, "I'm not a total idiot. I see well enough."

Peltzer's brow narrowed. "Of course, *Herr Oberleutnant.* Sorry—"

"I've flown the D.II before. At Adlershof, more than once or twice, I might add."

"Yes, sir. Of course you have."

Peltzer swung down off the stirrup, mumbling something bitter and unintelligible. He hustled up to the nose of the aircraft to begin the start-up procedures. Before takeoff, a great many things needed attention. The mechanics had worked all morning and through the late afternoon to get the Albatros assembled, typically a painstaking and monotonous task. They were just finishing up the final details, securing the flying wires when Wissemann had walked up.

A mechanic began filling water into the radiator and, according to strict procedure, would drain it every day thereafter. Then, after heating up the engine oil and filtering it through gauze, the mechanic poured it back in the crankcase. Peltzer poured eighty octane gasoline through a chamois, topping off the main and reserve tanks. In the meantime, Wissemann began the safety checks. He adjusted the seat cushion and inserted a ferry route air map into a wooden holder, clipping it into the cockpit's control panel. He smiled. The cockpit had the smell of brand-new varnished plywood.

The rigger finished tightening up the wing and airframe bracing wires. Contrary to popular belief, those wires were not supposed to "sing" in the wind when properly adjusted for good tension. The rigger had rechecked and adjusted all the turnbuckles until the flight controls moved freely with no slack in the linkages.

Oberleutnant Wissemann began his preflight ritual by sliding the seat backwards all the way and locked it in place with a thumbscrew, adjusting it to accommodate his lengthy frame. He placed both feet on the horizontal rudder bars and tested them for good resistance.

Then came the instrument check. Wissemann lifted the magneto switch as it hung on its tiny, linked chain and inserted it into a socket, making sure it was in the off position. Then he checked the switch positions for the engine-driven magnetos, turned them on, and moved the switch to the second position and engaged the starting magneto. He retarded the wooden knob of the spark control, checked the starting magneto, and made sure that the auxiliary throttle on the left of the control column moved through its full travel.

Wissemann scanned the instrument panel: tachometer—zero. Fuel pressure—zero. Valve gauge—on. All cockpit handles in the down position. He opened the brass fuel filter and drain cock, priming the engine for starting. The main petrol tank held eighty liters and the gauge read full. He twisted the water pump greaser can, and would repeat this with a half turn every ten minutes while in flight to ensure proper lubrication. No matter what the situation, he should always remember that. Wissemann checked the air pump and the compass, tapping the dial, and then reached up above his head and pulled the radiator cooling handle all the way back, to maximum ventilation. He reached past the breech of the left Maxim machine gun and turned the compression release gear handle to the right, to aid in starting the engine. It opened the exposed valves atop the engine. Peltzer turned the propeller, drawing just enough fuel air mixture into the cylinders. Wissemann turned the compression gear back to the left then opened the throttle slightly.

Peltzer then poured a mixture of oil and benzene into each of the primer cups of the exposed cylinder heads atop the Mercedes engine. Wissemann pulled the compression release gear to the left, once again. It was the same procedure for all the Albatros D scouts.

And just as Gutemann and Kindlich and their mechanics began the afternoon litany, Peltzer and Wissemann repeated the same monotonous exchange as well.

"Ready, sir?" Peltzer asked.

"Ready."

"Switch is off?"

"Switch is off."

"Free?"

"Free."

Peltzer turned the prop six times, priming each cylinder.

Wissemann nudged the compression release back to the right and switched the magneto key on, then turned the magneto crank as quickly as possible. Starting the Albatros did not require ground personnel to "swing" the propeller as with other aircraft. Instead, the left engine magneto was switched on and the starting magneto was hand-cranked from inside the cockpit; it sent an electrical current to the spark plugs that caused a continuous sparking discharge within the cylinders, which ignited the fuel air mixture, starting the engine.

After a few convulsive coughs, the Mercedes snarled with power. A jet of blue smoke belched from its exhaust pipe. A gale force slipstream flattened the icy grass about twenty meters back behind the tail plane. When the smoke finally cleared, Peltzer was standing, grinning in exultation, palms turned upward, nodding proudly.

"Listen to that engine purr... magnificent!"

While the engine warmed, Wissemann gradually moved the throttle up to 600-rpm. Both magnetos switches operated smoothly, and he revved the engine to full power. Peltzer and one of his assistants moved to the rear of the Albatros and leaned heavily on the leading edge of the tail assembly, making sure the tail didn't rise up as Wissemann increased the throttle. Satisfied both magnetos ran smoothly with no power loss, he ran each magneto separately. All the instruments read correctly. Then he reduced power. He was ready to taxi onto the field.

He gave a sweeping, double-hand wave, and the crew yanked the chain-linked chock blocks away. Peltzer and his assistant positioned themselves at the wingtips, held the cap strips tightly, and slowly pushed the Albatros upwind. With steady bursts of the throttle, the Albatros taxied forward into the wind, crabbing and wobbling on the uneven, frozen turf. The Albatros was ready for takeoff.

The *Jastaführer* gave the thumbs-up signal, pulled his goggles down over his eyes, and careened his head to the right so he could see past the blocky machine gun breeches and the engine's curved exhaust pipe, which was now exuding thick, noxious fumes. Holding the control column with forward pressure, he advanced the throttle to full and accelerated down the field. Pressure on the rudder bar told him that the rudder was taking effect—the tail began to rise as he eased off the stick. He was now rolling at a hundred kilometers per hour. And after about a two hundred meter run, with a quarter of the field to go, and the engine humming at 1,400-rpm, the little Albatros spurned the earth and buzzed into the air. The Mercedes engine settled into a steady rhythm as Wissemann adjusted the throttle well back to conserve fuel. Gutemann and Kindlich followed close behind.

After zooming past the hedgerows, and over the two lane highway that marked the far boundary of the airfield, Wissemann banked the Albatros and began a wide circuit around the aerodrome, climbing one hundred and eighty meters per minute. He saw the excess water vapor vent overboard from the radiator, as it cooled in the upper air, then reached up and closed the radiator shudders. As the flight progressed, he monitored the cooling efficiency by the sound of the engine and adjusted the shutters accordingly, as there was no temperature gauge.

Ten minutes later, at two thousand meters, he leveled off and reduced the rpm to a steady 1,300. Wissemann checked the gauges on the crude placard-like plywood panel, none of which were ever the same in the whole of the German Air Service. The Albatros was running smoothly. The little biplane responded well to the controls, bouncing upward, downward, or sideways, trembling whenever its nine hundred kilogram loaded weight collided with eddying currents of air, reacting more tempestuously when the slipstream got rougher or it hit an air pocket.

The Albatros D.II was well armed with twin Maxim machine guns, each equipped with five hundred rounds of 7.92-millimeter ammunition. The two guns, mounted on the decking in front of the pilot, were synchronized to fire independently or simultaneously. The bullets passed between the whirling propeller blades by means of a motorized synchronization gear, which actually operated both machine guns when a clear space appeared in the propeller arc at a maximum 450 rounds per minute. Reaching up to the cocking levers, on the outside of each breech of the Maxim machine guns, Wissemann charged—cleared and armed—both guns. With his thumbs resting on the molded trigger grips of the yoke on the control column, he fired a warming burst from each gun. The feed was good and the Hedtke synchronizing gear was working properly. A hang fire by a single bullet of just 1/250th of a second could shoot off one's propeller!

Gutemann and Kindlich followed suit and test fired their guns too. The rapid-fire bursts of machine guns was music to Wissemann's ears. Then the trio of Albatroses circled the airfield once more for good measure. All three aeroplanes were functioning properly. Three Mercedes engines were humming harmoniously.

Wissemann looked down upon the aerodrome beneath him and admired the white powdery snow that had blanketed the entire field. Winter's icy presence was still making itself felt here in the rolling meadows of the Champagne. The afternoon air was bitterly cold, and inside the cockpit, with the slipstream buffeting his face, it was even colder. The Bavarian aviator nestled down deeper in the cockpit. The miniscule celluloid windscreen offered little protection. And he knew the air temperature got thinner and even colder the higher he went. Above four thousand meters it could easily register minus 30-degrees centigrade!

The sky was a dreary gray that day, with widely scattered tufts of clouds hovering about the skyline. In the extreme reaches of the atmosphere, a milky scum of thin cirrus blotted out the sun. A thick haze engulfed the landscape below. In between were clouds as puffy as French pastries, and they masked most of the perceptible vista. At three thousand meters, the lateral panorama was vast. Wissemann clearly saw the curvature of the earth. The lowest cloud level was at less than a thousand meters, but these were thin and shapeless; blown, elongated wisps of sullied white vapor. They drifted across the sky obscuring much of the view below.

Wissemann signaled Gutemann, urging him to take the leading position, as they had agreed to do earlier that morning, and he took a place behind Gutemann's machine, slightly aft and to the right. Wissemann perceptions were those of a man in a labyrinth; he had to stick close to his leader, if for no other reason than to be finally led home. Bubi Kindlich's Albatros flew right echelon to his machine. Both alertly watched for Gutemann's hand signals.

As the three Albatroses clawed up to four thousand meters, above the uppermost level of clouds, the flat country stretching to the four horizons, Wissemann acclimated himself with the surroundings. He began taking his eyes from Gutemann's Albatros, stealing glances above, ahead, and below.

The earth was white, and misty patches lay in the hollows. Bluish veils of smoke clung, becalmed, around villages. Occasional flashes from firing artillery pieces, or windows, would recoil like glinting bursts. All the while, and unnoticeably, dimming light was fading from the west, defining golden halos on hilltops, dispelling mists, obscuring the general scenery.

The landscape required a keen eye for practical perception since, above a thousand meters, objects lost their color and depth. And with the landscape draped in a heavy white snow, everything looked nearly the same. The actual scenery had a stupefying amount of extra detail, an abundance of subdued color, of light and shade that made it difficult at times to correspond it with its map-printed equivalent. Highways, so significantly printed in red, were actually gray, obscure, and difficult to discern from other roads. Railways were not distinct black lines but tortuous ribbons even less well fixed.

Woods were not always patches of green, except in high summer.

Instead they appeared as black or dark-browns, blending sometimes inconspicuously into plowed fields that enclosed them. And of course cloud shadows often darkened parts of the countryside while casting others in high relief. Ground haze blurred the horizon and drew in the skyline for kilometers.

The *Kette* passed over the Ailette River, just a tiny, winding thread at four thousand meters, glistening silver in the faint sunlight. A shell-torn village swung into view and Wissemann knew it was Vailly. Its red-tiled roofs were mere faint dots against the snowy landscape. To the west, he observed, near the horizon, the town of Soissons and the majestic Aisne River.

The new *Jastaführer* was feeling quite content and anxious, all at the same time. Even though he'd flown countless reconnaissance and bombing marauds in the past, not to mention umpteen test flights and instructional sorties, he still felt very nervous.

He looked down several times at the control column. Those trigger grips were queer things, always right next to a man's thumbs, and yet not in the way. Would he use them today? He felt his skin prickle. His head bobbed about like a giddy schoolboy. Wissemann was finally where he wanted to be. Today... was the day of days!

THE TRIO OF ALBATROSES had circumnavigated all the waypoints of their patrol area in a mere thirty-five minutes. Now they approached the front lines. Their predetermined patrol route had taken them southwest near the village of Vouziers, then east to Warmerville. Further south, Wissemann noticed the great city of Reims, its majestic cathedral rising high above the mist. The historic French city lay just across the lines in enemy territory.

At Otto Gutemann's hand signal, the *Kette* descended lower to get underneath the patchy overcast that now seemed to stretch for kilometers. Once Gutemann got a few landmark bearings on their position, he knew exactly where they were. The trio continued their patrol of the Front.

Wissemann could now hear the faint thundering of artillery guns. He wondered if they were German or French. He soon got his answer. Suddenly, Gutemann rocked his wings and pointed southwest. He'd spotted something at about a thousand meters, flying a course due east—it was a lone enemy two-seater.

A lump of anxiety formed in Wissemann's stomach and soon found its way to his throat, all but choking him. The two-seater was meandering along slowly, an *Artilleriehäschen*—an "artillery rabbit."

He likened it to a fat Christmas goose waddling around for scraps. But in actuality, it was an artillery spotter directing a murderous artillery barrage into the German trenches. Wissemann knew it was signaling the French artillery gunners, via wireless Morse code, where to aim and fire their heavy batteries of cannon. The enfilade of French 155-millimeter shells exploded all along the German trench line. The wary Bavarian knew the poor potato-heads were catching hell.

Always the tireless tactician, Gutemann carefully scanned the sky above the two-seater for enemy scout planes that might be lurking in the overcast. This was a favorite ruse used by the French—luring unsuspecting German pilots into taking the bait of an easy victim. Once the bait had hooked its victim, the Frenchmen would zoom earthward, boiling down out of the clouds like furious falcons, bite off one of the Albatroses, and then vanish before anyone realized what had happened. Wissemann watched and waited eagerly as Gutemann searched the sky above.

After nearly a minute of searching, Gutemann signaled for the attack, certain that no French scouts lurked in the atmosphere above. Gutemann's Albatros decelerated, dropping back to Wissemann's position. The young officer pointed to Wissemann and yanked his fist down, directing the *Jastaführer* to go forward with the attack; he would get first crack at the enemy while Gutemann and Kindlich covered his flank.

Wissemann acknowledged with a snappy nod. He charged the twin Maxim machine guns nestled in the decking before him, pulled another notch in his safety belt, and pitched the little shark-like Albatros down in a steep, swooping dive. The engine's exposed rocker arms hammered steadily as he eased the throttle forward.

As the big Bavarian neared the enemy machine, he recognized the French aeroplane as a Dorand A.R. 2, a boxy two-seat biplane with a tractor engine, back-staggered wings and a rear gunner. This Dorand was a dirty, coffee-colored barge—a decrepit old bedspring sent out on another thankless artillery-spotting junket.

The *Jastaführer* half-rolled the Albatros over on its back and back-sticked the trim little bird into a dive. The Albatros responded instantly and plunged toward the two-seater. He approached the Dorand from a few hundred meters above and behind.

Of course, all this didn't go unnoticed by the French crew. The rear gunner swiveled his Lewis machine gun into action and began firing. Wissemann could clearly see the gunner tracking him through the machine gun's ring sights.

Undaunted by the Frenchman's gunfire, he accelerated to

maximum speed and quickly closed to within a hundred meters of the two-seater. He dropped slightly below the Dorand's tail, into the observer's blind spot, taking aim. His slitted blue eyes glared through the gunsight.

The French pilot, seemingly frozen in either terror or befuddled indecision, was flying the Dorand in nearly a straight line. Poor lad, Wissemann thought. He doesn't know what's about to happen. The *Jastaführer's* confidence wasn't hubris; it was calm assurance. He knew in this "safe zone" the gunner wouldn't be able to get at him, because the length of the fuselage and tail assembly blocked his line of fire. The disquieting prospect of shooting off one's tail plane, a very grim and fatal consequence, was not something the Frenchman was willing to risk. At fifty meters, Wissemann open fired. The sky was lit by the staccato crackle of guns as he raked the enemy's tail.

TOK-TOK-TOK! TOK-TOK-TOK—

Inexplicably, after twelve rounds, both guns jammed. He charged them again and thumbed the triggers. They refused to fire.

"Ach! Not now! Peltzer you idiot! You feckless, fat-fingered, nuts-and-bolts chaser! You are the world's worst mechanic!" Wissemann wrenched the Albatros over in a jerky bank to avoid a collision.

CR-RAT-TAT-TAT-TAT!

The gunner fired a perfectly aimed deflection shot. The trajectory riddled the Albatros from stem to stern. Caught betwixt the proverbial Scylla and Charybdis, the hemmed-in *Jastaführer* felt a torrent of bullets slam into his brand new Albatros. Centimeters in front of his eyes, the windscreen smashed to bits, and three holes appeared like magic in the cockpit flooring. At least a dozen more bullets perforated his wings, and there were more in the fuselage behind him. One slug smashed the tachometer. The glass face dissolved in a shower of glass dust.

With a silently muttered oath, Wissemann shoved the stick left, then right, weaving, trying to avoid the Frenchmen's bullets. Following a long overwrought moment of balky banks, curses and bitter-tongued invectives, he finally got out of range of the Frenchman's gunfire. He circled back towards the action.

In the meantime, *Leutnant* Gutemann, whose guns were working fine, circumvented the French aircraft with devastating results. His Maxims flickered deadly bursts from their flashing muzzles—the twin guns responded in a fearsome concerto. A massive cough of flame belched from the Dorand's engine. The flaming two-seater then slipped earthward, tumbling from the sky aglow with fire, like a carelessly dropped torch. Kindlich put in a few parting shots as it spun out of control, trailing a long, black column of smoke.

Then something ghastly occurred. Wissemann watched in shock as the occupants, both aflame, suddenly leaped from the extirpated machine, choosing a death of free fall, instead of one in a flaming coffin. Strangely, Wissemann's frustration turned to deep regret as he watched the two fiery bodies tumble head over heels and disappear in the milky haze below. Moments later, the Dorand crashed in a fiery cloud of rolling black smoke five kilometers south of Ramecourt.

Wissemann caught up with Gutemann and Kindlich, and the trio flew north, back to the aerodrome. Wissemann cursed his bad luck. He conceded reluctantly that his luck had been better than that of the two Frenchmen. While flying back to the aerodrome the scene of the flaming two-seater and its hapless crew replayed itself in his mind—a tragic tableau of flames, burning death, and sickly remorse. He vowed he would never forget it.

✠

WHEN WISSEMANN SAW THE FIELD AND HANGARS creeping toward his wings, he dropped down out of formation and began his approach. He noticed a fresh blanket of white powder covering the ground. It had snowed again at Pusieux Ferme, and the snowfall was still descending from the heavens. He was now bitterly cold, the drafty cockpit offering no respite from the biting wind. He wondered how much longer the winter would linger here in the gently sloping landscape of the Champagne, known more for its wine vineyards than its glacial temperatures.

The Champagne usually conjured up images of pure pastoral idyll; divergent landscapes, rolling plains giving way to lakes, water meadows to the south, dense oak forests and hills, like the Ardennes, in the north. That image, like spring, seemed very far away. Wissemann, as a former infantry officer, knew the thawing snow and ice would once more bring about relentless combative action in the form of another military offensive. There would be plenty of opportunities to score aerial victories. Even so, that little bit of solace couldn't warm his shivering bones this cold afternoon.

The new Albatros had performed well enough with the exception, of course, of its malfunctioning armament. Wissemann was extremely displeased with the gun's performance. He was more like infuriated. More than once during the flight home he'd tried clearing the jam, but to no avail. He had felt powerless and disgusted. Somehow, he thought this engagement should've yielded better results.

How many times had he envisioned, in his mind's eye, a glorious victory—the satisfaction of seeing a vanquished foe tumbling from the sky on fire or out of control? Alas, he had witnessed such a sight today. But not by his hand. The foe had fallen by someone else's sword. Indeed, Otto Gutemann's sword was very sharp today.

Wissemann throttled back the thrumming Mercedes engine to landing speed and came in low for an approach. He made the Albatros flair out, sigh into a wagtail slip, then drop delicately onto the frozen turf with a little thump. The wheels bounced once, gently, on the frosty turf, then settled smoothly on the ground. He revved the engine back up slightly once the tail skid made solid contact, and the Albatros taxied smoothly toward the hangars at one-third throttle.

The Albatros D.II didn't have wheel brakes, so the approach to the airfield tarmac was a very cautious one. Once in the dispersal area, Wissemann switched the magnetos off, and the propeller windmilled to a halt. Two mechanics helped guide the Albatros to the hangar. Wissemann's hands and feet were numb from the cold, and he longed to get back indoors. A fitter jumped up on the stirrup and unfastened the safety harness while Wissemann undid his chin strap.

Peltzer stood waiting for a moment, and then strode up aside the cockpit. "Well, *Herr Oberleutnant*," he asked. "How did she perform—"

"Horrendous!" Wissemann snapped. "Those blasted guns jammed during my attack. They must be checked thoroughly! I couldn't get them to clear—at all." The testy *Jastaführer* snatched his goggles off, hitched himself up out of the cockpit, and sat on the fuselage resting his feet on the seat cushion.

"Oh?" Peltzer stepped up on the stirrup, glanced over the twin machine guns, and saw the problem immediately. A section on both hemp-belted cartridges feeding into each machine gun had ripped, preventing the flow of bullets to the breeches. "Here's the problem, sir," he nudged one of the belts. "The ammo belts broke."

"Both of them? How did *that* happen?"

"Very bad luck?" Peltzer immediately thought better of that. "Um, faulty cartridge belts, maybe?"

"That's unacceptable. They must work—"

"I'll have this repaired straight away, sir."

"See that you do, Peltzer."

"I'll talk with your armorer, sir," Peltzer muttered assuredly, "and make sure this never happens again."

Wissemann spat. "I realize this is a brand new machine—a few bugs have to be worked out. But damnation! I must be able to depend on my equipment."

"Yes, yes, *Herr Oberleutnant*—"

"The enemy gives no quarter, Peltzer. Your negligence could get me killed, see!"

"I'm sorry, sir. It won't happen again."

Wissemann hopped overside to the icy ground and unbuttoned his jacket, then muttered rather arbitrarily: "The tachometer will have to be replaced. I took a few hits."

The hefty maintenance chief looked inside the cockpit and saw the shattered gauge. He also noticed quite a few bullet holes in the fuselage as well. The mechanic grunted dubiously. *Gott!* The new *Jastaführer* was certainly a "bullet-catcher." He counted at least twenty-two holes total!

Wissemann peeled his flight cap off and strode over to Gutemann's machine. "Well done, *Leutnant*," he said, patting the young officer on the shoulder. "Thanks for covering my pathetic marksmanship. Kindlich was right. You don't miss."

Gutemann grinned. "Well, it's not difficult at close range, sir."
The broad-shouldered Bavarian pulled two Halpaus fags from his cigarette case and popped one in his mouth. Wissemann gestured. "Care for a smoke, *Leutnant?*"

"No thanks, sir, don't smoke. But I'm dying for a strong drink."

"*Ach, ja.* We'll all feel better with something warm goose-stepping around inside us."

"What happened?" Gutemann inquired, "You had a sitting duck."

"My guns jammed—broken belt linkage. Damned bad luck." Wissemann stowed the extra cigarette and lit his up. He inhaled deeply. "Got off ten rounds and then—*kaput!*"

Bubi Kindlich came trudging up, his boots slogging heavily in the mud and snow. His face was red from the bitter cold, and he sniffled gracelessly, wiping drivel from a cherry-red nose. "*Herr Oberleutnant*, I t-thought you h-had him?" he stammered. "D-Did your guns—j-jam?"

"Yes, yes, my guns jammed." Wissemann's tone was acrid now.

"Don't fret, sir," Gutemann drawled. "It happens to everyone—"

"Let's just drop it for now, shall we, *Junge?*" Wissemann cut in tersely. "I think we could all use a strong drink and some hot food."

The blond-haired Gutemann ran clammy fingers through tousled bangs and cocked a keen and piercing eye at the *Jastaführer.* "Sure. Okay. Whatever, sir."

"We'll discuss it later over some cognac, eh?"

"Right."

"This cold weather is making me miserable."

"M-m-me t-too." Kindlich stammered.

Wissemann sniffled. His nose was running too now. He was tired and frustrated. The snow was coming down in huge flakes now. He just wanted to get indoors. "Let's go, lads."

"Sure, *Herr Oberleutnant.* Let's get inside. I'm starving."

"Y-yes—m-my ass is f—f-frozen—n-numb!"

The two young pilots burst into jocular laughter. Wissemann tried to smile. But he kept thinking about those two burning Frenchmen leaping from the Dorand. Ghastly business this war, he thought. He still hadn't become accustomed to such things. The trio loped back to the chateau. The snow began to fall heavily.

THIRTY MINUTES LATER... the three pilots took a car ride to the crash site. Wissemann was disturbed by what he found. When the Dorand had finally hit the ground, after a slow, winding death spiral, it had erupted in a ball of fire as it impacted, the fuel tank rupturing. The wreckage was still smoldering. What was left of the smoking residue, and still hot to the touch, hardly resembled an aeroplane. The engine block and crankcase, now a lump of fused fire-blackened sludge, was half-buried in the ground. Toy-like bicycle wheels of the landing gear, their frames burned down to fried spokes and buckled rims, lay sprawled about haphazardly. It was all quite surreal.

And not far from the crash site, they found the remains of one of the crewmen. The Frenchman had been reduced to a blackened, dwarf-like creature, surrounded by a small pool of melted fat, of which was now mostly frozen. Wissemann became ill. He nearly retched. Gutemann and Kindlich felt nearly the same.

Once young Gutemann had got what he'd come for—the battered remnants of the French observer's machine gun—a souvenir for the *Staffel* mess, the burial squad moved in, shoveling the remains of the charred Frenchman into a bag. The trio of pilots drove back to the aerodrome. Wissemann sat quietly in the car. The flaming two-seater scene played again in his mind, and so vivid this time, it sent grisly shivers up his spine.

Later that night, he thought about it again before he went to bed. And during the night, he awoke from a nightmare. He had dreamed of himself jumping from a flaming aeroplane!

"Was nicht ist, kann noch werden," the battle weary Bavarian soliloquized, sitting upright in bed, sweating profusely, thinking of death by fire. What isn't, still can be. Your day will come, he thought to himself. "Fret not, Willi dear."

Going down in flames was now his greatest fear. To be burnt alive was the worst possible fate. Willi Wissemann was so disturbed by his nightmare, when he awoke the next morning, he decided every day thereafter, he would carry his Luger sidearm with him on every flight. If his aircraft ever caught fire, he would perish by his own hand. A 9-millimeter slug would be his ticket to hell. There, he could burn for eternity.

Passed by FlugM Censor #2770
Frau Ilse Magdalena von Linkhof
c/o 7th Army Headquarters Laon
Berlin (Please forward)
....

Liebe Ilse!   28. Feb.1917

I hope to be with you very soon, Leibchen. I have a long leave coming up, and I will spend all of it with you. The loneliness of this wretched countryside infuses distaste in my very soul; it tugs on my heartstrings, as if I were a lifeless, wooden, marionette. The cold winds of spitefulness blow over me and force me to dig deep into the recesses of my soul. Yet I am only one man. But my will is strong, my heart is pure, and my aspirations are honest. Nevertheless, I need your sanction, your support... and I need your love. But I only ask for your patience. It is a grim existence for a man to face the trials of endless warfare, day in and day out, by himself. Kindred spirits can only defeat the forces of evil together, standing shoulder to shoulder, side by side, hand in hand. Only my indomitable spirit and hope will keep me alive. That hope is you. This nonsense will be over one day, be assured. Then we will know the true meaning of peace of mind. We will know it because our hearts will have endured the greatest test of all ...the test of time.

Herzlichst, Willi

Chapter 10

✠

MARCH 2, 1917. AFTER NEARLY TWO weeks of cold snowy weather, the skies over the Front cleared just enough to resume air operations. The spring thaw was still many weeks away, as the constant snow falls seemed to suggest; a winter mistral was still clawing at the countryside. On a frosty Friday afternoon, a determined *Oberleutnant* Willi Wissemann found himself patrolling the front lines near Moronvilliers. Three kilometers below, the French 4th Army, under General Anthoine, lay quietly, covered in snow and mud, finishing their breakfast before commencing the day's work of slaughter and futility.

In a few weeks the French Armies were rumored to be launching a new offensive along this sector. If the German High Command wasn't aware of it, Wissemann and his *Staffel* certainly were. French reconnaissance machines began a concerted effort in photographing the entire area. Lumbering Caudron and Farman two-seaters scurried over the German lines in small flights, hiding in cloud banks wherever they could, sometimes staying low to the ground, or flying so high no one could reach them. Occasionally, a lone two-seater would sneak into the rear areas for a peek. Wissemann found one such fearless crew this particular afternoon.

He spotted anti-aircraft bursts a few kilometers south of Mount Le Casque and signaled his two *Ketten* mates, Frankenberg and Fleischer. After an uneventful morning patrol, the trio went up again on another mission, hoping the afternoon would yield better results.

Wissemann glanced at the cockpit clock and noted the time: 1417 hours. The sky was clear with the exception of a wispy cirrus overcast, suspended in the upper atmosphere. The sun was bright against a blue-gray sky, and visibility was good. He flew toward the anti-aircraft bursts.

His Albatros was running smoothly, and he'd personally seen to the maintenance of his machine guns, much to his armorer's chagrin. He'd checked his guns and ammunition belts himself, inspecting every round carefully, going over them again and again, checking them for uniformity of weight and shape, making sure the empties ejected properly.

Each belt was now varied with his personal preference: a standard nickel-coated lead bullet, an armor-piercing bullet with a steel core, and a tracer. The tracer, one part magnesium to eight of barium peroxide in the base, made accurate shooting at close range easier. But the tracer often burnt itself out of shape, making trajectory unreliable. There was only one sure way of scoring hits.

"Get in close, and then, even closer!" Gutemann's Swabian drawl echoed inside his head. Wissemann had been advised to hold his fire until he could not miss. Only when the enemy machine turned the smeared isinglass of his tiny brass-bordered windscreen black with its looming silhouette would he press the trigger buttons.

Amid the anti-aircraft bursts, Wissemann noticed a tiny speck weaving through the haze, well above the German trench line. That speck, he quickly realized, was a Farman two-seater—an ungainly observation aircraft held together by a multitude of bracing wires and wooden struts. Amidst the wings, a peculiar bathtub-like fuselage contained a crew of two. The pilot sat in the bathtub just forward of a twelve-cylinder engine. The observer sat in the nose and operated a Lewis machine gun. The Farman was plodding along at about two thousand meters, busily photographing the fortifications below.

The eager *Jastaführer* eased the Albatros into a shallow dive, gently turned east, and put the sun at his back. This made the Albatros ostensibly "invisible" in the blinding rays of the sunlight. "Now get in close, Willi. No hurry," he said to himself. He grinned.

His two machine guns were ready, their openwork, air-cooling casings glinted dully in the afternoon sun. Everything was in order. He yanked the charging handles and reduced the throttle, then jerked the stick back. The Albatros answered buoyantly, and a second later, he was behind the French two-seater. Fleischer and Frankenberg flew close behind him. Hunched above the control stick and squinting into the gunsights for aim, Wissemann targeted the unsuspecting Farman.

It grew larger by the second inside the gunsight rings. He held his fire until he got within fifty meters, tapping the rudder bar, taking up the proper angle of deflection, finally thumbing both triggers. The control column vibrated in his hands and the twin machine guns burst into action, spewing hot tracer rounds at the French two-seater. The bullets streaked out toward the Farman like long, smoking fingers. The stream of gunfire thudded into the engine and bathtub-shaped cockpit, sending splinters and debris in every direction.

The startled Farman pilot banked violently to avoid the fusillade of gunfire, but it was already too late. The Farman skidded clumsily, yawing and slewing about in an aimless direction. The gunner was helpless; his machine gun was fixed to the front cockpit. Somehow he'd been convinced an attack might come from the front.

Sporting. Jolly. Idiotic!

Wissemann tripped another quick burst from the smoking Maxims. He saw the pilot bolt upright as a sheet of lead ripped through his body. Wissemann was so close now, less than twenty-five meters, the Frenchman's blood spattered on his windscreen. He grimaced. The taste of blood was real, but the revulsion was fleeting. The Maxims flashed again. The Farman's engine was hit. It began streaming oily black smoke. A fire? Wissemann thought worriedly. *Gott!* But the Farman did not burn. The embattled Bavarian Eagle cut the throttle back to one-third to stay behind the faltering two-seater. A final burst from his guns sent the flying bathtub plummeting down in a twisting nosedive. The main plane snapped off in the slipstream and drifted down after the falling two-seater like a wilted autumn leaf. The lattice-boomed fuselage broke into several pieces and disappeared in the ground haze. The cockpit nacelle crashed just north of Vaudesincourt near the Suippe River in an abandon beet field. Wissemann timed the crash at: 1419-hours.

A hoarse cheer loosened in his throat. *"Ein Luftsieg!"*

"OBERST THOMSEN, WILL SEE you now," said the shapely, blond secretary. "Go in. He's waiting."

"Danke." A scrawny-looking soldier got up from a chair.

"Your cap, please? Remove it," she demanded fussily.

"Oh, yes. Sorry."

The soldier removed his *Feldmutze* and winked, then paced from the antechamber into a spacious office. He saluted meekly and took a seat in front of a big oaken desk, waiting a moment, clearing his throat officiously as if to announce his arrival.

A tall heavyset figure stirred behind a desk, rubbing a double chin thoughtfully, grumbling. "Well, Gustav," said the heavyset figure. "What news have you, today?"

Gustav looked up meekly at the menacing figure. Beyond the desk, looking very grim and foreboding, stood a most august personage indeed: *Oberst* Hermann von der Lieth-Thomsen. He was standing, hands clasped behind his back, gazing out of a huge bay window overlooking the plaza of downtown St. Quentin. He was a friar-bald, thickset man in his early fifties, tall and brawny, a gray, well-trimmed mustache complimenting his rugged face; a hard, unyielding countenance of formidable authority. The brass buttons on his *Feldgrau* tunic fit snugly around a potbelly—an obvious sign of his great appetite. Thomsen cradled an old Meerschaum tobacco pipe in a weathered hand. Smoke curled up from the pipe and drifted to the ceiling, creating a ominous haze around his immense physique.

Oberst Hermann von der Lieth-Thomsen was all soldier.

"Well, *Herr Oberst*. Not much to report yet. He's just settling in."

"Hmm, well, keep me informed of anything unusual."

The burly Chief of Staff turned around and faced the young soldier, removing the pipe from his mouth. He did not salute the soldier, although he was quite aware of the noncom's limp-wristed adherence to protocol. Thomsen's contempt for this soldier's existence was quite evident. This soldier was barely just that, the old Prussian thought. He didn't have a high regard for reservist "part-timers" as he liked to refer to them. To Hermann Thomsen, the military was a full-time job and way of life. Not a carefree weekend on some local parade ground playing at soldier.

"Of course, *Herr Oberst*," the soldier replied.

Thomsen sneered. "I want to know every move that impudent devil makes, understand?"

"Yes, sir."

"That improvident lack-wit will run that *Jagdstaffel* into the ground given a little time—and a little help." Thomsen smiled slyly, a puff of smoke curling up from the corner of his mouth as he exhaled. He winked theatrically, jerking a little nod.

"A little help, sir?"

"*Verdammt!* You know what I mean."

"Yes, yes. I do?"

"He's an incompetent egomaniac who thinks very highly of himself!" Thomsen pounded the desktop with a heavy fist.

The soldier winced and fidgeted uneasily in his chair. "Doesn't he know General von Hoeppner? Aren't they good friends?"

"Hah! He thinks his association, his friendship, with General von Hoeppner will grant him immunity from my wrath. Well, he's sadly mistaken."

"What exactly do you want *me* to do, sir?"

"You will coerce certain individuals of his staff, make it perfectly clear to them, they will be handsomely rewarded for their help in this operation."

"In this... *operation*, sir? I'm not sure what you mean."

"Are you daft, man? You know exactly what I mean."

"I do?"

"Yes! Here's what I want you to do now." Thomsen's gaze became deadly serious. "Wissemann is an idealist, which is by and large commendable but occasionally awkward. You will be my eyes and ears and tell me everything."

"Oh. How will I do that, *Herr Oberst?*"

"You will systematically sabotage and subvert all his efforts through the dissemination of disinformation, misinformation, gossip, et cetera, et cetera and so forth. Create some scuttlebutt. Start a rumor mill. Do whatever you can, Gustav."

"A rumor mill?"

"*Mein Gott,* man! Spread rumors. File erroneous claims. Find some dirt on him. Dig into his personal life. Find out who he really trusts. Find out who hates his guts, besides me of course." Thomsen chuckled.

"Aha, I see now."

"Play on those things, Gustav. Do what you do best."

Thomsen smiled sinisterly; he had a broader plan. He plopped down heavily in his high-backed office chair, resting his elbows on the chair's armrests, supporting his chin on interlaced fingers, like a professor preparing to listen to a long dissertation.

"Oh, I see what you mean now, sir," the noncom replied. "Can I expect assistance? I mean... am I to do all this by myself?" Gustav adjusted his spectacles anxiously.

Thomsen grumbled quietly and shook his head in disgust. He'd already briefed the forgetful noncom days ago about his fellow "conspirators." Thomsen sighed and cursed to himself about the depreciating state of the Reserve Army and its pathetic recruiting policies. Ach! How did this man ever pass the basic aptitude tests for recruitment?

"Must I repeat myself? I am transferring a man from *Jasta 22.*"

"Oh. Of course."

"He's a bad hat, a maverick. The type Wissemann truly abhors."

"Ooh, he sounds like a real character."

"Yes! He's quite the rascal."

"What's his name—?"

"He's just the kind of rebel that will confront Wissemann's pretentious character and pompous attitude."

"What's his name, sir?"

"Don't worry about that right now. You'll find out soon enough, my little friend." Thomsen got up and paced out from behind his desk and stood next to the soldier. "You just get busy as soon as you can."

"And what about my compensation, sir? You promised."

Thomsen's eyes widened at the soldier's audacity. He slammed his pipe down hard on the desktop, glaring balefully at the rumpled soldier. How dare this little rat inquire about compensations, he thought, when good men were dying everyday for merely the satisfaction of serving the Fatherland!

"Dismissed!" Thomsen barked.

"But, sir—"

"Get out of my sight you insolent little twit! You'll get nothing if you fail."

"Nothing? But—"

"I'll send you back to the Russian Front. So help me God!"

"But, sir—"

"*DIS-MISSED!*" Thomsen's thundering dismissal reverberated ominously in the spacious office. "If that man so much as takes a dump on the crapper, I want to know about it!"

Startled, the soldier jumped up from his chair and darted out of the office.

Thomsen laughed haughtily. He adjusted his tunic and strode over to the full-length mirror mounted on the wall, humming tunelessly, grinning, admiring his portly reflection, nodding with marked approval.

"Hmm... handsome devil, you." He called for his secretary. "Greta! Make sure my dress uniform is ready for the ceremony on Sunday. I want to look my very best when His Majesty the Kaiser awards me the *Pour le Mérite.*"

"Of course, *Herr Oberst,*" Greta, his shapely blond secretary replied. "But which uniform? The dress-blue or the *Felgrau?*"

Thomsen sighed irritably. "The dress-blue, *Liebchen.*"

His tone rang with frustrated irony. He thought: one can't have brains and beauty, I suppose. He gazed in the mirror again, clicked his heels and snapped to attention, his conceit knowing no bounds. He stroked his graying mustache and rearranged the paltry strands of hair over his shiny, bullet-shaped head, trying to suck in his sagging gut but gave up quickly, as if the effort of holding it in was unnecessary or too tiring. The old Prussian groaned wearily.

"*Gott!* You're dealing with idiots, Hermann. Total idiots." He strode back behind his desk and plopped down heavily in his chair. He thought about Wissemann and scoffed derisively. "Idiots, indeed!

THE ALBATROS' ENGINE whined down as Wissemann reduced the throttle for the approach. The D.II glided to the edge of the snowy airfield and touched down gently. After a short run the little scout coasted for the maintenance shed. Two mechanics followed it closely. Wissemann carefully taxied in and then switched the magnetos off. The Albatros came to a halt just shy of the snow-covered tarmac, and the engine sputtered to a halt. Wissemann peeled his goggles and flight cap off, loosened his scarf, and undid the safety harness. He pulled himself up and sat down upon the cockpit coaming. He took a deep breath and then exhaled a contented, vaporous sigh.

Peltzer stood waiting on the flight line. "Well, *Herr Oberleutnant,* I can see by that look on your face—you had a successful patrol?"

"Indeed I did! Shot down a Farman near Vaudesincourt. It came down in pieces—one of those archaic '*Gitterrumpfs*' the French still fly," Wissemann replied with a broad smile. He raised a fist in the air and shook it. "Victory!"

"How many cartridges did you use, sir?"

"Three volleys. About, sixty rounds."

"Good shooting, sir."

"It doesn't take much at close range."

"Where about?"

"It fell behind our rear trench lines. I was amazed it didn't burn."

"Then the guns functioned properly, sir?"

"No problems at all."

"The cold does tend to make them jam at the higher altitudes—"

"Not today! They worked fine."

"Then I congratulate you, sir. Bravo!"

"Thank you, Peltzer. Providence smiles upon us both today."

Wissemann slid off the side of the fuselage and landed squarely on the frozen ground. He reached inside his jacket pocket for his cigarette case, pulled out a Halpaus and lit it. He took a deep drag, and then exhaled contently. "Now. I shall register a claim with *Idflieg.* And with any luck, 7th Army's observers saw the Farman crash."

"Then you'll have your first officially confirmed victory, sir."

"Right—the first of many, I hope."

Wissemann trusted he didn't sound too vainglorious, but he was feeling very confident. He felt exhilarated. At last, he thought, I have arrived. Yes! He was finally a true *Jasta* pilot—no longer an instructor or a glorified chauffeur for expensive cameras. A real combat pilot. A new phase of his military career was on its way. He remembered his days as a two-seater pilot; flying clumsy reconnaissance machines; dropping bombs; taking photographs; artillery spotting; all very mundane duties, but equally dangerous. He had come a long way. A certain level of fulfillment had now been reached.

"Geduld Willi, Rom ist auch nicht an einem Tag erbaut worden!" he soliloquized philosophically. Indeed, Willi. Rome wasn't built in a day!

He capered off to the Operations hut humming blissfully. The snowy turf crunched under his boots as he trudged across the field. The wind swirled bitterly. The cold air gave him a shiver. The weather was quite miserable—not the ideal conditions for air operations. Wissemann coughed and grumped: "Not the kind of weather for anything!" The shivering Bavarian took a final drag from his cigarette then tossed the smoldering butt to the ground. He finally reached the entrance of Operations after scads of cold, stiff strides. He went inside and found *Feldwebel* Schutzling hard at work typing up acquisition reports.

"Schutzling," Wissemann said, "please contact *Flugmeldedienst.*"

"Are you filing a claim, sir?"

"Yes. I shot down a Farman, somewhere behind our lines."

"Wunderbar!"

"Find out if they've located the wreckage of a Farman two-seater."

"Right away, sir."

"If so, send a man to retrieve a serial number... swatch."

"A *swatch*, sir?"

"Or some other part of the wreckage."

"Okay?"

"Get a souvenir from the crash site!" Wissemann clarified. After visiting the Dorand's grisly crash, he wanted no personal part in souvenir hunting.

"Of course, I see now. Where did it go down, sir? Which sector?"

"Near Vaudesincourt, close to the rail bridge over the Suippe."

Schutzling spun around in his chair and eyed a topographic map hanging on the wall above his file cabinet. He hopped up to get a closer look. "Well, let's see... that's south of Dontrien, I'm guessing?"

"Yes, yes, thereabouts. Find out, Schutzling."

"Will do, sir."

"Sixth Company Pioneers probably saw it go down."

"I'll check with them first, *Herr Oberleutnant.*"

"Excellent. Well, I'll be in the Kasino, if you need me, Schutzling. This calls for a little celebration." Wissemann smiled and tramped out the door. The door slammed.

The redheaded adjutant nodded duteously. But there was a frown on his pale face. He reshuffled the mounds of paperwork, stared at the clock on the wall, sighing detestably. Now he had one more task to complete, before he could relax with that nice little bottle of schnapps. He muttered bitterly. A frustrated fist came crashing down on the desktop. "Aghh! One more hour..."

LE GRAND SALON, or as the Germans had dubbed it, the "Kasino" was a well-known restaurant and bar on the outskirts of Laon, off the Rue de Bellevue, a place where the *Jasta* cadre adjourned after the day's duties. It had originally been owned and run by a local French family. But they had long since fled the premises after the Fatherland's occupation swallowed up the environs of Laon. The 7th Army Quartermaster currently ran it, and after a long day of fighting a war, it was a bustling scene of activity.

Willi Wissemann opened the door and went inside.

Smoke swirled through the rafters as cigarettes, pipes, and cigars, lit one after another, cloaked the ambiance with a nebulous haze. Officers and noncoms alike lounged around casually, hats perched askance on sodden heads, tunic collars loosened, exposed shirt tails hung over grubby trousers, suspenders drooped, wooly, sweat-stained sweaters reeked of fusty odors. This nonmilitary-like laxity comprised the uniforms of these bibulous denizens. Insistent music crackled from an old gramophone, and several soldiers tried, inharmoniously, to sing along. Wissemann winced; the cacophonous exhibition was quite comical if not grating

"Where's the real Schlusnus when you need him?" he quipped, laughing quietly, despite himself, closing the door behind him. He strode through the smoky den of merriment, making his way toward the bar at the center of the dining room.

Unteroffizier Karl Eduard Koehler, a gangling ramrod-type Tyrolean from Innsbruck, labored behind the counter, polishing beer mugs and humming tunefully. "Afternoon, *Herr Oberleutnant,*" he said, grinning cordially.

"Afternoon. How goes it with you, Koehler?"

"Oh, not so bad, sir. Just getting things in order. How about you?"

"Had a successful day for a change."

"Oh? What happened?"

"Bagged a two-seater," Wissemann replied gleefully. "The *Rothosen* are a stubborn lot. Thought they could get past me. *Tu as bu, ou quoit!*"

Like many German soldiers during the war, he dubbed French soldiers *"Die Rothosen"* among other things, since part of their uniform had once consisted of bright red pants. A mild appellation considering the French used harsher names like "Boche" for the Germans, a term loosely translated as "cabbage head."

The bold Bavarian took a cigarette from his case and popped it in his mouth. "A drink please, my man."

"The usual, sir?" Koehler asked. He struck a match, lighting Wissemann's cigarette.

"No, no. Let me have a shot of Irish. I'm turning over a new leaf."

"Irish? No cognac? Hmm, *must be* a special occasion."

Wissemann nodded. "Shot down my first enemy machine this afternoon. I'm waiting for the official confirmation from Army," he replied confidently, removing his leather jacket and sitting down on a wooden bar stool.

"Congratulations, sir! May I pour two—in honor of your victory?"

"By all means, Koehler—no one should ever drink alone."

Koehler poured the whiskey into two shot glasses, slid one over to Wissemann, and then held his up for a toast. He nodded and smiled. *"Prost, Herr Oberleutnant."*

"Prost!" Wissemann downed the shot in one gulp, slammed the glass down, motioning for another. Koehler chuckled merrily and refilled the glass. He reached into a tunic pocket and pulled out a pipe and began packing the bowl with tobacco. He watched Wissemann down the second shot with equal gusto.

"Ooh! Now that hit the spot, Koehler!"

"A third, *Oberleutnant?*"

"No, no. Not yet. I don't want to spoil the effect," Wissemann replied, his face now lighted with alcoholic bliss. "Hah! That's what my Ilse would say."

"Your fiancée?"

"Yes. I must write to Ilse and tell her of my recent success."

"Fiancée, eh?"

"Yes, my Ilse," Wissemann replied with a discerning grin. "She'd like to marry this summer. But, I think we should wait until this war is over."

"Ah, a June wedding—now that would be nice." Koehler smiled

"*Ja*. But I think she worries too much—that I might not return."

"It is a troublesome concern these days for the women folk, *Herr Oberleutnant*."

"Nevertheless, I wouldn't want to make a widow out of her, she is far too young for that."

Wissemann took a puff from his cigarette and then perched it on an ashtray, which was actually an old coffee tin. He thought about Ilse, his darling, *Liebchen*. She wasn't happy with his decision to return to the war. Ilse hoped he would've stayed at Stutthof. Perhaps be promoted to a flying desk? And thus cheat his way to an early retirement? *Nein!* He made a solemn vow to himself: I will never fly a desk. Never! He thought back to December. He'd been temporarily posted to Adlershof as a liaison officer for *Idflieg*. His technical and combat experiences served him well as a test pilot, befriending various aircraft manufacturing designers and engineering experts, learning plenty about aeronautics and aircraft production. During that period, he was offered a lucrative position at *Halberstadt Flugzeugwerke GmbH* as a military consultant. But he turned the generous offer down. Willi Wissemann wanted to fly single-seat scouts instead.

"Don't wait forever, *Oberleutnant*," Koehler warned. "Marriage is a wondrous thing."

"That's what I keep hearing."

"You might be an old man before this war is over."

Wissemann smirked. He assumed Koehler didn't know his age. After all, he didn't look thirty. Not yet at least—he hoped. He figured himself to be the oldest *Oberleutnant* in the German Air Service. Something he wasn't too proud of anymore.

"Old man?" Wissemann scoffed. "I only counted two gray hairs this morning!"

"Well, suchlike. She may not wait, sir," Koehler added.

"Ach, she'll wait—"

"A girl gets lonely."

"She does love me, I am certain. She will wait. She told me so."

"That confident, eh, *Oberleutnant*?"

"Well, we've known each other for a long time—"

"I do speak from experience, sir" Koehler interceded. "I let my girl get away. She eloped with a banker from Munich after I joined the army back in '14, a few months before the outbreak of the war."

Wissemann grinned and took another puff. "A banker? Hmm, sounds like she was after the money, my friend."

Koehler shrugged. "Maybe so."

"Most women want security, Koehler. A soldier? Well..."

"She said she wouldn't marry a soldier like her mother had done." Koehler poured Wissemann another shot then capped the bottle of Irish. He knew he could easily drink his ex-fiancée's memory off his mind; if he ever let himself slip that far again. However, it wasn't prudent while on duty, and certainly not in front of an officer. Later, once the bar closed, he could "reminisce" all he wanted.

"Well," Wissemann sighed. "I guess the world's on hold until the end of the war, aye?"

"Unfortunately."

"Who figured it would go on this long."

"Not much longer I hope. Germany can't afford it."

The concurring Bavarian nodded and slid his shot glass forward. Koehler grinned and doled out another shot. Wissemann slugged the Irish. He reveled in the warm stinging sensation it gave him. But he remembered Ilse's warning about drinking too much. Alcohol, he thought, liquid courage? Life at the front lines would be mercilessly tedious without it. The warm, numbing feeling of whiskey or cognac, or any other type of drink, was incomparable. Drinking or getting drunk was a soldier's ritual, dating back to the days of Caesar. It was expected. There was no such thing as social drinking; one either abstained or got blitzed. It was an escape from the maddening routine of life in the trenches—or in the air. It was an escape, if only temporarily, from the realities of death and endless slaughter. But there was no cheating destiny, no way to avoid the inevitable mortality of man. It was just a matter of when. But alcohol seemed to postpone that fate. It was the sole retreat from constant warfare, death, destruction and desperate loneliness. Willi Wissemann wondered if he was just being morbid or if these thoughts lurked in the mind of every serviceman. He trembled.

Wissemann scanned the smoky barroom. "Has Grimm been here yet? I haven't seen him since this morning."

"No, not yet. He'll be here soon. It's about time for his daily pint."

"Hm. Well, he was supposed to be back from St. Quentin by now."

"Oh?"

"I sent him out on a *spying* mission."

"Spying?"

Wissemann nodded. "I heard a rumor that a few of the new Albatros D. III scouts might pass through there on their way back to the factory for modifications."

"The D.III?"

"Correct."

"I thought *Idflieg* grounded all the new Albatros scouts."

"They did. But I still want them for my *Jasta.*"

"Isn't there some sort of danger, *Herr Oberleutnant?*"

"Danger?"

"I heard something about wing failure—at least that's been the rumor going around."

"Well, that's what the *Idflieg* investigation seemed to determine. Apparently, von Richthofen's bird suffered structural failure."

"Von Richthofen, having difficulty?" Koehler's eyes widened, faintly astonished.

"Uh-huh" Wissemann nodded. "The lower wing beam is apparently too weak for prolonged diving. It collapses under stress."

"That's not good."

"A nasty business for sure." Wissemann nodded reluctantly.

"What about von Richthofen? What does he say—?"

"Ach, von Richthofen! He certainly has the General Staff by the balls, does he not? Whenever their Prussian hero whines, they bend over backwards and grab their ankles!"

Koehler arched an eyebrow. "Sounds like you harbor a bit of contempt for our great von Richthofen," he said as carefully as he could. Karl Koehler thought Manfred von Richthofen was the envy of all German pilots. Maybe not, he pondered. Wissemann after all, was Bavarian, not Prussian; and certainly not of the aristocracy.

"I was at Döberitz for a spell," Wissemann said, "when von Richthofen came through for his training."

"Really?"

"He was a lousy pilot at best. He crashed on his first solo."

"Von Richthofen—crashed?" Koehler replied, rising to the bait.

"That's right," Wissemann replied with a cocky grin. "But lord knows, he's a crack shot—a hunter—a stalker. A very patient man, my Austrian friend."

"Patience is a virtue, as the saying goes."

"He waits for the perfect moment to strike. And then—" Wissemann demonstrated with animated gestures; his hand swooped down above the counter top like an aeroplane and toppled the ash can in a mock air attack. "Whoosh! *Rat-tat-tat-tat-tat*—he doesn't miss. That's his secret!"

Koehler's brows arched warily. Perhaps it was time to cut the pie-eyed officer off; the Irish seemed to be making him giddy and undignified. The wary Tyrolean covertly slid the bottle of Irish from the counter top and stowed it on a lower shelf, hidden from view.

"Richthofen was a pupil of Oswald Boelcke," he said uneasily. "He's learned his lessons well—"

"*Quatsch!*" Wissemann grumped. "Air combat is like a hunting trip for him. I believe the man has no personal fear whatsoever. It's all great sport for him."

Willi Wissemann cringed. He did admire von Richthofen, more for his exploits than for his social standing. The landed gentry or aristocracy always made him cringe a little bit. Perhaps it was their snobbish arrogance or their over-privileged status as Germany's upper class. Von Richthofen was a dead shot and a born leader, but he wasn't as bourgeois as many a Junker. Wissemann knew that. Was it just that Manfred von Richthofen was a Prussian aristocrat, and he a simple little commoner from the Allgäu? Perhaps.

"Well, *Herr Oberleutnant,* he is our leading ace."

"That he is."

"He's just like you, sir. An officer and a gentleman."

"Well, he was in the cavalry, and I in the infantry..."

"Twenty more victories and you might catch him."

"Twenty? Sure." Wissemann smirked. "That's easy enough."

"So. Here's to Germany's next aerial hero, Willi Wissemann!" Koehler retrieved the Irish and poured one more shot for the both of them; they clinked glasses together and drank a toast.

"*Here, here!*" Wissemann couldn't help but smile. He was well into the warming throes of bacchanalian cheerfulness now.

And the clock's slender hands ticked away another hour...

✠

THE FRONT DOOR FLEW OPEN and a gust of cold, winter air rushed in. It was *Unteroffizier* Grimm stumbling in clumsily.

"Close the goddamn door!" someone yelled.

"Piss off!" Grimm hissed viciously.

A peal of laughter erupted from a nearby card game.

The annoyed noncom slammed the door and sneered at the men and their card game, cursing quietly. Officers, the plague of all enlisted men everywhere!

Wissemann sniffed. "Speak of the Devil."

"Aha. There's the little blighter, now." Koehler grinned.

"Over here, Grimm!" Wissemann gesticulated drunkenly.

Grimm tramped over, saluted weakly, dropping a few pages from a manila folio in the process. More laughter erupted from the card game. He stooped over and picked them up, muttering a few inaudible expletives. Willi Wissemann smirked and made a limp gesture that could have hardly been interpreted as a return salute.

"At ease, *Unteroffizier*," he ordered softly.

"Having a rough day, Grimm?" Koehler jibed.

"Oh, why don't you just—"

"Got any news, Grimm?" Wissemann interrupted.

"Well—"

"What's going on up there in St. Quentin? Find anything?"

Grimm leered stonily at the simpering barkeep. "Well, sir. The weather is very bad, as you well know—"

"Oh, enough about the damn weather!"

"Well..."

"What did you find out? Anything?"

"Sorry, sir." Grimm shrugged. "They're really not saying much up there in St. Quentin."

"*Quatsch!* Out with it, Grimm."

"Sir, Army doesn't want information leaking out about the faulty wing problems. It's all hush-hush, you know. Top secret," Grimm equivocated, smiling proudly. He glanced at Koehler again; he couldn't resist giving him a self-satified smirk.

"Hush-hush? What do you mean?"

"Sir, they—*Idflieg*—says that if French Intelligence found out this information they might use it to their advantage—use the information as propaganda, possibly leak it to our press agencies."

"Oh, that's utterly preposterous." Wissemann scoffed.

"Huh, right," Koehler interjected dubiously, crossing his arms over his chest in a superior manner. "Only their Spad has a chance in hell against our Albatros, not their propaganda,"

"Did you submit the requisition request for spare parts, Grimm, while you were snooping around?" Wissemann asked, leering at the little noncom with doubtful eyes.

"Yes, sir. I did. *Tank Stelle-7* supplied mostly engine odds and sods, and so on and so on—"

"Better than nothing, I suppose," Koehler chimed.

"*Herr Oberleutnant,*" Grimm interceded. "I spoke with Peltzer. He assured me that he could fix the faulty wing chord if he could just get his hands on one of those new Albatroses."

"Well, *Unteroffizier* Grimm," Wissemann replied, a torrent of thoughts streaming through his mind. "Peltzer will have his chance when you get your scrawny little ass back to St. Quentin tomorrow morning."

"Tomorrow morning? But, sir—"

"*Verdammt!* We need new aircraft for *Jasta 23!*" He snarled, waving the surly noncom off in a patronizing manner, exploding, alcohol and outraged dignity speaking simultaneously.

Grimm frowned, seething petulantly. He opened his mouth to say something, but thought better of it. What good would it do? He grumbled, bitter to the core.

"Good-bye. Off you go," Wissemann said in a jeering tone.

"Tomorrow morning? But, but, it might to snow again!"

Wissemann sniffled, stiffening to the impertinent reply.

"DIS-MISSED."

Grimm's face soured; he stomped off, grumbling.

"And bring back some decent schnapps this time, will you!" someone wisecracked. Once again the card game erupted into irreverent laughter. But the little noncom wasn't having any of it. He slammed the door and was gone in a heated, snow-flurried animus.

Wissemann looked at Koehler despairingly.

"Hmm, bad news travels fast."

"Seems like it, sir."

"*Idflieg* is keeping things quiet, as usual."

"Typical, eh?"

"So what's your take on all this, Koehler?"

Koehler sighed thoughtfully. "Well, sir, my guess is this: Supreme Headquarters believes the D.III to be our new 'secret weapon.' They probably don't want to lose face with the enemy, and with our own pilots. I suppose if the enemy found out about our quandary, well, it would be an embarrassing blow to German invincibility." He had answered as artfully as he dared.

"Hah! German invincibility! That's a good one, Koehler."

"We do seem to have air superiority now, sir," Koehler remarked with vague assurance. "We don't want to lose it, even in spirit."

Willi Wissemann scoffed. Koehler's salutary observations didn't convince this bleary-eyed Bavarian. But it was true enough. Germany did have the edge in technology and held aerial supremacy, although it wasn't known as that yet. Morale was high and the air war was now front page news. All the combatant nations exalted their air heroes. High scoring aces were celebrities, much like famous opera singers and stage actors. Their faces were plastered all over newspapers, magazines, and postcards. They even received fan mail!

Thus, any breech in the assertion of total German supremacy was unacceptable. Imperial propaganda had to perpetuate the idea of total invincibility in its warriors and in its war machines. Anything less might undermine the perception of the *Luftstreitkräfte's* unshakable primacy. He reluctantly had to agree; Germany must maintain the upper hand, even if it had to resort to surreptitious means. The French and British must never suspect the mighty Albatros was a flawed war bird.

"Spirit?" Wissemann snickered. "As long as the spirits flow freely round here, morale is high, eh?"

"You got that right." Koehler nettled a brow. Wissemann's banal humor was getting a bit grating.

The pie-eyed *Jastaführer* set his glass down and shrugged into his jacket. "Well, I must get back to the aerodrome," he said. "Dirty business—this war."

"*Alles Gute.*" Koehler nodded politely.

"*Danke.*" Wissemann left some coinage on the counter, plopped his service cap upon his head, and traipsed off toward the door. He passed the card game on his way out, stopping, standing, hands in pockets, grinning.

Leutnant Eckhardt paused his deal and looked up at the *Jastaführer.* "Evening, sir. What's up?"

"Eckhardt..." he said, and then glanced across the table, "and the rest of you gentlemen—take it easy tonight, okay?" Wissemann urged. "Tomorrow is a busy day. Try to turn in early if possible?"

"Yes, sir. We'll make it a short night."

Eckhardt nodded and winked.

"Carry on, men."

Wissemann paced to the exit and pushed through the front door, stepped out into the frosty air and walked to the parking lot where his staff car was parked. He swiped the snow off the windshield of the Renault Tourer, cranked up the engine, and the little sedan rumbled to life. He sat in the front seat for a moment as the engine warmed up, thinking, wondering what Ilse was doing right now. He drifted off for a long pleasurable moment, warming to the image of his dear, sweet fiancée, sighing longingly. "Dear, dear, Ilse..."

He put the car in gear and accelerated, pulling up to the edge of the road, waited while a heavily laden truck roared by, then gunned the engine. The Renault quickly picked up speed, bumping and bouncing down the snowy, mud-caked road.

The late afternoon sun was just visible on the horizon. Thin clouds hovered in the brilliant pink-orange haze. The sky was clearing; tomorrow would be a good day for operations. And soon, the weather would be warming up for good, Wissemann contemplated. The warmer clime would be ideal for constant aerial operations.

Woe be unto the French two-seaters!

HOURS LATER, after an unappetizing meal at mess, Wissemann wandered back to his office for a final look into the day's events. Schutzling was about to lock up for the evening; he was filing a set of papers when Wissemann walked in.

"How were the cabbage rolls, sir?" Schutzling inquired.

"That was cabbage? Ugh! Utterly horrible!"

"Well, I guess I'll just head to the Kasino for my supper then," Schutzling replied mindfully then folded his arms across his chest and said: "Sir, your victory was confirmed by *Flugmeldedienst.* Congratulations. Well done."

"Oh?"

"Yes, sir. Call came in a couple of hours ago."

"Well, good. So, did we secure any souvenirs from it?"

"No, *Herr Oberleutnant.* Nothing yet."

"I see."

"I sent Hippel out to fetch some part of it earlier this afternoon. But he hasn't returned yet."

"Right. No hurry, I guess."

"Perhaps tomorrow?"

"Yes. Tomorrow." Wissemann sighed. *"Humph,* Hippel. He's in no hurry to get back here, I'm sure."

"I've already put in a request for your Ehrenbecher."

"You did?"

"Yes, sir. It should arrive in a couple of days."

The *Ehrenbecher* or "Honor Cup," as Wissemann recalled, was a silver cup awarded to airman for their first confirmed victory. It was a tradition started by Oswald Boelcke. Von Richthofen continued the trend for every British machine he'd shot down; he currently displayed twenty-one silver cups on the mantle above his fireplace.

Willi Wissemann nodded, impressed by Schutzling's efficiency. "Excellent. It'll make a fine paper weight for my desk." The *Jastaführer* smirked derisively.

"Paper weight?"

Schutzling shrugged and sighed. Why did he bother with such trivialities? If his *Jastaführer* didn't care for such honors, why should he? This Wissemann fellow was an odd one all right, he thought. He reached for his overcoat and cap hanging on the coat rack. He jangled the keys in his coat pocket, as if to alert Wissemann of his intentions, then looked up at the clock on the wall. "Will you be locking up, sir?"

"Yes. I won't be long."

"Well, I'll be off then. Good night, sir." Boot heels clicked.

"Goodnight, Schutzling."

Schutzling shuffled off. Wissemann sat quietly for a moment.

A second later he could overhear the weary noncom cursing the cold weather as he tramped away. The *Jastaführer* grinned merrily. Good 'ole Schutzling! He brushed his service cap back, rasping his forehead, reclining on the corner of the desktop, glancing over the confirmation report.

"Hmm, my first confirmed victory. *Wunderbar.*"

He was a bit amazed he wasn't more excited about it though. Had the thrill of victory already faded? Perhaps all those days in the trenches, the mindless killing, the senseless slaughter and now the faceless aerial enemy, had dulled his senses. Where, the grim warrior wondered—where was that brash, Teutonic pride? Where had it gone?

"*Hochmut kommt vor dem Fall,*" Wissemann uttered grimly. "Pride comes before the fall."

DEKE D. WAGNER

```
TO: Idflieg, Berlin.                    From: JASTA 23


        REQUESTING CONFIRMATION OF 1st VICTORY


Date:    2.Mar.1917.(Friday)
Time:    1419 Hours.
Place:   South of Vaudesincourt—rail bridge(Suippe).
Type:    Farman F.40, two-seater. Serial No.413. Renault
         motor-135 hp. Machine gun:(1)Lewis No.19644.


Occupants: Both killed. No identity disks. Names found
on maps were Clavier and Dufaux.


                      NARRATIVE:


At 1417 hours... I spotted black anti-aircraft bursts a
few kilometers south of Mount Le Casque and signaled my
two Ketten mates, Ltn. Frankenberg and Ltn. Fleischer.
I spotted an enemy reconnaissance machine. I made my
attack from the sun. I made two successive attacks and
on the second burst, the body of the machine broke in
half. The Farman fell smoking into our lines. The enemy
machine is lying near the rail bridge at Suippe, a few
paces behind the German reserve trench line.




                  Signed: Oblt. Wilhelm R. Wissemann
                    OBLT.WILHELM R. WISSEMANN
```

CONFIRMED
Kofl 7.Armee, Laon

Chapter 11

✠

MARCH 15, 1917. OBERLEUTNANT Wissemann's little, ragged-winged *Kette* of Albatroses and Halberstadts, climbed leisurely in a clear blue sky, some two thousand meters above Villers-le-Sec, a German airfield northwest of *Jasta 23's* aerodrome. His formation of five was linking up with a flight of six Rumpler two-seaters from FA-254, ready to escort them to an area north of Reims near the Brimont Fort. The Rumplers had been tasked with the job of bombing enemy trench positions. They took off in pairs, ascending slowly, soaring skyward, old battle wagons making a heroic showing as they buzzed off into the high blue. The Rumpler flight leader fired a signal flare and the droning two-seaters formed up at the predetermined altitude of three thousand meters, then proceeded to the target in formation.

In February and March the German Army's strategy in the Champagne was of a defensive nature. The Army High Command had decided to shorten the front line with a planned withdrawal. They named this newly prepared position the *"Siegfried-Stellung."* But the Allied Command mistakenly referred to it as the Hindenburg Line. This "misunderstanding" was perpetuated by a German deserter's erroneous statement to Allied intelligence. The areas evacuated were devastated—towns and villages razed. Roads were bombed and destroyed, wooded areas leveled, and water sources poisoned. The German code name for this special operation was "ALBERICH" after the deceitful dwarf of the German *Nibelungenlied*—an epic poem composed some eight hundred years earlier.

Wissemann's *Kette* made the final circuit of the aerodrome, while the last two-seater took off from the grassy field below. His *Kette* was amassed in a tight arrowhead: the *Jastaführer* at its apex, Schröder and Bubi Kindlich on the right flank, Gutemann and Frankenberg on the left. They climbed high above the Rumplers, following them closely. The ponderous formation of eleven German aircraft soared south towards Reims, dead set on bombing and do battle with their snail-eating antagonists.

Wissemann's *Kette* was comprised of three Albatroses and two Halberstadts. Both Halberstadts had twin machine guns instead of the customary one. They'd both been retrofitted at the Army flight depot before redeployment. Alas, they were not new machines though, "retreads" from AFP-7—patched, sewn and put into plumb. Peltzer had wryly commented: "Now those old buzzards have much sharper teeth." Things were looking up for the *Jasta!*

The formation of five single-seat scouts positioned themselves on the right flank and about a thousand meters above the two-seater flight, keeping a close vigil. In the big Bavarian's personal opinion, the Rumpler C.III was one of Germany's better utility aircraft, its 260-horsepower, 6-cylinder Mercedes providing decent high-altitude capabilities and excellent top speeds. Armed with a synchronized Maxim machine gun up front and one flexible Parabellum machine gun in the rear, it too was armed to the teeth. Added to that, it could carry four 50-kilogram bombs on center section under wing racks.

The wind whipped Wissemann's scarf backwards in the slipstream —a jaunty snapshot of a German aviator. The assiduous *Jastaführer* peered through a pair of tinted goggles, scanning the sky for trouble. It was a clear day with no clouds to obscure the view. The sun was shining brightly. The seemingly halcyon atmosphere offered very little turbulence, and it seemed to be a perfect morning. Perhaps too perfect, he pondered suspiciously. Willi Wissemann was always aware how quickly events could go from good to bad at a moment's notice.

It was late morning—just around ten o'clock, when Wissemann's eyes flickered over his control panel gauges for just a second, making sure the Albatros was operating at optimal efficiency. During these inchoate phases of every mission, he agonizingly obsessed over every little detail. Only during this fleeting moment of rapt concentration did the Bavarian take his eagle eye off the sky. But just for a second—

TAC-TAC-TAC ! TAC-TAC-TAC ! TAC-TAC-TAC !

Wissemann was abruptly jolted to attention by the disquieting thumping of gunfire. His head jerked around, seeing Gutemann's and Frankenberg's Albatroses turning out, beginning a rapid descent toward the Rumpler formation. A flight of four Nieuport scouts was attacking; Wissemann recognized their distinct silvery—*enduit metallisé*—wings and fuselages flashing in the sun. The Nieuports glistened in the bright sunlight like vicious, metallic birds of prey; their gaudy red, white and blue cockades gleamed dangerously. They zoomed down after the lead Rumpler in a headlong dive—four French scouts filed into a neat line astern formation, claws out, engines screaming, machine guns blazing. Wissemann fired a red flare and opened his throttle, signaling the *Kette* to follow him. The Mercedes engine roared to maximum power as he wheeled the Albatros over in a tight turn, following Gutemann and Frankenberg's descent. As always, the young Swabian was the first to see the enemy, he'd signaled the *Kette* for the counterattack a second before. However, Wissemann's unfortunate lapse in attentiveness had cost him crucial seconds of reaction time.

"*Verflucht!*" he swore. "Daydreaming again!"

The Nieuports zoomed over the lead Rumpler, their single Vickers machine guns chattering viciously, scoring lethal hits again and again. The Rumpler began to smolder from its engine compartment. And soon, a ragged gray smoke billowed out from its green and lilac painted fuselage—a long thin column. The observer was nowhere to be seen. Wissemann had to assume he'd been hit and had collapsed to the floor of the fuselage. The observers of the other Rumplers returned fire as the Nieuports flashed by. Meanwhile, Gutemann made contact with the leading Nieuport. He rolled sharply to the left and got behind the silvery scout, firing a quick, high-deflection burst that missed. The enemy flight leader's streamers, attached to the outer wing struts, fluttered boldly in the slipstream, betraying his identity. Gutemann hunched down behind his gunsights and kept visual contact with the Nieuport, unwilling to let it out of his sight for any reason. He knew that during the tumultuous action of a dogfight, it was easy to loose sight of one's adversary. He fired again.

TOK-TOK-TOK! TOK-TOK-TOK! TOK-TOK-TOK!

The Maxims burst to life and flashes flickered behind the whirling propeller. Tracers streaked and flecks of angry fire danced along the upper wing of the French scout. Young Gutemann's marksmanship was amazing. Frankenberg fired shots too when the trailing Nieuports whizzed by. But he missed, banking hard to stay with Gutemann. By now the riddled Rumpler was streaming dense orange flames, and it spun down out of formation. Wissemann saw its hapless crewmen leap to their doom. The remaining Rumplers herded together in a close formation for mutual protection. They continued on to the target area, climbing higher. Without escort, the two-seaters would be highly vulnerable to another attack. But they pressed on, confident in their own defenses.

The air battle had now reached its zenith. A twisting and turning vortex of Nieuports, Albatroses and Halberstadts, swirled about the sky in a savage imbroglio. Machine gun fire, with its shrill staccato clatter, rose above the drone of engines. Angry bullets zipped across the high blue in every direction. It was a deadly dogfight.

Gutemann, still locked on to the tail of the enemy flight leader fired at close range. A full volley of twenty-five rounds smashed into the fuselage, abaft the cockpit, wounding the enemy pilot. The Frenchman tried to skid the Nieuport into a slip-turn, kicking the rudder hard right, but Gutemann hung on, popping off short bursts. The Frenchman, Gutemann quickly realized, was a veteran.

Frankenberg hurtled after another Nieuport as it tried to disengage itself from the action. A third Nieuport, in turn, piled down on top of Frankenberg's Albatros and attacked him from the rear. Its single Vickers machine gun snapped out angry staccato bursts. The fourth Nieuport, obviously flown by a novice, panicked and banked about in an aimless pattern.

Wissemann alertly recognized Frankenberg's predicament and plunged headlong after the Nieuport, his Albatros's superior dive quickly planting him within range. He popped off a quick burst at one hundred meters, hoping more to scare the Frenchman off than actually score a hit. To Wissemann's elated surprise, flashes of tracer flickered all over the Nieuport's fuselage. The Frenchman wisely broke off his attack, yanking the Nieuport up in an artful half-loop, heeling up into the wind. Of course, much to Wissemann's despair, the excessive dive speed caused the heavier Albatros to overshoot— the Mercedes-weighted nose of the D.II did not pull up so easily. The nimble Nieuport slipped away without further damage. Wissemann's frustration was quite apparent now. A balled fist shook angrily.

A few meters away, Gutemann finished off the enemy flight leader. He squinted through the gunsight and let the belt run. The Albatros' twin machine guns made short work of the Nieuport's flimsy airframe. The now fatally wounded pilot lost control, spun around twice, and fell into a twisting death dive. The wings folded back, snapped off, and the naked fuselage plunged straight down. It crashed in a densely wooded area near Berry-au-Bac. This was the Swabian's sixth victory. Then he instantly banked back towards the fight, regaining some altitude in a climb, continuing his quest for the destruction of the French flight. He at once saw the solitary enemy machine lolling about below him and pitched the yoke forward, beginning a diving descent. The green-as-grass Frenchman had no idea where he was or realized that he was about to be attacked.

Wissemann and Frankenberg regrouped, racing back toward Gutemann and the wandering Nieuport. They had lost contact with the third Frenchman, who seemed to have vanished in the haze. Wissemann was quite furious by this time.

Gutemann pressed his attack now. He peered through the gunsights, taking careful aim, closing within twenty-five meters of the unsuspecting Frenchman. He squeezed both gun triggers. A fiery blur of copper spewed out from the twin Maxims. Gutemann's blazing guns caught the Nieuport as it whipped upwards for a half-loop. The Nieuport slid down on its tail, rolling over and over, then burst into a mass of flames, going down, trailing oily black smoke. The fire engulfed the engine and cockpit, trapping the pilot in a blistering inferno. Yet the kill still flew. But it was dead meat—a cold plate set up for the victory table. Gutemann fired a second volley from dead astern at point blank range. The smoking Nieuport crumpled into a twisted ball of wreckage and broke apart in several flaming pieces as it tumbled earthbound. Oily black smoke billowed out behind it. The long, black column of smoke alone marked its fatal passing.

The *Jastaführer* watched in silent awe.

The remaining Frenchman, seeing that he was now outnumbered, streaked away wildly, nearly losing control of his Nieuport as he made his getaway, some of the canvas wing surface on the Nieuport's lower wing tearing away in the wind, the fragile sesquiplane lower wing threatening to break. But somehow it held. Since the Frenchman was below the German flight, no one saw him escape. The battle was over—fought inside the seemingly eternal length of three minutes.

Wissemann, enraged by his awkward performance, banged balled fists against the cockpit coaming, his curses explicative and self-critical, chiding his amateurish reactions, condemning himself for being such a bumbling idiot. The niceties of flying meant nothing here, he knew. Excellent marksmanship is what really counted at the Front. He did manage to compose himself long enough though to fire a signal flare and regroup the *Kette*.

Otto Gutemann pulled along side Wissemann's Albatros, waving, flashing two fingers, signifying two victories. Wissemann nodded, acknowledging the victorious pilot with a thumbs-up gesture, then thrust his arm forward stiffly, bitterly, in the direction of the Rumplers, which were now just tiny silhouettes against the glowing blue horizon...

✠

THE FREEZING RAIN PATTERED incessantly at the windowpane and the sky thundered with ominous frequency. Ilse von Linkhof sat quietly in a living room, by a fireplace, warming her cold hands and feet. Another dreary day, Ilse thought to herself. Oh, how I wish Willi were here. Nearby, she could hear someone closing a door and shuffle down a long hallway. It was Ilse's mother. *Frau* von Linkhof entered the living room, strolling towards Ilse with a plodding gait of a thin, doddering woman of fifty-three years. *Frau* Helene von Linkhof wore her graying hair in a tight bun and was finely dressed in a dark blue dress and pearls. She smiled cheerfully when she saw her daughter. *Frau* von Linkhof reached out to hug her only child, her pride and joy.

"Ilse, dear... how are you, my sweet?"

Ilse rose from the chair, opened her arms and smiled. "Fine, mother dear. How are you?" She embraced her mother and kissed her forehead.

"I am well, my child. And to what do I owe this pleasure?"

"I want to talk to *Papi, Mutti*," Ilse said pertly.

"Ahh. Marten told me you were here. I was just in the study talking with your father," *Frau* von Linkhof replied.

Ilse listened politely. She smiled but said nothing.

"Will you stay for lunch, Ilse?"

"No. I'm sorry, *Mutti*. I have to get back to the schoolhouse before the children are dismissed for the afternoon."

"Oh, that's right, the children—"

"I want to talk to *Papi*," Ilse insisted sternly.

"Of course you do." Ilse's mother sat down behind a fine, teakwood coffee table. "But he's very busy, dear."

The von Linkhof home reflected opulence but there was a *gemütlich* air about every space. The room in which they sat was a combination den and family parlor. A broad-beamed fireplace was set as the centerpiece with bric-a-brac cabinetry buttressing both sides. It was faced by a hand-carved sofa made out of solid walnut complete with silk down-filled pillows. Spread about were three low tables that displayed an ancient sextant, a terrestrial globe, and open dictionary. A contemporary Odeon horn gramophone set in a walnut case stood between two French windows while a Blüthner grand piano glistened wide-legged in a room offering wall to wall bookcases.

Ilse sighed. "I know. But—"

"He's meeting with the Armaments Board today."

"He's *always* very busy."

"Papi' is going over notes for the meeting. Would you like some tea, dear?"

"No *Mutti*, I want to talk to *Papi*. Please!"

Ilse folded her arms about her bosom, frowning petulantly. *Frau* von Linkhof shook her head. She rang the service bell. A moment later, Marten Zangler, the old major-domo, tread wearily into the living room.

"Yes, *Frau* von Linkhof? " he said.

"Marten, please tell Gertrude to prepare some tea and *Keks.*"

"Immediately, *Frau* von Linkhof."

"Thank you, Marten."

Marten bowed and scurried away.

"I'll fetch *Papi*. Wait here, Ilse. He's a very busy man. Busy, busy!"

"Thank you, *Mutti*," Ilse replied meekly.

Ilse's mother hurried off to the study, calling her husband's name. "Konrad! Ilse is here!" Halfway down the hallway she stopped in front of the mansion's study. She rapped heavily on the fine wooden doors. "Konrad!"

"*Ach Gott!* What is it now, woman?" a gruff voice resounded from inside the study.

"Konrad? Come out, please," *Frau* von Linkhof begged.

"Can't I have a moment's peace, woman?"

"Konrad..."

"Don't you know that I have important business to tend to?"

"Please come out, dear."

"I'm working up the details for this proposal!"

"Konrad!"

"Confounded!"

There was a curious crash, then the cantankerous old man's head appeared from around an opened door. "What? What is it, dear?"

"Ilse's here. She wants to talk to you."

"What about?"

"She's upset," *Frau* von Linkhof whispered.

"Ilse, upset?" the old man scoffed facetiously. "That's absurd—"

"Konrad, come out this instant!" She tugged him on his book-ladened arm.

"*Ach,* all right already. Give me a moment!" He disappeared for a minute. There was a dull thud, then a reluctant muttering. Then the old man reappeared, stalking into the living room in an obvious animus of frustration. He sighed softly. "Yes?"

General Konrad von Linkhof, a short and stocky man with graying hair and a large mustache, was a War Academy graduate and former

Army railway director. He'd recently accepted the prestigious appointment of Deputy War Minister to the Prussian Cabinet and was a very busy man these days, having no time for nonsense. Konrad von Linkhof was regarded quite the eccentric among the German military, but was a proficient enough administrator with a moderate political agenda. At the beginning of the war, he'd headed the Army railway section of the General Staff, therefore responsible for timetabling and mobilization. His successful record had made him an ideal pick as deputy of the new War Office set up in November '16. It was created to reorganize the German war industry. Konrad von Linkhof was an austere and straightforward man, thus making him unpopular, and that eventually produced enemies amongst the industrialists. Even so, stepping on a few toes here and there never concerned him. He had a job to do, and he did it with all his will and fortitude, regardless of whose feathers he might ruffle. He loved his country and his family, especially adoring and treasuring his only child and daughter, Ilse von Linkhof. She was like a rare and fragile flower to him.

"*Papi!* I'm so glad to see you," Ilse chirped.

She jumped up from the high-backed chair, threw her arms around him, planting a big kiss on his rosy-red cheeks. He hugged her and whirled her around once, like a ballerina, admiring his daughter's elegant beauty.

"Princess! And I'm happy to see you too." General von Linkhof kissed his daughter's cheek. "So. What is so important that you must interrupt my work, dear? Tell me." He glanced at his pocket watch and noted the time.

Ilse turned around, returned to her chair, and sat down with folded arms. "*Papi,* I'm worried about Willi."

"Is that what this is all about—Willi?"

General von Linkhof scowled.

"*Papi!* Something could happen to him out there at the Front."

"Oh dear. Please—"

"He's put himself in harm's way again, and I am terribly worried."

General von Linkhof glanced at his wife standing next him, rolling his eyes testily. *Frau* von Linkhof shook her head and grabbed his hand, squeezing it firmly, causing some agonizing discomfort.

"*Autsch!* Let go of me, woman!" he bawled, grimacing with pain. The acerbated General jerked away from her grip, frowning crossly.

Ilse continued to pout. "Why is he back at the Front, *Papi?*"

"Princess, his instructor's term at Stutthof was completed—"

"I thought you fixed it, so he couldn't transfer out the flying school." Ilse's eyes became wide with suspicion.

General von Linkhof shook his head. "Ilse..."

Frau von Linkhof glowered at him distrustfully. "Konrad?"

Marten returned from the kitchen with a silver platter of tea and sugar *Keks.* He offered the General some refreshments. "Sir..."

"Not now, Marten. Not now!" Konrad von Linkhof said sharply, shaking his head.

"As you wish, sir." Marten turned to Frau von Linkhof. "Madam?"

"Danke, Marten. That'll be all. Set the tray on the coffee table."

The dutiful butler obeyed, set the tray down, bowed politely and left the room.

"Princess, I did all I could."

"Are you sure, *Papi?*"

"Willi's an officer, Ilse. He wanted a posting to a scout *Staffel.*"

"What?"

"I did all I could do—"

"I wish I could believe that!" Ilse snarled.

"Ilse, behave yourself!" her mother warned.

"We need smart, experienced officers on the front lines."

"I know, *Papi*, but—"

"Ilse, the Fatherland needs good men at the Front. He requested a transfer. There wasn't a thing I could do about it."

Frau von Linkhof frowned at the old man. She knew her husband disliked Willi Wissemann with a passion, and he particularly despised aviators. "Wars are not won with flimsy flying contraptions," he was once quoted as saying to a Berlin reporter, "but with infantry, artillery and cavalry!" Konrad von Linkhof was a staunch supporter of the "old ways", and he didn't embrace the new tools of warfare. Machines like aeroplanes, U-boats and machine guns were well beyond his out-of-date comprehension.

"*Papi,* I'm really worried."

"Ilse, please. Don't worry yourself."

"You're the Deputy War Minister. Can't you do something?"

"Princess, I'm sorry. There's nothing I can do now. What's done is done. Please believe me."

"Your father is right, dear," *Frau* von Linkhof implored.

"You must be strong and pray for him, Ilse."

"Papi, please..."

"All right! Enough now!"

"Papi..." Ilse began pouting.

"I must get back to work now, Princess." He glanced at his pocket watch again and sighed heavily. "Will you be staying for dinner?"

Ilse's face suddenly twisted up in a bitter scowl, her mouth clamping down in a hard line. She huffed heatedly and bolted for the door. A moment later a thunderous clangor shook the house as she slammed out the front door.

Frau von Linkhof scoffed. *"Ach Gott!* I swear, Konrad, you are impossible sometimes!" She stormed off after her daughter.

General von Linkhof rolled his eyes, now totally annoyed. "What? What!" he retorted, quite dumbfounded. "What in the world is wrong with everybody today?"

The door slammed again. There was an uncomfortable silence.

The old General shook his head. "Bah! Women! Sometimes I just don't understand them at all." He stomped back to his study, glaring at his watch, groaning miserably. "I don't have time for all this whiny nonsense!" General von Linkhof went back to his study and locked the doors behind him. "I have work to do!"

Marten Zangler returned to the living room to find an empty room of cold tea and a platter of untouched sugar *Keks.* He chuckled, picked up a *Kek* and took a bite of the sweetened biscuit.

"Mmm..." he mumbled with a mouthful of crumbs. "Where did everybody go? Oh, well. Can't let all this go to waste now, can we?" Marten poured himself some tea and sat down.

THE RUMPLER TWO-SEATERS began the mission by bombing the enemy trench lines at low altitude. Their bombs whistled shrilly as they fell through the open sky upon the enemy emplacements, exploding in fiery bursts, sending dirty fountains of earth high into the air. Even the roar of an aeroplane engine couldn't drown out these violent explosions.

Wissemann scanned the sky for enemy machines. For the moment, the atmosphere was clear. But anti-aircraft shelling began to detonate around the formation of German aircraft. It was an alarming event for some, but simply a nuisance to the more seasoned veterans of the *Kette.* Down below, unperturbed by the shelling, the Rumplers finished their bombing runs, inflicting moderate damage—knocking out a machine gun nest and an observation post. The Rumplers then ascended above the destruction, gaining altitude for the trip back home, reforming into a typical arrowhead formation. Wissemann signaled the *Kette.* It was time for *Jasta 23's* attack run.

Although not equipped with bombs themselves, they planned to impose damage with machine gun fire. The German scouts peeled out of formation—down, one after the other, line astern, for a low level strafing run of the trenches. This was a new tactic. Known as "trench-strafing" at that time, it later became known as simple ground attack.

Wissemann charged his guns, heeled over and bore down, his Albatros's engine shrieking a murderous death dirge, swooping down a hundred meters above the French trench line. Previously hidden details—gun pits, machine gun emplacements and doomed infantry in attack formation, individual men in their burdensome equipment—became visible. At the sudden sound of the screaming Mercedes engine, hapless French soldiers began to scamper for cover, like lice in the folds of a blanket, or more likely, Wissemann imagined, like flies on a dung heap.

Wissemann opened fire with both guns. A volley of tracer arched earthward. He didn't see the bullets impact; at ground level, the visibility was extremely limited, due to thick mist and smoke clouds leftover from the Rumpler's bombing attack. He was sure he hadn't hit anything. But *Oberleutnant* Willi Wissemann did not care. He was just completing the last phase of the mission at the behest of 7th Army *Kofl*. And since he generally hated this new trench-strafing business, he decided to make only one pass.

Machine gun and small arms fire began to pop around him. A few rounds tagged the Albatros but nothing apparently critical. He raked the crawling ground with burst after burst, diving to fire and zooming away until his belts were half gone. Seconds later, after traversing the entire section of French trench line, he yanked the Albatros into a steep climb. It was time to go home.

The *Kette* mimicked the *Jastaführer's* attack run. One by one, Gutemann, Kindlich, Frankenberg, and Schröder—the tail end of the formation—plunged down, each making diligent firing passes. Wissemann, still clawing for altitude, glanced over his shoulder to observe each pilot's attack. His hawks were doing well.

Then, inexplicably, Schröder's Halberstadt stalled upwards, stood on its tail, rolled over upside down, and nose-dived straight into the ground. Wissemann's heart sank. A dirty cloud of dust billowed up from the crash site. The Halberstadt's fuel tank erupted in flames, spreading quickly, consuming the wood and canvas aeroplane like a blazing bonfire out of control. Black smoke rolled up into the sky.

With a bitterly muttered oath, Wissemann slammed his fist on the side of the cockpit. He reached for his signal pistol and fired a green flare, signaling the *Kette* to regroup. Schröder must have been killed instantly, he realized. Only a mortal wound could've caused him to crash so suddenly, ending a brief and inauspicious career. He moped for the rest of the flight home. Schröder was the first casualty under his command. It was a bitter pill to swallow.

ONE HOUR LATER. At the aerodrome, the pilots gathered for the debriefing. Although the mission was deemed a success, no one felt any sense of achievement. Poor Schröder was dead, diffusing any exuberance they may have had. They congregated outside of the dispersal tent in a loose group, waiting for the *Jastaführer* to join them, for Wissemann was the last to land. He taxied up to the flight line and parked, the Mercedes shuddering to a stop as he switched off the magnetos. He sat for a long, silent moment.

A mechanic stepped up on the stirrup and undid his harness. "Sorry, *Herr Oberleutnant.* Just heard the news," he lamented.

The bereaved Bavarian pulled off his flying cap, biting at his nether lip, looking up, frowning, saying nothing. He pulled himself up and out of the cockpit and hopped to the ground. After removing the gloves from his hands and unbuttoning his jacket, he reached for the silver cigarette case, fumbling for a smoke. Peltzer, who had just walked up, struck a match and offered a light. Wissemann nodded his thanks as Peltzer lit the cigarette.

"What happened?" Peltzer asked, lighting his cigar.

"I don't know exactly," Wissemann replied.

"Ground fire?"

"Yes. Schröder *must've* been hit by ground fire."

"Dirty business, trench-strafing."

"We were all very low. We all took a few hits. He, well... must've taken a fatal one. A damned pity, really."

"I hope he didn't suffer much."

"I doubt it. It was over in an instant."

"That's reassuring."

"His Halberstadt flipped over dreadfully quick before the crash. And I'm afraid the poor boy was burnt to a cinder." Wissemann exhaled a sigh of smoke. He thought of that charred Frenchman again and trembled.

"That's horrible, terrible. Just a kid, he was."

"Yes, just a kid. I'll be busy writing his family tonight. Sadly, I can't even remember the poor fellow's first name."

Wissemann was suddenly very annoyed with himself; he felt completely ashamed. It was his job—his duty—to know all the men in his *Jasta*, and least of all, their first names. Alas, it was a minor thing to forget, but it bothered him gravely. Young Schröder was such a new addition to the *Staffel*, he'd never had the chance to converse with him besides a flight debriefing. Wissemann and Peltzer started walking toward the Dispersal hut. Each man racked his brains for the young pilot's name. It was Peltzer who finally remembered.

"Stefan! Stefan Schröder!" he spouted. "Yes, that's it."

"Yes—Stefan. You're right," Wissemann replied, nodding his head, still a bit dazed and shocked by the incident. As he approached the waiting group, Wissemann could see their dour expressions too. It spoke volumes about their feelings. It put him in a depressed mood.

Gutemann spoke first. "Don't know what to say, sir. I—"

"No need to say anything, Gutemann. It's been a tough day, all around," Wissemann interrupted, his voice full of remorse. He put a hand on the young pilot's shoulder, his brow narrowing. "Schröder is dead. There's nothing else to be said about it."

"You're right, sir," Gutemann replied, his voice trembling with awkwardness, trying to mask his feelings with an affected smile.

Wissemann clapped Gutemann on the back. "What about you, eh? Good shooting today!"

"Thank you, sir."

"Six victories, is it?"

"Seven, sir," Gutemann corrected.

"Oh? Seven. Right."

Gutemann nodded.

"I'm going to recommend you for the Iron Cross."

"The Iron Cross?" Gutemann gasped.

"Indeed. You've earned it, *Junge*." Wissemann proffered his hand.

Gutemann shook the *Jastafürer's* hand firmly. "Thank you, sir." His face suddenly blushed red, aware that everyone was staring at him—the latest winner of the Iron Cross 1st Class.

"Let's go inside, lads," Wissemann said.

Waiting inside the dispersal tent, *Leutnant* Rudi Bekemeir, the *Jasta* Recording Officer and supply clerk, among other things, labored quietly. Bekemeir typically kept track of the *Jasta's* victories, losses, missions, sorties, transfers, the distribution of alcohol chits and many other seemingly mundane statistics. He compiled the after-action reports and patrol information, writing it all down in the *Jasta's* official logbook. Later, he would send a report to *Kofl*, via courier.

He carefully took down each man's account of the mission and entered in it the logbook in the form of a short narrative. Then the *Jastaführer* scrawled his signature at the bottom to make it all official. Alas, the German Air Service always kept meticulous records!

Wissemann nodded. "Good work today, gentlemen."

"Yes. Excellent work." Bekemeir smiled.

"Let's try to forget about this, but not our fallen comrades."

"Yes, lads," Bekemeir agreed. "Schröder is in a better place now."

"Get some lunch and a nap, men," Wissemann advised. "There will be a volunteer patrol at fifteen hundred hours."

"Another patrol?" Gutemann's eyes brightened.

"I need one man to accompany me on a barrage patrol over the *Chemin des Dames* sector."

Gutemann immediately volunteered. "I'll go—"

"No, Gutemann. You're exempt. Take the rest of the day off."

"I-I'll go, s-sir," Kindlich interceded clumsily.

"Fine. Meet me here at fourteen-thirty."

"*Jawohl, Herr Oberleutnant.*"

"All right, gentlemen. Dismissed."

Gutemann nodded, yet was profoundly disappointed, wanting desperately to fly that mission. He shrugged his shoulders resignedly; perhaps Wissemann was just giving him the day off for all his hard work. Or maybe he was really upset by Schröder's death and didn't want to risk losing his best pilot as well. He wasn't sure. Sometimes he just didn't understand this new *Jastaführer's* reckoning.

The pilots dispersed and headed to mess for lunch.

Wissemann remained a moment to talk to *Leutnant* Bekemeir. "Rudi, please call AFP-7, posthaste," he said. "Make a requisition for a replacement pilot and machine as soon as possible, okay?"

"Right away, sir."

"Please gather Schröder's information, as well."

"Yes, sir."

"And prepare a statement for *Kofl.*"

Bekemeir nodded.

"I'll write his family and collect his personal effects."

"Right."

"Also... put in a recommendation for *Leutnant* Gutemann for the Iron Cross 1st Class. He shot down his sixth and seventh enemy machines today."

"Of course—"

"I witnessed both victories today."

"Right."

"Call *Flugmeldedienst* to corroborate the claims."

"Yes,sir."

"Got all that?"

"Yes, *Herr Oberleutnant.*" Boot heels clicked.

"That's all, then. Carry on."

"Very good, sir." Bekemeir saluted in acknowledgment.

"Thank you, Rudi—"

"Oh, sir..." Bekemeir said, suddenly remembering something. "There's a telegram in Operations for you. It's from Berlin, Schutzling says. I believe it's from your fiancée—Ilse von Linkhof?"

"Really? A telegram?" Wissemann's face lit up. "Ilse?"

"A courier dropped it off about a half-hour ago."

"Excellent!"

"Indeed," Bekemeir saluted and returned to his bookkeeping.

Willi Wissemann absently ignored Bekemeir's salute in his eagerness and dashed off to his office in search of the good news. Finally, some word from Ilse, he thought. I hope everything's all right. It had been a few weeks since he'd last heard from her. The mail and telegraph services to the Front seemed to have slowed to a snail's pace of late, a verity not unusual given the intransigent nature of war.

Moments later, he was standing in Operations. Schutzling was busily pecking away at his typewriter. The mustachioed adjutant knew immediately by the *Jastaführer's* blissful expression that Bekemeir had informed him of the telegram. He smiled.

"It's in your mail slot, sir," he pointed to the *Jasta* mailbox.

"Thank you, Schutzling."

"Sir." Schutzling jerked a nod.

An anxious Willi Wissemann snatched the telegram out of the slot marked—*JASTAFÜHRER*—and ripped open its contents. He strode into his office and closed the door behind him and sat down at his desk. He carefully unfolded the paper telegram. He paused a moment, caught his breath, held it, then sighed blissfully. He read silently...

```
IMPERIAL TELEGRAPH SERVICE
     BERLIN, GERMANY

Lieber Willi:                         15.MAR.1917

    I hope you are well and safe. I am dreadfully worried
about you and miss you very much. Please come home as
soon as you can. I am lonely without you here. I love you
very much darling. Please be careful at the Front!

                                              —Ilse
```

Wissemann read the telegram a second time, gazing at the framed picture of Ilse on his desk, smiling. If she only knew how much he missed her! After he read the note a third time, he folded it up, crammed it back in the envelope, storing it in his top desk draw. He reached into the bottom draw, pulled out a flask of cognac and a shot glass. He poured himself a liberal shot, then picked up the glass, contemplating its contents for a moment before quaffing it down.

Strangely, his mind drifted back to poor Schröder. The warm, blissful recollections of Ilse suddenly faded to regret. He set the glass down, pulled out a sheet of stationary and pen, and thought for a moment. He scribbled a line then paused, thinking back to that fated mission. "Aghh!" He crumpled the paper in a tight wad and swiped it from the desk, accidentally knocking Ilse's picture off the desktop. It hit the floor with a shrill crack, the glass shattering in a hundred shards. The frame was broken too.

"No! Ilse's picture! *Gott!* Willi, you are pathetic," he spouted furiously to himself. "Control yourself, you're acting like a silly little schoolboy."

Schutzling tapped on the door. *"Herr Oberleutnant?"*

"What?"

"Is everything all right in there? I heard glass breaking."

"Yes, yes! E-Everything is fine. Just another one of my clumsy mishaps," Wissemann muttered awkwardly, putting the flask and shot glass back in his desk. He took a deep breath and tried to compose himself.

"Are you sure?"

"Yes!" Wissemann shouted at the closed door.

"All right. I was just a little concerned—"

"Could you bring me Schröder's file, please. A dustpan and broom would be nice too. I have a little mess to clean up in here."

Wissemann bent down to pick up the remnants of the shattered picture frame, fishing the photograph out of the pile of broken glass, gazing thoughtfully at the photograph, realizing suddenly what a lucky man he really was. Marriage was the only answer to this wretchedness he felt. But alas, a wedding seemed so remote now. He was stuck here at the Front in a war with no end in sight.

Schutzling tapped on the door again. *"Herr Oberleutnant?* I have Schröder's file and a broom. Did you know that tomorrow would've been his twentieth birthday?"

Wissemann opened the door. "No, I didn't," he replied, quite discomfited. "I never actually spoke to Schröder—I mean, we never had a friendly conversation."

"Do you want me to write the letter for you?"

Schutzling gave Wissemann the personnel file.

"No. I'll—"

"Sir, I know it's an unpleasant task."

"No, no. I think I can handle it."

"Are you sure?"

"Quite sure. I've done it many times before."

"I did it for *Hauptmann* Traurig. He wasn't good at writing letters."

"No! I'll do it, Schutzling. However unpleasant, it is one of *my* responsibilities." Wissemann exhaled wretchedly. "But thank you, all the same."

Schutzling bowed his head. "As you wish, *Herr Oberleutnant.*"

Wissemann tossed the file on his desk and donned his service cap. "Only twenty? Poor boy," he grumped. Schröder was too young to die.

"Do you want me to sweep up this mess for you?"

"No, no. I'll clean it up later. I'm off to mess. I need to eat a bite."

"Very well, sir. I'm always here if you need me."

A SOPWITH RECONNAISSANCE AEROPLANE crept along at a dawdling 120-kilometers per hour, soaring four thousand meters over the town of Cernay, over a thick overcast. It was on a routine reconnaissance mission. The French observer loaded the cumbersome photographic plates into the surveillance camera and began a pictorial exposé of the city below, working methodically and deliberately, careful to tend to every detail. He occupied the rear seat of the British built biplane, where he could also operate the single Lewis drum-fed machine gun. He tapped the pilot on the shoulder to signify all was ready. The pilot nodded and eased the stick forward and the Sopwith descended into the clouds. A couple of seconds later, it emerged above the city. Eager to complete his work in a timely fashion, the French observer began photographing the shattered landscape below.

The once pastoral township of Cernay, had been pounded into a ruinous, bombed-out breadth of devastation. Its surrounding hills and woods were transformed into a splintered wasteland. Buildings and houses marked on the map as objectives and strong points belonging to local and well-known companies or chateaus, were no more. Like chalk marks wiped from a blackboard, they had wholly vanished from the murdered countryside. As for the stately and grand homesteads which had once given their names to the area, they too had suddenly disappeared, leaving only charred, naked outlines of brick-shattered foundations to mark the fact they'd ever existed.

Months and months of unrelenting bombardment had reduced the small French town into a gutted, pockmarked wilderness of red brick, tile and shattered glass. Cernay, like many other French towns in the region, had endured interminable shelling and destruction.

French Intelligence had ordered the two young Frenchmen in the air to gather information on the German withdrawal. The new French

Commander-in-Chief, General Robert George Nivelle, who had effectively "replaced" Marshal Joffre in December, had devised a new battle plan. The French forces would attack the German Army whilst the British, in the north, played a diversionary role for the offensive. Nivelle planned to use a deep-creeping artillery barrage to neutralize the German defenses and capture the enemy's complete defensive system. The principal attacks would occur at Soissons and Reims. However, dissension between Nivelle and British General Sir Douglas Haig, alerted the German Army of the coming attack. They promptly withdrew their forces to a newly fortified position, dubbing it the "Siefried-Stellung." That withdrawal was nearly complete now.

Not too far away, Willi Wissemann, while adjusting his goggles, spotted the silhouette of the French Sopwith against the opaque cloud base. He was about five hundred meters below it and flying in the opposite direction. He signaled his wingman, Bubi Kindlich, pushed the throttled to maximum, and climbed above four thousand meters. Kindlich flew close and to Wissemann's flank.

The pilot of the Sopwith immediately saw the two Albatroses and alerted his observer. The observer prudently left his camera and readied the Lewis gun. The pilot knew he had little or no chance against two well-armed Albatroses—his Sopwith couldn't out dive the German scout, nor did it have the power in its Clerget engine to climb away. The pilot and his observer would have to stand and fight; there was no other alternative in this gritty Frenchman's mind. He began some evasive maneuvering.

Wissemann turned toward the Sopwith and quickly worked out an angle of attack. He would approach it from slightly below and in the rear, attacking the Sopwith in its blind spot, where the Lewis gun couldn't hurt him. He saw the observer make a slight adjustment to his goggles, then his hands fell to the Lewis. Wissemann open-fired at a hundred meters, and when he got within fifty meters, he fired again. The French pilot cut the throttle and yanked the control stick back. This caused the nose to rise up and the tail to drop, giving his observer a clear field of fire. Wissemann stopped firing, swooped left and under, and was then up under the belly of the Sopwith. His guns stuttered murderously. The Sopwith canted up, and the Lewis spit down in his face. But the gunner's shots were wide. He'd missed.

The Sopwith was a huge silhouette above him for a brief moment, then it was gone. Wissemann's Albatros lurched forward, in front of the stalling Sopwith. The wily French pilot instantaneously advanced the throttle and pushed the control stick forward so that he had Wissemann's Albatros directly in front of him, only fifty meters away.

He took careful aim and fired the single Vickers machine gun. The sudden thumping of that gun was a starting realization for one, Willi Wissemann.

"*Verdammt!* That rascal has a machine gun up front!" he spouted.

If he hadn't known it before, he knew it now—this Sopwith was equipped with a front machine gun. Bullets sailed over his head, their whizzing akin to a swarm of angry bees. A bullet ricocheted off the coolant pipe of the wing-mounted radiator. There was a loud clang, but no apparent damage. Wissemann jerked the Albatros in an abrupt bank, peeling away from the Frenchman's gunfire.

By this time, Bubi Kindlich, right behind the Sopwith, pressed his attack. He caressed the trips of the twin Maxims and the barrels flickered savagely. Bullet strikes flashed all over the fuselage. He saw his tracers pour in the motor and rake the center section. An instant later the propeller disintegrated. Kindlich gave a shout of triumph as the Sopwith's riddled rotary engine coughed, sputtered, and belched black smoke. Kindlich ceased fire, temporally blinded by the smoldering plume, pulled up, and re-sighted his guns.

The fearless French observer was an excellent gunner, seizing the opportunity. He swiveled the Lewis, aimed, and fired, raking a surprised Bubi Kindlich's with exacting accuracy. Bullets smashed the Albatros' windscreen and knocked out one of its twin machine guns. Kindlich wisely broke off his attack, heeled over, upside-down, and tore away in the opposite direction, away from the withering barrage of bullets as the faltering Sopwith turned south for its front lines.

Wissemann yanked his Albatros around. He saw the Sopwith diving in a wide curve, trying to escape back to its own lines, an oily column of black smoke streaming after it. He rode the throttle to full power and raced after the Sopwith two-seater. He squeezed both thumb triggers and a hundred rounds streaked towards the target. He held the triggers down until both guns ceased firing—jammed!

The observer had held his fire until he saw the Albatros' twin machine guns flashing at about a hundred meters. The determined French observer had gotten off a volley too. His bullets found Wissemann's Albatros and the embattled Bavarian heard the—*tick-tick-tick*—of bullets holing it somewhere underneath.

But Wissemann's gunfire was lethal, devastating! Deadly!

He saw the rounds slam into the pilot's back and skull. A halo of pink mist appeared around the pilot's head and then swiftly dissolved in the slipstream. In mortal agony, the pilot jerked back on the stick and the Sopwith pitched upwards until it hung vertically, standing on its tail, stalling. Wissemann zoomed under the Sopwith, his upper wing nearly colliding with the tailplane of the Sopwith.

Suddenly, there was the sobering stench of leaking petrol. Instinctively, Wissemann switched the engine off, preventing a potential fire. The fuel-starved Mercedes sputtered to a halt, its prop windmilling silently, the wind in the wires the only sound now.

The smoking Sopwith flicked into a tailspin, the pilot dead at the controls. The unfortunate observer, pinned in his seat, struggled violently, holding on tightly, bitterly, for the last moments of his life, now in complete terror. He rode the doomed two-seater all the way down to the ground. He had no parachute, nor was he ever issued one. A fatal mistake! The Sopwith crashed on the outskirts of Cernay in a fiery, orange explosion, black smoke curling up in the pale afternoon sky amid an ominous, fireball, the observer dead and burned, the flames of Hell claiming his charred soul for all eternity.

Wissemann glided over the crash site, a feeble bird of prey. Now it was his turn to feel the effects of enemy gunfire, beginning a hapless descent to earth in powerless flight. He circled around a few times as he got closer to the ground, getting a lay of the land, finally spotting a sparsely sown beet field near a muddy highway. At three hundred meters, he began a long and slanting approach. He could see the ground was mostly flat and level near the center of the field, so he tried to steer his damaged bird there.

When he got below one hundred meters, he got a nasty shock. He saw telephone wires stretching across the road, obstructing his glide path. He shoved the control stick forward to avoid the wires but the damaged Albatros responded slackly, no power in its motor. He tore through, shredding the wires like spider webs, careening closer to the ground, much sooner than he'd intended. But the Albatros slewed out of the hasty slip-dive at fifty meters, leveling out under the careful touch of its Bavarian pilot. Up came the nose, but not soon enough.

The Albatros hit tail-low, striking with a resounding crunch, careening jerkily on a wheel, the force of the impact ripping the landing gear completely off, skidded, bounced once, turned sideways, tipped up on its nose, the propeller biting into the earth with a sickening thud, sending dirty snow and splintered wood whipping through the air, tossing Wissemann about violently, his knee slamming into the control stick, finally halting in a cloud of dust.

The broken tail section creaked perilously for a second, hanging, then broke off from the fuselage, crashing to the ground in a dull thud. Wissemann hastily undid the safety harness and crawled out of the wrecked single-seater, the stench of petrol thick and noxious in his nostrils, making him coughed hoarsely. He knew those fumes were intimation to a potential fire!

The wary Bavarian got away from the crashed aeroplane, limping, staggering, stumbling, finally collapsing from exhaustion about fifty paces from the Albatros. His knee throbbed painfully; blood seeped from a nasty gash. He snatched the goggles from his eyes and lay on his back panting, craning his neck to get a look at the wrecked Albatros, then heard the petrol tank ignite with a vile—*WOOF!*

The shattered Albatros began to burn, hot flames crackling and snapping with increasing ferocity. Soon a cloud of smoke boiled high in the sky. Wissemann frowned and shook his head warily.

"F-Flames," he gasped, anxious and full of dread. "*Gott!* Those damn telephone wires almost caused me to roast!" He closed his eyes and thanked Providence for sparing his life once again.

Kindlich's Albatros thundered by overhead. The youngster rocked his wings and flipped a brisk salute as he soared by. A relieved smile beamed from his pale face. He was glad the *Jastaführer* was alive. Willi Wissemann, still flat on his backside, could only manage a halfhearted wave, his trembling hand fluttering feebly.

As the rumble of Kindlich's Albatros faded away, Wissemann heard something else now, something troubling. He lay very still in that patchy beet field, breathing quietly, suddenly fearful of being captured. In his zeal to get his damaged Albatros earthbound, he'd forgotten to check his position over the front lines. Had he crash-landed in enemy territory? He heard the frantic banter of nearby voices... frantic, unrecognizable banter. Wissemann cursed.

"*Verdammt,* Willi! Where in the hell are you?"

Passed by FlugM Censor # 2701
Frau A.W. Schröder
c/o 7th Army Headquarters Laon
Jagdstaffel 23, Pusieux Ferme
Berlin (Please forward)

Liebe Frau Schröder   15.Mar.1917

    It is my sad duty to inform you that your son,
Stefan Schröder, was killed in action today. His
enduring dedication to his duty was an inspiration to
all of us. He served the Fatherland with fervor and zeal
beyond the expectations of the average soldier. His warm
smile and easygoing nature will not be forgotten. Stefan
was a dutiful officer and a good pilot; he always gave a
good account of himself in the battles he participated
in. Not once, ever, did he shy aware from danger or
disobey a direct order. Stefan was an exemplary aviator,
a young man you can be proud of, a German of good stock.
Do not fret; young Stefan did not suffer. He was killed
instantly, painlessly. I saw his final moment with my
own eyes, and that is the plain truth. I give you my
word as an officer and a gentleman.
    Unfortunately, he was shot down behind the enemy's
front lines, so the Army could not retrieve his body.
But rest assured, the French will bury his body and give
him a decent burial. Although we are their sworn
enemies, combatants on the field of warfare, the French
still recognize honor and propriety. I am positive of
this! I know this is not much solace for you; I
sympathize with your bereavement. You have my deepest
apologies. Your regret is mine. I will miss young
Stefan, as I miss my own fallen brother. I have reserved
my most tender thoughts for you, in your hour of great
despair. Please accept my most humble condolences.

Signed: *Oblt. W. R. Wissemann*
Oblt. Wilhelm R.Wissemann

Chapter 12

MARCH 19, 1917. WILLI WISSEMANN LAY awake in bed, his right knee still aching from the crash landing three days earlier. In the near distance, he could hear the nightly overture of artillery guns. This was a prelude to the long awaited French offensive, a protracted and terrifying declaration of the imminent assault. Artillery barrages of heavy 75-millimeter and 155-millimeter field guns were pounding German positions everywhere along the Front. Pulling himself from the bed, a weary Willi Wissemann limped to the balcony doors overlooking the courtyard. Along the horizon, he could see lights flashing, the telling signs of the artillery barrage. He lit a candle then a cigarette and stepped out on to the balcony. The air was cold and damp; a light breeze blew across the field. Wissemann stood in silence, clad in silk piebald pajamas, puffing the cigarette. The faint thundering and sporadic flickering illuminating the skyline was reminiscent of an outlying thunderstorm. It reminded him of his infantry days in the front lines; the early phases of trench warfare...

MAY 1915, THE SECOND BATTLE OF ARTOIS. Attached to the Bavarian 1st Reserve Battalion of the German Sixth Army as an executive officer, *Leutnant* Willi Wissemann waded in ankle-deep water, cowering anxiously in the muddy trench, as countless 75-millimeter shells whistled by overhead.

"*Leutnant! Leutnant!*" A grimy sergeant bellowed. "We must fall back to the secondary trenches, take up a defensive position or we'll be overrun by the French infantry!"

Willi Wissemann, tired, dirty and hungry, stood rigidly, his 9-millimeter Luger clenched in a mud-caked hand. He glared at the noncom with flinty eyes. "Stand fast, *Feldwebel!* Fix bayonets! We hold this position until reinforced!" Wissemann had to shout; the artillery barrage was deafening.

The bewildered noncom grimaced. "But sir! We'll be slaughtered if we don't withdraw to the secondary trenches!"

"We're getting slaughtered now, *Feldwebel!* We can't retreat any farther. We have to make a stand here. Hold the line!"

"But the *Hauptmann* said—"

"He's dead. I'm in command now!

"But *Leutnant*—"

"Get your fat ass down the line, *Feldwebel!* Spread the word! The French are coming!" The battle-hardened Bavarian shoved the portly sergeant backwards, knocking the *Picklehaube* helmet from his head. The stunned noncom gasped, fear in his eyes. Wissemann was making threatening gestures with his Luger.

"Pick it up. Move out, soldier!"

"Sir—"

"That's an order!" Wissemann had an insane look in his eyes.

The noncom cautiously picked up his helmet and moved away.

"*Herr Leutnant*—"

"MOVE OUT!" Wissemann cocked the Luger.

"*Jawohl! Jawohl!*" The startled noncom bolted down the trench, helmet in hand, quickly disappearing in the mist.

Then the artillery barrage ceased. Wissemann holstered his Luger and stared into a pair of field glasses affixed to the parapet, bracing himself for the assault. "Get ready men! Here they come!"

After a long, tense silence, Wissemann heard the distant crackle of German machine guns barking as advancing enemy troops began to tramp forward. All along the German trench line soldiers began firing their rifles. There was heavy ground fog that day, and it obscured the battlefield. It was difficult to see the advancing enemy troops in the haze. But facing the Germans that day were the French 33rd and 20th Corps. They stormed the German trenches and both armies soon became locked in bloody hand-to-hand combat.

Wissemann, standing flush with the parapet, seized a rifle, aimed, and fired. He picked off a Frenchman as he tried to breech the cordon of barbed wire, then fired again, and dropped another one; the *Poilus* were now advancing past the escarpment. He fell back to the opposite side of the trench when the French infantry flooded into the line, stabbing one with his bayonet. The soldier shrieked in agony and tumbled down in the muddy water. Wissemann bashed him in the back of the head with his rifle butt; his head cracked open like an eggshell. Blood spurted on Wissemann's face and uniform. Another Frenchman jabbed him from behind with a bayonet. He cried out in anguish, spun around, slammed the rifle butt squarely across the Frenchman's jaw, knocking him to the ground. Wissemann pulled the trigger, but the rifle jammed. He flung it down, drew his 9-millimeter Luger, and pumped three rounds into the dazed soldier. Another Frenchman came at him and he popped off three more rounds at him. He fell dead too. Wissemann crawled out of the trench and could see in the hazy mist, the silhouette of thousands of advancing enemy soldiers. He hadn't noticed that he was bleeding from the stab wound —he couldn't feel anything at that moment. He grabbed the whistle hanging around his neck and blew it three times.

"*WITHDRAW! WITHDRAW! RETREAT!*" he raged.

A bloodied, delirious Bavarian officer rallied his men back in retreat, hurling blasting expletives like a rapid fire cannon, hoarsely ordering his men to higher ground. He fired off two more rounds at the advancing Frenchmen, then withdrew to safer ground, trudging laboriously in the muddy terrain.

After an grueling trek, he made it back to the German rear trench, rounds whizzing by him all the while. He paused there a moment, gasping for breath, observing the hellish scene. Nearby, a German machine gun crew rattled off round after round, covering the German withdrawal with deadly accuracy. French riflemen dropped dead or wounded all along the overrun trench line. It was a massacre.

Wissemann retreated still further, to a reserve trench, just short of the high ground near Neuville-Saint Vaast, stumbling into a communications dugout, collapsing breathlessly, exhausted, spent, too tired to continue. He sat down on the ground, his head drooping wearily. A soldier approached him, noticing his bloody tunic. He grabbed Wissemann by the shoulder, bellowing for a stretcher-bearer.

"*Achtung! Sanitätsdienst! Achtung!*" the soldier shouted. "Hang on, sir! They'll be here in a moment!"

Wissemann threw off the man's arm and stood up, leveling hostile red eyes, seizing him by the coat lapels and shaking him violently. "*Verdammt!* I don't need a goddamned medico!" he roared. "Get on that blasted field telephone, why don't you! Call up Army, already! Now! I need reinforcements! Reinforcements! Reinforcements..."

"HERR OBERLEUTNANT, snap out of it!"

"Huh?"

"The French are here!"

"What did you say?" Wissemann stood dazed for a moment.

Inexplicably, *Feldwebel* Schutzling had suddenly materialized before him in a nightshirt and jackboots, shaking him briskly from his delirious reverie.

"Herr Oberleutnant! The French are here! Air raid!"

"Air raid?" Wissemann muttered dazedly, then awoke to full consciousness, spouting: *"AIR RAID!* Sound the alarm!"

The languid look had gone from his countenance. He'd been startled out of a nightmare and the bloody business of the past. His eyes were narrowed and hard now. He quickly followed Schutzling down the stairs, taking a pair of trousers with him. Outside he could hear the buzzing of aircraft and the stutter of machine guns.

Stopping at the bottom of the narrow staircase, Wissemann pulled the trousers on and popped the braces over his shoulders. He could hear the air raid siren wailing, putting the entire aerodrome on high alert. The now fully awake *Jastaführer* limped barefoot out the side door of the chateau, padding down the cobblestone walkway leading to the hangar area. The entire aerodrome was a scattered mass of frantic personnel. The crackling of machine gun fire echoed all across the aerodrome. The *crump-crump* of exploding bombs shook the ground. A hundred meters above him, a low-flying French two-seater suddenly roared by. Wissemann dashed for cover.

"Over here, sir!" *Leutnant* Gutemann yelled.

He was firing from one of the aerodrome's two machine gun emplacements. He blasted away at the unseen enemy, hosing the night sky with a 7.92 Parabellum machine gun. Angry tracers leaped across the sky, spent shells sprang from the smoking breech like a carnival popcorn machine. As Willi Wissemann hurtled the low sandbag wall surrounding the machine gun emplacement, landing on the slushy ground inside, he suddenly realized he'd run out barefoot. He cursed his stupidity and took cover behind the sandbags. The frosty turf crunched between his toes.

Gott! A fine night to go out on a barefoot stroll!

"Hmm, nice pajamas, Wissemann," Gutemann quipped.

"Have they done any damage yet?" Wissemann asked, not really hearing Gutemann's sardonic comment. "What's going on?"

"Hangar-2 was hit, sir."

"Verdammt!"

"But nothing was in it," Gutemann answered then continued firing the machine gun. "I don't think the French were wise to it."

"Idiotic snail-eaters!" Wissemann snarled.

"Can you hand me another magazine, sir? This one's almost out."

"Of course." Wissemann nodded.

He grabbed a magazine of 7.92 ammo, carrying it over to Gutemann. Another French machine zoomed down low, dropping a brace of bombs. There was a shrill whistling, then a thunderous roar. Wissemann could feel the earth shake through the soles of his bare feet. The ground erupted skyward and a fountain of earth rained down on top of the two men.

"Ach! That was too close!" Otto Gutemann howled, reloading the machine gun. He rose from his crouch and said to Wissemann: "Here, sir. Take over! I'm going to see if I can get airborne and knock one of these bastards down."

"Right!

"Wish me luck!" Gutemann leaped over the sandbag emplacement and raced toward Hangar-1, where he saw Peltzer and his crew pulling out his Albatros.

The barefooted Bavarian grabbed hold of the machine gun and started firing at the darkened silhouettes that buzzed overhead. A second later, Eckhardt and Winkler, both with smoking rifles in their hands, joined him. They hid behind the sandbags, taking pot shots at the swarming French two-seaters flying above them.

The wily Willi Wissemann scanned the sky, thinking.

He guessed the French squadron must have taken off in the darkened predawn hours and traversed German territory undetected. The French bombing squadron—single-engine Caudron two-seaters—assaulted the aerodrome like a swarm of angry bees circling round and round an agitated beehive. Their likely mission was harassment—harry the sleepy German aerodrome with small incendiary bombs and machine gun fire. Their main objective, Wissemann quickly realized, was to damage or destroy the aerodrome's main hangars and fuel dumps. This kind of thing was probably occurring at other German aerodromes too. This was in preparation for the French offensive.

Wissemann muttered a bitter curse.

A few paces away, Gutemann climbed in his idling Albatros and commenced takeoff procedures, Peltzer standing by at the ready. A Caudron made a diving bomb run on the aerodrome, releasing two bombs close to Gutemann's sputtering Albatros. The bombs exploded in a fiery blast of shrapnel, sending lead slugs ripping through the canvas wings of the Albatros, puncturing the gas tank. Peltzer leaped for cover, taking a fragment in the leg while diving away. Gutemann squirmed out of the cockpit, petrol squirting all over his legs and flying suit. He fell to the ground, stumbling to his feet as another bomb went off close by, destroying a supply truck parked near the Operations hut. The fair-haired young Swabian leopard-crawled away on hands and knees, all the way to the other machine gun emplacement, finally huddling behind some stacked sand bags, where *Leutnant* Bekemeir crouched behind the other machine gun, hammering away at the unseen French attackers.

"Take that, *Herr Rothosen!*" he spouted angrily.

Gutemann grinned wryly, gazing at his petrol soaked flying suit. "Ach! My new suit, ruined! Some wake-up call this turned out to be!"

Paying Gutemann no mind, Bekemeir grit his teeth anxiously, scanning the sky above, calmly lighting a cigarette, then slapped another magazine in the Parabellum. He locked his sights on the faint outline of another enemy machine, tracing it along the night sky, sighting it carefully, firing a long volley of tracer rounds. The flashing bullets arced upward, slamming into the French Caudron. Rudi Bekemeir watched in delight as the bullets struck, sparkling luminously against the engine cowling of the enemy aeroplane, ringing a neat little tune. The Caudron, apparently badly damaged, limped away, smoke trailing from its engine.

"Run, run, you slimy snail-eaters!" Bekemeir exclaimed, shaking a fist. "Run for home now!"

Then, one by one, all the Caudrons turned away and climbed for higher altitude, their machine guns spent, their bombs all dropped. And as the uproar slowly subsided, the French motors becoming a swiftly decreasing rumble, they soon disappeared in the predawn light leaving a wrecked and smoldering aerodrome in their wake.

AS THE SUN PEERED over the horizon, shedding more light onto the condition of the battered airfield, Wissemann could see the destruction fully. He had damage reports in hand as well now. He soon discovered that, though caught by surprise, the aerodrome had suffered only moderate damage—one old hangar destroyed, one utility truck destroyed, two aircraft damaged. The field itself had experienced the worst destruction. Pockmarked with numerous small craters and clumps of earth, up and down its length, it seemed doubtful to this *Jastaführer* that it would be operational today.

Peltzer was the only man injured in the attack. But his wound was negligible. It would keep him out of action for maybe a day or two.

The *Jasta's* dignity and sense of pride were the only real casualties. It was a "morale raid" designed to dampen German *esprit de corps.* Several pilots called for reprisals. But the cadre had been confined to just shaking their fists and swearing, muttering implacable threats of reprisal, mere blustered posturing.

Willi Wissemann shook his head in disgust and limped back to his quarters. He made his way up the stairs, strode into his room, and got ready for the day's duties. His feet were freezing cold from exposure; it could bring on a wretched chilblain if he didn't get them warmed up soon. And of course, he chagrined, the day's flight operations would probably be suspended, unless the field could be patched up quickly. And that... was doubtful.

"*Verdammt!*" he swore. "More difficulties!"

THIRTY MINUTES LATER... Willi Wissemann was sitting on his bed, rolling on his puttees, getting ready for the day, when he heard a knock on the door.

"Enter," he said.

It was Schutzling. "*Herr Oberleutnant—*" he said in a hesitant tone.

"What is it, Schutzling?"

Wissemann finished rolling his puttees and stood up.

"I know this is probably not a good time to mention this..."

"Now what?"

"But you told me to remind you of *Oberst* Thomson's inspection—scheduled for Wednesday."

"*Um Gottes Willen!* What time? This place is a shambles!"

"Thirteen hundred hours, sharp. After mess."

Wissemann began polishing his boots then slammed the brush down irately. "Inspection? Bah! What else could possibly go wrong?"

"And, uh... *Kofl* called a few minutes ago."

"*Kofl?* What—"

"He wants a barrage patrol over the Front by, oh-seven hundred."

"Of course! They want a patrol over the Front! *Gott!* Don't they know the situation here?" Wissemann jerked his boots on and began lacing them up.

"Yes, *Herr Oberleutnant,* they do. But—"

"What's our status, Schutzling?" Wissemann got up from his footlocker and reached for his shirt hanging on the bedpost.

"Actually, *Herr Oberleutnant,* the men have already started filling in the craters and moving some of the debris off the tarmac. We should be able to get a *Kette* airborne for the mission."

"Really?" Wissemann was quite surprised.

"Yes, sir. Only one machine suffered serious damage."

"Only one?"

"Those Frenchies didn't really do a thorough job, sir. They never even came close to the fuel dumps. I don't think they were really equipped for night operations."

"Hah, they could have fooled me."

"Their attack seemed clumsy—more random and uncoordinated."

"I see. Did Eckhardt's *Kette* suffer any casualties or damage?" Wissemann shrugged a shirt over his shoulders and pushed his arms through the sleeves.

"No. Only Gutemann's Albatros was damaged."

"Oh."

"Eckhardt said his *Kette* will be ready. He personally assured me."

Wissemann smiled. Schutzling's poise certainly amazed him. The bristling Bavarian buttoned his shirt and tugged at the sleeves. He stretched the suspenders over his shoulders and put his tunic on, methodically cinching up all eight brass buttons. The *Jastaführer* nodded confidently. Now he was ready for the day.

"Okay. Brief them on the barrage patrol, Schutzling."

"Yes, sir."

"Then get me some availability reports—"

"Of course."

"Meet me at mess in thirty minutes. We'll sort out this chaos."

"Jawohl, Herr Oberleutnant."

Boot heels clicked. Schutzling departed.

Wissemann stared in the mirror and combed his tussled hair. *"Ach,* I'll need a haircut," he said, scowling crossly. Then testing his French, said: *"Tu veux ma photo?"* He stroked the stubble on his chin, grimaced, reached for his shaving kit and began stropping his razor.

✠

AT MESS. "Now. Proceed to here, *Leutnant* Eckhardt, to Filain," Schutzling said, pointing to the grid map coordinates of the little French village. "Then, fly east—here, following the *Chemin de Dames* all the way to Craonne. Try to stay below two thousand meters."

"Right. Stay below two thousand meters," Eckhardt parroted.

"Enemy scouts have been harassing our troop columns along the road, *here....* making it very difficult for our supply trucks to get through."

"Right." Eckhardt nodded.

"Keep those enemy scouts off their backs! Got it?"

"Got it." Eckhardt cleared his throat gawkily. "Uh, Schutzling... I'm one man short, though."

"One man short?"

"Schäfer went on sick call this morning. Says he's got an 'ear infection'."

"Bean breeze! Ear infection, my eye," *Leutnant* Neubauer growled. "That sorry son-of-a-bitch is just hung over again!"

"Oh. Hung over." Schutzling replied, though not really surprised.

"He stumbled in from the *Kasino* on a late night bender," Neubauer imparted bitterly.

"*Ja! He* woke me up too," Fleischer added.

Schutzling yawned. "That's not surprising—"

"Came in at three in the morning."

Neubauer scoffed. "What a katzenjammered old cock!"

"And he owes me a lot of money," Fleischer threw in, adding insult to injury.

"*Lieber Gott!*" Schutzling snapped, shaking his head. "Will you ladies calm down!"

"Well, whatever the reason," *Leutnant* Eckhardt enjoined calmly, "he's in no condition to fly."

"Is he ever?" Fleischer scoffed.

"Who can replace him?" Eckhardt shrugged. "We could just fly as three, I suppose."

As the four men deliberated over Schäfer's condition, the *Jastaführer* appeared suddenly, pushing through the mess kitchen door, armed with his first cup of coffee of the day. He walked up to the table. Four men stirred to respectfully rise to attention but Wissemann forestalled their efforts with a halting hand.

"At ease, gentlemen." He sat down next to Schutzling, facing the other three men. "Have you worked out the details for the patrol yet?" he asked and sipped his coffee.

"Yes, sir, they have," Schutzling replied glumly. "Just one problem, though..."

"Oh? What's that?"

"Schäfer."

"Hmm... Schäfer, again." Wissemann groaned.

He was well aware of Schäfer's bibulous exploits by this time. Josef Schäfer was the *Jasta's* official drunkard. Every unit seemed to have one. He was a hard-boiled, hard-living alcoholic—something about him suggested violence. He often flew patrols in a hung over state or even quite inebriated. But it didn't seem to impinge on his flying skills. Schäfer may have had the reputation of an outlandish drunk, but he was still a competent and seasoned veteran with plenty of nerve—a pilot of steel resolve.

"We need a replacement, *Herr Oberleutnant*," Schutzling said.

"Right. A replacement." Wissemann stroked his chin cagily.

"We can't pull anyone from the escort flight either. They're already short a man, too."

The *Jastaführer* thought for a moment, his eyes kindling, grinning fearlessly. True, his knee was still hurting somewhat. Although the stitches were gone, a nasty scab still festered. But he didn't want anyone to know that. Moreover, he didn't want to appear weak and wounded or lose face with the men. He knew exactly who was going to fly in Schäfer's place, nodding, confident in his own abilities.

"All right. I will go," the battered Bavarian declared boldly. "Fleischer, will you fly as my wingman?"

"Um... of course. Certainly, sir," Fleischer replied, a bit surprised.

"What about your knee?" Schutzling asked. "Do you think it's healed yet?"

That was a damned good question; everyone was a bit stunned. They'd all heard the *Jastaführer* complain more than once in the last few days about the pain in his knee.

Schutzling was especially stunned. "Sir?"

Wissemann stroked his knee gingerly and slapped his thigh as if to show everyone he was okay. "It's fine! A little tender maybe. But I'll be all right. Don't you worry."

Schutzling and the three pilots exchanged quizzical glances. The red-headed adjutant shrugged apathetically. "Fair enough then. Takeoff is at oh-seven hundred, sir."

"Excellent." Wissemann jerked a nod.

"The *Jastaführer* will lead the patrol," Schutzling said. "That all right with you, Eckhardt?"

"All right by me," Eckhardt replied in a spiritless tone.

"I'll brief you, sir, on the details of the cleanup operation before you depart for the mission," Schutzling said, looking at his pocket watch. It was almost 0600-hours. "We've got an hour yet before takeoff, sir."

"*Wunderbar*, Schutzling," Willi Wissemann said and then turned to the gathered pilots. "Dismissed, gentlemen. That will be all."

The pilots rose dutifully and shuffled off to the dispersal tent.

Wissemann and Schutzling remained. They talked quietly.

"Sir..." Schutzling began, "I have a probable explanation for Schäfer's more than usual drunken behavior."

"Oh?"

"Yes, sir. We recently received word from Graves Registration on the demise of Schäfer's brother Johann. He was killed during an artillery barrage. Apparently, there wasn't much left of his mangled corpse when they buried him in some rotten mass grave. Schäfer's been extremely distraught ever since," Schutzling remarked, rather matter-of-factly.

"Really?" Wissemann pursed his lips dubiously. "Well, that might account for *some* of his behavior, I suppose."

"They were evidently very close. They were twins, I understand."

"Identical?"

Schutzling nodded.

"Twins, eh?"

"Just imagine—two Schäfers? Ach! One is trouble enough."

"Yes, a difficult thing, losing one's brother." Wissemann sighed.

"He's been very out of sorts, sir."

"I can imagine." Wissemann stared off into space, now in deep thought. He was thinking of his own long-lost brother.

"Sir, it's only a guess, but I believe he's very upset."

"I know."

"Perhaps you can let it go, sir? Just this time?"

"Okay. I'll let it go," he replied absently. "But just this time."

Josef Schäfer's demise brought back some painful memories. Wissemann's thoughts drifted back to another time, during the first weeks of the war—August '14—when he'd endured twenty agonizing days of worry after receiving news that his brother had gone missing in action. For three solid weeks there had been no news of his brother's whereabouts. Then, late one evening, a courier found Wissemann sitting in a dingy dugout deep in the trenches. Tired and dirty, eating his rations of beans and bread in the sweltering August heat, the exhausted Bavarian officer sat in solitary silence. At first he thought this little disturbance was just another order from Divisional Headquarters. He told the courier where he could "stick it." However, the courier insisted he read the letter. Wissemann snatched the letter from the courier's hand. He ripped open the envelope. It was from Graves Registration. His heart sank; he immediately realized his brother's fate. He sat stone-faced as he read the communiqué, finally learning the fate of his younger brother Christian. His brother had died in a British field hospital, wounded, captured in the Battle of Mons. Christian Wissemann was buried in an unnamed military cemetery somewhere in Flanders.

Wissemann wept. He thought of his poor mother. She would be

devastated. After losing her husband to cancer the year before, now she had lost her youngest son to a war she didn't understand. Poor *Mutti!* Wissemann whimpered. Later, when he visited her on his first leave, during Christmas, the grieving *Frau* Wissemann pleaded with her only living son to transfer out of the infantry if he could. Respectfully, Willi Wissemann promised her he would try to transfer into the newly forming Air Service. He eventually did apply for aviation training, after putting it off for many months due to a painstaking recovery from wounds received at the battle of Artois. Even so, he warned her, he knew the dangers aviators faced were just as hazardous as the infantry. But it was enough for her. She had entertained secret hopes back then that the war would end before he could complete his training. She knew not the hazards facing the fledgling German Air Service, during those incipient phases of aviation, where mechanical failure and human error accounted for more casualties than aerial combat ever did. In the end, he decided, it proved to be the wise choice. *Mutti* was right, once again!

In a calm Bavarian accent that didn't betray in the slightest degree the regret within him, he said: "Find out if Schäfer is eligible for leave, Schutzling."

"Leave, *Herr Oberleutnant?*" Schutzling replied, a surprised look on his pale face.

"Yes, leave. I'll approve two weeks. I think I know what he's been going through."

"Okay. I'll check his file, sir." Schutzling's surprise had blossomed into astonishment; he still couldn't figure out this *Jastaführer's* modis operandi.

"By the way, how is Peltzer? Was he badly injured?"

"No. Just a flesh wound, sir—in the thigh."

"Oh. Good."

"I sent him to a field hospital to have it patched up, sir. He could be back this afternoon."

"Excellent. Now we've got to get this rotten disaster area cleaned up. *Verdammte Rothosen!*

Schutzling nodded and moaned, sinking into a bitter reverie. Yes! What a damned mess it was. And there was still *Oberst* Thomsen's upcoming inspection too; no one was looking forward to that. The aerodrome was in total chaos after the Frenchmen's bombing attack. He secretly wished the inspection were under better circumstances. This was just the kind of thing Thomsen would hold against them—a bombed-out aerodrome.

He sighed. "And there's still Thomsen's inspection, mind you, sir."

"And this place is a bloody shambles," Wissemann grumbled. "*Gott!* Thomsen is going to have a field day."

"Probably so." Schutzling's foxy mustache twitched resentfully. "He'll try to find fault wherever he can—nasty, old son-of-a-bitch!"

Wissemann's eyes flickered with astonishment. He gazed at the red-faced, glowering adjutant, a little surprised by the embittered outburst. "Well, there is nothing to be done about it now. See that repairs continue while I'm out, Schutzling."

"*Jawohl, Herr Oberleutnant.* Good hunting." Schutzling got up from the table and headed out to the Operations hut.

Wissemann sat for a moment and then patted his tender knee and winced. His lips twisted painfully. "*Hals-und Beinbruch,* you old fool," he quipped and rose from the table, sauntering off to the dispersal hut. It was time to "clock-in." Time to earn his pay.

TWO DAYS LATER, the *Staffel's* relentless patrols over the Champagne had yielded only one enemy engagement; Eckhardt's *Kette* shot down a French two-seater, another ancient Farman artillery spotter. It was officially credited to *Leutnant* Neubauer. It was his second victory. Wissemann flew five sorties with his *Kette* during that span, and he never fired his machine guns once. The French squadrons had inexplicably curtailed their incursions over German territory. This was frustrating and Wissemann accepted it quite reluctantly.

FlugM had issued an intelligence communiqué days before, stating that the *Jastas* might experience a sudden lull in enemy air activity. Air Intelligence claimed the French didn't want to reveal their intentions so conspicuously by sending waves of reconnaissance aircraft over the lines. This would surely reveal their hand—a blatant announcement for an offensive. Wissemann had to laugh; every man down to the lowest potato-head knew an attack was coming. But by some unfathomable reasoning, the French wanted to pretend it was still a big secret. Did they really believe they'd fooled the German High Command?

Wissemann's "new" Albatros was performing well; it was actually Schäfer's machine, the oldest in the *Jasta.* Wissemann had adopted it after Schäfer left for leave a day earlier. Schäfer, looking forward to a much welcome respite from flying, took a train to his hometown, Volklingen, where he'd lived and labored as a steelworker before the war. Wissemann noted with pleasure that the aerodrome seemed a bit more at ease without the gritty noncom's presence.

The old Albatros, refitted with a new Mercedes engine, had more power than some of the newer machines of the *Staffel*—some of Peltzer's mechanical handiwork, Wissemann concluded. The old Albatros bore the scars of numerous enemy engagements as well as Schäfer's personal insignia, a cartoonish arm and hammer, smashing an absurd-looking snail.

It amused Wissemann how each pilot had their own symbol painted on the fuselage of their machines: Gutemann's blue firedrake and coat of arms; Kindlich's Edelweiss; Frankenberg's Star of David; Eckhardt's black and white "Yin-Yang." Neubauer's machine had a totally original design—a fountain pen breaking a sword in half. This, he explained, was the proverbial aphorism: "The pen be mightier then the sword." Prandzynski typically had nothing painted on his machine since he rarely flew the same aircraft more than a week. Winkler had a curious good luck symbol painted on his bird—a Hakenkreuz—something he'd apparently picked up during a family vacation in the Far East. The rest of the *Jasta* just used plain letters or stripes on their machines. Auersbach, the old-timer, for instance, had a giant-sized white letter "A" stenciled on his fuselage. Hah! How original, Wissemann mused ironically.

And he too, had considered a symbol for his machine. Maybe something silly like a bleeding heart might be appropriate—for his enduring love for Ilse. However, his original machine, wrecked in the crash landing, was written off, burnt to a cinder. He awaited a new machine from AFP-7. Till then, he would have to be content with Schäfer's "Snail" until a new machine was available for the *Jasta*.

By this time in the war, all German *Jagdstaffeln* had begun painting their aircraft in garish shades, most notably von Richthofen's *Jasta 11*. After von Richthofen's inspiring success and glaring red Albatros scout, *"Le Petit Rouge"*, his unit followed suit, and the entire *Jasta* was daubed in red too. Each *Jasta 11* pilot, however, retained some personal color besides the scarlet tint, applying a secondary color somewhere on the nose or tail assembly for personal identification. Only the great Manfred von Richthofen's Albatros remained entirely blood red. It was well known along the front lines over Flanders and the Somme.

Privately, Wissemann thought the red color was utterly ridiculous and in bad taste. He'd originally forbidden the *Jasta* to decorate their machines with gaudy paint jobs or emblems. However, he'd relented a little, allowing the pilots individual symbols for their aeroplanes with the limitation they restrain their designs to the fuselage. He promised them more latitude once the *Staffel* became equipped with the new Albatros D.III. However, Wissemann soon realized, allowing these minor liberties contributed immeasurably to morale. The pilots seemed happier and more at ease. They felt like the aeroplane really belonged to them—like a sports car or favorite horse. Except for the personal adornments, the Albatroses and Halberstadts retained their dull factory finishes—green and brown wing surfaces with all-natural wood-varnished or canvas fuselages. But Wissemann soon realized, the personal markings could identify each pilot's machine during wild melees over the Front. During the heat of a dogfight it wasn't always apparent who was who.

The markings seemed to remedy that problem.

Today, *Oberleutnant* Willi Wissemann sat at his desk reviewing the dossiers of three new replacements that had come in that morning. He scanned over their files, scrutinizing every detail, carefully noting each pilot's service record. The first two, Ziegler and Baer, were a couple of tyros from 7th Army *Flugpark*. The third, one *Leutnant* Heinrich Luddenvoss, a Saxon, was transferring in from *Jasta 24*, a unit currently operating at Mörchingen, in the Alsace-Lorraine.

The first two replacements were typical recruits sent by FEA— fresh young lion cubs full of piss and vinegar. Neither one possessed extraordinary flying skills, according to their dossiers. And neither man had any combat experience. However, the latter, *Leutnant* Luddenvoss, was already a veteran with five confirmed victories. This man also claimed another five victories, but *Idflieg* could not confirm these. All his victories were against enemy scouts. Luddenvoss obviously did not waste his time going after lumbering two-seaters. Instead, he preferred sparring with Spads and Nieuports. Although his stellar combat record seemed to speak for itself, his personal conduct did not. According to his former commander, he preferred to fly alone and hunt the enemy, avoiding *Jasta* patrol formations if he could. He didn't like to follow Army regulations either. "He comes and goes as he pleases," *Jastaführer* von Braun had written in the personnel file. "A dangerous man in the air and on the ground."

Nonetheless, the surly Saxon was apparently a dead shot and an excellent pilot with unparalleled acrobatic skills and a keen eye. Why transfer to this unit? Wissemann wondered. He read further and found this Luddenvoss chap to be a hard drinker and a womanizer. It seems he allegedly raped a young French girl in a neighboring town, and was also involved in several brawls with town locals, not to mention his own *Jasta* mates. He was an incorrigible nonconformist.

Wissemann shook his head, sighing wearily. "Why does trouble always find its way to me?"

Schutzling appeared in the doorway, knocking. *"Herr Oberleutnant,* the replacements are waiting outside. Also—I just got word from 7th Army *Kofl.* General von Hoeppner will also be present at this inspection. He's riding in with *Oberst* Thomsen. They'll both arrive at twelve hundred, sharp." The red-headed adjutant sounded nervous, his mustache twitching restlessly.

"General von Hoeppner?"

Schutzling nodded, grinning sickly. Wissemann stiffened, stood up, glanced at his pocket watch—1148 hours—grabbed his leather jacket and cap, and made his way to the door.

"Twelve? I thought the inspection was scheduled for thirteen hundred?"

Schutzling shrugged his shoulders. "Change of plans, *Herr Oberleutnant?*"

"Thomsen, that old schemer. Whatever!" Wissemann snapped. He exhaled wearily. "Assemble the men in parade formation."

"Already done, sir."

"Where would I be without you, Schutzling?"

Schutzling didn't say a word; he winked.

Wissemann nodded in genuine appreciation. He donned his cap and tramped out of Operations and marched across the field. The weather was damp, noticing the gathering gray clouds above his head, realizing some nasty weather was on its way. Schutzling paced close behind him, stepping in unison with his *Jastaführer.* It was now ten minutes to twelve when Wissemann approached the assembling group of men that comprised the rag-tag cadre of *Jasta 23.*

"*JAGDSTAFFEL TWENTY-THREE... ACH-TUNG!*" Schutzling barked.

The assembled *Jasta* personnel staggered to attention in a graceless unsynchronized movement. The weary Bavarian officer surveyed the formation of men with a discriminating eye. What a motley collection of oddballs, he thought. There's not a complete or regulation uniform amongst them. But Wissemann knew there was no standardized dress code for the *Luftstreitkräfte,* and each noncom or officer still wore the traditional uniform of his former branch of service. Yet they were still expected to adhere to the basic policies of military protocol; the usual spit and polish reserved for inspections was still a requirement.

Wissemann groaned, he didn't see too much of that.

And standing shoulder to shoulder, in a separate formation, stood two of the three new replacements, the third apparently still in transit. The two lion cubs stood rigidly at attention. Wissemann jerked a nod, directing his adjutant to give the next command.

Schutzling shouted: "*STAND AT... EASE!*"

The gathered formation fell into a more relaxed posture.

The *Jastaführer* then individually addressed each one of the new replacements. The first man bolted to attention and popped off a crisp salute when his new commander addressed him. Wissemann returned the salute, then shook the youngster's hand and gave him a few words of encouragement. The same exchange was repeated with the second man. Both lads seemed like decent chaps, he realized. But Willi Wissemann was already worrying that they lacked the requisite aggressiveness typically seen in a successful German *Jagdflieger*.

Only time would tell.

AS WILLI WISSEMANN was preparing to give an informal inspection of his *Jasta*, a grungy, mud-spattered officer was racing down the Charleville-Laon highway astride his V-twin motorcycle. He crouched low over the gas tank, goggled, clad in puttees, and buttoned up in a short-waist leather jacket. The machine was a 1915 Wanderer, a scourge to all meandering poultry and the two-wheeled inspiration of every French schoolboy along the roadway. Every muscle tensed with achy tautness as he gripped the low-angled handlebars—lean hard muscle—muscle stiffened by months of aerial combat. Slewing in a turn, he gassed the motorcycle down a soggy thoroughfare, leading to the Operations hut, then turned sharply left and skidded to a stop atop the tarmac in front of a large canvas hangar. He paused a moment, revving the motor obnoxiously, gazing at the throng of gathered *Feldgrau* assembled on the field—until they took notice—then lowered the parking rack and shut the motor off. He removed his gloves with studied care and folded them over the handlebars. He slipped the goggles up above the bill of his service cap and climbed off, then lit a cigarette and inhaled a lungful.

Although he was a veteran officer, he slouched heedlessly, both hands in pockets; a blowsy-looking man who had found no opportunity to shave and whose uniform clung to him with the intimacy of a thing lived in; a tatty leather jacket fit snugly over his broad shoulders; a tunic collar hung limply, unbuttoned; hair was greasy and unkempt. His boots were muddy, evidently from the long, sloughy trek from Flanders. The smoldering cigarette hung carelessly from his lips. He strode over to the man in charge.

"Is this Pusieux Ferme airfield?" he asked casually.

"Yes," Wissemann replied. "This is Pusieux Ferme, *Jagdstaffel 23*."

"I thought so."

"And... you are?"

"*Leutnant* Heinrich Luddenvoss—late of *Jasta 24*—Alsace Sector."

No "sir" or salute followed the statement.

Wissemann frowned. "*Leutnant* Luddenvoss, of course."

"What's all the hubbub about, eh?" *Leutnant* Luddenvoss looked around curiously.

"Inspection," Wissemann replied, gazing at the young officer's disgraceful attire, appalled. He restrained a spiteful impulse and made a vague gesture to the two new tyros. "Take a place next to one of those two lads, please."

"Right." Luddenvoss strode over and stood shoulder to shoulder with the taller of the two replacements. Cigarette smoke wafted over the taller young mans face, filling his nostrils. He slowly edged away from Luddenvoss, grimacing with disgust.

Wissemann marched up to Luddenvoss, paused for a moment before he spoke, waiting a long minute, hoping to jar the stubborn Saxon to his senses before finally saying: "Please come to attention, *Leutnant* Luddenvoss," his voice calm and polite. Wissemann immediately sensed an air of raw arrogance in this new officer.

The surly Saxon took a final drag of his cigarette, flicked it to the ground and slowly came to attention. He averted his gaze, though, staring languidly at some distant object, avoiding the *Jastaführer's* flaring eyes.

Wissemann studied the veteran officer with roving eyes, examining the shabby Saxon's appearance with wary inspection. Heinrich Luddenvoss was a slender man with a swarthy complexion, shaggy brown hair and features which might have been cut from stone. He was not particularly tall but possessed the physique of a seasoned wrestler—muscular, taut and powerful. Cold blue eyes bespoke raw courage. The long line of his unshaven jaw betrayed a mulish stubbornness. A man of action, plainly, on whom subtle, diplomatic phrases would be wasted.

Wissemann came directly to the point.

"Did you lose your shaving kit, *Leutnant*?" His tone was cold and patronizing. "We normally shave before inspections around here. It's a troublesome practice, I know. But, it's a requirement."

"Well, uh... I rode my motorcycle all the way in from Riencourt early this morning—didn't have the time, I guess?" Luddenvoss answered in a slow, cool drawl.

"Didn't have time—*what*?" Wissemann rejoined, trying to remind the belligerent officer of his superior rank.

Luddenvoss's eyes flickered with false obfuscation. "What?"

"*MENSCH!*" Schutzling interjected loudly. "You will refer to the

Jastaführer as—*Herr Oberleutnant* or sir—understand!" He folded both arms over his chest, posturing superiorly.

Wissemann waved the well-meaning adjutant off. "Please, Schutzling. Let me handle this, all right?" he snapped, frowning, his patience diminishing with every second. He cleared his throat and stepped closer, toe-to-toe, with the refractory Heinrich Luddenvoss. "*Leutnant* Luddenvoss, regardless of your past combat record or your disdain for military protocol, you *will* adhere to military regulations while you are part of my *Jasta*. Understand?"

Luddenvoss looked at him mockingly, but said nothing.

Schutzling, arms still crossed, brows nettled, glared at Luddenvoss and weighed him up. What an arrogant little piece of dung, he thought. An officer? Indeed, not!

"You *will* follow orders and you *will* conduct yourself like a decent German officer," Wissemann continued, his tone crisp and even. "I'm not a strict disciplinarian, nor a stickler for regulations. However, I do expect my officers to set examples for the rest of the *Staffel*. I have been thoroughly briefed, with full details, on your military and moral delinquencies, jail time, how many times you've been drunk, arrests and everything else. Oh, yes, I know everything about you, *Leutnant* Luddenvoss... and I couldn't care less!"

"Uh? Couldn't care less—?"

"I want men that are tough, love to fly, fight to win, and who'd rather die than give up. Now, that's asking quite a bit. But no more than you're capable of, if you'll accept the responsibility. Do I make myself clear, *Leutnant* Luddenvoss?"

"Right. Right. Got it," Luddenvoss muttered, his tone sour with deepening reproach.

"We're here to fight, *Leutnant*—shoot down enemy machines, bomb, destroy, kill and cripple the enemy. Nothing more. Above all, we are all still officers and gentlemen."

"Gentlemen? In this pesthole? Hah—"

"I know the war isn't a jolly little beer fest down here on the Champagne. Nevertheless, we are all expected to pull together and make the best of it, right? Without order there is chaos. Without law there is anarchy. Do you understand?"

Mein Gott! Luddenvoss thought. Spare me the philosophic cow plop, will you please!

"*Leutnant* Luddenvoss... did I make myself clear?"

"Yes," Luddenvoss hissed, his lip curled in scorn.

"*Yes*, what?" Wissemann hinted.

"Yes, *Herr Oberleutnant*?"

"That's better."

Luddenvoss rolled his eyes and sighed.

"We'll not have this conversation again. Got it?"

"Got it!" replied the Saxon, sneering crossly now, the disgust on his face matching the spittle he tasted in the back of his throat.

"Good. I endeavor to believe your career will be a productive one here at *Jasta 23, Herr* Luddenvoss," Wissemann articulated earnestly, smiling, stepping back, now fully satisfied.

"Sure, whatever you say, *Herr Oberleutnant.*" Luddenvoss' tone was steeped in derision.

"And you had better button up that collar, *Leutnant!*"

The Bavarian *Jastaführer* smartly about-faced and marched to the head of the formation.

"Jump off, already," the Saxon uttered sotto voce. He scoffed and lackadaisically fastened his collar, his actions seeming more like insolence rather than an affirmation to a direct order. Luddenvoss slouched back to his normal, careless bearing, legs spread wide.

Willi Wissemann stood for a long moment, reviewing the motley collection of pilots and mechanics, then frowned grimly. But when he spoke, it was distinct and confident, giving an unusual clarity to every syllable. "Good afternoon, gentlemen. As you all well know, *Oberst* Thomsen will be here very shortly to begin an inspection of this aerodrome. I realize that the last few days have been very interesting —trying—to say the least. Yet, I am very proud of your progress, especially since the unexpected visit the other morning from the snail-eaters. I am particularly proud of the enlisted cadre for doing such a fine job. Men... you have performed well, superbly, in getting this airfield back in shape for operations. Well done, gentlemen! You've all earned an extra chit in your alcohol ration."

There was a feverish buzz of voices. Heads bobbed up and down in approval; an extra alcohol ration was much appreciated.

Wissemann waxed on. "Progress has been slow but we have moved forward nonetheless. Let's keep up the good work..." He paused for a moment when he saw *Oberst* Thomsen's motorcade coming through the main entrance. Two Mercedes staff cars, escorted by two noisy motorcycle mounted troops, followed by a third vehicle, made up General von Hoeppner and Thomsen's official procession. The two staff cars parked near the tarmac.

"JAGDSTAFFEL—ACH-TUNG!" Wissemann bellowed huskily.

The ragged *Staffel* snapped to attention as Wissemann about-faced. The air became choked with anxiety—all awaited General von Hoeppner and *Oberst* Thomsen. And soon, both of the ranking staff officers were out of their cars and making their way toward the formation. Von Hoeppner was leading the group of officers with *Oberst* Thomsen following close behind.

Wissemann gazed fondly upon the approaching figure, a man now well known to all members of the German Air Service. General Ernst von Hoeppner was an averaged-height slender man. Grayish hair and a thin mustache complemented his rugged features. His eyes sparkled with a marked youthfulness, unusual for a man of fifty-six years. His uniform was immaculate and neatly pressed. And he still wore the spurs of a cavalry officer on highly polished boots. Von Hoeppner carried a riding crop and displayed the epaulettes of *General der Kavallerie* upon his shoulders. He was commander in chief of the *Luftstreitkräfte* and trod with the self-assured gait of a Prussian aristocrat. The old general, pacing steadily, negotiated the muddy field towards Wissemann and his awaiting *Jasta* with apparent ease, while his orderlies and junior staff members struggled to keep up. Von Hoeppner approached the waiting *Jastaführer.* He was smiling.

Wissemann saluted crisply. Boot heels clicked. "Good afternoon, *Herr General,*" he said amiably. "Welcome to Pusieux Ferme, happy home of *Jagdstaffel 23.*"

"Afternoon, Willi." General von Hoeppner nodded and returned the *Jastaführer's* salute. "Good to see you again."

"Likewise, *Herr General.*"

"You're looking fit, Willi."

"Thank you, *Herr General.*"

Von Hoeppner proffered his hand. A brisk handshake followed.

Schutzling, standing close by, was somewhat amazed that General von Hoeppner referred to Wissemann by his first name. Perhaps, he thought, this *Jastaführer does* have a few friends in high places. That was very reassuring. He grinned jovially. Hmm, things weren't so bad after all! He sighed happily, relieved.

"Stand at ease, Willi. Please," von Hoeppner insisted.

"Yes, sir—"

"Let's forgo the seriousness of procedure for once, shall we?"

"Yes, *Herr General.* By all means."

"I'm here on official business, of course. But there's no need for all this parade ground fanfare. Put your men at ease, Willi."

"At once, *Herr General,*" Wissemann said with a smile. He smartly about-faced and barked out the General's orders. "*Jagdstaffel...* STAND AT... EASE!"

The *Jasta* reshuffled in a more relaxed position and began muttering quietly amongst themselves. Wissemann turned around casually and faced the General once more. He clasped his hands behind his back and stood legs spread apart. Von Hoeppner stood relaxed too, his fine greatcoat draped over his shoulders, friendly eyes beaming brightly underneath the lee of his peaked service cap.

A light drizzle began falling from the sky.

"By the way, how's the leg, Willi?" Von Hoeppner asked. "Heard you had a nasty crack-up the other day."

"It's healed nicely, sir. It was only a minor injury. Nothing at all."

"Good, good. Glad to hear it."

"Thank you for asking, sir."

"I understand the French recently paid your aerodrome an unexpected visit, Willi." Von Hoeppner looked around, pursing his lips with amazement. "But things seem in order, though."

"Yes, *Herr General*. The French caught us with our pants down."

"Willi..." General von Hoeppner said then sighed wearily. "Oh, never mind." He had changed his mind suddenly. Von Hoeppner had thought about telling the dutiful Bavarian he didn't have to go through all the histrionics of military protocol. A simple "General" or "sir" would suffice. Nevertheless, he knew Wissemann probably wouldn't be comfortable with all that. He decided to leave it alone. "I'm sure you have things well under control, yes?"

"Yes. Of course, sir."

"No major catastrophe, I hope?" von Hoeppner smiled, tapping the mud from his boots with the riding crop.

"No serious damage, *Herr General*."

"Excellent."

"Just a little blemish on our pride, that's all."

Von Hoeppner looked around again and surveyed the aerodrome, quite impressed by Wissemann's confidence and the apparent tidiness of the field. *Oberst* Thomsen, standing close by, who obviously thought otherwise, interjected tersely.

"Wissemann," he growled, "This *Jasta* will be relocated soon."

"Really?" Wissemann replied, truly uninterested.

"Yes. So don't get too attached to this location."

"Why? Whereabouts, sir?"

"When I have definitive information, I will convey it to you."

Wissemann reluctantly nodded. "Of course, *Herr Oberst*."

"In the meantime, I suggest you get this damnable disaster area straightened out!"

The Bavarian Eagle grit his teeth and sighed, a bit riled. He really wanted to tell the old son of a bitch to piss off. But instead, he decided this wasn't the time or place for blatant candor. Would there ever be?

Willi Wissemann tried to focus on the positive side of things. "Know your enemy, know yourself," he quipped coolly. "And you can fight a hundred battles without disaster."

"Mind your tongue, Wissemann!" Thomsen snapped.

Von Hoeppner put his hand on Wissemann's shoulder. "Oh, never mind all that, Willi," he said, glaring coldly at *Oberst* Thomsen. "I have some *real* important news for you." The General motioned to one of his subordinates. "*Leutnant* Dietrich, my brief case, please..."

Leutnant Dietrich held out the briefcase, and General Hoeppner released the catches of the leather case, opened it, and pulled out a black, gold-trimmed jewelry box. Then the General produced an envelope from his coat pocket and gave it to his aide. He nodded once.

Wissemann's eyes narrowed. What was the General up to?

"Read the citation to '*Hauptmann*' Wissemann, Dietrich."

"Yes, *Herr General,* at once," *Leutnant* Dietrich saluted crisply, clicked his heels, opened the envelope. He cleared his throat and read aloud: *"To Wilhelm Reinhardt Wissemann, Jastaführer, Jasta 23 (active) Officer of his Majesty's Imperial German Air service: an exemplary pilot of the highest degree, a constant example of verve, spirit, and admirable fighting ardor. The Chief of the General Staff of the Luftstreitkräfte, General Ernst von Hoeppner, by virtue of the powers which are conferred to him by the German Army and the Supreme Warlord, Kaiser Wilhelm II, bestows the honorable rank of Hauptmann upon you, Wilhelm Reinhardt Wissemann, in recognition of your long and loyal service to the Fatherland, the German Army, the Imperial Air Service and the peoples of greater Germany."*

Wissemann had stood stiffly, listening carefully as the General's adjutant recited the heady words of the type-written encomium in a slow scholarly cadence, pausing dramatically after each line, giving prideful solemnity to every syllable. The *Jastaführer's* eyes grew wider as each line was read and a tight grin of elation began to form on his lips. His face beamed with the ruddy tint of humility, his heart drubbed fast, his chin rose, his posture was ramrod straight, his chest swelled outward. He sighed happily; his great day had come. The Gods of War had finally heard his prayers. Destiny had found him!

"Congratulations, Willi. This was long overdue," General von Hoeppner said and presented Wissemann with his captain's pips.

Wissemann, quite stunned, didn't quiet know what to think, much less what to say. "Well, thank you, General von Hoeppner. I am... -honored." He stammered. The baffled officer's saluted crisply and clicked his heels, his face suddenly ruby with embarrassment. Von Hoeppner returned the salute and then proffered his hand amiably. Both men shook hands like two doting brothers. Wissemann noticed

Oberst Thomsen whispering something to one of his aides in the entourage, scowling with deepening pretense, shaking his head with disapproval.

Wissemann smiled proudly. Well, well, well... the old Prussian isn't too happy about all this, he thought, basking in his little moment of triumph. Too bad, *Herr* Windbag!

Oberst Thomsen interceded icily. "Now that we've finished with these pettifogging proceedings. I would like to commence with the inspection. Without delay!"

"All in good time, *Oberst* Thomsen. Don't diminish Wissemann's achievement. You were once a young officer yourself, remember?" von Hoeppner reproached the plump colonel in a jovial tone.

Thomsen frowned. General or not, he would not let von Hoeppner rebuke him so artfully. "I have other aerodromes I have to visit today! My time is very valuable!"

The drizzle swelled into a light rain. The sky rumbled with distant thunder. Faint flashes of lightning flared on the horizon. The weather was turning foul again.

"I'm sorry, Willi. *Oberst* Thomsen obviously does not share in our enthusiasm."

"No matter." Wissemann winked. "I'm sure *Oberst* Thomsen has more important things to do."

Thomsen knew sarcasm when he heard it. "Wissemann! Call your men to attention. That's an order!"

"*Jawohl, Herr Oberst!*" Wissemann permitted himself a little smile.

"Congratulations, Willi," von Hoeppner said. "I'll leave you with the inspection now, and *Oberst* Thomsen."

"Thank you, *Herr General.*"

"I shall inspect your mess facilities, Willi, and see what's stewing for lunch."

"That's an excellent idea, *Herr General.*"

"Carry on, Willi."

"Enjoy your lunch, sir."

"I believe I will."

"I'm sure *Feldwebel* Rummer has prepared something sumptuous for today's 'festivities'." Wissemann saluted. Boot heels clicked.

Von Hoeppner touched the brim of his cap with his riding crop, and then departed with both of his aides, walking to the mess kitchen in careful strides. Wissemann about-faced, yet again, ready to bring the *Jasta* to attention. Thomsen stalked around to face him and waited for his command.

"*ACH-TUNG!*" he barked. Once again the *Staffel* snapped to attention. He stood rigidly, starched and uncomfortable in a freshly pressed uniform, angry, a sudden wave of annoyance washing over him. *Oberst* Thomsen was trying his best to ruin his special moment of glory. The *Jastaführer* growled and bit at his nether lip. Damn you! He thought. You sorry old son of a bitch!

Thomsen waited until the General was out of earshot to address Wissemann. He leaned in close and snarled in his typically grating way. "Wissemann, I want you to know something. I did not approve of your promotion. Nor did I approve of your assignment to this *Jasta*. And as a matter of fact, I do not approve of anything you do!"

"*Herr Oberst—*"

"But since the General seems to favor you—if you think you're putting something past me, think again! I've been in this Army a long, long time, Wissemann. And I've seen the likes of your kind come and go many times before. You *will* follow my orders. I know what I'm doing, you idiot. I know how things are supposed to be done. Understand?"

The incensed Bavarian's eyes narrowed, feeling the color creeping in his face deepen under the impact of that scornful broadside, regarding Thomsen with an expression that hinted at some deep inner loathing. He reluctantly nodded. "You are right, *Herr Oberst*," he replied glibly.

Oberst Thomsen's forefinger fluttered with minatory insistence. "And one thing more, Wissemann. It is not essential for you to ever... EVER—inform me that you think I am right. We will assume it!"

"Yes, sir."

"Begin the inspection!"

"*Jawohl, Herr Oberst!*"

Wissemann's face was a brilliant pink now. Whilst Thomsen's invective was offensive and unkind, he still managed to pop off a crisp salute, then paced smartly to the first rank of assembled men, the *Staffel* standing at a attention, their faces calm and expressionless. All except for one, of course—*Leutnant* Luddenvoss. The seedy Saxon from Leipzig grinned haughtily, his ice-blue eyes beaming with satisfaction. His thoughts: Revenge is sweet sometimes!

Deutsche Luftstreitkrafte
KOGUNLUFT, BERLIN

General Order: _No. 101_
Supreme Headquarters Staff
Kreuznach, Germany
21. March. 1917

7th Armee, Jasta 23, Laon (Champagne)

To: Wilhelm Reinhardt Wissemann, Jastaführer,
Jasta 23 (active) Officer of his Majesty's
Imperial German Air Service

An exemplary pilot of the highest degree. A constant example of nerve, spirit, and admirable fighting ardor. The Chief of the General Staff of the Luftstreitkräfte (Kogenluft) General Ernst von Hoeppner, by virtue of the powers conferred to him by the German Army and the Supreme Warlord, Kaiser Wilhelm II of Germany, bestows the honorable rank of Hauptmann upon: Wilhelm Reinhardt Wissemann *in recognition of his long and loyal service to the Fatherland, the German Army, the Imperial Air Service and to the peoples of greater Germany.*

General Ernst von Hoeppner,
Kogunluft, Luftstreitkrafte

General Ernst von Hoeppner

Chapter 13

✠

MARCH 26, 1917. *TAC-TAC-TAC-TAC-TAC-TAC!* Willi Wissemann glimpsed over his shoulder as a single Vickers machine gun, hammering viciously, its glowing white tracers zipping downwards, hissing by perilously close, its .303 bullets seemingly singing, hammering out a horrid death chant, the smoking barrel tellingly flashing like the breath of some xanthous, fire-breathing fiend, missed its intended target, Wisseman's head, by only a few centimeters.

"*Verdammt!*" he cursed. "Where the hell did he come from?"

Wissemann stabbed the rudder bar, side-slipped the Albatros left, then right, momentarily avoiding the Frenchman's gunfire. But a series of dull thuds raked the fuselage and cockpit a second later, and then another red-hot stream whizzed by his ears. A meter in front of his eyes, the rear view mirror exploded to bits, six holes appeared like magic in the cockpit flooring, at least a dozen bullets perforating his wings, and there were more in the fuselage behind him; his chinstrap was hanging loose, bullet cut. He shoved the stick over and barrel-rolled, cutting the throttle, causing the speedy Spad overshoot and bank away. Advancing the throttle back to full power, Wissemann zoomed to within twenty-five meters behind the Spad. His lips parted in a grim smile. He took aim and tripped the thumb triggers.

Click—Click. Nothing!

"Curses!" The *Jastaführer* spat testily. He'd forgotten to charge his guns in the heat of the excitement! Now the Spad was getting away.

Wissemann cleared his guns. But before he could realign his sights, another Albatros muscled in behind the scarpering Spad and fired. Wissemann recognized the Albatros D.II's distinctive green and yellow stripes. Luddenvoss! His marksmanship was unmistakable. The flaming snouts of his twin Maxims caught the French scout square in the fuel tank—a perfectly aimed deflection shot.

A flag of flame fluttered from the Spad's engine and cockpit; the French biplane twisted down in a mad spiral, smoke rolling from its innards, Luddenvoss continually blasting away until the wings broke off and fluttered away in the slipstream. Then the victorious Saxon zoomed up in a masterly half-loop and roll, saluted, and banked away in search of other prey. Wissemann jerked his head about, seeing the vortex of twisting and turning aircraft: Albatroses, Spads, Nieuports, Halberstadts. Some twenty opposing aircraft had stumbled in each other's path over the sleepy village of Allemant.

A real hot dogfight indeed!

Quickly rebounding from his amateurish gaffe, Wissemann latched onto the tail of another Spad that had darted in front of him, closing the gap to twenty meters, ripping a quick burst from his guns, a torrent of 7.92-millimeter tracer slugs that smashed headlong into the Spad. Willi Wissemann could see the Frenchman's head screwing around, looking, searching, trying to find the origin of his attacker.

"*Ach, ja!* How quickly the tables turn," the *Jastaführer* quipped, an implacable grin toying with his features. "Hah hah! Now *you* are in a pickle, *nicht, Herr Rothosen?*"

Wissemann was leaning into his sights as his thumbs closed down tight on the stick triggers, pressing them, holding them, firing. *TOK-TOK-TOK! TOK-TOK-TOK!*—his twin guns stuttered. Twenty rounds; he saw them go straight in the Spad. The Spad veered from its straight course, flying crazily now, queerly for a few seconds, then fluttered earthward lazily, like a dead bird. He had scored! He pressed the triggers again, dishing out another twenty rounds, nudging the rudder to readjust for proper deflection, targeting the Spad's engine compartment for good measure.

Tracer flickered again, the flecks of flashing flame dancing along the Spad's fuselage, the bullet-riddled aeroplane careening over lamely, upended, its engine smoking copiously. And without warning, its fuel tank suddenly exploded, the flaming wreckage wafting wildly through the sky. Wissemann grimaced as he staggered through the debris shower, feeling a few pieces of the disintegrating Spad bounce off his Albatros, wondering what kind of damage had been done to his bird. Enveloped in a ball of fire, the remaining part of the Spad's fuselage, with the pilot still trapped inside, fell like a meteorite, streaking across the sky.

An Albatros went to pieces off to his left; it hurtled earthward in several twisted clusters of canvas. Wissemann couldn't make out whose it was. *"Gott!—"* once more, he heard the nerve-racking chatter of gunfire. Another Spad was snapping at his heels!

He yanked the Albatros over in a half-roll, abruptly back-sticking in a dive. The engine stalled briefly as he slid into the long escape dive, trying to flee into the clouds, plummeting a thousand meters. The Mercedes engine quickly recovered from its little hiccup, roaring back to full power as the Albatros regained level flight. The air speed gauge read two hundred and fifty kilometers per hour, the wildly vibrating needle going ever higher until finally, it was jammed against the peg. The Albatros had exceeded its maximum dive speed. But Wissemann needed every ounce of power to escape the much faster Spad, needing just a second to get in a cloud and disappear in the murky haze below. Schäfer's old "snail" certainly was fast!

Once inside the safety of the cloud, Wissemann sighed with relief. The Frenchman wouldn't be able to find him in here. He eased the throttle back, and seconds later, emerged from the cloud at two thousand meters. Suddenly, he heard the sound of another aircraft engine close by. He glanced over his shoulder and got quite a shock. The Frenchman was still there; he was closing in for the kill! He heard the Vickers machine gun thumping, saw the bullets sailing through the rigging. Something nipped at his helmet, feeling the hot breath of death as a sizzling bullet cut across the leather, just missing a killing crease of his skull. Now you're in a terrible pickle, Willi Wissemann!

UNTEROFFIZIER GRIMM snaked quietly through the crowded mess tent, adjusting his spectacles, searching the teeming canvas facility for a familiar face. The din of conversation was deafening and the air was thick and smoky as two infantry companies consumed their meager breakfast chow. Muddy-looking coffee and biscuits were the main fare for the morning meal. Breakfast also included a mystery meat of questionable variety, Grimm reckoning some old mare must have gotten the chop. As he held his briefcase tightly under an arm, plodding through the cramped tent, he accidentally bumped into a burly sergeant seated at the head of a long table.

"Ach! Watch where the hell your going, asshole!" the ruffled noncom growled as warm coffee dribbled down his chin.

"Sorry, *Feldwebel,* didn't mean to..." Grimm patted the noncom on the shoulder, making a glib apology, smiling artfully.

The noncom noticed Grimm's Air Service ribbon. "Hey, you're

from that *Jagdstaffel* up the road, aren't you?"

"Yes, yes. *Jasta*—"

"You aviators get all the good grub, don't you?"

"Hmm?" Grimm shrugged. "Uh, can you tell me where I can find, *Leutnant* Frantz? He's with the 14th Reserve Corps, I think,"

The sergeant gazed inquisitively at Grimm. "Frantz? What in the hell do you want to talk to him about?"

"I have official business with him. He's expecting me."

The grubby-looking noncom studied Grimm's face with careful inspection. Humph, he's probably one of them, he thought. "Down at the other end—with all the other part-timers."

"Rotten *Wackes* more like!" a scrawny private exclaimed.

A collective laugh erupted from the grimy group of soldiers. Grimm nodded nervously, making his way between tables and chairs, forcing himself through, getting odd looks as he went. A few bustled seconds later, he made it to the opposite end of the tent and found *Leutnant* Frantz, who was sitting at a corner table with four other noncoms. Grimm saluted and introduced himself.

"Morning, *Herr Leutnant*. I'm *Unteroffizier* Gustav Grimm, orderly clerk of *Jagdstaffel 23*. We spoke on the telephone yesterday?"

"Yes. I remember," *Leutnant* Hugo Frantz replied.

Frantz was a thin man from Strasbourg, sporting a bristly mustache and close-cropped haircut. He wore an expression of total exhaustion, having just spent twenty straight days in the front lines without a break from action. His wan complexion and red nose suggested a man under the duress of a chronic grippe. He returned Grimm's salute with halfhearted effort, too weary for the earnestness of military etiquette.

"Have a seat, please. Would you care for some coffee or some of the wonderful chow our cooks have whipped up?" Frantz said in a obviously sarcastic tone, directing Grimm with a indifferent gesture.

"Uh, no thank you, sir. I've already eaten," Grimm replied uneasily. "Some coffee, perhaps?"

"Meyer," Frantz motioned to his orderly. "Would you please bring this gentleman a tin of coffee?"

"*Jawohl, Herr Leutnant*." The orderly nodded and disappeared into the crowd of soldiers.

Grimm removed his cap and took a seat at the table. Frantz spread his elbows out on the tabletop and made a little steeple with his fingers. "Well, now, *Unteroffizier* Grimm. What brings you to our dirty little corner of the world, hmm?"

"Well sir, I am here on behalf of *Oberst* Hermann Thomsen, Chief of Staff to General von Hoeppner of the Air Service."

"*Oberst* Thomsen?" Frantz's eyes narrowed in curiosity, a face slightly suffused with the effects of the smoke-filled tent, not really sure who *Oberst* Thomsen was, nor did he care, and he certainly wasn't familiar with the hierarchy of the German Air Service. But then most German infantryman, noncoms especially, regarded the *Luftstreitkräfte* with a high degree of contempt these days.

"Do you recall serving with an officer named Wilhelm R. Wissemann?" Grimm asked, cutting to the chase.

"Hmm... Wilhelm R. Wissemann?" *Leutnant* Frantz's mind stirred thoughtfully.

"I believe you were both attached to the First Bavarian Reserve Corps, May '15, during the battle of Artois."

"Artois. An officer, you say?"

"Yes, a *Leutnant* at that time."

"Maybe. Why?"

"We—I mean the Air Service—sir, is just trying to collect some general information about him." Grimm fidgeted absently with his briefcase. "His service record, past history, family background, etc. You know, standard procedure stuff."

"Standard procedure?" *Leutnant* Frantz began to sense an odd tack in the questioning.

"*Ja,* standard procedure, sir," Grimm echoed. "Any information on Wilhelm Wissemann would be helpful."

Frantz squinted suspiciously. "Well... I knew him at the War Academy in Munich," he began. "We were both cadets there in '05. Later on, we met again at the Battle of Artois. His battalion and mine were both overrun in the attack. We were both wounded, and we convalesced at the same hospital in St. Quentin."

"I see. H'mm, St. Quentin, eh?"

"Is he in some kind of trouble?"

"Well, no... not yet."

Frantz cocked his head askew, puzzled, saying nothing.

Grimm continued: "Did you know his family?"

"Family?"

Grimm fidgeted, clearing his throat gawkily. "I mean like, his parents... or grandfather, perhaps?"

"Grandfather?" The puzzled officer shook his head. Why is this idiot asking such trifling questions, Frantz thought? What is this seedy little character getting at? But then his supple mind began to grasp the implication of Grimm's questioning. His lip curled up in a bravura of contempt. "So. *Unteroffizier* Grimm, tell me. Who sent you on this fool's errand? Hmm?"

"Fool's errand, *Herr Leutnant?*"

"What are you getting at, *Unteroffizier?* Come to the point."

"*Oberst*—the General Staff, I mean—is trying to ascertain if he's... of French descent."

"What? French? You can't be serious?"

"Uh, well—yes."

Frantz swore under his breath, stiffening. "So, you think he's a spy... is that it? For France? Is that what your getting at?"

"Spy? No, no, not at all—"

"Aha, I see what you getting at now."

"*Herr Leutnant—*"

"We Alsatians are Germans too, see? We fight for the Fatherland just like the rest of you—Prussians, Bavarians and Saxons—the whole damn lot of you!"

"No, no. You misunderstand, *Herr Leutnant.*"

"I understand quite clearly! We've died in the service of this country too. We've all fought against the enemies of *Deutschland*, not just for ourselves, for all German people!"

"What's he talking about?" one of Frantz's subordinates asked.

Leutnant Frantz scoffed bitterly. "Ever since that nonsense back in '13, Germany is still up in arms. Everyone with French roots or French background is suspect these days," he waxed resentfully.

"You mean the 'Saverne Affair', sir?" another noncom asked.

"Exactly!" *Leutnant* Frantz retorted excitedly. "The German Intelligence Agency is investigating anyone who might have ties to the Alsace and France."

"Please, sir," Grimm begged. "I'm not with German Intelligence."

"Nah-nah," Frantz continued unabated. "Anyone from Alsace-Loraine who is suspected of French heritage is being weeded out."

"Unbelievable!" the noncom protested.

"That's why we're being transferred to the Russian Front in two weeks. Nice, eh?" Frantz glared at Grimm with loathsome eyes.

"*Leutnant* Frantz," Grimm pleaded. "It's not really like that—"

"In the atmosphere of growing prejudice," Frantz declared. "I've seen the war as an opportunity to prove my—*our commitment*—I should say, to the Fatherland. We are Germans too, you idiot!"

Frantz's voice rose to the level of embittered fervor as he bolted up from his chair, knocking it over, the two companies of hungry soldiers suddenly silencing their chatty conversations and laughter, every man looking up now, glaring at the infuriated officer. A sudden silence fell upon the men and the mess tent, all held their breath.

Grimm felt ill at ease as a mess tent of curious eyes fell upon him. He got up from his seat, clutching his briefcase anxiously, his face growing hot with mortification. "Really, *Herr Leutnant.* I'm just here at the behest of the General Staff—"

"Go to hell!" Frantz bawled. "Tell the General Staff they can go to hell too! I'm not going to take the blame for the collapse of morale. Nor should any Alsatian!"

"No one is blaming you, sir," Grimm whispered loudly.

"This Wissemann fellow isn't even French, and you people hound him like he's a common criminal. Ridiculous!"

Grimm leered at the table of men staring at him, not liking their glances, their baleful eyes seemingly divesting him of what little humility he had left. He edged away from the table.

"Leave now, *Unteroffizier,* before I forget I'm an officer!" Frantz shouted, pointing angrily towards the exit.

Grimm stood frozen in stupefaction a moment, nodding slowly, sighing heavily. The orderly returned from the kitchen with his cup of coffee, oblivious to what had just transpired.

"Your coffee, *Unteroffizier,*" the orderly offered.

Grimm frowned, easing away.

"Forget it," Frantz snarled crossly. "This wag is leaving now!"

"Sorry, guess I can't stay," Grimm muttered sheepishly. "Actually, I prefer tea." He turned on a heel and slithered off for the exit.

Mindful of limited time and their empty bellies, the two infantry companies went back to their clamor and conversation as if nothing had ever happened. Frantz's staff mumbled disbelievingly, shaking their heads. Frantz stormed out of the tent, angry and annoyed.

THE CLOUD WAS MURKY. The baffled Bavarian pilot, temporarily blinded by the murkiness of the bloated cumulus, twisted his head around frantically, still hearing the Frenchman's engine droning behind him. But at least the shooting had ceased, for the moment. That was reassuring! He hurled the Albatros in a tight turn and flew faster, and the sound of the Spad's motor grew fainter.

A second later, he emerged from the cloud deck at five hundred meters. Disoriented, he bent over his compass, assessing his heading. He swore in disgust; the compass had been shattered by a bullet! He would have to guess his way back, and the sky was thick with clouds. He flew beneath the billowing mountains of mist, peering down, sussing out some landmarks that might guide him. But he didn't recognize a one. He checked his route map for a clue. He shrugged, clueless, seemingly lost for the moment—

TAC-TAC-TAC! TAC-TAC-TAC! Bullets slammed into his Albatros, its windscreen exploding in a shattered blur of shards. He took evasive action, feigning left, then right, wildly, hoping to confuse the enemy's aim. But the Frenchman kept firing and scoring hits. For the first time in his flying career, Willi Wissemann felt the cold, clammy hands of the Grim Reaper clawing at his soul.

"Do something, Willi. *Schnell!*" he said to himself.

Wissemann cut the throttle, stomped hard on the rudder bar, yanked the control column back, and the tail yawed sideways. The Albatros rolled—a slow corkscrew—reducing its forward momentum, almost stalling in a dangerous spin. The Spad, unable to maintain position on Wissemann's tail, zoomed up, slewing gracelessly in front of the Albatros. Now Wissemann had a chance to inflict a reprisal. The Spad twisted and turned to evade fire, just as the Albatros had done only seconds before. Wissemann aimed and fired.

TOK-TOK-TOK! TOK... click-click. Both guns jammed!

Wissemann recharged the guns and pressed the triggers.

Click-click...

"Tender-hearted Jesus—these guns are cursed!"

Gott! A damned rotten situation! If he ever got his hands on his armorer—but there was no time to waste on angry thoughts. Willi Wissemann wheeled the Albatros up in a chandelle—a climbing turn—braking off his attack, madly hammering at his gun breeches.

The foxy Frenchman took note of the German's predicament and soared up after the Albatros, his Spad's eight-cylinder motor roaring powerfully. Wissemann, in his fury to free his jammed machine guns was flying a straight line, a very foolish course. He was furious, gnashing his teeth, cursing God, the Kaiser, the Spandau engineers, the expletives flying from his mouth like machine gun fire.

Suddenly, in a brief moment of clarity, it occurred to him to look around. He was startled to see the Spad flying parallel to him now, the Frenchman staring curiously at him, goggles up, grinning. Wissemann could see his eyes; they were affable orbs. Then Wissemann noticed the faded red stork painted on the fuselage as well as the French phrase: *LE VIEUX CHARLES—Old Charlie*—scrawled in thick black letters in front of a tricolor red, white and blue banner. Wissemann's stomach soured with fear, his mouth went sticky dry.

"Old Charlie? *Lieber Gott... GUYNEMER!*"

The Bavarian Eagle sat motionless, awestruck and fearful. He gazed back at the Frenchman, seeing a consumptive-looking little man with a pencil thin mustache staring back at him. *L'As des as!*

Capitaine Guynemer waved amiably, then pointed to his single Vickers machine gun, making a sour face—then gestured thumbs-down. Wissemann was puzzled. What was Guynemer trying to say? Wissemann didn't understand what was happening. This is just a bad dream, he thought. I will wake up soon, roll out of bed, hit the floor then have my morning coffee. But this was no dream, only cold stark reality! Then it abruptly dawned on him.

"His machine gun must be jammed!"

Guynemer smiled, flashing a toothy grin. *"Ça gaze, monsieur?"* He put a slender finger to pursed lips and shook his head, mouthing silently: *"Shhh! Ce n'est pas la mer à boire!"* The wily Frenchman flipped a chivalrous salute. *"Bonne chance!"* he said, and heeled "Old Charlie" over in a tight bank, peeling away, heading back to French territory.

Wissemann had understood perfectly; *Capitaine Guynemer* had bid him good luck, telling him it wasn't the end of the world. Wissemann smiled timidly, returning the salute, his heart drubbing frantically, sweat draining down his forehead, feeling exhausted, his bladder suddenly aching to be relieved. This was unbelievable!

The great *Capitaine* Georges Guynemer, the deadliest guns in all France, had given him quarter. The legendary French ace was as notorious for his gallantry as he was for his victory total. Wissemann knew Guynemer had well over thirty official victories, and probably just as many unofficial. Georges Marie Ludovic Jules Guynemer, whose name echoed like sword blows on a fine suit of armor, was France's greatest aerial hero.

Willi Wissemann had fought the French ace of aces to a draw—a victory with the taste of defeat. He felt drained, his hands clammy and shaky, his legs rubbery. This would be a grand tale for the mess. Would anybody believe it? Hah! He gassed the Mercedes, setting a course for home, humming tunelessly, a sick smile creasing his trembling lips. *"Gott sie Dank, Willi.* You are a very lucky man today."

LEUTNANT LUDDENVOSS CONTEMPLATED SILENTLY. He eyed his half-empty glass of cognac, relaxing in a dark corner of the Kasino, sitting away from others, having a solitary drink. He was on his third neat one, a cigarette burning in his fingers, wondering if he should have a fourth. He typically preferred to be alone, in the air and on the ground. Only the company of a woman really suited him. But, since his deviant misdeeds in Mulhouse and his clash with the local authorities there, he'd refrained from female contact. Heinrich Luddenvoss just wanted to be left alone these days; he didn't enjoy the banal ways of fellow squadron mates, so unruly in their attempts to blow off steam. He didn't like to participate in *Jasta* formations, mess conversations either, and wouldn't have anything to do with anyone else. And while he would've preferred the company of equals, he had to admit reluctantly, he had no equals. It was the same here in France as it had been in Africa. Men fought, men drank, men died. He thought back to a hot August night in East Africa...

After the wireless station at Dar es Salaam had been destroyed by ship-to-shore gunfire, via two British cruisers, sudden, uncontrollable circumstances forced a disinclined *Unteroffizier* Luddenvoss into the sweltering countryside alone. All that he possessed was a 9-millimeter sidearm and two bottles of Martell. Wandering aimlessly for ten days through the African bush, he finally came upon a German outpost, nearly dead from dehydration and exposure. Luddenvoss recovered. His situation improved, but only a little; the Allied blockade of Zanzibar made life unbearable during the East African campaign.

A month later, he was heading home for Germany on the cruiser, *Königsberg,* when two British monitors sank it after blockading the cruiser in the Rufiji River. He survived a near drowning and was once again cast into the harsh African environment—alone. Yet, once again, the stalwart Saxon survived.

Finally, after another year in Tabora, General Paul von Lettow-Vorbeck finally answered his requests for transfer, and a newly commissioned Heinrich Luddenvoss returned to Germany in late '15 for flight training. He never returned to Africa. He flew Aviatik two-seater machines for a time, and later, Eindeckers over Verdun. He flew alone, stalking French reconnaissance aeroplanes. His early victories went unconfirmed, but that didn't matter to him. The mere thrill of victory was always enough to satisfy him.

Eventually the confirmations came. He began to develop a taste for Nieuports and Spads, and the French scouts fell like flies. He soon became a local celebrity in the quiet little Alsace sector. And with fame came the women. His tiny billet in Habsheim saw more action than any battlefront ever did. Then one night during a steamy liaison in Mulhouse, things got out of hand. He was quite drunk and the young French maiden suddenly quite unwilling. But the sinful Saxon was never one to take no for an answer, he always took what he wanted. Luddenvoss essentially forced himself on the young woman. The local Alsatian authorities got involved, then eventually the 19th Army *Kommandeur.*

Luddenvoss was reprimanded but not charged. His file was sent to Supreme Headquarters in Berlin. That's when *Oberst* Thomsen became aware of the recalcitrant *Leutnant* Heinrich Luddenvoss.

The old Chief of Staff had a special way of dealing with young mavericks. Luddenvoss grinned, remembering—

"Evening, *Leutnant*... may I join you for a drink?"

Hauptmann Wissemann stood before him with a nearly full bottle of Courvoisier. Luddenvoss said nothing, but with a faint nod, directed Wissemann to the chair across from him. He struck a match and calmly lit a cigarette, inhaling deeply.

"*Danke.*" Wissemann sat down. He uncorked the bottle and poured Luddenvoss a shot, then poured himself one.

"Hmm," the Saxon grunted approvingly.

"Just in time, eh, *Leutnant?* Your glass was just about empty."

"Timing—*is* everything."

Luddenvoss' eyes flickered eagerly at the shot of cognac, as Wissemann slid the glass over to him. Luddenvoss picked it up, took a sip, and moaned with approval, savoring the sharp bite of the vintage Courvoisier. Wissemann picked up his glass. The two drank, assessing each other over the rim of their glasses. Exhaling in a long sigh of cognac-fueled contentment, Wissemann sank back in his chair.

"*Your* timing is impeccable," he said. "I might add."

"My timing?"

"You polished off that Spad quite handily."

"I did, didn't I. Why didn't you? You had him cold."

"My guns jammed, Luddenvoss," Wissemann lied, eyes dropping, unwilling to admit the awful truth—he'd forgotten to charge his guns before firing; a novice's mistake.

Luddenvoss finished his shot of cognac and set the glass down. He took a deep drag from his cigarette and considered the peace feeler—making up his mind to reject it. Luddenvoss reached for the bottle, exhaling a cloud of smoke. "Do you mind?" he asked.

"By all means, *Leutnant.*"

Luddenvoss poured himself a liberal shot, eyeing the golden-brown liquid glowing in the glass like a scientist examining a rare specimen, swirling it around gently, breathing in its alcoholic aroma, then gulping it down greedily.

"The Storks play for keeps, *Hauptmann,*" he quipped capriciously. "Those were Guynemer's chums we fought today."

"Yes, I know. They are formidable foes—"

"Formidable?"

"The Storks are the elite of the *Service d' Aéronautique,* you know."

"*Humph,* doesn't make a damn bit of difference to me. Even the likes of the Storks fall victim to my excellent marksmanship."

The Saxon stared at the bottle of Courvoisier, Wissemann stared at Luddenvoss. Both sensed a hint of contempt in the other.

Luddenvoss was undoubtedly an excellent shot and a first-rate pilot, Wissemann conceded, but his hubris certainly wouldn't endear himself to his prim sensibilities. Excellence aside, the proprieties of gentlemanly conduct had to be observed at all times.

"Well…" Wissemann said with a strained smile. "The better part of valor is discretion, *Leutnant* Luddenvoss."

"Hmm?"

"I see modesty isn't one of your finer qualities."

Luddenvoss chuckled.

Wissemann was acutely aware of Luddenvoss' condescending style by now, and he certainly didn't appreciate the snotty attitude either; he didn't have to take such disrespect from a subordinate. All the same, he reluctantly had to concede, feeling obligated to pursue a more positive course with him. He wanted to befriend the young Saxon and affirm that old truism "no man is an island."

"I locked horns with *Capitaine* Guynemer today. Now there's a valorous gentleman," Wissemann relayed in a halfhearted spirit. "A very merciful man, too, it seems. Don't you agree, Luddenvoss?"

"Merciful? That's an outdated notion for these times."

"With *Capitaine* Guynemer, mercy seems to be a passion. With me, it's merely good manners. You may judge which is the more reliable."

Luddenvoss did not comment, smirking, the recusant airman deciding to maintain his aloof attitude, which he knew would infuriate this puritanical officer, or at least ruffle his feathers a bit.

The sudden silence unnerved Wissemann. He took a cigarette from his sterling case and searched for a matchstick. But Luddenvoss magically produced a lit match and set the *Jastaführer's* cigarette aglow, before he could locate one. Wissemann nodded his thanks, sensing the young man's eyes probing him, exhaling a sigh of smoke, squinting through the haze, thinking of something clever to say.

"Timing *is* everything," Wissemann reiterated, coolly.

Another ceasefire was in the air.

"So what happened, today?"

"What do you mean?"

"Your Albatros was all shot up when we got back."

"Ah, Guynemer is a plucky devil. He almost had me. But his gun jammed at the crucial moment."

"Lucky for you."

"That's the only thing that saved my sorry heinie today."

"Hmm. Fortunate.

"Fortunate, indeed."

"Now Baer... he could have used a little luck today," Luddenvoss quipped callously. "Poor, luckless bastard."

"What happened to *Leutnant* Baer? He was your responsibility."

Luddenvoss paused before answering, weighing the gravity of the question, evaluating Wissemann's real intent. What was Wissemann getting at? What did he want? Why was he patronizing him with idle conversation? Luddenvoss had protested being assigned the rookie Baer, arguing it was a silly practice, coupling a tyro with a veteran. It made no sense at all! It only slowed him down, kept him from scoring more victories. He had no desire to show a tyro the ropes, especially when an outfit like the Storks appeared on the scene. He had his own neck to worry about, not some snot-nosed kid. The surly Saxon stroked the stubble on his chin, contemplating the answer, his eyes eluding Wissemann's questioning stare.

"Guess he strayed too far during the fight," he replied absently, snorting, staring at the tip of his cigarette.

"You guess?"

"He couldn't keep up, *Hauptmann.* Then I lost sight of him. One of Guynemer's hawks got him, I suppose," Heinrich Luddenvoss replied, his tone obdurate and unyielding.

Wissemann grumbled. He should have known better than to entrust the life of a tyro with a loner like Luddenvoss. It was a stupid decision, which he now regretted. He really wanted to tear into the snotty Saxon but he really couldn't hold the apathetic officer accountable, realizing that new replacements were often difficult to rein in during a dogfight, and in the heat of battle, new pilots often lost their nerve and panicked.

"*Nah ja,*" he conceded meekly. "The new ones, they can't help it."

"Can't help it?"

"They lose their nerve during the first combats."

Luddenvoss snorted. "It's a cruel world isn't it, *Herr Hauptmann?*"

Wissemann's eyes clouded. "Cold and cruel."

Luddenvoss grinned.

"We lost Eckhardt, too," Wissemann imparted grimly. "An old hand. He'll be sorely missed—"

"Well, we all have to go sometimes, I suppose. Fate isn't choosey."

"Gutemann says he went down behind enemy lines, still under power, smoking badly." Wissemann dragged on his cigarette, eyeing the Saxon for a reaction. "Perhaps he lives..."

Luddenvoss shrugged. "The breaks, eh?"

"Hmm." Wissemann sighed fractiously.

"Well, I avenged him. I shot down a Spad."

"Did you now?"

"Kindlich can corroborate it. That makes—eleven for me now."

"Eleven?" Wissemann's brow narrowed. "No. I believe that's—*six* for you. We only count confirmed victories here in *Jasta 23, Leutnant*." His patience was wearing thin. Remain calm, Willi. Remain calm...

"Whatever. Six, then." Luddenvoss smiled coolly. Personally, he didn't really care about such things; he was only testing Wissemann's mettle, see how far he could push the *Jastaführer*, figuring he ought to be seething by now. He took another drag from his cigarette, basking in mute amusement.

A stiff silence ensued.

Wissemann struggled to hide his annoyance, thinking furiously, trying to find a new tack for the conversation. He shot back his cognac, then blurted out: "I claimed a Spad, too!"

"Two-for-two. Not bad against the Storks, for *this* pathetic mob."

Wissemann's face was raging hot now, finding himself struggling desperately to mask his irritation, his vein attempts at befriending Luddenvoss failing miserably. He truly despised the man's blatant contempt and felt his control cracking, his forces crumbling. The smoldering Bavarian decided to cease his childish fencing—use a more traditional method incorporated by commanding officers—the blunt and direct approach. He leaned forward, leveling flaring eyes, glaring balefully, letting the cognac do the talking for him.

"You know something," he said, his brow narrowing in a scowl, "let's get this understood right now, *Leutnant. DO NOT* try any of your smart-alecked antics with me. Understand? Other commanders may have let you get away with bloody blue murder, but not under my watch. No, sir. Take note—"

"Calm yourself, *Hauptmann*—"

"I'll bounce you out of my *Jasta* so fast, your feet won't even touch the ground, *Leutnant!*"

"Look here—"

"It's probably too much to ask of you, eh? For you to show the slightest bit of interest or concern for those around you? Hell, I doubt you're capable of showing any emotion at all." Wissemann seized the armrests of his chair and leaned forward. "You're just a cold, callous old fish—*Herr Luddenvoss!*"

The churlish Saxon sank back in his chair, grinning back at the fuming *Jastaführer*, amused. "If you say so—*sir*."

Wissemann threw caution to the wind. "You know something, *Leutnant*, I misjudged you. I thought maybe under that tough exterior a real man existed. Bah! You're just a self-absorbed little shit!"

Wissemann scooped up the bottle of cognac, slapping the cork home petulantly. Heinrich Luddenvoss sat expressionless for a moment, snorted, then reached for his service cap. Well, there goes the free drinks, he thought. Time to fly the coop.

"Well, it's getting late," he said, his tone playfully sarcastic "It's been nice chatting with you, really."

"Uh, before you go, *Junge,* I want you to know something." There was a disrespectful timbre in the *Jastaführer's* tone. "I've decided to suspend your privileges for solitary patrols, in lieu of your... defiant attitude tonight, *Leutnant.*"

"What?" Luddenvoss muttered, a bit stunned.

"Starting tomorrow, you'll fly in my *Kette.* Once you have proven to me you can fly and fight as a team member, *Leutnant,* participate in *Jasta* briefings and debriefings and such, I'll consider reinstating your solo patrol privileges."

Luddenvoss scoffed carelessly. "Pissed off, are you now?"

"If you disobey me," Wissemann cut in, *"I WILL* take disciplinary action against you, *Leutnant* Luddenvoss. Your listless attitude had better change or—"

"Or what?" Luddenvoss eased up from the table, sneering.

Wissemann jerked up, his face flushed with vexation. The eyes of the two men clashed. There was mutual dislike in that exchange. The music, the chaotic banter of the Kasino, the card games, everything, suddenly ceased, as all eyes fell upon the two men, an awkward silence infusing the smoky barroom. The tension was electric!

Don't loose your control, Willi, Wissemann said to himself. You're losing it. Stay calm. Stay calm! He lifted his chin stiffly, staring at the seething Saxon, his eyes flashing with fire. But he wisely forced himself to cool from the heated parley, taking a deep breath, sighing, straightening his tunic tails. He calmly eased himself into his chair.

"Dismissed—*Leutnant,*" he ordered evenly, a crisp drawl that didn't quite mask the cold fury underneath.

"Ta, ta, Hauptmann," Luddenvoss quipped, walking away, humming quietly to himself. And in an attitude of chesty contempt, rolled his eyes at Kindlich as he strutted by his table. Kindlich and Gutemann had been in earshot of the heated exchange.

"N-nighty-n-night, *J-Junge,*" Luddenvoss stammered mockingly, then disappeared in the throng of men crowding the doorway.

Gutemann shook his head, watching the sassy Saxon saunter off in a slapdash manner. "Ach! What an *Aschloch!*" he spouted.

"That's putting it mildly," Wissemann replied.

"May I join you, *Herr Hauptmann?*"

"Yes, please do. You too, Kindlich." Wissemann gestured. "Take a seat, gentlemen."

"Who d-does he... t-think h-he is," Kindlich stammered.

"An arrogant asshole! That's who," Gutemann explicated.

The two young officers sat down. Gutemann and Kindlich were drinking beer, each holding a large tankard in their hands, clumping them down clumsily on the tabletop. Wissemann noted both lads were clearly deep into their own cups. He grinned suavely, trying to mask his own crapulence.

The still stewing *Jastaführer* nodded in agreement. "That he is, Gutemann. He's an excellent pilot."

"You really think so, sir?" Gutemann replied, surprised.

"Yes. Unfortunately."

"He-he's j-just a—" Kindlich tried to say.

"A great marksman?"

"W-Well..."

"Alas, we do need his talents in this *Jasta.*"

"Do you really think he's that good, *Herr Hauptmann?*"

"I do, Gutemann."

There was a hint of regret in that tone. As much as he despised the arrogance of Heinrich Luddenvoss, his pompous attitude, his loner mentality, his surly personality, Wissemann did marvel at the Saxon's piloting prowess. It was a pity, he contemplated; why was such natural talent always wasted on such reprehensible rogues? The bleary-eyed Bavarian poured himself another shot of Courvoisier, slugged it back and took a deep breath. Finally, he had calmed down after his exchange with the Saxon.

"He bagged a Spad today. Only used fifteen rounds," Wissemann stated matter-of-factly.

"Fifteen rounds?"

"Indeed. I spoke with his armorer this afternoon," Wissemann explained. "Luddenvoss personally inspects both of his machine guns before every sortie, Gutemann, checking each cartridge individually for uniformity and defects."

The *Jastaführer* spoke in tones of veiled admiration, trying to appear none too enthusiastic about Luddenvoss' apparent abilities; he couldn't help but admire the young maverick's skill. Even after their heated exchange, Wissemann was still hoping to make a positive impression on him. It would not be an easy task. He lit another cigarette, contemplating a possible plan of action, wondering how he was going to penetrate that Saxon's thick skull!

Otto Gutemann carped: "He has a nasty habit of pissing on the undercarriage of his Albatros before each flight. Disgusting idiot!"

"Yes, I noticed that, too," Wissemann replied, grinning. The wily *Jastaführer* understood that all pilots had preflight rituals based on their beliefs of luck and fate. "We all have our own quirky little superstitions, I suppose."

"I guess so. But that's just disgusting!"

"T-that's r-ridiculous... j-just s-stupid."

Willi Wissemann wanted to change the subject, hearing enough about Luddenvoss for one night. He puffed his cigarette thoughtfully, wisely reversing the tack of the conversation. "Did anyone see Eckhardt make a forced landing in No-Mans Land? Or behind the French front lines?"

"I saw his Albatros smoking badly, sir," Gutemann answered.

"Was he burning? On fire?"

"I don't think so, sir. His propeller was windmilling, tacking over. I think the engine might have just conked out."

Kindlich imparted clumsily: "He d-disappeared in the-the g-ground haze—h-heading for enemy l-lines."

"Are you sure, Kindlich?" Wissemann asked.

"W-well, I d-don't really know f-for, c-cer-cer... sure."

"Well, until we get official word from *Flugmeldedienst*, we'll have to list him as missing in action. Until then, let's hope for the best."

Wissemann took a thoughtful drag from his cigarette. The trio sat quietly for a moment, each man recollecting the last time they saw the luckless *Leutnant* Ludwig Eckhardt alive.

"Poor Baer, only lasted a week," Gutemann uttered arbitrarily.

"*Nah-ja.*" Wissemann exhaled frustratedly. "Putting him with Luddenvoss was a bad mistake. I should've known better."

"He never said a thing about signals, directions, tactics—*nix.*"

"He-he, j-just g-grabbed him by-by the j-jacket lapels and-and spouted awful obscenities at him."

"*Ja,* something like: '*Stay outta my way, boy'* or '*don't do anything stupid',*" Gutemann elaborated in an acidic Saxon drawl, trying to imitate Luddenvoss' gruff timbre. He shrugged. "Well, something like that, I think."

"The p-poor m-m-man was... t-terrified of him."

"Gutemann..." Wissemann announced suddenly, placing a gentle hand on the lad's shoulder, "I'm going to put all the newcomers in your *Kette* from now on. I know you'll teach them the basics. Young Ziegler seems to have potential, eh?"

"He does. Seems like a decent flier. He's a lousy shot, though."

"Oh." Wissemann chagrined.

"He had a Nieuport dead in his sights yesterday—completely missed! Unbelievable. I swear, he was close enough to spit on him, sir. But incredibly, he missed!"

"Well, work with him, eh? Take him up to the gunnery range at AFP-7, Gutemann, when next you get the chance," Wissemann said, finishing off his cigarette, stubbing it out in an ashtray. "We must nurture these tyros. We must!"

"Of course, sir" Otto Gutemann replied. "I have a day off coming up—Wednesday. I'll take him then." He slugged back a foamy mouthful of beer, nodding affirmatively.

"Excellent. Good man." Wissemann uncorked the bottle of cognac and poured yet another shot. "I'll see that you're amply rewarded."

"A toast!" Gutemann jerked his beer stein high in the air. "To your third victory, *Herr Hauptmann?*"

Wissemann raised his glass. *"Prost!"*

"M-May there be-be many more, s-sir."

Kindlich raised his stein too, and all three clinked them together.

The *Jastaführer* quaffed down the cognac in one gulp, feeling very merry by this time, vintage cognac always having a special way of raising his spirits. "Yes, Kindlich, may there be many more..."

Chapter 14

✠

APRIL 15, 1917. THE BLUE AND GOLD medal glistened in the morning rays of sunlight like expensive jewelry. "Congratulations Hermann on your recent decoration," said Deputy War Minister Konrad von Linkhof to *Oberst* Thomsen, both men relaxing comfortably inside von Linkhof's palatial Reichstag office, located on Wilhelmstrasse. "A well deserved honor for such a fine gentleman."

"Well, thank you, Konrad. I appreciate that very much."

"But don't you have to shoot down sixteen enemy machines to qualify for it?"

"Twenty! We've raised the requirement again."

"Again?"

"That's right. Besides, I couldn't fit my fat ass into the cockpit of one of those little scouts," *Oberst* Thomsen joked, laughing spiritedly. "Good god, man. I'd never get off the ground!"

Both men laughed with delight.

Oberst Thomsen had just recently received Germany's highest military honor, the Order *Pour le Mérite*—known to the rest of the world as the "Blue Max." The Kaiser had awarded it to him for outstanding service in the development of the *Luftstreitkräfte*.

Although von Linkhof and Thomsen seemed outwardly amused, both realized a darker topic lurked in the back of their minds. Konrad von Linkhof knew he could not put off the inevitable; it was time to get to the business at hand. His expression was grim, his eyes clouding with worry. He gave *Oberst* Thomsen a special report.

"Read carefully, Hermann," he said gloomily. "I'm afraid its bad news for the Fatherland."

"Indeed. Very bad." Thomsen took the report and began to leaf through it.

"That's the official war report, compiled by the War Cabinet, and it also includes the latest *FlugM* intelligence." Konrad von Linkhof sank back into his plush office chair and sighed. "Now the Fatherland is truly involved in a world war."

Thomsen read the report with growing concern. It was indeed bad news, bad news for the Fatherland. The United States had declared war on Germany and her allies on April 6. The declaration came after the Americans received a decoded intercept of the Zimmerman Telegram from British Intelligence. Germany had tried to influence Mexico into attacking the United States. German foreign secretary, Arthur Zimmermann, sent a telegram to Heinrich von Eckhardt, the German minister in Mexico, in anticipation of Germany resuming unrestricted submarine warfare on February 1, a calculated act the German High Command feared would draw the neutral United States into the war on the side of the British and French. Whether it did or not, the intercepted communique managed to have the same effect.

"*Herr* Zimmerman didn't even deny it, Konrad, when confronted. Did he?" Thomsen asked.

"No! That man is a complete idiot."

Thomsen read on. British Naval Intelligence intercepted the telegram. It had been transmitted by radio across two telegraph routes, under the cover of diplomatic messages by two neutral governments, Sweden and the United States. Germany lacked direct telegraphic access to the Western hemisphere because the British had cut the German cables in the Atlantic and shut down German stations in neutral countries. This forced Germany to use British and American cables instead, despite the risk of interception.

Thomsen shook his head in total disbelief. How could Zimmermann have been so careless?

The encrypted messages had traveled over cables that passed through British territory, and as a result, was intercepted by British intelligence. President Wilson responded by asking Congress to arm American ships so that they could defend themselves from potential German submarine attacks. A few days later on April 2, Wilson asked Congress to declare war on Germany. Four days later, Congress complied, bringing the United States into the war.

Thomsen sighed. He knew America had nearly limitless resources.

The telegram was not the only reason for the United States' entry into the war, Thomsen found out in the report. German U-boats had been very busy against Allied shipping. Previously, German U-boats sank United States ships, vessels that carried many American citizens. The most well known, of course, was the *RMS Lusitania*, torpedoed off the coast of Ireland in May '15. Although Thomsen, like many other high-ranking Germans, viewed this as a travesty, he reluctantly realized this was the result of total war. Most officials in the High Command believed the ocean liner had been carrying munitions for the Allied war effort. It was a propaganda windfall for the Allies. Other lesser-known ships sunk were the *SS Housatonic* in February '17, in the Bay of Biscay and the *SS California*, also off the Irish coast.

Perceived as especially deceiving, the telegram was sent to the German embassy in Washington via the United States embassy in Berlin, and the American-operated cable from Denmark. Once the American public believed the telegram to be genuine, it was inevitable that the United States would join the war.

Thomsen closed the report, chucking it onto von Linkhof's desk, grumbling, shaking his head in dismay. "This whole thing is a fiasco, Konrad," he asserted bitterly.

"That's putting it mildly," Deputy Minister Konrad von Linkhof agreed. "And Ambassador Eckhardt failed in his attempts to urge Mexico to broker an alliance between our government and Japan."

"That plan was doomed from the start too."

"No matter how generous an offer, our financial support is worthless if Mexico is unable to acquire arms, ammunition and other war supplies."

"That's not so difficult to fathom, Konrad."

"Truly. The English, unfortunately, are the only sizable arms manufacturer in the Americas. Thankfully, American industry hasn't geared up for war yet."

"Well, why can't we ship our own supplies to them?"

"The Royal Navy controls the Atlantic sea lanes, U-boats be damned. So we couldn't possibly supply a sizable quantity of arms to *Presidenté* Carranza." Von Linkhof sank back in his chair, hands folded, his mind in deep thought.

"Right. Mexico's attempts to retake its former territories would mean a very long war with the more industrially powerful United States," Thomsen remarked dryly. "I don't think Mexico is capable of sustained warfare."

"Like you said, Hermann, it was a plan doomed from the start."

"Have we received official word from *Presidenté* Carranza yet?"

"He formally declined Zimmermann's proposals yesterday."

"Alas, there's no immediate threat. The American military is small and obsolete. It'll take some time before their weight can be felt, my friend"

"I hope you're right, Hermann. Time is all we have right now."

"They practically have no air service to speak of either. And Russia," he guffawed, "will soon be out of the picture. Then we'll be able to divert all our forces against the French and English. We'll crush them in one final victorious offensive!" Thomsen raved, shaking a fist in the air.

Still dejected, the Deputy War Minister sighed and decided to shift the conversation to yet another problem. "Let me change the subject a moment, Hermann. What have you been able to find out about the Albatros recall?"

"Well, Konrad. All the new Albatros D. III's have been sent back to the factory for modifications, refitted of sorts, and will then be forwarded to the various Army *Flugparks* for redeployment," Thomsen explained.

"How were they modified?"

"A makeshift method is being used to strengthen the lower wing —extra bracing wires, an auxiliary bracing strut, I'm told."

"Right. And what do Thelen and his engineers have to say?"

"Nothing really. They say the Albatros, like all new prototypes, isn't immune to technical problems."

"Why didn't Thelen just continue with the successful D.II wing design?"

"The V-strut designed was apparently copied from the French. The idea was taken from the Bébé—the Nieuport 11—a nimble but somewhat fragile scout aeroplane. It gave our Eindeckers much trouble. The French design worked well enough for the next Nieuport production model, as well— the 17C—except for one drawback."

"And what was that?" von Linkhof wondered.

"Occasionally, the lower wing breaks in flight."

"*Occasionally?* That's not very practical."

"This is termed 'wing flutter,' Konrad. Vibration, over stressing the wing—pulling up too fast or diving too steeply. For the French, apparently, this drawback was an acceptable risk."

"But not for our pilots, *nicht?*"

"Well," Thomsen shrugged abjectly. "Our pilots simply have to be careful putting the aircraft through violent maneuvers."

Von Linkhof scoffed. "Not always an easy task in aerial combat."

"Indeed!" Thomsen exclaimed. "The inherent wing defect in the Albatros has just been shrugged off by the designers and engineers.

Everything has a breaking point, they claim."

"That's preposterous! Unacceptable!" von Linkhof bolted up from his chair, turned about, and stared aimlessly out the window. He contemplated the consequences for rushing the prototype Albatros D.III into production. It should've been apparent to him from the start that aircraft design and production was still an imperfect science; aeronautical engineering was still in its infancy. Hell, he thought, aeroplanes hadn't even been armed at the beginning of the war. It wasn't until some French ex-tennis star had strapped a machine gun onto his aeroplane, shot down three German aircraft, with crude deflection plates bolted onto the propeller, before anyone in the German High Command even took notice.

"Ach! Those idiots at *Albatros Gesellschaft* don't have to fly them," von Linkhof groused, "Of course *they're* not worried."

"My thoughts exactly," Thomsen replied.

"Why hasn't Anthony Fokker come up with something respectable lately? Those damned D.II and D.III biplanes he came out with last summer were—well, horridly obsolete. Down right inferior."

"Anthony Fokker says he's been working on a triplane design, Konrad. He seems to have won von Richthofen's endorsement."

"Von Richthofen?"

"*Ja,*" Thomsen replied. "Von Richthofen claims the British Triplanes *play* with our new Albatros."

"So why did they change the Albatros design in the first place?"

Thomsen racked his brain for an answer. He tried to recall what the engineer from *Albatros Gesellschaft* had told him. Thomsen had received a two hundred page—*Technische Berichte Apr/1917*—report detailing the engineering aspects of the new Albatros D. III. Thomsen hadn't bothered to read it through fully, just skimming through it. He did remember one point though: *Herr* Thelen's designers much admired the lower wing configuration of the Nieuports.

"*Herr* Thelen and his engineers studied the Nieuport designs and copied their sesquiplane wing design," Thomsen replied.

"Sesquiplane?"

"The lower wing is smaller than the upper wing."

"Oh." Von Linkhof nodded. "Go on."

Thomsen sighed, then took a deep, hesitant breath.

"C'mon, Hermann. What's the problem, here?"

"Well, the benefits of a smaller, lighter wing are: better maneuverability, an unobstructed lower vision, and of course, better aerodynamics. The thirty percent smaller wing is supposed to decrease the weight of the Albatros."

"Really? Is the Albatros that heavy?"

"The Mercedes six-cylinder engine is *quite* heavy, Konrad. Therefore, Thelen tried other ways to reduce the overall weight. Cutting the lower wing beams from two to one—reduces the weight. But creates a smaller wing loading factor." Thomsen shrugged. "Or something like that?"

"Hmm, is that such a good idea?"

"On paper the idea seems good enough."

"On paper..." Von Linkhof scoffed.

"That's engineers for you, Konrad."

"Idiots, more like!" Von Linkhof shook his head disgustedly. "And connected by triangular outboard struts, just like the French scout, the Albatros looks a bit like the Nieuport?"

"Well, sort of. The Brits have nicknamed it the—*V-strutter*—so say the intelligence blockheads at *FlugM*." Thomsen smirked haughtily.

FlugM, or more aptly, *Flugmeisterei*—German Air Intelligence—kept him constantly inundated with the absurd as well as the important regarding enemy activity. Thomsen viewed the various intelligence agencies, and there were quite a few, with growing contempt, being a victim of their overwrought machinations once too often. *Oberst* Thomsen's traducements and disrespect for the "stuffed shirts" at Air Intelligence were boundless.

"*Puh*, the English and their silly nicknames," von Linkhof quipped.

"The big difference between the Nieuport and the Albatros is, of course, weight, my friend."

"How much weight?"

"The Nieuport weighs in at about four hundred and eighty kilos. The Albatros checks in at nearly eight hundred and eighty-five, fully loaded. The Albatros is probably the heaviest scout at the Front."

"So why then, do the wings... break off?"

"According to the 'geniuses' at Johannistal, the Nieuport can't approach the diving speeds required for the wings to flutter and break off. However, the Albatros with its sturdy plywood fuselage can. Prolonged dives can result in disaster."

Von Linkof's chin jerked up crankily. "And what does *Herr* Thelen and his engineers have to say about that, hmm?"

"Well..." Thomsen paused for a moment, trying to remember a technical calculation from the factory report. "Oh, yes, now I remember. And I quote: 'The four-and-a-half times loaded wing safety factor can be easily exceeded in combat by speeds exceeding 250-kilometers per hour.' There!" He held up the substantially thick paper report. "I'm quoting *Herr* Thelen's analysis verbatim, Konrad."

"So..." Von Linkhof sighed. "In short: the new D.III design characteristics favor structural failure?" He returned to his chair, completely disgusted.

"That about sums it up, Konrad. The Albatros D.III incorporates a unusually fast diving speed, significant wing under-camber, a weak lower wing, incorrect wing loading estimates and insufficient safety factors. It's all here in this tedious technical report." Thomsen plopped the two hundred page ream down on von Linkhof's desk.

"Unbelievable! Unbelievable!" von Linkhof exclaimed.

"All those factors add up." Thomsen sighed and folded his hands together on his lap. "Well, anyway, we'll have to double production with the Americans coming into the war now. General von Hoeppner has already suggested it to the War Cabinet."

"General von Hoeppner has already sent me the proposal. And the Cabinet has decided to call it the *Amerika Programm.* It should take effect by mid June," Von Linkhof grumbled, shaking his head in disgust. All this technical stuff was mind boggling and confusing. There was no easy fix to the problem. Unfortunately, the German pilots would just have to make due. And that was ridiculous.

Ludicrous! Ludicrous! Ludicrous! he thought bitterly.

He sat quietly for a long moment, his concentration beginning to drift, another thought coming to mind, something more personal. "So. Tell me, Hermann. Have you found out anything about Willi Wissemann's background? Did the investigation reveal anything?"

"Well, sort of," Thomsen replied. "His grandfather was Alsatian, born in Colmar. He married a German woman from Offenburg. Then they moved to Kempten in 1865. A year later, Wissemann's father was born. Five years after that, Wissemann's grandfather fought in the war against France—winning the Iron Cross, 1st Class, for bravery." The old Prussian frowned, folding his hands, utterly disappointed. His findings had only proved one thing—Wissemann was truly German.

"So? Is Wissemann of French descent or not?"

"Well, distantly, Konrad. But not in the truest sense."

"Nah-ja," von Linkhof rejoined, exhaling wearily. "Unfortunately, the ancestry investigations have lost impetus now that the United States has declared war on Germany."

"Well, it never really proved anything in the first place."

"But there must be something we can do, Hermann! That man must not marry my daughter. We must find a way to discredit him, tarnish his image, ruin his reputation."

"What were you thinking?"

"We must make Ilse see the real Willi Wissemann!" An angry fist came down on von Linkof's desktop. "A low-born commoner! Ach! A rotten—*Hochstapler*—for God's sake!"

"An imposter? Really?

"A fraud!"

"Indeed." Thomson smirked. "There's always a chance he could fall in battle?"

"And there is always the possibility he may not! He's been wounded umpteen times already. The man seems indestructible." Von Linkhof's fist shook angrily.

"Come, come now, Konrad. No man is indestructible. Don't be so dramatic."

"Well..."

"He is a bit of an idiot. An 'accident' could be arranged."

Von Linkhof paused a moment, surprised by Thomsen's sinister suggestion. "No, no, Hermann! Ilse would be devastated if he perished mysteriously."

"Well, I've been toying with an idea that might work." There was a heinous gleam in *Oberst* Thomsen's eye. "Surely your daughter couldn't love a traitor of the Fatherland. Could she?" The old Prussian smiled evilly.

Von Linkhof cocked his head, puzzled. "A traitor? What in blazes do you mean?"

"As you probably well know, Konrad. We have a large spy network operating in Paris. And from time to time, they pick up and drop off spies at clandestine locations near Paris."

"Really? And how do they get past the French defenses?"

"They use captured Allied aircraft—operate under the cover of darkness, etc. etc."

"Aha. And how do you intend to turn Wissemann into a traitor?"

Thomsen chuckled. "One of our spies in Paris is a double agent, I'm told by Intelligence. They've suspected him for quite sometime now. He's definitely spying for the French," he explained. "Other contacts in Paris alerted Intelligence a year ago about his spurious identity. With a skillful campaign of disinformation, they discovered many crucial errors in the information he was relaying to the High Command. Certain things just didn't add up."

"And this agent is *still* operating?" Von Linkhof was aghast.

"Well, yes. Of course."

"Why hasn't he been eliminated?"

"Because he still serves a useful purpose to the Fatherland."

"Where are you going with all this, Hermann? Come to the point!"

"Patience, Konrad. Patience," Thomsen rejoined evenly. "We have special *FlugM* aerial units that operate directly with our Secret Service Office."

"*FlugM* operates aircraft?" von Linkhof asked. "I didn't realize—"

"That's right." Thomsen unfolded both hands in his lap, clearing his throat. "Now listen carefully. Here's the plan..."

WILLI WISSEMANN WATCHED THE CAUDRON tumble down out of control; it was his second victory of the day and the first "double" of his career. Earlier that morning, he'd shot down a pesky little Nieuport-11 patrolling low over the Chemin des Dames for his fourth confirmed victory. In that same engagement, Luddenvoss dispatched two other Nieuports, both in flames. *Leutnant* Fleischer shot down the old Dorand artillery spotter the trio of Nieuports had been escorting.

Wissemann's Caudron crashed two kilometers north of Bétheny in a cloud of smoke and flames. By French standards, he was an ace now. And according to a French newspaper, among other comforts, he would be automatically issued a three-day pass and a cash bonus from the Michelin Tire Company. Hmm, he wondered. Could a German airman qualify for such an auspicious award? The big Bavarian chuckled. Nevertheless, by German reckoning he needed ten victories to claim the honorary title of *"Kanone."* Five more to go!

Wissemann fired a green flare and the *Kette* reassembled.

His flight of six Albatroses had ambushed a trio of Caudron two-seaters on their way back from a bombing sortie. The French Caudrons had just hit the road junction at Craonne, an intersection choked with German supply wagons and infantry soldiers. 7th Army *Flugmeldedienst* had alerted the *Jasta* via telephone, and Wissemann's *Kette* took off immediately to intercept them, the call coming in at 1730-hours. The *Kette* of six searched the skies for nearly an hour before they finally caught the Caudrons trying to cross the front lines.

Of course, Luddenvoss was the first to spot them. He didn't bother to signal the rest of the *Kette.* Instead, he instantaneously broke formation, peeling off in a hasty zoom-dive. That dive brought his Albatros within point-blank range for a quick attack against three unsuspecting Caudrons. Wissemann, after noticing the Saxon's speedy onrush, signaled the *Kette.* Five Albatros scouts zoomed down in the wake of an impetuous Heinrich Luddenvoss. Luddenvoss closed on the leading Caudron and fired two bursts of ten rounds from a pair of well-aimed Maxims. He scored lethally.

Seriously damaged, the lumbering Caudron immediately staggered out of formation and fell in a long inverted dive, breaking apart on the way down. And Wissemann, who had now ranged the enemy formation, bore in close at thirty meters. He blasted a long volley of fifty rounds. The observer never had a chance to retaliate. In a firestorm of streaking lead, both observer and pilot were hit and killed instantly. The Caudron stalled, rolling sideways, tumbling earth bound, spun down out of control. Winkler and Auersbach shot down the third Caudron, both claiming to have put in the fatal burst. A "friendly" coin toss later, would determine who got full credit.

Wissemann was quite pleased—it had been a textbook-styled attack. And what's more, seven enemy aircraft had been added to the *Jasta's* score card for the day. A successful day indeed! *Jasta 23* was finally shaping up. He banked his Albatros northward, and the rest of the *Kette* followed suit. The *Jastaführer* marshaled them into a broad arrowhead, and like a flock of wild geese on their way to summer sanctuary, winged back to base.

The sun was setting, illuminating the horizon in a pink-orange glow. It was a marvelous thing to behold. The puffy clouds reminded Wissemann of French pastries he'd sampled in a Parisian café, while strolling along the *Champs Elysées* one day before the war. How could one think of the horrors of war in the midst of such natural beauty? And looking off to his right, in the distance, he could see the Cathedral of Reims. It was but a faint silhouette in the fading light of dusk but still magnificent! He checked his fuel gauge.

"Time to go home."

OBERST HERMANN THOMSEN plopped down in his chair after pacing around von Linkhof's office anxiously for fifteen minutes, explaining his mad scheme in detail.

"There, Konrad. It's foolproof." The old Prussian nodded, sneering pridefully. "I've thought of every detail. It'll go like clockwork. Everything's been worked out."

"It sounds like a devilish plan, Hermann," von Linkhof replied, but still not quite convinced. "Are you sure it will work?"

"*Hah-hah-hah!*" Thomsen belly-laughed. "It's certain to work."

"And if he returns?"

"*Quatsch!* He will not return."

"But, what if—"

"He will be shot as a traitor!"

"Shot? And how do we get him to accept such an undertaking?"

"Leave that to me, Konrad. He won't be able to resist such a task. His deep sense of pride and duty will override his better judgment."

"How can you be so sure, Hermann?"

"Trust me, Konrad. I know Willi Wissemann."

"All right then," von Linkhof said, rising to his feet. "Put the plan in operation, let me know how it falls into place. But let's keep it between just us two. Okay?"

"Of course, of course." *Oberst* Thomsen nodded. "I'll use the 'special' channels of communication. Secrecy is my specialty. No one will ever know you were involved, or I, for that matter."

"Good enough, Herman," von Linkhof concluded, proffering his hand in friendship. "Well, I have a Cabinet meeting in ten minutes... we'll talk again later. Good day, my friend."

"Good day, Konrad."

Both men shook hands.

With the meeting concluded, *Oberst* Thomsen left von Linkhof's office. As he traipsed down the steps of the War Ministry building in his heavy, lumbering gait, a wicked thought occurred to him. The new Albatros scout was a problematic and hazardous machine, and Willi Wissemann was just as troublesome. The old Prussian smiled deviously. He threw his head back in evil laughter. "Sometimes, Hermann," he said to himself, "your cunning is astounding!"

He went back inside and made a quick phone call.

THE *KETTE* WAS CIRCLING THE AERODROME. As he made his final approach, Wissemann noticed several ominous-looking thunderheads forming along the horizon. In the fading light of evening, these massive clouds almost seemed black. The *Jastaführer* sighed—a bad weather front was moving in. This would obviously curtail operations for a few days. More rain! He muttered to himself. The weather here at the Front was a maddening factor sometimes.

He touched down and taxied towards the dispersal hut. The wind was picking up, and the rain was starting to fall in fine droplets. He throttled back and shut the engine off.

Vizefeldwebel Peltzer was standing inside the canvas hangar. The illumination of naked electric bulbs silhouetted his hefty frame and trademark cigar which was clenched firmly in his mouth. Peltzer had a curious grin on his face. He was standing next to a brand new aeroplane. "Good evening, *Herr Hauptmann!* Wonderful weather we're having, eh?" He said.

Wissemann dashed from his Albatros to the safety of the hangar as the icy rain began to fall even harder. The other members of the *Kette* parked their machines and scurried for cover as the fitters and riggers worked fast and feverishly, hauling the six Albatroses underneath the cover of the hangars.

"What's this?" Wissemann said, as he peeled off a water-soaked flight cap.

"It's a present from General von Hoeppner. A factory fresh D.III!" Peltzer replied.

"From General von Hoeppner? Really?"

"That's right."

"I'll be damned. It *is* a new Albatros! From AFP-7, Laon?"

"*Ja*. Gutemann picked it up after you left for the intercept."

"I see. Excellent."

"By the way, did you find them, the Caudrons?" Peltzer asked.

"Yes! We bagged all three."

"All three? My, my. Now that *was* a successful—"

"*Gott!* A brand new Albatros D.III," Wissemann cooed. "It's a fine-looking machine." His eyes were wide with awe. He could barely contain his excitement. The sleek new Albatros was a good-looking machine, its streamline, almost shark-like appearance, made the hair on the back of his neck stand up.

"Since Schäfer's back from leave, *Herr Hauptmann*, he'll want No. 1045 back." Peltzer was referring to the serial number stenciled on the horizontal tailplane of Schäfer's old Albatros. Albatros—No. D.1045/16—was a model produced in August 1916 and built by L.V.G. or *Luft Verkehrs Gellschaft GmbH*, one of Germany's largest aircraft manufacturers, located at Johannistal, near Berlin.

"Fine. He can have that old bed-spring back," Wissemann quipped as he stroked the smooth, wood-lacquered finish of the new D. III's fuselage. "Is this one mine, Peltzer?"

"Yes, *Herr Hauptmann*, it is. And we'll be receiving two more tomorrow, I understand. And three the day after that. It has a few new modifications from the previous D.III model." Peltzer sighed. "However, I'm not sure they resolved the wing problems."

"Really?"

"Yes, sir. The main spar in the lower wing is still subject to crack or break," Peltzer replied gravely. "So, you'll just have to be careful."

"It looks lighter than the D.II."

"Lighter and faster, sir. A bit more maneuverable, too. You'll fly rings around the enemy."

Thunder rumbled. Peltzer groaned as he looked upon the stormy skies, realizing the gathering thunderheads and accompanying rain would probably suspend air operations for a few days. Foul weather was always a frustrating factor here at the Western Front.

"Well, you might have to wait a day or two, before you test her out, sir," Peltzer added. "This weather front looks bad."

"I noticed." Wissemann shrugged. "Whatever."

The "Inseparables" Otto Gutemann and Bubi Kindlich, came dashing in from the rain, joining Wissemann and Peltzer underneath the cover of the canvas hangar, cringing chillingly from the icy rainfall. Thunder cracked loudly and the horizon flickered with lightning. Gutemann smiled, rainwater dripping down his nose.

"What do you think, *Hauptmann?*" he said. "It's about time, *nicht?*"

"*Ja,* it's about time alright. Now, if the damn weather would just cooperate, we could find out how this new bird performs." Wissemann walked around the Albatros admiring its sleek lines, his hand caressing the fuselage, his eyes beaming with glee.

Peltzer began an impromptu technical briefing. "For today's standards, gentlemen..." he said, beginning a lengthy mechanical discourse, the trio of pilots listening carefully. The new Albatros D.III was very similar to the preceding D. II model. But there were a few major modifications." His mechanically inclined mind had quickly absorbed the contents of the Albatros manufacturer's manual, and he astutely relayed his conclusions to the pilots. "This latest Albatros is a compact and streamlined machine, its wooden fuselage a semi-monocoque configuration formed by spruce longerons and plywood formers. The outer covering of the shaped birch panels screw in place, whereas other manufacturers used laminated strips. This eliminates the need for internal bracing."

"That's the same Mercedes as in the D.II, isn't it?" Gutemann asked, pointing to the six-cylinder engine.

"Yes, sir. The 160-horsepower Mercedes D.IIIa inline—fits in the nose with the cylinder heads, now exposed—for easier maintenance."

Wissemann patted the wooden propeller made of laminated ash, walnut and mahogany. He walked to the rear of the Albatros, remarking on the tail construction. "The tailplane, it's the same as the old D.II?"

"Essentially. It's integrally built into the fuselage, sir—skinned with plywood, just like the D.II."

"Hmm, it's very streamlined looking," Wissemann noted.

"It is. The horizontal tailplane is framed in wood and enclosed in fabric. The rudder and elevators are constructed of steel tubing and covered in fabric."

Wissemann smiled. "I like the new mainplane design. Now the wings look like a *real* albatross."

"Uh-huh. The D.III's two-box spar upper wing has interior spars made up of plywood ribs. The leading edge-strip of plywood capping, with a trailing edge of wire, gives it a unique scalloped effect," Peltzer pointed out. "The surface is doped fabric as well, and the ailerons are framed in steel tubing."

"And I see it has a newly configured radiator, too." Wissemann eyed the angled metal 'plumbing' of the new Albatros keenly.

"That's right. The radiator is now offset to the right."

"Thank God! Now we don't have to get scalded by boiling water if we take a hit in the radiator."

"And the new angled radiator pipes don't hamper aiming, *Herr Hauptmann*," Gutemann threw in. "A very wise modification, if you ask me, sir."

Wissemann nodded. "Indeed." He kicked the tires and smiled.

"A pair of steel-tubed V-chassis makes for a solid landing gear."

"I see."

"A triangular ash tail-skid under the tailplane section augments the wheels. It's enclosed in an aerodynamic fairing, sprung with an elastic shock cord." Peltzer grinned proudly.

"The new Albatros D.III is definitely a sophisticated piece of machinery, that's for certain," Wissemann remarked, stepping up on the stirrup, looking inside the cockpit. "Ah, at least the cockpit configuration is the same. And of course, the machine guns?"

"Yes, the same. Like all Albatros models before, it's armed with a pair of LMG 08/15 synchronized Maxim machine guns, Light Machine Gun, Model—"

"I know what it stands for, Peltzer."

"They were updated in '15," Petlzer continued unabated, "when they became standard on the Eindeckers."

"That I knew as well, Peltzer." Wissemann rolled his eyes.

Peltzer grumbled, half-annoyed. "It also has the new improved Hedtke synchronizing gear, sir. It's been modified to increase rate of fire by a third."

"Now *that*, I didn't know!" Wissemann chuckled.

"Yes, she's quite the warbird, the D.III," Peltzer puffed his cigar proudly. "This is definitely the Fatherland's best scout aeroplane yet produced, *Herr Hauptmann*."

Gutemann added: "You'll be surprised to know too, sir..."

"What's that?"

"The D.III has power to spare," Gutemann elaborated. "I gave it a little workout on the way back from Laon. Remarkable! A speedy little bird, *Herr Hauptmann*."

"I can hardly wait!" Wissemann gasped. "Well, let's get inside and have some supper, shall we, gentlemen? I'm starved."

"But, sir, I still have a few things to go over—"

"Peltzer, thank you for your informative and... in-depth briefing. Let's discuss the finer details over a nice bottle of cognac and a hot meal. What say you, eh?"

"Very well, sir," Peltzer replied, a bit crestfallen.

The motley group of men slipped into the darkening light as the rain continued to pelt the scenery around them. They dashed to the chateau laughing, now soaking wet to the skin.

Thunder rumbled, lightning flashed.

The Gods of War were elated!

To: Idflieg, Berlin   From: JASTA 23

        REQUESTING CONFIRMATION FOR 5th VICTORY

        Date: 17.Apr.1917
        Time: 1821 Hours
        Place: N.of Bétheny
        Type: Caudron G.4, two-seater.

No details to report. Enemy machine crashed in trench zone. Destroyed by shellfire. Occupants: SLt. Guillaume, Sgt. Depardieu. Both killed. Buried by XX Korps, 7. Army, Witry. ID disks sent to Red Cross HQ, Berlin.

        NARRATIVE:

    At 1730 hours...message came through that enemy two-seaters had been seen at 2,000 meters altitude after bombing road junction at Craonne. I took off with five comrades. After nearly an hour, Ltn. Luddenvoss spotted the enemy two-seaters, heading southeast near the lines. After a quick zoom-dive I attacked a Caudron at close range and fired 50-rounds. Suddenly he made uncontrolled curves and crashed to the ground. After crew was removed by German infantry units, French artillery shelled the wrecked machine.

                    (Signed) Wilhelm R. Wissemann
                    HAUPT. WILHELM R. WISSEMANN

TWO DAYS LATER... A candle flickered gently in the mild evening breeze. Willi Wissemann sat quietly at his roll-top desk, pen in hand, writing a letter to Ilse. It was nearly ten o'clock and the rains had finally ceased, the weather front finally moving on. But it had taken the warm air with it, it seemed. He got up and closed the bedroom window, feeling a chill from the damp air. The weather was still wet and cooling and the aerologists at *Wetterdienst* had predicted cold conditions for the next few days. This wasn't good news for the *Jasta;* the men became restless with too much idle time on their hands. Scout pilots were high-strung thrill seekers that needed a challenge all the time. Hair-raising dogfights, high speed aeroplanes, the constant threat of death, gave these men a fine edge.

So, Wissemann organized a football match earlier that afternoon, in the hopes that some spirited competition might promote better *Jasta* morale—help the men blow off some steam. The game pitted the officers against the noncoms, Wissemann as the referee. It was a closely contested contest. Of course, when the officers won, a scuffle broke out after a disputed penalty kick. The officers won the match two goals to one. However, the noncoms didn't see it that way. They protested the game. A brawl ensued. Two men were hurt bad enough to spend a day in the local field hospital. After that, there were no more foot ball games.

The day before that, Wissemann tried to put a musical band together. He let *Leutnant* Winkler handle the arrangements since he was the most accomplished musician. Impromptu auditions were held. Not really a musician himself, Wissemann was just content to sing along occasionally. Gutemann, as it turned out, had a splendid singing voice. The Swabian's nearly operatic tenor thrilled and awed the *Jasta* cadre. Even the drunken "Ironman" from Völklingen, Josef Schäfer, contributed a tune or two on his ragged old concertina.

But of course, as always, the performance generated into a drunken singalong and alcohol-infused drinking bout. Soon tempers flared, and the after-hours activity evolved into a raucous free-for-all. Although this was a normal occurrence for most squadrons stationed at the Front, French or German, Wissemann chagrined, alcohol seem to be the defining element in everything occurring after off-duty hours. It was a discouraging fact of military life.

The *Jastaführer* had, in the past, tried to limit the consumption of alcohol by restricting the cadre to the aerodrome during heavy action periods. But this failed miserably. Trouble soon arose when pilots, wretched from constant flying, illicitly slipped off in the night in search of something to wet their alcoholic cravings. Nothing seemed to work. Wissemann soon rescinded the order. And this Bavarian gentleman was more than aware of his own propensity for drinking, often worrying that the effects of a demanding command and the constant exposure to air combat would whittle away his genteel and well-mannered military bearing. The men must never see their commander stumbling about in a drunken stupor. Even if they didn't like him, they must respect him. He had to strive constantly to set a good example "a guiding beacon for the men."

It wasn't an easy task being a good squadron leader. There was more to being a *Jastaführer* than just ordering people around, signing documents, meting out discipline, leading combat formations. It was like being the head of a large family or an executive of a small firm. He had to lookout for his "children" his "colleagues," make sure everyone understood their role and was properly cared for. Although there was a job to do, a war to fight, people would always remain people, there would always be everyday annoyances and troubles outside the sphere of daily combat and military protocol. A *Jastaführer* was a combat leader, a father figure, and above all, an example of inexorable military discipline. Ach! He sighed. Never an easy job.

He paced the floor of his quarters stiffly, trying to concentrate on his letter. He stopped, thought for a moment, smiled, and then as if suddenly inspired, sat back down at the desk and resumed his writing. Moments later, he finished. Wissemann sealed the treacly little billet doux and placed it in a box with cheese and chocolate. He sat for a moment in thought, recapping the day's events. What in the world was I thinking? A football match pitting the officers against the noncoms? Ridiculous idea, Willi. How utterly ridiculous!

Indeed. Anxiety was a constant verity plaguing every man at the Front, he concluded. It reared its ugly head in the most unusual way sometimes. Most often, the common soldier vented his frustrations the best way he knew how—restless aggression. Airmen were no different. *Gott!* And how very anxious he was to fly that new Albatros. Soon, Willi, soon, he said to himself. Five more would be coming in two days. The bad weather had delayed their delivery. And the crafty *Jastaführer* decided to allocate them among the men, according to seniority, not rank or combat record. Luddenvoss would probably object, but Wissemann figured he could use the new Albatros as leverage—get the rebellious Saxon to toe the line—

There was a thunderous knock on the door!

"*Herr Hauptmann!* Sorry to disturb you, sir," Schutzling shouted from behind the closed door.

"What is it, Schutzling?"

"There seems to be some trouble down at the Kasino."

Wissemann opened the door."Trouble? What's going on?"

"Schäfer and *Leutnant* Luddenvoss have been arrested by the military police for fighting. Please, come quickly!"

"Fighting? Where are they now?" Wissemann asked.

"The Kasino. The military police are about to haul them off!"

The *Jastaführer* yanked limp suspender straps over his shoulders, grabbed his cap and tunic and darted out of the room. Schutzling led the way down the staircase, Wissemann close behind him. Downstairs, the idling Renault staff car waited with Grimm at the wheel. Both men scrambled into the staff car, then all three sped off to the Kasino.

Upon arriving, they found a scene of chaos and confusion. The military police had Schäfer and Luddenvoss bound and restrained as a throng of boozy onlookers gawked and jeered, taunting the two troublemakers. An overanxious Wissemann leaped out of the Renault, even before it came to a complete halt, and stalked up to the mob of onlookers, addressing the military policeman, an *Oberwachmeister*.

"I am *Hauptmann* Wilhelm Wissemann—*Jasta 23*."

"Oh?"

" I'm the commanding officer of these two men."

"*Herr Hauptmann*—*Oberwachmeister* Gruber, at your service, sir" he said with a snappy salute. Boot heels clicked.

"What's the trouble?"

A flustered Willi Wissemann did not return the salute.

"Both men are under arrest for disorderly conduct. Brawling, sir."

Gruber was a tall, lanky NCO with a bright red mustache and piercing blue eyes. He wore a M1916 field tunic with a dark green collar piped in red and the duty gorget bearing the Roman numeral XII, his original corps, and his personal police number. He was armed with a 9-millimeter Luger and a bayonet hung at his side. He eyed Wissemann with caution, seeing this officer was overly excited and annoyed. He didn't want to provoke another altercation in an already busy evening of arrests and investigations.

"I'm taking these men to the Laon jail for the evening—"

"Hold on just a minute, my man."

"Hmm?"

"Let me speak to them for a moment. Please?"

"Uh... of course, sir. Go right ahead."

The gangly military policeman stroked the reddish stubble on his chin and sighed heavily. He ordered the crowd to move back, out of the way, giving *Hauptmann* Wissemann some room. Four guards, two restraining Schäfer and Luddenvoss respectively, manhandled the two airmen, shoving them forward so that the *Jastaführer* could get a better look at them.

Willi Wissemann gazed at the two scalawags suspiciously, frowning. Schäfer was obviously drunk and struggling to maintain his balance. The two military police officers had only to restrain him with light force. His face was bloody and his right eye was swollen, as well as his lower lip. He also seemed to be missing a tooth. Luddenvoss, on the other hand, appeared unscathed. The simmering Saxon stood quietly, composed, displaying his customary arrogant expression. Wissemann could see blood on his clenched fists and smelled the liquor from his winded breathing.

He addressed Luddenvoss first.

"What happened here?"

"Nothing, really," Luddenvoss replied

"Nothing?"

"Just having a good time until this... *JACKASS*, ruined— "

"You b-bastard!" Schäfer ranted drunkenly. "Who in t-the hell do you think you are—"

"Silence, Schäfer!" Wissemann roared, his head snapping about. "I'm talking to Luddenvoss now. You'll have your turn in a moment." He turned back to the Saxon. "Please continue, Luddenvoss."

Leutnant Winkler suddenly stepped forward, shoving his way past the bibulous throng, addressing Wissemann in a slow, sottish drawl. He'd been drinking too. *"Herr Hauptmann (hic)* I saw the whole thing," he said with a quirky hiccup.

"Really?" Wissemann could smell the liquor on Winkler's breath. "All right. Explain."

"Schäfer here, as you can see, is quite drunk."

"Yes. Go on..."

"He confronted Luddenvoss *(hic)* after his girl ditched him."

"Aha..."

"You see, sir," Winkler slurred drunkenly. "She *(hic)* ditched him for Luddenvoss' company."

The drunken crowd of men booed and jeered. The womanizing Heinrich Luddenvoss was not a popular man, but neither was a raunchy little barfly that slept around with every Fritz in town.

"Josef Schäfer's a disgusting drunk—treats me bad!" a petite, dirty-looking French girl spluttered in inarticulate German.

The crowd erupted into raucous laughter.

"Silence! *Mein Gott!*" Wissemann bellowed.

The boozy crowd hushed, then settled to a restless murmur.

Then Wissemann said: "Winkler, go on. Continue."

"Well, sir. Schäfer here took the first swing, missing quite badly, I must say. Then Luddenvoss (*hic*) just let him have it. I guess Schäfer had it coming, you know," Winkler explained then shrugged his shoulders as if he weren't sure what had actually happened.

The Ironman from Völklingen was scowling at Winkler now, seething heatedly for being ratted out.

Wissemann shook his head. His temper was rising as fast as the temperature was dropping. Little snowflakes began to fall from the sky, the aerologists seemingly correct for a change, the weather turning icy-foul again. He grumbled and eyed the Saxon officer with misgivings, somehow, knowing Luddenvoss was to blame for this altercation. He stared into a pair of baleful, unblinking eyes, eyes bloodshot and unyielding, eyes simmering with hatred.

"Is this true, Luddenvoss?"

Luddenvoss stood silent for a long moment.

"Well...?"

"Schäfer is an idiot," Luddenvoss replied, finally. "I told him to buzz off. But he wouldn't let it go. Genevieve prefers my company, see? But he insisted. That dirty *schweine* took a swing at me, and I let him have it. Schäfer started it—I finished it." Luddenvoss grinned cynically. "Like Winkler said... he had it coming."

Wissemann sighed irritably, gazing into the throng of gathered men, his volatile spirits sagging as his searching eyes found nothing, nothing but rosy, bleary-eyed faces sullen with cheap beer and distilled spirits. All of them seemed to be slightly intoxicated. He saw Peltzer and their eyes met. Peltzer nodded languidly, his expression seemingly saying: *It's all true, Herr Hauptmann. It's all true.*

Wissemann glared at the drunken noncom from the Saar. "All right, Schäfer. Is that how it happened? Did you take a swing at Luddenvoss? Did you try to assault him physically?"

Josef Schäfer teetered back and forth drunkenly, mumbling incoherently. "*Herr Haupt*—I, I'm... ooh... so sorry, but-but... oh my— I'm gonna—ugh-h-h-h..."

The Ironman turned a sickening pallid of pale, moaning, coughing once, drooping over. Then in a seemingly uncontrollable yawn, retched on the ground right in front of Willi Wissemann's feet. The wary *Jastaführer* jumped backed instinctively, his boots nearly splattered by a sickening surge of vomit.

Wissemann stood dumbfounded a moment, glowering, groaning, shocked to utter disbelief, shaking his head, rasping his forehead as if he were trying to restrain a massive migraine.

The crowd grumbled and hissed, sickened by the sight of that nauseous deluge, a collective and disgusted moaning reverberating through the throng, a sobering reminder to them all about drinking too much. But not Luddenvoss, he was laughing. Laughing hard!

Wissemann was seething. "Ach! Take them away, Gruber. I'll deal with these drunken half-wits tomorrow morning."

"Yes, sir." Gruber gave a nod, saluting respectfully.

He then ordered his men to load the two troublemakers into a waiting police lorry. Luddenvoss went willingly, but Schäfer had to be manhandled into the lorry. He had passed out cold, unconscious, after his sickening torrent. Wissemann and Schutzling returned to the staff car and drove back to the aerodrome. In the car, the *Jastaführer* ordered swift, punitive action.

"Schutzling, put both men on report," he snapped. "They're both to see me the moment they return from jail. Schäfer is restricted to his billet until further notice. I want a full account of this little episode entered in their personnel files and the disciplinary report on my desk first thing tomorrow morning!"

"*Jawohl, Herr Hauptmann,*" Schutzling obeyed. "I'll send the truck and retrieve them from Laon tomorrow morning. I'll have the paper work ready for your signature."

"Good! I will not tolerate outright insubordination any longer!"

Schutzling nodded in compliance.

Grimm smiled cynically as he steered the Renault back to the aerodrome, observing Wissemann's angry expression in the rearview mirror, smiling, his eyes flashing with elation.

"*Hm-hm-hmm...*" came the evil chuckle.

NEXT MORNING, WISSEMANN, ordered by *Kofl* to fly a barrage patrol over the St. Souplet Sector, in the vicinity of the Bazancourt-Challerange Railway, rose at the crack of dawn. The weather was decent enough, the wind minimal, only a light snow had fallen the night before—the ceiling was at least a good three thousand meters. Three new Albatros D.III scouts lined the edge of the tarmac near the hangars, along with two older D.II's and one ancient Halberstadt. Peltzer's ground crew had worked feverishly before daybreak to prepare the machines for the dawn patrol. As *Jastaführer,* he rarely flew the dawn perambulation, but since he was two men short, he really had no choice. Just as well, Wissemann conceded, he needed to air out his frustrations anyway. Schäfer and Luddenvoss wouldn't be back until late morning, so he had a little time before those two bibulous "blockheads" returned from Laon.

"Perhaps..." Willi Wissemann confided to his mirrored reflection that very morning, "I'll have a Frenchman for breakfast—clear my head of these problems. Nothing like the thrill of combat to revitalize the senses, get the heart pumping." His reflection winked back. *Ja!*

Accompanying the *Jastaführer* on this early morning excursion were Auersbach, Fleischer, Neubauer, Prandzynski the Austrian, and a new replacement named, Emil Metzger. While Wissemann was at the message center getting an update on the weather, the four pilots gathered in the mess. Auersbach, Fleischer, Neubauer sat restlessly playing a friendly game of skat, while the Austrian fidgeted with his medals, which hung in a neat row on his leather jacket.

Metzger was the last one to arrive. He strode in cautiously, being the new man always an awkward situation, feeling uncomfortable and unwelcome. The trio of card sharks hardly noticed him when he came in. Only Prandzynski acknowledged him—a faint smile and a nod, then he went back to fondling his decorations.

Metzger coughed insistently, clearing his throat, announcing himself. "Morning, gents," he muttered timidly. "I guess we're all waiting for the *Jastaführer?* Is that right?"

"That's right! Have a seat, boy," Auersbach, the old-timer, snarled without looking up.

"How old are you anyway, Metzger?" Neubauer asked.

"Nineteen."

"Menschenskind!"

"More lambs for the slaughter," Auersbach chuckled, slapping down a winning trump. Fleischer and Neubauer grumbled as they went down in defeat, yet once again.

Metzger found a seat, a sheepish, emasculated grin distorting his pale features. He was quite jittery, this being his first patrol. He drummed nervous fingers on the tabletop, staring at the clock on the wall. It was only a few minutes after five o'clock and he was already terribly exhausted from lack of sleep. Pre-patrol anxiety had kept him up nearly all night. He exhaled worriedly and nibbled at a fingernail.

"You should eat something, Metzger," Prandzynski suggested.

"Oh, no, I c-couldn't. My stomach is in knots."

"Quatsch!" Auersbach snapped. "Don't listen to him, better just have some coffee, *Junge*. A bundle of nerves and a full stomach, will just make a mess of things up there."

"Huh?"

"The first bit of turbulence and... *whoops!*"

"Excuse me?"

"You'll have a nice little pool of puke in the cockpit!"

Metzger grimaced.

Prandzynski shook his head. "Advice from the wise old owl?"

"You just keep that packing crate of yours on an even keel, *Herr Holzkopf!*" Auersbach muttered bitterly. "You crack up one more machine and we're going to send your sorry ass back to Sarajevo."

"Promises, promises."

"That old Halberstadt he flies won't last much longer," Fleischer waded in spitefully. "He nearly tore the landing gear off yesterday on a hedgerow."

"*Gott!* Was it six or seven bounces, Prandzynski?" Auersbach chuckled maliciously.

The Austrian sneered, flicking his thumbnail against his upper teeth, affecting a soured face. "You just watch the *Jastaführer's* hand signals, sweetheart," he shot back. "Left hand signals mean bank left —not right. You blind old bat!"

"At least I know *how* to bank—without stumbling all over the sky, you Austrian blockhead!"

"Bah! Look who's talking—"

"Oh, you're a grand ace, Prandzynski," Auersbach replied in a spiteful tone. "Why, you deserve the Croix de Guerre!"

"Enough, you cackling hens!" Neubauer roared. "*Gott Verdammt!* Shut up and let's play cards already."

"Sorry, Your Excellency, didn't mean to—"

"So, what do you think of our new *Jastaführer* so far," Fleischer drawled to Neubauer, changing the subject inexplicably.

Neubauer rolled his eyes. "I don't know? He's okay I suppose."

"He's more uptight than Traurig ever was, that's for sure."

"Indeed." Neubauer nodded. "I hope he loosens up soon."

"*Ja,* Luddenvoss and Schäfer really got under his skin, it seems," Fleischer affirmed.

"Ach! Wissemann has no more control over this *Jasta* than the Kaiser has over this war," Neubauer intoned acerbically. He reshuffled the cards and cut the deck, then dealt out ten cards each. "C'mon you dimwits, make your bids. We haven't much time."

Metzger stared at the three men in disbelief, sitting quietly, listening. He was far too new to the *Jasta* to participate in such conversation, much less idle gossip. He knew he had to be cautious, fully aware that in the Air Service, the sensible man by no means ever committed himself on the subject of the commander until the local environment was thoroughly sniffed out. Why were these men so down on *Hauptmann* Wissemann, he wondered? Was he not their commanding officer? Didn't that merit a certain degree of respect? Metzger couldn't understand it. He swallowed uncomfortably, his throat bone dry now. He glanced up at the door, abruptly shocked—

"*ACH-TUNG!*" he shouted shrilly.

All five men sprang up into heel-clicking ramrods. An annoyed looking *Hauptmann* Wissemann stood framed in the doorway, the weather report in his hand, an unhappy look on his face, gazing at the group of firebrands with loathing in his eyes. He was already fully dressed and ready for the patrol. He'd been waiting for the five men at the dispersal hut for nearly fifteen minutes. Wissemann smartly strolled into the mess amongst them, frowning, shaking his head in disgust, glaring at each airman with deepening annoyance.

"I hate to break up your little *Kaffeeklatch*, ladies," he growled. "But I do believe we have a mission to fly this morning!"

"Um, sorry, sir," Auersbach stammered. "We were just about to—"

"Get out! Move your asses to the flight line. *NOW!*"

All five men scrambled for the doorway. Wissemann waited a second then called out to Metzger as the teenager made for the door. Metzger turned back, facing Wissemann with fear in his eyes.

Wissemann stalked up to him; he had a stern look on his face. "*Leutnant* Metzger," he said. "You are new to this *Jasta,* and have a lot to learn yet. I suggest you develop a sensible degree of rectitude and a thick skin. Do you hear me? Understand?"

"*Jawohl, Herr Hauptmann—*"

"These men are all troublemakers. They have no sense of duty or propriety, they're not your friends, they will not help you in anyway."

"I know, *Herr Hauptmann.*"

"I hope so."

"I'll do my best, s-sir."

"Keep your eyes on me today, at all times. Understand?"

"Yes, *Herr Hauptmann.*"

"Watch my hand signals."

"Yes, sir—"

"If we run into trouble this morning, specifically enemy scouts, run for home. Do not engage the enemy. Understand?"

"Understood—"

"*DO-NOT-ENGAGE-ENEMY-SCOUTS!*"

"Yes, yes, Herr—"

"You are worth more alive than dead. And I want your machine back in one piece too. We cannot afford to lose any equipment. Especially you!"

"Jawohl, Herr Hauptmann."

"The German taxpayer has spent far too much money on your flight training to lose you so needlessly. Keep your wits about you—in the air and on the ground. Is that clear?"

"Jawohl, Herr Hauptmann. I will. I will!"

Metzger's heart was racing madly now.

"Good. Dismissed."

Metzger bolted for the door after a stiff salute. He ran all the way to the flight line. Wissemann muttered exasperatedly, pacing for the door. He hoped he'd made a positive impression on young Emil Metzger. The *Jastaführer* sighed. "We shall see." He slammed the door and headed to the field, hoping this day would yield better results than the previous two. He scoffed inwardly—running a front line *Jasta* seemed like a lot more than he'd bargained for. Indeed!

WILLI WISSEMANN'S EYES SWEPT the skies again. Yes—there! He could see faint anti-aircraft bursts billowing around four, twin-engined devils of the old Caudron type: ugly, yellow winged insects hightailing it home from Dontrien. The ungainly-looking two-seaters were stumbling back to their 'drome after bombing the rail bridge spanning the Suippe River. Wissemann couldn't tell if the Caudrons had escort though. He'd have to get closer.

At the *Jastaführer's* hand signal, the *Kette* accelerated to full war power, making a wide turn towards the north. Prandzynski, of course, wheeled his ancient Halberstadt around in a clumsy bank. They were only a thousand meters higher than the tightly grouped French two-seaters, so Wissemann decided to assault them with a frontal attack. Wissemann signaled Metzger to stay close to him as they approached the Caudron formation. He searched the sky again above the two-seaters for a possible escort. *Nix!*

Wissemann was certain the enemy had made a grave mistake in sending their bombers out without proper escort. Poor slobs! Now there was a bum job, steering a cold-meat crate across the sky into German territory. With a hasty arm signal—a bent arm over his head—he signaled his airmen to form a line astern formation. The aeroplanes banked inwards, behind him, one after the other, lining up in a trail formation. It was a clumsy maneuver, but within a couple of seconds, they had managed it. Prandzynski lazily took up the tail end slot in the slower Halberstadt. Wissemann shook his head disgustedly.

"Ach! Something must be done about the Austrian!"

He glanced back at Metzger. The youngster was still clinging to his tail. Good, he thought. He's a fine fellow for following my orders so exactly. Perhaps there is hope for this young tyro after all.

Each pilot followed the man in front of him, their engines droning in concert, but their maneuvers lacking synchronicity. Now the observers of the Caudrons were swinging their Lewis guns into action, their motions suggesting well-timed cohesion.

Where? Where is the escort for this graceless flock of geese, Wissemann wondered? He repeated his investigation of the sky above and around. Nothing. Come now! If you hide much longer, my dear Frenchmen, we will have these fat birds for breakfast! Come now! Your poor comrades need you!

Wissemann shook his head in utter disbelief and signaled for the attack. He raised an arm then jerked it down, his hand balled in a tight fist. The *Kette* pitched down and began a long zooming dive towards the bow of the Caudrons. The French observers began to fire. Oh, let them fire, he thought. Let them waste their precious ammunition. They won't hit anything. They're still out of range.

"Fire away, you silly Frenchmen!"

The two formations accelerated closer and closer. The converging speed was tremendous. It would have been very hard for the Frenchmen to hit anything at that speed and angle, and sure enough, bright yellow needles of tracers zinged above and away from the swarm of attacking scouts. The observers' hastily aimed volleys were nowhere near Wissemann's bloodthirsty war eagles.

The *Jastaführer's* strategy was sound.

As his dive steepened, Wissemann lined his sights up on the leading Caudron. He saw that the Frenchmen were flying in a close diamond formation, for mutual protection, the fourth machine following directly behind the leader, the other two slightly abaft the leading aircraft. All four were painted a dull, mustard yellow.

Each man in the *Kette* had been previously instructed on the line astern attack approach: the leader would guide the formation to the target, firing first, then each pilot would follow up with a quick burst. In this way, the leading enemy aircraft would be pummeled by six successive attacks, ensuring a quick kill. And by taking out the enemy flight leader first, the remaining Frenchmen would be too confused to fight effectively. Then, the *Kette* would pull up, turn about, spreading out for another attack, this time on the stern of the confused two-seaters, hopefully shooting the Caudrons down from behind.

Just as Wissemann was about to fire, he heard an earsplitting—**CRACK!** At first, he thought he'd taken a hit from German anti-aircraft, gunners too exuberant to cease firing once the German airmen began their attack. It couldn't possibly be the French gunners. He was still a good three hundred meters away from them. As he glanced to his right, he saw the trouble. A large section of fabric had ripped away from the lower wing. He could see that the exposed wing beam had collapsed, broken in half under the strain of the dive. It was vibrating dangerously, bending backward in the buffeting slipstream, threatening to break off completely. Wissemann eased the stick back in a long, shallow climb. He waved the formation onward.

"Attack! Attack!"

But to Wissemann's dismay, their reactions were slow, confused, disorderly, each man having a different interpretation of the signal. Young Metzger, following the order to the letter, continued diving. Auersbach and Neubauer climbed upward, mimicking Wissemann's pullout, flying close aside his Albatros. Fleischer dived onward behind Metzger, and Prandzynski, of course, just leveled off in utter confusion. He threw his hands up briefly, as if disgusted, then banked idly in the direction of the Caudrons.

The men's reactions were deplorable. Wissemann cursed. But he was too exasperated with the details of his own dilemma, having no time to experience the full effects of his annoyance. Wissemann felt the controls growing soggy as he wrestled for control, the machine beginning to slew in a wide circle. He leveled off at two thousand meters and began circling around. He'd have to get to the ground quickly before total disaster struck!

Auersbach and Neubauer swiftly learned the reason why the *Jastaführer* had pulled up so unexpectedly out of his attack run before closing the deal. Both men saw the fluttering lower wing of his Albatros, both men grimaced in horror. Auersbach fearfully checked his own wings as did Neubauer. Their wings were fine.

Metzger and Fleischer, in the meantime, continued with the attack, Metzger's attack run feeble at best. He opened fired too soon, before he even had the Caudron properly sighted, his second gaffe occurring seconds later. After holding the triggers down too long, both his guns jammed. He climbed up over the Caudrons prematurely, under a withering fusillade of fire. His Albatros was hit many times. Fleischer, on the other hand, never even fired a shot. He'd forgotten to charge his guns before the attack. His twin Maxims were strangely silent when he depressed the trigger buttons. The French gunners put a few bullets in his Albatros too. He hastily broke off the attack after realizing his amateurish blunder, blaspheming furiously.

Wissemann gripped the control stick with both hands, trying to maintain control. The mighty Bavarian was equal to the necessity, hand and foot moving together, timed to the split second, his response to this emergency instantaneous and instinctive, and even more important than the mind and body, which could react instantly, was the automatic accuracy of his flying skills.

Somehow, the crippled Albatros maintained aerodynamic lift, beginning a controlled, spiraling descent from two thousand meters. The Albatros shuddered and bucked like a feral horse as a cursing Willi Wissemann rode it down to the ground. And since a light fog obscured most of the landscape, he decided to head towards the bombed rail bridge. The billowing smoke columns from the Caudron's bombing attack were still visible, they would be his unlikely beacons. He was almost certain there would be a road, a pasture or a field near by, where he could land safely.

Wissemann jerked his eyes back to the fluttering beam. More fabric had stripped away revealing the skeleton-like ribs and spars of the wing. The V-strut was the only thing holding the Albatros' wing together, and it was bending dangerously now. If it broke free, he worried, it might collapse and take the upper wing with it. All would be lost. Then the Valkyries could spirit him away to Valhalla.

By this time, the rest of the *Kette* had abandoned their attacks on the two-seaters, the Caudrons escaping without taking a single bullet. The *Kette* milled around loosely watching the *Jastaführer's* damaged Albatros glide round and round in wide circles, dropping ever so slightly. Auersbach realized that Wissemann had to fly at minimum speed and angle to keep the pressure off the broken wing. He knew it was a laborious, superhuman task and he didn't envy Wissemann's predicament one iota. He bit his lip and gnashed his teeth every time the Albatros's wing fluttered, threatening to break off. Neubauer and the rest of the *Kette* all shared the same sense of dread, following Wissemann all the way down.

Finally, after a long, tedious, gut-wrenching descent, Wissemann was down to a hundred meters. His whole body ached. His arms and hands throbbed painfully. But he held on tightly to the control stick. Wissemann spat, feeling his strength wane, knowing he had to get down soon! Down! Down! He yanked his goggles up, sweat draining across his forehead into his eyes, nearly obscuring his vision.

But at long last he could see a dirt highway materializing beyond the spinning blades of his propeller. Murky ground fog obscured the details of the road, but it seemed wide enough to fit the nine-meter wingspan of the Albatros. He eased the throttle back to landing speed. The wing was writhing violently now, completely stripped clean of its mauve-green fabric. "Just a few seconds more," he pleaded. "Just a few seconds more. Almost there!"

Suddenly, a large truck loomed ahead. It was blocking the road! A collision seemed imminent. *Gott!* Wissemann's heart nearly pounded out of his chest. He hastily switched the motor off and braced himself for a crash. The wheels of the Albatros kissed the ground once and then settled in the muddy roadway, wobbling roughly. Then came another loud—**CRACK!** The lower wing had finally given way, taking the strut with it. The control stick went limp. But it didn't matter; the Bavarian Eagle was safely on the ground now. The Albatros swanned onwards a few meters more, dragging the remnants of the broken wing behind it before it halted directly in front of the truck, the gray spinner of the propeller hub clipping the top of the truck's radiator, bending its shiny Daimler hood ornament backwards.

Wissemann's head drooped in total exhaustion, spent, tired, weary, his whole body drenched in sweat, his neck taut and rubbery, panting in exasperated relief. Soldiers began piling out of the truck, gathering around the cockpit. They all had incredulous looks on their pale faces. Few had ever been this close to an aeroplane before.

As Wissemann unfastened his harness, climbing out, more and more soldiers began to gather around. They were part of an infantry battalion—a lengthy convoy that stretched some five hundred meters long. The obliging soldiers helped Wissemann to the ground as he clambered down from the cockpit. The soldiers were awestruck. The questions began to fly in quick succession.

"Are you okay?"

"What happened?"

"Were you shot down?"

Wissemann smiled for the first time since the beginning of the long ordeal. The ground felt good under his feet. "Yes, I'm fine. Thank you, gentlemen," he replied, prying the sticky goggles from his forehead, peeling the sweaty flight cap from his scalp. "Its good to be back on terra firma."

"Ho! That was some landing. You almost ran out of roadway!" a soldier babbled excitedly. "You're quite the lucky airman, sir."

The blessed Bavarian chuckled. He strode around the front of the Albatros, ducking under the nose, striding over to the side of the road to better observe the damaged wing. It looked like a splintered piece of firewood kindling with a wrinkled bit of canvas twisted around it. He rolled his eyes, whistling in a low pitch, amazed.

"Lucky? Maybe," Wissemann said with a cagey grin and snort. He nodded, winking playfully, then quipped: "Any landing you can walk away from—is a good landing."

293

Chapter 15

✠

APRIL 20, 1917. HAUPTMANN WILLI WISSEMANN sat at his decrepit little office desk reading a field report from Supreme Headquarters. He studied the report with deepening interest, reclining uncomfortably in a canvas camp chair, smoking a cigarette, sipping bitter coffee. He glanced up at the window as the wind and rain buffeted the thinly paned glass, shaking his head, cursing the abysmal conditions. The weather had been bad, increasingly bad. The *Jasta* was grounded.

Ten days after diversionary attacks by British forces at Arras, nineteen divisions of the French 5th and 6th Armies, led by General Mazel and General Mangin, attacked the German line along an eighty kilometers stretch, from Soissons to Reims. An imposing amount of firepower had been concentrated on the German lines. The 7th Army, under General von Boehm, had had little difficulty holding their positions. Field commanders situated on the high ground of the banks of the Aisne River, had positioned nearly one hundred machine guns for every thousand meters of front line barbwire and were well entrenched. The report stated that on the first day of combat alone, the French suffered an estimated forty thousand casualties, and lost over a hundred vehicles and lightly armored tanks. Nivelle's creeping barrage, poorly executed, had failed miserably at covering the advance of the French infantry.

On the second day, the document reported, the French 4th Army, led by General François Anthoine, launched an attack east of Reims towards Moronvilliers. General Fritz von Below's 1st Army easily repelled this assault. It became known as "The Battle of the Hills."

Undaunted by these setbacks, the French continued to order full-scale attacks, making some small gains to the west of Soissons. A four-kilometer stretch of the Chemin des Dames was captured. Wissemann noted a pattern—these smaller, scaled-back attacks seemed more successful than the larger ones. He laid the report down, sipping his coffee, grumbling remorsefully.

"The *poilus,* those poor poor sheep," he said. "They've won nothing worthy for their spilled blood!"

The *Jastaführer* glanced over *Kofl's* Air Activity report, scoffing bitterly. For the past four days, the weather had been sporadic, air operations had been limited. Heavy ground fog had curtailed flights on the opening day of the attack and rain and snow had prevented patrols in many sectors of the Front. Neighboring *Jasta 32* did manage to engage and shoot down two enemy artillery spotters near the *Bois en Escalier* Woods, but that was all. Wissemann sighed; his *Staffel,* only able to wage a limited defense against the French artillery spotters and bombers, came back from their few patrols without ever having made contact with the enemy. It was quite frustrating.

Wissemann looked up at the calendar on the wall and frowned. Today was his birthday. Thirty years? Where had all the time gone, he wondered? He was getting older and none the wiser, he agonized. And a well-meaning *Oberfeldwebel* Schutzling had blatantly reminded everyone about his birthday too. This, Wissemann surmised, was due to Ilse's well-timed telegram and package the day before. Schutzling had the mess prepare a special cake for the occasion. Wissemann was only mildly enthusiastic. He hated birthdays, especially his own!

Later that evening, there was a little party. It was a simple affair, just the way he wanted it, and the more incorrigible members of the *Staffel* stayed away; inveterate misanthropes like Luddenvoss and Schäfer could have cared less. Wissemann relaxed with Schutzling, Gutemann, Kindlich and Peltzer in the mess, while the rest of the cadre sat around playing cards, talking quietly, sharing several bottles of cheap cognac. And as the evening progressed, Schutzling became very merry, even a little tipsy. Eventually, he tried to get the men to join in on a chorus of "Happy Birthday" for the *Jastaführer.* However, it only annoyed Wissemann. He angrily stalked out of the mess and retired to his quarters for the evening.

Schutzling shrugged, unperturbed.

"Oh, well. We tried," he remarked, and poured himself another shot. "More cognac for the rest of us!"

The men cheered, the bottles emptied, glasses filled.

And it was another restless night for the *Jastaführer.*

✠

THE DOOR TO OPERATIONS slammed hard. *Oberfeldwebel* Albrecht Schutzling, ubruptly disturbed, gazed up from his typewriter—then winced. *Leutnant* Heinrich Luddenvoss came tramping in. He had just returned from a morning barrage patrol and had two losses to report. Two new replacements had been shot down in a fight with a French patrol. His gaunt face showed neither remorse nor pity.

Schutzling leered uneasily at the officer.

"You're late, *Leutnant*," he said. "The *Jastaführer* wanted to see you over an hour ago."

"Well, some of us are fighting a war, you know."

"Go in. He's waiting. And I'd button up that collar if I were you."

The surly Saxon growled and stalked off, an aggravated hitch in his gait. A sullen Heinrich Luddenvoss jerked the door open and found *Hauptmann* Wissemann sitting at his desk, poring over combat reports. Wissemann looked up, glancing at the clock on the wall, then regarded Luddenvoss with a disdainful stare.

"Don't you ever knock?" Wissemann shook his head. "Sit down."

Luddenvoss did not reply. He haphazardly collapsed in the camp chair facing Wissemann's desk and gazed at the other with an absent stare. Wissemann scribbled a few more notes, closed the file folder and set his pen down. He paused a moment, measuring up the ill-natured Saxon, a scornful gaze sullying his features.

"So," he began. "How many did we lose today, Luddenvoss?"

"Two."

"Who'd we lose?"

"Müller and, uh..." Luddenvoss shrugged. "Don't recall the other man's name. Sorry."

Wissemann grumbled. "Both of the new replacements? What—"

"We found and attacked the artillery spotter. Those tyros were supposed to wait upstairs while Winkler and I dispatched the two-seater. They got all impatient when a trio of Spads decided to make trouble. Then the whole *Kette* mixed it up in a wild dogfight with the French patrol. Later on, when everyone had cleared out and the *Kette* reformed—they were gone, missing," Luddenvoss explained.

Wissemann made a face, sighing. "Did they fall on our side?"

"Don't know."

"Did your *Kette* bag the artillery spotter?"

"Yes—"

"And I suppose you shot it down?"

"Of course."

"What about the Spads?"

"Metzger flamed one. That kid is going to be good if he sticks around long enough. I think he understands the game now."

"Metzger?" Wissemann scoffed.

"That's right. He's got a bit of a wild streak though. He was supposed wait upstairs with the new replacements. He's the one who led them into the dogfight with the Spads."

"Why didn't you just take Metzger down with you? Leave Winkler with the new men. Instead, you took Winkler with you. Two old hands trying to pad their score, eh? We must nurture novices like Metzger."

"He disobeyed my order to hold formation. It's not my—"

"Not your fault? You blame Metzger for their deaths, don't you?"

"No, I mean—"

"*YOU* are to blame for the losses, Luddenvoss, not Metzger."

"Me?"

"Correct! You should encourage him, not blame him."

"What? You want me to hold his hand, now?"

"I'm not asking you to hold anybody's hand, Luddenvoss. I have one responsibility as *Jastaführer*—shoot down enemy aeroplanes. That's the job. If this youngster can get victories, I won't get in the way—as long as he keeps his nose clean."

"Well, you can wipe it for him. I'm not the one. No sir—"

"There are a lot of men sacrificing their lives to win this war, Luddenvoss, even if they don't know why they fight."

"*Hauptmann,* spare me the—"

"But not you, Luddenvoss, eh?" Wissemann waxed bitterly. "You relish the danger. It's all fun and games for you. You gamble your life just to see if your number comes up—a roll of the dice, hmm?"

"I'm sorry... sir?" Luddenvoss replied lamely, a remorseless reply if there ever was one. "I-I feel... bad, about the losses."

Wissemann gasped, stunned, his eyes smoldering orbs now. He shook his head in disgust. Luddenvoss wasn't really sorry, he thought. If apologizing to the *Jastaführer* got him off the hook, got him off his back, then he'd figure that was the clever thing to say. Remorse? That wasn't a typical Luddenvoss attribute. Ach! Spurious sentimentality only infuriated him more. Wissemann leaned forward.

"My dear, *Leutnant* Luddenvoss," he rejoined acidly. "Don't pretend to care about those men's lives. A comrade's passing never caused you to shed a tear. It's always been about you, eh? Hasn't it? Your score... your fight... your personal war?"

"A summary of my past history?" Luddenvoss replied scornfully.

"Past history? Recent events, my egocentric friend!" Wissemann shot back. "Men like you never grow up. They just grow old and die."

"If you say so, *sir.*"

"I do say so."

"Is that all?"

"Dismissed." Wissemann's hand fluttered indifferently.

Luddenvoss rose slowly, saluting casually—more of a kiss-off rather than a salute—and reached for the door. Wissemann grumbled, returned the gesture with a simple nod, then went back to his reports. Luddenvoss opened the door, paused, thought a moment, then heeded Wissemann with a rueful gaze.

"*Herr Hauptmann.* Listen, I... uh—"

"Get out!" Wissemann snarled. "And close the door."

The door slammed noisily.

Heinrich Luddenvoss strutted past Schutzling, who was still pecking away at his typewriter. The Saxon stopped, regarding the noncom with seething contempt.

"Typing more goddamned reports, Schutzling?" he rumbled.

"No. I'm writing a letter to my wife. I write everyday."

"Only once a day? Luddenvoss huffed. "You're slipping, old man."

UNTEROFFIZIER GRIMM PARKED the old Daimler truck next to Operations, got out, directing the new replacement pilots to the farmhouse, shielding his eyes against an icy buffeting wind. The three pilots heaved their kit bags over their shoulders and shuffled aimlessly across the field, laughing and giggling like little school girls on holiday. Grimm shook his head in disgust.

"Blockheads," he whispered, shrugging carelessly. He called out to the replacements, pointing. "There, to the left, ladies. It's the only *real* structure on the aerodrome."

The wind howled as he trudged over to the noncoms billets with a brown package in his hand, holding the package tightly, cradling it in his arm. Snow was starting to fall again and the gray overcast seemed like it was about to unleash another withering snowstorm. The weather was foul again. No one had gotten off the ground in nearly a week, not even the French. Grimm loathed the bad weather more than anyone else. No flying meant pilots sat around and grumbled and complained about everything. There was an old *Jasta* expression: "Fair weather is flying weather; flier's weather is foul. The sun may fade, the winds blow cold, but it never rains on the Kaiser's Army."

This was definitely flier's weather!

As orderly clerk to adjutant Schutzling, Grimm received all kinds of odd requests. Every time he left for the supply depot or the Army *Flugpark*, someone, namely officers, always had some strange request. Today it was Schäfer's bottle of schnapps. It constantly amazed Grimm that Schäfer was still with the *Jasta*. How could anyone survive a war by just depending on wits and luck alone? And the Ironman was as witless as they came. His "luck" was something more like clumsy happenstance. Clearly, the Gods of War had taken him for a pet.

The ex-boxer often flew and fought in a state of total drunkenness or in the throes of a hangover. But he'd been in the *Jasta* longer than anyone—eight months. He'd logged more flying hours, flown more missions, had more combats, gone through more machines than anyone could remember, either wrecking them or bringing them back so badly shot up they couldn't be repaired, Peltzer once remarking that Schäfer had destroyed more German aircraft than French; he was at least an enemy ace three times over! But as a German airman, Josef Schäfer could only claim, officially, three victories.

Unteroffizier Gustav Grimm found the irascible Ironman's tent and announced his arrival by jerking on the tent flap heavily. "Got your schnapps, Schäfer. Are you decent?"

A voice rumbled. "Hah! Me, decent? That's an understatement."

"Well...?"

"Come in, you little jackass."

Grimm slithered through the tent flaps and went inside. He found Schäfer sitting in his long underwear and trousers, limp braces draped over a grimy undershirt. The cold never seemed to bother him. While other pilots bundled up like oversized teddy bears for every flight, the Ironman from Völklingen always went aloft in a thin, short-waist leather jacket. He seemed oblivious to the elements.

"You owe me twenty Marks, Schäfer," Grimm announced. "This stuff isn't cheap, you know."

"Twenty Marks? For that swill? That's damned outrageous!"

"I'm but a poor, old soldier, *Junge*—my grateful Emperor only pays me two marks a day." Grimm grinned glibly.

"*Quatsch.*"

"Look you idiot, it took some doing just to get *this* stuff." Grimm shook the paper-bagged bottle. "Take it, or leave it."

"Idiot?" Schäfer snorted. "You're talking to a superior—you noncommissioned half-wit."

"You outrank me, sure—but a superior?" Grimm scoffed.

"Careful, you."

"Do you want it or not?"

"All right, all right," Schäfer groused wretchedly. "Damn, but this is highway robbery."

The besotted noncom reached into a kit bag, pulled out a wadded up bill and gave it to the gritty noncom. Grimm unfolded the bill and smiled. He stuffed it into a coat pocket and then handed Schäfer the bottle of schnapps, still wrapped in the brown paper. The shaky Josef Schäfer immediately uncorked it and took a long, sloppy swig.

"Ugh!" he spat. "This is the worst... oh, what the hell." He tilted the bottle upright and took a deep pull from the bottle. He belched, his potbellied paunch rolling foully.

Grimm snickered. "You better ease off there, *Junge*."

"Why?" Schäfer smacked his lips.

"You might want to make it last, at least for a little while."

"I'm not worried. As long as there's money, there's booze."

"This is true. But, when I'm not around anymore..."

"There'll be some other slob to step and fetch it for me."

"Slob?" Grimm scoffed. "Such contempt. Keep it up, Schäfer."

Schäfer made a little face. "What's the news on the weather? What's our fearless leader saying, hmm?"

"He says he won't tolerate drunkenness in his *Jasta* anymore."

"Very funny." Schäfer shook his head. "The man gives himself airs. I know he drinks on the quiet."

"And expensive cognac, at that," Grimm chuckled. "Anyway, the forecast is more snow—and heavy, unrelenting hangovers due to tawdry schnapps."

It was Schäfer's turn to chuckle. He took another healthy swig.

"So. Sit tight, *Junge*." Grimm jerked a nod. "Nobody's going anywhere for a few days."

"Damn filthy weather," Schäfer grumped. "Damn filthy war."

"Oh, its not so bad, really. I've—"

"And to fight alongside a pattycake like Wissemann. Ach! I've died and gone to hell." Schäfer belched again.

"He keeps turning up like a bad penny, doesn't he?"

"I thought *Oberst* Thomsen was going to run him out of the Air Service? What happened?"

"Wissemann has friends in high places. Namely, certain generals."

"What generals? "

"Von Hoeppner, you *Dummkopf!*"

"Oh. How does he know von Hoeppner?"

"Von Hoeppner got him this posting." Grimm nodded. "They're good friends, you know."

"Wissemann? Von Hoeppner?" Schäfer shook his head "Beanbreeze! Our *Jastaführer* is the General Staff's worst nightmare."

"Not anymore," Grimm said and sat down on a wooden crate, tired of waiting for Schäfer to offer him a seat. "He's quite the Headquarters pet now."

"*Humph!* He's just been lucky. Once he really locks horns with a *Oberst* Thomsen—he's done for, my bootlicking little friend."

"Perhaps..."

"Or some Frenchy from the Storks flames his sorry heinie!"

"Well, that Caudron he bagged a few days ago makes... five victories for him. He's an ace now, as they say. And that's more than you, my drunken friend."

"Ah, but I've never been shot down. Never!"

"Not yet, eh?" Grimm smiled affectedly.

"Not in a hundred and fifty-one combat missions."

"Well, you'll meet your match, too, old cock, one day." Grimm rasped his chin thoughtfully. "Hmm, one hundred and fifty-one, eh? You're certainly due for a thrashing then."

"Get out of here—before you jinx me!"

"Aw, don't get cranky now. You know how—"

"When will you head back to Laon?"

"Why?"

"Because this bottle will be empty by tomorrow, Grimm. I'll need another." Josef Schäfer shook the already half-empty bottle of schnapps for emphasis.

The seedy little corporal's eyes widened. "Oh, sure." He scoffed. "Old Grimm—good enough to put up with your flap and run your errands, aye? Like a good little cabin boy? Well, don't be so sure."

The Ironman reached into his pants pocket, pulled out a rumpled roll of bills and waved them back and forth, trying to entice the incensed noncom. Schäfer nodded confidently. "As long as there is plenty of *this*, my indigent little friend," he muttered tauntingly. "You'll step and fetch it every time. And you know it's true."

Grimm's eyes narrowed. He bolted up, irked by Schäfer's arrogant reproach. But, he knew the unscrupulous wag was about right.

The Ironman winked. "Am I right?"

Grimm recovered, smiling thinly. He snatched the roll of bills from Schäfer's hand and turned for the exit. "*Ja*—right."

Schäfer cleared his throat and quipped: "That's fifty Marks, my greedy comrade. I want something worthy for my wares this time, all right? No more pig swill, eh?"

"Oh, don't you worry, *Junge*," he answered archly. "I've got just the stuff for you."

The seedy little noncom threw the tent flap aside and stomped out onto the snowy field, heading back to Operations, groaning crankily. Why did he subject himself to such indignity? Why did he put up with such lowborn scum like Schäfer. He squeezed the roll of bills clutched tightly in his hand and grinned.

"Money. That's why. Glorious money!"

Gustav Grimm had no compunction about extorting exorbitant amounts of cash from his *Jasta* comrades. His base pay wasn't nearly enough to cover all his expenses. And his markup on alcohol and other specialty items was high, high enough for him to pocket the equivalent of a month's pay. He was even known to pimp out whores to pompous Prussian officers, servicemen too proud to scrounge around for their own *"Düfte Bienen."* He snorted callously. He'd really made those haughty officers pay through the nose. And now, that fat old Prussian, *Oberst* Thomsen, had another project for him. This was turning out to be a profitable little war, he thought. Transferring to the Air Service was the best damn thing he'd ever done!

ANOTHER ETERNAL FORTNIGHT PASSED. On May 5th the weather warmed and the skies cleared. All twelve machines of the *Jasta* left the ground; six new Albatros D.III's and six Albatros D.II's. Wissemann led the full-strength formation. It was only his sixth sortie in two weeks. The 7th Army *Kommandeur* had requested a patrol of full force over the front lines. "Secure local air superiority in your sector!" the *Kommandeur* had ordered implacably.

At four kilometers up, the air was nearly 30-below freezing. The Bavarian Eagle sat stiffly in his brand new Albatros, shivering, trembling, from the cold air that whipped around the cockpit. It didn't seem to matter how many layers of extra clothing he wore, he always felt dreadfully cold. Before each patrol, Wissemann typically put on several layers of outer flying gear to contend with the freezing temperatures, dressing carefully and meticulously, following a strict practice from which he seldom deviated. This was based on personal experience, the time of year and, like some pilots, superstition.

On this particular wintry morning, his outfit consisted of a thick cotton vest, long woolen underwear, a wool shirt, and his *Feldgrau* tunic. Over that, he wore a heavy leather jacket that hung to his knees. To keep his feet and legs warm, he put on a pair of silk hose Ilse had sent him, a pair of cotton ones, and finally, a pair of heavy woolen stockings which came up to his knees. Next came thick cord breeches protected by knee-length, fur-lined Schmidtt boots.

Even after all this extra insulation, his feet, all wrapped up in their new wool acquisitions, still went numb in the freezing cold. A woolen cap with a long back flap, something Ilse had knitted for him, covered his flying cap. Around his neck, he wore a gaily-colored red and white silk scarf, a birthday present from Ilse. The bright two-toned pattern attracted playful pokes from the *Staffel* personnel. But Wissemann took it all in stride though—silk didn't irritate his neck as he constantly screwed his head about searching the deadly skies of the Champagne.

On his hands, Wissemann wore triple layered wool gloves. But before putting them on, he smeared his face with whale oil, thoroughly rubbing it into his cheeks, forehead and nose. Once done, he wriggled his hands into his lucky fur-lined leather gauntlets.

Next came the goggles. These fit tight and snug around his eye sockets, causing a bit of discomfort. Better to be too tight than too loose, though; his eyes could easily tear up if the cold air seeped into the edges of the goggles. Underneath his goggles he wore a fleece-lined leather mask, over his nose and cheekbones. This shielded his face from the wind blasts of the open cockpit. He routinely blew through the mask's nose slits, attempting to dismiss genuine feelings of claustrophobia, which he never really shook off no matter how many times he wore it.

The formation of Albatroses hovered at four thousand meters, above a milky layer of altostratus that obscured most of the landscape below. Wissemann scanned the sky with careful scrutiny, while the patrol flew east, parallel to the front lines. Down below the icy Suippe River cut through the frozen landscape, its muddy waters stretching across the front lines to the city of Aubérive. The *Jasta* routinely patrolled along this area—from Nauroy to Vaudesincourt—about five kilometers. This was their route today, back and fourth for an hour, then back to the aerodrome for a late breakfast. Down below, lay the entrenched German 1st Army, under the command of General von Below. And on the other side of the lines, the French 4th Army. And somewhere down there in between, a bloody battle raged—a cold, thankless bloody battle.

Gott! Spring has forgotten to come, Wissemann thought. Old Man Winter ravages the countryside yet one more day. Oh, how I miss those carefree summers on the Bodensee!

He glanced over his left shoulder, observing *Leutnant* Luddenvoss, Winkler, and Ziegler, all maintaining steady formation. Then he gazed to his right and saw Neubauer, Frankenberg and Schäfer. He looked up above his head; Gutemann's *Kette* soared a thousand meters higher and slightly aft. A perfectly arrayed combat formation.

As he held course, Wissemann constantly searched the sky around him. Left to right, then up, then down, and back again. He'd repeated this ritual so many times that his neck became sore and his elbow ached from gripping the control stick too tightly. He wondered if the other men in the *Jasta* felt as miserable as he did. Constant open cockpit flying had its drawbacks; the continuous exposure to the elements could definitely take a toll on a man's constitution. Combat patrols, like everything else in his life, had become mundane and routine, something to be dealt with, something to be endured, something to be tolerated.

Wissemann signaled for a turn. He searched the sky again.

"Nothing!"

The *Jastaführer* ruminated idly about his thirtieth birthday. Why did he get so irritated with Schutzling? Was he truly worried about getting older? Thirty wasn't really "old" at all. Or was it? That was rather a joke, he thought. But he felt no desire to laugh. That very morning in the mirror, at the outer corner of his eyes, he noticed jagged little crows' feet, like those normally seen on a middle-aged man. He worried only a little less, realizing it was just caused by constant squinting and staring into the sun. So he told himself.

But those lines could also hint at a more serious problem. After so many missions, combat fatigue would eventually take its toll. The usual indications of combat fatigue were: constant headaches, shaky or trembling hands, twitchy eyelids, irritability, lapses in memory and even blurred vision. Too little action had a similar effect. It was quite obvious to him how tenuous one's chances really were out here at the Front. Was his mind starting to slip?

"Snap out of it, Willi," he cautioned himself. "Pay attention to the sky or you'll not live to see thirty-one!" He scanned the horizon. Nix.

Athletic competitions and after-hour activities could alleviate some stress. But most pilots were either too tired or disinterested in such things to participate. He tried to keep every man on a strict rotation of days off and regularly scheduled leaves. But with the French offensive in high gear, no one would be allowed time off.

He steered the D. III through the sky with apparent ease. The new Albatros was sleek and streamlined, a veritable pleasure to fly. It responded instantly to the controls and handled like a high-powered sports car. Peltzer had briefed the entire *Jasta* on its strengths and weaknesses after the *Jastafürer's* unfortunate incident. And in the interest of greater safety, the assiduous maintenance chief had also instructed the machine shop to fashion and weld on small auxiliary braces, connecting the leading edge of the main V-shaped inner-plane struts to the wings leading edge. This, Peltzer had affirmed, would strengthen the main chord and reduce wing flutter. Or so he hoped.

Once again, Wissemann ordered a slow turn.

"Where is *Herr Rothosen?*" he asked, then grumbled: "Sitting fireside, lounging, sipping hot coffee, that's where!"

So. The sky was empty this morn, a dull and uneventful patrol so far. Nevertheless, the *Jagdstaffel* droned on along its patrol route, intersecting all its mission waypoints. A strong headwind from the west made it difficult at times, but the flight was going routinely.

The new man, Metzger, was having trouble keeping station, constantly drifting behind. Wissemann tirelessly coaxed him along, knowing it was crucial for new pilots to make it through their first few flights without too much anxiety.

It was usually the *Jastaführer's* responsibility to see that every new pilot in the *Staffel* flew a few familiarization flights before flying actual combat missions. But this was only possible as long as there was time. In addition, and as long as he wasn't distracted by staff duties and paperwork—and there was a lot of paperwork—he liked to personally take every new man up for a few flights. Unfortunately, the distractions of reequipping a *Jasta* and imparting disciplinary action, mainly meaning Schäfer and Luddenvoss, had prevented him from taking Metzger up. Instead, he had let Gutemann take the tyro aloft a few times. Otto Gutemann was an excellent pilot and Metzger would learn much from the studious second-in-command. But Wissemann would've preferred to groom the newcomer himself.

His thoughts drifted back to that night at the Kasino. Since the French had launched their attack the very next morning, every *Jasta* had gone on high alert, every man and machine was needed. So, Wissemann initially delayed his inquiry into the Luddenvoss and Schäfer affair. However, as the days progressed and the weather worsened, it was quite clear no one would get airborne for at least a week. But nevertheless, the *Staffel* was still required to remain on standby until the weather did improve.

Therefore, on Thursday, the 26th of April, he had addressed each man individually. Schäfer, finally temperate enough to admit to his foolishness, apologized. But the surly Saxon, on the other hand, maintained a cavalier attitude; he vowed that if Schäfer ever came near him again, he would do his worst. Wissemann had planned to ground both officers. But with the French offensive in high gear, every man was expected to fly, everyday, weather permitting. Both men were barred from the Kasino, though, until the situation cooled off. Wissemann was well aware that their resentments could affect air operations. But so far, nothing had happened.

He scanned the skies again. His brow narrowed. "Aha!"

About a kilometer away, high above the village of Beine, he noticed four specks drifting to the southwest towards the front lines. *Herr Rothosen?* But his excitement quickly turned to disappointment, realizing that if these were indeed enemy machines, German anti-aircraft gunners would've already opened up on them. But he saw no such shell bursts, and assuming that they were German two-seaters on their way to French territory, he dejectedly watched them disappear into a cloud bank.

He turned his eyes back to the formation. Luddenvoss signaled. He had seen the four specks too. And had he made the same assumption, Wissemann wondered? No. He wasn't budging from his position. Their eyes locked. He studied the truculent officer's face for a long moment. Luddenvoss grinned coldly. Then, a second later, his eyes widened as if he'd just seen a ghost. He gestured frantically.

Wissemann whipped his head around to observe a thin, black column of smoke arching across the sky. One of those four specks was falling out of control—on fire! The jumpy *Jastaführer* glanced up to see Gutemann's lads already peeling away for the attack. Wissemann signaled his *Kette* to follow suit. Dive! But not too steep or too fast. The Albatros' wings must be remembered. Twelve Albatroses charged headlong in hot pursuit at two different altitudes.

A second speck fell out of control, disappearing in the cloud deck below. And as his formation drew nearer, Wissemann saw that he was indeed correct; those specks were definitely German two-seaters, Rumplers; slender crates with mottled green and purple paint jobs. A formation of Nieuports—he counted six of the silvery scouts— buzzed around the Rumplers like a swarm of angry hornets. The Rumpler gunners swiveled their Parabellums around madly, spraying the sky with smoking bullets. But their aim was pathetic. They were obviously inexperienced or too frightened to cause the Frenchmen any alarm. The Nieuports attacked with near impunity.

Now Wissemann could hear the fusillade of machine gun fire as his *Jasta* engaged. Gutemann and Bubi Kindlich made first contact and fired at long range. They weren't really trying to hit anything; they were just trying to frighten the Frenchmen off.

Gutemann closed the gap quickly and fired again, this time at point-blank range. His surgical-like gunfire sawed the Nieuport's red white and blue rudder in half. The empennage snapped off and the stricken machine tumbled down helplessly, spinning wildly around without a tailplane to stabilize it.

The skies turned into a deadly circus of somersaulting aeroplanes, like maddened acrobats hurling flaming confetti at each other, like crazy clowns rolling and tumbling, laughing, cursing, crying.

Wissemann, Luddenvoss and Schäfer were nearly parallel to each other when they closed in for the attack. Wissemann pulled the charging handles of his own twin Maxim machine guns and took careful aim at a Nieuport. At the same time, Luddenvoss attacked the one in front of him. Schäfer, who was apparently coming in too fast, overshot his target. Suddenly, gracelessly, the Ironman barrel-rolled his aeroplane up and over Wissemann's Albatros. The big Bavarian cringed as Schäfer's headlong maneuver put him just over wing-top, just a few uncomfortable meters away.

"*Dummkopf!* Watch out!" Wissemann shouted across the gap, instinctively shoving the control stick forward to avoid a collision. He felt a sudden and sickening falling away in the pit of his stomach as his Albatros lurched down. He winced and caught his breath.

Schäfer completed the barrel roll and clumsily dropped in behind Luddenvoss' machine, now attempting a difficult thrust at a darting target. It was a high-angled deflection shot from at least two hundred meters away. Somehow he managed to hit the dancing Nieuport. But a few rounds slammed into Luddenvoss' Albatros, too.

The stunned Saxon screwed his head about wildly, thinking an enemy scout had surprised him. He side-slipped, trying to roll out of Schäfer's line of fire. But more bullets slammed into Luddenvoss' upper wing, ricocheting off the radiator head, chewing up canvas and wood. The savvy Saxon back-sticked into a masterful retournment—applying full rudder, looping over, rolling the aircraft, coming over the top. He soon saw who was firing at him. Suddenly the two parts of his afeared brain seemed to come together and at least a portion of the rotten truth began to dawn on him. "*Schweine!*" Luddenvoss circled around abaft Schäfer's tail. He cleared his guns for action.

Meanwhile, Schäfer zoomed in and finished off the Nieuport; it burst into flames and nose-dived out of control. Wissemann wasn't exactly sure what had happened. His attention had been split between attacking his target and watching Schäfer from the corner of his eye. Nevertheless, he lost contact with his quarry. The Nieuport skirted into the cloud deck below, disappearing from sight. The remaining Frenchmen, seeing themselves totally outnumbered by a squadron of Albatros, retreated, scattering off to the four winds.

The *Jastaführer* signaled the *Jasta* to reform—a green flare arched across the sky. But before Luddenvoss took his place in formation, he flew alongside Schäfer's Albatros. A minatory finger jutted out accusingly. The seething Saxon drew a forefinger across his throat, a threatening gesture, if their ever was one. The Ironman threw his head back, having a good laugh.

Wissemann, outraged by this juvenile display, fired a quick burst from his Maxims, trying to get their attention, directing Luddenvoss to get back in formation with a frenzied wave. The Saxon just glared back at Wissemann for a moment, scowling, then flicked his Albatros over on to its back, diving away in the direction of French lines. The embittered Bavarian beat enraged fists on the gun butts of his Maxims, then fired off a flare to get Luddenvoss' attention. But the wayward officer was long gone.

"*Verfluchter, kerl!*" Wissemann cursed. "Get back in formation! Dear God! Am I leading children?" The *Kette* returned to base with one less a man, and one man very angry. Wissemann was beside himself.

THE ALBATROS' WHEELS had barely touched the ground and Willi Wissemann was already overside stalking towards Schäfer. The pugnacious Ironman was just strolling off to his quarters, quite oblivious to the frantic footfall behind him. In a few lanky strides Wissemann was within arm's reach of Schäfer.

"*Feldwebel* Schäfer! Just a moment, please," he barked, seizing the surly sergeant by the shoulder. "What in the hell were you doing out there, eh? You reckless wag!"

"Pardon me, sir?" Josef Schäfer replied, seemingly oblivious to what the other meant. He turned about and smiled. "Did I do something wrong, sir?"

"You know damn well what I am talking about."

"Sir?"

"*Verdammt,* Schäfer! What kind of shooting was that?"

"What do you mean, sir?"

"You could've hit Luddenvoss!"

Wissemann stared into Schäfer's eyes.

They were puffy and bloodshot.

"Oh, Luddenvoss?" Schäfer replied, a pixilated reply replete with a touch of naivety. "*Hauptmann...* he turned into my line of fire."

"Schäfer!"

"I was aiming at the Frenchy. Honest—"

"*Quatsch!* That was a damned risky shot to try at that angle, Schäfer. Since when did you become such a great marksman, eh?"

"Sir, I was only trying to help out Luddenvoss."

Wissemann scoffed. "I find that very hard to believe."

"Did you think I was trying to shoot—*him?*"

"I think you had aspirations."

"Now really, *Hauptmann,* I'm shocked! What kind of man do you think I am?" The burly noncom's reply sounded stilted and insincere.

You are a liar and a drunk! Wissemann thought to himself, then said: "Do you take me for a fool, Schäfer?"

"Herr Hauptmann, really—"

"You nearly collided with me with your acrobatic antics!"

"Acrobatic antics?" Schäfer frowned. "I was just trying to reduce my forward momentum."

"Nonsense! You were—"

"I was going to overshoot that Nieuport."

"Schäfer, you are a reckless excuse for a pilot."

"I'm sorry I startled you—"

"Startled me? You scared the hell out of me!"

"Herr Hauptmann, I-I..."

"You are grounded, Schäfer."

"Grounded?"

"Grounded! You are finished in this *Staffel,* Schäfer."

"What do you mean?"

"I'm going to have you transferred!"

"What? No!"

"Yes! As soon as I can get the paperwork completed."

"I beg you. Please, *Hauptmann,* I'm—"

"Consider yourself under arrest, Schäfer. You are confined to quarters until further notice."

Schäfer sighed heavily, a faint hint of alcohol souring his breath.

Bessoffen kerl! Wissemann's eyes widened. "And—you have been drinking on duty! Schäfer—"

"Sir, I can explain—"

"That will go on my report, as well."

"Oh, no, sir. Please..."

"You are in deep trouble, my friend. Deep trouble! Dismissed."

"But, sir—"

"DIS-MISSED!"

"Bah!" Schäfer grumbled, finally giving up his false facade.

"You are dismissed, Schäfer!" Wissemann raged.

"To hell with this!" The angry Ironman spun around and stamped off to his quarters, mumbling obscenities under his breath.

Some of the mechanics had gathered around to watch the confrontation. They grinned and elbowed one another, enjoying the little showdown. Peltzer was there too. He flicked his cigar to the ground, folding his arms over his chest, grinning.

The Bavarian officer, sensing the amusement of his gathered ground crew, wheeled around, glaring at the motley throng. "What in the hell are you men staring at? Get back to work. *NOW!*"

They obeyed, though reluctantly, striding off, mumbling, nodding their heads, laughing. It was a good little show while it lasted, they all agreed wholeheartedly.

Vizefeldwebel Max Peltzer trudged up to Wissemann with a perplexed look on his pudgy face.

"What's going on, sir," he asked. "What happened?"

"I'll explain later."

"Later?" Peltzer frowned.

"When Luddenvoss returns, have him report to me, immediately."

"Yes, sir."

"This nonsense will cease today. *Bei Gott!* I've had enough!"

"Luddenvoss? Nonsense? What's going on, sir? What happened?"

Peltzer didn't like being left out when it came to *Staffel* scuttlebutt. Damn! *The Jasta* is falling apart again, he thought silently.

Of course, Wissemann was too irritated to discuss anything with him at that moment, his was face red, his temper was flaring.

"I'll be in my office," he snapped.

"Right."

"I have a few transfer orders I must file with the *Kommandeur!*"

"Yes, sir. What—"

"Place a guard on Schäfer's quarters, Peltzer. He is not to leave. Under no circumstances!"

"Yes, *Herr Hauptmann.* Right away." Peltzer's eyes clouded. Man! What is he's so pissed off about, the befogged mechanic wondered? What in the hell happened out there today?

Wissemann stripped the flight cap from his head, loosening his scarf, stalking off to Operations, suddenly feeling ill and achy. He reached into a pocket and pulled out a handkerchief, wiping the drivel from his nose, coughing roughly.

"*Wunderbar!* Now I'm coming down with a blasted cold. What else now? *Verdammt!* What else!"

Peltzer stood silently a moment, sighing heavily. Here we go again, he thought. Back to where we damned started! He walked back to Maintenance seriously thinking about getting utterly blotto.

Wissemann, a man at the end of his proverbial rope, a man ready to explode like a powder keg of dynamite, a man on the verge of a nervous breakdown, was ready to mete out some serious discipline. Schäfer and Luddenvoss were done, gone, finished—transferred!

IT WAS ALMOST 0900-hours when the telephone on the *Jastaführer's* desk suddenly rang. Wissemann's brow nettled suspiciously. He wasn't expecting a call at this hour. Perhaps it was *Flugmeldedienst* calling to confirm the results of the morning patrol? He cleared his throat, snatching the handset up, placing it on an ear.

"*Hauptmann Wissemann, Jastaführer, Jasta 23...*"

"Good morning, *Hauptmann* Wissemann," a raspy voice replied.

"Morning. How may I help you?"

"*Hauptmann* Wissemann... this is Major Bruno Reinhardt here, *Stabsoffizier der Flieger, Flieger Abteilung Nr. 99*, Sivery Aerodrome. I'm with *FlugM*." Major Reinhardt had just explained that he was a staff officer, Army Aviation, Flying Section No. 99, Secret Service. *FlugM*, or *Flugmeisterei*, was Germany's Air Intelligence agency, oft working in conjunction with the German Secret Service.

Wissemann was speechless. The Secret Service? Really?

"Hello?" Reinhardt urged impatiently. "Can you hear me?"

Wissemann's stupefaction had created an awkward pause.

"Yes, yes. *Fl. Abt. 99*, Sivery?" Wissemann replied in a puzzled tone, thinking: why would they be contacting *me*?

"Correct. So you've heard of us then?"

"Of course, of course, *Herr Major.*"

"Splendid."

"Your flying section handles covert operations and long-range reconnaissance. Am I right?"

"H'mm, something like that."

"So, what's on your mind, Major?"

"*Kogunluft*, Chief of Staff, *Oberst* Hermann Thomsen, suggested you might be available for a special mission, Wissemann."

"*Oberst* Thomsen said—what?"

"He said I should give you a call—you'd be a perfect candidate for our operations."

"Me? I don't understand?"

"You speak fluent French, don't you?"

"Well, yes, I do. But—"

Reinhardt's tone sharpened. "Look, Wissemann. I don't have a lot of time here..."

"Right. Go ahead, sir."

"Now listen... one of our pilots has come down with influenza and will be unable to fly a important mission tomorrow night. The rest of my section is scheduled for a special night recon over an enemy aerodrome. I can't spare a man right now. I need a replacement."

"I see. You need a pilot?"

"Experienced pilot! We need someone to fly an agent to Paris."

"Paris?" Wissemann's eyes widened.

"To a clandestine location outside the city limits."

"Really? That's quite a long trip."

"Two hundred and ten kilometers round trip to be exact."

"Aha. So, what would I be flying for such a mission?"

"I understand you're familiar with Sopwith two-seaters?"

"Well, yes. I used to test fly captured enemy aircraft when I was posted at Adlershof, for a short time—"

"You were at Adlershof?"

"Yes, sir. During my instructor's term at the Stutthof Flying School, I was ordered to Adlershof last December for a short stint of duty. I test flew enemy machines assessing their performance, combat capabilities, endurance, etc. etc. I spent a full month at the Adlershof test facility."

"Good, good. Then you are more than qualified for this mission."

"What time is the mission scheduled?"

"Tomorrow—twenty-two hundred hours."

"Tomorrow? I see."

"You would fly to a secluded field outside Paris. There's a little chateau nearby. Our Secret Service agent will rendezvous with operatives waiting there. He'll slip into Paris for an exchange and return in roughly an hour."

"An exchange, sir?"

The Major chuckled. "Sorry, *Hauptmann*, that's all I can tell you. The rest is classified information. You understand, right?"

"Right. Classified." Wissemann frowned.

"It's for your own protection. The less you know about the details, the safer you'll be in the event of capture and interrogation."

"Capture and interrogation?" Wissemann sighed uncomfortably. "Uh, yes. I understand."

"Excellent."

"And what will I do while the agent is in Paris?"

"Stand by the aeroplane until he returns. Simple enough, eh?"

Wissemann groaned. "Hmm, I don't know?"

"Will you accept the task, *Hauptmann*? Will you fly the mission?"

"Well, simple or not, there's always the chance something might go wrong, sir."

"True."

"What happens if he doesn't get back in an hour?"

"Take off with out him. Assume something went wrong."

"Uh-huh..."

"Don't stick around—get the hell out of there."

"I see. Will I be able to refuel there? That's a long flight."

Wissemann rasped his chin thoughtfully. He knew the Sopwith two-seater only had a three and a half hour flight endurance. Not enough for a round trip.

"Of course. There will be fuel stores available at the landing field for the return trip."

"Aha..."

"Everything you'll need, *Hauptmann* Wissemann, will be at your disposal, let me assure you"

"Right." Wissemann nodded suspiciously.

There was a brief pause, then the Major sighed heavily.

"Look, *Hauptmann* Wissemann," he said testily. "I can't reschedule this mission. It's all set for tomorrow night. We need someone who's experienced, someone who we can trust and rely on, someone whose integrity goes beyond question—"

"Like a pilot who knows Sopwith aircraft, a pilot that happens to speak fluent French?"

"Precisely!"

"I don't know, sir. Let me think about it—"

"Come on, man. Can the Fatherland count on your help?"

The wary *Jastaführer* sighed, thinking about the consequences. Operating so far behind enemy lines was risky business, failure meant capture, capture meant spending the war as a POW, and spies were always shot. But could he really refuse? The urge to do his duty had always beset him, he felt obligated somehow. Yet, for some strange reason, the whole mission seemed quite suspicious. He funked, sighing warily. "No," Wissemann replied firmly.

"Why not?"

"Well, I'm not a spy, Major Reinhardt. I-I'm a combat pilot. I don't know the first thing about espionage and all that kind of stuff."

"You don't have to. One of our agents will be your companion—a man whose made countless trips into Paris."

"I see. What about getting out?"

Reinhardt chuckled. "Shall we discuss exfiltration once we know your willing to... infiltrate?"

Wissemann fell silent, brooding thoughtfully.

"The mission is really quite simple, you know," Reinhardt added. "You'll fly under the cover of darkness, work with experienced agents, fly French aircraft, etc. etc and so forth."

Wissemann exhaled resignedly "Well, all right, Major Reinhardt— you can count on me, I suppose."

The Major laughed. "Why? For patriotic reasons?"

"Well..."

"You can't count on the Army to rescue you if you're caught."

"I didn't think I could."

"*Hauptmann*, this is exceptionally hazardous duty. You have only the agent in Paris and the man you fly with for help. So, do you still want to go?"

"I do. And my reasons, Major Reinhardt, are personal."

"Of course. Welcome to the fold, *Hauptmann.*"

"Right. Thanks?"

"I'll send a staff car to fetch you tomorrow morning. Our chief intelligence officer, *Kapitänleutnant* Klimke, will brief you with all the details on the way back."

"Sure." Wissemann grimaced, having second thoughts already.

"These missions are quite routine, *Hauptmann*. We've done this sort of thing many times over. There's really no cause for alarm."

"Good enough, then."

"Well, thank you for your cooperation, *Hauptmann* Wissemann. Best of luck. Good-bye now."

"*Good-bye.*"

Willi Wissemann hung up the telephone. He sat in deep thought for a moment, considering it quite strange that *Oberst* Thomsen would recommend him for such a mission. He'd always thought the old Prussian had it in for him. Maybe not. Maybe he was finally softening up a little? Hah! But routine or not, he chagrined, something could always go wrong. And with his luck, he could count on it!

Schutzling was standing in the doorway.

"Sir," he said. "Luddenvoss just landed a few moments ago."

"Aha! Now begins the real fun."

Wissemann stood up, deciding he wouldn't wait; he would meet Luddenvoss on the tarmac. He coughed roughly as he reached for his leather jacket and cap, beginning to feel a bit feverish and congested, an aggravating grippe completely plaguing him now. He sneezed, trembling with a sudden chill. He reached for his handkerchief.

"*Gesundheit!*" Schutzling said. "Are you all right, sir?"

"*Danke.* I'm fine. Just coming down with a blasted cold, I guess."

Indeed. Wissemann had felt the symptoms of influenza coming on for days now. But he'd convinced himself not to fret about it, determining not to let a little thing like the flu get in his way or stop him from completing his duties. Personal discomfort mattered not to him anymore. There was too much to do now.

"I have some aspirin powders, sir?" Schutzling offered.

"Yes, aspirin..."

"Hot tea might be good, too."

"Fine. I'll take them when I'm finished dealing with the devil."

A MINUTE LATER, *Hauptmann* Willi Wissemann was marching down to the tarmac where the "devil's" Albatros was now parked. *Leutnant* Luddenvoss was just climbing out of the cockpit when the other approached. The ailing *Jastaführer* stood and waited as the roguish pilot pulled his helmet and goggles off. Two clean circles encased his eye sockets, grimy soot covered the lower half of his face, the telltale signs of furious aerial combat; Luddenvoss had apparently found and engaged another French patrol. He eyed the stiff figure waiting for him on the tarmac as an orderly helped him remove his flying suit. Before Wissemann even had a chance to start in on him, Luddenvoss turned about abruptly, his face beaming with hostility.

"*Herr Hauptmann*," he growled. "When a man takes a swing at me, that's one thing. But when he takes a shot at me—that's another thing completely!" The angry officer spat and turned to walk away.

Wissemann trailed after him. "Just a minute, Luddenvoss!"

The *Jastaführer* paused a moment, wanting to make sure he addressed the situation with all the facts straight in his mind, not wanting to complicate things by being too rash. He thought: was Schäfer just careless or did his actions really contain malice? His reaction to questioning seemed to suggest the former, but Wissemann wasn't sure. Would Luddenvoss try to seek revenge? Probably. He did seem to make that quite clear. Wissemann had witnessed the threatening gesture after the fight with the Nieuports. That was certainly an apparent enough indication.

The big Bavarian caught up with the surly Saxon. "Luddenvoss, you will not take personal action against Schäfer. Understand?"

"*Humph!*"

"This matter will go before the jurisdiction of a military court."

"Huh—"

"Understand? Is that clear, *Leutnant* Luddenvoss?"

Wissemann stepped in front of Luddenvoss, blocking his path, standing toe-to-toe with him. He folded his arms over his chest. The surprised Saxon balked and looked away. He spat on the ground.

"You saw it yourself, sir," he explained. "Schäfer deliberately fired at that Nieuport knowing full well he might hit me. In fact, I

315

think he *wanted* to hit me."

"Yes. I saw —"

"He can't face me like a man down here on the ground. So he tries to shoot me in the back, up there!"

Luddenvoss was standing spread-leg, his face a demonic mask of fury. Willi Wissemann was standing stiff and straight, his face wiped clean of all expression.

"Your testimony will be recorded as such, Luddenvoss, in a court martial proceeding—"

"Ach! Don't give me that guardhouse lawyer *quatsch,* Wissemann!"

"Listen to me, Luddenvoss—"

"Schäfer has it coming, *sir!* Mark my words. Court martial or not, he's a dead man!" Luddenvoss' face contorted angrily. His eyeballs shifted excitedly from side to side.

"Luddenvoss, watch your tongue—"

"So help me God!"

The exasperated *Jastaführer* swallowed hard, gnashing his teeth, his patience and better judgment dissolving with every second. The circumstances, the weather, his weakening constitution and just plain old ire, were whittling down his gentlemanly forbearance. Then, something snapped somewhere, Willi Wissemann seemed to melt into a boiling heap of vindictiveness. He grabbed the young officer by the jacket lapels and shook him violently.

"Nothing doing!" he raged. "You will do nothing. Do you hear me? Nothing. Nothing!"

Startled by Wissemann's sudden spittle-flecked tirade and seizure, *Leutnant* Luddenvoss reacted instantly, instinctively, shoving Wissemann backwards. "Unhand me, damn you!"

Wissemann stumbled backwards, slipped, and fell to the muddy ground with a slushy thud. Luddenvoss' finger wagged threateningly.

"Don't ever grab me like that again, *Hauptmann,* or—"

"*VERDAMMT NOCH MAL!*" Wissemann shrieked, staggering up from the ground, flinging mud from his fingers, breathing in throaty gasps. He swore angrily, spat, shaking his fist at Luddenvoss, his face turning bright red. "You... you are finished, Luddenvoss!" He gasped again, nearly choking. "Do you hear me? F-Finished! You, my rebellious f-friend, will never fly in this *Staffel* again!"

The smoldering Saxon glared at Wissemann uneasily. He'd not intended to shove him. Once again, he reacted on his baser instincts; it was far too late for regrets now. He shook his head regretfully, knowing full well that shoving a superior officer was the same as striking one; the consequences were just the same—court martial.

Luddenvoss tried to apologize. *"Herr Hauptmann... I'm—"*

"Get out of my sight, Luddenvoss!" Wissemann wheezed.

"Sir, please—"

"Go to your quarters straightaway, until I send for you! When it's time for your—arrest!"

"But I have one more mission scheduled for the day?" the Saxon replied sheepishly,

"NO! You are confined to quarters!"

"Wait a minute, sir—"

"Get out of my damn sight before I, I... I...*uh-h-h-h*—" Wissemann suddenly looked as if he were choking, his little tirade causing a violent coughing spasm. He bent over in agony, pounding his chest, gasping for breath.

Luddenvoss grinned arrogantly, turned on a heel and strode off to his quarters. "Whatever."

Schutzling, who had come down to the tarmac only a moment earlier, leaned over the *Jastaführer's* crooked frame and offered some assistance. "Sir?" he said. "You all right? Shall I call the medics— "

"N-No, no! A red-faced Willi Wissemann spouted, coughing uncontrollably now, gasping for breath. He collapsed to a knee, staring at the ground, wheezing, shushing the noncom away with angry gestures. "Aghh! J-Just—get—away from me! Leave me. *GO!*"

AN OPEL STAFF CAR sped down a rain-soaked highway. Along the shoulders of the road, columns of dirty German soldiers marched along in an aimless gait, each heavily laden with combat gear. Wissemann shook his head. Poor potato-heads, he thought. I certainly don't envy them. He gazed up at the sky as the sun showed itself for the first time in days, peeping radiantly from behind giant-sized cumuli. The weather seemed to be clearing up, and he swore he'd seen some blossoms on the poplar trees lining the road.

"Finally," he uttered quietly. "Spring is making an appearance."

"I'm sorry, what was that?" a deep voice asked.

"Nothing. Nothing, sir"

Hauptmann Wissemann sat in the backseat of a staff car while *Kapitänleutnant* Sepp Klimke briefed him on the mission for the coming night. Klimke was a balding, thirty-three year old naval officer with the equivalent rank of army captain, and a veteran of numerous bombing sorties over France and England. He'd led several Zeppelin airship raids over London, commanding the L-14 on most of them. He was an expert on night flying and an experienced pilot.

"Are you all right, *Hauptmann?*" *Kapitäinleutnant* Klimke asked, noticing Wissemann wiping his runny nose with a handkerchief.

"For the most part, I guess."

"Are you sure? You don't sound too good."

"I'm fine, sir. Really. I think my cold is getting worse, though," Wissemann replied, blowing his nose again, inelegantly cramming the handkerchief back into a pocket.

"A cold?"

"Unfortunately. After this mission I'll need to take a little rest."

"*Ja.* Dirty weather has made everything quite miserable."

"*Quite*—miserable."

Klimke handed Wissemann a grid map and pointed out the waypoints for the flight to Paris. "Look here... the route is quite simple, *Hauptmann.* Just follow this southwesterly course to Épernay," he explained, indicating with a pen.

"Right—Épernay."

"Then, follow the Marne River all the way to Paris, along—here. A little moonlight should help guide the way. Stay low, about five hundred meters, and stay out of the clouds if you can. Things get a bit confusing up there at night." Klimke gestured firmly.

"Right."

The Opel's axle groaned as the staff car slammed into a pothole, jostling the occupants about in a rough manner. The driver peered over his shoulder, smiling sheepishly.

"Sorry, gentlemen," he apologized. "These roads are awful!"

Wissemann and Klimke grinned, readjusting their crooked service caps, and went back to their conversation.

Wissemann stared out the window at the cloudy sky. "What do the aerologists say about the weather tonight?" he asked.

"Oh, it'll be alright—partly cloudy for most of the evening, I'm told," Klimke replied, sounding quite confident. "Some precipitation is expected later on, but you'll be back by then."

But Wissemann did not share in that confidence. The possibility of inclement weather was never reassuring for an airman. He looked at the typewritten orders, glancing over the weather report, then read the equipment information section.

"I see that I'll be flying a Sopwith two-seater," he noted uneasily.

"Correct. And complete with French insignia."

"Hmm, very thorough."

"The front machine gun has been removed to save weight."

"And the rear gun?"

"You'll have the customary Lewis gun in the rear."

"Good. We might need it."

"Oh, I seriously doubt it, *Hauptmann*."

"That's reassuring." Wissemann's reply was flatly ironic.

Klimke opened a gold cigarette case and offered: "Cigarette?"

"Thank you." Wissemann took the fag. "Who's the passenger?"

"Agent Fritz Weinhofer."

"Fritz Weinhofer? A good agent?"

"One of the best, Wissemann—operating in Paris before the war. He's a very capable man." Klimke lit Wissemann's cigarette.

"Can he operate a machine gun?" Wissemann grimaced in a sigh of blue smoke, overly anxious about the mission. He didn't like working in strange situations, or with strange people, for that matter.

"Please. You needn't worry, *Hauptmann*."

"Well, I can't help it, I guess."

"This is all very routine, I assure you. Relax." Klimke smiled. "There won't be enemy scouts patrolling around after dark or anytime later than twenty-three hundred hours."

"I hope your right, *Kapitänleutnant*."

"The French don't like groping around in the dark too much." Klimke laughed. "Well, maybe in the bedroom, perhaps!"

Wissemann didn't laugh, frowning instead, making a little face, not so sure of Klimke's glib assertion. The French were always unpredictable. *"Humph!* Tell that to the Frenchmen that bombed my aerodrome a few weeks ago." He scoffed. "Damnable *Rothosen!*"

"Ach, don't worry, *Hauptmann*."

"I'm sorry, sir. It's been a tough week."

"I understand."

"I guess I really shouldn't worry, eh?"

"No you shouldn't. It's all quite routine."

"Yes, I suppose you're right." Wissemann exhaled nervously. "I've flown countless missions deep into enemy territory. Many times, in fact, when I was a reconnaissance pilot. Once within ten kilometers of Paris. This is no different, I suppose."

"Now that's the spirit, *Hauptmann* Wissemann. Just another day's —night's work—I should say." He slapped the nervy Bavarian officer on the knee, nodding, laughing merrily.

Willi Wissemann drew heavily on the cigarette. He grimaced. It tasted foul and acrid. But the tobacco was fresh enough, he knew.

Damn! That old sick feeling was back again. He sighed worriedly as the Opel staff car raced down the muddy road to Sivery at full speed, hitting every bump, pothole and dip along the way.

"The cruel skies give no one a second chance," Mars whispered.

Liebe Ilse !   6. May. 1917

   I do not know how to begin. . . .so much has happened in the last few days. I'm sorry I have not written sooner, but things are very busy here at the Front. I suppose I could lament on the weather as I always do, but I will spare you the trivialities of the conditions here. I'm eating well enough. Nevertheless, the food is, well, Army food ! Rummer, our cook does his best at disguising the portions. Still, as you predicted, I have dropped in weight considerably. Withal, do not be alarmed Liebchen, my spirit still has a hearty appetite. I can survive on a steady diet of coffee and cigarettes as long as I have the strength and will to continue.

   As you may already know, my promotion to Hauptmann has finally gone through! My new shoulder boards will go nicely with my Iron Cross, 1st Class, yes? I shall receive it any day now for my fifth official victory. I shot down two Frenchman in one day, one in the morning and one in the evening. Have you seen the recent reports about von Richthofen? He had a stellar month against the English in Flanders. He shot down twenty-one enemy machines. He recently surpassed Boelcke's record of forty victories. There's no stopping "Le Petite Rouge".

   The Jasta is shaping up nicely. We recently acquired an "old hand" from Jasta ███. Oberleutnant ████████ He is an excellent pilot and a remarkable marksman, but a wholly insubordinate individual. I'm afraid that things have come to a head. I've tried to be congenial to him, but he has rejected my camaraderie. I must find a way to bring him around, or else his manner will poison the rest of the Jasta.

   I'm enclosing a few of the "delights" that we enjoy here at the Front. Mainly some fine Brie and some Swiss chocolate "borrowed" from the Quartermaster's commissary. Thank you for the wonderful wool cap and stockings. They will keep me warm from the frigid temperatures we fliers have to endure, due to the extreme heights we are forced to operate.

                                        Yours truly, Willi

Book Three

✠

Eagle's Odyssey

May 1917
Sivery Aerodrome
Lorraine Sector

Chapter 16

✠

MAY 7, 1917. A COOL NIGHT HAD SETTLED over the embattled purlieu of France, and the spirits of vanquished airmen lingered longingly amid the moonlit shadows of canvas hangars. It had rained earlier that day, and in the depressions of the tarmac remained reflective little pools of water. The air was stirred by the faint breeze drifting in from the west, rippling the puddles of this shoddy tableau, mirroring its secretive scenes. Wissemann mounted the aeroplane, like a knight throwing a leg over the withers of a favored warhorse, and nestled into the cockpit, ensconcing himself squarely amidst an archaic array of gauges, switches and valves. A mechanic labored over him, strapping him in, while another shuffled to the nose of the two-seater Sopwith and seized the wooden propeller. Wissemann and mechanic barked the usual litany, and shortly, the 9-cylinder Clerget sputtered to life.

Once the Sopwith was throbbing with full power, the mechanics yanked the chocks away, Wissemann guided the slender, snub-nosed aeroplane down the darkened airfield. Seconds later, he was airborne. He tinkered with the fuel mixture briefly then ascended to one thousand meters altitude.

He was quite nervous. But once comfortably airborne, he calmed his nerves with a neat shot of cognac from a flask of cheap, junky stuff he'd bought at the Kasino, and it did the trick. Wissemann smiled anxiously, grinning with comprehension; it'd been a long time since cognac had given him such a glow as had the wine of adventure.

He smiled, suddenly realizing the soothing humming of the Clerget motor—its constant pounding and vibrations probing deep into the fillings of his teeth—did more for his nerves then any cognac could. It was good to finally get underway.

It was barely past midnight as he guided the tetchy little Sopwith across the ink-black sky, higher and higher and further away from Sivery, the secret aerodrome of *Fl. Abt. 99*, hidden deep inside German held territory. Destination: Paris!

Also aboard the two-seater was his tight-lipped passenger, Agent Fritz Weinhofer, who sat stiffly in the observer's seat of the British built biplane. Wissemann, always an astute officer, assessed Agent Weinhofer as quite unimpressive, an odd looking individual, a small, frail man with a twitchy little mustache. How he'd survived as a spy this long was anybody's guess. Wissemann leered back at Agent Weinhofer, wondering how this feeble little creature could possibly be an operative of the renowned German Secret Service.

After a mild protest from Weinhofer, Wissemann climbed to three thousand meters, disregarding orders to stay low. He wanted to get as high above the Front as he possibly could, where the droning revolutions of the Sopwith's rotary would not be heard. Minutes later, he crossed the front lines north of Verdun and proceeded southwest to Épernay, dropping back down to the prescribed five hundred meters. A mollified Agent Weinhofer sighed restlessly and snuggled down into the cockpit.

The Sopwith was performing perfectly.

A refulgent moon lit up the Marne River, just as *Kapitäinleutnant* Klimke had said it would, and Wissemann followed its meandering path through the countryside, its cold waters glistening in the pale moonlight. He'd done very little night flying during his two-year career as a pilot, and for very good reasons. Most aviators rarely flew once the sun went down. Things looked very different at night. Typically, airmen used maps or local landmarks to orient themselves, but in the darkness of night, those landmarks weren't so easily visible. Nor did the maps offer much help. And the old Sopwith? Well, it only had a directional compass, that was all. Wissemann was quite thankful this cool, dark night, for the moon and its radiant attributes. It was a welcomed beacon.

After a trouble-free hour and thirty minute flight, the unlikely pair of Germans arrived at their destination. Wissemann landed the Sopwith safely in a patchy beet field parallel to a narrow roadway just a few kilometers east of Paris. He noticed a strangely glowing skyline. He had assumed the City of Light would have been blacked out because of war. Not so. Wise to the Parisian proclivity of unbridled gaiety and its love of nightlife, he knew the good people of Paris could never allow something like a silly little war to get in the way of their everyday lives. Singing, dancing, drinking, eating, making love, celebrating—everything had to continue. The pilot chuckled; sometimes the French were as arrogant as any German.

Once the Sopwith's noisy rotary engine shuddered to a halt and the wheel chocks were set in place, Agent Weinhofer bounded from the rear cockpit. An idling car was already waiting for him. And before the little man darted off for his destination, he gave Wissemann terse, laconic instructions. A determined expression beset his pale face.

"Wait here," he ordered. "Back in an hour!" Weinhofer sprinted to the waiting sedan. He slid into the backseat and was immediately driven away.

Wissemann watched the sedan accelerate down the road and disappear into the darkness. Moments later, another man came out of the farmhouse. Wissemann felt tense and ill at ease, not sure whom he could trust.

The man approached him slowly.

Wissemann kept a wary hand on his 9-millimeter Luger, just in case. He wouldn't hesitate to use it if the need suddenly arose. He whispered his line. "Poincaré is a bigot."

The stranger spoke his line, muttering in a hoarse Breton dialect. "Clemenceau is the man in chains." He stepped out from the shadows.

Wissemann recognized him, remembering him from the Secret Service briefing. He'd seen all the dossiers of the men participating in the mission, complete with current photographs and sobriquets. The mission, as it had been explained to him, was an exchange of military intelligence. He got no further information than that. Klimke had simply stated that certain aspects of the mission were confidential and on a "need to know" basis, and he didn't need to know.

"*Bonjour, monsieur. I* am Agent Z," said the man.

"*Salut, Enchanté,*" Wissemann replied. He knew "Agent Z" was just a sobriquet, a codename.

"*Alright, this way, monsieur,*" said Agent Z. "I'll assist you with the refueling and such."

"Of course." Wissemann nodded. "All right, lead the way."

Agent Z led him to a barn, where he was instructed to wait. Waiting was always the most nerve-wracking part of any mission, and this situation was no different.

Damn! Willi Wissemann grumped silently. Those pesky old

butterflies were fluttering about his gut again!

Agent Z offered him something to eat.

A jittery Wissemann refused politely. "Thanks. But no," he said. "Couldn't eat a thing right now."

"Oh, I understand. Too nervous, eh?"

Wissemann sighed. "Shouldn't we go ahead and refuel the aeroplane?"

"Sure, in a moment. Relax for a minute, that was a long flight."

"Relax? Sure."

"How about a drink?" Agent Z pulled a green bottle of mineral water out of a haversack.

"Hmm, got anything stronger?" Wissemann asked.

"Of course." The compliant agent reached into a jacket pocket and tossed over a flask. "Take a deep pull, my friend."

The thirsty pilot unscrewed the top, sniffed the contents, and smiled. "Schnapps?" Wissemann took a hearty gulp then gave it back to the agent. He suddenly remembered the flask of cognac; but he was saving that for the return flight. *Merci, monsieur. That's really what I needed."* His face flushed a pinkish glow as the bite of needful spirits took effect.

"Hals und Beinbruch," Agent Z uttered, in a sharp Berliner's accent, revealing his German heritage. He took a swig from the flask then replaced the cap and stashed it back into his breast pocket.

"Ah, your deutsch makes me feel a lot more comfortable," Wissemann replied in his typically prim Bavarian accent. A reassured grin formed on his face. And from that moment on, both men gladly cast aside their Gallic patois and spoke in High German.

"I take it, this is your first operation with *FlugM?"* Agent Z asked.

"Ja."

"Do you normally fly with a *Jagdstaffel* ?"

"Uh, just trying to do my part."

"Aha! A patriot, then?"

"Not exactly." Wissemann shook his head, scoffing softly. He felt more like a high-flying chauffeur than some high-flown nationalist. He coughed roughly—that feverish grippe was beginning to take hold of him. He plopped down on an old wooden box, a light sweat breaking out on his forehead, his breathing became laborious strained. He could feel his temperature rising ever higher.

"Got the bug, eh?" Agent Z said. "The weather's been dreadful around here lately."

The Bavarian sniffled and nodded, reaching into a jacket pocket, pulling out his cigarette case. He offered Agent Z a smoke. *"Willst du eine Zigarette, mein Herr?*

"No thanks. Don't smoke."

"Good man. It's a nasty habit. But, you know how it is?"

Agent Z's head bobbed in agreement, grinning. He rifled through a brown paper bag and pulled out a sandwich and began eating.

Wissemann lighted a cigarette and puffed quietly, thinking to himself: I hope Agent Weinhofer gets back sooner than later. This is absurd! What in the hell am I doing here? Disgusted, he rose to his full height, the cigarette dangling from his lips. He gestured impatiently to Agent Z, saying: "C'mon. Let's get that machine refueled, eh?"

Agent Z frowned. "Oh, all right." He bagged his sandwich and got up. "You worry needlessly, my friend—"

"Let's just get it done now."

Agent Z led Wissemann to a shed where a cache of 10-liter petrol cans was stored. A moment later, both were striding from the shed to the Sopwith two-seater, each burdened with two full petrol cans, and began the refueling process, an interminably laborious task.

Lightning suddenly flickered. Thunder rumbled.

Wissemann's eyes jerked to the sky as cold petrol spilled over his hand drenching his tunic sleeve, gushing over an already full tank, stinging his nostrils with acrid forty octane fumes.

"*Verdammt!*" he swore. "They said no rain! No rain!"

Wissemann capped the Sopwith's tank as rain began to fall, and fall steadily. He stared up at the darkened sky and wondered if all aerologists were just a bunch of bumbling stuffed shirts with meaningless meteorological degrees. And yet as the rain fell in steady droplets, he began reviewing the past few hours in his mind. He'd always felt suspicious about fortuity; would it manifest itself as ill-timed luck or would it bestow an unpredictable grace? As it appeared, luck had been on his side thus far. But the synchronicity of a timely rendezvous, mechanical efficiency, good intelligence, and above all, agreeable weather, had given him a sick feeling inside; was it unusual luck or a fateful harbinger of some unseen doom? Perhaps. But then the peril of the situation struck him all at once. Wissemann gladly heeded the sudden spatter of falling rain, welcoming it as a sign of normality. But his mind kept wondering back to thoughts of catastrophe as he dashed back to the barn, his face glistening with angry dampness, his leather jacket shiny with rainy wetness.

Agent Z followed closely.

Once inside the barn and out of the rain, they sat and waited.

"Damnable French weather!" Wissemann spouted.

"Oh, don't worry, my friend," Agent Z affirmed as he supped on his half-eaten sandwich. "This will pass. It's just a little shower."

But the rain fell harder and heavier and Wissemann began to pace about, back and forth, more anxious than ever, puffing a cigarette like a condemned madman, smoking one after another, even though his distaste for them deepened with every puff. He glanced at his pocket watch for the tenth time then gazed out of the barn doors at the glistening field. It was getting soggier by the second. He shook his head in disgust and stalked back to the rear of the barn where he unbuttoned his fly, relieving himself in one of the empty horse stalls.

He stood for a moment in deep thought. What if Weinhofer doesn't get back in time? What then? What if I take off, like Major Reinhardt instructed, and he's just running late? What if he's just had car trouble? The pilot sighed heavily. What if? What then? What If... It was all quite maddening! He finished his business and buttoned up his trousers—

"*Mein Herr,* come quick!" Agent Z shrieked suddenly. "I see lights. Agent Weinhofer is coming back. Look there!"

The big Bavarian hustled back to the front of the barn. He peered carefully out the two barn doors, which were now fully open. Indeed! There were headlights of an approaching car. They flashed twice as the car neared the entrance of the field. The signal! Both men sprinted out to the Sopwith and commenced start-up procedures. Wissemann climbed in the cockpit and Agent Z took a position at the prop as the black sedan sped up the gravel driveway, skidding to a halt, sending rocks flying through the air. The Sopwith, which was at that moment, just belching to life, shuddered and shimmied, the cold Clerget rotary struggling to crank up. Thunder clapped and the rain continued to fall in heavy sheets.

Agent Weinhofer dashed up to Wissemann. "Hurry, let's get out of here!" he shouted frantically. "I'm being followed!"

"What!" Wissemann yelled back in a shocked voice.

His eyes jerked to the roadway. Sure enough! The German aviator saw three sets of headlights, growing more rapidly in size every second as they approached the field. Agent Weinhofer hastily climbed into the observer's seat and jerked his flight helmet on. Wissemann primed the fuel cock for takeoff, then yanked the goggles over his eyes, then placed both feet on the rudder bars, clutching the control stick tensely, ready for takeoff. "Get that Lewis gun ready, *Herr* Weinhofer!" he ordered "We may need it!"

Wissemann's voice was scarcely comprehensible under the roar of the steadily thrumming Clerget engine. He increased the fine-fuel adjustment to full, and signaled Agent Z to remove the chocks, just as the headlights, now recognizable as black police sedans, broke through a gate at the far end of the field, racing straight for the Sopwith. Wissemann heard the faint crackle of gunshots and thought he saw Agent Z fall to the ground, firing his sidearm in retort. But he wasn't sure; the penetrating white beams from the car's headlights were nearly blinding. He threw an arm up against the bright lights, shielding his eyes, and guided the Sopwith down the rain-soaked field, directly towards the oncoming cars. Bullets whizzed by his head as he slewed the Sopwith down the field, keeping it on a collision course with the police sedans.

"Hang on, *Herr* Weinhofer. This is going to be close!" he shouted.

Wissemann gripped the stick firmly, accelerating down the wet field still fumbling with the fuel regulator. Closer and closer, he converged with the three sedans, feeling bullets bouncing off the Sopwith now. Suddenly, a sharp stinging pain bit into his right shoulder; blood spurted from a nasty bullet wound then quickly dissolved in a pink mist in the prop wash.

"*Aghh-h-h-h-h-h!*" He gasped, blood spattering all over the cockpit and instrument panel. He grasped at his injured shoulder, instinctively yanking the stick back at the same time. The Sopwith flitted into the air just as the landing gear cleared the roof of the first oncoming car. But the engine was still sputtering, the Clerget still choking for fuel, still gasping for air, struggling for power, spinning weakly, but gaining altitude nonetheless.

"Airborne!" Wissemann exhorted grimly.

Agent Weinhofer pelted the passing sedans with the Lewis gun. Miraculously, he hit one of the drivers with his hastily aimed volley, killing him outright. The car swerved and flipped over, cartwheeling out of control across the field trailing a welter of debris. Then, inexplicably, the Sopwith's Clerget engine, choked for lack of fuel, spluttered, misfired and died. The aeroplane canted up and over the hedgerow at the far end of the field in a near stall. Wissemann, stricken with dread, frantically fumbled with the fuel mixture as his consciousness faded. But his adjustments failed miserably.

The prop ticked over twice, then shuddered to a halt.

"What's the matter?" Weinhofer yelled at the top of his lungs.

"Damnation!" shrieked Wissemann. "We're—going—to... crash!"

Blood had leaked from his shoulder at an alarming rate, and he had steadily weakening from the loss of it. Now his only thought was to get the Sopwith's nose pitched down before he passed out, before it stalled and fell tail first into the ground, killing him outright.

Gritting his teeth hard, he forced his all but limp arm to obey his will and the powerless Sopwith pitched, nose-down, from a paltry one hundred meters altitude. The balky biplane descended into the opposite field at the edge of a hedgerow and crashed.

Wissemann's ears were full with the sound of rending timber and the tearing of canvas as his head smacked into the windscreen; he fell slack in the seat. Agent Weinhofer wasn't so lucky. He somersaulted over the top wing, head over heels, thudding into the ground with a muted crack, dying instantly when he landed too heavily on his neck and shoulders. In a haste to get airborne, he'd forgotten to strap on his safety harness!

The two remaining police sedans plowed back across the soggy field towards the wrecked aeroplane, as several other Army staff cars swarmed in from the main road. The rain fell in great sheets and thunder rumbled as Parisian Gendarmes began to assemble around the crash site. And soon they were accompanied by the Deuxième Bureau. The Frenchmen began sifting through the wreckage as the rain continued to fall in great chiseling beads.

So the moon, like a glowing phantom, disappeared silently behind a cloud, taking the light with it. It was as if a stagehand had dropped the curtain on some tragically enacted tableau. However, there was no great applause, no encore. Only the crack of thunder and the flash of lightning. The gods of war were not amused.

And somewhere deep in Germany two old men laughed cynically, mooning over a glass of vintage wine, their voices echoing wickedly through the halls of the Reichstag. They were amused. Then, quietly, unceremoniously, total darkness fell upon the countryside.

ILSE VON LINKHOF SCURRIED UP THE STEPS to her parents' home; the Linkhof mansion was located on Berliner Strasse in the affluent borough of Charlottenburg. She held a small box in her hand and was very excited. She slammed the door and stripped her coat off, hurriedly hanging it on the coat stand, then dashed into the living room. "*Mutti, Mutti!* It's a package from Willi!" She scurried to the chair by the fireplace and sat down. Ilse carefully removed the string and wrapping of the parcel.

"Heavens, child! What is it?" her mother inquired curiously. *Frau* von Linkhof donned her spectacles and leaned over the chair to get a better look.

"It's from Willi," Ilse said. "Look, he sent chocolate and some French brie!"

"My, my. So he has."

"And there's a letter, too. Willi writes so infrequently."

"Well, I'm sure he's very busy at the Front, dear. He has many responsibilities."

"I hope he's all right."

"Of course he is, dear."

Ilse slipped a finger under the edge of the envelope, slit it open and unfolded the letter. Her eyes widened with glee as she read.

"*Ach, Gott! Mutti!* He's been promoted to *Hauptmann.*"

"Really?"

"I'm so happy for him! He has waited so long for this."

"*Hauptmann,* eh? Wonderful!"

"And he says that he'll receive the Iron Cross too, soon!"

"The Iron Cross? Such a fine accolade for a young officer."

Ilse read every line aloud with hurried but careful articulation. *Frau* von Linkhof smiled cheerfully while Ilse read, her head bobbing in joyful understanding.

"Aha. Does he say when he might take leave and see you, dear?"

"No." Ilse replied dolefully.

That amort feeling was tugging at her heartstrings again; she was really starting to feel the heartache from his absence. And her worries for his safety were mounting as well, remembering what her father had told her, only days ago, about the war in France.

"No one will be granted leave for a long time. *Papi* told me the French Army launched a great military offensive in Willi's sector."

"Another offensive?"

"I hope he's careful out there at the Front."

"My dear, don't worry so much. You mustn't think about it. He's in the Air Service now. The dangers are a lot less."

Frau von Linkhof knelt next to her daughter, clutching her hand, holding firmly, staring into Ilse's weepy eyes, smiling. Ilse smiled too, and then embraced her mother.

"I miss him so much. Why, *Mutti?* Why does my heart ache so?"

"Come, come now, dear. Willi will be fine. He is a very cautious and wary young man, you know that. He doesn't take foolish risks." Frau von Linkhof hugged her daughter tightly for a moment, then got up and sat down on a Turkish divan. "This war will end soon. The fighting must end sometime. It must!"

"Why must people fight?" Ilse questioned bitterly. "Why is there so much hatred in the world these days?"

"Alas. We live in troubled times, my child."

"Why can't Germany be at peace with France and England?"

"Because, dear. Frenchmen and Englishmen are restless and

ambitious sorts."

"And what is this war going to solve? Nothing, I fear."

"I don't know, Ilse. European history is written in the blood of warfare. That's just how—"

"Always war, war and more war!"

Frau von Linkhof frowned reproachfully.

"Ilse, please. Calm down. Stop all this grumbling."

"I'm sorry, Mutti. I'm just worried sick."

"Well, there's nothing to be done about it."

"Yes there is! The Kaiser could call a truce. England and France might agree to it. They're reasonable people, *Mutti.*"

"Ach, the Kaiser and his cabinet know what's best for Germany, dear. Believe me. He'll guide the Fatherland through this temporary predicament. He is a resourceful man, our Kaiser."

Ilse sighed, exasperated, and thought: temporary predicament?

Ilse von Linkhof wasn't totally naive about world politics. She was fully aware of the warmongering nature of the Prussian aristocracy. After all, her father was a general in the Prussian Army. She knew the gist of things. She and Willi had talked often about the causes of the war. And although she didn't always agree with his biased political point of view: the upper class always ruthlessly exploited the proletariat, they had a reasonable and comparable understanding about economics and the social structure of Germany, England, France and Russia. She knew Germany as well as Europe would be socially transformed by the outcome of the war. Already, the Fatherland was beginning to feel the pinch of social unrest as the rationing of goods began to cause labor strikes and food riots, due to the British blockade of German ports.

"The Kaiser is clueless, *Mutti,*" Ilse shot back audaciously.

"Ilse!"

"He doesn't really care about the common people. If he did, he would make peace and end this horrid war."

"Don't let your father hear you talking like that, dear. Please!"

"I don't care." Ilse petulantly crossed her arms over her bosom.

"He would be highly annoyed, to say the least."

"But it's true, *Mutti—*"

"Enough! Enough of all this political gossip!" *Frau* von Linkhof exclaimed, her hands fluttering dismissively. She took a deep breath sighing, sinking back in her chair trying to calm herself.

There was a long moment of silence as both women slowly mellowed, composing themselves. Then *Frau* von Linkhof cleared her throat and said, finally, as calmly as she could: "Now. Would you like a cup of tea, dear?" She rose to her feet, still staring at her daughter with deepening concern.

Ilse continued to sulk silently. She knew it was a fruitless cause to discuss politics with either of her parents, especially her mother. Her mother only humored her, and that simply frustrated her more. No one cared to hear what a dainty little schoolteacher had to say, particularly when it came to politics. Ilse stared absently out the window, distressed by her quandary. A bitter frown contorted her usually cheery face.

Frau von Linkhof sighed. "Ilse, did you hear me—"

"Yes, yes, *Mutti!* I'll have some tea. Thank you."

Ilse folded the letter in half and put it back in the envelope. She sank back in her chair, folding her arms over her bosom, reminiscing —it was more like pouting. She really felt like crying. Oh, Willi, I wish you were here. I miss you so much, she thought to herself.

"That's a dear. No more worrying about Willi or talk of war."

"Yes, *Mutti,*" Ilse said quietly, resigning herself to her mother's wary insistence.

"Your father will be home soon. So, behave yourself, please?"

"*Yes...*" Ilse hissed.

"Marten!" Frau von Linkhof called to the household butler. "We'll take our tea now."

"Of course, *Frau* von Linkhof, immediately," Marten replied. The old butler had been dutifully waiting beyond the periphery of their conversation. The faithful house servant bowed his head in obeisance and disappeared down the hallway.

Ilse's mother turned back to her daughter and clapped her gently on the shoulder. "Please, dear," *Frau* von Linkhof begged. "Don't concern yourself with the trivialities of social turmoil and politics."

"All right," Ilse agreed reluctantly.

"You have your children—your students—to worry about."

"Yes. My students. They're a handful sometimes."

"Oh?"

"Quite."

Frau von Linkhof decided to change the subject. "So, how was your field trip to the *Tiergarten* today?" She said, sitting down again on the cushy chesterfield across from Ilse. She folded trembling hands in her lap, just a little bit unnerved by Ilse's behavior.

"Oh, it was fine, *Mutti,* I suppose," Ilse replied, shrugging, her face brightening a little.

"Anything special happen?"

"A scuffle broke out between two boys. Little Klaus Jedermann is such a bully. He picked a fight with one of the new boys."

"*Ach, Gott!* I hope no one was hurt?"

"No. Not really. Just a bloody nose."

"A bloody nose?"

"Oh, it was nothing, *Mutti.* I sent them back to the headmaster, *Herr* Erlenmeyer, so he could deal with them." Ilse smiled. "It was some argument about von Richthofen, I think?"

"Manfred von Richthofen?"

"All the boys idolize him, you know."

"Willi regards him very highly too, doesn't he?" *Frau* von Linkhof quipped. She was trying to be funny and ironic, knowing Willi didn't care too much for the man known as Germany's greatest air hero.

Ilse nodded, smiling

"Yes. But you would never hear him admit it!" she chuckled.

"Silly Willi!" *Frau* von Linkhof laughed.

"Yes. Willi is such an impossible prude sometimes."

"Well, Ilse, sometimes men don't like to confess their adoration of valorous celebrities," *Frau* von Linkhof said in a lighthearted tone. They both laughed for a long moment. Ilse had tried to hold back a smile, but her mother, as usual, had found a way to cheer her up. Ilse was truly grateful for loving parents, although they often seemed old fashioned and stodgy. But they were usually very wise in their perception of the world. Ilse was thankful for their wisdom.

"Maybe I'll bring the children the chocolate and cheese."

"Good idea."

"I think they'll like that."

"And tell them about Willi, for heaven's sake!" *Frau* von Linkhof suggested. "I'm sure the boys would love to hear a story about one of Germany's latest air heroes."

"*Ja!* That's a wonderful idea, *Mutti.* I'll do that."

"Young boys love stories of heroes and gallant deeds of daring."

"Willi? He's a hero isn't he?" Ilse implored playfully.

"Of course he is, my dear."

Marten returned with the tea tray, and mother and daughter began their afternoon ritual. Ilse sipped the hot tea charily, her thoughts wondering back to Willi again. She could see his smiling face, remembering their last day together. They'd leisurely strolled along the *Kurfüstendamm* admiring the fine shops along the vast storefront. Later, they had enjoyed a festive evening at the Deutsches Opernhaus, cheering Beethoven's Fidelio. It all seemed like such a distant age now. Was it all just a dream, she wondered?

"Willi told me in his letter—one of his new pilots is causing him some concern. He's a little worried something awful might happen. He thinks the new officer may... to use his word 'poison' the rest of the *Jagdstaffel.*"

"Oh, really? What's the troublemaker's name?"

"I don't know, *Mutti.* It was censored—blacked out."

"Oh. Well, that's not surprising."

"Why do they do that? Why do they bowdlerize personal letters?"

"For very good military reasons, dear."

"It doesn't seem fair." Ilse sighed and took another sip of tea.

"I thought your father explained all that to you, dear."

"*Papi* doesn't tell me anything, *Mutti.*"

"It's for security reasons, Ilse."

"Security reasons?"

"That letter passes through many hands before it reaches yours."

"I know—"

"Sometimes what we may think of as trivial, could be regarded as important information to others. Spies are everywhere, you know," *Frau* von Linkhof explained further.

"I suppose you're right."

"A letter from a front line aviation unit would definitely attract a spy's attention, my dear."

"That's true, *Mutti.*"

"That's why your father insisted you get an anonymous post office box."

"He certainly did. But still, it doesn't seem right, censoring." Ilse von Linkhof frowned disapprovingly. "It's just plain nosy!"

"Finish your tea, Ilse." *Frau* von Linkhof stirred her cup. "Then let's take Pritzel for a quick walk before your father gets home."

"Where is he? That little rascal," Ilse wondered.

"Ach! That poor dog has been cooped up in the house all day."

Pritzel was Ilse's pet Scottish Terrier. Wissemann had given the dog to her as a Christmas gift two years earlier. Pritzel was a pet she dearly loved, and an animal her father practically despised. Little Pritzel was a constant household reminder to General von Linkhof of the man he detested the most... Willi Wissemann!

"*Komm, kleines Hündchen!*" Ilse called out to her pet terrier. "Where are you? Pritzel?"

A furry black Scottish Terrier came trotting into the room. He stretched his legs and back, then barked.

"*Na bitte?*" *Frau* von Linkhof smiled.

Pritzel hopped up in Ilse's lap, sniffing the envelope, panting.

"Oh, Pritzel. You miss Willi too, don't you?"

FELDWEBEL ALBRECHT SCHUTZLING hung up the field telephone, tugging at his mustache uneasily, shaking his head in utter disbelief. That telephone call had been from 7th Army *Kofl*. They'd just informed him *Hauptmann* Wilhelm Wissemann was missing in action and presumed dead. But they weren't exactly sure. Even if he had survived, Schutzling reasoned, he would be a POW for the rest of the war. *Kofl* also notified him that *Leutnant* Otto Gutemann was to take command of the *Jasta*. *Oberst* Thomsen would be at Pusieux Ferme in a couple of days to oversee the transfer of power, promoting Gutemann to *Oberleutnant,* brevetting him, officially, as *Jastaführer*. Schutzling picked up the handset and rang up the maintenance hangar. A moment later, the phone was ringing.

"Maintenance—this is Peltzer."

The telephone line crackled with static.

"Peltzer—Schutzling here." His voice warbled with uneasiness. "Is *Leutnant* Gutemann around?"

"He's just finishing up a technical briefing. Something wrong?"

Peltzer detected the anxiety in Schutzling's voice.

"K-*Kofl* just called. *Hauptmann* Wissemann is missing in action."

"What? Missing in action?"

"Presumed dead, I'm afraid. It came over the wire this morning."

Peltzer was suddenly stunned to silence. He swallowed gawkily, his throat becoming bone dry, his forehead breaking out in a cold sweat. He could only manage a muffled grunt. *"Uh, um..."*

"Please tell *Leutnant* Gutemann to come to Operations as soon as possible, Peltzer. He is to take Wissemann's place as *Jastaführer.*"

"A-As soon as possible. R-Right—"

"He will take command of the *Jasta* immediately. *Oberst* Thomsen will be here Thursday, at thirteen-thirty hours, for Gutemann's field promotion to *Oberleutnant...*"

Peltzer dropped the handset, his arm limp with shock.

Schutzling paused a moment. "Peltzer? Are you there? Peltzer!"

There was a long silence.

The stumped mechanic, suddenly a bit choked up, cleared his throat, finally raising the handset back to his ear, answering hoarsely. "Yes, yes. Right away... I'll send him along." Max Peltzer hung up the telephone. He chucked his cigar down in an angry fury. Wissemann, missing? His mind raced worriedly. He could hardly believe it!

Peltzer strode up to Gutemann, who was just wrapping up a briefing with the *Staffel* mechanics and pilots.

Peltzer cleared his throat intrusively. "H'mm, excuse me, sir?"

Pilots, mechanics, fitters and armorers, were all gathered around in a semicircle, sitting on empty ammo crates. Gutemann was standing, facing them, reviewing a technical manual. He paused for a moment, regarding the intrusive noncom with venomous eyes.

"What is it, Peltzer?" he asked, lowing the manual to his side.

"Uh, *Herr Leutnant...*"

"What?"

The astute, young Swabian realized something was wrong, the assembled men knew it too. Anyone could read Peltzer's face—the struggle that was going on within him.

"What's the matter?" Gutemann asked.

"S-Sir..."

"Speak, man! What has happened?"

"*Herr Leutnant.* Um..." Peltzer muttered, his voice trailing off .

"*Mein Gott,* Peltzer! Out with it!"

"Schutzling just rang, sir," Peltzer motioned feebly. "You are to return to Operations immediately!"

"Why?" Gutemann tossed the technical manual down, still glaring at Peltzer with questioning eyes. "What the hell is going on?"

"*Hauptmann* Wissemann is missing in action, *Herr Leutnant!* Go to Operations. Immediately!"

Peltzer, now suddenly overcome with terrible grief, nudged the young officer, jerking his head in the direction of Operations. Tears were welling up in his eyes and he hid his face with a trembling hand, feigning a sudden coughing spasm. *Gott!* What's the matter with you, he said to himself. Get a hold of yourself, Max!

Gutemann's eyes flashed with leery apprehension. "C'mon, men. To Operations! Quickly!"

He dashed out of the hangar and ran back to the operations hut with the *Jasta* cadre close on his heels. Peltzer trailed after them, clumsily, still trying to pull himself together. Within minutes, all of *Jasta 23* knew what had happened. Mechanics, fitters, armorers, clerks, cooks—everyone, now converged into the little courtyard surrounding the Operations hut.

Vizefeldwebel Max Peltzer, feeling strangely weary, plopped down on the steps while everybody else scrambled to get inside, slumping down on his haunches, cupping his chin in greasy, oil-stained hands, muttering miserably. "Wissemann, missing?" He moaned sickly.

Chapter 17

✠

MAY 9, 1917. *"MONSIEUR* WISSEMANN, are you awake?" a kindly voice articulated in soft-spoken French. A sleepy-eyed Willi Wissemann stirred, dazed and confused, blinking owlishly. He sat up and tried to piece together his senses, grumbling, coughing, rubbing his swollen eyes. As he focused, the fog slowly dissipated, a slender young woman draped in white stood before him. A cloying smile and placid face stared back at him. Was she an angel? Was he in heaven?

"Where am I?" he asked, suddenly realizing he was laid out in starched, cotton sheets. No, he wasn't in heaven, that was for sure. Something more like hell probably. Moaning voices echoed around him, the pervading stench of carbolic and ether hung heavy in the air, the bitter taste of blood lingered in his mouth, his shoulder throbbed painfully. Yes, this was hell all right—an army hospital.

"Hôspital d'instruction des Armées du Val-de-Grâce, Monsieur Wissemann," the "angel" rattled off in carefully formed syllables, standing at the foot of the bed, hands folded reverently. Alas, she was no angel, not in the literal sense, at least. But she was beautiful, a beautiful Benedictine nurse; the next best thing.

"Hospital? What the... how did you know my name?" Wissemann replied in French, albeit with a thick German accent, his words slurred and clumsy; he was still in a semi-conscious daze, his head still aching horribly. He rasped his forehead and discovered a thick bandage around his skull. His shoulder was bandaged as well. Eventually, as he regained all cognizance, he ruefully remembered the circumstances that had brought him to this pathetic state.

"Ooooh..." he moaned miserably.

"That's right, *Monsieur* Wissemann," the kindly nurse said. "When the Gendarmes pulled you from the wreckage of your aeroplane, they found your pilot's certificate and your identification papers."

"Hmm? My what?"

"Your identification papers. That's how I know your name: *Hauptmann* Wilhelm Reinhardt Wissemann," the nurse explained in gentle tones, her voice barely rising above the din of a busy hospital.

"Oh, I-I see. Y-yes..." Wissemann sputtered dizzily. "And what's your name, Sister?"

His eyes began to focus, gazing upon her winsome features.

"I am Sister Anne Marie Coudouret, a Benedictine here at the Val-de-Grâce."

"Val-de-Grâce?"

"Oui, monsieur. The Val-de-Grâce is a military hospital located in the 5th arrondissement of Paris, France. It was built by order of Queen Anne of Austria, wife of Louis the Thirteenth," Sister Coudouret kindly elaborated.

"I'm in a church?"

"Well, it's actually, a hospital."

"Oh, I see."

"After the birth of her son Louis the Fourteenth," the Sister continued unabated, "Queen Anne, previously childless after twenty-three years of marriage, showed her gratitude to the Virgin Mary by building a church on the land of a Benedictine convent. Louis himself is said to have laid the cornerstone for the Val-de-Grâce in a ceremony that took place in 1645, when he was only seven years old."

"And why are you telling me all this?"

"It is required by the abbess," she replied flatly. "The church of the Val-de-Grâce was designed by François Mansart and Jacques Lemercierand and is considered by some as Paris's best example of baroque architecture. Construction began in 1645 and was completed in 1667. And the Benedictine order of nuns provided medical care for injured revolutionaries during the French Revolution. Thus the Val-de-Grâce was spared the desecration and vandalism that plagued other more famous churches, like Notre Dame. Furthermore—"

"Were you ever a tour guide, Sister?" Wissemann quipped, grimacing at the absurdity of the situation, flat on his back, a prisoner of war, and somehow, the student of some Benedictine nurse's cockamamie history lesson.

"No, but I was a schoolteacher before the war," she replied courteously, then waxed on with her historical discourse. "And furthermore, Notre Dame was looted and turned into a warehouse, as St. Eustach was used as a barn, and neither was spared the indignation of the Revolutionaries. As a result, the Val-de-Grâce's exquisite interior was one of the few unspoiled remnants of Paris's pre-Revolution grandeur. Following the Revolution the building became a military hospital—as it is today."

She smiled, bowing her head.

"*Voilá!* Very nice, Sister. Very nice." Wissemann smirked, clapping mockingly. "Now. How long have I been here?"

"Two days, *monsieur*. Don't you remember? It was Sunday morning when you arrived."

"*Two days? Sacre bleu!* I'm sorry, Sister. I don't remember a thing." With great difficulty, Wissemann tried to raise himself to an elbow, but the pain was too great. "*Agh-h-h...* my shoulder!" He sank back in the pillow grimacing painfully.

"You are lucky, *monsieur*. That bullet went clean through."

"Lucky?"

"Quite—it only broke your collarbone. Likewise, that nasty gash on your forehead occurred when your head apparently hit the windscreen of your aeroplane."

"I vaguely remember that."

"You suffered a terrible concussion."

"Ah. That explains the splitting headache."

"But you'll be fine in a week or so. "

"My thick German skull saved me again."

"And... you have influenza."

"Heigh-ho! You're full of good news, Sister."

"Bed rest is what you need, *monsieur*."

Sister Coudouret glared suspiciously at Willi Wissemann. She thought she'd seen and heard it all by now. As a nurse, she'd witnessed men in their worst state of mind. Some had been in denial, some in the throes of depression, others shocked to silence. But this one, she quickly realized, was reacting quite oddly to his injuries. His sense of humor seemed to border on sarcasm. Young Sister Coudouret was a bit naive, not used to heady irony or cynicism.

"*Eh bien*," Wissemann shrugged. "Well, if I didn't have bad luck, I'd have no luck at all."

"Bad luck? The Lord will watch over you now."

"Will he now?" Wissemann managed a little grin.

"You're in good hands here at the Val-de-Grâce, Monsieur Wissemann." She motioned to one of the orderlies. "*Corporel...?*"

"*Bien sûr, ma sœur.*" A young noncom in a ratty uniform and soiled apron tramped in and brought a tray of food to Wissemann's bedside.

"Would you care for soup and bread?" Sister Coudouret asked.

"Not hungry."

"You need to eat something," she said as she adjusted his pillow so that he could sit up and eat. "You're very weak, *Monsieur* Wissemann."

"No, thank you, Sister. I'm not hungry."

"You should eat. You must regain your strength."

"No!" Wissemann leered irritably at the orderly, waving him off.

The orderly scowled, gazing quizzically at Wissemann, then to Sister Coudouret. She dismissed the orderly with a jerk of her head. *"Tant pis...* leave the tray. He doesn't feel like eating now."

"Whatever." The orderly shrugged, obeyed, tramping away, vanishing down a dimly lit hallway, his boots reverberating noisily in the grand expanses of the church corridor.

That echoing footfall, ringing in the recesses of the Bavarian's aching head, somehow reminded him of his predicament. He wasn't with his *Staffel* anymore, nor was he in Germany; his precious Ilse was far, far away. His world had turned upside down, upended, collapsed. He was a pitiably wounded POW now, a captive of France, a prisoner his own foolish pride. Wissemann rasped his head, sighing, thinking. Had Providence totally forsaken him? Had the gods of war given up on him? Perhaps.

He gestured to Sister Coudouret—the sudden yearning for the taste of tobacco harrying him. "I don't suppose you smoke, Sister?"

"Non!" Sister Coudouret spouted objectionably. "Smoking is not permitted in the recovery ward, *Monsieur* Wissemann."

"Oh."

"But maybe, if you eat your soup and behave yourself, I could arrange to have someone escort you to the courtyard for a smoking break." She gave a reassuring nod, looking very serious.

"Magnifique! Splendid!"

"I'm sure one of the orderlies can spare a cigarette or two."

"Thank you, thank you. You're very kind, Sister—a saint!"

"But only if you eat your soup, *monsieur*."

"It's a deal, Sister."

"It is ratatouille. It's very good today."

"Ratatouille?" Wissemann grimaced. He hated vegetable stews.

"Oui." Sister Anne Marie Coudouret smiled sweetly.

Wissemann nodded resignedly, regarding the Sister with a surreptitious gaze. She was a petite woman in her mid twenties, with big, brown eyes and dark auburn hair, which she kept pinned back tightly and partially hidden in a plain white wimple. Even in her dowdy Benedictine habit, Wissemann found her to be rather attractive. He couldn't help but notice her buxom figure; Anne Marie had curves in all the right places.

Lieber Gott, Willi! The bewitched Bavarian cursed to himself, feeling a bit disgusted for thinking such puerile thoughts. Willi Wissemann's gentlemanly sangfroid seemed to have vanished temporarily. Well, he chagrined, he hadn't seen a woman since he'd left for the Front more than four months ago. Indeed, Anne Marie was certainly a comely angel of mercy, a beautiful figure of grace and goodwill.

"Okay, Sister. You win. Agreed. I'll eat the soup."

Wissemann leaned over, took up the spoon and slurped a big mouthful, nodding artfully, masking his distaste, reluctantly choking down the tepid, foul-tasting stew. It was quite bland!

"*Miam-miam!* Excellent. Scrumptious!"

"Eat all of it, *Monsieur* Wissemann."

"Of course."

"I'll be back to check on you in an hour or so." She bowed and turned to walk away.

"*Pour l'amour de Dieu!* You can knock off all that 'Monsieur Wissemann' nonsense, *bien?*"

"Hmm?" She said, glancing back over her shoulder.

"*Bitte ruf mich an, Willi! Um Gottes willen!*" Wissemann yelled out to her in German, begging her to call him Willi, for God's sake!

She stopped for a moment, spun around, temporarily stunned by his sudden, German parlance. She smiled and bowed her head reverently. "*Sprechen Sie bitte langsam, Willi,*" she rejoined in German, asking him to slow it down a bit.

"Huh?" Wissemann's jaw dropped.

"*Ich spreche nicht sehr gut Deutsch!*" She winked playfully and darted off down the corridor.

"*Hah-hah-hah!* I knew it." Willi Wissemann slapped a knee, shaking his head in disbelief. "*Gott!* She speaks German. And better than she thinks, I daresay!"

"MMM... SHE'S A REAL LOOKER, that Sister Coudouret," a hoarse voice croaked from the next bed.

Wissemann jerked his head around and saw a gaunt, older man sitting sideways in his bed, legs hanging overside. His striped pajamas were billowy and ill fitting, his face pallid and whiskery, his skin wan and waxy—a wizened old front-hog if there ever was one.

He proffered his hand amiably. *"Feldwebel* August Steiner, 4th Army, 24th Reserve Corps," he said. "Glad to meet you, sir. What was your name again?"

"Hauptmann Wilhelm R. Wissemann, *Jasta*—" he hesitated for a moment, suddenly wary of giving too much information.

"Oh, there's no secrets here, sir. We're all Germans in this room." Steiner smiled affably, noting Wissemann's apparent apprehension. "You can call me Vati, if you like. All the young ones do."

"Okay—Vati." Wissemann nodded. *"Jasta 23*—7th Army."

"Ach ja! An aviator. I should've guessed."

Wissemann probed "Vati" Steiner's face. He seemed genuine enough. But the wily Bavarian was keenly aware that sometimes the enemy planted operatives within POW compounds in an effort to gather information, often using casual and informal methods to trick POW's into revealing military bases, units strengths, new weaponry and so on. Was this man a spy? No, Wissemann decided. Steiner seemed harmless enough. But just in case, he decided to maintain a distant level of cordiality, and at the same time, keep his wits about him. Willi Wissemann didn't trust anyone.

"They keep all us German POW's in this ward, until we're well enough to be transported to a regular prison camp," Steiner explained. "Officers and noncoms alike."

"I see."

"There's only twelve of us, now."

"Twelve?"

"Yes. One of the youngsters died last night."

"Died?" Wissemann grimaced.

Steiner nodded dolefully. "Uh-huh. Both his legs were blown off. I thought that poor pup would never stop whining. Only eighteen, he was. Just a boy, really."

The old-timer sighed glumly, scratching the gray stubble on his chin, a forlorn gaze in his ancient face. Wissemann's eyes flickered over Steiner's thin, grizzled frame. Steiner, wearing tatty, over-sized pajamas, sitting in the bed silently, staring at the floor, had a despairingly look on his face. Vati Steiner was swarthy and rugged, with a gray and thinning hairline. Lines etched deep around his mouth and forehead bespoke of years of harsh toil and backbreaking labor. His eyes were tired and bloodshot, his head bobbed nervously. He constantly tugged at his face and whiskers. Vati Steiner was, no doubt, a worn out old front hog. Wissemann figured he was miserably ill and speculated he was probably suffering from shell shock—a condition not always apparent to "modern" military doctors.

"How long have you been here?" Wissemann asked.

"A couple of weeks, I guess. Got half my foot blown off."

Steiner propped his bandaged foot up so Wissemann could see it better. Wissemann scrutinized the bandaged stump, which he could see was darkly stained with blood. He saw the old-timer was missing all his toes and half a foot and the bloodied stump reeked faintly of gangrene. Steiner patted his foot tenderly. "Well, they say I'll be able to walk again... without too much trouble. I hope." He put his foot down and leaned back into a pillow.

Wissemann nodded grimly. "Fourth Army, eh? That's in Flanders, isn't it, Steiner?" He said, not really all that curious, but more as an attempt to check the validity of Steiner's affirmations.

"H'mm," Steiner nodded. "Ypres sector."

Wissemann smiled. "Ypres, aye?"

Steiner gave a nod and cleared his throat. "The English sent me to a dressing station in Rouen. Then here, once I was bandaged up and well enough to move. The Limeys were going to send me straight to a prison camp, but a nice Red Cross nurse intervened. Something about the Geneva Convention, she said. She had me transferred into French custody. She saved my sorry old ass, that's for damned sure. Not all the Frenchies are pigs, I suppose."

"Interesting."

"How did you come to the Val-de-Grâce, *Hauptmann?*"

"Aeroplane crash, special mission," Wissemann lamented. "It's a long story."

"We've got nothing but time." Vati Steiner grinned.

"So. How did you get captured, Steiner?" There was a suspicious gleam in Wissemann's eyes. His brow drew down and those blue eyes narrowed. He was still not convinced Steiner was on the up-and-up.

"Well..." Steiner said with a grave sigh, realizing Wissemann was still distrustful, shrugging carelessly, not really caring anymore if this officer didn't believe him. "When I—my Company—I should say, attacked the British trenches, I was hit, halfway across No-Man's Land. I tried to limp back to our lines, but I was captured during the Limey counterattack, stumbling around in the muck on my bloodied stump. They took me prisoner and brought me back to their trench. And, then... well, it's a long story. But here I am."

Steiner winked, knowing Wissemann still didn't believe him.

The cynical Bavarian turned away from the pale face that lay revealed, a lucid realization registering in his mind. This man was no spy, not even someone under the pressure of French intelligence threats. He acquiesced, finally relenting, deciding Steiner was all right. He smiled and gave a resigning little nod.

"I see. And how long have you been in the Army, Steiner?"

"Seventeen years regular—three years reserve."

"A lengthy career. Impressive."

"I thought I'd be able to retire quietly. But, of course when the war started in '14, I went back to active duty." Steiner gazed at his bandaged stump. "I guess my soldiering days are finally over."

"It would seem so."

"When this mess is all over with, Wissemann, I'll go back to my farm and live a peaceful life, I swear. Just the wife and me. I'm just an old pensioner biding my time." Steiner sighed heavily, scratching his chest. "No more blood and bombs for me—just peace and quiet."

"Any children?"

"No. Wife lost the only one at childbirth."

"That's sad."

"Very sad. She couldn't have anymore after that. What about you Wissemann, married?"

"Not yet. My fiancée and I were going to wait until the end of the war. But... I don't know what's going to happen now."

Wissemann laid his head back down on the pillow and thought about his career. What would happen now? He wondered. Is the war really over for me? Will I ever fly again? Ach! I must find a way to get out of here as soon as I'm able. I must get back to Germany and Ilse. Somehow! Wissemann exhaled gloomily, unsure of the future.

"*VERDAMMT!*" VATI STEINER swore and pointed, suddenly. "Here comes that dandy-assed French Intelligence officer again."

"Huh? Who?" Wissemann jerked his chin over a shoulder.

"He's been waiting for you to wake up, Wissemann, ever since the orderlies brought you in here. He's an arrogant little son-of-a-bitch, that's for damn sure! Watch yourself, sir."

"I will. Thank you."

"Well, it's nap time for me," Steiner declared, slipping under the covers, feigning unconsciousness.

Wissemann propped himself up, holding the soup bowl steadily on his lap, as the dapper French officer stalked down the hallway, glowing resplendently in a horizon blue uniform and highly polished riding boots, his head topped-off in the traditional Kepi service cap, his neck ruff glistening with the rank of an army captain. His finely trimmed mustache and round spectacles gave him a decidedly insensate look. He was brandishing a swagger stick in one hand and a leather briefcase in the other, walking in an assured, unwavering gait.

Wissemann suddenly felt very self-conscious. Frail and pathetic, was a better description, as he lay in his bed, banged up, bruised and bandaged. This was quite unbecoming of an officer, he mused vainly. He mussed his greasy bangs back, and closed the top button of his hospital fatigues, trying to give the illusion of an upstanding German.

The Frenchman stopped at the foot of his bed.

"*Bonjour, Monsieur Wissemann,*" he said in a nasally tone. "I see you've regained your faculties." The officer spoke in a sharp Parisian accent, arrogant in its effect, crisp and businesslike. His smile had the kind of merciless charm only the truly insincere possess; a little bit of snobbery always made him feel like a high-minded ranker.

Wissemann didn't reply. His lips tightened, his eyes closed to slits.

"I am *Capitaine* Henri Perrin of the Deuxième Bureau—French Army Intelligence," said the Frenchman crisply. "I'd like to ask you a few questions, *Monsieur* Wissemann. If you don't mind?"

Wissemann looked up at the Frenchman, still holding the bowl of soup under his chin, smirking. This wag, he thought, apparently knew he could speak French. But then, he was in Intelligence, he would certainly know that. What else did he know, Wissemann wondered.

"You may ask me anything you like, *Capitaine...*"

"Excellent. Now, listen—"

"However, you will only get my name, rank and serial number," Wissemann retorted evenly, his French syllabication sounding as vitriolic as ever. "And I believe you already have that information."

He purposely slurped his soup as Steiner rolled over, moaning bogusly. Perrin chuckled and removed his Kepi, smoothing his hair to one side. He smiled broadly, displaying a flawless set of white teeth. "Hmm, we do have that information, *monsieur.*"

"Good. Glad to hear it. Then you won't need—"

"Even so, it would be in your best interest to cooperate with us."

"Really?"

"Really. And we shoot spies, you know."

Perrin patted his pistol for effect.

Wissemann scoffed, unimpressed.

"You can hardly call me a spy, *Capitaine*. I'm just a pilot."

"Just a pilot, eh? Oh, you're a spy, *monsieur.*"

"I haven't the foggiest idea what you're talking about."

"Yes you do. You're an aviator, true. But a spy, as well."

"I was merely the driver, a chauffeur, so to speak. Nothing more."

Wissemann tilted the bowl back and drank the broth down with sudden, palpable delight. He wiped his mouth on a shirtsleeve, set the bowl on his lap, then defiantly folded his arms over his chest. There was a venomous glint in the Bavarian's eyes.

"Taxi driver?" Perrin chuckled.

"Yes!" Wissemann hissed.

"You were working undercover for the German Secret Service, transporting a well-known operative, flying appropriated French aircraft, operating from surreptitious locations over French soil. Very subversive actions, *monsieur*."

"*Humph!*"

"That makes you a spy. A criminal in the eyes of France—"

"*Tut-tut*," Wissemann snickered mockingly. "I was just the chauffeur, *Capitaine*. I'm not a spy, I assure you."

"Well, then. Spy or not. Chauffeurs, taxi drivers, pilots—whatever. I assure *you*, they all get the same punishment. A quick, all-expenses paid trip to St. Laurent."

"St. Laurent?" Willi Wissemann was well aware of the infamous French penal colony in South America, and he wasn't the least bit intimidated. He scoffed jeeringly. "Is that where I'm going, *Mon Capitaine*, *Ile du Diable*?"

"No. Devil's Island is only for French criminals."

"Well, that's a pity. I was hoping—"

"You will most likely be sent to the prison camp at Barcelonette, or the one in St. Nazaire. That is, of course, if we don't stand you up in front of a firing squad first."

"*Hah-hah-hah!*" Wissemann guffawed. But inside he was just a little bit worried. "Sorry, I can't help you, *Capitaine*. I'm only a German officer, and I expect to be treated as one."

"You'll be treated like a German spy—"

"I am *NOT* a spy, *Capitaine*. I'm a soldier, an aviator. A faithful citizen of the Fatherland!"

"*Sacre Bleu!* Then you're an accessory to the crime of spying."

"Oh, go away, please," Wissemann rejoined, his hand fluttering dismissively. "You have all the information you're going to get out of me today. So leave me alone."

"Oh, we have ways of making people talk."

"You're just wasting your time with me."

"We shall see about that, *monsieur*."

"Whatever you say, *Capitaine*."

"Once you've fully recovered, French Intelligence *will* interrogate you most thoroughly. Most thoroughly!"

"Just piss off, eh? Will you? You've spoiled my lunch. *Au revoir!*"

"*Monsieur* Wissemann—"

"French arrogance just makes me want to retch."

"French arrogance?" Perrin's eyes flared.

At that very moment, Sister Coudouret returned, alarmed by Perrin's sudden presence. She confronted him in no uncertain terms.

"*Capitaine!* I told you yesterday that he was not to be disturbed."

"Sister, I was only—"

"He's not well. Please, do not disturb him. When he is better, you may question him at length. But not here in this ward. Leave, now. *Allez! Allez!*" Sister Coudouret pointed angrily to the exit.

"Sister, this man is a German spy, and—"

"Leave, *monsieur!*"

Capitaine Perrin huffed irritably, jerking his Kepi back on his head, his face flushed with embarrassment. He wasn't accustomed to being dressed down by Benedictine nurses, or much less, any woman. It was an emasculating experience. "Very well," he snapped petulantly, wagging a finger at the chesty German officer. "I shall return in a week, I assure you, *monsieur* Wissemann. I'll glean the desired infor—"

"Get out," Sister Coudouret spouted. "Please go!"

Perrin huffed, totally incensed. He stalked off angrily, shaking his head in frustration, his tap-shod boots echoing urgently as he stalked off down the hallway.

Wissemann smiled; he'd certainly approved of Sister Coudouret's curt castration; Perrin definitely left a few kilos lighter. She was a feisty little woman and he was really beginning to like her.

"Very nice, Sister.

"I'm sorry, *monsieur*—I mean, Willi. Did he upset you?"

"Oh, no. Not at all. Everything's fine, Sister."

"Are you sure?"

"Yes, I'm fine."

"*Capitaine* Perrin is a nuisance. I don't like him coming in here."

"I understand him, Sister, this *Capitaine* Perrin. He's just trying to do his duty, I suppose, just like you and I. But he's just being a great big jackass about it. Do not be troubled, Sister."

Sister Coudouret nodded. "Well, I suppose you're right, *monsieur.*"

"The soup was delicious, by the way. Now... if I only had a cup of coffee. That would be so—"

"Coffee? Of course, of course! I'll fetch the orderly. He'll bring you a cup, and some cigarettes, too." Sister Coudouret had composed herself suddenly; that happy expression returned to her winsome face. "Then the orderly will escort you to the courtyard, all right?"

"Can I go too?" Vati Steiner interjected, throwing off the sheets, fully "awake" now. He sat up, sliding into his hospitol slippers.

"*Ja.* You can go, too, *Herr* Steiner," she articulated evenly in her halting German. Sister Coudouret bowed her head and then left to find the orderly.

Wissemann smiled, broke off a piece of bread and gulped it down. He handed the other half to Steiner, who was grinning contentedly.

"That was good, *Junge.* You certainly tore a strip off of that smug, little snail-eater," Steiner sniggered. "Damn good!"

"Well, he deserved it. Cursed wag!"

"Ooh, but he's gonna make your life even more miserable now."

"Ach..." Wissemann scoffed. "Piss on him."

Chapter 18

✠

MAY 17, 1917. A WEEK LATER, Willi Wissemann found himself sitting in an old wicker chair facing the sun, relaxing in the enclosed courtyard of the hospital, smoking a cigarette and sunning his bones in the warm sunlight. He was quite content to be outside, enjoying the spring sunshine and warming temperatures, taking particular pleasure in a pack of Gauloises cigarettes an orderly had so graciously given him. On his lap lay a stack of magazines. He'd been perusing through some French publications, one of special interest to him "*La Guerre Aerienne*," a magazine about the air war. He thumbed through it with mild curiosity. It was quite out of date, but he was glad, nonetheless. It was something to occupy his restless mind.

Vati Steiner laid on the ground next him, resting his backside, his injured foot propped up on a knee, hands folded behind his head, staring up at a cloudless sky. Sister Coudouret had promised to bring him a copy of "*Das Illustrierte Blatt*," a German publication from Frankfort, his hometown. But he dared not hope for such a luxury. Even though the curvacious Anne Marie seemed to have connections with every Red Cross inspector that passed through the hospital, he knew it would be near impossible to acquire.

As a savvy Bavarian officer, Willi Wissemann knew by now the Red Cross had informed German authorities, who in turn, would notify his mother about his whereabouts and condition. Ilse would soon know as well. Both would be heartbroken, they would worry hopelessly about him. Ilse would fret ever more knowing her "Willi dear" languished in a French prison camp.

He drew on the cigarette and blew a long plume of smoke.

He'd thought of her every day since his departure in December. And it made him even more miserable that he might not see her for a very long time. Maybe never. Not a moment had passed that he didn't think about her. Everything reminded him of Ilse, memories became painful, his heart ached inexorably—something more wretched than any war wound. His soul felt empty and hollow.

He tossed the magazine down next to Steiner. "Here. Read this pulp. What a load of cow-plop!"

Vati Steiner craned his neck to see, shielding his eyes from the sunlight. "Ah-huh. I read that one already. Damned snail-eaters—all evil lies!" Steiner simpered mockingly, thumbing his nose. He went back to his lazy daydreaming.

"Well, I'm sure our magazines tell the same specious stories about this *Glorious War*," Wissemann declared cuttingly, extinguishing his cigarette butt underneath a boot heel.

"Of course, *Herr Hauptmann*," Steiner jeered.

"Clever journalist... Idiots!"

"And the fine folks back home believe every word of it. Sad."

"Fifteen *pfennigs* for a few pages of journalistic pulp."

"The world is drowning in duplicity, sir."

"It's a fine age we live in, eh Steiner?" Wissemann readjusted his sling, pulled the brim of his service cap down over his brow and yawned. "Let's hope we survive it."

Steiner scratched his bandaged stump. "Well, we won't die of starvation, that's for sure," he said.

"No. I think not."

"That was some lunch, hmm, Wissemann?"

Steiner smacked his lips superciliously.

"It was—"

"Real meat with those haricot beans. Nice!"

Wissemann had only known the old noncom for a week now, but he was beginning to realize that August Steiner had quite a dry sense of humor, often commenting on anything and everything with biting irony. One could never be sure whether Steiner was being serious or not. What did he mean by "real meat" anyway?

"Not bad at all."

"Not bad at all, sir."

"A little gristly, tho'. Some old mare must've gotten the chop. "

Steiner chuckled. "I'll bet you aviators eat pretty well, eh?"

The old-timer had heard plenty of rumors of wild parties and the plentiful fare on aerodrome mess kitchens. He truly believed all pilots enjoyed clean sheets, good food, regular showers and a real roof over their head—all the things the infantryman did not have. He didn't begrudge the Air Service for its luxuries but only wished he'd accepted the offer presented to him two years before, when the Army first petitioned for volunteers. Only after he'd wasted away in the mud and rain-saturated trenches of Flanders for a year did he realize the folly of his decision. *Na-ja*, hindsight is always—oh, never mind, Vati, he grumbled to himself.

"We do well enough, I suppose." Wissemann nodded. "But it's not what you think, Steiner."

"No way. Really?"

"H'mm. We get rationed slop too, sometimes."

"Oh, c'mon, sir. I can hardly believe that."

"Not everything's so wonderful. I assure you."

"Well, I guess I had my chance," Steiner admitted.

"What chance was that?"

"In '15… I could've joined the Air Service. But I thought it was for the youngsters, the daredevils. It never occurred to me that an old-timer like myself could bum around an aerodrome, engaged in light duties and such. Oh, no. I had to be the hero and stay in the infantry. What a damn old fool I am." Steiner propped himself up on his elbows, shaking his head disgustedly.

Wissemann frowned, thinking to himself: And what a fool I am. Special missions? *Gott!*

Steiner scratched his balding pate and spat. *"Puhh!* I don't give a rat's ass anymore, Wissemann."

"What do you mean?"

"It's all over for me now anyway."

"I don't understand? You mean, give up?"

"Well, just stay alive, wait for the war to end. That's my motto."

Wissemann leaned forward, eyeballing the old noncom. "Is it not the duty of every good German soldier," he said in all seriousness, "to try and escape?"

Steiner shot Wissemann a cockeyed glance, smiling grimly, defiantly. "Escape? On this useless stump, *Herr Hauptmann? Quatsch!"* He shook his bandaged foot, emphasizing the point.

Wissemann nodded. "I see what you mean. That's how you got caught in the first place."

"Right. Now you're getting it, sir."

"But when it heals…"

"Mein Gott! When it heals? That's a laugh."

"What about your duty?

"Duty? I'm gonna do my 'duty' as a human being and stay alive."

"That's a bit selfish, don't you think."

"Selfish? It's not for my sake, sir. But for my poor old wife."

"Ah, I see now—"

"She doesn't deserve to be a widow. Not yet, not at forty-one."

"And what about the Fatherland, Steiner?" Wissemann cajoled, relishing in antagonizing the old-timer. But he had to admit, though he hadn't really thought about it much himself; he wouldn't get far with a lamed arm and cracked skull.

"The Fatherland? The Fatherland can kiss my—" Steiner caught himself, refusing to be baited. "Well..."

"Careful, Steiner." Wissemann grinned.

"*Ach*, I've done my duty for Germany, sir. Three years of bloody trench warfare. That's enough for me, see?"

"No, no, my friend. You're just getting started—"

"I'm finished, I tell you. *Kaput!*"

"Nonsense. Your as fit as a fiddle."

Steiner stood up, balancing himself on his crutches. He knew when he was being taunted, but he took it all in stride. Nothing could shake his steadfast bearing. He knew he'd done his duty many times over, the days of sacrificing one's self for king and country were long gone, his life was his own now; he would do as he pleased. He turned to Wissemann with a smile.

"Well, I'm headed to the latrine," he announced. "Those beans kind of filled me up, if you know what I mean?" Vati Steiner winked elaborately.

Wissemann grinned. "Yes, Steiner. You *are* full of beans. You old-graybeards. Hah!"

"I'm stopping by the mess. You want anything, *Junge?*"

"No, I'm fine. You go ahead. Enjoy yourself." Wissemann picked up another magazine, thumbing through the pages.

Steiner hobbled over to the courtyard gate, where a French sentry stood by, guarding the exit. Steiner stopped, waited, glaring impatiently as the guard unlocked the wrought-iron gate and then let him pass. He smirked at the sentry, gesticulating with a mocking gesture. *"J'en ai assez, j' abandonne!"* Steiner bellowed, limping down the hallway to the latrine.

Wissemann laughed and went back to his magazine. But his laughter faded quickly; he looked troubled, thinking. Could I escape? Is it possible? He groaned—he'd have to figure something out soon.

Capitaine Perrin had so bluntly informed him, just the day before, all German prisoners at Val-de-Grâce were to be transferred to a POW camp within the week. They were to be relocated to Barcelonette—a remote little town in the Southern French Alps. It was a highly isolated camp and reputedly escape-proof.

Wissemann sighed. His injuries had healed well enough, time was running short, he needed to work out a plan, and soon. He speculated warily: Once the interrogations commenced in earnest, he'd be at the mercy of Perrin's unrelenting wrath. Willi Wissemann knew he was innocent of spying, but how would the French see it? Would they treat him like an officer, would they treat his commission with respect and honor? Probably they needed a scapegoat, now that Fritz Weinhofer was dead. That mustachioed little agent had thwarted French Intelligence for a long time; his clever wheeze had succeeded in neutralizing their espionage efforts. They wanted someone to prosecute, for the French needed to save face now. Wissemann was in a precarious situation. He exhaled apprehensively, sick with worry.

His stomach churned, those haricot beans playing havoc on his bowels. He held his breath and broke wind, clearing his throat at the same time, trying to drown out the noise, laughing to himself, looking around sheepishly. *Phew!* No one had heard.

"Oh, Vati Steiner, if you only knew me better. An officer, yes. A gentleman...well?" He leafed through the magazine again, frowning in disapproval, shaking his head. "Rubbish! Just plain rubbish!"

CAPITAINE PERRIN PACED back and forth stiffly. He was "locked-in" in a boxy interrogation room on the second floor of the French War Ministry building in Paris. At the far end of a long wooden table sat a German officer. The officer sat quietly in a chair, arms folded across his chest in a resentful posture. A brand new pack of Gauloise cigarettes lay before him—a little carrot to sweeten the proceedings. Perrin donned his spectacles, turned to the officer, and there was once again a droning, syllabic nasal exchange.

"So you expect me to believe that, *monsieur?*"

"Believe what you like, *Capitaine*. I am innocent."

"You knew nothing of the documents Agent Weinhofer carried with him? That's hard to believe—"

"Nothing."

"You're lying."

"Even if I did know something, *Capitaine,*" the German officer retorted in flawless French, "do you seriously think I'd tell you?"

"Let me remind you of something. You could be shot as a spy."

"Me? An agent of Wilhelmstrasse? Don't be ridiculous."

"Yes," Perrin snorted. "I think you're an undercover agent."

"I don't care what you think," the German officer replied defiantly. "I'm innocent, I tell you."

"So. You knew nothing at all?"

"Nothing."

Perrin smiled villainously. "Then I'll have to subject you to a more drastic means of interrogation."

The German scowled contumaciously. "I'm afraid that kind of talk doesn't amuse me."

"I'm not trying to amuse you—"

"As an officer of the Imperial German Air Service, I... *Hauptmann* Wilhelm Reinhardt Wissemann... am protected by incontestable legal conventions under the precepts of civilized warfare."

Perrin sighed, rolling his eyes in the French manner. "Lest I remind you, *Hauptmann* Wissemann—those conventions you so deliberately hide behind are for soldiers in uniform. Not spies in civilian attire, mind you."

Wissemann shook his head in protest, now drumming his fingers anxiously on the table. "I *WAS* in uniform—"

"Silence!"

Wissemann fidgeted in his seat. "I was told by superiors it wasn't necessary or safe to know the nature of the mission. I was a last minute replacement for the flight."

Perrin returned to his seat and began rifling through a file folder lying on the table. He pulled a yellowed slip of paper out from a heap of documents and gave it to Wissemann. Wissemann took the slip of paper and read it. It was an intelligence intercept decoded by the Deuxième Bureau. He glanced over the document, smiling scornfully, then tossed it aside in a gesture of dismissive contempt. The lanky Bavarian guffawed.

"*Tu as bu, ou quoit!*" he quipped.

"Do you find something amusing?" Perrin said, readjusting his spectacles.

"Yes, quite. It's preposterous nonsense, that intercept. What sort of game are you playing, hmm?"

"Game? This is no game. This is war."

"I'm not as dim-witted as you may think, *Capitaine.*"

"That intercept was decoded only hours before your secret rendezvous outside of Paris. Let me read it to you, just in case you misunderstood something."

"Do as you like." Wissemann rolled his eyes.

Perrin stood up abruptly, paced around to the end of the table and seized the yellowed copy from Wissemann.

He adjusted his spectacles and sniffed haughtily, staring at the paper, nodding superiorly, holding it up, posturing as if he were about to read a bit of romantic prose, then began to read the Deuxième intercept. His voice was precise and monotonous. He said:

```
From: Secret Service HQ, Berlin
      Ministry of War
      2335 Hours 6 May, 1917
      (1st from Paris #5750-Deuxième Bureau)
-------------------------------------------------
To: Kommandeur de Flieger (Kofl)
    1st Army, 3rd Army, 7th Army, 9th Army.

Intercept immediately Sopwith two-seater aircraft
leaving vicinity of Sivery/Verdun. Occupants-double-
agents: (Agent-Y) Haupt. Wilhelm R. Wissemann and
(Agent-X) Fritz Weinhofer—have appropriated classified
battlefield documents detailing German unit strengths
and artillery locations, are attempting to deliver such
to French Intelligence. STOP AT ALL COSTS! The
assailants are considered dangerous and traitors and
criminals of the German Empire. Use all means
necessary; ruthless, merciless, summary—immediate
retaliatory action is required. Conspirators have
commandeered Allied aircraft for this purpose. Stop at
all costs.


Oberst Hermann von der-Lieth Thomsen, Kogenluft,
General Konrad von Linkhof, Deputy War Minister
```

The words had spewed from the little Frenchman's mouth like an over-rehearsed recital, giving unnecessary emphasis to every syllable. He'd paced around with his hand in his tunic pocket, as if it gave the narration some special credence.

That nasally drone only made Wissemann want to retch; it was redundant as it was mawkish. He was a captive audience to some Frenchman's melodramatic recital, and the document, like Perrin, was unbelievably and equally absurd. Wissemann shook his head and thought: What a self-absorbed idiot! He scoffed. "There isn't a grain of truth in it, Perrin. Just a lot of theatrical trimming."

"Oh? Well, it's the truth, all right, Wissemann."

"Nice diction, though. You obviously missed your calling."

The Frenchman's lips tightened. "Now. Why would German Intelligence issue such an urgent message, if it were not true? They've implicated you as a traitor, *monsieur.*" Perrin returned to his chair.

The brash Bavarian was suddenly silent.

"Perhaps you are playing games with me?" Perrin continued.

Wissemann rolled his eyes again.

"It is unfortunate your colleague, Agent X, Fritz Weinhofer, didn't survive the crash."

"Unfortunate?"

"Perhaps I'd be asking *him* all these questions."

"Perhaps you're just wasting your time, *Capitaine.*"

"And your other accomplice, Agent Z—or Rudolf Müller, as he is better known, is being interrogated by our people right now. He'll soon relent and divulge everything he knows." Perrin folded his hands, grinning complacently.

"Agent Z? He's... alive?" Wissemann replied, surprised.

"Aha. Very much alive."

"But, how—"

"If he implicates you, then you are in serious jeopardy."

Perrin plucked a cigarette from his golden tobacco case and lit it. He blew the smoke in Wissemann's direction, taunting the stubborn German officer.

Wissemann smiled. "Oh, you're bluffing, *Capitaine.* I saw Agent Z go down, shot dead."

"Shot dead, eh?"

"Dead men make poor witnesses." Wissemann folded both arms over his chest and glared calmly at the Frenchman. "You're just bluffing, Perrin. Bluffing, I say."

But it was Perrin's turn to smile.

"*Now, now, monsieur,*" the Frenchman rejoined mockingly. "Would we have gotten this far with me bluffing. He's alive—and we have offered him a deal if he cooperates with us."

Perrin puffed his cigarette confidently.

"A deal? *Bah!* A deal with the devil."

Perrin laughed. "You think you're so clever, don't you?"

"Clever and innocent, *Capitaine.*"

"Well, you'll find out soon enough."

"*Humph!*"

"You've been implicated by your own intelligence people as a double agent, and a traitor Wissemann. So, it's just a matter of time before we learn the whole truth."

"The truth?" Wissemann scoffed. "Why does everyone put so

much stock in the truth? Why is truth considered to be so bright and shining and wonderful, hmm? Truth can be more rotten and destructive than any lie!"

"But the liar will die one day, and the truth... it never dies."

"Ach, don't urge truth onto me, *Capitaine.* I've seen it, the filth, the death, the misery, what one man does to another. There's your truth, man!" Wissemann shot back hotly.

"Indeed. Very philosophical."

"You're an idiot, Perrin."

"Oh? Well, you'll tell us the facts, eventually. We have methods."

"I've told you everything I know. There's nothing more to tell."

"We shall see—"

"And that little intercept of yours... well, it's a felonious concoction created by your Intelligence people, no doubt. It fools no one. Especially me." The Bavarian's voice was controlled but as cold as a French jail.

"*Tais-toi,* Wissemann!"

"You'll have to do better than that, I'm afraid, *Capitaine* Perrin."

Willi Wissemann was nearly at his wits' end. He knew full well that Perrin would be persistent, and he doubted the intercept he'd read was genuine. But he had not counted on Agent Z still being alive. Wissemann knew he personally had nothing to hide. However, Agent Z, in his desperate attempts to bargain for his own life, might rat him out by concocting some rotten lie or half-truth. Then again, Wissemann suddenly realized , Agent Z could've been working for the French all along. Or perhaps Perrin was after some other information; maybe since Weinhofer was dead, the French needed a scapegoat, someone to make headlines for the Paris Press. Things were getting confusing! Wissemann decided to call the Frenchman's bluff.

"All right. Bring him in then. Let's see what you've got, *Capitaine,*" Wissemann demanded confidently.

Perrin snickered haughtily. He called to the soldier waiting outside the door. "Guard—bring the prisoner in now."

"*Oui, mon Capitaine,*" the guard replied and marched off.

"You will have your proof in a moment, *Hauptmann* Wissemann."

"Whatever." Wissemann cupped his hands, staring absently at the ceiling tiles, pursing his lips, pretending not to be worried.

"Go ahead, have a smoke, those cigarettes are for you," Perrin offered, gesturing with an upturned hand.

Wissemann hesitated.

"Go on. Take them..."

The Bavarian shrugged and obliged himself to a cigarette, fearing he had nothing to lose by smoking one of the Frenchman's cigarettes.

Perrin struck a match. Wissemann waved him off.

"No thanks," he said. "I've got a light."

"Suit yourself, *monsieur*." Perrin squelched the match.

Wissemann produced a matchbox from his tunic pocket, struck a match, lit the cigarette, filled his lungs, then exhaled slowly. "Hmm... not bad. Of course, Halpaus is a much better brand," he quipped sardonically. "But... these will suffice for now, I guess." The big Bavarian took another deep, anxious drag, feeling his nerve cracking just a little bit. Things were getting a bit ticklish!

The Frenchmen's eyes blazed, then cooled. "You think I have a dirty job, don't you?"

Wissemann snorted, cigarette dangling. "There are no *clean* jobs in wartime, *Capitaine*."

A minute later, the guard returned with the prisoner, Rudolf Müller—a.k.a. Agent Z. His hands were bound, and he drooped his head pitifully. Wissemann was a little distressed, Müller looked battered and beaten, his lower lip was bloody and split, blood oozing slowly down his cheek from a ragged laceration under his eye. His nose appeared to be broken, plainly, all results of harsh interrogation methods. Although Müller did not speak, Wissemann saw something in his eyes, a glimmer of hope, a gleam of honor that spoke volumes of his fidelity to the German espionage effort. Müller was a loyal agent and German through and through, Wissemann realized. He would die for the Fatherland if necessary. Müller grinned tightly and winked. Perrin ordered him out of the room.

"You see, Wissemann, he is indeed alive," the Frenchman said. "And as you can see by his condition, he'll not last much longer. He'll soon tell us what we want to know."

Capitaine Perrin's conceited threats didn't frighten Wissemann in the slightest. But he was surprised to see Müller alive. Even so, that didn't influence his attitude. He knew the French officer would be hard pressed to implicate him as a spy, his storied combat record spoke for itself; the fearless Bavarian knew French Intelligence was certainly aware of his military exploits. They probably knew his *Jasta* number, the aerodrome from which he operated, and most likely, they even knew his personal victory score. German Intelligence possessed the same meaningless information on French Air Service personel as well. But the intercept had apparently befuddled the snail-eaters—it befuddled Wissemann! But French Intelligence, he knew, would make its own suppositions, assuming it was either just another German ruse, or more clever disinformation, diverting them from more important things like new aircraft and personal strengths.

"Talk, talk, talk!" Wissemann snarled. "He will say nothing,"

"We shall see. "

"You're really a tiresome little man, Perrin, you know that?" Wissemann rejoined, his patience thinning, blowing smoke from his nostrils, studying a fingernail.

Perrin chuckled haughtily, closing the file folder.

"So. I'm getting on your nerves, eh? Good."

"Piss off, Perrin."

Perrin snorted. "We'll continue this melodrama tomorrow."

"Melodrama? Whatever—"

"Alright, we're finished for today."

Perrin gave a curt nod then called for the guard. The door swung open and the guard strode in. He poked Wissemann with his rifle, rousing the Bavarian from his chair. Wissemann growled, Gauloises in hand, and got up. A moment later, he slammed out the door and was escorted down the hallway to a waiting lorry. Perrin sat quietly for a moment, thinking, shuffling some papers.

Another French officer came in and sat down next to him. It was Perrin's superior, Commandant Rousseau. He'd been eavesdropping on the interrogation. "Capitaine Perrin," he said. "Do you really think this Wissemann knows anything?"

"I think he does, sir."

"Well, I don't think so. Take a look at this."

"Hmm?"

Rousseau presented Perrin with an Intelligence dispatch. "We just received some new information about an hour ago."

"Let me see that."

Perrin adjusted his eyeglasses, seizing the dispatch.

"As it turns out, *Hauptmann* Wissemann really is a pilot."

Perrin glanced over the dispatch. "How did you come by this information, sir? If I may ask?"

"Apparently our agents in Berlin have uncovered some sort of 'intrigue' involving Wissemann." Rousseau clamped down on his cigar and nodded.

"Intrigue, *mon Commandant?*" Perrin was perplexed.

"It's something. But we're not sure what yet."

"What do you mean, sir, exactly?"

"Wissemann is, somehow, connected to Deputy War Minister, Konrad von Linkhof, who is in turn, good friends with *Oberst* Hermann Thomsen, Chief of Staff to the German Air Service. Thomsen also happens to be Wissemann's commanding officer. Both names have appeared in several dispatches—something about faulty aircraft wings? Redeployments? Structural failure? God only knows. It's probably just more Boche disinformation. Damned sausage-eaters!"

"Really?"

"Uh-huh." Rousseau nodded. "It's nothing, I'm sure."

"Very odd, sir."

"*Oui*, it's an odd bit of news, I know," Rousseau said. "However, I think this Wissemann fellow might be some sort of troublemaker. He's apparently ruffled some feathers in the German hierarchy—someone in the Prussian High Command doesn't like him."

"I see..."

"And Fritz Weinhofer, as you well know, was a double agent."

"Right, of course."

"The Germans didn't trust him anymore than we did, someone blew the whistle on him. We received an anonymous telephone call the night Wissemann and Weinhofer were captured."

"Yes, my desk received that call too, sir. It's all very strange."

"I suspect this whole mess may have been an elaborate set up, Perrin." Rousseau waved his cigar about, scowling. "Some of our best agents are all suspects now—the General Staff is in an uproar. It's a grand fiasco, if you ask me."

"A fiasco, sir?"

"Unfortunately." Rousseau scoffed bitterly. "Wissemann may be guilty for being German, but I doubt he's a spy."

Perrin laughed haughtily. "Well, being German certainly makes any man guilty in my eyes."

Rousseau stroked his goatee, unamused. "Uh, well. He's actually part French, believe it or not. Anyway, he doesn't strike me as the secret agent type, *Capitaine*. He's too starchy."

"I see. What about his involvement as an accomplice?"

"I don't think we can try him under the traditional auspices of espionage, he's just a regular flying officer. And Wissemann has an impeccable combat record and long service history."

"All right, sir. Good enough then," Perrin replied, a bit crestfallen. "Well, I still have Müller to interrogate. That might garner some useful information." Perrin carefully placed the dispatch into his attaché case, still quite pleased with himself.

"Well, good luck with that, *Capitaine*. You'll need it."

"Thank you, *mon Commandant*." Perrin jerked a nod. "I'll get something out of our... AGENT Z."

"Fine. And I suggest you take the heat off of Wissemann for a while, let him get comfortable, let his wounds heal. Then later, we'll take him to Compiègne—interrogate him for possible information on the German War Ministry. If he knows anything in that respect, we'll find out then."

"*Oui, mon Commandant.*"

"*Continuez, Capitaine.*"

Both men stood up. Perrin nodded, saluting snappily. Rousseau returned the salute and left the room. Perrin pondered for a moment, baffled, smoothing his little mustache bemusedly.

"What are those rotten Boche up to, I wonder?"

OTTO GUTEMANN SAT QUIETLY at a table in the mess picking at his shriveled cabbage rolls, having no appetite for Rummer's over-cooked creations. He should've been a happy man. He'd recently been promoted to *Oberleutnant* and *Jastaführer*. The General Staff had also awarded him the Iron Cross. In addition, he led the *Staffel* with twelve confirmed victories. But none of these honors meant a thing to him.

He pushed the plate aside and stared out the window. It seemed since *Hauptmann* Wissemann's disappearance, a gloomy funk had descended upon the aerodrome. Even the dispute between Schäfer and Luddenvoss had cooled off. *Oberst* Thomsen had dismissed the initial charges filed by Wissemann, and now neither man faced disciplinary action from Supreme Command. Thomsen had informed Gutemann to simply separate the two agitators into two different *Ketten*. His orders were explicit: separate flight groups, and, whenever possible, separate missions. No additional disciplinary actions were issued. None.

Ironman Schäfer, banned from the Kasino, stayed in his billet most of the time now, drinking by himself. Luddenvoss went about the usual business of shooting down the French scourge, wholesale. A tight race soon developed between Gutemann and Luddenvoss for the title of leading ace of the *Jasta*. Just a day before, Luddenvoss had shot down his eleventh confirmed victory, a Dorand two-seater. It was the start of a fierce rivalry. But Gutemann did not relish the competition.

The young Swabian watched from the window as the afternoon patrol returned from a mission. He counted the machines as they pulled up to the flight line. One hour ago, six machines of Fleischer's *Kette* had taken off for an escort mission over Reims. Now they were back. Only five, Otto Gutemann said to himself. One of the new replacements must have been shot down. The thought brought a fresh crease to his forehead.

The disillusioned officer reluctantly got up from the table and headed to Operations. Every time a machine was lost or a pilot killed, the incident generated a mound of paperwork. Everything had to be accounted for—in triplicate. Gutemann loathed administrative work, but it was something a *Jastaführer* had to deal with every day. The Imperial German Air Service was notorious for its meticulous record keeping. Otto Gutemann didn't like sitting behind a desk, he only wanted to fly his Albatros and do combat against the French.

"*Herr Oberleutnant*," *Feldwebel* Rummer said as he walked by. "You didn't finish your lunch. Are you all right, sir?"

"I'm fine, Rummer—just sick of cabbage rolls."

"Sorry to hear that, sir. But that's all we have right now."

"That's what you said yesterday."

"Dinner will be better. I promise you."

"Sure it will."

"I've secured a reserve of bratwurst from the Quartermaster's commissariat in St. Quentin. It'll be a first-rate meal."

"*Mmm...* sounds delicious," Gutemann replied, cynically.

Rummer shrugged his shoulders. "Well, there's always the cabbage, sir," he said.

"Right. Cabbage," Otto Gutemann shook his head in disgust. He strode to the exit hands buried in pockets, frowning, his head drooping low. "Afternoon, Rummer."

"Afternoon, sir."

Gutemann walked down the hallway and exited through the side door, making his way to Operations. Time for more mundane paperwork, he thought bitterly. As he entered the hut doorway, he nearly collided with an excited Adjutant Schutzling.

He huffed, barking crossly at the adjutant.

"What is it, Schutzling!"

"*Herr Oberleutnant,* I just got a telephone call from *FlugM.*"

"And..." Gutemann folded arms over chest.

"They told me that *Hauptmann* Wissemann is alive!"

"Alive?"Gutemann's eyes kindled.

"He is convalescing in a hospital in Paris."

"In Paris?"

"Yes, sir. The Red Cross conveyed the information to the War Ministry this morning."

Schutzling handed Gutemann his handwritten notes.

"Convalescing? Did they state the severity of his injuries?" Gutemann asked, as he glanced over the notes.

"No, sir. But they did say he'd fully recover within a few weeks."

"So he is alive? That *is* good news," Gutemann remarked with pronounced relief, a thin smile creasing his lips.

"Good news, indeed, sir."

Gutemann sighed. "But now he'll just rot in some lousy French POW camp for the remainder of the war. That's a damned shame."

"A damned shame, alright. He was an excellent officer."

Gutemann went into the office and sat down behind his desk, the old desk Wissemann once occupied. He turned and called out to the ginger-haired adjutant.

"Schutzling…"

"Sir?"

"Please type up a bulletin for the *Jasta*, would you?" Gutemann asked. "I think the men might like to know *Hauptmann* Wissemann is still alive and well. They'll appreciate that, I think. He wasn't here long, but he definitely left a positive impression on all of us."

"*Jawohl, Herr Oberleutnant.* I'll do it immediately."

Schutzling sat down and loaded his typewriter with a fresh sheet of paper, and began pecking away at the new assignment.

The door swung open and *Leutnant* Eduard Fleischer stumbled in, still in flying leathers, wearing a grim expression on his face. "Well, we lost another one today," he announced dolefully.

"I saw," Gutemann said. "Who was it?"

"*Leutnant* Ziegler—shot down."

"How'd it happen?"

"The Storks bounced us over Witry on our way back from Reims. Poor slob, he never saw it coming." Fleischer stripped his flight cap from his head. "A bad way to go, not seeing the man that did it—"

"Any Frenchmen shot down, Fleischer?" Gutemann questioned. "Or was it just one sided?"

"No. The Storks were in and out before we knew what hit us, sir."

"Of course." Gutemann shook his head grimly.

"Those Spads are just too fast, sir."

"More excuses. Anything else?"

"We did catch an ancient Farman on its way back from our lines. *Leutnant* Winkler shot the bastard down. He burned beautifully," Fleischer replied, grinning gleefully.

"All right, then," Gutemann replied, somewhat placated. "Gather up Ziegler's personal effects. I'll inform *Kofl* immediately."

"Yes, sir."

"Schutzling… have AFP-7 send up another replacement."

"Of course, *Herr Oberleutnant.*"

Otto Gutemann glared at Fleischer. "Did our recon plane complete its mission? What happened?"

"Well..."

"Did it show up at all?"

"No, sir," Fleischer replied flatly. "We waited at the rendezvous point, but it never appeared."

"Unbelievable."

"Well, we patrolled over Reims without it, sir. The anti-aircraft was absolutely murderous!"

Otto Gutemann was well aware of Fleischer's cowardly nature, knowing the fearful flight leader would avoid a dogfight if he could. He scowled and said: "Next time, if that happens, don't cross over into enemy territory. Patrol over the front lines instead. Understand?"

"Yes. I'll make a note of it." Fleischer sneered.

"We're not up there for target practice, you know." Gutemann jerked his head to the ceiling to emphasize the point.

"Agreed, *Herr Oberleutnant.*" There was a small degree of indignation in Fleischer's tone. He wiped the sweat from his brow, plopping down in the chair in front of Gutemann's desk, restless, an inquisitive look besetting his hazel eyes.

Gutemann looked up from his paperwork, gazing questioningly. The young *Jastaführer* cleared his throat. "Do you have anything else to add, Fleischer?"

"Well..."

"That'll be all then, *Leutnant* Fleischer. Go have some lunch or something. Dismissed."

"Um, uh... sir—"

"What? Speak, man!"

"I heard a little latrine rumor, sir." Fleischer fidgeted. "Is—is Luddenvoss going to be transferred to another *Jasta*? Is it true?"

Gutemann leered at Fleischer. "No. Nothing's been confirmed. It's just a rumor. Forget it. *DIS-MISSED!*"

The chickenhearted Fleischer scowled, got up jerkily, saluting, leaving Gutemann's office in a hurry. Schutzling glared at him curiously as he passed by his desk. Fleischer shrugged as he exited the Operations hut, frowning, slamming the door behind him.

Schutzling rose from his typewriter, sauntering up to Gutemann's door, a look of hopeful delight beaming from his face. "Well. That's the first I've heard of that. Anything of it, sir—"

"You too, Schutzling? Get out!"

Gutemann bolted up from his desk and slammed the door in the nosy adjutant's face, rattling the frame noisily.

A ruffled Schutzling huffed, returning to his desk, continuing his typing assignment. "Ach!" he scoffed. "Damnable snotty officers!"

Chapter 19

✠

MAY 30, 1917. WILLI WISSEMANN sat quietly in the musty cell, staring at the cold plate of food, not the slightest bit hungry, the carefully prepared meal not to his liking. Outside, he could hear the shouts and barks of the French sergeant preparing his squad for the task at hand. The sounds of shuffling feet and clicking rifles sent a chill up his spine. How had it come to this, he wondered? How had that little rat, *Capitaine* Perrin, changed the lesser charge of simple accessory, to one of political espionage? How had everything gone from bad to worse in just a few days time?

Wissemann shook his head, disgusted.

"So... is this suppose to be our last meal?" said Rudolf Müller, standing, hands in pockets, frowning.

"Humph," Wissemann scoffed. "It *is* our last meal."

Müller sat down at the table across from the dejected looking Bavarian, gazing at the fine plate of baked hen, assorted vegetables, fresh bread, cheese, wine and coffee. "And what the hell are we suppose to eat it with, eh? Our hands?"

"The guards said we couldn't have any knives or forks."

Müller tore a leg off the hen, bit into it, and swallowed. "You think they put anything in the food?"

"First they poison us, then they shoot us?"

Müller spat. "I bet they put something in it!" He tossed the half-eaten leg back onto the plate, grimacing.

"Why would they do that?"

"I don't know? To make us groggy, or something?"

"And why would that be bad, Müller?"

"I don't want to be drugged, see. I getting out of here, somehow. I can't be slowed down by some—tainted baked bird."

"How are you going to get out of here, hmm?" Wissemann asked, a cigarette burning in his mouth now, his face grim and indifferent. "Smash your way through those stone walls? Break down that iron door? Tell me, how?"

"We've got to get out of here, Wissemann. They're going to kill us if we don't!"

"Have you got an idea?"

"No. But there has to be a way. I mean—"

"How many guards do you think they've got out there?"

"I don't know? Maybe a squad—two squads?"

"They'll shoot us dead before we got two steps from this place."

"Well, I'm getting out of this, I tell you! I'm not going to die in this rotten country. I guarantee you of that, Wissemann."

"There's no way out, Müller. We are doomed, I fear."

"But that French Major, Rousseau, said he would submit our appeal to the French High Command—see if our sentence could be commuted to a lesser charge..."

Wissemann grinned derisively, smoke jetting from his nostrils. "The only way we're getting out of this, my friend, is in a pine box."

The bolt to the cell door suddenly rattled, the door swung open, creaking ominously at its rusted hinges. An elderly priest in a long, black cassock strode in, a bible cupped in his hand, a solemn look on his face. He removed his hat, dropping it to his side.

"Good morning, my sons," he said. "I am Father Guerin."

"What's the word, Father?" Müller asked, turning around in his seat, gazing at the old Catholic priest with hopeful eyes.

"Bad news, I'm afraid," replied the priest. "*Capitaine* Perrin asked me to tell you to prepare yourselves for the worst."

Müller gasped miserably. Wissemann stiffened.

"I spoke with Commandant Rousseau, he's been in contact with Army Headquarters, but he was unable to convince General Nivelle, or anyone else in the High Command, to commute your sentence to a lesser charge. Same thing at the War Ministry, no one will budge."

"How much time do we have?" Wissemann asked.

"Time enough to prepare yourselves, my sons."

Wissemann scowled. He dropped his smoldering cigarette to the floor and crushed it out with a boot heel. So this is it, eh? He thought. My last hours on earth spent in a dank old jail cell awaiting execution.

Müller began sobbing. "I don't want to die! I don't want to die!"

"Oh, for God's sake," Wissemann snarled. "Get a hold of yourself."

"Have faith in the Lord, Müller. He will see you through this."

Müller sniffled pitifully, eyes full of dread. "I don't want to die!"

"You want to give your confession, *Hauptmann?*" the Father asked.

"To be quite honest, Father, I'm not a very religious man," Wissemann replied, standing up, exhaling guiltily. "I realize you're just trying to be helpful, and I appreciate that... praying now would only make me feel like a hypocrite, I'm afraid."

"Oh, that is a lamentable attitude, my son. Our Lord-God is always willing to hear your prayers."

"Well, would you take this letter, Father?" Wissemann reached into his tunic pocket and pulled out a folded piece of paper. "It's to my fiancee. I've tried to explain all this, but I know she won't understand it."

"Of course, my son. I'll make sure that she gets it." Father Guerin took the folded letter and placed it inside his bible.

"Would you hear *my* confession, Father?" Müller said.

"Yes. Have faith in the Lord, my son. Death awaits us all."

Müller got up and knelt down on the floor in front of Father Guerin, and made the sign of the cross over his chest. "In the name of the Father, the Son and the Holy Ghost..."

Wissemann grumbled, shaking his head sullenly, embittered by the priest's glib mutterings. "That's really prophetic: *Death awaits us all,*" Willi Wissemann rejoined bitingly, scowling. "Oh, that's *really* prophetic, Father."

Müller rose, leering at Wissemann with stunned eyes.

"Afraid to die, Müller? Afraid your luck will fail you now?"

Father Guerin stood up, frowning. "I understand your pain, my son, but do not let it harden your heart."

"*Do not let it harden my heart?*" Wissemann returned angrily. "This war has—*broken*—my heart! It has destroyed my family, killed my friends, ruined my life, ruined my relationship! Ruined my country, for God's sake!"

"Calm down, Wissemann," Müller interjected, standing between him and the priest. "He's only here to help us—"

"Ach, spare us the sanctimonious blather, Father!" Wissemann spouted. "Get out of here with your pat little answers, will you? Stop torturing us—God does not care if we live or die now!"

"I am here to help you, my son. With all my power—"

"Power?" Wissemann scoffed. "You haven't any power!"

"God has power, my son."

"He does, does he? Don't make me laugh!"

"You can still be saved."

"Saved? I can be saved?" Wissemann laughed mirthlessly.

"Listen, my son," Father Guerin said, holding his bible close to his chest. "God works in mysterious ways. We can never really know what his plan for us is until we give ourselves completely to his divine love and fellowship."

"Oh, shut up, Father!" Wissemann spun about and began pacing around, hands jammed in his pockets. "All those poor souls, dead on the battlefields of the Champagne and Somme—was that God's plan? Did all those men die because our Creator 'works in mysterious ways?' Is that the answer for everything? Do you mystics know anything, of how the world really works? Is everything just left up to fate and circumstance? When things fail, it's God's divine will? When things work out, it's God's divine love? Bah! Rubbish!"

"Please, my son," said Father Guerin, placing a gentle hand on Wissemann's shoulder. "You must have faith—"

"Faith? Faith in what? In my eminent death!" Wissemann shrugged Father Guerin's hand from his shoulder. "Is this war the result of, *His... divine will?* Nonsense, I say! Just plain nonsense!"

The door swung open again. The sergeant of the guard was standing in the doorway, eyes flaring, jaw pulsing, pistol drawn. "Quiet in here! Damn you! Quiet!"

"Everything's alright, sergeant," Father Guerin assured.

"Okay, Father. But your time is up," the burly, bearded sergeant replied. "They're ready for these two now."

Wissemann's stomach sank, his face paled fearfully. Müller burst into tears, crumbling to the floor, face down, burying his head in his arms. Father Geurin knelt next to him, patting him on the back.

"Pull yourself together, man," he said. "Rise, my son—"

"I don't want to die!" Müller sobbed. "Please save me, O Father!"

Wissemann's eyes flared. "He can't save you! No one can, now!"

Several armed guards stamped in, the sergeant directing them to the two prisoners. He waved his pistol at Müller. "Get up," he snarled. "Act like a man or we'll drag you out of here like a dog."

"No! No! No..."

"Seize him!"

Two guards shoulder-slung their rifles and reached down, jerking Müller upright to his feet. Müller reluctantly straightened himself, still sobbing pathetically, sniffling, practically crying. The sergeant sneered, disgusted by the man's cowardly display. He stepped forward, backhanding Müller, bloodying his nose, snapping his head sideways. Müller staggered clumsily

"Shameful!" he growled. "Damned shameful!"

Wissemann lunged headlong, intent on retaliation, raising a fist in sheer fury. But before he even moved one step forward, the sergeant had his pistol cocked, his arm extended, a finger hooked around the trigger, pointing it directly at Wissemann's face.

"Stand down, Boche!" he ordered. "Or I'll kill you here and now!"

Father Guerin lurched forward, intervening. He eased the sergeant's arm down, moving in front of Wissemann, protecting him.

"No, sergeant!" he urged. "That would be tantamount to murder."

"Oh, spare me the trouble, Father," Wissemann snapped. He jerked away from the Catholic priest and strode to the doorway. "Let's get this over with, shall we? This is pure hell, it is! Heaven must surely await me after all this!"

The guards shuffled forward, boxing Wissemann in, their rifles drawn, worried that he might try to escape. Müller was shoved forward at rifle point, and escorted to the doorway.

"Your confession, Wissemann?" Father Guerin urged. "Please, my son. Let me hear your confession."

"Forget it, Father," Wissemann said. "I have nothing to confess."

The sergeant stalked out the door. "Detail—forward!" He barked, leading the group of men onto the prison's main parade ground.

The guards shouldered their rifles, marching out stiffly, both prisoners aligned in the middle of their tight formation. All along the fringe of the main thoroughfare, French soldiers stood at attention, rifle butts perched next to their boots, indifferent expressions on their faces. Snare drums banged out an ominous cadence, adding to the general gloom of the proceedings. Political dignitaries and high-ranking officers stood by in casual knots, smoking cigarettes, chatting softly, watching intently. All were anticipating the next few moments.

Wissemann marched forward steadily, chin held high, lips pursed arrogantly. His eyes were complacent, his face was calm. But inside, his heart drubbed fearfully. He wasn't really ready to die, not yet. But he was willing to sacrifice himself for his country, although this was never the way he thought he'd go. He'd always pictured himself going down in flames in a burning aeroplane, after doing glorious combat with enemy fliers. But this? Death by firing squad? It had never occurred to him, not even during all the heated conversations with Perrin. He'd never taken the little Frenchman's threats seriously. Now, he realized how stupid he'd been, how stubborn he'd acted— constantly depending on his wits, and the protection of his military commission, depending on the precepts of civilized warfare, leaning on the good will of other gentlemanly officers. How ludicrous!

"*Humph!*" he grunted. And muttered to himself: "You are a grand old fool, Willi Wissemann. A grand old, foolish fool!"

Behind him, Müller paced slowly, still muttering woefully, his face a red mask of tears and remorse. Father Guerin walked with him, side by side, still clutching his bible, still clutching to his religious ideals, maintaining a solemn but stern countenance. He tried to console the blubbering Rudolf Müller, grasping his arm, nodding.

"I don't want to die, Father," Müller cried. "Why must I die? I only did as ordered... I'm just a poor, obedient soul..."

"Do not question the will of God, my son—"

"I did my duty! I only did as I was ordered," Müller sobbed meekly, clutching the priest's arm, tears streaming from his eyes.

"You served your country bravely. Show some courage now in the face of your enemies. Be strong! God is with you."

"Oh, Father I am scared!"

"Courage. Brace yourself, man," Father Guerin urged, his voice stern and even now.

Wissemann saw *Capitaine* Perrin standing at the end of the long rank of helmeted troops, bedecked in a fine, horizon blue uniform, his face beaming with haughty disdain. He smiled at Wissemann as the tall Bavarian marched by, chuckling, pushing off on the balls of his feet, restless, but nonetheless elated. Wissemann did not look at him. He kept his head stiff and face-forward, unwilling to acknowledge Perrin in any way, unwilling to give him any satisfaction.

The grim detail paced onward, finally reaching the end of the gravel thoroughfare. Two tall, wooden posts stood ominously apart, stacks of piled sandbags behind them, all stacked nearly as high as the wooden posts.

"Detail—halt! barked the sergeant. "Forward—face!"

"Oh, God! Please save me! Save me! Save me!"

"Brace yourself, my son. Have courage."

"Secure—prisoners!"

The sky was gray and the air was cool. The wind blew chillingly as the guards broke formation, seizing both Müller and Wissemann, jerking them around roughly, binding their hands, preparing them for the execution—standing them up against the posts. The drummers continued to drum their snares, beating out a doleful cadence, their strident strikes echoing in the wind, their drumsticks sounding the death knell for two unfortunate Germans.

A lieutenant approached Wissemann. "Blindfold?"

Wissemann scowled, shaking his head.

The lieutenant paced up to Müller. "Blindfold?"

"I don't want to die! Please, God! Save me!"

The lieutenant grimaced, tying the blindfold over Müller's tear-soaked eyes, knotting it off tightly. He paced away.

"Detail—at-ten—tion!" barked the lieutenant. "Forward—march!" Another formation of riflemen tramped forward, marching out in front of the secured prisoners, rifles on their shoulders, stamping in place once they aligned themselves, about thirty fifty paces away, the lieutenant marching in place with them.

"Detail—halt," he commanded. "Left—face!"

The detail of sixteen men pivoted smartly at the command, now facing Wissemann and Müller, standing at attention. The sergeant paced up and down, near the two bound Germans, making a last minute check, while Father Guerin continued uttering his grim supplications, his bible open, his head bowed reverently. Müller continued balling unabashedly, crying like a little child. Wissemann stood tall and straight, his eyes piercing, his chest swelled with pride. Or with what little was left of it. He didn't care anymore. He was ready to die now—his soul be damned. *Humph!* The Gods be damned! His time was up, it was time to finally dance with the devil.

Capitaine Perrin paced ahead, pivoting, hitting every turn with unnecessary precision. He stopped, standing before Wissemann and Müller, his face gleeful with smiles. He unfolded a piece of paper and began reading, his tone glib and full of smug self-assurance.

"In the name of the Republic and the French people... Wilhelm Reinhardt Wissemann—Rudolf Albert Müller... both of the German Secret Service... having been found guilty of spying and espionage... are to be executed immediately by firing squad... in accordance with official judgment of a military tribunal." He smiled, refolded the rescript, and about-faced crisply. He stepped off and marched back to his place among the officers of his company. Commandant Rousseau was standing by, gazing sternly, dressed in a resplendent red and black uniform. But he was not smiling.

Father Guerin strode up to the sobbing Müller, making the sign of the cross over him, then moving in front of Wissemann, doing the same. Wissemann scoffed, shaking his head, unmoved by the simple religious gesture. Guerin then retook his place at the fringe of the thoroughfare, still chanting his supplications.

The drums abruptly ceased.

"Ready..." the lieutenant spouted, drawing his saber, raising it into the air, ready to drop it at the final command. "Aim..."

Wissemann tensed, the sounds of his own heart drubbing loudly in his ears, the last seconds of his life about to be snuffed out by a French firing squad, Death's bony fingers clawing at his soul.

"*FIRE!*"

"*Agh-h-h-h-h-h-h-h-h-h-h...!*

✠

ILSE VON LINKHOF sat in her parents' mansion, her face wet with tears. A telegram had just been delivered by special courier. She'd read the telegram over and over and still could not believe it. Willi Wissemann had been officially listed as a POW by the War Ministry, after it received word from the Red Cross detailing his convalescent condition. She was sad beyond consolation. Poor Willi was locked away in some dirty old camp somewhere, possibly sick, emaciated, wounded, distraught and war weary. Ilse couldn't stop crying. Her face was flushed; her eyes were puffy and red. She felt sick, and it seemed as if her heart would burst with anguish. A bitter stiffness steeped her petite figure; her heart ached and her head throbbed with grief. Ilse felt as if her world had come to an end suddenly.

"There, there now, Ilse," *Frau* von Linkhof said reassuringly, swanning into the living room with a handkerchief. "Don't you fret so much, hmm?"

"*Ach, M-Mutti!*" Ilse burst into a spasm of tears. "He's g-gone!"

"Oh, dear. Please get a hold of yourself. He is not dead. He's a POW. That means he'll return to you... in time."

"He could die in one of those camps. I've heard horror stories!"

Frau von Linkhof handed Ilse the hanky. "Here, wipe your face, dear. Those tears don't become you. Cheer up."

"Never! I'll be sad forever."

"Stop it, Ilse. Willi is alive, for God's sake! That's more than I can say for many others. So many have died, but *he* lives. Be assured."

"I know, I know, *Mutti*. I should be grateful." Ilse dabbed her eyes, sniffling miserably, trying to compose herself. "It's just so terribly horrid. I'll worry endlessly about him. I know I will."

"Once your father finds out what camp he's been sent to, you can write him. The Red Cross will convey all your correspondence, and they'll relay his letters to you as well. It'll be heartbreaking but not the end of the world, my dear." *Frau* von Linkhof sat down next to Ilse and gave her a loving hug.

"Oh, Mutti," Ilse sniffled. "Why did Willi have to go back to the Front? Why! Why couldn't he have just stayed put?"

"Willi is an officer, my sweet, and an aviator too. He is destined to be daring and bold. He demands it of himself, as the Fatherland demands it of him. He's bound to his duty, which is instilled by the indomitable German spirit of obedience and propriety. It's men like him who have made our country strong and enduring..."

Ilse spluttered. "Wha—M-Mutti?"

"You know all this, Ilse. Willi is a man like no other. A hero, a Teutonic warrior, an iron fist against the enemies of Germany."

Astonished, Ilse caught her breath. She'd never heard her mother say such things before. And certainly not about Willi. "Why, Mutti... I did not realize you felt so strongly about him. I'm surprised."

"I've always felt that way about Willi." She stroked Ilse's hair, smoothing it adoringly. "He's a fine man. And it doesn't matter if he isn't of our class, dear. He has plenty of admirable qualities I've not seen in many a 'noble' Prussian, I'd say."

"Really?"

"Yes, dear."

Ilse was speechless.

"Your Willi Wissemann is a fine, noble gentleman through and through, Ilse."

Stunned, Ilse said: "*Gott, Mutti.* You really like him, don't you?"

"From the first day I met him." *Frau* von Linkhof nodded. "He will make a fine husband. He certainly will. Because... he truly loves you."

Ilse's eyes glistened with tears again. "Oh, *Mutti!*" She embraced her mother like she never had before. "I love you, sweet mother."

"I love you too, my dear." *Frau* von Linkhof patted Ilse's back and gently rocked her daughter from side to side. "Just keep the faith, my girl. Willi will return to you. He will. Then all will be well. Be assured, my sweet. Be assured." A single tear drained down the old mother's cheek. It was a tear of joy. *Frau* von Linkhof was smiling.

✠

"WILLI! WILLI!" a voice echoed inside Wissemann's head. Sister Coudouret was suddenly hovering over him, patting his cheeks frantically, trying to rouse him from a horrid dream.

"What? Huh? Sister?" A languid Willi Wissemann felt a tender hand on his forehead, a soft gentle caress. He slowly opened two eyes sticky with sleep. He heard a familiar voice.

"Willi... you were dreaming."

"What? What did you say?"

Puffy blue eyes reluctantly focused in the bright afternoon sunshine. The hospital room was awash in a penetrating light; Sister Coudouret had drawn the curtains and was leaning over him, her hand cradling his neck as she adjusted his bandage.

"I said—you were dreaming, Willi."

"Dreaming? Oh—"

"You look much better this morning." She touched his cheek with one of her wonderfully soft hands, her brown eyes flickering with deep, earnest warmth. "Your fever seems to have subsided, Willi."

"I do feel better," he said. "I was having an awful nightmare."

"I'm sorry. What about—?"

"What time is it?"

"Nearly 1 o'clock. You slept for twelve hours, Willi."

"Twelve hours?"

"You must've really been tired." She smoothed his covers.

"Twelve hours? *J'y crois pas!*"

"Yes, Willi. I came by last night and checked up on you, around midnight."

"You did?"

Anne Marie nodded. "The evening duty nurse alerted me to your coughing spasms."

"Oh, yes. I remember now."

"But when I got here though—you were fast asleep."

Wissemann coughed and cleared his throat.

"When can I get out of this infernal sickroom? I feel better now."

"Well, today I suppose, Willi. If you really feel up to it."

The determined Bavarian rolled back the covers. Indeed, he felt far stronger since that fateful night outside Paris. His shoulder was feeling much better, his pneumonia was waning, he felt renewed. He propped himself up on an elbow, rose from the bed, sliding into the hospital slippers sitting by the bed. He stretched and yawned.

"I'm well enough, Sister. Time to get up."

"Willi..." Anne Marie muttered haltingly, "this may come to you as good news or bad news. I don't know."

"What do you mean?"

"They're transferring you to a POW camp tomorrow."

"Already?"

"*Capitaine* Perrin came by this morning with the paperwork."

Anne Marie nodded, arms folded over her bosom, a doleful expression suddenly tormenting her beautiful face. Wissemann plopped down on the bed, perplexed.

"Tomorrow?" he said. "Where?"

"I believe Perrin said Barcellonette? It's in the mountains near—"

"I know where it is!" Wissemann snapped. "But I'm not well yet."

"I know, Willi. Nevertheless, since we've received so many wounded troops from the Front lately, Perrin decreed there isn't room for German prisoners anymore."

"*Capitaine* Perrin! That, that—goddamned little son-of-a—"

"Willi! Watch your language, please!"

"Sorry. Sorry." His hands fluttered apologetically, blushing shamefacedly "When do we go, Sister?"

"You and the rest of the POW's are being transferred, tomorrow."

"*Sacre bleu!*"

"Perrin would have you convalesce in a prison infirmary."

"Great. I might as well be dead then."

"I'm sorry, Willi," she said, misty eyed, standing at the foot of the bed now.

"I'm sorry too, Sister." Wissemann sighed. "Look, I didn't mean to snap at you just now. I'm just a bit annoyed now, that's all."

"It's all right, Willi. I understand."

The anxious Bavarian got up from the bed, reaching for the hospital robe hanging on his bedpost. He tied it shut as best he could with his good arm, removing the canvas sling accordingly. He mussed the tousled locks out of his face. "Where is *Feldwebel* Steiner?"

"He's waiting for you out in the courtyard. He, too, stopped by this morning, Willi."

As she stepped forward and adjusted the collar of his robe, an overwhelming sense of sorrow came over her. She had grown very fond of this German officer over the past few weeks. Now she felt an unusual sense of emptiness. Why, she wondered? Was this the last time she'd see him? What would happen to this poor man? She tried to hold back her tears, but Anne Marie Coudouret felt her heart sinking, and despite her best efforts, began to sob quietly. Trembling hands tried to manipulate Wissemann's collar, eyes full of tears cried.

"Sister? Are you crying?" Wissemann turned around to face her.

Crimson with tears and contorted with fretfulness, Anne Marie returned his perplexed gaze with a sorrowful one. Wissemann was stunned to silence. He placed both hands on her shoulders and tried to console her, his own face suddenly reddening with grief.

After a long moment, he said: "Dear Sister, please don't cry."

"Oh, Willi. I'll m-miss so you v-very much," she stammered. "I'm afraid I've grown quite f-fond of you." Tears coursed down her cheeks in great gushing drops.

The saddened Bavarian's eyes glazed over too, his face becoming flushed and hot, fighting back tears, trying to smile. Anne Marie had been his angel of mercy these long frustrating weeks. He hadn't realized it until now, that he'd formed the deepest affections for her, and she for him. Somehow she'd seen through all his morose moods, his odd behavior, his acerbic dialogue. She'd gazed deep into his heart, looking past his bitterness, seeing a warm and compassionate man inside, seeing the real Willi Wissemann, understanding the genial and tenderhearted man he really was.

"Anne Marie..." he began. But she forestalled his words with a loving embrace, holding him very close. They stood this way for a long time. She was stiff with grief and sorrow. Wissemann kissed her forehead, then gently detached himself. He hadn't realized until that moment just what his imprisonment had cost him—physically and emotionally. He held her hands at arms length, gazing into her watery, red eyes, smiling dolefully. "I'll miss you too, Anne Marie." Wissemann swiped a tear from his eye. "Very much so..."

✠

A CONTENTED VATI STEINER SAT IN THE HOSPITAL COURTYARD on a wooden bench, enjoying the warm afternoon, observing several other German prisoners scuffling about in a loosely organized soccer match. He shook his head in ill-tempered disgust.

"C'mon, Klein! My dead mother can kick harder than you can."

Young Klaus Klein chuckled. "Oh, really? Can she suck a—"

"What in the hell are you doing?"

"Keep your seat, old man," Klein snapped back.

"Keep it up, *Junge!* And I'll box those little monkey ears of yours."

"Hah! Watch and you just might learn something."

Steiner scoffed and took a drag from his cigarette. *"Quatsch!"*

Klein dribbled clumsily, tripped, and fell face down amidst a dirty cloud of dust. The ball squirted obliquely into the sidelines.

Steiner threw his hands up in laughter. *"Ahh-hah-hah-hah-hah!"*

"Oh, shut up old man!" Klein bolted up, dusting off his pants.

"And they call your generation the Iron Youth? Bean breeze!"

Steiner suddenly noticed Wissemann standing at the wall, waiting for the guard to unlock the gate. He stood up, balancing himself on his crutches, yelling: "Over here, *Hauptmann!* Over here, sir!"

Wissemann looked over, nodded and waved. He traipsed across the dusty courtyard, then stopped a moment, intercepting the foul ball that had bounced in his direction. He dribbled it twice between his feet, and then, like a pro, side-kicked it back into play. The motley group of prisoners cheered as they chased after the ball. Kurt Klein marveled at Wissemann's agility with just a little jealousy.

"Wow! Nice play, *Hauptmann,*" he said. "Very nice play!"

Wissemann winked and smiled, scurrying over to Steiner, plopping down on the bench exasperated. *"Phew!"*

"Not bad, sir. Not bad at all," Steiner said, offering Wissemann a cigarette. "Smoke, sir?"

"Oh, no. I better not. Sister Coudouret would have a fit if she knew." Wissemann adjusted his sling and took off his service cap.

"Gott... am I ever out of shape!"

"Fine. One more for me." Steiner lit a cigarette for himself.

"So. What's this I hear about a transfer?"

"That's right, sir. Tomorrow morning—zero-six hundred."

"That's a bit early."

Steiner grinned uneasily. "Yes, it's off to the Alps with us."

"Hmm, Barcellonette. Not my idea of a summer resort."

"Looks like the Frenchies are really taking a licking at the Front. Their wounded are coming in by the truck load."

Steiner pointed. Wissemann looked and saw a bloc of lorries pulling onto the hospital grounds, stopping near the emergency entrance. Wounded Frenchmen, some on stretchers, some on their feet, some being carried, began filing into the emergency room amidst a flurry of clamor. Medics scuffled about purposefully, shouting, barking, giving heated commands. It was confused disorder.

"I see."

"They're kicking us out to make room."

"The French are falling back, eh?"

"That's right, sir. Heard a little rumor, too."

"A rumor? What kind of rumor?"

"French troops are just giving up, sir. Mutiny, they say."

"Mutiny?"

"Ja! That's what I heard. The Brits are falling back too. And the Russians have had it as well, it seems. They've got a full-blown revolution on their hands now. They've been crying for change and a new world order, while we're still dying for the old one. Praise be! This rotten war will be over soon."

Steiner laughed, seemingly enjoying relaying the grim news.

Wissemann rested an elbow on the backrest and contemplated the rumors. Europe was coming apart at the seams, it appeared, while he languished in a French hospital; he didn't like being left out of those cataclysmic events, somehow; he had to get back into the thick of things; he had to escape and get back to Germany. He just had to! Nothing else mattered now.

"Sounds like all hell is breaking loose, Steiner."

"It certainly is, sir."

"Any news about our counteroffensive?"

"No. But it's safe to say the French are finished."

"How are our soldiers doing, I wonder?" Wissemann watched the football bounce over the fence.

"Look at these idiots!" Steiner exclaimed, watching the game in utter dismay. He turned back to Wissemann. "Well, sir, according to the scuttlebutt I've heard, they're holding the line. They haven't given up one millimeter of ground. They've kicked the damned snail-eaters back across the lines. Maybe all the way to Paris."

"So, Germany is winning, aye?" Wissemann nodded thoughtfully. "That's good news, Steiner."

"It would appear so, sir. We won't have long to wait in a POW camp, I think. The war has finally seen its end."

"Did you see Perrin this morning? I heard he paid us a little visit."

"*Ja.* I don't trust that little bastard—too smooth by half. He told us we were being transferred by lorry, first thing in the morning, to our new home." Steiner ashed his cigarette. *"Gott!* I'm gonna miss this place. At least the food was decent here."

"Any more details than that?"

"Well, only one."

"What?"

"Perrin said he'd be making several other stops to pick up more prisoners—"

"More prisoners?"

"Close to Compiègne, I think."

"Compiègne, you say?"

"*Ja.* While you were fast asleep, sir, *Capitaine* Perrin informed me and the rest of the fellows of our sudden departure. A convoy of lorries will transport us near French General Headquarters in Compiègne. There, they'll pick up a few more prisoners and then proceed to Soissons for one more stop. After that, Perrin said we'd take a nice long train ride through the Alps to our new home—beautiful Camp Barcellonette."

"Hmm. Interesting." Wissemann's mind began to stir.

Steiner noticed the Bavarian's thoughtful expression. "If you're contemplating escape, *Hauptmann,* forget it," the old noncom cautioned. "They're going to have us in shackles and under heavy guard. Perrin promised us."

"I figured as much. But I can't help it. I want to get back into the war, Steiner."

"Back into the war?"

"I want to see Germany again. Most of all, I want to see my girl."

"Well, can't blame you for that last part, *Junge.*"

"I don't want to spend the rest of the war in some rotten prison camp just biding my time." Wissemann fidgeted with his bandage.

"You've already served your country loyally, sir. Why risk further trouble for yourself?"

"I know it sounds absurd—"

"Absurd? It's downright ridiculous."

"Perhaps, Steiner. But it's the duty of all captured soldiers—especially officers—to try an escape," Wissemann explained. "It's ingrained in our minds. It's a natural instinct."

"*Quatsch!* There are times when reason is an even better guide than instinct, Wissemann."

"As an officer, Steiner," Wissemann waxed on, "I've lived only for the honor of serving my country in times of war. I've spent the better part of my adult life preparing for it. I'm doing my duty as a citizen of the Empire, a subject of the Kaiser... for whose divine mission no forfeiture is too great."

Steiner scoffed. "That rather sounds like something you learnt from a book, sir."

Wissemann folded his arms over his chest and shrugged. "Well, it's what I live for."

"What?" Vati Steiner replied, incredulous. "You really believe in all that romantic nonsense, don't you?""

"It's not romantic nonsense, Steiner."

"Bah!" Steiner shook his head. "You're a true Victorian, sir."

"Honor's a personal thing, I guess," Wissemann gestured imploringly. "You make it sound so meaningless... so futile."

"I'm no idealist, *Hauptmann*. However, in battle, in the presence of others, we're expected to be brave. The Gods of War insist upon it."

"They do insist..."

"Well, *Junge*, whoever they are, the Gods, they've taken little interest in this old man's hopes." Steiner eyed his bandaged foot. It was ripe with stench. It seemed to be getting worse by the day.

"They have their ways, I suppose," Wissemann mused.

"Armies weren't meant to cower in filthy, rat-infested trenches."

"True. I fought in the trenches just as you did, Steiner. I saw the carnage, the fear, the destruction. That's why I got into the Air Service, to get away from all that."

"I don't blame you there, sir—"

"You know, the stagnation—the needless waste of life."

"Needless waste of life? *Gott!* That's putting it mildly."

"Well, there are better ways to fight more meaningful battles—"

"Aha. And you think you can turn the tide of war in your little aeroplane, don't you?"

"No. But the war is different up there."

"How? Tell me, sir. What's it like—flying a combat aeroplane?"

"Well—"

"C'mon, sir. I really want to know. Tell me."

"All right." Willi Wissemann nodded, staring up at the clouds, smiling. "Imagine yourself, Steiner, in a fast motorcar... driving 100-kilometers per hour, zooming down a highway..."

Steiner grinned. "Yes, a fast motorcar. Go on, sir. I'm listening."

"Stick your head out the window. Now, imagine yourself going twice that fast. And imagine it's zero degrees outside, and it's difficult to breathe—the air's thin and it's cold. Add in the fact that you're sitting right next to a full tank of highly inflammable aviation fuel..."

Steiner grimaced. "Sounds dangerous."

"It is, Steiner. Very dangerous." Wissemann nodded. "But that's what it's like." He paused a moment, then said: "Now. Imagine that someone is shooting at you—trying to kill you. You have no parachute, no armor, nothing to protect you, really, only your wits and your two machine guns. Sound like fun?"

"Hmm, does sound a bit dicey, sir."

"But it has an air of gallantry, reverence and sport about it. There are certain rules that every pilot abides by, friend or foe."

Steiner shook his head, folding his arms, looking up to the sky.

"Rules? That's idiotic. This is war, not a game of cricket."

"Men abide by the principles of chivalry in the skies, Steiner."

"Chivalry?" Steiner had to laugh. "Where ever did you pick up such a dusty old phrase like that?"

"You know, like knights of the air—"

"Knights? Chivalry? Aristocratic cow-plop, my naive friend."

"It's a contest of wills—"

"Bah!" The old noncom was not convinced. "So, it's like a great tournament for you, isn't it? Jousting about up there like knights of old. Well, those steeds you gentlemen steer about the sky are barely airworthy. I seriously doubt aeroplanes can affect the outcome of *this* war," Steiner remarked cynically.

Old Vati Steiner was no idiot, he'd read plenty of articles, overheard the conversations of many a high-ranking officer, often bitter and defamatory philippics on the progress of the air services. The aeroplane had yet to reach its peak as an essential instrument of war. Even Vati Steiner, a lowly noncom, knew that. The "limits of modern day air power" was yet a feeble and emergent science plagued by imperfect aeronautical engineering and consistent human error—so said a famous general in 1914.

"Wars are decided by blood and iron. By infantry, artillery, naval power—von Bismarck had it right!"

"There's a code of conduct we airmen abide by."

"Code of conduct?" Steiner almost fell out of his seat. "You poor fool. That's ancient history. You're out of touch—you and your 'codes of conduct'. Outdated!"

"Not outdated, Steiner—emergent."

"*Mein Gott!* It's a new kind of world, *Hauptmann*—kill, maim, destroy. And maybe that's the way it should be, because man doesn't deserve anything better."

"Do you really believe that?"

"I do."

Wissemann sneered. "I'll be damned to hear you chide a code that better men have lived and died by—"

"The code? The code! How much does the code ask of a man?"

"Everything—if that man's a real soldier. His life."

"His life? You think that's the most a man can loose?"

"What do you mean?"

"What about a man's family?" Vati Steiner replied. "His wife? His children? What about their lives? What do *THEY* get when a man sacrifices his life, eh?"

"Well..."

"How many lives for one man's life."

Wissemann was silent.

"*His life,*" Steiner echoed. "Maybe that's the answer... for heroes!"

"Everyone must die one day—even the greatest of heroes."

"*Mein Gott!* Don't give me that hero manure, Wissemann. Maybe the Kaiser has to shovel it to keep his job, but it just makes me sick to my stomach to hear you say it!"

"Easy, my old friend. His Majesty would be mightily disappointed to hear you talk like that."

"Bean breeze! Kaiser Wilhelm is a mustachioed brat. Him and his upper-class cronies are totally insufferable. They always cloak their rotten doings in the trappings of altruism and self-righteousness, always putting up this glib front of self-defense, always claiming what they do is in the interest of the common folk."

"Steiner, listen—"

"I think your pretensions towards heroism, *Junge,* are a form of mental disease induced by your vanity." Vati Steiner spat. "There is no *raison d' être* in dying honorably—"

"If we fight without honor, *Herr* Steiner," Wissemann waxed on, unperturbed, "if at the last moment we wane, it's all without meaning, wasted." Wissemann crossed his arms defiantly.

"Oh, folly! Words are poor security, Wissemann."

"Perhaps. But sometimes those 'words' are all we have left."

"If you try to escape, you'll die."

"Maybe. But—"

"And I can promise you this, sir. The medals they give to dead heroes are all made of brass." Vati Steiner got up hastily, fumbling for his crutches. "All they do is add weight to your coffin!"

Wissemann shook his head. "It's my sworn duty, Steiner. One must respect those who try. Maybe my death is inevitable. Perhaps for a brief moment, between escape and death, I'll be a soldier again."

"A soldier? A dead soldier! It's insane to try an escape. You'll be shot, killed, and to what end? It's an escape from reality," Steiner huffed. "Always the knight in shining armor, eh? The Bavarian ace of the high blue fails at his duty, so he flies out to meet his doom. Bah!"

"I only want to do my duty as an officer, as a man—"

"It's all a delusion, sir."

"Delusion?"

"Perhaps that's not the right term," Steiner said thoughtfully. "I'm not an educated man. It's... it's the hope that there's always one more chance—*that* is the delusion."

"Aha. Go on, Steiner."

"Nah, I've said too much already, really."

"Tell me what's really on your mind."

"Let's just drop it, sir—"

"Come, come, *Herr* Steiner," Wissemann said with a censorious gleam in his eye. "Don't stop now, please continue—"

"Ach! This idea... this idea of escape—it's a fantasy. Give it up!"

"Don't talk rot, Steiner."

Vati Steiner grumbled irritably, his bitterness quickly fading to contempt. He gave Wissemann's face a wary inspection, folding his hands in his lap, measuring up the officer with grave misgivings. After a long pause he spoke. It was a calm and deliberate statement.

"It's a strange, stubborn conviction you keep, *Junge*..."

Wissemann's brow narrowed. "Huh—?"

"...to believe that existence has a purpose."

"Is that so crazy an idea, Steiner?"

"A sane man would've learned to let it go a long time ago."

"As you have!" Wissemann snapped. "What drove it out of you?"

Steiner bit down angrily, turning to walk away. Wissemann stood up, realizing he had infuriated the old man. He put a gentle hand on Steiner's shoulder. "Look here, Steiner. I'm sorry."

"Please, sir. Just drop it. The war will be over soon."

"Steiner—"

"We'll all be home by Christmas, for God's sake!"

"I must be faithful to my cause—devoted to my duty."

"Your cause? Your duty? Now you're talking rot, Wissemann." Steiner cooled a bit, sighing resignedly. "You and I love life, sir. It's true. But you want to fight for it, to kill for it, even die for it. I just want to live it, *Junge.* "

"We must keep faith, Steiner—"

"Faith? God in heaven! Damn you and all your rotten codes of conduct, Wissemann!" Steiner snarled. "You make me sick with all your heroics—there's a stench of death about you, you carry it on your shoulders like the pestilence. Dogfights, death, heroics! They go well together, don't they? With you, it's one thing or the other, destroy the enemy or destroy yourself. This war is just a game for you. You and *Capitaine* Perrin are two peas in a pod. Mad for heroism —and for what? How to die like a gentleman, how to die by the rules. *Gott!* The only important thing is how to live like a decent human being!" The old noncom shoved his way past the Bavarian officer.

Wissemann tried to console a Steiner. He reached out to him. "Steiner? Steiner? *Feldwebel* Steiner! Vati! Wait!"

"Damn you! Leave me alone!"

Steiner jerked away and hobbled down the walkway.

Wissemann frowned dejectedly as the old man limped away, angry and frustrated. He groaned glumly and shrugged.

"Well, Willi. You've done it again, it seems," he said to himself. "That's twice in one day." He plopped down on the bench, cheering the clumsy footballers. "C'mon, Klein! C'mon! Let's really see something now!"

Chapter 20

✠

JUNE 1, 1917. A PROCESSION OF TWO DE DION lorries and a Renault staff car crept down the highway trailing thin banners of dust. Perrin sat in the back seat of the staff car carefully watching the road; he didn't want to miss the turnoff for his next stop, Compiègne. The sun, hidden by an overcast sky, made for a dreary day, casting irregular patches of dull shadows over the landscape, adding to the general gloom of the trip. A light drizzle fell from the sky. And somewhere in the distance, artillery guns rumbled ominously.

It all made *Capitaine* Perrin very tense. His little convoy was running an hour behind schedule; he had hoped to get to Compiègne by 9 o'clock. Now it was already well past ten. Once there, he'd have to quickly put his charges aboard a train bound for Reims, along with five other POWs, and then send them on to the prison camp at Barcellonette. But the roads were choked with columns and columns of *poilus,* horses, wagons and dilapidated camion. Traffic had slowed to a perpetual standstill on the narrow highway to Compiègne.

The bedraggled remnants of Mazel's 5th were trudging back to the Front, as if they barely had the strength left to drag themselves forward, the first ranks of men lining up mechanically, trying to give an illusion of a force still unbroken. Behind them, stumbled a pathetic band of soldiers caked with mud and blood. Their faces were drawn and gaunt, brooding men, consumed by the task of marching, seemingly aware of their own pathetic existence. The footfall of ten thousand muddy feet tramped out a sad and sorry cadence.

Wissemann and Steiner hovered uncomfortably inside the dingy prison lorry, along with eleven other men. Perrin had ordered all thirteen Germans into one vehicle so that when he made subsequent stops, the new prisoners could be easily loaded into the other.

"Orderly little groups of Boche,"   the little Frenchman had quipped maliciously.

Vati Steiner sighed wearily as he peered out a tiny hole in the side of the lorry. A wave of anger washed over him as the lorry suddenly hit a pothole, jolting him harshly. *"Gott!* What's taking so long? Where in the hell are we going, anyway?"

"Can you see anything, Steiner?" Wissemann asked. "What's going on out there?"

"Ach! Just lines of filthy *poilus* hoofing it back to the Front—"

The lorry came to a sudden halt, breaking hard. The imprisoned Germans lurched forward, tripping, tumbling head-over-heels into a tangled heap of bodies, struggling to maintain their balance, laying motionless and helpless for a moment, cussing, cursing, groaning.

"Verdammt, Klein!" Steiner growled. "Get off of me!"

Young Kurt Klein tried to balance himself as he crawled over the pile of bodies. "Sorry. Sorry, Steiner," he apologized.

"Autsch!" Wissemann yelped, an elbow grinding him in the chest, grimacing painfully as he held his breath until everyone had crawled off and regained their footing. Outside, he could hear loud voices yelling, and wondered what was going on. He could hear Perrin's unmistakably nasally voice amongst the din of road traffic, barking out heated orders, cursing a blue streak.

"Sacre bleu!" Perrin roared. "What in the hell is going on! What's the hold up!"

Up ahead, an exhausted horse had apparently collapsed in the middle of the road, blocking the passage of traffic. Curious *poilus* congregated around the animal, creating an impassable bottleneck. Thoroughly annoyed, Perrin hopped out of the Renault and stalked up to the mob of gathered men. A skinny little corporal was kneeling over the groaning dobbin, caressing its nose, trying to rouse it to life.

"Easy, Marianne. Easy there, old girl," said the corporal to the worn-out old horse. "Rest quietly now."

Perrin huffed, booting the exhausted animal with a hostile kick. "Get this damned animal off the road! *Tout de suite!"* he snarled.

"Mon Capitaine, she's—"

"Move! I don't have all day to waste. That's an order!"

"Calm down, *mon vieux,"* The skinny corporal cautioned.

"Damn you! I gave you an order!"

"The poor animal is exhausted. She needs to rest a moment."

"I don't care!"

"*Mon Capitaine,* please—"

"If you don't get that wretched animal off the road right now, I'll, I'll—*agh-h-h-h!*" Perrin was beside himself.

"Sir, we'll have her up in just a few minutes."

"I don't have a few minutes!"

The filthy mob of soldiers stared crossly at him. The company's senior NCO, a pudgy-looking staff sergeant, noticed Perrin's spotless uniform and polished boots. *Regardez-moi ça!* Here was another one of those dandy rearguard officers, he thought, replete with the stench of fine cologne and a cleanly pressed uniform.

"*Tous droits, Capitaine.* Just back off a moment, sir," the sergeant warned. "It's just a helpless animal. No need to talk that way about it." The bearded noncom shoved a grimy finger into Perrin's face. The gathered infantrymen nodded in accordance, mumbling their displeasure.

Perrin's eyes flared with fury. "How dare you affront an officer of the Republic!"

"Now look here, sir—"

"Are you disobeying a direct order, sergeant?"

"Just give us a damn second to move the animal, sir."

"I can have you arrested for insubordination!"

"*Capitaine*—" he started, but Perrin interjected.

"I'll haul your fat ass off to jail, right now, sergeant!" Perrin edged closer to the pudgy NCO.

Back at the truck...

Vati Steiner was still peering through the hole, observing the confrontation. He watched Perrin's exchange with curious eyes. The Frenchman's face was glowing red.

"What's going on out there?" Wissemann asked.

"I think a horse must've died or passed out," Steiner replied. "Not sure though."

"Is that why we've stopped?"

"*Ja.* It's in the middle of the road, it seems. Perrin is arguing with one of the noncoms. And he's mad as hell, too. I swear, that man is such a jackass."

"That's officers for you, eh, Steiner?" Wissemann threw in sardonically.

Steiner shot Wissemann a sour look. He grumbled then continued staring out the hole. He saw Perrin pacing back in forth, cursing angrily. Perrin motioned for two of his men to come forward. They marched up stiffly, rifles in hand. The French officer glared angrily at the sergeant. Vati Steiner heard him shout, loud and clear:

"Sergeant! If you don't get this goddamned animal of the road immediately, I will place you under arrest!"

Perrin stepped brim to brim with the grubby noncom. The sergeant swallowed hard and cleared his throat, his obstinate resolve seemingly vanishing against Perrin's vitriolic broadside. He backed away, acquiescing sheepishly.

"Okay-okay—*bon m'sieu,*" he croaked.

"A wise decision, sergeant!"

The sergeant turned to the gathered men. "All right, you heard the *Capitaine.* Move it now! Get this beast off the road."

The noncom's command was direct enough, plain enough. But no one moved a muscle. Only the little corporal stirred, standing up, staring blankly at Perrin.

"When she's rested a while, *Capitaine,*" he said, his tone indifferent and noncommittal, "then we'll move her."

"Pure insolence!"

The fuming French officer's eyes narrowed, his patience finally boiling over. He shoved his way past the corporal, nearly knocking the spindly-framed soldier to the ground. Perrin snatched the pistol from his holster, chambered a round and fired a bullet into the poor horse's head, blood, brains and bone splattering everywhere. The brilliance of the discharge coupled with a reverberating echo, startled the soldiers, jolting them luridly in their boots. The bullet had brought an abrupt silence to the tormented animal's whimpers, but now the thunderstruck soldiers ears were thick with hoofbeats of hatred. They glowered at the haughty officer, eyes intent on revenge.

Henri Perrin holstered his smoking sidearm, his foxy mustache twitching, his lips curving into a sick smile. "*Voilá!* Now she can rest for eternity." He nodded complacently, swabbing the blood droplets from his eyeglass lenses with a handkerchief, sighing crossly, as if the tiny droplets had caused him some tremendous inconvenience.

"*Mon, Capitaine!* Why did you do that?" The corporal cried, the dejected noncom collapsing to his knees, sobbing.

The soldiers began mumbling inaudibly, leering at Perrin with venomous eyes, moving closer to him, frowning, rifles drawn, bayonets pointing perilously close. Perrin backed up.

"H-How d-dare you," he stammered bitterly. "Stand down!"

He teetered backwards precariously, trying to maintain his balance. His hand frantically scrabbled for his sidearm—*THUNK!* A muffled hammer blow resounded, much like the sound of an egg breaking. One of the soldiers had cracked Perrin across the forehead with the butt of his rifle, knocking the officer to the ground. Perrin's head began bleeding profusely.

"Ah-h-h-h-h-h-h!" He shrieked in horror.

The soldiers surrounded the prostrate officer, and one by one, slowly at first, then more quickly as each second elapsed, they began stabbing away at the shrieking officer with their bayonets, piercing him until his screaming ceased. A full minute elapsed, then there was eerie silence. A maimed, French officer—a lifeless, bloodied pulp—lay in the road, an ugly red stain spreading around his motionless body. Perrin's men stood by, aghast, staring in abject terror, unable to move or speak.

Back at the truck...

Vati Steiner had watched all this in disbelieving horror. *"Um Gottes Willen!"* He swore. "I can't believe it! Perrin is... is..."

"What? What happened?" Wissemann implored.

"Dead. Perrin is dead. They—*murdered* him."

Wissemann scrambled up to see out the tiny hole. He saw a throng of French soldiers rolling a dead horse off the roadside into a ditch next to a bloody, inanimate body—Perrin's body. The sergeant of the murderous band then barked out orders to his men, ordering them to commandeer the three vehicles idling along the roadside. Perrin's remaining men, including the lorry driver, had recovered from their shock, and fled into the nearby woodlands, disappearing with amazing alacrity, discarding their weapons as they went. A moment later, Wissemann heard the back door of the lorry rattle as someone unlocked the door. He and his fellow Germans cowered fearfully, huddling closer together. The door clanged open.

"All right, get out of there, you pigs!" the sergeant demanded.

Wissemann hobbled out first, his shackles rattling noisily on the metal truck bed. He hopped to the ground. Vati Steiner and the rest of the men clambered out clumsily, each muttering in disquieted murmurs and groans, now terribly fearful for their lives.

"Mon dieu! It's just a bunch'a rotten Germans," a French soldier quipped exasperatedly.

"Aghhh! It certainly does smell like bunch of rotten Boche!"

"Any of you pigs speak French?" the sergeant queried, his dialect abstruse and barely discernible, speaking in some foul-mouthed argot Wissemann hardly understood. The sergeant eyed the prisoners suspiciously—he didn't trust Germans, or for that matter, any officer.

Wissemann studied the man's face and accent, figuring him for a Corsican. *"Oui, sergeant.* I am *Hauptmann* Wissemann, the senior officer," he replied in shaky French.

"*A Capitaine?* Speak up! Where were they taking you?"

Wissemann edged forward, approaching the Corsican sergeant cautiously. "We are prisoners of war, sergeant. We're being transported to Barcellonette—"

"Barcellonette? *J'y crois pas!*" the sergeant snorted, annoyed with Wissemann's answer. "That's hundreds of miles from here! Why in the hell would they take you this way?" He spat on the ground, scratching his head dumbly.

Willi Wissemann was close enough to the sergeant to smell the pungent stench of wine on his breath, realizing the Frenchman was quite soused. Wissemann tried to explain, wary of the man's drunken state. "We were going to Compiègne, to pick up other—"

"*Ta gueule!*" the sergeant interrupted crossly. "I really don't give a damn. My men and I are confiscating these vehicles, we've had enough of this bloody war. We're going back to our homes."

"*Déserteurs!*" Klein blurted out, a French term he'd heard more than a few times lately.

"Shut—up!" Steiner whispered, jabbing an elbow in Klein's chest.

"Deserters?" The Corsican reached for his sidearm and unsnapped the holster flap. "Why, I ought to—"

"Easy, sergeant. He didn't mean anything by it," Wissemann cautioned, stepping forward, blocking the Frenchman's path.

The Corsican drew his pistol. "I've had just about enough of—"

"What do you plan to do with us, sergeant?"

"Puh! Let's just kill em'! They're just a bunch of filthy Germans," an impatient infantryman suggested.

"*Oui!* Who gives a damn anyway," another yelled out.

"*Viens, mon vieux.* Let's get on with it. Stop wasting time."

"Wait. Wait! J-Just a minute!" Wissemann stammered.

"Quiet!" the sergeant barked. "I can't think."

"We're soldiers just like you, sergeant. You can't just kill us like that. That would be murder."

Steiner seized Wissemann by the coat sleeve, jerking him to one side, whispering in his ear. "Easy, *Hauptmann.* Don't rile up this bunch of cutthroats. You saw what they did to Perrin. Ease off, all right?"

Wissemann pushed Steiner away. "Let me handle this!"

"That idiotic officer had it coming!" The sergeant bellowed; he'd apparently overheard Steiner's muffled remarks. He grabbed the old-timer by the shirt collar, jerking him about, choking him harshly. The Corsican, it seemed, understood German quite well!

"*Non-non-non! S'il vous plaît!* Don't—" Steiner begged.

"We're not cutthroats or murderers. We are soldiers—men!"

"*Oui, oui,* sergeant!" Steiner croaked fearfully. "We are s-soldiers too... poor German s-soldiers."

"We've been pushed beyond our limits," the sergeant explicated heatedly. "We won't fight anymore!" He stroked his tatty beard uneasily and spat, shoving Steiner back into the crowd of cowering German prisoners. Gimpy old Vati Steiner stumbled and fell.

"Sergeant, please," Wissemann pleaded. "Don't kill us!"

"Shut up! I can't th—"

"We're *your* prisoners now, sergeant. We'll follow your orders. We surrender willingly to you."

The poor sergeant looked completely bewildered now; he'd seen enough of death and war. He didn't especially hate anyone in the army, he didn't even hate Germans, he hated war; the fighting, the killing, the blood, the death, the wasted lives of men for a mere meter of earth. He was weary, hungry, spent, he just wanted to go home. Sergeant Jon Paul Duvalier was tired, tired of war, tired of hating. But still, there existed some humane urge in his conscience. He holstered his pistol, sighing wearily, sick and tired of army life.

"*Pour l'amour de dieu!*" he muttered resignedly. "Alright, then. Just to show you I'm still a decent man, *Hauptmann,* I'm going to let you and your men go."

"W-What's that sergeant?" Wissemann stammered incredulously. He could hardly believe his ears. "Say again—"

"I'm letting you go, I said!" the sergeant threw his hands up brokenly. "I don't have the means to keep or take prisoners anyway."

"*Merci! Merci!*" Wissemann gasped.

"Private Mansard," the sergeant commanded tersely, pointing to one of his subordinates. "Unshackle these Germans."

"*Hein? Non, mais t'es pas bein, mon vieux!*" the shocked private replied, staring quizzically at the sergeant. "What! Let them go?"

"That's right, let them go. Do it—*NOW!*"

The confused private shuddered at the unbelievable command. He scratched his head, shrugged, then began unshackling Wissemann and his comrades, the rest of the Frenchmen watching uneasily as the Germans shook off their shackles.

"All right, you slugs!" Duvalier barked to his men. "Move out! Nothing to see here now."

The grungy Frenchmen stood around, stock-still and stupid, in utter disbelief, grumbling, muttering, gazing about dumbly.

"*MOVE OUT, I SAID !*"

Like a dazed herd of cattle, the French troops began to shuffle off down the road. Some of them climbed into the lorries and the staff car. They began rifling through the supplies Perrin's men had left behind, talking quietly amongst themselves, hoarding their booty with furtive pride. The sergeant approached Wissemann.

"Listen up, Boche," he said. "I really don't give a damn one way or the other about you or your comrades. The Front is *that* way," the sergeant said with a jerk of his thumb.

The anxious Bavarian nodded. "Yes. *That* way."

The sergeant spat. "If you make it across, fine. If you don't, I don't care either. You'll all be dead soon enough, anyway."

"I see," Wissemann sighed grimly.

"Or maybe you'll just get captured again."

"I hope not—"

"There are several battalions of French regulars in this area."

"Right. I'll keep that in mind—"

"Just remember this, Boche. I'm not letting you and your men go because I feel sorry for you. I do it because I'm sick of war—I don't want anymore blood on my hands, understand?"

"I understand." Wissemann replied warily, knowing full well what became of mutinous soldiers once they were brought to justice. "Your troubles have just begun, my friend."

The sergeant stared at Wissemann blankly; it was a dull, vacant expression, a haunted look lingering in his pale brown eyes. Then, without saying a single word, he turned and walked away.

Steiner grabbed Wissemann, pulling him aside, his eyes clouded with confusion. "They're just letting us go?" he said disbelievingly. "What a mutinous rabble."

"So it seems, Steiner."

"We must get into the woods and hide, sir."

"Right." Wissemann agreed. "We can't be too far from the front lines—I can hear the guns."

"This is unbelievable! The war is truly coming to an end."

Wissemann huddled the men together on the shoulder of the road and said: "Listen, lads. If we are going to survive, we have to split up in groups of two. Lay low until dark—stay off the main roads. We can't be more than ten kilos from the Front." He turned to Steiner. "Vati, I want you to come with me." Wissemann placed a gentle hand on Steiner's shoulder. "We'll be all right, you and I—"

"No, Wissemann. I'll only slow you down."

"Steiner—"

"I can't move too fast on this damned thing!" he shook his crutch in protest. "You and Klein go. I'll be fine by myself."

"Steiner, you're coming with me." Wissemann seized the old man.

"No, no, no, nothing doing! I'm going to surrender to the next group of Frenchmen I come across—give my self up." Steiner frowned, "I'll never make it on this bum foot."

"That's ridiculous. The French are murderous scum. You saw—"

"*Nein!* It's useless. I promised my wife I'd stay alive."

"Listen, Steiner, this is no time to argue."

"I want to see her again when this war is over, Wissemann. I can wait a few more months."

"No! I'll see you through, I promise, Steiner." Wissemann huffed. "This war may not end for another year yet. Who knows for sure, maybe never. Come on, Steiner. Don't be a old fool now."

Vati Steiner shook his head, grumbling heavily. "Wissemann, you stubborn so-and-so, listen..."

"Shut up, old man. You're coming with me. That's an order!"

"Sir—" Steiner sighed abjectly, knowing Wissemann was probably right. The war could go on for another year or more, maybe longer. And if he hung around in these parts long enough, he thought warily, he'd likely run into another gang of mutinous Frenchies. They might not be so kindly to a solitary, gimpy old German like himself. Steiner shivered at the thought. "You're one stubborn son of a bitch, you know that, Wissemann?" he muttered resignedly, acquiescing to the circumstances, finally giving in to the Bavarian's wishes.

"I know." Wissemann jerked a nod. "C'mon, lets go."

The liberated gang of Germans stole off into the woods, Steiner slowly hobbling behind. He shook his head wearily, muttering a little prayer, then remarked dispiritedly: "*Gott...* I hope I don't regret this."

✠

THE ALBATROS' ENGINE sputtered, coughed, belching black smoke. A Spad closed in for another attack, ready to deliver the *coup de grâce*. However, when the French pilot squeezed the trigger, his machine gun jammed. As the Frenchman pulled the charging handle, attempting to clear his disabled gun, he was suddenly silenced—hit by a single bullet—shot through the back of the head. He collapsed in his seat and the Spad lurched over in a tailspin.

The victorious German pilot swooped over in a half-loop and roll, saluting his vanquished foe, then waved to the pilot in the stricken Albatros, which was now falling earthward, trailing an oily column of smoke, still under control but nevertheless, out of the fight.

"*Alles Gute, mein Herr,*" he quipped and flew away. A moment later, he disappeared in the haze of the encroaching darkness.

Alas, the German pilot in the faltering Albatros was too consumed with his dilemma to reciprocate the chivalrous gesture, reluctantly guiding his smoking aeroplane down to the darkening landscape below. Down! The ground, obscured by the dim evening shadows, was dull and featureless. Down! The twisted twilit details of the countryside were hard to distinguish. Down! He muttered a silent prayer. As the pilot finally managed to nurse his damaged bird down to five hundred meters, the engine completely seized, the prop ticking over silently, the buffeting slipstream the only sound heard. The pilot circled anxiously, looking for a safe place to land, not recognizing the terrain, fearing he may have drifted too far over the front lines into enemy territory. The protracted battle with the Spads had evidently fouled his sense of direction—now that the sun had set and darkness was fast approaching, little could be seen or recognized. The pilot drew a fearful breath, bracing himself for the crash.

Actually, he was near the small town of Laffaux, northeast of Soissons, which was at least two kilometers behind enemy lines. And when he finally crashed-landed near a bombed-out champenoise church, he realized his erroneous reckoning, all too late.

The smoking Albatros skidded into a dense poppy field, bouncing once, upending itself, burying its nose deep in the soft ground before coming to a canvas-tearing, wood-rending halt. The pilot unbuckled his harness and leaped from the smoldering wreck, scampering across the open field towards a cemetery. He glanced at his watch: it was nearly 2100-hours. He reached for his Mauser sidearm, chambering a round, figuring he might need it if a French patrol appeared.

The pilot gazed across the poppy field, seeing the silhouetted gravestones, which were barely visible beyond the wrought iron fence that framed the church grounds. The pilot was certain the French had seen him go down; soldiers had surely been dispatched to search for him. The young pilot sighed; he had to get inside that church, he had to find sanctuary from the probing eyes of France. He bolted up and dashed across the field. A few strides in and—*Gott!* He stumbled into an unseen ditch, falling, twisting his ankle, rolling to the bottom, head over heels, cursing profanely.

He sat up and rallied his senses, seizing his ailing foot with a muddy hand. He took a deep breath and gingerly unlaced the boot to examined his ankle. "*Autsch!*" he shrieked in agony.

And the light had all but faded. "*Lieber Gott!* Can't see a damn thing," the young pilot cursed.

He peered over the rim of the ditch, scanning the road that ran parallel to the church. Nothing, no one. No one had heard his mournful cry. He slipped his muddy boot back on and hobbled out of the ditch, stumbling up the steep embankment, limping towards the church grounds. The pilot pushed his way through the iron gate into the cemetery, carefully stepping between the tombstones, trying to avoid walking on the actual grave plots. Superstitious and wary, he didn't want to burden his bad luck any further!

Finally, after a breathless dash to the back door of the church, he'd reached his destination. He rested a moment on a rusted metal railing, gasping for breath, leaning heavily against it. Then, with an ear pressed to the wooden door, he listened quietly. The pilot listened for just a moment, then reached for the doorknob and gave it a turn. Was it unlocked? It was! After deciding no one was there, he opened the door, but gradually. It creaked noisily at the hinges. He grimaced, stopping, holding the door steady. He squeezed through the half-opened entrance, and paused, standing flat against the wall, panting.

"Ach! Calm down, Franz," he said to himself, crouching silently inside the tiny vestibule, composing himself, rallying his senses. His heart was racing madly.

After regaining some of his nerve, he cautiously limped across the floor to another doorway. He opened the door and peered into an inner sanctum, his apprehension quite evident as he glared into the dusty darkness. Thankfully, no one was there. And up above, the pilot saw the open sky through a hole in the roof. An artillery shell had probably caused that, he thought. The stars were already twinkling in the purple twilight. Darkness at last!

He stumbled around, groping searchingly, finally finding a chair next to a table. He sat down. After removing his jacket and flight cap, the young pilot began looking around. In the fading light, he spied the waxy remnants of a candle and lit it with a match he produced from his jacket pocket. The match strike generated an incandescent flash of light that illuminated the tiny room, casting a shadowy glimmer, revealing the spartan features of the inner sanctum.

"Hmm, not much after all the looting, eh?" he said with a chuckle. "Not even the inviolability of sanctuary is left untouched by warfare." With the same match, he lit a cigarette. He sat calmly for a moment, looking up at the sky through that gaping hole, contemplating his situation. "What have you gotten yourself into, *Junge?*"

He grinned, shrugging, pulling his boot off again, peeling off the puttee this time. The pilot gazed at his swollen ankle, probing it with gentle fingers, wincing at the sharp pain. *"Ooh!* Well, it's not broken," he muttered in deep relief. "Thank God!"

He glanced up, gazing at a faded painting. Christ was hanging crookedly on the wall. The pilot smiled; there was solace in that kind, lopsided face, the discolored, impassive expression of the Savior seemingly giving the young man some hope. He seized the frame and leveled the picture.

"There! One good turn deserves another."

He scrounged around and found a strip of cloth from a ceremonial vestment and tied it tightly around his ankle. He nodded, smiling at the faded painting. *"Gott sie dank!"*

The hopeful pilot reached into his jacket pocket and pulled out a map, spreading it out over the table, smoothing out the wrinkles and creases with clammy fingers and palms. Straining his eyes in the dimly lit sanctum, he scanned over the crinkled route map.

"Hmm... could be here at—Missy? Or here at—Laffaux?" He scoffed. "Hah! Do I really know?"

The pilot sighed resignedly, never one to have a great sense of direction. He took another drag from his cigarette, exhaling, listening. He could hear the distant thunder of artillery guns and the crackle of machine gun fire. And as the echoing sounds of artillery faded, he suddenly heard a faint drone—the drone of a vehicle engine —and it sounded like it was coming nearer!

"Verdammt!" He cursed. "The Frenchies have already found me?"

The pilot jumped up and darted to a side window, catching a glimpse of a utility truck zooming by at great speed. It skidded to a halt, overshooting the entrance, backed up, then roared into the front entrance of the church, tires spewing a wake of mud. The pilot grabbed his boot and jerked his jacket on, crumpling the map, cramming it in a pocket. He blew out the candle, which he'd nearly forgotten about, and crushed out his cigarette. He drew his Mauser pistol, releasing the safety catch, and crept up to the doorway.

The nervous pilot gazed into the main sanctuary. He heard voices muttering in indiscernible and frantic phrases. One of the large double doors of the church swung open slowly; two men stood silhouetted in the doorway. One of the two men seemed to be in excruciating pain. He fell to a knee, grasping at his chest. The taller man hefted his arm up under the other's shoulder and dragged him to the last row of pews, laying him down on his back.

The pilot observed the two figures, watching the taller man struggling to remove the wounded man's tunic, watching all of it with a pounding heartbeat, standing frozen in fear, not knowing what to think about it. Who were these men? What was going on here? And where was the French patrol?

As the pilot leaned in closer, to get a better look, the rotted door jamb unexpectedly gave way. The pilot lost his balance and stumbled to the ground, his Mauser pistol errantly going off, cracking shrilly, the bullet ricocheting off the stone wall.

Startled, the tall man dropped to the floor, cowering behind a pew, the concussive discharge echoing loudly in the cavernous sanctuary, stunning him in a paralyzing fear. The young pilot hurriedly bolted to his feet and scrambled back into the sanctum. A full minute went by... then another.

Finally, the taller man rose from behind the pew. *"M-Monsieur,* do not shoot!" he demanded, speaking in a fearful voice, his French reverberating shakily. "We are unarmed!"

"Huh?" The pilot sat up against the wall, thinking to himself. Where have I heard that voice before? It sounded very familiar, that voice having a distinct twang of German in it. Suddenly, it seemed unlikely that it was someone from a French night patrol. But where had he heard it before, the pilot ruminated furiously, racking his thick skull for an answer.

A cry of anguished torment bellowed out; the wounded one was calling out to his friend. *"Hauptmann...* p-please. I'm hurt... bad."

Hauptmann? the pilot thought. *Gott!* They must be German.

"Achtung! Identify yourself—*Hauptmann!"* the pilot anxiously shouted back in German, emphasizing the man's rank, testing the truth of the word to himself.

The tall man froze, dumbfounded. Was it a trick, he wondered? Another German in a French church... behind the front lines? Impossible! "What are the chances?" he whispered to himself, then yelled back hesitantly: "I am... *Hauptmann* Wilhelm R. Wissemann! Who the hell are you?"

The young pilot's jaw dropped in disbelief. "Unbelievable!" He gasped. "Willi? Willi Wissemann? Is that really you?"

"Y-Yes! W-Who are you?"

"It's me, Willi! Franz! Franz Zemke!"

"Franz Zemke? Here?" Wissemann's eye's flickered disbelievingly; he was downright flabbergasted. *"Mein Gott!* Incredible!"

He dusted off his tunic and moved to the main isle. Zemke got up too, clambering onto the pulpit. In the dim half-light they approached each other, both men smiling broadly, embracing each other like two long lost brothers. It had been quite a long time since they last seen one another—maybe a year? This was strange indeed !

"How in the hell are you, Willi?" Franz said, clapping Wissemann on the back as the two men embraced firmly.

"Well, I'm still alive, Franz. Just barely, though." Wissemann smiled. "And you, Franz?"

"Doing about the same, I guess."

"Good, good. Glad to hear it."

"This is unbelievable! What happened? How did you—"

"*Hauptmann, p-please?*" the wounded man cried out again, gasping a fountain of blood, shivering uncontrollably as life slowly drained from his body. That wounded man... was poor old Vati Steiner.

Wissemann dashed to his side, crouching down next him. He began unbuttoning his tunic, and explained to Zemke, how Steiner had become wounded—shot in the back as they fled from the French.

"Earlier today, Franz," he explained, "my old friend here and I commandeered a French lorry at an unguarded motor pool. We then posed as Frenchmen, using blue overcoats and helmets we'd stolen—and made our way to the Front. We passed undetected through one checkpoint, Steiner as the driver, me as a French officer. But we ran into trouble at the next one. A suspicious sentry asked for our identification papers. I rattled off in French that we didn't need any papers. I explained, we were with French Intelligence—on a mission to interrogate prisoners at the Front. I guess that little bastard noticed my coat bore the insignia of an artillery officer, quite unusual for an 'Intelligence man.' He got a little leery, I guess, and phoned his headquarters..."

"Then what happened?"

"Steiner got a bit nervous when one of the sentries tried to initiate small talk. Poor old Steiner neither speaks nor understands French too well. When the guard pressed him for an answer, I told him to mind his own damn business. Well, Steiner panicked and gassed the truck, crashing through the barricade, running down one of the guards. Gunfire ensued—"

"And I-I was d-doing damned fine... up until then," Steiner spluttered, raising his head slightly. "S-Steering and clutching... with half a frigging foot. Not too s-shabby, eh, *Hauptmann?*"

"Not too shabby, Vati. Sorry about the bullet—"

"I knew you'd get me killed—you b-bloody-minded... so-and-so." Steiner managed a grim smile. "Goddamn you, Wissemann!"

"I'm sorry, Vati." Wissemann frowned.

"For all the rotten luck." Zemke shook his head pitifully.

"Hmm," Wissemann grumbled. "Bullets whizzed by us as we sped away, one striking Steiner in the back, just above his heart. He doubled over, nearly crashing the truck. I grabbed the wheel just in time and drove the rest of the way here."

"A harrowing escape, no doubt," Zemke replied, shaking his head in utter disbelief.

"Indeed." Wissemann groaned. "That was just a half-hour ago, my friend. I'm sure the snail-eaters are on to us now."

He leaned in closer to the dying old-timer. Steiner's tunic was soaked blood-red, his face pale and clammy, his lips caked with dried blood. Wissemann gripped the old man's hand firmly; he knew Steiner wasn't going to make it.

And Steiner seemed to know it too. "I g-guess this is the end of the road... f-for old Vati Steiner, eh?" he gurgled pitifully.

"Shhh—nein, nein, Vati. You'll be all right. Jut hang on."

Zemke knelt down near Steiner, gazing at the old soldier, his own eyes bloodshot and tired. He sighed heavily, knowing the old fellow didn't have much longer. And he knew too it was already high time to move on, a French patrol would surely be after them now. Sadly, he relized, he and Wissemann would have to leave Steiner behind, if they hoped for any chance of escape.

Steiner's eyes welled up with tears. "Go, Hauptmann. L-Leave me. This is the... end of the l-line for old Vati Steiner."

"Nonsense! Hang on, old man," Wissemann uttered, realizing it was an unsatisfactory response, feeling feeble and helpless, seemingly having exhausted all his resolve in extracting just that.

" I—I can't go any f-further... leave me. Go on, save yourselves."

"No—"

"He's right, Willi. We'll have to leave him," Zemke interjected.

"Verdammt! We can't. I-I promised—"

"Go on, you damn fool!" Steiner sputtered dazedly. "I'm as—good as dead now! I told you I'd only s-slow you down—ugh-h-h-h..." The old-timer gulped and coughed up a mouthful of blood.

"C'mon, Willi! The French will find him. They'll give him a proper... I mean—they'll patch him up. They'll take care of him."

The big Bavarian knew what Zemke had meant; they could leave Steiner behind and the French would find him and take care of him. The snail-eaters were damnable pigs, sometimes, but he knew, at the very least, they were still humane—they'd care for a wounded man, even if he wasn't a Frenchman.

He held Steiner's hand to his chin, murmuring gently: "Sein Leben hängt an einem seidenen Faden." Wissemann began sobbing.

"W-Wissemann," Steiner sputtered, "...there's a l-letter in my coat pocket. It is to my, my... wife. P-Please make sure she receives it when you get across. I know you'll make it. I just know you will, sir."

"Sure, Vati. Sure."

"I'm s-sorry I doubted your doggedness. You were right all along."

"What are you talking about, Vati?"

Steiner gasped. "You were... right. It is b-better to die a soldier—than live like a d-damn prisoner."

"I'm sorry, Vati, Wissemann apologized, his eyes misting over. "I should've let you stay behind, like you wanted to. Forgive me. I was wrong—"

"*Quatsch!*" Steiner croaked. "I die a soldier now, with h-honor. As it—should be... " he coughed, trembling convulsively. Then his eyes went blank, expiring, whispering the final reply: "Since when is forgiveness a better quality than... loyalty."

Wissemann lips tightened. Tears drained down his cheeks.

"Steiner?" He shook the old man. "No, no. No!"

Zemke and Wissemann gawked stiffly, saddened. Vati Steiner was dead now, and the Valkyries were surely looming over his expired body, ready to take his soul up to Valhalla—the Great Hall of Heroes.

Zemke tugged at Wissemann's arm. "C'mon, Willi. He's dead. We've got to get out of here!"

"Yes. We go now."

Wissemann gently closed Steiner's lifeless eyes, then reached into his pocket and retrieved the letter, stashing it carefully in a tunic pocket. He sighed gloomily, feeling responsible for the old man's death, feeling shame, guilt, and remorse. His "doggedness" had gotten another man killed, his vainglorious tenacity had victimized yet another. Wissemann's head drooped miserably.

"Alright, let's go, Willi. C'mon!"

Wissemann nodded. "Right."

Both men got up, standing there side by side, brooding a moment. Franz Zemke cleared his throat awkwardly, staring at Wissemann with longing eyes. "Wait..." he said hesitantly. "Shouldn't we at least say something for the old man?"

"Say something?"

"Like a prayer, perhaps?" Zemke shrugged. "I don't know?"

"A prayer?"

The Bavarian frowned; he was never one for religious utterances. But he thought about poor Steiner, knowing he was a fine fellow, a decent and practical man, possessing an earthy wisdom that no book or any damned military code could ever come close to. He deserved better than fate had given him. Steiner had wanted no praise, no medals, no accolades, nothing of the sort. He just wanted to live, to spend the rest of his days in peace and in the arms of his loving wife. Damned war! Wissemann cursed inwardly. It takes everything from everyone. And for what? Nothing but death and destruction!

"I know, Franz," Wissemann said at last. "Vati Steiner does deserve something, eh?"

"He does."

Willi Wissemann bowed his head, pausing, thinking. Now he could really feel the effects of weariness he'd been fending off since his escape, utter exhaustion finally catching up with him. He grit his teeth and mustered every ounce of resolve he had left, knowing he still had a long way to go yet. Alas, nothing ever came easy for him.

He drew a heavy sigh, and after a brief moment of contemplation, he uttered a brief supplication for the old man's soul. "For as much as it has pleased Almighty God, to take unto himself, the soul of our dear brother departed, we entrust his body—unto your Kingdom, O Lord. Amen." It felt artificial and stilted, but it was the best he could do.

"Amen," Zemke echoed. "May he rest in peace."

"Peace?" Wissemann frowned dispiritedly. *"Humph!* He found little enough of it during this lifetime."

"The French will give him a decent burial, right?"

"Well, we can hope."

Wissemann laid his bloodied overcoat over Steiner's body. He shook his head in despair, gazing at the lifeless body of one, *Feldwebel* August Steiner—Division Supply Clerk, Fourth Army, 24th Reserve Corps, and at forty-six years old—a faithful and honorable son of the Fatherland. "Rest in peace, old father," he said. "Rest in peace."

"C'mon, Willi. This place is going to be crawling with Frenchmen any minute now."

"Right!"

Wissemann nodded, regarding Vati Steiner one last time, then collected his resolve. Zemke jerked his boot on and hurriedly laced it up. Then the two men scurried out of the church and into the truck. Wissemann started the motor, jamming the accelerator to the floorboard as the truck tore out of the muddy lot onto the darkened roadway. Franz Zemke clapped Wissemann on the shoulder.

"Gott! I never thought I'd see you here. Of all the rotten places."

Wissemann was amazed too. "Small world, isn't it?"

"Small world indeed, and no error, Willi."

But the Gods of War were hardly amused.

Chapter 21

✠

JUNE 5, 1917. THE LAST SUPPLY TRUCK was finally unloaded. *Vizefeldwebel* Max Peltzer and his work gang had labored diligently since four o'clock in the morning, getting the new aerodrome set up for operations. *Jasta 23's* new locality, Chéry les Pouilly, was just a few miles northwest of Laon, adjacent to a thickly wooded area. It was also the aerodrome of another Bavarian *Staffel, Jasta 32.* It was twice the size of the aerodrome at Pusieux Ferme and could easily accommodate two squadrons. The 7th Army Engineers had constructed wooden building facilities including a new mess kitchen and a row of enlisted huts, all built adjacent to twelve new hangars. The officers now took quarter in a huge maison bloc chateau across the main road. The new mess also contained a recreation area and bar for after-hours relaxation.

Oberst Thomsen had finally decided to move *Jasta 23* to the new airfield because FA-215, a reconnaissance section, would be setting up shop at Pusieux Ferme. FA-215 needed to be closer to the Army Photographic Headquarters in Laon. The punctilious Prussian Chief of Staff had determined provisioning two *Jastas* would be logistically easier at one aerodrome.

"Let's go see what's for lunch at the new mess, aye?" Peltzer said. "I'm starving."

"Maybe Rummer can take a few lessons from *Jasta 32's* cook," *Leutnant* Rudi Bekemeir replied, rubbing his hands together eagerly. "I hear he was a hotel chef in Munich."

"I would hope so. I'm so tired of that slop Rummer shovels out."

"*Ja-ja!* How many dishes can one make out of cabbage?"

Peltzer grumbled, turning to the work gang and waving, whistling. "C'mon, lads! Forget that for now. Let's go eat."

"*Jawohl!*" *Gerfreiter* Hippel retorted, comically flexing his muscles.

"Hippel, you hairy little monkey!" Peltzer barked grumpily. "Put your shirt back on! Nobody wants to see your furry little chest."

The sweaty cluster of men laid their burdens down and trudged after Peltzer and Bekemeir, who were already heading off to mess. They kidded and joked with one another. Hippel, always the *Staffel* prankster, tripped up one of the newcomers. The new fellow tumbled head over heels and a raucous chorus of laughter erupted.

Peltzer looked on wearily; sometimes he felt like a manager of a traveling circus. "C'mon you bunch of apes!" Peltzer shouted.

Hippel laughed and began imitating a monkey, hopping around on his knuckles, scratching his head and grunting apishly.

Bekemeir and Peltzer shook their heads.

"Bloody idiot," Bekemeir remarked bitterly.

He and Peltzer quickened their pace across the field. A moment later, they were shuffling through the double doors of the new facility. Inside, a hungry crowd was already gathering for afternoon mess. The building was so new that Peltzer could still smell the fresh paint. It even overpowered the aroma of the afternoon meal. Peltzer shook his head, grumbling.

"Don't know what smells worse," he said, making a little face. "Rummer's lentil soup or the paint fumes."

"Well, you've got to hand it to him, Peltzer. He does try."

Peltzer scoffed, quipping sardonically: "*Ja*, he'll certainly win the *Field Kitchen Assault Badge*, that's for damn sure!" He decided then and there that Rummer's soup was much fouler!

Max Peltzer had determined long ago that German Army chow was France's greatest weapon. What had Napoleon once said? An army travels on its stomach? Hah! The German Army must travel on its liver. Tots of booze seemed to be dolloped out more often than a decent tin of soup or a fresh piece of bread. "Iron Rations"—potato rind bread and chestnut-leaf tobacco? Ugh!

And here in the Bavarian sector, things were quite spartan as well. Officers of both *Jasta 23* and *32* dined together at a large table near the front of the hall, along with noncoms and enlisted men. Alas, a separate facility for officers was not available. The noncoms ate on one side of the building while the enlisted ate on the other. Peltzer had to laugh. You'd never see that arrangement in a Prussian *Jasta*. Never! Ah yes, he mused, the advantages of noble birth.

The hungry mechanic ambled up to the serving line. He could see

Leutnant Fleischer's *Kette* had already gathered for their preflight meal. They were discussing the latest gossip with *Jasta 32's* morning flight which had recently returned from a patrol. Their conversations were quite animated. Peltzer considered them dubiously.

Officers? *Quatsch!* They seemed more like little schoolboys, chattering, cheering, bragging, masking their frail insecurities with lusty bravado—children, for God's sake. These young men only saw themselves covered in glory. How sad, Peltzer thought. He could only picture them covered in dirt.

"I swear to you, Fleischer," Krauss affirmed. "That was *Lieutenant* Dorme, Luddenvoss shot down a couple of days ago."

"Who is Dorme?" Braun, one of the new replacements asked.

"He was an ace with the Storks," Neubauer replied.

"But some fellow from *Jasta 9* claims to have shot him down too," Krauss added. Krauss was a *Kettenführer* from *Jasta 32.*

"Well, whoever it was, he sure smoked Zemke's tail feathers!" Fleischer exclaimed.

"Did Zemke crash land behind French lines?" Neubauer asked.

"Luddenvoss thinks he got down alive," Winkler interjected.

"Wasn't he one of Wissemann's old buddies?" Fleischer asked.

"Yes. Just got here two weeks ago," Krauss informed the others. "He only had ten missions under his belt—but had already scored three confirmed victories."

"Three? Not bad," Winkler said. "Not bad at all!"

"If Zemke is still alive," Neubauer said. "He can certainly thank Luddenvoss for it."

"How many victories does Luddenvoss have now?" Braun asked.

"Seventeen, officially. Of course he'll tell you he's got more. But who's counting, eh?"

"Three more and he wins the *Pour le Mérite*," young Braun chirped obsequiously.

"*Quatsch!* He'll win the 'Order of Despot First Class' if he doesn't stay out of trouble. Maybe he'll get transferred instead. Gutemann could authorize it."

"Really?" Fleischer rasped his chin thoughtfully.

"I think Gutemann's had enough of *His Royal Arrogance*," Winkler replied, winking at the toadying tyro. "Steer clear of that wag, see?"

"And where is Gutemann?" Fleischer asked.

"Sulking in his office again, I imagine."

"He's hardly ever seen anymore, except before a sortie."

Neubauer grinned. "You mean—*Herr Professor?*"

"Ooh, that's cruel!" Fleischer quipped.

"Well, ever since he notched his thirteenth victory, Gutemann seems to have lost his nerve," Neubauer said observantly. "He hasn't scored since."

"So? He's been in a slump of late," Winkler countered, shrugging his shoulders. "He'll get back on track."

"Sure—right." Neubauer scoffed dubiously, scowling. "Nah-nah-nah, the competition between Luddenvoss is too much for him."

"You think?" said Fleischer.

"*Ja!* Running the *Jasta* is distracting him."

"He's not the born leader type," Winkler interjected. "He'd rather fly a patrol everyday—not be bothered with shuffling papers."

"Can't say I blame him." Fleischer shrugged. "Who wants to be a pencil-pusher, anyway?"

Everyone laughed.

"And he doesn't like dealing with characters like Schäfer or Luddenvoss, either," Fleischer added, then dropped his voice to a whisper. "I think he's afraid of the Saxon."

"*Nein!*" Winkler snapped. "He's not afraid of Luddenvoss, you lily-livered little *Dummkopf!*"

"What then?"

"*Herr Professor* has just found it easier to leave him alone," Winkler elaborated. "Let him be—let him blast the snail-eaters out of the sky wholesale."

Krauss said: "Well, our *Jastaführer* is one tough *Scheisskerl!*"

"Really?" Fleischer said, irony spoiling his tone.

"*Ja.* He doesn't tolerate disobedience one damn bit." Krauss pushed the cold bowl of lentil soup away. "Ugh! And he won't tolerate this slop either."

The officers burst into raucous, red-faced laughter.

Max Peltzer had to laugh too. He completely agreed with Winkler and Neubauer. Gutemann was certainly struggling in the position of command. With Wissemann gone, Thomsen had thrust him into the difficult job of *Jastaführer*. This was a void the young officer could never adequately fill. Executing the duties of command seemed too much responsibility for him, too much accountability. Peltzer, more than once heard the young *Jastaführer* say that he worried he was sacrificing some moral sense of his character. It was contrary to his beliefs to send men out in flimsy wood and canvas fighting machines, to fight the enemy and die in battle for the Fatherland. That wasn't his idea of good moral conduct, although he willingly did it himself. And the conscientious Swabian had also once admitted to Peltzer, in a rare moment of frankness, that he admired men like Wissemann and

General von Hoeppner for their capacity to lead, but he just couldn't see it in himself. He'd be a happier man following orders instead of giving them.

Peltzer grumbled. Bean-breeze! If Gutemann's expensive training hadn't taught him that war was blood, bullets and pine boxes, then he'd been cheated. Ach! Things were in a pickle. If men like Otto Gutemann were losing their will to carry on, then the war was truly lost. The weary maintenance chief sighed. Gutemann's decline would only spell disaster for himself and for the *Jasta*. He'd tried to advise the young officer, but Gutemann had only rejected his advice. Peltzer soon realized that Gutemann would never accept his help, as it would signify some weakness in his character, perhaps undermine his position as an officer; he was just too proud. Or just too pig-headed! *Gott!* That poor boy needed someone's help.

Alas, Peltzer's hands were tied. He couldn't waste time thinking about Gutemann's quandary, he had his own duties to worry about. His one job as maintenance chief was to keep the *Jasta* running on all cylinders, all the time. The hefty noncom had decided long ago not to tiptoe around officers, always reminding them of the costs and counts of warfare. Officers had their jobs and he had his.

And that was that... Q.E.D.

AFTER A DAY AND NIGHT of hiding out, Wissemann and Zemke trekked to the rear area of the French 6th Army and rested for the evening, bivouacking in a deserted storage cellar in a bombed-out longhouse near the town of Laffaux. Rummaging through storage bins in the cellar, they found a stockpile of potatoes and canned meat. They dined ravenously, both men laughing later, imagining the dejected faces of the returning Frenchmen. Those poor *poilus* would certainly cuss the abhorrent wags that had stolen their stash of provisions!

As Willi Wissemann and Franz Zemke settled in for the night, they exchanged stories about their recent past while sharing a bottle of cheap Burgundy, something they'd found among the hidden rations.

"What ever happened to Hochstetter, Franz?" Wissemann asked.

"Well, Willi, as you may know, FA-4b transferred to Krilov—the Russian Front—in September, not long after you left."

"Oh, that's right."

"One cold afternoon in October, he was flying a bombing mission over Rovno—headquarters for the Russian 8th Army—when his machine got hit by anti-aircraft, forcing him to crash land behind enemy lines."

"Was he killed?"

"No, no. But his observer was."

"That's rotten. He never had much luck with observers."

"Hochstetter made it all the way back to German lines before a Russian sniper got him, as he tried to swim across the Styr River."

"That's quite a swim."

"And he almost didn't make it, Willi."

"What happened?"

"German infantry pulled him out of the water with three bullet holes in his back."

"Wow! Hochstetter is indestructible, that fine gentleman."

"True." Zemke took a swig of wine. "Well, they finally got him to a field hospital near Kovel, and just in time. He'd lost a lot of blood."

"Good 'ole Hochstetter."

"Last I heard, Willi, he was back in Germany working as a aeronautics adviser for some aircraft manufacturer in Johannistal."

"Good for him. He deserves a nice job like that."

Wissemann grabbed hold of the wine bottle and took a big gulp.

"So. What about you, Willi? How did you get captured?"

"Ach, Franz. It's a long story. I don't really—"

"C'mon, Willi. What happened?"

"Oh, all right." Wissemann sighed. "I volunteered for something I should've just kept my pompous snoot out of. A special mission, if you will. I was transporting a Secret Service agent into Paris. Everything went wrong. It ended up in a great big mess, Franz."

"That's unfortunate."

"Quite! If I ever get out of this conundrum, Franz, and get back to Germany, I think I'll take it easy for a while. Marry Ilse, settle down, keep my big nose out of trouble."

"Sounds like a good plan, Willi."

"And you, Franz. A scout pilot now, eh?"

Franz smiled. "It took some doing, but I finally got qualified."

"Good for you. Score any victories?"

"Three—two Nieuports and a Dorand."

"Bravo, Zemke. Bravo!"

Zemke began reminiscing about his days at Colmar Nord, an aerodrome where he'd trained with a home defense *Staffel*, earning a certification for scout pilot status. He thanked Wissemann for his advice—suggesting flight training. His conversion from observer to pilot had taken the better part of six months. And so, after a brief stint in a training squadron, Zemke transferred to *Jasta 32*.

Wissemann told him more of his adventures. Zemke marveled at the big Bavarian's wild escapades, the secret mission, the peculiar escape from captivity, hardly believing that the *poilus* had just let a bunch of German prisoners go. Wissemann assured him it was quite true. Perhaps the rumors were correct—maybe the French Army was in a state of open rebellion? The nearer to the front lines they got, the more amazed they became. The ramshackle condition of the French rearguard was appalling. Was the French Army really ready to give up? It certainly looked that way.

Wissemann's brow narrowed. "I'm really baffled, Franz. Why do the rear areas we've been close to—seem so empty, deserted?

"Don't know, Willi."

"And where *is* the French Army?"

"I don't know that it either. It's all very strange."

"Something is amiss here."

"The French can't be this demoralized, can they?"

Wissemann smiled. "Perhaps, Franz, it's some kind of ruse the snail-eaters are perpetrating—trying to fool our reconnaissance efforts? Maybe they're just hiding?"

Zemke shrugged, taking up the bottle of Burgundy.

"Well, I know for a fact, Willi," he declared with assurance. "They took a lot of casualties during their offensive."

"I know, I heard. It was horrible."

"But can they be this worn down?"

"It's quite possible." Wissemann hunched his shoulders, lighting a cigarette, inhaling, smoke jetting from his nostrils. "And you say German ground units made no concerted counterattacks?"

"Nothing of significance, Willi."

"Hmm?"

"Only isolated retaliation. They were just token assaults against local strong points and observation trenches."

Franz Zemke knew this because he'd flown more than a few ground attack missions in support of the infantry during his short stint at the Front. The German Army had maintained its defensive posture in an effort to wear down the French forces. When the time was right, the German High Command would launch a counter offensive. Now would be the perfect time to strike, Zemke thought. So what in the hell were they waiting for?

"Vati Steiner was probably right," Wissemann reasoned.

"Oh? What did Steiner have to say?"

"Maybe the French divisions have just given up, Franz. Mutiny!"

"Mutiny? *Quatsch!*"

Both men laughed lustily.

Neither knew it at the time, but in fact, a full-scale mutiny was taking place within the French Army. The French troops at Chemin des Dames had suffered a steadily growing number of desertions since late April. Those individual desertions were now turning into widespread mutiny. Thousands upon thousands of soldiers were leaving the front line trenches and marching to the rear areas. The French Army was in turmoil!

A distraught French General sent a dispatch to Paris detailing the situation. Things were deteriorating fast, and fed up soldiers were plainly quitting the fight. Something had to be done immediately!

```
From:  GENERAL CHARLES MANGIN.
       COMPIÈGNE, G.Q.G (CHAMPAGNE SECTOR)
       FRENCH 6th ARMY HEADQUARTERS/STAFF
       7.JUNE 1917


To: FRENCH WAR MINISTRY (Paris)...URGENT!...TOP SECRET.

    Following the failure of General Nivelle's spring
offensive and the loss of over 270,000 men, widespread
mutiny has been reported. Many units refuse to return to
the Front...Fifty-four Divisions now involved. Only two
reliable divisions stand between the German Army and
Paris. Court-martials and executions (by firing squad)
have commenced in earnest. Sincerely suggest suspending
further offensive initiatives for remainder of year.


Signed: GENERAL CHARLES MANGIN,
        FRENCH GROUPE D'ARMEES
```

General Charles Mangin, G.Q.G.

DURING THE NIGHT, Wissemann and Zemke left the dank little basement and drove closer to the front lines in the old truck. After a bumpy drive down a few deserted back roads, they ditched it—after a flat tire and bent axle rendered it useless. Just as well, they reasoned, they'd have to continue the journey on foot anyway. So close to the front lines, they didn't want to draw attention to themselves, walking would offer better opportunities for stealth and concealment. They skulked through thick woods and hedgerows until they came in sight of the French reserve trenches, just a short distance from No-Man's Land. And there they waited until 0300-hours...

As the tightlipped Bavarian crouched in a dense thicket, he could hear the cannonade of high-caliber artillery firing somewhere close by. The sky was black with a starry darkness, a slight breeze rustled the catkin flowered poplar trees beside him. Near the horizon, he could see the dim outline of Allemant—a small village just on the other side of the lines—his proposed destination. The occasional star shell illuminated the devastated landscape along the Aisne front line, arching high over No-Man's Land, sputtering and sparkling, their incandescence casting ominous shadows on the cratered earth below.

Zemke exhaled nervously. "Okay, Willi. Let's get on with it, eh?"

Both men bolted up and moved forward. And after sneaking past dozing sentries with relative ease, the two German officers crept up to a support trench occupied by a medical unit. They overpowered and reluctantly killed a pair of medicos who were casually snacking on their rations. Wissemann and Zemke confiscated their coats and medical armbands then hastily disposed of their bodies. Wissemann struggled to button up the French tunic over his *Feldgrau*, as it seemed a size too small. Franz Zemke looked absurd in his oversized French uniform, the huge helmet nearly swallowing up his little head.

The uniforms reeked horribly and were dirty and bloodstained. But neither man cared. As long as they could fool the French *poilus* into thinking they were fellow soldiers—medicos—the outfits were good enough. Zemke grabbed one of the nearby canvas stretchers, to complete the little charade. Wissemann confiscated a revolver he found lying on a table, checked the cylinder—six rounds—then stuffed it in his pocket. He whispered:

"If anybody stops us, Franz, let me do the talking." Wissemann winked. "Just follow my lead, eh?"

"*Oui, mon vieux,*" Zemke replied, testing his French.

Although his expression was a mask of mocking humor, his face grimaced underneath with grievous pain. His ankle was still tender from his fall, causing him to hobble along on it gingerly. But he was determined not to let it slow him down.

Together the two men plunged into the narrow maze of crooked trenches, traversing this labyrinth of fortifications and its muddy duckboards, acutely aware of the consequences of detection, acutely aware that their chances of getting across were remote indeed. However, not a soul seemed to notice them, nobody said a word to them, nobody seemed to care. Onward they went, closer to the front lines. Closer, closer. Ever closer to freedom. Yes, freedom!

As they approached the forward trenches, the shelling grew louder. But the initial bombardment of the great French offensive had long ceased its relentless barrage. Only sporadic shelling, by both sides, interrupted the silence of night. Wissemann chagrined. Both armies participated in a sadistic, ritualistic tactic known as "sleep deprivation bombardment" lobbing the occasional salvo into enemy lines at hourly intervals, disrupting the sleep of already frightened and exhausted men. Those bastards, they'd murdered sleep! If they couldn't blast the poor slobs into little bits, they'd haunt their dreams with nightmarish shelling. Artillery—the scourge of the foot soldier.

A far off crackling of machine guns echoed through the night air, Wissemann and Zemke heard the whistling of nearby shells too. They were close to the guns. Too close? Wissemann studied the trenches and tried to work out the details of their planned escape. Zemke's map had come in quite handy as they plotted the shortest and least dangerous route across No-Man's Land, earlier that day. But he was a bit stunned by the condition of the French trench system. Everything seemed to be in extreme disrepair. Putrid puddles of standing water were everywhere, there were dilapidated dugouts, partially collapsed ramparts, decayed wooden battlements—just general disorder. Compared to the German fortifications he'd lived and fought in two years prior, the conditions here were pitiful. The French seemed to be totally oblivious to all this.

Both men trudged along for a full thirty minutes before a portly sergeant finally halted them. The sergeant's wide girth unwittingly blocked their path through the narrow trench. There seemed no way of getting past him without some sort of interaction. He regarded them casually and without suspicion.

"*Excusez-moi, mon vieux,*" he said politely, rasping his ratty goatee. "Do any of you fine gentlemen happen to have a smoke?"

"*Non, désolé,*" Wissemann apologized nervously. "I'm fresh out."

"*Merde!* Nobody can help out a poor old man tonight."

"Perhaps you should check with—"

"*Attendez!* What outfit are you fellows with?" he asked suddenly.

"Um..." Willi Wissemann's mind went blank. He smiled falsely, clearing his throat, stalling to find an answer.

The ever-attentive Zemke interrupted his abated cerebration, reaching into his coat pocket, grinning. "*Voilà,* sergeant," he said in flawless French, tossing his remaining pack of Gauloises cigarettes to the pudgy *poilus.* "Keep them, *mon ami.* I'm trying to quit."

"*Merci! Merci!* God bless you, man!" the elated sergeant howled. He happily tramped off down the narrow trench whistling a happy tune, coveting his newly acquired smokes.

Wissemann breathed a sigh of relief. *"Phew!* That was unnerving."

Franz Zemke chuckled. "Got your tail covered, Willi. Just like the old days, eh?"

"How did I ever get along without you?"

"Yes, how did you?"

Wissemann grinned, eyes kindling. "Your French has really improved, Franz. I'm impressed."

Zemke winked. "You owe me a pack of cigarettes."

Wissemann nodded, and resumed their trek.

Many minutes later, they came upon a remote redoubt occupied by a single sentry. The sentry stood attentively at the rampart aiming his 8-millimeter Lebel rifle through a tiny wood-framed slit. He regarded them dejectedly.

"Sacre bleu!" He snarled. "You're not my relief."

"Uh... no. Sorry," Wissemann replied dumbly, gazing at the young sentry, figuring him to be no more than eighteen years old. He shook his head in disbelief. The French were really scraping the bottom of the barrel these days.

"I suppose you're here for Clousiot, then?" said the kid snottily.

"Clousiot?" Wissemann and Zemke traded awkward glances. Then it suddenly dawned on him—the young soldier was referring to his and Zemke's appearance as medicos. "Yes, yes! We're here for Clousiot? Where is—"

"He's out there, you idiot!" the soldier said, pointing. "He's been moaning all night, poor bastard."

"Where, exactly?"

"There!" The snotty sentry pointed again. "Just beyond the wire!"

Wissemann stared at his best friend with weary apprehension, thinking: What had they gotten themselves into?

Zemke shrugged, seemingly aware of Wissemann's thoughts.

The Bavarian officer remembered during his stint in the infantry, both sides had observed a reciprocated "cease-fire" during battlefield evacuations of wounded men, mainly meaning the stretcher-bearers and medicos that attended them. He shuddered—were those little truces still observed, could a man in a medical corps uniform walk out into the abyss of No-man's Land and not be shot at? He knew things had changed dramatically over the course of the war, things like unrestricted submarine warfare, aerial bombing of civilians, chemical weaponry, population-starving naval blockades. Outright brutality was the order of the day now!

"Well, Zemke. What do you think?" Wissemann whispered.

"What do you mean, Willi?"

"Will our German brothers take a shot at a couple of 'French' stretcher-bearers?"

"That's a damned good question, I'd say."

"But what choice do we have?"

"None, Willi. We've come too far to turn back now."

Indeed, they had come too far to turn back now, Wissemann agonized. If they lingered any longer in this labyrinth of enemy trenches, their little ruse would surely be discovered. What is more, he and Zemke could be summarily executed for posing as medical personnel. Both were taking grave chances. This was a pivotal moment—no time for a weakening resolve, no time for hesitation, no time for one's balls to shrink up and disappear!

He stepped on the first rung of the ladder leading to the top of the parapet, his apprehension quite evident now. His hand trembled and his throat became choked with fear. Zemke stood beside him, his heart pounding inexorably, his face etched in dread. Wissemann paused, seized a trench periscope and glanced through it, studying the darkened landscape near the wire. He could see a pile of bodies lying amidst a tangled heap of barbed wire. He saw the body of one Frenchman still breathing, but only faintly. Clousiot! He estimated the distance to the wire at about two to three hundred meters.

Suddenly, there was an earthshaking crump of artillery then the thumping of machine gun fire. Wissemann shivered.

"C'mon, you two. Go on!" The young sentry jerked a thumb at the two disinclined medicos. "He won't last all night!"

"Okay! Here we go," the Bavarian "medico" replied.

The two Germans quickly scaled the ladder and dashed pell-mell into the darkness, zigzagging as they went, carrying the stretcher between them, pacing themselves as if they were a competing relay team, breathing short bursts, crouching as low as possible to the ground. They made it in record time.

Wissemann knelt next to the wounded Frenchman, Clousiot. He was moaning deliriously, laying supine in the mud, covered in dirt and dried blood. He was missing half a leg, one arm was bleeding out and his face was partially burned. Wissemann looked around and saw other dead and dismembered bodies laying about in various phases of decay. He tried breathing through his mouth as the putrid odor of human decay was quite overpowering; the stench was unbearable.

Franz Zemke grumbled. "*Verdammt!* Papa always told me never to trust a living soul and walk carefully among the dead. But this? This is ridiculous!"

Willi Wissemann peered hopefully into the cold darkness toward German lines—no response yet from the German gunners. That was good. Perhaps he and Zemke had a chance. Zemke pointed to a large shell hole athwart of their position, suggesting they take cover there. Wissemann blindly turned away from the pale face that lay revealed, an anguished sob rumbling from his lips. Poor Clousiot—he would not live to see the dawn—

TOK-TOK-TOK-TOK-TOK-TOK-TOK-TOK-TOK-TOK!

The frenetic stammering of a machine gun shattered the silence. A volley of bullets churned up the ground near them, spewing mud in their faces. Wissemann and Zemke flopped face down in the muck as more bullets whizzed over their heads. *Mein Gott!* German gunners were shooting at them. Idiots! Blockheads! Rotten potato-heads!

Wissemann swiped the mud from his face. "This is madness!"

Chapter 22

✠

JUNE 8, 1917. OTTO GUTEMANN heeled his brand-new Albatros up into a zooming climb. The tattered Nieuport below him was coming apart, riddled with smoking bullet holes. A lower wing snapped off, taking a strut along with it and a piece of the upper wing. The Frenchman looked absolutely desperate as his head jerked up and around, searching for the cause of his sudden predicament. Up above, he saw an Albatros, its guns still smoking. In turn, Gutemann gazed down into the Nieuport's cockpit and saw the Frenchman jerking his goggles off, revealing a shocked, pale-white face. Death was clawing after him and he knew it. He saluted as his plane went to pieces. Gutemann returned the salute.

Elsewhere in the dawn sky, Heinrich Luddenvoss whirled around in violent combat with another Frenchmen. Albatros and Nieuport were circling in the familiar death dance of a dogfight. Guns crackled and engines roared. Luddenvoss had come to grips with the French flight leader, a feisty snail-eater with tricolor streamers and stripes of red, white and blue, an ace, to be sure. Luddenvoss, in his trademark green and white striped D.III, banked around smartly as he tried to draw a bead on the silvery Nieuport, his guns stuttering sporadically.

But the Frenchman would not falter, flicking his Nieuport up into a fanciful loop-and-roll, dropping down behind Luddenvoss' Albatros, peppering it with .303 gunfire. The Vickers spat out twenty rounds that punched neat little holes in the Saxon's wings. Luddenvoss, in turn, jerked his crate over, upside down, diving for the deck, his Mercedes 6-cylinder howling powerfully. Down he went, the Nieuport snapping at his tail, its Vickers hammering madly.

Had Heinrich Luddenvoss met his match? It seemed so. The Frenchmen wanted to notch another victory and the green and white Albatros looked like the next likely candidate. He wanted the Saxon's blood, he wanted revenge for years of German occupation, he wanted death for the green and white Boche!

A deadly hail of bullets raked through Luddenvoss' center section. To say that he was caught utterly unawares seemed absurd. Yet such was the case. In thinking of other matters, he'd completely forgotten himself; his position had become threefold precarious. His unforeseen defeat made him fearful, he felt alone and the Frenchy was upon him! With numb fingers he jerked the controls. The Albatros answered, but slowly, clumsily—damaged.

With a lightning dive, the Nieuport flashed past his tail, zooming down to rain a hail of lead from above. The bullets spattered through the windscreen, demolishing what was left of his instrument panel. Luddenvoss gave tongue to a cry of despair as he tried a tight spiral. The Nieuport whipped around, turning, and raked him viciously. Luddenvoss kicked into a side-slip. The Frenchman pounded him with crushing effect, hungry for his prey, determined not to let it escape him, his single Vickers blazing a fiery song of death, his tricolor Nieuport a flashing sword of destruction.

With a frantic jerk at the stick, Luddenvoss hauled his Albatros out level. His hope was gone, doom was staring him in the face, defense was as impossible as escape. It was too late to signal for help now, even had he been able to do so. There were some specks, far to the north, which might be Albatroses, but his nerve was gone, he couldn't even signal if he wanted to. He dodged a rattling burst from behind and knew that the next would finish him.

Luddenvoss slumped over the controls, hoping only for a quick and painless death, finding himself frozen to his controls, stupefied with fear. Such an outcome to the battle had never entered his mind. Of course, as far as his career was concerned, it made little difference. He was going down, not wounded, but killed, a crash landing on German soil, a bone-jarring death!

In the next second, everything seemed to change suddenly. A sound came to his ears that sent a surge of astonishment through his numb frame. The crackle of guns, but not the Vickers of the Frenchy. Other guns, closer—behind him! He jerked upright and twisted about in his seat. His eyes widened at what he saw. Gutemann's Albatros was bearing down on the tricolor Nieuport!

Otto Gutemann had seen all this from above. He'd winged-over in a dive, coming down after the Frenchman, closing quickly. His heavier Albatros easily closed the gap and Gutemann bore-sighted the Nieuport at fifty meters. Now the Maxims spoke deftly, spouting out flaming bullets that slammed into the fuselage and tail plane of the French biplane. The sudden blast of fire disconcerted the Frenchman who had not thought to check his tail. He'd made a momentary error. But the Frenchy, no fool, whipped his bird up into another masterful maneuver and adroitly drew a bead on Gutemann's blue and white lozenge-painted tail plane. In response, the jaunty Swabian, equal to the task, wheeled his Albatros up and about, just as the Frenchman fired. A stream of bullets sailed past harmlessly.

In the meantime, Luddenvoss, pulling out of his plunge, peered upward. He had recovered from his dive and was climbing back up, leveling off at two thousand meters. A fresh wave of choler gripped him. He saw Gutemann tuck in behind the Frenchman's Nieuport and give him a quick burst, chewing up the rudder, shredding canvas. Luddenvoss growled, that Nieuport was *his* quarry, and he wouldn't relinquish it so easy. He accelerated across the sky and muscled his machine in between Gutemann's Albatros and the Nieuport, blocking the Swabian's sight, bumping in to him, wheel against wing—just a little kiss—cracking a spar, tearing some fabric loose on Gutemann's upper wing. It didn't affect the performance of Gutemann's machine but it frightened him to near panic. He jerked his Albatros up, out of Luddenvoss' way, throttling back swiftly, realizing he'd just narrowly escaped a career-ending collision.

Luddenvoss straightened up, shoving the stick, beginning a hard turn to the right. Before he realized it, he found his sights sweeping along a high-backed, narrow fuselage, marked by a painted replica of a crude-looking stork. With instantaneous reaction, his thumbs clamped down on the triggers and his Maxims spoke. His very first bullet must have found the mark. The Nieuport never dodged at all, it slid up on a wing, rolled over onto its back, tracers tearing at its cockpit, and then fell drunkenly into a spin.

Down went the ace of the Storks, Luddenvoss in hot pursuit. Halfway to the ground, the Nieuport seemed to right itself, as if its pilot had suddenly recovered consciousness. But Luddenvoss, diving madly, like he was riding a thunderbolt, cut loose another burst, putting an end to any further resistance. The lamed Nieuport burst into flames, gushing fiery smoke. It canted over, spinning down in slow, lazy spirals, trailing a long plume of black smoke behind it. With a rending crash, it struck a treetop, somersaulted, and lay still. Fire then consumed the wrecked remains of the Nieuport, burning wildly, blackening everything to a crisp. The Frenchman never got out.

Seconds later, the once gaily painted Nieuport, now just an ugly black smudge on the green and dun landscape of the Champagne, exploded, its petrol tank erupting. Fire boiled up from the crash site as curious Feldgrau-clad infantrymen scurried all around it, gawking in stupefied awe, grimacing at the grisly sight.

This was the Saxon's eighteenth victory.

Gutemann was fuming mad as he wielded his flare gun, rallying his scattered *Kette*, preferring to aim it at Luddenvoss instead. That brassy Saxon had usurped his authority once again, this time nearly knocking him out of the sky, literally. Nah-nah! Gutemann grumbled. This would not stand. Luddenvoss was in for some real trouble now, the young Swabian vowed, plotting revenge. That damned man was going to get what was finally coming to him. A quick dive out of the sun had yielded two victories, two victories that should've been Gutemann's, two that would've broken his slump with a much needed double-kill. But Luddenvoss had thwarted that feat with a greedy grab, padding his own score with another victory.

All the way back to the aerodrome, the young *Jastaführer* glared across the gap at the Saxon, cursing bitterly, vowing vengeance. Something was going to happen, Gutemann just knew it!

"SO! OUR GERMAN BROTHERS ARE AWAKE," Wissemann growled. He and Zemke hastened to a shell crater, crawling, rolling, elbows over shoulders, dragging the stretcher. Wissemann slid down in the giant shell hole, and to his surprise and utter revulsion, landed upon a dead body. Zemke lost his footing, tumbling down the inside of the crater, splashing into a shallow pool of water.

A star shell suddenly fizzled high overhead, illuminating the landscape below. Wissemann's stomach clabbered with repugnance, the dead body was a decapitated German soldier, he saw the faded Feldgrau, the torso already infested with maggots. Willi Wissemann put a trembling hand over his mouth and gagged, bile rushing up into his throat, burning acidulous and vile. He gulped, suppressing it with a begrudging swallow. Then he heard a muffled grunt coming from the bottom of the crater. It was another German soldier, seriously wounded—but alive!

The soldier gazed up dazedly at the two "Frenchmen" sighing resignedly. "T-Take me back to your l-lines... *monsieur,*" he babbled clumsily in French, glaring at the befuddled faces before him.

"Huh?" Wissemann uttered, spitting sour bile from his lips.

"I'm your... p-prisoner," the man stammered. "Help me."

"What?" Wissemann looked at his bloody blue tunic, suddenly realizing the wounded man had mistaken him for a Frenchman.

He growled bitterly and stripped off the disguise, discarding the helmet. He yanked a rumpled Bavarian crush cap from his pocket and clapped it on his head. "I am German, *Um Gottes willen!*" the Bavarian declared proudly in Deutsch. "See here! I've escaped from the damnable French, I have!"

"Hallelujah! My prayers have been answered!" The wounded soldier exclaimed elatedly.

Zemke hunched closer. "Is he hurt badly?"

Wissemann looked the poor soldier over. He saw that a bullet had destroyed his knee, pus and blood had coagulated in a nasty-caked mess, and the bone was shattered. Wissemann had seen this kind of thing before. It looked hopeless, amputation would be necessary—if he survived. But he didn't want to trouble the soldier further by telling him the inevitable.

"Um... It's not so bad, really." The kindness in Wissemann's tone hid a falsity that a hard man dared not admit. "What's your name, lad?" he asked.

"Falkenhayn. 7th Army Pioneers."

"Ah, an engineer."

"Where did you men come from?"

"It's a long story, *Junge.* How far is it to your trench?"

Falkenhayn's eyes flickered. "Five hundred meters, maybe?"

"Five hundred meters? Right."

"Aha! You're an aviator, *ja?*" Falkenhayn asked, recognizing Wissemann's pilot badge dangling from his uniform tunic.

"I am—"

"We're both pilots," Zemke put in, fingering his own badge proudly. "How long have you been out here, Falkenhayn?"

"Since, since the counterattack l-last evening."

"*Gott!* Last evening? You've been out here far too long, lad," Wissemann replied uneasily. He looked at Zemke with troubled eyes.

Zemke stared questioningly. "What do you have in mind, Willi?"

The beetle-browed Bavarian reflected lugubriously on the irony of the events. He and Zemke had posed as medicos, dragging along a stretcher to uphold the ruse, but never in his wildest dreams did he think he'd actually have to perpetuate it. It seemed he was always in the wrong place at the wrong time. Why had fate plopped him into this particular crater? Had it mysteriously put him here for a reason? For young Falkenhayn? Wissemann grumbled, cursing the Gods of War. By Mars, his escape plan hadn't included a rescue attempt!

Moreover, here beside him was Franz Zemke. A strange twist of fate had placed him in a church, the very church he'd stopped at. Was fate mocking him? Wissemann swallowed, thinking hard. Steiner was dead and the rest of the hospital prisoners were surely captives of war by now. Falkenhayn was wounded, Zemke was hobbling about on a sore ankle, he himself was still recouping from his own injuries. What a convoluted mess I've gotten myself into, Wissemann groaned inwardly, his head throbbing furiously.

Suddenly, Steiner's old argument replayed itself in his mind, an intolerable tableau that clouded his brain, the old man's accusative voice echoing shrilly inside his skull. "Hero? Where are your codes of conduct now, Willi Wissemann? Where are they, eh? Hmm...?"

Oh, shut up, old man! Wissemann uttered silently, then regrouped his senses. Nah-nah, young Falkenhayn will not be left behind. I will not leave another man to die in France—

"Willi?" Zemke's eyes were wide with wonder.

"Sing o' German brothers of mine, so long as a drop of blood still glows..." Wissemann began to chant quietly, gazing up at the heavens, spurning the cold hand of Death, a wave of stern resolve washing over him. What forces were watching over him, he wondered? Was it God? Was it Providence? Who, or what was it?

"It's my destiny to survive this damned war," he said to himself. But he knew he needed a little bit of luck for a change—

"WILLI!"

"Huh... hmm...? Oh. Right! Let's get him on the stretcher."

"Wake up, damn you! Let's go!"

They struggled for a moment, hefting young Falkenhayn onto the stretcher. He wasn't a big man but his body, all limp and prostrate, was nigh impossible to control, and climbing up a steep muddy incline of a bomb crater with a full load, wasn't an easy thing either. Zemke grimaced as his sore ankle bore the brunt of the weight.

Wissemann poked his head over the edge, surveying the terrain, but only saw darkness. "Into the cauldron we press on..." he intoned morbidly, then muttered: "Here we go, Franz!"

They scrambled out of the crater, nearly stumbling, nearly falling back in the shell hole. Wissemann groaned painfully and recovered his balance, bolting up, scurrying across the pock marked waste of No-Man's Land. Falkenhayn was heavier then he'd imagined and his arms and legs quickly grew weaker. Franz Zemke struggled to keep up too, managing well enough though, keeping the stretcher level and moving forward. Both men were spent, yet both kept pace, moving ever closer to freedom. The Fatherland was a few steps closer now!

GUTEMANN'S ALBATROS touched down last. The rest of the *Kette* had already landed and the pilots were dispersing slowly for the debriefing. All except for Luddenvoss, that is. He was already on his way to his billet, stamping out a steady cadence, longing for a celebratory shot of cognac, elated with himself. Eighteen victories now, two more, he ruminated, and the fabulous *Pour le Mérite* would be his. Then perhaps, command of his own *Jasta?*

"Certainly not, "he muttered to himself with a laugh. "Supreme Headquarters would never allow it. Never!"

He ambled across the field, heading to the Officers' barracks, a multi-room chateau just across the roadway from the airfield. He went inside, pulled his jacket and flight cap off, and sat down on a chair next to his bed. He reached for the bottle of Martell, uncorked it, pouring a shot in the glass sitting on his nightstand. He raised the glass high and then quaffed it down, sighing gleefully.

"Ahh! Two more snail-eaters to go." He reached for the bottle and proceeded to pour himself a second shot.

"Luddenvoss!" a voice cried out suddenly. It was Otto Gutemann. He pushed open Luddenvoss' door and closed it behind him. Sprawled out in the only chair was a brawny man with a sooty complexion, shaggy black hair, features which might have been cut from granite, a crass, bloody-minded man, plainly, on whom subtle phrases would be wasted. Gutemann came straight to the point.

"Luddenvoss, I have a bone to pick with you."

"Huh? What the hell are you talking about?"

Gutemann explained the situation. "You nearly knocked me out of the sky today, Luddenvoss, trying to pad your score again. I won't have it, I tell you. Your reckless abandon nearly cost me my life. "

The leery-eyed Saxon spread his elbows on the armrests and stared at Gutemann. "That Nieuport was mine. You knew that." He paused, his thin lips curling in scorn. "I was just claiming what was rightfully mine, see?"

"Bah! Rightfully yours? You're quite full of yourself, aren't you?"

"Listen you. It's all fair game out there. I finished that Frenchy off, you're just pissed you didn't do it sooner. Don't be a spoilsport, boy." Luddenvoss smirked devilishly.

Gutemann's jaw clenched down. *"Ja,* I could've shot him down. Easily! But I was busy saving your sorry heinie, now wasn't I?"

"Don't know what you're talking about." Luddenvoss poured a shot and settled back into his chair, smirking coyly. He gestured to the bottle of Martell. "Have a drink, boy?"

"No. You're coming with me, Luddenvoss."

"Am I?" Luddenvoss grinned.

"The military constabulary has been summoned. You're going to the clink, my friend."

"Really?" Luddenvoss scoffed. "And if I don't—what are you going to do about it?" His eyes burned with fearless daring.

Gutemann returned his stare without batting an eyelash. With clenched fists, he measured the point of that blunt jaw. "I might smash you on that big mouth of yours," he riposted coolly.

Luddenvoss, a full twenty kilos heavier of the two, almost gasped. But he could not quite conceal the gleam of admiration in his eye. "Hah!" he snorted. "A lot of good that would do you, my friend!"

Just what Otto Gutemann was thinking to himself. He might get in one good crack, yes, but after that? Luddenvoss would soundly pound him to a pulp, and quite within his rights, too. Besides acting in self-defense, Luddenvoss was a an officer, and striking an officer was a capitol offense. The German Air Service did not like its commissioned officers, its "gentlemen" settling their disputes with fisticuffs.

"I appeal to your sense of honor then, Luddenvoss. Don't be a jackass now. Let's settle this like gentlemen, hmm?"

"Like gentlemen?"

"Come quietly—"

"Listen, you little pip-squeak," broke in the tousled-haired Saxon. "You got plenty of nerve talking to me like that. But you're banging that thick skull of yours against a wall. It's no use, boy. If you think I'm going to make a martyr out of myself to suit your sick sense of duty, you're crazy."

"Luddenvoss, listen—"

"Nah! I haven't gotten where I am in the Air Service by asking other people to do me favors. No, sir!"

"Luddenvoss—"

"What I've got, I had to fight for, and I'm going to fight to keep it. That Nieuport was mine. Stay out of the way next time."

Gutemann bit at his lip. His eyes became embittered slits.

"Oh, I know what you're thinking, boy," Luddenvoss waxed on. "You think you pulled me out of a jam out there, don't you? You thought that Frenchy had me. Well, you're wrong, boy."

Gutemann didn't bridle at "boy."

"Stop calling me that—"

" I had everything under control, see!"

"You have no honor or humility, do you, Luddenvoss?"

"Ach, don't give me that honor and humility cow-plop—why you sound just like that damned Willi Wissemann idiot. He was full of himself, too."

Though discouraged, Otto Gutemann was far from giving up. But he saw that to argue with Heinrich Luddenvoss was useless. He turned and opened the door, on his way out.

But the Saxon's voice recalled him. "Whoa, there!"

Luddenvoss was up now. He followed Gutemann out into the hallway and down the steps to the foyer of the chateau. A small group of men had gathered there. Kindlich, Winkler, Peltzer, Schäfer and Schutzling were all there. So were a few men from *Jasta 32*.

"You've got some guts, for a little guy, Gutemann," Luddenvoss raved on heatedly. "Maybe you never liked me, but let me tell you, the men in *Jasta 23* always swear by me." He looked around. "Right, my fine gentlemen?"

No one responded, there was only silence. Even the overtly gregarious Josef Schäfer was strangely reticent for a change.

"I doubt that," Gutemann replied. "They've all been begging me to transfer you for weeks."

Luddenvoss chuckled. "You want to transfer me? I'll settle for a transfer, if you say so. I'd love to ditch this weak-kneed outfit and go join up with a good *Staffel?* I'll bet von Richthofen and his bunch would take me."

"Von Richthofen? Hah! He doesn't allow scoundrels in his *Jasta*, my friend. No matter how many victories they have." Gutemann turned to face the Saxon, who was standing right in front of him now.

Luddenvoss' face did not change, but his eyes burned with fire. "Go to hell," he said bluntly, sneering. He turned to walk away.

"Well, if I were you, Luddenvoss"—Gutemann's voice took on a mean-spirited tone—"I'd just leave, quit, desert, before Supreme Headquarters hears about all this. Take the coward's way out, why don't you?"

Luddenvoss spun around. "That's enough out of you!"

"Coward!"

"Damn you!" Luddenvoss lunged forward and landed a heavy right fist on Gutemann's jaw, sending the fair-haired lad tumbling to the floor, sprawling him out on his backside. "Shut your damned mouth! You boot-licking little—"

"Luddenvoss!" Schutzling protested.

Gutemann sat up, blinking dazedly, codling his jaw "Ooh... that's the end of you, my friend. That's the end. You better get out of here, while you still can, you dirty *schweinehund*—"

"It's a little late for that!" a voice snarled.

Everyone snapped to at the sound of that gruff voice. No one had seen or heard General von Hoeppner arriving at the field. He darted into the foyer with several Prussian military policemen behind him. He'd witnessed the whole incident.

"Luddenvoss, you're under arrest!" Von Hoeppner jerked his head and the military policemen seized the surly Saxon, hauling him away. "I was just in the neighborhood when your call came in, Gutemann. It's a good thing I was at 7th Army Headquarters, I see."

With Kindlich's help, Gutemann got to his feet, replying: *"Ja,* and I'm glad you were, *Herr General.* Luddenvoss is one belligerent *schwein.* That damned rascal has been a thorn in everyone's side since the day he joined the *Jasta."*

"Well, he's going away for a long time. Striking a superior officer, that's a court-martial offense. He's done, I tell you. Done!"

Everyone smiled. Otto Gutemann nodded joyfully, rasping a swollen jaw, smiling too. *Ja,* all was well now. *Wunderbar!*

"HANG ON, *JUNGE.* We're almost there," Wissemann grunted to the wounded Falkenhayn. Another star shell burst in the sky above them. A volley of machine gun fire erupted and sizzled by. At once, Wissemann and Zemke ducked into another shell hole—just a mere hundred meters from the German trenches.

"Verdammt! Those are German gunners firing at us again, Willi!" Zemke exclaimed excitedly.

"I know! Guess they don't care we might be medicos."

"Well, they can't really see us too good in this darkness, Willi."

"Then we'll have to let them know we're German—somehow."

"And how do we do that?"

"I'll call out to them. Maybe luck is on our side tonight."

"Luck?" Zemke scoffed. *"Gott!"*

Wissemann crawled up the side of the crater and rolled on his side. He swallowed hard. His throat was parched but he managed to articulate evenly. "Don't shoot! We're Germans! German airmen—shot down. Hold your fire!"

But there was no answer.

Zemke shook his head dejectedly. "They can't hear you, Willi. C'mon, man. Louder. Louder!"

Willi Wissemann moaned weakly—sick, spent, out of breath, well beyond the limits of his physical endurance, thoughts of dread taunting his worried mind. He cleared his throat and inhaled deeply.

"*DO—NOT—FIRE!*" he shouted. "We are German! Do you hear? German!" His voice echoed across the ground, a voluminous deutsch utterance of desperation.

Zemke nodded. "That should do it."

"What's the password?" A voice echoed back.

Wissemann's head collapsed in disgust. Password? Had they come so far, had they been so fortunate, had they struggled so desperately, to be held up at the threshold of freedom, by a frigging password? Ach! This was too much. Wissemann was feeling hopeless.

"S-Siegfried..." Falkenhayn croaked, breaking the tense silence. "Siegfried is the password, sir."

Wissemann's eyes widened with anticipation, nodding. He drew himself up stiffly and yelled: "Siegfried!"

Again there was silence.

"*SIEG-FRIED!*" His voiced reverberated ever louder.

Damn! Wissemann's whole body ached all over, his heart drubbed furiously in his chest, his lungs still tingled with pneumonia. His hands trembled, his eyes burned with fatigue, his mind raced worriedly. The only thing intact, the only thing left, the only thing keeping him going, was his indomitable spirit to survive.

"That was yesterday's password—friend!" a gruff voice sounded back distrustfully. "What's today's password, eh?"

Wissemann shook his head in disbelieving anguish.

Franz Zemke sighed brokenly. "We must surrender, Willi," he explained. "It's the only way. We must, sadly, surrender our sorry selves as... rotten Frenchmen!"

"Frenchmen?" Wissemann scoffed bitterly.

Both men exchanged doleful glances; they reluctantly had to agree, surrender was the only way. Wissemann began to rummage around for something suitable to surrender with—something white.

"If we make it through this, it'll be a miracle."

Then something occurred to him. Mumbling inaudible curses, he unbuttoned his tunic and pulled it off. He tugged at a shirtsleeve of his white uniform shirt, until it tore loose from the shoulder seam.

Zemke found a fire-charred, shovel handle in a rubble pile and handed it to him. "Here, tie it to this, Willi."

"This is bizarre! Surrendering to our own countrymen as the enemy!" Willi Wissemann spouted angrily as he tied the tattered half of the white shirtsleeve to the handle. He then stuck the white "flag of surrender" up and waved it about slowly, back and forth.

"We give up! Do you hear! We surrender!"

Several seconds ticked by. Then a minute. Then another.

There was no response. The silence began to erode Wissemann's already waning forbearance. He waved the "flag" about wildly.

Zemke moved to the edge of the crater and peered over the rim.

"What's the matter with those idiots!"

"We surrender! For God's sake! *WE SURRENDER! WE SURRENDER!*" Wissemann cried out, nearly incoherently, his eyes flushed with tears as he glared into the darkness. Sweat broke out from every pore on his ashen face. He looked as if he was about to cry.

Zemke gazed at him, worried. "Willi, are you all right—"

"Come out, slowly!" the gruff voice replied, finally. "Throw down your weapons!"

Wissemann let out a relieved sigh. *"Gott... at last."*

Zemke's eyes widened with hope.

The gruff voice bellowed again. "If you try any tricks, my friends, our machine gun will cut you to pieces!"

Wissemann's hands trembled. He nodded to Zemke and flung the French revolver into the black abyss. "All right! We're coming out now!" he shouted. "Don't shoot! We're unarmed!"

"We have a wounded man here," Zemke announced.

"No tricks, you!" The voice replied. "Come forward! Slowly!"

Another star shell exploded high above them, bathing the landscape in a gloomy light, the shadows stirring across the cratered earth, bending and distorting as the shell arched across the dim sky. Two dog-tired aviators grabbed the stretcher and the helpless Falkenhayn, and clambered out of the crater. Wissemann huffed exhaustively, staggering forward, his heart pumping the last ounces of strength into his long legs. As he neared the trench line, he could see coalscuttle helmets of the German infantry peering over the ramparts. He smiled, finally relieved, his great ordeal soon over. At last, he would be home. At last, he would see his beautiful Ilse again.

"I've returned to the Fatherland," he rejoiced. "Finally—"

A rifle cracked, sharp and dry. Wissemann heard the agonized cry. Then another shot rang out. He felt a stinging, searing heat lance into his left thigh just below his rump, a bullet ripping into his flesh. He collapsed, tumbling to the ground in a limp heap, moaning, clutching his leg in excruciating pain, feeling the red life force swiftly drain from him. What had gone wrong? Who had fired the shot? This was all wrong. No—No!

Wissemann regained some of his composure and crawled towards Zemke's writhing body. He could see his friend's head covered in blood; he was screaming uncontrollably, his hands were trembling convulsively, his face was white as a ghost. He was dying!

And he screamed. Oh, how he screamed! The screaming! The shrieking! Madness! Madness! Insanity!

When Wissemann finally reached Zemke's convulsing body, he saw the faint silhouette of a man crawling across the ground a few meters away. Who? A sniper! The teenaged rifleman had found them. He'd apparently stalked them across No-Man's Land when they'd callously abandoned his comrade, Clousiot. He despised all deserters and mutineers. He knew not their identity, probably, he did not care, nor did it matter. They were cowards. They deserved to die!

The German machine gunners opened up.

The young rifleman slithered backed to his trench, crawling like a snake amidst the fusillade of flaring gunfire. Then the French gunners opened up. A barrage of bullets crisscrossed No-Man's Land. A full-scale exchange of machine gun fire and mortars soon commenced. A German infantryman found Willi Wissemann and dragged him, blood-soaked and delirious, back to the safety of German lines. Wissemann closed his eyes and began sobbing quietly. He had made it back, he had returned. He was home... at last. What would become of him now?

The star shell fizzled out, darkness returned to the Front.

And the Gods of War wept as the Valkyries flew west.

Willi Wissemann returns in:

"Only the Eagle Dares"

WISSEMANN'S
OFFICIAL VICTORIES

(HAC/UTD)

1917

NO.	DATE	TIME	TYPE SHOT DOWN	LOCATION
1	2 Mar.	1419	Farman F 40	Vaudesincourt
2	15 Mar.	1625	Sopwith (two-seater)	Near Cernay
3	26 Mar.	0613	Spad 7	Allemant.
4	17 Apr.	0832	Nieuport 11	Chemin des Dame
5	17 Apr.	1821	Caudron G 4	N. of Bétheny

* List does not include unconfirmed aircraft shot down.

HISTORICAL NOTE

WHAT HAPPENED IN EUROPE a century ago has had a profound effect on the history of the world as we know it today. World War One was the first of its kind in the history of warfare. According to the politicians, it would be also the last—the "war to end all wars" they'd said. The aeroplanes flown by daring young men were machines constructed mainly of canvas and wood—flimsy, fragile flying machines fashioned in fabric and wire. They carried machine guns and bombs into an atmosphere of clouds and falling climates, an arena never before experienced by mankind. Those delicate biplanes, and yes, sometimes monoplanes, offered little or no protection to the men who flew them. Their machines bore no protective armor and pilots were not typically issued parachutes. Much later, in the waning months of the conflict, German airmen were given such safety devices. But many preferred to fly without them.

The airmen that took part in "dogfights" were mostly young, well-educated men. They perished in battles like no other soldiers before them. Much has been written about the chivalrous nature of the aerial combats fought over the fields of France and Belgium—sportsmanship, unwritten codes of conduct, knightly principles supposedly adhered to by these jousting "Knights of the Air." Yet, in reality, most pilots fought these deadly dogfights by the only real rule of warfare—kill or be killed.

The romantic aura of the air war lies primarily in the minds of fiction writers and filmmakers. The real myth is the idea that these dogfights were fought under the rules of chivalry—a medieval principle governing knighthood and knightly conduct. World War One was a dirty, underhanded conflict in more ways than one. The utilization of gas, unrestricted submarine warfare, small scale strategic bombing, and population-starving naval blockades, ushered in a new era of warfare. The aerial dogfights over the Somme and Champagne were just a hint of what was to come two decades later: armadas of multi-engined, metal-winged bombers escorted by sleek, heavily armed, high-powered fighter planes. The days of the lone air ace were over before they had began.

General Ernst von Hoeppner was a real person. So were Oberst Hermann Thomsen and Max Immelmann. And so, of course, were Capitaine Guynemer, *Kapitäin* Peter Strasser, and *Rittmeister* Manfred von Richthofen, the "Red Baron." As for the the other characters—they are composite creations of the author's mind. All military equipment, weaponry, locations, air terminology, German phrases, words and ranks, squadrons, *Jastas*, air groups (the Storks, Hawker's RFC SQD No. 24), are all real and authentic. The French mutinies of 1917 actually occurred.

—Deke D. Wagner

APPENDIX

AEROPLANE PROFILES
SPECIFICATIONS AND DATA OF SELECTED
GERMAN, FRENCH AND BRITISH AIRCRAFT
OF WORLD WAR I (1914-1918)

APPENDIX

ALBATROS D. II

Engine:	160-hp, liquid-cooled, six-cylinder, Mercedes D.III, inline
Wingspan:	27 ft. 11 in. (8. 05 m)
Length:	24 ft. (7.33 m)
Weight:	1954 lbs. (888 kg)
Max Speed:	109 mph. (175 km/h)
Ceiling:	17,060 ft. (5,200 m)
Armament:	2-forward-firing 7.92 mm Maxim machine guns
Endurance:	1 hr. 30 min.

Single-seat scout (1916-17). In 1916 German aerial domination had been lost to the Allied air services. German pilots requested an aircraft that was more powerful and more heavily armed. By April 1916 Robert Thelen and his engineers had developed the Albatros D.I, which featured a 160-horsepower Mercedes engine and twin forward-firing machine guns. Alongside the development of the D.I, Thelen had built the Albatros D.II which appeared on the Western Front in September 1916. D.IIs formed part of the early equipment of German Jastas—the first specialized fighter squadrons in the German Air Service. Famous pilots included Oswald Boelcke (Jasta 2's first commander) and Manfred von Richthofen. With its high speed and heavy armament, the D.II won back air superiority from Allied fighter types such as the Airco D.H.2 and Nieuport 11. After a successful combat career in the early Jagdstaffeln, the D.II was gradually superseded by the Albatros D.III.

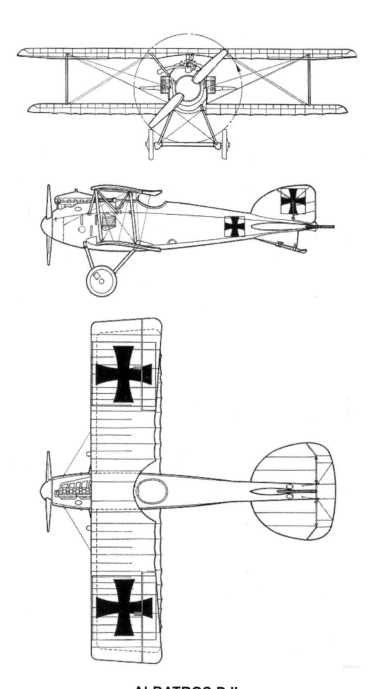

ALBATROS D.II

APPENDIX

ALBATROS D. III

Engine:	170-hp, liquid-cooled, six-cylinder, Mercedes D.IIIa, inline
Wingspan:	29 ft. 8 in. (9. 05 m)
Length:	24 ft. 5 in. (7.33 m)
Weight:	1949 lbs. (886 kg)
Max Speed:	115 mph. (180 km/h)
Ceiling:	18,044 ft. (5,500 m)
Armament:	2-forward-firing 7.92 mm Maxim machine guns
Endurance:	2 hrs.

Single-seat scout (1917). One of the most successful of its line—excluding its propensity for shedding a lower wing in prolonged dives. First deployed on the Western Front in December 1916. One of the first truly modern biplane fighters of the war. The powerful, twin-gunned Albatros D.III represented two revolutionary design philosophies: maneuverability and firepower. It became the mainstay of the German Air Service during all of 1917. Initially withdrawn for nearly two months (Feb-Mar) due to structural issues, but returned to wreck havoc on the RFC, during what became known as "Bloody April."

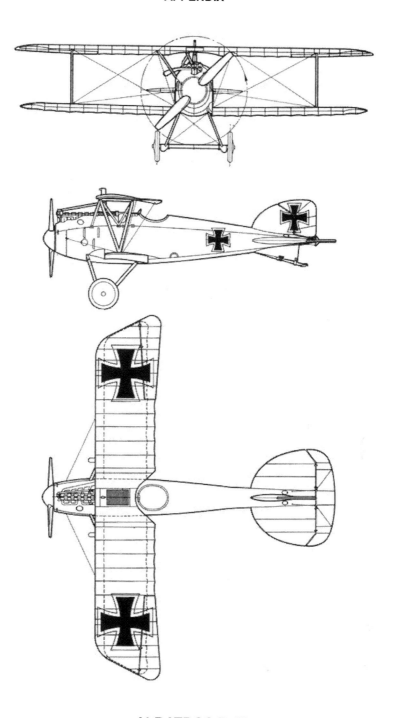

ALBATROS D. III

HALBERSTADT D. III

Engine:	120-hp, liquid-cooled, six-cylinder, Mercedes D.II, inline
Wingspan:	28 ft. 10 in. (8. 8 m)
Length:	23 ft. 11 in. (7.3 m)
Weight:	1696 lbs. (771 kg)
Max Speed:	90 mph. (145 km/h)
Ceiling:	13,123 ft. (4,000 m)
Armament:	1-forward-firing 7.92 mm Maxim machine gun; later models had two.
Endurance:	1 hr. 30 min.

Single-seat scout (1916-17). The first Halberstadt and went into service in the summer of 1916. While quite successful early on, it was later out-classed by the emergence of the Spad-7 and the Nieuport-17, and was finally replaced by the Albatros D.I and D.II. Early models suffered from having only one machine-gun and an underpowered engine. Later, two machine guns were added at the factory, giving the Halberstadt greater firepower.

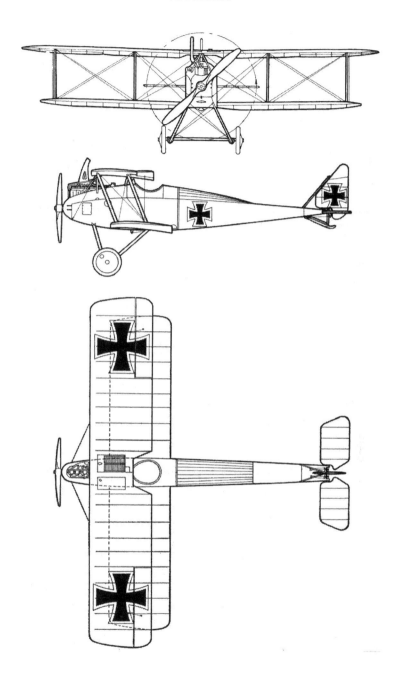

HALBERSTADT D. III

APPENDIX

FOKKER D. II

Engine:	100-hp, 9-cylinder, air-cooled rotary, Oberursel
Wingspan:	30 ft. 10 in. (9.41 m)
Length:	23 ft. 7 in. (5.77 m)
Weight:	1289 lbs. (586 kg)
Max Speed:	93 mph. (150 km/h)
Ceiling:	13,125 ft. (4000 m)
Armament:	1-forward-firing 7.92 mm Maxim machine gun
Endurance:	1 hr. 30 min.

Single-seat scout (1916). The Fokker D.II was a single seat scout aircraft developed before the Fokker D.I. It was based on the M.17 prototype, with single-bay unstaggered wings and a larger fuselage and shorter span than production D.Is. Using a (100 hp) Oberursel U.I, the D.II was underpowered, though the single 7.92 mm machine gun was normal for 1916. The German Army purchased 177. In service, the D.II proved to be little better than the earlier Eindecker fighters. In particular, it was outclassed by the Nieuport 11 and 17. A few D.IIs were used by the *Kek* and early *Jagdstaffeln* alongside the Halberstadt D.II. Later on, the twin-gunned Fokker D.III supplemented the early *Jastas* as well. But these early Fokker biplanes were deemed inferior and quickly discarded when the new Albatros fighters came out.

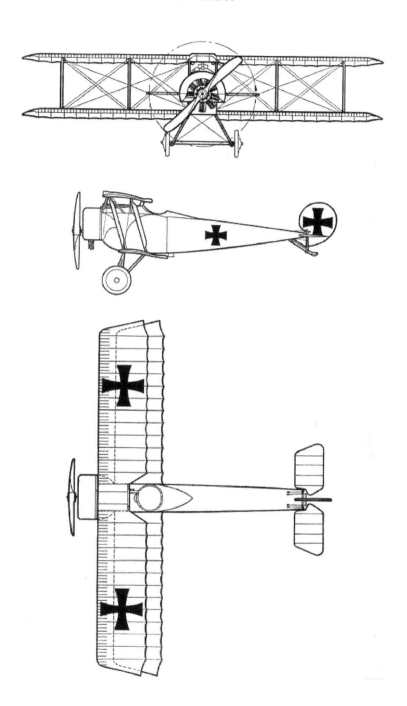

FOKKER D. II

FOKKER E. IV "Eindecker"

Engine: 160-hp, Oberursel 14-cylinder, two-row air-cooled rotary
Wingspan: 30 ft. 10 in. (9.41 m)
Length: 23 ft. 11 in. (7.3 m)
Weight: 1342 lbs. (610 kg)
Max Speed: 106 mph. (170 km/h)
Ceiling: 12,992 ft. (3,950 m)
Armament: 2 or 3 forward-firing 7.92 mm Maxim machine guns
Endurance: 1 hr. 30 min.

Single-seat scout (1915-16). First appeared at the Front in December 1915. Its predecessor (Model E. III) was one of the first German scouts to have a fixed machine-gun synchronized to fire between the propeller blades. The Eindecker, which simply means "monoplane" revolutionized the air war in August 1915, as it was the combat first aircraft with a synchronized machine-gun. Given the Fokker designation of M.15, the E.IV was essentially a lengthened Fokker E.III powered by the 160 hp Oberursel U.III two-row, 14-cylinder engine. The more powerful engine enabled the Eindecker to carry two or three 7.92 mm machine guns, thereby increasing its firepower and providing redundancy if one gun jammed, a common occurrence at the time. The E.IV was a troubled design that never achieved the success of its predecessor. Oswald Boelcke and Max Immlemann scored their first victories in the Eindecker series

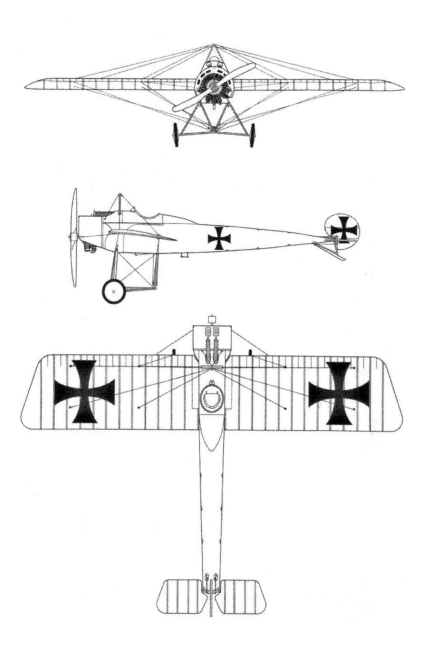

FOKKER E. IV "Eindecker"

BRISTOL SCOUT D "Bullet"

Engine:	80-hp, Le Rhône 9-cylinder, air-cooled rotary
Wingspan:	24 ft. 7 in. (7.49 m)
Length:	20 ft. 8 in. (6.3 m)
Weight:	1,250 lbs. (567 kg)
Max Speed:	100 mph. (156 km/h)
Ceiling:	16,000 ft. (4,877 m)
Armament:	one .303-caliber. Vickers machine gun, or one upper wing mounted .303 Lewis machine gun
Endurance:	2 hrs.

Single-seat scout of (1915-16). Great Britain's first aircraft in service with a fixed machine-gun. After three previous variants the Bristol Scout model D, which had modified structure and tailplanes, was first deployed in November 1915. A speedy and maneuverable machine for its time. This however was not enough to make the small biplane an efficient warplane. By late summer of 1916 it was withdrawn from service in favor of more modern aircraft. Wissemann's first victory, although officially unconfirmed, was against a Bristol Scout.

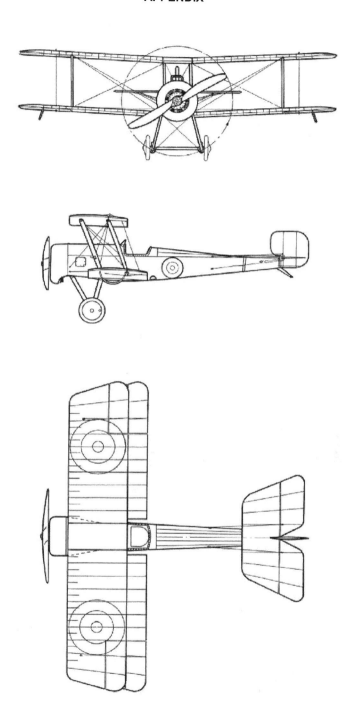

BRISTOL SCOUT- D "Bullet"

APPENDIX

DE HAVILLAND D.H. 2 "Airco"

Engine:	100-hp, Gnome-Monosoupe 9-cylinder, air-cooled rotary
Wingspan:	28 ft. 3 in. (8.61 m)
Length:	25 ft. 2 in. (7.68 m)
Weight:	1,441 lbs. (653 kg)
Max Speed:	93 mph. (150 km/h)
Ceiling:	14,000 ft. (4,267 m)
Armament:	one flexible .303-caliber Lewis machine gun.
Endurance:	2 hrs. 45 mins.

Single-seat scout (1916-17). The ungainly yet nimble D.H.2 wrested air superiority from the Germans over the Somme in early 1916. With a rear-mounted rotary engine "pusher" it afforded its pilot excellent visibility and eliminated the need for a synchronized machine-gun. It was more than a match for the Eindecker and anything else the German's could put into the air until the emergence of the Albatros D-series, most notably the Albatros D.II. The infamous Major Hawker of RFC SQD. No. 24 flew D.H. 2 scouts.

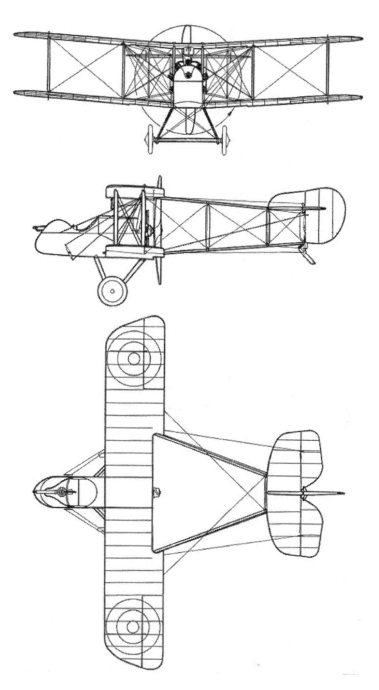

De HAVILLAND D.H. 2 "Airco"

R.A.F. F.E. 2b

Engine:	160-hp, Beardmore 9-cylinder, air-cooled rotary
Wingspan:	47 ft. 9 in. (14.55 m)
Length:	32 ft. 3 in. (9.83 m)
Weight:	3,337 lbs. (1,378 kg)
Max Speed:	91 mph. (147 km/h)
Ceiling:	11,000 ft. (3,335 m)
Armament:	one forward-firing Lewis machine gun.
	one rear-firing Lewis machine gun.
Endurance:	2 hrs. 30 mins.

Two-seat fighting scout (1916-17). Another rear engine "pusher-type" machine employed on the Somme battlefront by the British. Later in 1917, as the F.E. 2 became obsolete, it was relegated to night-bombing and escort missions, as well as reconnaissance sorties. It was a unwieldy and ponderous machine and fell easy victim to the more superior Albatros D-series. Altogether some 1,939 of these machines were built, including 386 long-span F.E. 2d models. Know affectionately as "Fee" by British aircrews.

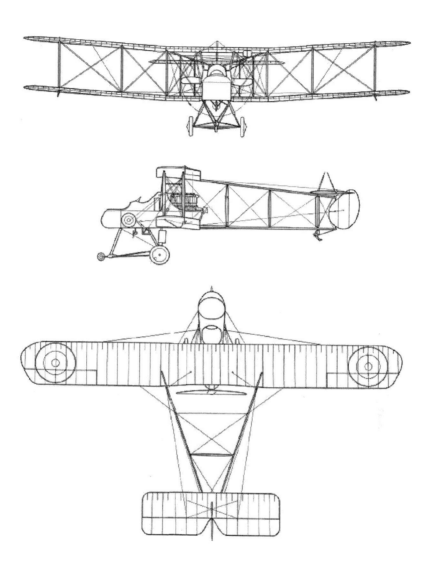

R.A.F. F.E. 2b

NIEUPORT 11 *Bébé*

Engine:	80-hp, Gnôme-Monosoupape 9-cylinder, air-cooled rotary
Wingspan:	24 ft. 9 in. (7.55 m)
Length:	19 ft. 11 in. (5.8 m)
Weight:	1060 lbs. (480 kg)
Max Speed:	97 mph. (156 km/h)
Ceiling:	15,090 ft. (3,500 m)
Armament:	1-flexible-Lewis, drum-fed, .303 Cal. Machine gun mounted on top wing.
Endurance:	2 hrs. 30 mins.

Single-seat scout (1915-16). Nicknamed *Bébé* (Baby), because of its small size. It became France's answer to the German's Fokker Eindecker. The Nieuport 11 was very popular with the French squadrons and with the Americans of the *Lafayette Escadrille*—the United States of America's first, all-volunteer, all-pursuit squadron (1916-1917).

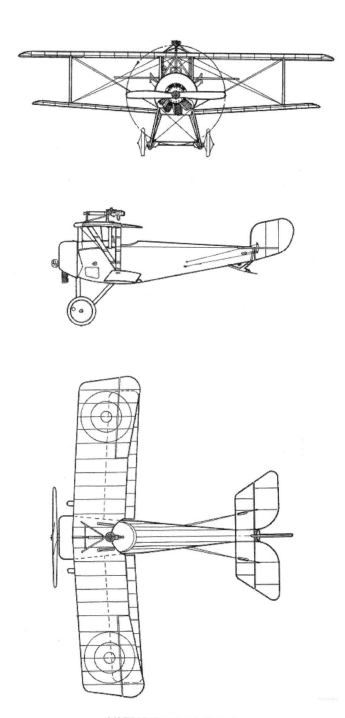

NIEUPORT 11 Bébé

NIEUPORT 17

Engine:	110-hp, Le-Rhône 9-cylinder, air-cooled rotary
Wingspan:	26 ft. 10 in. (8.17 m)
Length:	18 ft. 11 in. (5.77 m)
Weight:	1246 lbs. (565 kg)
Max Speed:	110 mph. (156 km/h)
Ceiling:	17,390 ft. (3,500 m)
Armament:	1-forward-firing Vickers .303 Cal. Machine gun.
Endurance:	2 hrs.

Single-seat scout (1916-17). Probably the most popular Allied fighter of the war. Successor to the Nieuport 11. Very maneuverable, but like all Nieuport designs, could not take much battle damage. Used extensively by British squadrons, although only armed with a single wing mounted Lewis gun. It Was eventually replaced by the Nieuport 24, which resembled it closely in appearance and performance. Aces, Bishop, Ball, and Guynemer, all started out in the Nieuport 17 scout.

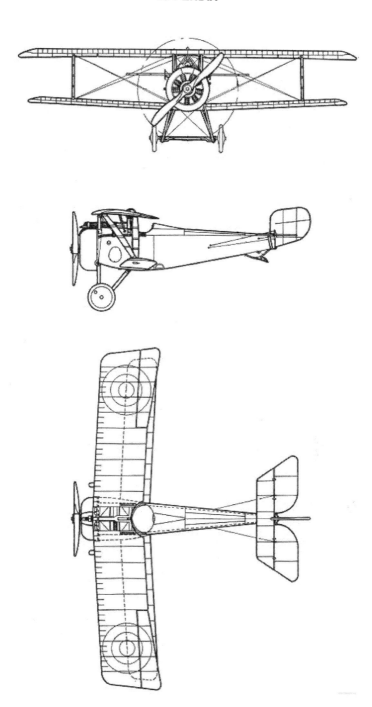

NIEUPORT 17

SPAD 7

Engine:	150-hp Hispano-Suiza, V8-cylinder liquid-cooled inline
Wingspan:	25 ft. 10 in. (7.77 m)
Length:	20 ft. 1 in. (6.13 m)
Weight:	1550 lbs. (703 kg)
Max Speed:	120 mph. (192 km/h)
Ceiling:	18,000 ft. (5,485 m)
Armament:	1-forward-firing Vickers .303 Cal. machine gun.
Endurance:	2 hrs 15 mins.

Single-seat scout (1916-17). SPAD (Société Pour L'Aviation et ses Dérivés). The Spad 7 was one of the mainstays of the French Air Service. Also used by the British and American units. A very rugged aircraft known more for its structural strength than its mediocre maneuverability. Like its successors, the Spad 7 was renowned as a sturdy and rugged aircraft with good climbing and diving characteristics. It was also a stable gun platform, although pilots used to the more maneuverable Nieuport fighters, found it heavy on the controls. Like all Allied types of the period, it suffered from its single Vickers machine-gun. The Spad 7 was Georges Guynemer's favorite mount.

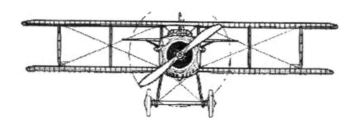

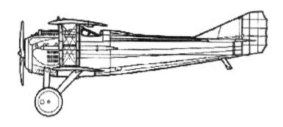

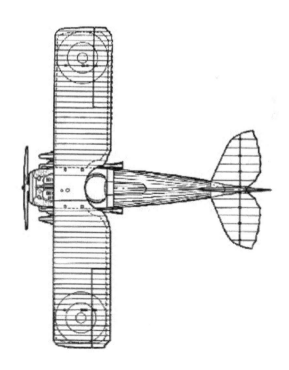

SPAD 7

LFG ROLAND C. II "Walfisch"

Engine:	160-hp, liquid-cooled, six-cylinder inline, Mercedes D.III
Wingspan:	33 ft. 8 in. (10.3 m)
Length:	25 ft. 2 in. (7.70 m)
Weight:	2,831 lbs. (1,284 kg)
Max Speed:	102 mph. (165 km/h)
Ceiling:	13,100 ft. (4,000 m)
Armament:	1-forward-firing 7.92 mm Maxim machine gun
	1-flexible, rear-firing 7.92 mm Parabellum
	4-12.5 kg bombs carried under the fuselage
Endurance:	4 hrs.

Two-seater recon-bomber (1916). Because its fuselage resembled a fish, it was nicknamed "Walfisch" by the Germans. Allied pilots had much respect for this rugged aircraft. Wissemann flew a Roland C.II when he was assigned to FA-4b on the Somme battlefront. The Roland C.II was a product of *Luftfahrzeug G.m.b.H.* of Berlin-Charlottenburg, and abbreviated to LFG. There existed at the same time another manufacturer *Luft-Verkers G. m.b.H.* of Johannisthal Berlin abbreviated LVG. Since the two abbreviations were too similar for the marketing folks at LFG, it was decided to add "Roland," after the French medieval hero, to their name. Thus it became LFG Roland.

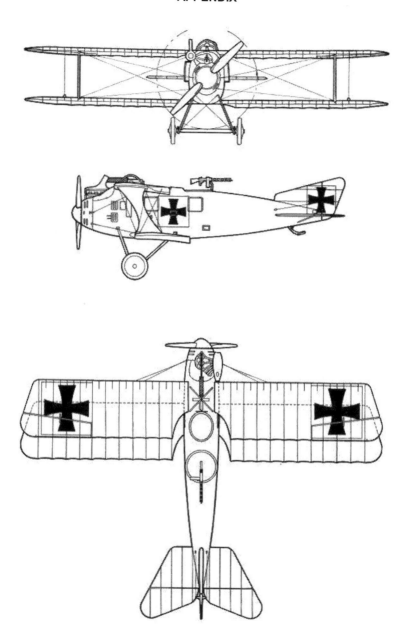

LFG ROLAND C.II "Walfisch"

RUMPLER C. IV

Engine:	260-hp, liquid-cooled, six-cylinder, Mercedes
Wingspan:	41 ft. 8 in. (12.70 m)
Length:	25 ft. 2 in. (7.70 m)
Weight:	3,439 lbs. (3119 kg)
Max Speed:	101 mph. (162 km/h)
Ceiling:	21, 056 ft. (6,400 m)
Armament:	1-forward-firing 7.92 mm Maxim machine gun
	1-flexible, rear-firing 7.92 mm Parabellum
Endurance:	3 hrs. 30 mins.

Two-seater reconnaissance/bomber aircraft (1917-18). Excellent aircraft all-around. Developed from the previous C.III model. Its high-altitude capabilities made it ideal for long-range reconnaissance work. Well-liked by German aircrews and proved a very feisty opponent for any attacking French or British scout. Could carry a formidable bomb load as well.

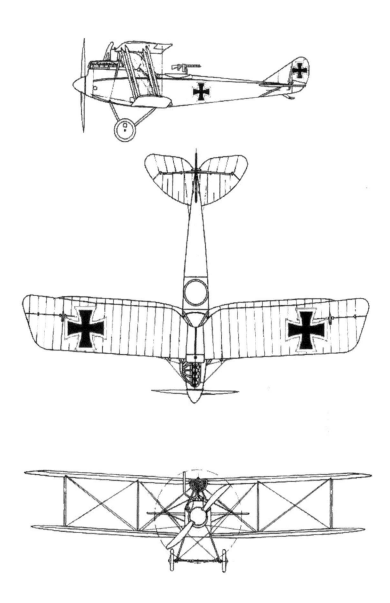

RUMPLER C. IV

ALBATROS C. III

Engine:	160-hp, liquid-cooled, six-cylinder inline, Mercedes
Wingspan:	38 ft. 4 in. (11.69 m)
Length:	26 ft. 3 in. (8 m)
Weight:	2,977 lbs. (1,353 kg)
Max Speed:	88 mph. (140 km/h)
Ceiling:	11,155 ft. (3,400 m)
Armament:	1-forward-firing 7.92 mm Maxim machine gun
	1-flexible, rear-firing 7.92 mm Parabellum
	220 lbs (100kg) bombs.
Endurance:	4 hrs.

Two-seater recon-bomber aircraft (1915-17). Stable and reliable utility aircraft, early workhorse of the German Air Service. Von Richthofen began his career in a C. III, as did Herman Goering and Ernst Udet—the latter—the second highest scoring German ace of the war with 62 victories. Succeeded by the equally successful C.V model.

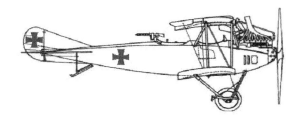

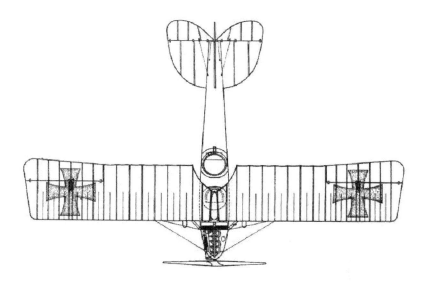

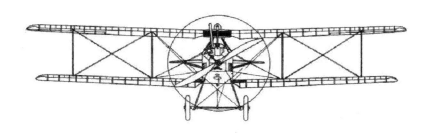

ALBATROS C. III

SOPWITH "1 ½ Strutter"

Engine:	130-hp, 9-cylinder, air-cooled Clerget rotary
Wingspan:	33 ft. 6 in. (10.21 m)
Length:	26 ft. 3 in. (8 m)
Weight:	2149 lbs. (975 kg)
Max Speed:	100 mph. (155 km/h)
Ceiling:	15,500 ft. (4,730 m)
Armament:	1-forward-firing .303 cal. Vickers machine gun
	1-flexible rear firing .303 cal. Lewis machine gun
Endurance:	3 hrs. 30 mins.

Two-seater recon-bomber aircraft (1916-17). It is significant as the first British designed two-seater tractor scout, and the first British aircraft to enter service with a synchronised machine gun. It was given the name "1½ Strutter" because of the "one-and-a-half" (long and short) pairs of cabane struts supporting the top wing. As well as serving with the Royal Flying Corps, it also saw widespread but rather undistinguished service with the French Air Service—*Aéronautique Militaire.*

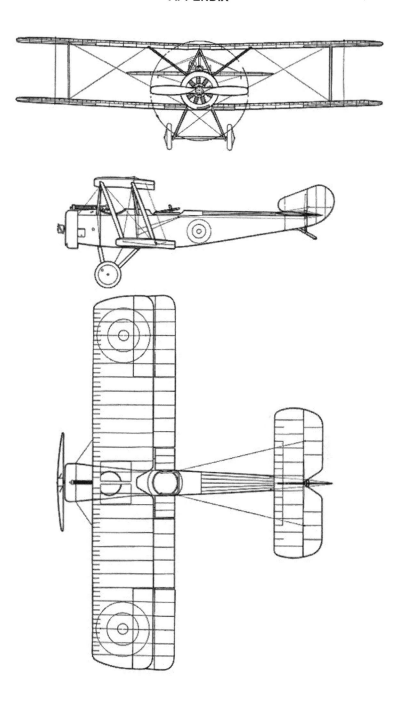

SOPWITH "1 ½ STRUTTER"

FARMAN F. 40

Engine:	135-hp, 12-cylinder, air-cooled Renault Vee piston
Wingspan:	57 ft. 9 in. (17.6 m)
Length:	30 ft. 4 in. (9.25 m)
Weight:	2469 lbs. (1120 kg)
Max Speed:	84 mph. (135 km/h)
Ceiling:	13,100 ft. (4,000 m)
Armament:	1-flexible forward-firing .303 cal. Lewis machine gun.
Endurance:	2 hrs. 30 mins.

Two-seat pusher recon/bomber aircraft (1915-17). The "Shorthorn" was an improved version of the "Longhorn." It first appeared at the Front in 1915, a year after its predecessor, and served with the Russian and Italian air services as well as the French. Popularly dubbed the "Horace Farman" it had an overall smoother outline and smoother crew nacelle. A pair of upper tail booms supported a horizontal tailplane and a curved fin. The aircraft went into production in early 1915. Wissemann's first official victory was scored over a Farman F. 40

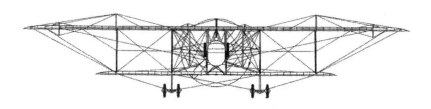

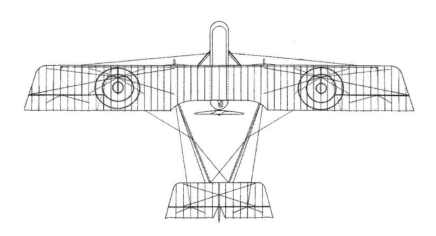

FARMAN F 40

CAUDRON G .4

Engine:	2 x 80-hp, 9-cylinder, air-cooled Le-Rhône rotary
Wingspan:	56 ft. 5 in. (17.20 m)
Length:	23 ft. 10 in. (8.60 m)
Weight:	2600 lbs. (1,612 kg)
Max Speed:	77 mph. (124 km/h)
Ceiling:	13,100 ft. (4,000 m)
Armament:	1-flexible .303 cal. Lewis machine gun
	250 lbs. (113 kg) of bombs
Endurance:	3 hrs. 30 mins.

Twin engine, two-seater, recon/bomber (1915-17). French biplane with twin engines, widely used during World War I as a bomber aircraft. It was designed by René and Gaston Caudron as an improvement over the Caudron G.3. The aircraft employed wing warping for banking. The first G.4 was manufactured in 1915, both in France, England and in Italy. The Caudron G.4 was used as a reconnaissance/ bomber, ranging deep into Germany itself. Later, when Germany developed a strong fighter force, the Caudron was relegated to night bombings sorties. By mid 1917, the Caudron G.4 was in use by Belgium, France, Finland, Italy, England, and the United States.

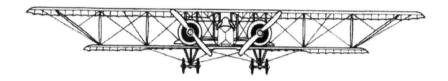

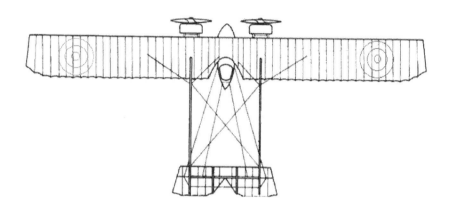

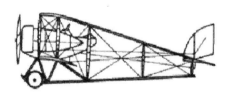

CAUDRON G. 4

GLOSSARY

> Familiarity with these terms will be useful in reading this novel about World War I aviation, the German Air Service and the role of the fighter pilot. These terms are by no means 100% accurate but regarded by most historians as generally correct.

AA, ack-ack (anti-aircraft) pertaining to artillery designed for use against aircraft, a general term also used for all ground guns aimed at aircraft.

Abteilung – section, unit or detachment.

Ace – term to denote a pilot who had five victories against the enemy. A word invented by the French—originally to denote a sports star. Not used by the British.

Ach! - an informal interjection or mild expletive.

Achtung! - Attention!

Aerodrome – An airfield, generally makeshift or temporary.

Aeroplane - British spelling of airplane; used in this novel to add historical flavor.

AFP - *Armee Flug Park*: Army Flight Depot.

aileron – moveable wing portion used to generate roll.

Albatros Gesellschaft GmbH – Premier German aircraft manufacturer; products carried name, ie; Albatros D.II or D.III.

Adlershof – German aviation test facility near Berlin.

altimeter – An instrument graduated and calibrated to indicate the height above sea level.

Amerikaprogramme – America Program; a concerted production increase.

Armee – Army.

Artilleriehäschen – "artillery rabbit" airman's slang for artillery spotter.

Auf Wiedersehen - Good-bye.

bank – to dip wings in a left or right attitude.

Barrel-roll – a combat maneuver in which an aeroplane makes a complete rotation on its longitudinal axis while following a helical path, approximately maintaining its original direction.

Bayern Bluse – The basic Bavarian uniform tunic.

B.E.2 - British two-seat recon/artillery-spotter aircraft.

Bébé – (Baby) Nickname for the Nieuport 11 single-seat scout.

Benzol – German fuel additive.

Bitte – please.

Bitte shön – you're welcome.

Boche – derogatory French word for a German.

Bogohl - the *(Bombengeschwader der Obersten Heeresleitug)* the bombing wing under direct control by the German Army's High Command in World War I.

Bubi – German for: boy, lad, baby.

Castor oil – Bean derived lubricant especially suited for rotary engines.

ceiling – the maximum altitude at which an aircraft can operate under specified conditions.

Croix de Guerre - (Cross of War) is a military decoration of France.

Danke – thank you.

GLOSSARY

De Havilland – Designation for a popular fighting aeroplane (D.H. 2), named for its designer.

Deuxième Bureau – French Secret Service agency.

DFW – *Deutsche Flugzeug Werke*; German manufacturer of recon/bombing aircraft.

D.H. – De Havilland D.H. 2

Dogfight – Multiple aircraft involved in an aerial melee.

dope – a chemical solution brushed or sprayed on the "skin" of aeroplanes to tauten and waterproof the fabric.

Dreidecker – German word for triplane.

Dufte Bienen – "fragrant bees" ie; prostitutes.

Dummkopf! – Blockhead!

Ehrenbecher – Cup of Honor for the victor in aerial combat; usually silver.

Eindecker – revolutionary German monoplane fighter of 1915-16.

Eisenkruez I/II Klasse – Iron Cross 1st & Second Class. Basic field awards for bravery for regular servicemen, officers, and airmen.

elevator – An adjustable horizontal surface at the tail of an aeroplane, operated remotely from the cockpit control column to incline or pitch the tail (reverse the nose) upward or downward in flight.

Entschuldigen Sie - excuse me.

FA - *Flieger-Abteilung*: Flier Detachment.

FA(A) - *Flieger-Abteilung (Artillerie)*: Flier Detachment (Artillery).

FE – Fighter Experimental.

FEA - *Fliegerersatz-Abteilung*: Replacement Detachment.

Feldgrau - "Field-gray" basic German uniform.

Feldmutze - field cap.

Feldwebel – Sergeant

FFA - *Feldflieger Abteilung*: Field Flier Detachment

Flamed - to shoot down an enemy aircraft in flames.

Fliegertruppen – Flying Troops; original name of German Air Service.

Flugbenzin - a fuel blend of 60/40, Benzol and gasoline which was effectively a higher octane fuel. This fuel enabled the Germans to develop over-dimensioned and over-compressed aircraft motors.

FlugM – *Flugzeugmeisterei*: German Air Intelligence Bureau.

Flugmeldedienst – Flight Reporting Service; front line observers.

Flugzeugführer – early designation for flight-leader.

FS - *Fliegerschule*: Flight School

front-hog – derogatory nickname for crusty front line soldiers.

Gefreiter – Private First Class

General der Infanterie – General

Generalleutnant - Lieutenant General

Generalmajor – Major General

Goettingen – German wind tunnel test facility.

Gitterrumpf - (lattice-tail) German airman's slang for pusher aircraft.

Gott! - German exclamation for: God!

Gott im Himmel! – exclamatory expression: God in Heaven!

GLOSSARY

GmbH - The acronym "GmbH", which is written after the name of a company, designates a company as private in Germany. The letters stand for *Gesellschaft mit beschränkter Haftung* which, translated literally, means a "company with limited liability".

Hakenkreuz – swastika.

half loop – a climbing-roll primarily used to change direction and altitude.

Hals und Beinbruch - a good luck saying akin to "break a leg."

hangar - A large shed used to house aeroplanes during maintenance and non-flying periods.

Hauptmann – Captain

Herr – Sir.

Hochstapler - imposter; a fraud; a lower-class social climber.

horsepower – A unit of measure to designate the power of aircraft motors and other engines; equivalent to 550 foot pounds-per-second or 745.7 watts.

Idflieg - (*Inspektion der Fliegertruppen*) Inspectorate of Flying Troops: the bureau of the German Empire that oversaw German military aviation prior to and during World War I.

Incendiary – A shell, bomb, or bullet containing substance that burns with an intense heat when triggered by timing, impact, or other means.

Ja – yes.

Jagdflieger – Fighter Pilot.

Jasta - short version for *Jagdstaffel* (Hunting squadron)

Jastaführer - Squadron Leader.

JastaSch - *Jastaschule*: Fighter Pilot School

Jawohl – yes (indeed).

JG - *Jagdgeschwader*: Fighter wing

Junge – young man/ lad.

Kagohl – the tactical bomber wing under direct control by the German Army High Command in World War I.

Kaiser (the German Emperor) specifically to designate Wilhelm II, also the King of Prussia.

Kanone – German pilot with ten aerial victories.

Kapitänleutnant – Imperial German naval rank equivalent to a British Navy Lieutenant or Army Captain.

Kasta - *Kampfstaffel*: tactical bomber squadron.

Kavallrie – Cavalry.

KEK- *Kampfeinsitzerkommando*: Combat single-seater command, a predecessor to *Jasta* units.

Kette – a three or six plane flight formation.

Kettenführer – Flight-leader

KG - *Kampfgeschwader*: tactical bomber wing

Kofl – *Kommandeur de Flieger*: Officer in charge of all flying units assigned to a particular Army.

Kogenluft – *Kommandeur General de Luftstreitkräfte*: Commanding General of the Imperial German Air Service; essentially, General Ernst von Hoeppner.

Kommandeur - Commander

GLOSSARY

Korvettenkäptain – Imperial Naval squadron commander, equivalent to Lieutenant Commander or Army Major.

Kriegministerium – Imperial German War Ministry.

Landwehr, or *Landeswehr,* term used in referring to militias.

Le Rhone – French manufactured rotary engine.

Leutnant – 2nd Lieutenant

Lewis gun – A light air-cooled, gas-operated machine-gun with a circular magazine, used on many French and British aircraft. Named after its inventor, I. N. Lewis.

Lieber / Liebe – Dear (gender oriented).

Lieber Gott! – German exclamation for: *Dear God!*

loop – an impressive maneuver at an airshow, practically useless in air combat. Aircraft loops over upside down, losing a great deal of altitude.

Luftstreitkräfte - (Air Strike Force). In English language sources it is usually referred to as the "Imperial German Air Service" although that is not a literal translation of either name.

Major - Major

Mannschaften - The German Rank and File.

Marine - *Marine-Flieger:* Naval pilots

Mein Gott! - My God!

Mercedes – German engine and automobile manufacturer.

Nacelle- part of the aircraft fuselage or wing which accommodates crew.

nein – no.

nicht – not.

Nieuport – Manufacturer of French scout aircraft.

No-Man's Land – The area between the German and Allied front line trenches. It was pockmarked, scarred and cratered by incessant shelling.

Oberfeldwebel - Staff-Sergeant

Oberleutnant - Lieutenant

Oberst – Colonel

Oberursel – German manufacturer of troublesome rotary engines.

observer – Individual aboard a two-seat aeroplane typically assigned the duty of photo-recon, bombing and the manning of defensive armament.

Patato-head – nickname for German foot soldiers.

petrol – British term for gasoline.

pitch – Nose down or change of attitude.

Poilus – *(pwaa'loo)* an informal term for a French infantryman, meaning, literally, hairy one.

Pour le Mérite – German decoration also known as the "Blue Max." Highest award given by Imperial Germany; typically pilots with twenty victories.

Quatsch! – Nonsense; baloney; bullshit; etc.

retournment – a looping, aerial maneuver used to get on an enemy's tail.

Richthofen – Manfred von, the "Red Baron." Highest scoring ace of the war.

Rittmeister – Cavalry Captain

roll – Wing tip rotation of ninety degrees or more.

Royal Flying Corps – (RFC) The British military air service.

GLOSSARY

rudder – The fin of the vertical-stabilizer of an aeroplane used to change direction while in flight.

Schweine! - German word for: swine, pig, hog, etc.

Schweinehund! - German exclamation for bastard; a derogatory term.

scout – (Fighter) Typically a single-seat biplane armed with machine-guns.

Service d' Aéronautique – The French Air Service.

sesquiplane – unique design where lower wing is smaller than upper wing.

side-slip – a maneuver used to lose altitude quickly without gaining speed.

slip-turn – a flat turn performed solely with the rudder, using no ailerons.

sortie – a mission flown by one aircraft.

Spad – (acronym) *Societe Pour l' Aviation et ses Derives;* French aircraft manufacturer; especially the Spad 7 fighting scout.

spin – An aeroplane's vertical descent while spiraling; sometimes out of control.

Stabsoffizier der Flieger – *(Stofl)* Staff Officer for Aviation within an Army.

staffel – (squadron) German Air Service *Jagdstaffel.*

stall – The condition of an aeroplane that has been caused to fly at a greater angle than the angle of maximum lift, thus causing loss of control and a downward spin.

Startwärter – a member of a pilot's ground crew; fitter, rigger, armorer, etc.

stick – The control column in an aircraft's cockpit used to operate the ailerons and elevators.

Storks – *(Cicognes)* The elite French fighter squadrons.

Technische Berichte - technical reports.

two-seater – (Recon/Bomber) Typically a machine with a pilot and observer.

Unteroffizier - Corporal

UR-2 – Troublesome German rotary engine.

Vati – German for "father" or "daddy."

vic – a formation of three aircraft arranged in a tight wedge.

Vickers – name for British .303-cal. machine gun.

Verdammt! - a German exclamation. Literally: *dammit!*

Vizefeldwebel - Sergeant Major

Wackes – a derogatory term for a native Alsatian; was considered inflammatory enough that German military regulations prohibited its use.

Werke – Works; an industrial site, e.g. where aeroplanes are manufactured or processed.

Wetterdienst – Weather Service.

Wie gehts? - How are you?

wingover – means of reversing direction, usually in a dive.

wireless – Any communications system such as radio, that requires no wires or other connections between sending and receiving stations and is operated through the use of electromagnetic waves.

Wunderbar – wonderful.

yaw – Angular offset of aircraft nose in a left-right sense.

GERMAN AIRCRAFT
DESIGNATION SYSTEM

DURING THE FIRST WORLD WAR, German aircraft officially adopted for military service, were allocated a designation that included (1) the name of the manufacturer (2) a function or "class" letter, and (3) a Roman numeral. The three-part system was needed for a specific designation to simplify logistics support of the many types of aircraft in operation—especially as *Luftstreitkräfte* squadrons were, more often than not, equipped with several different types.

A - Single-engine monoplane without armament.
B - Single-engine biplane without armament; pilot sits in rear cockpit.
C - Single-engine biplane two-seater with armament.
D - Single-engine single-seater with armament.
E - Single-engine single-seater monoplane with armament.
F – Single-engine single-seater triplane with armament.
G - Biplane with more than one engine with armament
R - Biplane with three to six engines with armament.
Dr - Single-engine single-seater triplane with armament.
CL - Light C-category aeroplane, two-seater with armament.
GL - Light G-category aeroplane with armament.
N - Single-engine Night aeroplane with armament.
J - Infantry aeroplane; two-seater armored biplane with armament.
L - Multi-engine biplane with armament.
S - Single-engine armored two-seater biplane with armament.
DJ -Single-engine single-seater, armored with armament.

Note: The first two Fokker Triplanes carried the F category marking but all subsequent aircraft of this configuration were designated Dr and the F category was no longer used. The E category marking was revived in August 1918 with the arrival of the Fokker E.V, when this type re-appeared after technical problems had forced its removal from the Front it was designated D. VIII, so plainly the biplane restriction of this category had to be removed.

ABOUT THE AUTHOR

DEKE D. WAGNER was born in Mississippi and raised in Georgia. The son of an American Air Force sergeant and a German mother from Hesse-Darmstadt, Deke grew up having a keen interest in aviation and his German heritage. At the tender age of ten years, he read Manfred von Richthofen's autobiography, *Der Rote Kampfflieger* (The Red Air Fighter) and has ever since been enthralled with tales of air aces and air combat. After high school and a stint in the Army Reserve, Deke attended art school but made little progress. He spent the next two decades pursuing a semi-professional musical career as a singer/songwriter before attempting his first novel—***The Eagle and the Albatros.*** Deke also enjoys playing guitar and recording original music. He currently resides in Atlanta, Georgia. This is his first novel.

37446172R10271

Made in the USA
Lexington, KY
02 December 2014